LILIAN JACKSON BRAUN

THREE COMPLETE NOVELS

Also by Lilian Jackson Braun

THE CAT WHO COULD READ BACKWARDS
THE CAT WHO ATE DANISH MODERN
THE CAT WHO TURNED ON AND OFF
THE CAT WHO SAW RED
THE CAT WHO PLAYED BRAHMS
THE CAT WHO PLAYED POST OFFICE
THE CAT WHO KNEW SHAKESPEARE
THE CAT WHO SNIFFED GLUE
THE CAT WHO WENT UNDERGROUND
THE CAT WHO TALKED TO GHOSTS
THE CAT WHO LIVED HIGH
THE CAT WHO KNEW A CARDINAL
THE CAT WHO MOVED A MOUNTAIN
THE CAT WHO WASN'T THERE
THE CAT WHO WENT INTO THE CLOSET
THE CAT WHO CAME TO BREAKFAST

THE CAT WHO HAD 14 TALES
(Short Story Collection)

LILIAN JACKSON BRAUN

THREE COMPLETE NOVELS

The Cat Who Knew Shakespeare

The Cat Who Sniffed Glue

The Cat Who Went Underground

G. P. PUTNAM'S SONS NEW YORK

G. P. Putnam's Sons
Publishers Since 1838
200 Madison Avenue
New York, NY 10016

Published simultaneously in Canada

Library of Congress Cataloging-in-Publication Data

Braun, Lilian Jackson.
[Novels. Selections]
Three complete novels / Lilian Jackson Braun.
p. cm.
Contents: The cat who knew Shakespeare—The cat who sniffed glue—
The cat who went underground.
ISBN 0-399-13984-2
1. Detective and mystery stories, American. 2. Qwilleran, Jim
(Fictitious character)—Fiction. 3. Journalists—United States—
Fiction. 4. Cats—Fiction. I. Title. II. Title: Cat who knew
Shakespeare. III. Title: Cat who sniffed glue. IV. Title: Cat who
went underground.
PS3552.R354A6 1994 94-10502 CIP
813'.54—dc20

Printed in the United States of America
1 2 3 4 5 6 7 8 9 10

DEDICATED TO

EARL BETTINGER, THE HUSBAND WHO . . .

CONTENTS

The Cat Who Knew Shakespeare

ONE

IN MOOSE COUNTY, four hundred miles north of everywhere, it always starts to snow in November, and it snows—and snows—and snows.

First, all the front steps disappear under two feet of snow. Then fences and shrubs are no longer visible. Utility poles keep getting shorter until the lines are low enough for limbo dancing. Listening to the hourly weather reports on the radio is everyone's winter hobby in Moose County, and snowplowing becomes the chief industry. Plows and blowers throw up mountains of white that hide whole buildings and require the occupants to tunnel through to the street. In Pickax City, the county seat, it's not unusual to see cross-country skis in the downtown shopping area. If the airport closes down—and it often does—Moose County is an island of snow and ice. It all starts in November, with a storm that the residents call the Big One.

On the evening of November fifth, Jim Qwilleran was relaxing in his comfortable library in the company of friends. A mood of contentment prevailed. They had dined well, the housekeeper having prepared clam chowder and escalopes of veal Casimir. The houseman had piled fragrant logs of applewood in the fireplace, and the blaze projected dancing highlights on the leather-bound books that filled four walls of library shelves. From softly shaded lamps came a golden glow that warmed the leather furniture and Bokhara rugs.

Qwilleran, a large middle-aged man with a bushy moustache, sat at his antique English desk and tuned in the nine o'clock weather report on the radio—one of numerous small portables deployed about the house for this purpose.

"Colder tonight, with lows about twenty-five degrees," the WPKX meteorologist predicted. "High winds and a good chance of snow tonight and tomorrow."

Qwilleran flipped off the radio. "If you guys don't object," he said to the other two, "I'd like to leave town for a few days. It's six months since my last trip Down Below, and my cronies at the newspaper think I'm dead. Mrs. Cobb will serve your meals, and I'll be back before the snow flies—I hope. Just keep your paws crossed."

Four brown ears swiveled alertly at the announcement. Two brown masks with long white whiskers and incredibly blue eyes turned away from the blazing logs and toward the man seated at the desk.

The more you talk to cats, Qwilleran had been told, the smarter they become. An occasional "nice kitty" will have no measurable effect; intelligent conversation is required.

The system, he had found, seemed to be working; the pair of Siamese on the hearth rug reacted as if they knew exactly what he was saying. Yum Yum, the affectionate little female, gazed at him with an expression that looked like reproach. Koko, the handsome and muscular male, rose from the spot where he had been lounging in leonine majesty, walked stiffly to the desk, and scolded with earsplitting yowls. "Yow-ow-OW!"

"I was expecting a little more understanding and consideration," the man told them.

Qwilleran, at the age of fifty or so, was coping with a unique midlife crisis. After a lifetime of living in large metropolitan areas, he was now a resident of Pickax City, population 3,000. After a career as a hardworking journalist getting by with a modest salary, he was now a millionaire—or billionaire; he was not quite sure. At any rate, he was the sole heir to the Klingenschoen fortune founded in Moose County in the nineteenth century. The bequest included a mansion on Main Street, a staff of three, a four-car garage, and a limousine. Even after a year or more he found his new lifestyle strange. As a newsman he had been concerned chiefly with getting the story, checking the facts, meeting the deadline, and protecting his sources. Now his chief concern, like that of every other Moose County adult, seemed to be the weather, especially in November.

When the Siamese reacted negatively to his proposal, Qwilleran tamped his moustache thoughtfully for a moment. "Nevertheless," he said, "it's imperative that I go. Arch Riker is leaving the *Daily Fluxion,* and I'm hosting his retirement party Friday night."

In his days of frugal bachelorhood in a one-room apartment, Qwilleran had never hungered for money or possessions, and among his fellow staffers he was not noted for his generosity. But when the Klingenschoen estate finally stumbled through probate court, he astonished the media of the Western world by inviting the entire staff of the *Daily Fluxion* to a dinner at the Press Club.

He planned to take a guest: Junior Goodwinter, the young managing editor of the *Pickax Picayune,* Moose County's only newspaper. Dialing the newspaper office, he said, "Hi, Junior! How would you like to goof off for a couple of days and fly Down Below for a party? My treat. Cocktails and dinner at the Press Club."

"Oh, wow! I've never seen a Press Club except in the movies," said the editor. "Could we visit the *Daily Fluxion* offices, too?"

Junior looked and dressed like a high school sophomore

and exhibited an innocent enthusiasm that was rare in a journalist with a *cum laude* degree from a state university.

"We might sneak in a hockey game and a couple of shows, too," Qwilleran said, "but we'll have to keep an eye on the weather reports and get back here before snow flies."

"There's a low-pressure front moving down from Canada, but I think we're safe for a while," Junior said. "What's the party all about?"

"A retirement bash for Arch Riker, and here's what I want you to do: Bring a *Picayune* newscarrier's sack and a hundred copies of your latest issue. After the dinner I'll say a few words about Moose County and the *Picayune,* and that'll be your cue to jump up and start distributing the papers."

"I'll wear a baseball cap sideways and yell, 'Extra! Extra!' Is that what you want?"

"You've got it!" Qwilleran said. "But the authentic pronunciation if 'Wuxtree!' Be ready at nine o'clock Friday morning. I'll pick you up at your office."

The early-morning weather broadcast on Friday was not encouraging: "A low-pressure front hovering over Canada increases the possibility of heavy snow tonight and tomorrow, with winds shifting to the northeast."

Qwilleran's housekeeper expressed her fears. "What will you do, Mr. Q, if you can't get back here before snow flies? If the storm is the Big One, the airport will be closed for goodness knows how long."

"Well, I'll tell you, Mrs. Cobb. I'll rent a dogsled and a pack of huskies and mush back to Pickax."

"Oh, Mr. Q!" she laughed. "I never know whether to believe you or not."

She was preparing an attractive plate of sautéed chicken livers with a garnish of hard-cooked egg yolk and bacon crumbles, which she placed on the floor. Yum Yum gobbled her share hungrily, but Koko declined to eat. Something was bothering him.

Both cats had the shaded fawn bodies and brown points of pedigreed seal-point Siamese: brown masks accentuating the blueness of their eyes; alert brown ears worn like royal crowns; brown legs elegantly long and slender; brown tails that lashed and curled and waved to express emotions and opinions. But Koko had something more: a disconcerting degree of intelligence and an uncanny knack of knowing when something was . . . *wrong!*

That morning he had knocked a book off a shelf in the library.

"That's bad form!" Qwilleran had told him, appealing to his intelligence. "These are old, rare, and valuable books—to be treated with respect, if not reverence." He examined the book. It was a slender leather-bound copy of *The Tempest*—one of a thirty-seven-volume set of Shakespeare's plays that had come with the house.

Experiencing slight qualms, Qwilleran replaced the book on the shelf. It was an unfortunate choice of title. He was determined, however, to fly Down Below for the party, despite Koko and Mrs. Cobb and the WPKX meteorologist.

An hour before flight time he drove his energy-efficient compact to the office of the *Picayune* to pick up Junior and the sack of newspapers. All the buildings on Main Street were more than a century old, constructed of gray stone in a variety of inappropriate architectural styles. The *Picayune* headquarters—squeezed between the imitation Viennese lodge hall and the imitation Roman post office—resembled an ancient Spanish monastery.

A satisfying smell of ink pervaded the newspaper office, but the premises had the embalmed look of a museum. There was no ad taker at the scarred front counter. There was no alert and smiling receptionist—only a bell to ring for service.

Qwilleran perused the silent scene: wooden filing cabinets and well-worn desks of golden oak . . . dangerous-looking spindles for spiking ad orders and subscriptions . . . old copies of the *Picayune,* yellow and brittle, plastered on walls that had not been painted since the Great Depression. Beyond the low partition of golden oak and unwashed glass was the composing room. A lone man stood before the typecases, oblivious to everything except the line of type he was setting with darting movements of his hand.

Unlike the *Daily Fluxion,* which had a metropolitan circulation approaching a million, the antiquated presses of the *Picayune* clanked out thirty-two hundred copies of each issue. While the *Fluxion* adopted every technological advance and journalistic trend, the *Picayune* still resembled the newspaper founded by Junior's great-grandfather. Four pages, printed from hand-set type, carried classified ads and social gossip on the front page. Pancake breakfasts, ice cream socials, and funerals were covered in depth, while brief mentions of local politics, police news, and accidents were relegated to the back page or omitted entirely.

Qwilleran banged his fist on the bell, and Junior Goodwinter came pelting down the wooden stairs from the editorial office above, followed by a large white cat.

"Who's your well-fed friend?" Qwilleran asked.

"He's William Allen, our staff mouser," said Junior casually, as if all newspapers had a mouser on the staff.

As managing editor he wrote most of the copy and sold most of the ads. Senior Goodwinter, owner and publisher, spent his time in the composing room, wearing a leather apron and a square paper hat folded from newsprint, setting foundry type in a composing stick while wearing an expression of concentration and rapture. He had been setting type since the age of eight.

Junior called out to him, "S'long, Dad. Back in a few days."

The preoccupied man in the composing room turned and said kindly, "Have a good time, Junior, and be careful."

"If you want to drive my Jag while I'm gone, the keys are on my desk."

"Thanks, Son, but I don't think I'll need it. The garage said my car should be ready by five o'clock. Be careful, now."

"Okay, Dad, and you take care!"

A look of warmth and mutual appreciation passed between the two, and Qwilleran momentarily regretted that he had never had a son. He would have wanted one exactly like Junior. But perhaps a little taller and a little huskier.

Junior grabbed a sack of newspapers and his duffel bag, and the two men drove to the airport. Together they were a study in generation gap: Qwilleran a sober-faced man with graying hair, luxuriant moustache, and mournful eyes; Junior a fresh-faced excited kid in running shoes. Junior opened the conversation with an abrupt question:

"Do you think I look too young, Qwill?"

"Too young for what?"

"I mean, Jody thinks no one will ever take me seriously."

"With your build and your youthful face, you'll still look like fourteen when you're seventy-five," Qwilleran told him, "and that's not all bad. After that, you'll change overnight and suddenly look like a hundred and two."

"Jody thinks it would help if I grew a beard."

"Not a bad idea! Your girl comes up with some good ones."

"My grandmother says I'd look like one of the Seven Dwarfs."

"Your grandmother sounds like a sweet person, Junior."

"Grandma Gage is a character! My mother's mother, you know. You must have seen her around town. She drives a Mercedes and honks the horn at every intersection."

Qwilleran showed no surprise. He had learned that longtime residents of Moose County were militant individualists.

"Have you heard from Melinda since she left Pickax?" Junior asked.

"A couple of times. They keep her pretty busy at the hospital. She'll be better off in Boston. She'll be able to specialize."

"Melinda never really wanted to be a country doctor, but she was hot to marry you, Qwill, and move into your mansion."

"Sorry, I'm not good husband material. I discovered that once before, and it wouldn't be fair to Melinda to make the same mistake again. I hope she meets a good man her own age in Boston."

"I hear you've got something going with the head librarian now."

Qwilleran huffed into his pepper-and-salt moustache. "I don't know what your picturesque expression implies, but let me state that I enjoy Mrs. Duncan's company. In this age of video-everything, it's good to meet someone who shares my interest in literature. We get together and read aloud."

"Oh, sure," said the younger man with a wide grin.

"When are you and Jody thinking of marrying?"

"On the salary Dad pays me I can't even afford an apartment of my own. I'm still living with my parents at the farmhouse, you know. Jody makes twice what I do, and she's only a dental hygienist."

"But you own a Jaguar."

"That was a graduation present from Grandma Gage. She's the only one in the family with dough anymore. I'll inherit when she goes, but it won't be soon. At eighty-two she still stands on her head every day, and she can beat me at push-ups. People in Moose County live a long time, barring accident. One of my ancestors was killed when his horse was spooked by a big flock of blackbirds. My Grandpa Gage was struck by lightning. I had an aunt and uncle that were killed when their car hit a deer. It was November—rutting season, you know—and this eight-point buck went right through the windshield. The sheriff said it looked like an amateur ax murder. Right now, according to official estimates, there are ten thousand deer in this county."

Qwilleran slowed his speed and started looking for signs of wildlife.

"It's bow-and-arrow season, and the hunters are making them nervous," Junior went on. "Early morning or dusk—that's when the deer bound across the highway."

"All ten thousand of them?" Qwilleran reduced his speed to forty-five.

"It sure is a gloomy day," Junior observed. "The sky looks heavy."

"What's the earliest the snow ever flies?"

"Earliest storm on record was November 2, 1919, but the Big One usually doesn't hit until midmonth. The *worst* on record was November 13, 1931. Three low-pressure fronts—from Alaska, the Rockies, and the Gulf—slammed into each other over Moose County. Lots of people lost their way in the whiteout and froze to death. When the Big One hits, you better stay indoors! Of if you're caught driving, don't get out of the car."

Despite the hazards of the north country, Qwilleran was beginning to envy the natives. They had roots! Families like the Goodwinters went back five generations—to the time when fortunes were being made in mining and lumbering. The most vital organizations in Pickax were the Historical Society and the Genealogical Club. On the Airport Road, history was unreeling: abandoned shaft houses and slag heaps at the old mine sites . . . ghost towns identifiable only by a few lonely stone chimneys . . . a crumbling railroad depot in the middle of nowhere . . . the stark remains of trees blackened by forest fires.

After a few minutes of silence Qwilleran ventured to ask Junior a personal question. "As a graduate of J-school, *cum laude,* how do you feel about the *Picayune?* Are you living up to your potential? Do you think it's right to hang back in the nineteenth century?'

"Are you kidding? My ambition is to make the *Pic* into a real newspaper," Junior said, "but Dad wants to keep it like it was a hundred years ago. He was counting on us kids to keep up the tradition, but my brother went out to California and got into advertising, and my sister married a rancher in Montana, so I'm stuck with it."

"The county could support a real newspaper. Why not start one and let your father keep the *Picayune* as a hobby? You wouldn't be competing; the *Pic* is in a class by itself. Did you ever consider anything like that?"

Junior threw him a look of panic, and the words tumbled out. "I couldn't afford to start a lemonade stand! We're broke! That's why I'm working for peanuts. . . . Every year we go further in the hole. Dad's been selling our farmland, and now he's mortgaged the farmhouse. . . . I shouldn't be telling you this. . . . Mother's been after him for a long time to unload the paper. . . . She's really upset! But Dad won't listen. He keeps right on setting type and going deeper in the red. He says it's his life—his reason for living. . . . Did you ever see him set type? He can set more than thirty-five letters a minute without looking at the typecase." Junior's face reflected his admiration.

"Yes, I've watched him, and I'm impressed," Qwilleran said. "I've also seen your presses in the basement. Some of the equipments looks like Gutenberg's winepress."

"Dad collects old presses. He has a whole barnful. My great-grandfather's first press operated with a treadle like an old sewing machine."

"Would your rich grandmother come to the rescue financially, if you wanted to start a newspaper?"

"Grandma Gage won't fork over any more dough. She's already bailed us out a couple of times and paid our insurance premiums and put three of us through college. . . . Hey, why don't you start a newspaper, Qwill? You're loaded!"

"I have absolutely no interest in or aptitude for business matters, Junior. That's why I set up the Klingenschoen Memorial Fund. They handle everything and give me a little pocket money. I spent twenty-five years on newspapers, and now all I want is the time and the quietude to do some writing."

"How's your book coming?"

"Okay," said Qwilleran, thinking of his neglected typewriter and cluttered desk and disorganized notes.

At the airport they parked in the open field that served as long-term parking lot. The terminal was little more than a shack, and the airport manager—who was also ticket agent, mechanic, and part-time pilot—was sweeping the floor. "Are we gonna get the Big One?" he asked cheerfully.

When the two newsmen boarded the twin-engine plane for the first leg of their journey, they were smart enough to avoid personal conversation. There were fifteen other passengers, and thirty ears would be listening. Moose County had a grapevine that disseminated more news than the *Picayune* and transmitted it faster than WPKX. Judiciously, Qwilleran and Junior talked about sports until the small plane bumped to a landing in Minneapolis and they boarded a jet.

"I hope they serve lunch on board," Junior said. "What are we having for dinner at the Press Club?"

"I've ordered French onion soup, prime rib, and apple pie."

"Oh, wow!"

There was a layover in Chicago before they took off on the final leg of the journey. By the time they landed and rode the coach to the Hotel Stilton and tuned in the weather reports, it was time to go to the Press Club.

"Will the sportswriters be there?" Junior asked.

"Everyone—from the top executives to the newest cowboy. I suppose they're called copy-facilitators now."

"Will they think it's corny if I ask for autographs?"

"They'll be flattered," Qwilleran said.

At the club Qwilleran was treated as a returning hero, but he reminded himself that anyone would be a hero if he staked the entire staff to dinner and an open bar. A photographer gave him a chummy poke in the ribs and asked how it felt to be a millionaire.

"I'll let you know next year, on April fifteenth," Qwilleran replied.

The travel editor wanted to know how he enjoyed living in the outback. "Isn't Moose County in the Snow Belt?"

"Absolutely! It's the buckle of the Snow Belt."

"Well, anyway, you lucky dog, you've escaped the violence of the city."

"We have plenty of violence up north," Qwilleran informed him. "Tornadoes, lightning, hurricanes, forest fires, wild animals, falling trees, spring floods! But nature's violence is easier to accept than human violence. We never have any mad snipers picking off kids on the school bus, like the incident here last week."

"Do you still have the cat that's smarter than you are?"

Around the Press Club, Qwilleran had a reputation as an amateur detective; it was also known that Koko was somewhat responsible for his success.

Qwilleran explained to Junior, "Maybe you didn't notice, but Koko's picture is hanging in the lobby, along with the Pulitzer Prize winners. Someday I'll tell you about his exploits. You won't believe it, but I'll tell you anyway."

During the happy hour Junior met the columnists and reporters whose copy he read in the outstate edition of the *Fluxion,* and he could hardly control his excitement. The guest of honor, on the other hand, was noticeably subdued. Arch Riker was glad to cut loose from the *Fluxion,* but the occasion was saddened by the recent breakup of his marriage.

"What are your plans?" Qwilleran asked.

"Well, I'll spend Thanksgiving with my son in Denver and Christmas with my daughter in Oregon. After that, I don't know."

After the prime rib and apple pie, the executive editor presented Riker with a gold watch, and Qwilleran paid a tribute to his longtime friend. He concluded with a few words about Moose County.

"Ladies and gentlemen, most of you have never heard of Moose County. It's the only underground county in the state. Cartographers sometimes forget to put it on the map. Many of our legislators think it belongs to Canada. Yet, a hundred years ago Moose County was the richest in the state, thanks to mining and lumbering. Today it's a vacation paradise for anyone interested in fishing, hunting, boating, and camping. We have two unique features I'd like to point out: perfect temperatures from May to October, and a newspaper that hasn't changed since it was founded over a century ago. Junior Goodwinter, the youngest managing editor in captivity, writes all the copy himself. In an age of satellite communication it's not easy to write with a goose quill and cuttlefish ink. . . . May I introduce Junior and the *Pickax Picayune!*"

Junior snatched his baseball cap and sack of papers and dashed about the dining room shouting, "Wuxtree! Wuxtree!" while throwing a clutch of papers on each table. The guests grabbed them and started to read—first with chuckles, then with guffaws. One page 1, in column 1, they found the classified ads:

> *FOR SALE:* Used two-by-fours in good shape. Also a size 14 wedding dress, never been worn.
>
> *HURRY!* If your old clunker won't make it through another winter, maybe you'll find a better clunker at Hackpole's Used Car Lot, or maybe you won't. Can't tell till you look 'em over.
>
> *FREE:* Three gray kittens, one with white boots. Almost housebroke.
>
> *JUST ARRIVED:* New shipment of long johns at Bill's Family Store. Quality ain't what it used to be, and prices are up from last year, but what the heck! Better buy before snow flies.

Sharing the front page with these examples of truth-in-advertising were news items with headlines an eighth of an inch high.

> RECORD NEARLY BROKEN
> There were 75 cars in Captain Fugtree's funeral procession last week—longest since 1904, when 52 buggies and 37 carriages paraded to the cemetery to bury Ephraim Goodwinter.
>
> BRIDAL SHOWER GIVEN
> Miss Doreen Mayfus was honored at a shower last Thursday. Games were played and prizes awarded. The bride-to-be opened 24 presents. Refreshments included sausage rolls, pimiento sandwiches, and wimpy-diddles.
>
> ANNIVERSARY CELEBRATED
> Mr. and Mrs. Alfred Toodle celebrated their 70th wedding anniversary at a dinner given by seven of their 11 children: Richard Toodle, Emil Toodle, Joseph Toodle, Conrad Toodle, Donna Toodle, Dorothy (Toodle) Fugtree, and Estelle (Toodle) Campbell. Also present were 30 grandchildren, 82 great-grandchildren, and 13 great-great-grandchildren. The dinner

was held at the Toodle Family Restaurant. The sheet cake was decorated by Betsy Ann Toodle.

During the uproar (everyone was reading aloud) the Press Club manager sidled up to the head table and whispered in the host's ear. "Long distance for you, Qwill. In my office."

Before hurrying to the phone, Qwilleran shouted, "Thanks for coming, everyone! The bar's open!"

He was absent from the dining room long enough to make a few phone calls of his own, and when he returned he dragged Junior away from a group of editors and reporters.

"We've gotta get out, Junior. We're going home. I've changed our reservations. . . . Arch, tell everyone goodbye for us, will you? It's an emergency. . . . Come on, Junior."

"What? . . . What?" Junior spluttered.

"Tell you later."

"My sack—"

"Forget your sack."

Qwilleran hustled the young man down the steps of the club and pushed him into the cab that waited at the curb with motor running.

"Hotel Stilton on the double," he yelled to the driver as the cab shot forward, "and run the red lights."

"Oh, wow!" Junior said.

"How fast can you throw your things in your duffel, kid? We've got seven minutes to pack, check out, and get up to the heliport on the hotel roof."

Not until they had piled into the police helicopter did Qwilleran take time to explain. "Urgent phone call from Pickax," he shouted. "The Big One is moving in. Gotta beat it—personal emergency. Get ready to run. They're holding the plane."

When they finally buckled up on the jet, Junior said, "Hey, how did you swing that deal? I've never been on a chopper."

"It helps if you've worked at the *Fluxion,*" Qwilleran explained, "and if you've cooperated with Homicide and plugged the Police Widows' Fund. Sorry to spoil the rest of our plans."

"That's okay. I don't mind missing the other stuff."

"We can make a fast connection in Chicago and then catch the TGIF commuter out of Minneapolis. We're lucky it worked out that way."

For the rest of the flight Qwilleran was reluctant to talk, but Junior couldn't stop. "Everybody was great! The sportswriters said they'd get me into the press box any time I'm in town. . . . The guy that runs the "Newsroom Mouse" column is going to write up the *Picayune* on Tuesday, and that's syndicated all over the country, you know. How about that? . . . Mr. Bates said I could have a job any time I want to leave Pickax."

Qwilleran reserved comment. He was familiar with the managing editor's promises; the man had a short memory.

Junior chattered on. "They hire a lot of women at the *Fluxion,* don't they? On the desk, general assignment, heads of departments, photographers. Do you know that redheaded photographer—the one with green stockings?"

Qwilleran shook his head. "She's new since I left the paper."

"She's a photojournalist, and she free-lances for national magazines. She might come up to Moose County next spring and do a picture story on the abandoned mines. Not bad!"

"Not bad," Qwilleran echoed quietly.

He was still abnormally quiet when they boarded the tiny commuter after midnight. He occupied the window seat, and when he turned to listen to Junior he could see a man sitting across the aisle, holding an open magazine. The passenger stared at the same page throughout the flight.

He isn't reading, Qwilleran thought. He's listening. And

he doesn't belong up here. No one in Moose County has that buttoned-down cool.

At the airport terminal the stranger went to the counter to rent a car.

"Junior," Qwilleran muttered, "who's the guy in the black raincoat?"

"Never saw him before," Junior said. "Looks like a traveling salesman."

The man was no traveling salesman, Qwilleran told himself. There was something about his walk, his manner, the way he appraised his surroundings . . .

As they drove back to Pickax in the early hours of the morning, Junior finally showed signs of running out of exuberance, and he noticed Qwilleran's preoccupied silence. "Anything wrong at your house, Qwill? You said it was an emergency."

"It's an emergency, but not at my house. Your mother called my housekeeper, and Mrs. Cobb phoned the Press Club. You're needed at home in a hurry. There's no storm moving in; I lied to you about that." Qwilleran made a right turn at the traffic light.

"Hey! Where are you going? Aren't you dropping me at the farm?"

"We're going to the hospital. There's been an accident. A car accident."

"*My dad?*" Junior shouted. "How serious?"

"Very bad. Your mother's waiting for you at the hospital. I don't know how to say this, Junior, but I've got to tell you. Your dad was killed instantly. It was on the bridge—the old plank bridge."

They pulled up at the side door of the hospital. Junior jumped out of the car without a word and bolted into the building.

TWO

MONDAY, NOVEMBER ELEVENTH. "Heavy cloud cover throughout the county, with promise of snow before nightfall. Present temperature in Pickax, twenty-two degrees, with a windchill factor of ten below."—So said the WPKX meteorologist.

On Monday morning the schools, stores, offices, and restaurants of Pickax were closed until noon—for the funeral. The day was cold, gray, damp, and miserable. Yet, crowds milled about the Old Stone Church on Park Circle. Other onlookers huddled in the little circular park—shivering, stamping feet, swinging arms, clapping mittened hands together, anything to keep warm, and that included a furtive swig from a half-pint bottle in desperate cases. They were expecting to see a record broken: the longest funeral procession since 1904.

Police cars blockaded downtown Main Street to facilitate the formation of the procession. Cars bearing purple flags on the fender were lined up four abreast from curb to curb.

Qwilleran, moving through the crowd in the park, watched faces and listened to the low, respectful hum of voices. Small boys who climbed on the fountain for a better view were shooed away by a police officer and admonished if they shrieked or raced through the crowd.

Gathered inside the church were the numerous branches of the Goodwinter clan, as well as city officials, members of the Chamber of Commerce, and the country club set. Outside the church were the readers of the *Picayune:* businessmen, housewives, farmers, retirees, waitresses, laborers, hunters. They were witnessing an event they would remember all their lives and describe to future generations, just as their grandparents had described the funeral of Ephraim Goodwinter.

Among them was one man who was obviously foreign to the scene. He wandered through the crowd, glancing alertly in all directions, studying faces. He was wearing a black raincoat, and Qwilleran hoped it had a heavy lining; the cold was bone chilling.

A hunter in orange-and-black camouflage was mumbling to a man who wore a feed cap and had a cheek full of snuff. "Gonna be a long one. Longer than Captain Fugtree's, looks like."

The farmer shifted his chew. "Near a hundred, I reckon. The captain had seventy-five, they said in the paper."

"Lucky they could bury him before snow flies. There's a Big One headed this way, they said on radio."

"Can't believe nothin' they say on radio. That storm from Canada blowed itself out afore it got anywheres near the border."

"Where'd it happen?" the hunter asked. "The accident, I mean."

"Old plank bride. It's a bugger! We been after the county to get off their duff and widen the danged thing. They say he rammed the stone rail, flipped head over tail, landed on the rocks in the river. Car caught fire. It's a closed casket, I hear."

"They should sue somebody."

"Prob'ly goin' too fast. Mebbe hit a deer."

"Or coulda been he was on a Friday night toot," the hunter said with a sly grin.

"Not him! *She's* the one that's the barfly. With him it was never nothin' but work work work. Fell asleep at the wheel, betcha. Whole family's jinxed. Y'know what happened to his old man."

"Yeah, but he prob'ly deserved it, from what I hear."

"And then there was his uncle. Somethin' fishy about *that* story!"

"And his grandfather. They never got the lowdown on what happened to him. What'll they do with the paper now?"

"The kid'll take over," the farmer said. "Fourth generation. No tellin' what he'll take it into his head to do. These young ones go away to school and get some loony ideas."

Voices hushed as the bell began to toll a single solemn note and the casket was carried from the church, followed by the bereaved family. The heavily veiled widow was accompanied by her elder son. Junior walked with his sister from Montana. On the sidewalk and in the park the townspeople crossed themselves and men removed their headgear. There was a long wait as the mourners moved silently to their cars, directed by young men in black car coats and ambassador hats of black fur. At a signal, men in uniform fell into rank and hoisted brass instruments. Then, with the Pickax Funeral Band playing a doleful march, the long line of cars started to move forward.

Qwilleran pulled down the earflaps of his winter hat, turned up his coat collar, and headed across the park to the place he now called home.

The Klingenschoen residence that Qwilleran had inherited was one of five important buildings on the Park Circle, where Main Street divided and circumvented a little grassy plot with stone benches and a stone fountain. On one side of the circle were the Old Stone Church, the Little Stone Church, and a venerable courthouse. Facing them across the park were the public library and the K mansion, as Pickax natives called it. A massive cube of fieldstone three stories high, the mansion occupied its spacious grounds with the regal assurance that it was the most impressive edifice in town, and the costliest.

For a man who had chosen to spend his adult life in apartments and hotels, always on the move like a gypsy, the palatial residence was a discomfort, an embarrassment. Eventually Qwilleran would deed it to the city as a museum, but for five years he was doomed to live with the Klingenschoen brand of conspicuous consumption: vast rooms with fourteen-foot ceilings and ornate woodwork; crystal chandeliers by the ton and Oriental rugs by the acre; priceless French and English antiques, and art objects worth millions.

Qwilleran solved his problem by moving into the old servants' quarters above the garage, while the housekeeper occupied a sumptuous French suite in the main house.

Housekeeper was a misnomer for Iris Cobb. A former antique dealer and appraiser from Down Below, she now functioned as house manager, registrar of the collection, and curator of an architectural masterpiece destined to become a museum. She was also an obsessive cook who liked to putter about the kitchen—a dumpy figure in a faded pink smock. Despite her career credentials the widowed Mrs. Cobb baked endless cookies and pies with which to please the opposite sex, and she was inclined to gaze at men worshipfully through her thick-lensed eyeglasses.

Mrs. Cobb had a hearty oyster stew waiting for Qwilleran when he returned from the funeral. "I looked out the window and saw all the cars," she said. "The procession must be half a mile long!"

"Longest in Pickax history," Qwilleran said. "It's not only the funeral of a man; it may turn out to be the funeral of a century-old newspaper."

"Did you see the widow? She must be taking it terribly hard." Mrs. Cobb related emotionally to any woman who lost a husband, having experienced two such tragedies herself.

"Mrs. Goodwinter's three grown children were with her—also an older woman, probably Junior's Grandma Gage. She was tiny, but as straight as a brigadier general. . . . Any phone calls while I was out, Mrs. Cobb?"

"No, but a busboy from the Old Stone Mill brought over some pork liver cupcakes. It's a new idea, and the chef would like your opinion. I put them in the freezer."

Qwilleran grunted in disgust. "I'll give that clown an opinion—fast! I wouldn't touch a pork liver cupcake if he paid me!"

"Oh, they're not people food, Mr. Q! They're for the cats. The chef is experimenting with a line of frozen gourmet dinners for pets."

"Well, take a couple out of the freezer, and the spoiled brats can have them for supper. By the way, have you noticed any books on the floor in the library? Koko is pushing them off the shelf, and I don't approve of his new hobby."

"I tidied up this morning and didn't notice anything."

"He's particularly attracted to those small volumes of Shakespeare in pigskin bindings. Yesterday I found *Hamlet* on the floor."

Behind Mrs. Cobb's thick lenses there was a mischievous twinkle. "Do you think he knows I've got a baked ham in the fridge?"

"He has devious ways of communicating, Mrs. Cobb, but that would be a new low," Qwilleran said. "What is today? Monday? I suppose you're going out tonight. If so, I'll feed the cats."

The housekeeper's face brightened. "Herb Hackpole is taking me out to dinner—somewhere special, he said. I hope it's the Old Stone Mill. They say the food's wonderful since the new chef took over."

Qwilleran huffed into his moustache, a private sign of disapproval. "It's about time that skinflint took you out to dinner! It seems to me you always go over to his place and cook for him."

"But I like to!" Mrs. Cobb said, with her eyes shining.

Hackpole was a used-car dealer with a reputation for being obnoxious, but she found him attractive. The man had red devils tattooed on his arms and wore his thinning hair in a crew cut, and he often neglected to shave, but she liked men in the rough. Qwilleran recalled that her late husband had been an uncouth lout and she loved him deeply. Now, since starting to date Hackpole, her round cheerful face had become positively radiant.

"If you want to have someone in for dinner," Mrs. Cobb said, "you can serve the baked ham, and I'll make the ginger-pear salad you like, and I'll put a sweet potato casserole in the oven. All you have to do is take it out when the bell rings." She was acquainted with Qwilleran's helplessness in the kitchen.

"That's very thoughtful of you," he said. "I might invite Mrs. Duncan."

"Oh, that would be nice!" The housekeeper's expression was conspiratorial, as if she sensed a romance. "I'll set the marquetry table in the library with a Madeira cloth and candles and everything. It will be nice and cozy for two. Mr. O'Dell can lay a fire with those applewood logs. They smell so good!"

"Don't make it too obviously seductive," Qwilleran requested. "The lady is rather proper."

"She's a lovely person, Mr. Q, and just the right age for

you, if you don't mind me saying so. She has a lot of personality for a librarian."

"It's a new trend," he said. "Libraries now have fewer books but a lot of audiovisuals . . . and champagne parties . . . and personality all over the place."

After lunch Qwilleran walked around the Park Circle to the public library, which masqueraded as a Greek temple. It had been built by the founder of the *Picayune* at the turn of the century, and a portrait of Ephraim Goodwinter hung in the lobby, although it was partly obscured by a display of new video materials and there was a slash in the canvas that had been poorly repaired.

The after-school crowd had not yet swarmed into the library with homework assignments, so four friendly young clerks rushed to Qwilleran's assistance. Young women were always attracted to the man with a luxuriant moustache and mournful eyes. Furthermore, he served on the library's board of trustees. Furthermore, he was the richest man in town.

He asked the clerks a simple question, and they all dashed away at once in several directions—one to the card catalogue, one to the local-history shelf, and two to the computer. The answer from all sources was negative. He thanked them and headed for the chief librarian's office on the balcony.

Carrying his lumberjack mackinaw and woodsman's hat, Qwilleran bounded up the stairs three at a time, thinking pleasant thoughts. Polly Duncan was a charming though enigmatic woman, and she had a speaking voice that he found both soothing and stimulating.

She looked up from her desk and gave him a cordial but businesslike smile. "What a pleasant surprise, Qwill! What urgent mission brings you up here in such a hurry?"

"I came chiefly to hear your mellifluous voice," he said,

turning on a little charm himself. And then he quoted one of his favorite lines from Shakespeare. *"Her voice was ever soft, gentle and low—an excellent thing in woman."*

"That's from *King Lear,* act five, scene three," she replied promptly.

"Polly, your memory is incredible!" he said. *"I am amazed and know not what to say."*

"That's Hermia's line in act three, scene two, of *A Midsummer Night's Dream.* . . . Don't look so surprised, Qwill. I told you my father was a Shakespeare scholar. We children knew the plays as well as our peers knew the big-league batting averages. . . . Did you go to the funeral this morning?"

"I observed from the park, and it gave me an idea. According to the phalanx of eager assistants downstairs, no one has ever written a history of the *Picayune.* I'd like to try it. How much is there to work with?"

"Let me think. . . . You could start with the Goodwinters in our genealogical collection."

"Do you have back copies of the newspaper?"

"Only for the last twenty years. Prior to that, everything was destroyed by mice or burst steam pipes or mismanagement. But I'm sure the *Picayune* office has a complete file."

"Is there anyone I could interview? Anyone who would remember back sixty or seventy-five years?"

"You might check with the Old Timers Club. They're all over eighty. Euphonia Gage is the president."

"Is that the woman who drives a Mercedes and blows the horn a lot?"

"A succinct description! Senior Goodwinter was her son-in-law, and since she has a reputation for brutal candor, she might supply some choice information."

"Polly, you're a gem! By the way, are you free for dinner tonight? Mrs. Cobb is preparing a repast that's too good for a lonely bachelor. I thought you might consent to share it."

"Delighted! I must not stay too late, but I hope there will be time for reading aloud after dinner. You have a marvelous voice, Qwill."

"Thank you." He preened his moustache with pleasure. "I'll go home and gargle."

Turning to leave, he glanced across the balcony to the reading room. "Who's that man over there—with a pile of books on the table?"

"A historian from Down Below, doing research on early mining operations. He asked if I could recommend any good restaurants, and I suggested Stephanie's and the Old Stone Mill. Do you have any other ideas?"

"I think I do," said Qwilleran. He clapped his hat on his head at a wild angle and clomped around the balcony in his yellow duck boots, stopping at the table where the stranger was seated.

In a parody of a friendly north-country native he said, "Howdy! Lady over yonder says yer lookin' fer a place to chow down. Fer a real good feed y'oughta try Otto's Tasty Eats. All y'can eat fer fi' bucks. How long y'gonna be aroun'?"

"Until I finish my work," the historian said crisply, bending over his book.

"If y'wanna shot-na-beer y'oughta try the Hotel Booze. Good burgers, too."

"Thank you," the man said in a tone of dismissal.

"I see y'be readin' 'bout them ol' mines. M'grampaw got killed in a cave-in back in 1913. I weren't born yit. Seen any ol' mines?"

"No," the man said, snapping his book shut and pushing his chair back.

"Nearest hereabouts be the Dimsdale. They got a diner there. Good place t'git a plate o' beans 'n' franks."

Clutching his black raincoat, the stranger walked rapidly to the stairway.

Pleased with the man's exasperation and his own performance, Qwilleran straightened his hat, bundled up his mackinaw, and went on his way. He knew by the man's obvious lack of interest that he was not what he claimed to be.

At 5:30 Herb Hackpole arrived to pick up his dinner partner, parking in the side drive and tooting the horn. Mrs. Cobb scurried out the back door as excited as a young girl on her first date.

At 5:45 Qwilleran fed the cats. Pork liver cupcakes, when thawed, became a revolting gray mush, but the Siamese crouched over the plate and devoured the chef's innovation with tails flat on the floor, denoting total satisfaction.

At 6:00 Polly Duncan arrived—on foot—having left her small six-year-old maroon car behind the library. If it were seen in the circular driveway of the K mansion, the gossips of Pickax would have a field day. Everyone knew what everyone else drove—make, model, year, and color.

Polly was not as young and slender as the career women he had dated Down Below, but she was an interesting woman with a voice that sometimes made his head spin, and she looked like a comfortable armful, although he had not tested his theory. The librarian maintained a certain reserve, despite her show of friendliness, and she always insisted on going home early.

He greeted her at the front door, a masterpiece of carving and polished brass. "Where's the snow they promised?" he asked.

"Every day in November WPKX predicts snow as a matter of policy," she said, "and sooner or later they're right. . . . This house never fails to overwhelm me!"

She was gazing in wonder at the foyer's amber leather walls and grand staircase, extravagantly wide and elaborately balustered. The dazzling chandelier was Baccarat crystal. The rugs were Anatolian antiques. "This house doesn't belong in Pickax; it belongs in Paris. It amazes me that the Klingenschoens owned such treasures and no one knew about it."

"It was the Klingenschoens' revenge—for not being accepted socially." Qwilleran escorted her to the rear of the house. "We're having dinner in the library, but Mrs. Cobb wants me to show you her mobile herb garden in the solarium."

The stone-floored room had large glass areas, a forest of ancient rubber plants, and some wicker chairs for summer lounging; the winter addition was a wrought-iron cart with eight clay pots labeled mint, dill, thyme, basil, and the like.

"It can be wheeled around during the day to get the best sunlight," he explained. "That is—if WPKX allows us to have any."

Polly nodded approval. "Herbs like sun but not too much heat. Where did Mrs. Cobb find this clever contraption?"

"She designed it, and a friend of hers made it in his welding shop. Perhaps you know Hackpole, the used-car dealer."

"Yes, his garage has just winterized my car. How do you like your new front-wheel drive, Qwill?"

"I'll know better when snow flies."

In the library the lamps were lighted, logs were blazing in the fireplace, and the table was laid with a dazzling display of porcelain, crystal, and silver. The four walls of books were accented by marble busts of Homer, Dante, and Shakespeare.

"Did the Klingenschoens read these books?" Polly asked.

"I think they were primarily for show, except for a few racy novels from the 1920s. In the attic I found boxes of paperback mysteries and romances."

"At least someone was *reading*. There is still hope for the printed word." She handed him a book with worn and faded cover. "Here's something that might interest you—

Picturesque Pickax, published by the Boosters Club before World War One. On the page with the bookmark there's a picture of the *Picayune* building with employees standing on the sidewalk."

Qwilleran found the photo of anxious-faced men with walrus moustaches, high collars, leather aprons, eyeshades, arm garters, and plastered hair parted in the middle. "They look as if they're facing a firing squad," he said. "Thanks. This will be useful."

He poured an aperitif for his guest. Dry sherry was her choice; one glass was her limit. For himself he poured white grape juice.

"*Votre santé!*" he toasted, meeting her eyes.

"*Santé!*" she replied with a guarded gaze.

She was wearing the somber gray suit, white blouse, and maroon loafers that seemed to be her library uniform, but she had tried to perk it up with a paisley scarf. Fashion was not one of her pursuits, and her severe haircut was not in the latest style, but her voice. . . ! It was ever soft, gentle, and low, and she knew Shakespeare forward and backward.

After a moment of silence during which Qwilleran wondered what Polly was thinking, he said, "Do you remember that so-called historian in your reading room? He had a pile of books on old mining operations. I doubt that he's telling the truth."

"Why do you say that?"

"His relaxed posture. The way he held his book. He didn't show a researcher's avid thirst for information, and he wasn't taking notes. He was reading idly to kill time."

"Then who is he? Why should he disguise his identity?"

"I think he's an investigator. Narcotics—FBI—something like that."

Polly looked skeptical. "In Pickax?"

"I'm sure there are several skeletons in local closets,

Polly, and most of the locals know all about them. You have some world-class gossips here."

"I wouldn't call them gossips," she said defensively. "In small towns people *share information*. It's a way of *caring.*"

Qwilleran raised a cynical eyebrow. "Well, the mysterious stranger had better complete his mission before snow flies, or he'll be cluttering up your reading room until spring thaw. . . . Another question. What will happen to the *Picayune* now that Senior's gone? Any guesses?"

"It will probably die a quiet death—an idea that has outlived its time."

"How well have you known Junior's parents?"

"Only casually. Senior was a workaholic—an agreeable man, but not at all social. Gritty likes the country club life—golf, cards, dinner dances. I wanted her to serve on my board of trustees, but it was too dull for her taste."

"Gritty? Is that Mrs. Goodwinter's name?"

"Gertrude, actually, but there's a certain clique here that clings to their adolescent nicknames: Muffy, Buffy, Bunky, Dodo. I must admit that Mrs. Goodwinter has an abundance of grit, for good or ill. She's like her mother, Euphonia Gage is a spunky woman."

A distant buzzer sounded, and Qwilleran lighted the candles, dropped a Fauré cassette in the player, and served dinner.

"You obviously know everyone in Pickax," he remarked.

"For a newcomer I don't do badly. I've been here only . . . twenty-five years."

"I had a hunch you were from the East. New England?"

She nodded. "While I was in college I married a native of Pickax, and we came here to manage his family's bookstore. Unfortunately it closed soon after—when my husband was killed—but I didn't want to go back east."

"He must have been very young."

"Very young. He was a volunteer fire fighter. I remember one dry windy day in August. Our bookstore was a block from the fire hall, and when the siren sounded, my husband dashed from the store. Traffic stopped dead, and men came running from all directions—running hard, pounding the pavement, pumping their arms. The mechanic from the gas station, one of the young pastors, a bartender, the hardware man—all running as if their lives depended on it. Then cars and trucks with revolving lights pulled up and parked anywhere, and the drivers jumped out and ran to the fire hall. By that time the big doors were open, and the tanker and pumper were moving out, with men clinging to the trucks and putting on their gear."

"You describe it vividly, Polly."

Tears came to her eyes. "It was a barn fire, and he was killed by a falling timber."

There was a long silence.

"That's a sad story," Qwilleran said.

"The fire fighters were so conscientious. When the siren sounded, they dropped everything and ran. In the middle of the night they'd wake from a sound sleep, pull on some clothes, and run. Yet they were criticized: arrived too late . . . not enough men . . . didn't pump enough water . . . equipment broke down." She sighed. "They tried so hard. They still do. They're all volunteers, you know."

"Junior Goodwinter is a volunteer," Qwilleran said, "and his beeper is always sounding off in the middle of something. . . . What did you do after that windy day in August?"

"I went to work at the library and found contentment here."

"Pickax has a human scale that is—what shall I say?—comforting. Tranquilizing. But why are we all obsessed with the weather reports?"

"We're close to the elements," Polly said. "The weather affects everything: farming, lumbering, commercial fishing, outdoor sports. And we all drive long distances over country roads. There are no taxis we can call on a bad day."

Mrs. Cobb had left the coffee maker plugged in and pots of chocolate mousse in the refrigerator, and the meal ended pleasantly.

"Where are the cats?" Polly asked.

"Shut up in the kitchen. Koko has been pulling books off the shelf. He thinks he's a librarian. Yum Yum, on the other hand, is just a cat who chases her tail and steals paper clips and hides things under the rug. Every time my foot comes down on a bump in the rug, I wince. Is it my wristwatch? Or a mouse? Or my reading glasses? Or a crumpled envelope from the wastebasket?"

"What titles has Koko recommended?"

"He's on a Shakespeare kick," Qwilleran said. "It may have something to do with the pigskin bindings. Just before you arrived, he pushed *A Midsummer Night's Dream* off the shelf."

"That's a coincidence," Polly said. "I'm named after one of the characters." She paused and waited for him to guess.

"Hippolyta?"

"Correct! My father named all of us after characters in the plays. My brothers are Marc Antony and Brutus, and my poor sister Ophelia has had to endure bawdy remarks ever since the fifth grade. . . . Why don't you let the cats out? I'd like to see Koko in action."

When they were released, Yum Yum walked daintily into the library, placing one paw in front of the other and looking for a vacant lap, but Koko flaunted his independence by delaying his entrance. It was not until Qwilleran and his guest heard a *thlunk* that they realized Koko was in the room. On the floor lay the thin volume of *King Henry VIII.*

Qwilleran said, "You have to admit he knows what he's doing. There's a gripping scene for a woman in the play—where the queen confronts the two cardinals."

"It's tremendous!" Polly said. "Katherine claims to be a poor weak woman but she blasts the two learned men. '*Ye have angels' faces, but heaven knows your hearts!*' Do you ever wonder about the true identity of Shakespeare, Qwill?"

"I've read that the plays may have been written by Jonson or Oxford."

"I think Shakespeare was a woman. There are so many strong female roles and wonderful speeches for women."

"And there are strong male roles and wonderful speeches for men," he replied.

"Yes, but I contend that a woman can write strong male roles more successfully than a man can write good women's roles."

"Hmmm," said Qwilleran politely.

Koko was now sitting tall on the desk, obviously waiting for something, and Qwilleran obliged by reading the prologue of the play. Then Polly gave a stirring reading of the queen's confrontation scene.

"Yow!" said Koko.

"Now I must go," she said, "before my landlord starts to worry."

"Your landlord?"

"Mr. MacGregor is a nice old widower," she explained. "I rent a cottage on his farm, and he thinks women shouldn't go out alone at night. He sits up waiting for me to drive in."

"Have you ever tried your Shakespeare theory on your landlord?" Qwilleran asked.

After Polly had said a gracious thank-you and a brisk good-night, Qwilleran questioned her excuse for leaving early. At least Koko had not ordered her out of the house, as he had done other female visitors in the past. That was a good sign.

Qwilleran was removing the dinner dishes and tidying the kitchen when Mrs. Cobb returned from her date, flushed and happy.

"Oh, you don't need to do that, Mr. Q," she said.

"No trouble at all. Thank you for a superb meal. How was your evening?"

"We went to the Old Stone Mill. The food is much better now. I had a gorgeous stuffed trout with wine sauce. Herb ordered steak Diane, but he didn't like the sauce."

That guy, Qwilleran thought, would prefer ketchup. To Mrs. Cobb he said, "Mrs. Duncan was telling me about the volunteer fire department. Isn't Hackpole a fireman?"

"Yes, and he's had some thrilling experiences—carrying children from a burning building, reviving people with CPR, herding cows from a burning barn!"

Interesting if true, Qwilleran thought. "Bring him in for a nightcap next time you go out," he suggested. "I'd like to know how a small-town fire department operates."

"Oh, thank you, Mr. Q! He'll be pleased. He thinks you don't like him, because you took him to court once."

"Nothing personal. I simply objected to being attacked by a dog that should be chained according to law. If you like him, Mrs. Cobb, I'm sure he's a good man."

As Qwilleran was locking up for the night, the telephone rang. It was Junior Goodwinter's voice, crackling with excitement. "She's coming! She's flying up here tomorrow!"

"Who's coming?"

"The photojournalist I met at the Press Club. She says the *Fluxion* is running the column tomorrow, and it'll be all over the country this week. She wants to submit a picture story to a news magazine while it's hot."

"Did you tell her . . . about your father?"

"She says that will only make it topical. I have to pick her up at the airport tomorrow morning. We're going to get some Old Timers who used to work at the *Pic* to pose in the shots. Do you realize what this could do? It'll put Pickax on the map! And it could put the *Picayune* back in business if we start getting subscriptions from all over."

Stranger things have happened, Qwilleran thought. "Call me tomorrow night after the shoot. Let me know how it goes. And good luck!"

As he replaced the telephone receiver he heard a soft sound, *thlunk,* as another book landed on the Bokhara rug. Koko was sitting on the Shakespeare shelf, looking proud of himself.

Qwilleran picked up the book and smoothed the crumpled pages. It was *Hamlet* again, and a line in the first scene caught his eye: " *'Tis now struck twelve; get thee to bed.*"

Addressing the cat he said, "You may think you're smart, but this has got to stop! These books are printed on fine India paper. They can't stand this kind of treatment."

"Ik ik ik," said Koko, following his remark with a yawn.

THREE

Tuesday, November twelfth. "Snow flurries during the day, then falling temperatures and winds shifting to northeast." So said WPKX, and Mr. O'Dell, the houseman, waxed his snow shovels and checked the spark plugs on his snowblower.

It was the day after the pork liver cupcakes had made their successful debut, and Qwilleran planned to lunch at the Old Stone Mill—to report results to the chef, and to solve a mystery that had been bothering him.

Who was this chef?

What was his name?

Where did he come from?

What were his credentials?

And why had no one seen him?

The restaurant was an old gristmill with a giant waterwheel, recently renovated with good taste. The stone walls and massive timbers were exposed; the maple floor was sanded to the color of honey; and every table had a view of the mill wheel, which creaked and turned incessantly although the millstream had dried up seventy years before. The food, everyone had always said, was abominable.

Then the restaurant was purchased by XYZ Enterprises,

Inc., of Pickax, developers of the Indian Village apartments and condominiums on the Ittibittiwassee River. The firm also owned a string of party stores in the county and a new motel in Mooseville.

One day at a Chamber of Commerce meeting Qwilleran was approached by Don Exbridge, the X of XYZ Enterprises. He was a string bean of a man, six-feet-five, with a smile that had made him popular and successful.

"Qwill, you have restaurant connections Down Below," said Exbridge. "Where can we get a good chef for the Old Stone Mill? Preferably someone who enjoys the outdoors and doesn't mind living in the boonies."

"I'll give it some thought and get back to you," Qwilleran had promised.

Then the wheels started turning in his mind: Hixie Rice, former neighbor Down Below . . . member of a select gourmet group . . . loved to eat, and her figure proved it . . . clever young woman . . . unlucky in love . . . worked in advertising and promotion . . . used to speak French to Koko. Why, Qwilleran wondered, were all the clever ones in advertising while all the hardworking serious thinkers were in journalism, earning less money?

The last time he had heard from Hixie, she was dating a chef and was taking courses in restaurant management. And that was how Hixie Rice and her chef happened to land in Pickax. Immediately they replaced the dreary menu with more sophisticated dishes and fresh ingredients. The chef retrained the existing kitchen staff, locked up the deep fryers, and rationed the salt.

When Qwilleran went to lunch at the Old Stone Mill on Tuesday, he hardly recognized the former member of the Friendly Fatties. "Hixie, you're looking almost anorexic!" he said. "Have you stopped putting butter on your bacon and sugar on your hot fudge sundae?"

"You won't believe it, Qwill, but the restaurant business has cured my obsession for eating," she said. "All that *food* turns me off. Fifteen pounds of butter . . . a two-foot wheel of cheese . . . two hundred chickens . . . thirty dozen eggs! Have you ever seen two hundred *naked chickens,* Qwill?"

In losing weight, Hixie had also lost her wheezy high-pitched voice, and her hair now looked healthy and natural instead of contrived and varnished. "You're looking great!" he told her.

"And you look *super,* Qwill. Your voice sounds different."

"I've stopped smoking. Rosemary convinced me to give up my pipe."

"Do you still see Rosemary?"

"No, she's living in Toronto."

"All our old gourmet gang is scattered, but I thought you two were headed for holy bondage."

"There was a personality clash between Rosemary and Koko," he explained.

Hixie seated him near the turning mill wheel. "This is considered a choice table," she said, "although the motion of the wheel makes some of our customers seasick. It's the *creaking* that drives me up the wall, and the tape recording of a rushing millstream has a psychological effect on diners. They're wearing out the carpet to the rest room." She handed him a menu. "The lamb shank with ratatouille is good today."

"How about the fresh salmon?"

"It's off the blackboard. You're a little late."

"It was premeditated," Qwilleran said. "I'd like to talk with you. Can you join me?"

He ordered the lamb, and Hixie sat down with a glass of Campari and a cigarette. "How did Koko and Yum Yum like the cupcakes?" she asked.

"After they ate the things they chased each other up and down stairs for two hours, and they're both neutered! Have you discovered a feline aphrodisiac?"

"That's only the first of several frozen catfoods we want to market. The XYZ people are backing us financially. Fabulous Frozen Foods for Fussy Felines! How does that sound?"

"When are you and your partner going to come over and speak French to Koko? You haven't seen the magnificent dump I live in."

"It's difficult to socialize," she apologized. "We work such *rotten* hours. They never told me about that in restaurant school. I'm not complaining; in fact, I'm *deliriously* happy! I used to be a loser, you know, but all that has changed since I've found a wonderful man. He's not a drunk; he doesn't do drugs; and he's not some other woman's husband."

"I'm very happy for you," Qwilleran said. "When am I going to meet the guy?"

"He's not here right now."

"What's his name? What does he look like?"

"Tony Peters, and he's tall, blond, and *very* good-looking."

"Where did he learn to cook?"

"Montreal . . . Paris . . . other good places."

"I'd like to meet the guy and shake his hand. After all, I'm responsible for bringing you both to this northern paradise."

"*Actually,*" Hixie said, "he's out of town. His mother had a stroke, and he had to fly to Philadelphia."

"He'd better get back before snow flies, or he'll have to make the trip on snowshoes. The airport closes down after the Big One. Where are you living?"

"We have a *super* apartment in Indian Village. Mr.

Exbridge pulled strings to get us in. There's a waiting list, you know."

"And what do you do on your day off?"

"Tony's writing a cookbook. I check out the competition around the county."

"Have you made any interesting discoveries?"

"Next to the Old Stone Mill, Stephanie's has the best food," Hixie said, "but their chef has some kind of mental *block*. I ordered a stuffed artichoke and got a stuffed *avocado*. When the waiter insisted it was an artichoke, I grabbed my plate and stormed out to the kitchen to confront the chef, and that arrogant *clod* had the nerve to tell me I didn't know a stuffed artichoke from a stuffed crocodile! I was furious! I informed him that an artichoke is a member of the thistle family, and an avocado is a pear-shaped fruit that gets its name from the Nahuatl word for testicle, although I assume he wouldn't know anything about *that!*"

"How did he react?"

"He picked up a cleaver and started flattening chicken breasts, so I retreated before I became a homicide statistic."

Later that afternoon Qwilleran sat at his desk in the library and wondered about Hixie and her mysterious companion. Koko jumped to the desktop, sat tall, and cocked his head expectantly.

"Do you remember Hixie?" Qwilleran asked him. "She was taking French lessons and used to say, '*Bonjour, Monsieur Koko.*' She always got involved with marginal types of men, and now she has this invisible chef. There's something strange about him, and yet his kitchen is turning out great food. I brought you a chunk of lamb shank in a doggie bag. Hixie was glad you liked the cupcakes."

Koko wriggled his posterior, squeezed his eyes, and murmured a falsetto "Ik ik."

At that moment Mrs. Cobb peered inquiringly into the room.

"I heard you talking and thought you had company, Mr. Q. I was going to suggest some tea and cookies. I've just baked butterscotch pecan meringues."

"I'm only having an intelligent dialogue with Koko, as Lori Bamba recommended," he explained. "I feel like an idiot, but he seems to enjoy it. By the way, I'll accept some of those butterscotch things, but make it coffee instead of tea."

She bustled off to the kitchen, and Qwilleran went on. "Well, Koko, today was the big shoot at the *Picayune* office. For Junior's sake I hope something good comes of it. I wonder if the Old Timers held together long enough for the picture taking. They probably had to prop them up with two-by-fours and baling wire."

The day passed without the snow flurries predicted on the radio, but the temperature was dropping rapidly. Qwilleran was listening to the late-evening weathercast when Junior finally telephoned. His voice had none of the excitement of the previous day. He spoke in a minor key. Qwilleran thought, Something went wrong; the redhead failed to show; she decided it was no-story; she forgot her camera; her plane crashed; the Old Timers had heart attacks.

"Have you heard any rumors?" Junior was saying.

"About what?"

"About anything."

"I don't know what you're talking about, kid. Are you sober?"

"I wish I weren't," Junior said glumly. "Mind if I come over to see you? I know it's late . . ."

"Sure, come along."

"I'm at Jody's place. Okay if I bring her, too?"

"Of course. What do you two want to drink?"

"Make it coffee," Junior said after a moment's hesitation. "If I drink when I'm down, I'm liable to cut my wrists."

Qwilleran filled a thermal server with instant coffee and had a tray waiting in the library when the red Jaguar pulled into the drive.

Tiny Jody, with her straight blond hair and big blue eyes, looked like a china doll. Junior looked like an old man.

"Good God! What's happened to you?" Qwilleran said. "You look ghastly, Junior." He waved the young couple into the library.

Junior flopped on a leather sofa. "Bad news!"

"Didn't the shoot work out?"

"Oh sure, but a lot of good it will do. I feel like a fool, getting her to fly up here for nothing."

"You're talking in riddles, Junior. Let's have it!"

In her little-girl voice Jody said, "Tell Mr. Qwilleran about your mother, Juney."

The young newsman stared at Qwilleran for a silent moment before blurting out the news. "She's selling."

"Selling what?"

"Selling the *Picayune.*"

Qwilleran frowned. "What is there to sell? There's nothing there but a . . . well . . . a quaint idea."

"That's the worst part," Junior said. "The *idea* and all those years of tradition are going down the drain. She's selling the *name.*"

Qwilleran could neither believe nor comprehend. "Where does she expect to find a buyer?"

Jody piped up, "She's already got a buyer. XYZ Enterprises."

"They want to make it an advertising throwaway," said Junior, looking as if he might cry. "One of those free tabloids with junky ads and ink that comes off on your hands. No news matter. I tell you, Qwill, it's a kick in the gut."

"Has she a right to sell the paper? What about your father's will?"

"He left everything to her. All the assets are jointly held anyway—such as they are."

"Juney," said the small voice, "tell Mr. Qwilleran about your dream."

"Yeah, I've been dreaming about my father every night. He's just standing there in his leather apron and square paper hat, all covered with blood, and he's telling me something, but I can't hear it."

Qwilleran was trying to sort out his thoughts. "This has happened very fast, Junior. Your father was buried only yesterday. It's too quick a decision for a bereaved spouse to make. Have you suggested that to your mother?"

"What's the use? When she makes up her mind to do something, she does it."

"How do your brother and sister react?"

"My brother went back to California; he doesn't care. My sister thinks it's a crime, but she doesn't have any clout. Not with *our mother!* You've never met her."

"Was it her idea? Or did XYZ make an offer?"

Junior hesitated before answering. "Uh . . . I don't know."

"Why is she in such a hurry to sell?"

"Well, the money, you know. She needs money. Dad had a lot of debts, you know."

"Did he carry decent life insurance?"

"There's a policy, but it's not all that great. Grandma Gage has been keeping up the premiums for years, just to protect my mother and us. . . . The house is being sold, too."

"The farmhouse?"

"Isn't that sad?" Jody put in. "It's been in the Goodwinter family a hundred years."

Qwilleran said, "A widow should never make such a quick decision to change her lifestyle."

"Well, it's mortgaged, you know," Junior said, "and she never wanted a big house anyway. She likes condominiums. She wants to unload the house before snow flies—doesn't want to be stuck with a big place in the country during the winter."

"That's understandable."

"She's going into an apartment in Indian Village."

"I thought there were no vacancies out there."

Jody said, "She's moving in with a *friend,*" and Junior scowled at her.

"Can she find a buyer for the house that fast—without selling at a sacrifice?" Qwilleran asked.

"She's got a buyer."

"Who? Do you know who it is?"

"Herb Hackpole."

"Hackpole! What does a single man want with a big farmhouse like that?"

"Well, he's been wanting a place in the country, you know, so he can run his dogs. He has hunters. There's no acreage, but he'll be getting a good big yard and two barns."

"And what about the furnishings? You said your parents had a lot of family heirlooms."

"They're going to be auctioned off."

Jody said, "Juney had been promised his great-grandfather's desk, but that's going to be sold, too."

In a tone of defeat Junior said, "If they can squeeze in the auction before snow flies, they'll attract dealers from Ohio and Illinois and get the high dollar."

"And what about the antique printing presses in the barn?"

Junior shrugged. "They'll be sold for scrap metal. They figure the price by the ton."

The three of them fell into three kinds of silence: Junior,

depressed; Jody, sympathetic; Qwilleran, stunned. Senior Goodwinter had been killed Friday night and buried Monday, and this was Tuesday.

"When did you hear about these drastic decisions, Junior?"

"My mother called me at the office this afternoon—right in the middle of the shoot. I didn't say anything to the photographer. Do you think I should have told her? It might kill the story—or take the edge off it. She left an hour ago. I drove her to the airport."

Suddenly Junior's beeper sounded. "Oh no!" he said. "That's all I need! A stupid barn fire! Take Jody home, will you, Qwill?" he called over his shoulder as he raced out of the house. The city hall siren was screaming. Police sirens were wailing.

It was then that Qwilleran realized he had forgotten to pour the coffee. "How about a cup, Jody? If it isn't too cold."

The tiny young woman curled up on the sofa, cradling the big mug in her small hands. "I feel so sorry for Juney. I told him to go Down Below and get a job at the *Daily Fluxion* and forget about everything up here."

"No one should act on impulse at a time like this," Qwilleran advised.

"Maybe he could get an injunction to stop her from selling—or postpone it until she's thinking straight."

"Won't work. She'd have to be proved mentally incompetent. It's her own property now, and she can do whatever she wishes."

At that moment Mrs. Cobb, in robe and bedroom slippers, made an abrupt appearance in the doorway. "Look out the window!" she said in alarm. "There's a fire on Main Street! It looks like the lodge hall's on fire!"

Qwilleran and Jody jumped up, and all three of them hurried to the front windows.

"That's Herb's lodge," Mrs. Cobb said. "This is their meeting night. There could be thirty or forty people in the building."

"I'll drive down and see," Qwilleran said, "Come on, Jody, and I'll take you home afterward. Out this way . . . back door . . . car's in the garage."

Downtown Main Street was filled with flashing blue and red lights. Traffic was rerouted, and fire trucks were parked in an arc, training their headlights on the center of the block. The pumpers were working, and fire hoses were pouring water on the roof of the three-story lodge hall. Beyond that building there was an orange-red glow with flames leaping upward—then a hiss of steam—then a cloud of smoke.

Qwilleran parked, and he and Jody walked closer.

"It's the *Picayune!*" he shouted. "The whole building's on fire!"

Jody started to cry. "Poor Juney!" she kept saying. "Poor Juney!"

"They're hosing down the lodge hall to keep it from catching," Qwilleran said. "The post office, too. The newspaper plant is going to be totaled, I'm afraid."

"I think that's what his father was trying to tell him in the dream," she said. "Can you see Juney?"

"Can't recognize anyone in those helmets and rubber coats. Even their faces are black. Dirty job! The white helmet is the fire chief, that's all I can tell."

"I hope Juney doesn't do anything crazy, like running into the building to save something."

"They're trained not to take foolish risks," Qwilleran assured her.

"But he's so impulsive—and sentimental. That's why he's taking it so hard—his mother selling the *Pic,* I mean." A sudden look of horror crossed her face. "Oh, *no!* William

Allen's in there! They always lock him up for the night. I'm going to be sick. . . ."

"Easy, Jody! He may have escaped. Cats are clever. . . . Come on. We can't stay here. It's icing up, and you're shivering. The men will be on the job for hours, mopping up and looking for hot spots. I'll drive you home. Will you be all right?"

"Yes, I'll wait up till Juney comes home. He's been staying at my place since his father died, you know."

At the K mansion Qwilleran found Mrs. Cobb at the kitchen table, still in her pink robe, drinking cocoa and looking worried. "There's no news on the radio," she said anxiously.

"It wasn't the lodge hall," Qwilleran told her. "It was the *Picayune* building. It's gutted. More than a century of publishing destroyed in half an hour."

"Did you see Herb?" She poured a cup of cocoa for Qwilleran. It was not his favorite beverage.

"No, but I'm sure he was there, swinging an ax."

"He shouldn't be doing such strenuous work. He's over fifty, you know, and most of the men are much younger."

"You seem unusually concerned about him, Mrs. Cobb." He gave her a searching look.

The housekeeper lowered her eyes and smiled sheepishly. "Well, I admit I'm fond of him. We always have a good time together, and he's beginning to drop hints."

"About *marriage?*" Qwilleran's dismay showed in his brusque question. As a housekeeper she was a jewel—too valuable to lose. She had spoiled him and the Siamese with her cooking.

"I wouldn't stop working, though," Mrs. Cobb hastened to say. "I've always worked, and this is the most wonderful job I ever had. It's a dream come true. I mean it!"

"And you're perfect for the position. Don't rush into anything, Mrs. Cobb."

"I won't," she promised. "He hasn't come right out and asked me yet, so don't you say anything."

She refilled her cocoa cup and carried it upstairs, saying a weary good-night.

Qwilleran made his nightly house check before setting the burglar alarm and locking up. Then he retired to his own quarters over the garage, carrying a wicker picnic hamper. Indistinct sounds came from inside the hamper, and it swung to and fro vigorously as he carried it.

The four-car garage was a former carriage house built of fieldstone—the same masonry that made the main house spectacular. There were four arched doors to the stalls, a cupola with a weather vane on the roof, and a brace of ornate carriage lanterns at each corner of the building.

Upstairs the interior had been refurbished to suit Qwilleran's taste—comfortable contemporary in soothing tones of beige, rust, and brown. It was quiet and simple, an escape from the pomp and preciosity of the K mansion.

In the sitting room there were easy chairs, good reading lamps, a music system, and a small bar where Qwilleran mixed drinks for guests. He himself had not touched alcohol since the time he fell off a subway platform in New York, an experience that had been permanently sobering. Nor had he ever ridden the subway again.

The other rooms were his writing studio, his bedroom, and the cats' parlor, which was carpeted and furnished with cushions, baskets, scratching posts, climbing trees, and a turkey roaster that served as their commode. There was also a shelf of secondhand books bought at the hospital bazaar for a dime apiece. There were books on first-year algebra and English grammar simplified. There was a collection of famous sermons. Other titles were *The Burning of Rome* and *Elsie Dinsmore* and Vergil's *Aeneid.* Koko could push them off the shelf to his heart's content.

Qwilleran opened the wicker hamper in the cats' parlor and invited two reluctant Siamese to jump out. Why, he asked himself, did they never want to get into the hamper? And when they were in it, why did they never want to get out? Koko and Yum Yum finally emerged cautiously, a performance they had repeated every night for the last year, stalking the premises and sniffing the furnishings as if they suspected the room to be bugged or booby-trapped.

"Cats!" Qwilleran said aloud. "Who can understand them?"

He left the Siamese to their own peculiar occupations—licking each other, wrestling, chasing, biting ears, and sniffing indiscreetly—while he tuned in the midnight news in his sitting room.

"The offices and printing plant of the *Pickax Picayune* were destroyed by fire tonight. The building is a total loss, according to fire chief Bruce Scott. Twenty-five fire fighters, three tankers, and two pumpers from Pickax and surrounding communities responded to the alarm and are still on the scene. No injuries have been reported. Elsewhere in the county, the Mooseville Village Council voted to spend five hundred dollars on Christmas decorations—"

He snapped off the radio in exasperation. The same fifteen-second news item would be repeated hourly without further details. Listeners would not be told how the fire had started, who reported it, what records and equipment had been destroyed, the age of the building, its construction, the problems encountered in fighting the fire, precautions taken, the estimated value of the loss, the insurance coverage.

Without doubt the county needed a newspaper. As for the fate of the *Picayune,* it was regrettable, but one had to be realistic. The *Pic* had been a relic of the horse-and-buggy era. It was Senior's sentimentality and self-indulgence that had bankrupted his newspaper. Typesetting was his obsession, his reason for living, to quote Junior.

Reason for living? Qwilleran jerked to attention and combed his moustache with his fingertips. If the newspaper had truly been on the brink of failure, could Senior's accident have been a suicide? The old plank bridge would be a logical place for a fatal "accident." It was well known to be hazardous. Senior was a cautious, sober man—not one of the Friday-night drunks or speeding youths who usually came to grief at the bridge.

Qwilleran felt a tingling sensation on his upper lip, and he knew his suspicion was valid. There was something uncanny about his upper lip. A tingling, a tremor, or simply a vague uneasiness in the roots of his moustache told him when he was on the right scent. And now he was getting the signal.

If Senior had intended to take his own life, a staged "accident" would avoid the suicide clause, provided the insurance policy had been in effect long enough. Didn't Junior mention that Grandma Gage had been paying the premiums for years?

An "accident" might pay double indemnity to the widow, or even triple indemnity, although that would be a gamble: There would be a thorough investigation. Insurance companies objected to being fooled.

Perhaps Senior feared something worse than losing the newspaper. He had taken desperate measures to keep the *Picayune* afloat—selling the farmland, mortgaging the farmhouse, begging from his mother-in-law. Did his desperation lead him into something illegal? Did he fear exposure? How about the man in the black raincoat? What was he doing in Pickax? Senior's death had occurred only a few hours before the stranger arrived on the plane. Did Senior know he was coming? And why was the visitor hanging around? Were others implicated?

And now the *Picayune* offices had been destroyed. It was curious timing for such a disaster. Was there something in the basement of the building besides presses and back-copy files? Was it incriminating evidence that had to be eliminated? Who knew what was there? And who threw the match?

Qwilleran roused himself from his reverie and flexed the leg that was going to sleep. He was getting some weird notions. What had Mrs. Cobb put in that cocoa?

From the cats' parlor down the hall came a muffled but recognizable sound: *thlunk!* It was followed by another *thlunk*—then again *thlunk thlunk thlunk* in rapid succession. It was the sound of books falling on a carpeted floor. Koko was bumping his private collection.

FOUR

WEDNESDAY, NOVEMBER THIRTEENTH. "Continued cold, with overcast skies and snow showers accumulating to three to four inches."

"Overcast!" Qwilleran bellowed at the radio on his desk. "Why don't you look out the window? The sun's shining like the Fourth of July!"

He turned his attention back to Tuesday's *Daily Fluxion,* which had given good space to the story about the *Pickax Picayune.* It was not entirely accurate, but small towns were glad of any attention at all in the metropolitan press. Then he tried to read about the disasters, terrorism, crime, and graft Down Below, but his mind kept drifting back to Moose County.

Snow or no snow, he wanted to drive out in the country, look at the old plank bridge, visit the Goodwinter farmhouse, meet the widow. He would take flowers, offer condolences, and ask a few polite questions. It was an approach he had always handled well on the newsbeat. Sad eyes and drooping moustache gave him a mournful demeanor that passed for deep sympathy.

In the county telephone book he found Senior Goodwinter listed on Black Creek Lane in North Middle Hummock. On the county map he cound find neither. He found Middle Hummock and West Middle Hummock. He found Mooseville, Smith's Folly, Squunk Corners, Chipmunk, and Brrr, which was not a misprint; the town was the coldest spot in the county. But North Middle Hummock was not to be found. He took his problem to Mr. O'Dell, who knew all the answers.

Mrs. Fulgrove and Mr. O'Dell were the day help at the K mansion. The woman scrubbed and polished six days a week with almost religious fervor; the houseman handled the heavy jobs. Mr. O'Dell had been a school janitor for forty years and had shepherded thousands of students through adolescence—answering their questions, solving their problems, and lending them lunch money. "Janitor" was a revered title in Pickax, and if Mr. O'Dell ever decided to run for the office of mayor, he would be elected unanimously. Now, with his silver hair and ruddy complexion and benign expression, he superintended the Klingenschoen estate as naturally as he had supervised the education of Pickax youth.

Qwilleran found the houseman lubricating the hinges on the broom closet door. "Do you know the location of Senior Goodwinter's farmhouse, Mr. O'Dell? I don't find North Middle Hummock on the map."

In a lilting voice the houseman said, "The divil himself couldn't find the likes o' that on the map, I'm thinkin', for it's a ghost town fifty year since, but yourself can find it, for I'm after tellin' you how to get there. Go east, now, past the Buckshot Mine, where the wind will be whistlin' in the mine shaft on a day without wind, and there'll be moanin' from the lower depths. When you come to the old plank bridge, let you be wary, for the boards rattle like the divil's own teeth. Keep watch for a lonely tree on a high hill—the hangin' tree, they're callin' it—for then you're comin' to the church where me and my colleen got ourselves married by the good Father Ryan forty-five year since, God rest her soul. And when you come to a deal o' rubble, that's all that's left o' North Middle Hummock."

"I feel we're getting warm," Qwilleran said.

"Warm, is it? There's a ways to go yet—two miles till you set eyes on Captain Fugtree's farm with the white fence. Beyond the sheep meadow pay no mind to the sign sayin' Fugtree Sideroad, for it's Black Creek Lane, and the Goodwinter house you'll be seein' at the end of it. Gray, it is, with a yellow door."

As Qwilleran set out for a North Middle Hummock that didn't exist and a Black Creek Lane that was called something else, he marveled at the information programmed in the heads of Moose County natives for instant retrieval. If Mr. O'Dell could recite the directions in such detail, Senior Goodwinter, who had driven the tortuous route every day, would know every jog in the road, every pothole, every patch of loose gravel. It was not likely that Senior had wrecked his car accidentally.

Qwilleran heard no whistling or moaning at the Buckshot Mine, but the old plank bridge did indeed rattle ominously. Although the parapets were built of stone, the roadbed was a loose strip of lateral planks. The "hanging tree" was well named—an ancient gnarled oak making a grotesque silhouette against the sky. Everything else checked out: the church, the rubble, the white fence, the sheep meadow.

The farmhouse at the end of Black Creek Lane was a rambling structure of weathered gray shingles, set in a yard covered with the gold and red leaves of maples. Clumps of chrysanthemums were still blooming stubbornly around the doorstep.

Qwilleran lifted a brass door knocker shaped like the Greek letter *pi* and let it drop on the yellow door. He had taken the risk of dropping in without an appointment, country style, and when the door opened he was greeted without surprise by a pleasant young woman in a western shirt.

"I'm Jim Qwilleran," he said. "I couldn't attend the funeral, but I've brought some flowers for Mrs. Goodwinter."

"I know you!" she exclaimed. "I used to see your picture in the *Daily Fluxion* before I moved to Montana. Come right in!" She turned and shouted up the staircase. "Mother! You've got company!"

The woman who came down the stairs was no distraught widow with eyes red from weeping and sleeplessness; she was a hearty type in a red warm-up suit, with eyes sparkling and cheeks pink as if she had just come in from jogging.

"Mr. Qwilleran!" she cried with outstretched hand. "How good of you to drop in! We've all read your column in the *Fluxion,* and we're so glad you're living up here."

He presented the flowers. "With my compliments and sympathy, Mrs. Goodwinter."

"Please call me Gritty. Everyone does," she said. "And thank you for your kindness. Roses! I love roses! Let's go into the keeping room. Every other place is torn up for inventory. . . . Pug, honey, put these lovely flowers in a vase, will you? That's a dear."

The hundred-year-old farmhouse had many small rooms with wide floorboards and six-over-six windows with some of the original wavy glass. The mismatched furnishings were obviously family heirlooms, but the interior was self-consciously coordinated: blue-and-white tiles, blue-and-white calico curtains, and blue-and-white china on the plate rail. Antique cooking utensils hung in and around the large fireplace.

Gritty said, "We've been hoping you would join the country club, Mr. Qwilleran."

"I haven't done any joining," he said, "because I'm concentrating on writing a book."

"Not about Pickax, I hope," the widow said with a laugh. "It would be banned in Boston. . . . Pug, honey, bring us a drink, will you? . . . What will you have, Mr. Qwilleran?"

"Ginger ale, club soda, anything like that. And everyone calls me Qwill."

"How about a Coke with a little rum?" She was tempting him with a sidelong glance. "Live it up, Qwill!"

"Thanks, but I've been on the wagon for several years."

"Well, you're doing *something* right! You look wonderfully healthy." She appraised him from head to foot. "Are you happy in Moose County?"

"I'm getting used to it—the fresh air, the relaxed lifestyle, the friendly people," he said. "It must be a comfort to you, during this sad time, to have so many friends and relatives."

"The relatives you can have!" she said airily. "But, yes—I am fortunate to have good friends."

Her daughter brought a tray of beverages, and Qwilleran raised his glass. "With hope for the future!"

"You're so right!" said his hostess, flourishing a double old-fashioned. "Would you stay for lunch, Qwill? I've made a ham-and-spinach quiche with funeral leftovers. Pug, honey, see if it's ready to come out of the oven. Stick a knife in it."

The visit was not what Qwilleran had anticipated. He was required to shift abruptly from condolence to social chitchat. "You have a beautiful house," he remarked.

"It may look good," Gritty said, "but it's a pain in the you-know-what. I'm tired of floors that slope and doors that creak and septic tanks that back up and stairs with narrow treads. God! They must have had small feet in the old days. And small bottoms! Look at those Windsor chairs! I'm selling the house and moving to an apartment in Indian Village—near the golf course, you know."

Pug said, "Mother is a champion golfer. She wins all the tournaments."

"What will you do with your antiques when you move?" Qwilleran asked innocently.

"Sell them at auction. Do you like auctions? They're the major pastime in Moose County—next to potluck suppers and messing around."

"Oh, *Mother!*" Pug remonstrated. She turned to Qwilleran. "That big rolltop desk belonged to my great-grandfather. He founded the *Picayune.*"

"It looks like a rolltop coffin," her mother said. "I've been doomed to live with antiques all my life. Never liked them. Crazy, isn't it?"

Lunch was served at a pine table in the kitchen, and the quiche arrived on blue-and-white plates.

Gritty said, "I hope this is the last meal I ever eat on blue china. It makes food look yukky, but the whole set was handed down in my husband's family—hundreds of pieces that refuse to break."

"I was appalled," Qwilleran said, "when the *Picayune* offices burned down. I was hoping the paper would continue to publish under Junior's direction."

"Poo on the *Picayune,*" said Gritty. "They should have pulled the plug thirty years ago."

"But it's unique in the annals of journalism. Junior could have carried on the tradition, even if they printed the paper by modern methods."

"No," she said. "That boy will marry his midget, and they'll both leave Pickax and go Down Below to get jobs. Probably in a sideshow," she added with a laugh. "Junior is the runt of the litter."

"Oh, *Mother,* don't say such things," Pug protested. To Qwilleran she said, "Mother is the humorist in the family."

"It hides my broken heart," the widow said with a debonair shrug.

"What will happen to the *Picayune* building now? Were they able to salvage anything?"

"It's all gone," she said without apparent regret. "The building is gutted, but the stone walls are okay. They're two feet thick. It would make a good minimall with six or eight shops, but we'll have to wait and see what we collect on insurance."

Throughout the visit thoughts were racing through Qwilleran's mind: Everything was being done too fast; it all seemed beautifully planned. As for the widow, either she was braving it out or she was utterly heartless. "Gritty" affected him less like a courageous woman and more like the sand in the spinach quiche.

Returning home, he telephoned Dr. Zoller's dental clinic and spoke with the young receptionist who had such dazzlingly capped teeth.

"This is Jim Qwilleran, Pam. Could I get an appointment this afternoon to have my teeth cleaned?"

"One moment. Let me find your card. . . . You were here in July, Mr. Q. You're not due until January."

"This is an emergency. I've been drinking a lot of tea."

"Oh. . . . Well, in that case you're in luck. Jody just had a cancellation. Can you come right over?"

"In three minutes and twenty seconds." In Pickax one was never more than five minutes away from anywhere.

The clinic occupied a lavishly renovated stone stable that had once been a ten-cent barn behind the old Pickax Hotel in horse-and-buggy days. Jody greeted Qwilleran eagerly. In her long white coat she looked even more diminutive.

"I've been trying to reach you!" she said. "Juney wants

you to know that he's flying Down Below to see the editor who promised him a job. He left at noon."

"Well, that's the end of the old *Picayune,*" Qwilleran said.

"Fasten your seat belt. You're going for a ride." She adjusted the dental chair to its lowest level. "Is your head comfy?"

"How late did Junior stay at the fire scene?"

"He got in at five-thirty this morning, and he was beat! They had to stay and watch for hot spots, you know. . . . Now open wide."

"Salvage anything?" he asked quickly before complying.

"I don't think so. The papers that weren't burned were soaked. As soon as they knocked the fire down they let Juney go in with an air pack to see if he could find a fireproof box that belonged to his dad. But the smoke was too thick. He couldn't even *see*—Oops! Did I puncture you?"

"Arrh," Qwilleran replied with his mouth full of instruments.

Jody's tiny fingers had a delicate touch, but her hands were shaking after a sleepless night.

"Juney says they don't know what caused the fire. He didn't let anyone smoke when they were taking pictures. . . . Is that a sensitive spot?"

"Arrh arrh."

"Poor Juney! He was crushed—absolutely crushed! He's really not strong enough to be a nozzleman, you know, but the chief let him take the hose—with three backup men instead of two. It made Juney feel—not so helpless, you know. . . . Now you can rinse out."

"Building well insured?"

"Just a tad wider, please. That's it! . . . There's some insurance, but most of the stuff is priceless, because it's old and irreplaceable. . . . Now rinse."

"Too bad the old issues weren't on microfilm and stored somewhere for safety."

"Juney said it would cost too much money."

"Who reported the fire?" Another quick question between rinses.

"Some kids cruising on Main Street. They saw smoke, and when the trucks got there, the whole building was in flames. . . . Is this hurting you?"

"Arrh arrh."

She sighed. "So I guess Juney will take a job at the *Fluxion,* and his mother will sell everything." She whipped off the bib. "There you go! Have you been flossing after every meal like Dr. Zoller told you?"

"Inform Dr. Zoller," Qwilleran said, "that not only do I floss after meals but I floss between the courses. In restaurants I'm known as the Mad Flosser."

From the dental clinic he went to Scottie's Men's Shop. Qwilleran, whose mother had been a Mackintosh, was partial to Scots, and the storekeeper had a brogue that he turned on for good customers.

Throughout his career Qwilleran had never cared much about clothes, being satisfied with a drab uniform of coat, pants, shirt, and tie. There was something about the north-country lifestyle, however, that sparked his interest in tartan shirts, Icelandic sweaters, shearling parkas, trooper hats, bulky boots, and buckskin choppers. And the more Scottie burred his *r*'s, the more Qwilleran bought.

Entering the store, Qwilleran said, "What happened to the four inches of snow we were supposed to get today?"

"All bosh," said Scottie, shaking his shaggy head of gray hair. "Canna believe a worrrd of what they say on radio. A body can get better information from the woolly caterpillars."

"You look as if you lost some sleep last night."

"Aye, it were a bad one, verra bad," said the volunteer fire chief. "Didna get home till six this mornin'. Chipmunk and Kennebeck sent crews to help. Couldna do it without 'em—or without our women, God bless 'em. Kept the coffee and sandwiches comin' all night."

"How did Junior take it?"

"It were hard on the lad. Many a time I been in the newspaper office to pass the time o' day with his old man. A fire trap, it was! Tons of paper! And them old wood partitions—dry as tinder—and the old wood floor!" Scottie shook his head again.

"Any idea how it started?"

"Couldna say. They'd been takin' pictures, and it could be a careless cigarette smolderin'. There's a flammable solvent they always used for cleanin' the old presses, and when it hit, it raced like wildfire."

"Any suspicion of arson?"

"No evidence of monkey business. No reason to bring the marshal up here to my way o' thinkin'."

"But you saved the lodge hall and post office, Scottie."

"Aye, we did indeed, but it were touch an' go."

On the way home Qwilleran stopped at the public library to check the reading room. The man who claimed to be a historian was not there, and the clerks had not seen him since Tuesday morning. Polly Duncan was not there either, and the clerks said she had left for the day.

For dinner that night Mrs. Cobb served beef Stroganoff and poppy-seed noodles, and after second helpings and a wedge of pumpkin pie, Qwilleran took some out-of-town newspapers and two new magazines into the library. He drew the draperies and touched a match to Mr. O'Dell's expert arrangement of split logs, kindling, and paper twists. Then he sprawled in his favorite lounge chair and propped his feet on the ottoman.

The Siamese immediately presented themselves. They knew a fire was being lighted before the woodsy aroma circulated, before the crackle of the kindling, even before the match was struck. After washing up in the warmth of the blaze, Koko started nosing books and Yum Yum jumped on Qwilleran's lap, turning around three times before settling down.

The female was developing an inordinate affection for the man. She was brazenly possessive of his lap. She gazed at him with adoring eyes, purred when he looked her way, and liked nothing better than to reach up and touch his moustache with a velvet paw. True, he called her his little sweetheart, but her obsessive desire for propinquity was disturbing. He had mentioned it to Lori Bamba, the young woman who knew all about cats.

"They go for the opposite sex," Lori explained, "and they know which is which. It's hard to explain."

Yum Yum was dozing on his lap, a picture of catly contentment, when Qwilleran heard the first *thlunk*. There was no sense in scolding Koko. It went in one pointed ear and out the other. When reprimanded in the past, he had not only resented it; he had found his own ingenious way of retaliation. In any argument, Qwilleran had learned, a Siamese always has the last word.

So he merely sighed, transferred his lapful of sleeping fur to the ottoman, and went to see what damage had been done. As he expected, it was Shakespeare again. Mrs. Fulgrove had been rubbing the pigskin bindings with a mixture of lanolin and neat's-foot oil, to preserve the leather, and both ingredients were animal products. But whatever the explanation for Koko's special interest in these books, two of them were now on the floor, and they happened to be Qwilleran's favorite plays: *Macbeth* and *Julius Caesar.*

He leafed through the latter until he found a passage he liked: the conspiracy scene, in which men plotting to assassinate Caesar meet under cover of darkness, shadowing their faces with their cloaks. "*And let us bathe our hands in Caesar's blood up to the elbows, and besmear our swords.*"

Conspiracy, Qwilleran reflected, was Shakespeare's favorite device for establishing conflict, creating suspense, and grabbing the emotions of the audience. In *Macbeth* there was the conspiracy to murder the old king. "*Who would have thought the old man to have had so much blood in him?*"

A tremor on Qwilleran's upper lip alerted him. Was the *Picayune*'s double tragedy the result of a conspiracy? He had no clues—only the sensation in the roots of his moustache. He had no clues and no logical way to investigate.

Years before, as a prize-winning crime reporter, he had developed a network of anonymous sources. In Moose County he had no sources. Although the natives were notorious gossips, they avoided gossiping with outsiders, and Qwilleran was an outsider even after eighteen months in their midst.

He glanced at the calendar. It was Wednesday, November thirteenth. On the evening of November fourteenth he would have seventy-five certified gossips under his roof—all the best people, drinking tea and socializing.

"Okay, old sleuth," he said to Koko. "Tomorrow night we cultivate some sources."

FIVE

THURSDAY, NOVEMBER FOURTEENTH. The weather was cooperating with the major social event of the season—not too cold, not too windy, not too damp. On Thursday evening seventy-five members of the Historical Society and Old Timers Club would view the Klingenschoen mansion for the first time, and the residence would become officially the Klingenschoen Museum.

Ever since inheriting the pretentious edifice Qwilleran had considered it an absurd residence for a bachelor and two cats. He proposed, therefore—with the cooperation of the Historical Society—to open the mansion to the public as a museum two or three afternoons a week. When the mayor announced the news at a council meeting, the citizens of Pickax were jubilant, and the guests invited to the preview felt singularly honored.

Qwilleran's day began as usual in his garage apartment. He tuned in the weather report, drank a cup of instant coffee, dressed, and walked down the corridor to the cats' parlor.

"Commuter Special now leaving on track four," he announced, opening the wicker hamper.

The Siamese sat nose-to-nose on the windowsill, enjoying

the thin glimmer of November sunshine and ignoring the invitation.

"Breakfast now being served in the dining car."

There was no response, not even the flicker of a whisker. Impatiently Qwilleran picked up one animal in each hand and deposited them unceremoniously in the hamper.

"If you act like cats, you get treated like cats," he explained in a reasonable voice. "Act like courteous, cooperative, intelligent beings, and you get treated accordingly."

There were sounds of scuffling and snarling inside the hamper as he carried it across the yard to the main house.

It was Mrs. Cobb's idea that the Siamese should spend their days among the Oriental rugs, French tapestries, and rare old books of the mansion. "When you have valuable antiques," she explained, you have four things to fear: theft, fire, dry heat, and mice."

At her urging Qwilleran had installed humidity controls, a burglar alarm, smoke detectors, and a direct line to the police station and fire hall. Koko and Yum Yum were expected to handle the other hazards.

When Qwilleran arrived at the back door with the wicker hamper, the housekeeper called out from the kitchen, "Would you like a mushroom omelette, Mr. Q?"

"Sounds fine. I'll feed the cats. What's in the refrigerator?"

"Sautéed chicken livers. Koko would probably prefer them warmed with some of last night's beef Stroganoff. Yum Yum isn't fussy."

After he had finished his own breakfast—a three-egg omelette with two toasted English muffins and some of Mrs. Cobb's wild haw jelly—he said, "Delicious! Best mushroomless mushroom omelette I've ever eaten."

"Oh dear!" The housekeeper covered her face with her hands in embarrassment. "Did I forget the filling? I'm so excited about tonight, I don't know whether I'm coming or going. Aren't you excited, Mr. Q?"

"I feel a faint ripple of anticipation," he said.

"Oh, Mr. Q, you must be kidding! You've worked on this for a year!"

It was true. To prepare the mansion for public use, the attic had been paneled and equipped as a meeting room. A paved parking lot was added behind the carriage house. Engineers from Down Below had installed an elevator. A fire escape was required in the rear. For barrier-free access there were such accommodations as a ramp at the rear entrance, a new bathroom on the main floor, and elevator controls at wheelchair height.

"What's the order of events tonight?" Qwilleran asked Mrs. Cobb. She had chaired the Historical Society committee on arrangements.

"The members will start arriving at seven o'clock for a conducted tour of the museum. Mrs. Exbridge has trained eighteen guides."

"And who trained Mrs. Exbridge? Don't be so modest, Mrs. Cobb. I know and you know that this entire venture would have been impossible without your expertise."

"Oh, thank you, Mr. Q," she said, flushing self-consciously, "but I can't take too much credit. Mrs. Exbridge knows a lot about antiques. She wants to open an antique shop now that her divorce is final."

"Don Exbridge's wife? I didn't know they were having trouble. Sorry to hear it." Qwilleran always empathized with the principals in a divorce case, having survived a painful experience himself.

"Yes, it's too bad," Mrs. Cobb said. "I don't know what went wrong. Susan Exbridge doesn't talk about it. She's a very nice woman. I've never met *him.*"

"I've run into him a couple of times. He's an agreeable guy with a smile and a handshake for everyone."

"Well, he's a developer, you know, and I take a dim view of *them.* We were always fighting developers and bureaucrats Down Below. They wanted to tear down twenty antique shops and some historic houses."

"So what happens after the tour of the museum?"

"We go up to the meeting hall, and that's when you make your speech."

"Not a speech. Just a few words. Please!"

"Then there'll be a brief business meeting and refreshments."

"I hope you didn't bake seventy-five dozen cookies for those shameless cookie hounds," Qwilleran said. "I suspect most of them attend meetings because of your lemon-coconut bars. Will your friend be there?"

"Herb? No, he has to get up early tomorrow morning. It's the start of gun season for deer, you know. How about the cats? Will they attend the preview?"

"Why not? Yum Yum will spend the evening on top of the refrigerator, but Koko likes to parade around and show off."

The telephone rang, and Koko sprang to the desk in the kitchen, as if he knew it was a call from Lori Bamba in Mooseville.

Lori was Qwilleran's part-time secretary, a young woman with long golden braids tied with blue ribbons that tantalized the Siamese.

"Hi, Qwill," she said. "Hope I'm not interrupting something crucial. Isn't this the big day?"

"You're right. Tonight we go public. What's the news from Mooseville?"

"Nick just phoned me from work and said I should call you. Someone's camping on your property at the lake. On his way to work he saw an RV parked in the woods there. He wondered if you had authorized it."

"Don't know a thing about it. But is it all that bad? There's a lot of land there that isn't being used." Qwilleran had inherited the lake property along with the mansion in Pickax: eighty acres of woodland with beach frontage and a log cabin.

"It isn't a good idea to encourage trespassers," Lori said. "They could leave a lot of litter, cut down your trees, set the woods on fire . . ."

"Okay, okay, I'm convinced."

"Nick said you should call the sheriff."

"I'll do that. Appreciate your interest. How's everything in Mooseville? How's the baby?"

"He finally said his first word. He said 'moose' very distinctly, so we think he'll grow up to be president of the Chamber of Commerce. . . . Do I hear Koko talking in the background?"

"He wants to have a few words with you."

Qwilleran held the receiver to Koko's ear, which flicked and swiveled in excitement. There followed a series of "yows" and "iks" and purrs of varying intensity and inflection.

When the conversation ended, Qwilleran said to the housekeeper, "The English language has six hundred thousand words. Koko has only two, but he gets more music and meaning out of 'yow' and 'ik' than some of our learned friends get out of the whole dictionary."

"That Lori certainly has a way with cats," Mrs. Cobb said with a trace of envy.

"If Lori had lived in Salem three hundred years ago, she would have been burned at the stake."

The housekeeper looked saddened. "I don't think Koko likes me."

"Why do you say that, Mrs. Cobb?"

"He never talks to me or purrs or comes to be petted."

"Siamese," Qwilleran began, clearing his throat and selecting his words carefully, "are less demonstrative than other breeds, and Koko in particular is not a lap cat, although I'm sure he likes you."

"Yum Yum rubs against my ankles when I'm cooking and jumps on my lap sometimes. She's a very sweet kitty."

"Koko is less emotional and more cerebral," Qwilleran explained. "He has his own attributes and personality, and we have to understand him and accept him for what he is. He may not make a fuss over you, but he respects you and appreciates the wonderful food you prepare."

He extricated himself from this ticklish dialogue with a sense of relief. Koko had alienated more than one woman of his acquaintance, and a standoff between a temperamental cat and a superlative housekeeper was much to be avoided.

From the library he telephoned the sheriff's office, and within a half hour there was a brown uniform at the back door.

"Sheriff's department, sir," said the deputy. "Got a report on the radio about your property east of Mooseville. No RV in your woods, sir, although there were recent tire tracks and a couple of empty cigarette packs. He buried the butts, so he knows something about camping. They were Canadian cigarettes. We get a lot of Canadian tourists here. No sign of poaching. No break-in or vandalism at your cabin. Gun season starts tomorrow, sir. If you don't want trespassers with rifles, you ought to have your property posted."

The day wore on. The weather held. Excitement mounted. Mrs. Cobb put sugar in the soup and salt in the applesauce. Koko's tail was stepped on twice.

At seven o'clock every light in the mansion was turned on. Eighty tall narrow windows glowing with light on a wintry night created a spectacle that Pickax had never before seen, and traffic cruised around the Park Circle to gawk.

When the guests arrived they were greeted by Qwilleran

and the officers of the Historical Society. Then they moved from room to room, marveling at the richness and palatial dimensions of the interior. The drawing room, with its twin fireplaces and twin chandeliers, had a fortune in oil paintings on the crimson damask walls. The dining room, designed to seat sixteen, was paneled in carved walnut imported from England in the nineteenth century. The visitors were so entranced by the museum that Koko went unnoticed, although he strutted in their midst and struck statuesque poses on the carved newel post and the antique rosewood piano.

At eight o'clock the meeting was called to order in the third-floor assembly room. Nigel Fitch, a trust officer at the bank, rapped the gavel and asked everyone to rise for a moment of silent tribute to Senior Goodwinter. Then the thanking began. First the president thanked the weatherman for postponing the snow. He thanked Qwilleran for making the mansion available as a museum.

Qwilleran rose and thanked the society members for their encouragement and support. He thanked XYZ Enterprises for donating labor for the construction projects. He thanked the CPA firm for computerizing the museum catalogue. Particularly he thanked Mrs. Cobb for establishing the museum on a professional level. Then she thanked the four committees that had worked on the preview. The president kept glancing toward the elevator expectantly.

During the transaction of old and new business Polly Duncan, representing the public library, proposed an oral history project to preserve the recollections of Old Timers on tape. "It should be handled by someone with interviewing skills," she specified, glancing at Qwilleran. He said he might give it a try.

Nigel Fitch, who usually chaired a brisk meeting, was proceeding at a leisurely pace. "We're expecting the mayor," he explained, "but he's been delayed at the city hall."

Whenever Fitch glanced toward the elevator, all heads in the audience turned hopefully in the same direction. At one point there were mechanical sounds in the elevator shaft, and a hush fell in the meeting hall. The doors opened, and out stepped an Old Timer, tall and thin and nattily dressed. He gave the president a cheerful salute and walked to an empty seat with a disjointed gait, like a robot.

"That's Mr. Tibbitt," whispered a woman next to Qwilleran. "A retired school principal. He's ninety-three. A dear old man."

"Mr. President," said Susan Exbridge, "I would like to make a proposal. The Singing Society will present Handel's *Messiah* at the Old Stone Church on November twenty-fourth, exactly as it was performed in the eighteenth century, with singers in period costume. We had planned a reception for the performers afterward, and this museum would be a marvelous place to have it, if Mr. Qwilleran would consent."

"Okay with me," said Qwilleran, "provided I don't have to wear satin knee breeches."

And still the mayor did not arrive. Looking frequently at his watch, Fitch invited discussions on raising the dues, recruiting new members, and starting a newsletter.

Finally the telltale hum in the elevator shaft was heard, followed by a click as the car reached the third floor. All heads turned in anticipation. The elevator door opened, and out walked Koko—his tail perpendicular, his ears proudly erect, and a dead mouse gripped in his jaws.

Qwilleran jumped to his feet. "And I want to thank the vice president in charge of extermination for his diligence in eliminating certain museum hazards."

"Meeting adjourned," shouted Fitch.

During the social hour the banker said to Qwilleran, "That's a remarkable cat you have. How did he do it?"

Qwilleran explained that Mr. O'Dell was downstairs, and

he had probably put Koko in the car, pressed the button, and sent him up—for laughs.

Actually Qwilleran thought nothing of the kind. Koko was capable of boarding the car, stretching to his full length, and reaching the controls with a paw. He had done it before. The cat was fascinated by push buttons, keys, levers, and knobs. But how could one explain that to a banker?

When the mayor finally arrived, he cornered Qwilleran. "Say, Qwill, when is this town going to emerge from the Dark Ages?"

"What do you mean?"

"Did you ever hear of a whole county trying to function without a newspaper? We all knew Senior was a nut, but we thought Junior would take over and make it go. He's a bright kid; I had him in poli sci when I was teaching. But I suppose you've heard Gritty's selling the *Picayune* to you-know-who. They'll make a mint of money on it—as an ad sheet, that's all—and we still won't have any news coverage. Why don't you start a paper, Qwill?"

"Well, it's like this. I used to think I'd like to own my own newspaper and my own four-star restaurant and my own big-league ball club, but I've had to face the fact that I'm not a financier or an administrator."

"Okay. How about your connections Down Below? I know you lured that young couple up here to turn the Old Stone Mill around."

"I'll think about it," Qwilleran promised.

"Think fast."

Over the cups of weak tea and mildly alcoholic punch there was no lack of chatter:

"Incredible collection of antiques!"

"How do you like this weather?"

"A memorable evening! We are indebted to you, Mr. Qwilleran."

"Snow's never been so late."

"What are you doing for Thanksgiving?"

"Would you like a twelve-foot Christmas tree for the museum, Qwill? I have a beauty on my farm."

"Charming place for a wedding. My son is being married soon."

There were no theories about Senior's accident or the *Picayune* fire, however, despite Qwilleran's leading questions. He was still an outsider. Although an eavesdropper by profession, he heard nothing that suggested illegal activity or conspiracy.

While he felt an underlying disappointment, he noticed that Mrs. Cobb was unusually elated. She talked vivaciously, laughed much, and accepted compliments without blushing. Something wonderful had happened to her, he guessed. She had won the state lottery, or she was a grandmother for the first time, or the mayor had appointed her to the Commission on Preservation. Whatever the reason, Mrs. Cobb was inordinately happy.

Then Qwilleran observed a pair of Old Timers sitting in a corner with their heads together. A frail woman dependent upon a walker was listening to an old man with a cane as he talked about the *Picayune* fire. Qwilleran inquired if they were enjoying the party.

"Good cookies," said the man, "but they shoulda put somethin' in the punch. Glad it didn't snow."

"We don't get out much after snow flies," said his companion. "I never saw such a grand house!"

"Couldn't hear a word at the meeting, though."

The woman sniffed. "Amos, you always sit in the back row, and you always complain you can't hear."

Qwilleran asked their names.

"I'm Amos Cook, eighty-eight," the man said. "Eighty-eight and still cookin'. Heh heh heh." He jerked his thumb. "She's a young chick, eighty-five. Heh heh heh."

"I'm Hettie Spence, and I'll be eighty-six next month," she said. The Old Timers flaunted their ages like medals. "I was a Fugtree before I married Mr. Spence. He had the hardware store. We raised five children of our own—four of them boys—and three foster children. They all went to college. My eldest son is an ophthalmologist Down Below." She spoke with a fluttering of eyelids, hands, and shoulders.

"My grand-niece married one o' them," Amos put in.

"I wrote the obituaries for the *Picayune* before my arthritis got too bad," Hettie said. "I wrote the obituary for the last of the Klingenschoens."

"I read it," said Qwilleran. "It was unforgettable."

"My father wouldn't let me go away to college, but I took correspondence courses, and—"

Amos interrupted. "Her and me was in the pictures they took before the fire."

"How did you enjoy it?" Qwilleran asked. "Was the photographer good? How many pictures did she take?"

"Too many," he complained. "I got awful tired. I just had a gall bladder operation. She went click-click-click. Not like the old days. In them days you had to watch the birdie till your face froze, and the man had his head under a black cloth."

"In those days we had to say 'plum' before he snapped the picture," Hettie said. "We never had girl photographers then."

"Wouldn't let me smoke my corncob. Said it would fog up the pictures. Never heard anythin' so silly."

Qwilleran asked what time they left the newspaper office.

"My grandson picked us up at six," Amos said.

"Five," Hettie corrected him.

"Six, Hettie. Junior took the girl to the airport at half past five."

"Well, my watch said five, and I took my medication."

"You forgot to wind it, and you took your pill too late. That's why you got a dizzy spell."

Qwilleran interrupted. "And the fire broke out about four hours later. Do you have any idea what caused it?"

The old couple looked at each other and shook their heads.

"How long had you worked at the *Picayune*, Mr. Cook?"

"I was a printer's devil when I was ten, and I stayed till I couldn't work no more." He patted his chest. "Weak ticker. But I got to be head pressman when Titus was alive. We had two men and a boy on them handpresses, and it took all day to print a couple of thousand. The paper sold for a penny then. You could get a whole year for a dollar."

Qwilleran remembered the book Polly had given him. "Would you good people come downstairs and look at an old picture of *Picayune* employees? You might be able to identify them."

"My eyes aren't very good," Hettie said. "Cataracts. And I don't move so fast since I broke my hip."

Nevertheless, Qwilleran conducted them to the library and produced his copy of *Picturesque Pickax*. He flicked on the tape recorder, and the interview was later transcribed by Lori Bamba.

Question: This is a picture of Picayune *employees, taken sometime before 1921. Do you recognize any of the faces?*

Amos: I'm not in the picture. Don't even know when it was took. But that's Titus Goodwinter in the middle—the one with the derby hat and handlebar moustache.

Hettie: He always wore a derby hat. Who's that next to Titus?

Amos: The one with arm garters? Don't know him.

Hettie: Was he the bookkeeper?

Amos: No, the bookkeeper has those black things on his sleeves. Bill Watkins, his name was.

Hettie: Bill was the sheriff. His cousin Barnaby kept

books. I went to school with him. He was killed by a runaway horse and wagon.

Amos: It was the sheriff that tried to stop a runaway, Hettie. Barnaby was shot in the head with a rifle.

Hettie: I beg to differ. Barnaby didn't believe in firearms. I knew his whole family.

Amos: (loudly) I didn't say he had a gun! Some hunter shot him!

Hettie: I thought the sheriff always carried a gun.

Amos: (louder) We're talking about the bookkeeper! Barnaby! The one with black sleeve things!

Hettie: Don't shout!

Amos: Well, anyway, the one with the derby hat is Titus Goodwinter.

Was Titus the founder of the newspaper?

Amos: Nope. Ephraim started the paper way back. Don't know when. Had a big funeral when he died. Hung himself.

Hettie: Ephraim *hanged* himself, or so they said.

Amos: On a big oak tree near the old plank bridge.

Is that when Titus started to manage the newspaper?

Amos: No, the oldest boy took over, but he got throwed by a horse.

Hettie: Millions of blackbirds rose out of a cornfield, and his horse bolted.

Amos: The blackbirds in them days was like the mosquitoes we got now.

Hettie: Titus ran the paper after that. My, he was spoiled! Once when the creek was swollen, his horse wouldn't cross it, and Titus jumped off in a rage and shot him.

Amos: His own horse! Shot him dead! That's Titus in a derby hat. Always wore a derby hat.

Who's the fierce-looking man at the end of the row?

Amos: That's the fellah that drove the wagon, eh, Hettie?

Hettie: That's Zack, all right. I never liked him. He drank.

Amos: Killed Titus in a fight and went to prison. Good

driver, though. Had a pretty daughter. Ellie, her name was. Worked at the paper for a spell.

Hettie: Ellie folded papers and made tea and swept up.

Amos: Throwed herself in the river one dark night.

Hettie: Poor girl had no mother, and her father drank, and her brother was a bully.

Amos: Titus took a shine to her.

Hettie: He was always a ladies' man—him and that derby hat and big moustache.

End of interview.

Nigel Fitch interrupted the dialogue, saying he was ready to drive the two Old Timers home. All the guests were drifting out, reluctantly. Plucking Polly from the departing crowd, Qwilleran invited her to stay for an afterglow.

"One little glass of sherry, and then I must leave," she said as they went into the library. "Did you object to my involving you in the oral history project?"

"Not at all. It might prove interesting. Did you know that Senior's father was murdered and his grandfather hanged himself?"

"The family has had a violent history, but you must remember that this was pioneer country like the old Wild West, but at a later date. We're more civilized now."

"Computers and video recorders do not a civilization make."

"That's not Shakespeare, Qwill."

"I visited Mrs. Goodwinter yesterday," he said. "She was hardly one of your traditional widows, ravaged by grief and sedated by the family physician."

"She's a courageous woman. When they named her Gritty, they had reason."

"She's made some rather sudden decisions—to sell the house, auction the furnishings, and let the antique presses go for scrap metal. It's less than a week since Senior died, and the auction posters are all over town. That's too fast."

"People who have never been widowed are always telling widows how to behave," Polly said. "Gritty is a strong woman, like her mother. Euphonia Gage should be on your list for an oral history interview."

"What do you know about XYZ Enterprises?"

"Only that they're successful at everything they undertake."

"Do you know the principals?"

"Slightly. Don Exbridge is a charming man. He's the promoter, the idea person. Caspar Young is the contractor. Dr. Zoller is the financial backer."

"That figures. I suspect he's made a fortune in dental floss," Qwilleran said. "Do X, Y, and Z all belong to the country club?"

He had made a study of the clique system in Pickax. Everything depended on which club one joined, which church one attended, and how long one's family had lived in Moose County. The Goodwinters went back five generations; the Fitches, four.

"I must leave now," said Polly, "before my landlord calls the sheriff and they send out the search posse. Mr. MacGregor is a nice old man, and I don't want to upset him."

After she left, Qwilleran wondered if the fine hand of XYZ Enterprises had guided Mrs. Goodwinter's decisions. They all belonged to the club. They golfed. They played cards. That was the way it worked.

He also wondered if Polly really had an elderly landlord named MacGregor monitoring her activities. Or was it a manufactured excuse for leaving early? And why was she so reluctant to stay late? She was afraid of something. Gossip, perhaps. Pickax imposed a Victorian code of propriety on its professional women, and they took pains to preserve appearances, even though they were privately living in the late twentieth century. Polly's landlord, Qwilleran suspected, might be more than a landlord.

SIX

FRIDAY, NOVEMBER FIFTEENTH. It was the opening day of gun season for deer hunters. At the Klingenschoen Museum it was the morning after the preview, and Mrs. Cobb was still elated and a trifle giddy.

Qwilleran complimented her on the success of the evening. "Everyone praised the museum and the refreshments, not necessarily in that order," he said. 'We've been offered a twelve-foot Christmas tree for the foyer, and the Fitches would like to use the museum for their son's wedding."

"It would be a beautiful setting for a wedding," she said, adding playfully, "Koko could be ring bearer and carry the ring on his tail."

"You're making jokes this morning," Qwilleran said. "You must be feeling good."

She looked at him coyly. "What would you think about having two weddings here?"

"You?"

Her eyes were glowing behind the thick lenses. "Herb is buying a hundred-year-old farmhouse. He called me just before the preview and said he thought we should get married."

"Hmff," Qwilleran said, then searched for something

more agreeable to say. "It's the Goodwinter place. I've seen it. It's a gem!"

"He got a good buy because she's in a hurry to sell before snow flies."

"It's overdecorated, but you'd know how to correct that."

"It will be fun to restore it and furnish it with primitives."

"Does Hackpole like antiques?" Qwilleran asked dubiously.

"Not really, but he says I can do anything I want. His chief interest is hunting and fishing. He has cabinets full of guns and hunting knives and fishing rods. He wants to give me a rifle—a .22 rimfire, whatever that is—for squirrels and rabbits." Her pursed lips expressed disapproval.

"It's hard to imagine you tramping around the woods, taking shots at small animals, Mrs. Cobb."

She shuddered. "Herb was telling me how he field-dresses a deer, and it turned my stomach. By the way, he wants to know if you like venison. He always gets his buck, and he says the meat is delicious if the deer bleeds to death slowly. The heart should keep pumping blood out of the tissues." She quoted without enthusiasm.

"Hmff," Qwilleran said again, his down-turned moustache drooping more than usual. He was not happy with the turn of events. A housekeeper who worked an eight-hour shift and then went home to cook for her husband would be quite different from the live-in housekeeper who had spoiled him and the cats with her cooking during the last eighteen months. Yet he knew that Iris Cobb, twice widowed, yearned for a husband. Too bad she hadn't found one better than Hackpole.

True, he made a good living—in used cars, auto repair, welding, and scrap metal. True, he was a volunteer fire fighter, and that was to his credit. He had fabricated Mrs. Cobb's mobile herb garden in his welding shop; he had picked the berries for her wild haw jelly; he was an expert woodsman. Yet, all around town Hackpole was considered obnoxious. He seemed to have no friends, except Mrs. Cobb, and this inept Romeo now wanted to give her a .22 rifle! Poor woman! She had hoped for a certain expensive silk blouse for her birthday, and Hackpole had given her an expensive Swiss army knife. The man aroused Qwilleran's curiosity.

How had he arranged the purchase of the Goodwinter house so fast? He was hardly a member of the country club clique, but he might have connections with XYZ Enterprises. His welding shop probably had the contract for the balcony railings on the Mooseville Motel and the Indian Village units.

Then the telephone rang, and Qwilleran took the call in the library.

A little-girl voice said, "Mr. Qwilleran, this is Jody. Juney came back from Down Below last night. He didn't get hired."

"Did he see the managing editor?"

"Yes, the man who promised him a job. He said they'd just hired three new women reporters and there was no opening at the present time, but they'd keep him in mind."

"Typical!" Qwilleran muttered. "Typical of that guy."

"Juney tried the *Morning Rampage,* too, but they're cutting down their staff. He's terribly depressed. He got in late last night and didn't sleep at all."

"With his academic record he'll have no trouble getting located, Jody. Newspapers send scouts to college campuses every spring to recruit top students. He's tried only one city. He should start cranking out résumés to mail around the country."

"That's what I told him, but he wouldn't listen. He left early this morning and said he was going hunting. He said he'd go to the farmhouse and pick up his brother's rifle—if his mother hasn't sold it already. That's why I'm worried. Juney isn't much of a woodsman, and he isn't crazy about hunting."

"Just getting out in the woods will be good therapy, Jody. It'll sharpen his perspective. And the weather's not bad. Don't worry about him."

"Well, I don't know . . ."

"When Junior gets back, we'll get together and have a talk."

Qwilleran had made an afternoon appointment with Junior's Grandma Gage for an oral history interview, but he had an hour to kill, and he felt restless. Mrs. Cobb's announcement had distressed him, and Junior's disappointment made him vaguely uncomfortable, so he took his own advice: He drove out into the country.

It was a gray day, not likely to cheer one up, and without snow the terrain looked dreary. Traveling north to Mooseville, through good hunting country, he glanced down side roads, looking for Junior's car. Here and there a hunter's car or pickup was parked well off the shoulder in a desolate wooded area, but there was no sign of a red Jaguar. He caught glimpses of a blaze-orange figure crouching in a cornfield or entering the woods, and he heard rifle shots. He was glad he had worn his own blaze-orange cap.

Arriving at his property on the lakeshore, he followed the winding dirt road that led to the cabin. He saw the tire tracks where the camper had parked. Then he went up to the log cabin overlooking the lake. With the windows shuttered, power turned off, and water system drained, it was colder inside than out. On the beach the snow fences were in position. The lake looked grim and ready to freeze. Altogether the scene was bleak and lonely. He heard rifle shots in the woods and hurried back to his car.

On the way to his appointment with Euphonia Gage he took a detour down MacGregor Road, looking for the cottage where Polly claimed to be living under the watchful eye of her elderly landlord. There were no habitations on this country road—just open fields interspersed with patches of woods. There was no traffic except for one car with a buck tied to the roof. The driver gave Qwilleran a happy grin and a **V** sign.

Suddenly there was a jog in the road, and the pavement gave way to gravel. A little farther on, two mailboxes on cedar posts marked a long driveway bordered with shrubs. It led to a cluster of buildings: a substantial stone farmhouse, a tiny frame cottage in the rear, some sheds, and a weathered barn sagging limply to the ground. The names on the mailboxes were MacGregor and Duncan.

No car was in sight. No farm machinery. No barking dog. But a goose rounded a corner of the main house and honked in a menacing manner. With extreme caution and with one eye on the bird, Qwilleran stepped out of the car and moved toward the side door of the farmhouse. There was no need to knock. He had already been announced.

"What do you want?" screamed a querulous voice. An old man, frail and stooped, appeared in the doorway, wearing three sweaters and some knitted leg warmers over his trousers.

"Mr. MacGregor? I'm Jim Qwilleran. Just want to ask you a question, sir."

"What are you selling? I don't want to buy anything."

"I'm not a salesman. I'm looking for a hunter who drives a red Jaguar."

"Red what?"

"A red car. Bright red."

"I don't know," the old man said. "I'm color-blind."

"Thank you anyway, Mr. MacGregor. Good day."

Still watching the goose, Qwilleran backed away. He had determined that Polly really lived in a cottage adjoining a farmhouse belonging to an elderly landlord named MacGregor. Satisfied, he drove back to town. The cottage, he remarked, was incredibly small.

At two-thirty he rang the doorbell of a large stone house on Goodwinter Boulevard, to interview the eighty-two-year-old president of the Old Timers Club. The woman who came to the door was the right age, but he doubted that she could do headstands and push-ups.

"Mrs. Gage is in her studio," the woman said. "You can go right in—through the front parlor."

A gloomy cave of dark velvet, heavy carved furniture, and black horsehair upholstery led into a light, bright studio, unfurnished except for two large mirrors and an exercise mat. A little woman in leotard, tights, and leg warmers sat in lotus position on the mat. She rose effortlessly and came forward.

"Mr. Qwilleran! I've heard so much about you from Junior! And of course I've read your column in the *Fluxion.*" Her voice was calm but vibrant. She threw on a baggy knee-length sweater and led him back into the suffocating front parlor.

She was petite but not frail, white haired but smooth skinned.

"I understand you're president of the Old Timers Club," he said.

"Yes, I'm eighty-two. The youngest member is automatically appointed president."

"I suspect you lied about your age."

Her pleased expression acknowledged the compliment. "I intend to live to be a hundred and three. I think a hundred and four would be excessive, don't you? Exercise is the secret, and *breathing* is the most important factor. Do you know how to *breathe,* Mr. Qwilleran?"

"I've been doing my best for fifty years."

"Stand up and let me place my hands on your rib cage. . . . Now breathe in . . . breathe out . . . inhale . . . exhale. You do very well, Mr. Qwilleran, but you might work on it a little more. Now, what can I do for you?"

"I'd like to turn on this tape recorder and ask you some questions about the early days in Moose County."

"I shall be happy to oblige."

The following interview was later transcribed:

Question: When did your ancestors come to Moose County, Mrs. Gage?

My grandfather came here in the mid-nineteenth century, straight out of medical school. He was the first doctor, and he was treated like a blessing from heaven. There were no hospitals or clinics. Everything was primitive. He made house calls on horseback, sometimes ahead of a pack of howling wolves. And once, after a forest fire, when all the trails were impassable, he chopped his way through fifteen miles of debris with an ax in order to treat the survivors. They were burned and mutilated and blinded, and there were no medicines except what he brought in his knapsack.

What kind of medicines did he have?

Grandfather mixed his own and rolled his own pills, using herbs and botanicals like rhubarb powder and arnica and nux vomica. Some of his patients preferred old-fashioned remedies like catnip tea or a good slug of whiskey. They never paid for his services with money. They'd give him two chickens for setting a broken bone or a bushel of apples for delivering a baby.

What kind of cases did he handle?

Everything. Fever, smallpox, lung disease, surgery, dentistry. He pulled teeth with a pair of "twisters." And there were plenty of emergencies caused by spring floods, poisonous snakes, sawmill accidents, kicking mules, saloon brawls. Amputations were very common. I have his collection of saws, knives, and scalpels.

Why so many amputations?

There were no antibiotics. An infected limb had to be cut off, or the patient would die of blood poisoning. Grandfather talked about performing surgery by candlelight in a log cabin while a member of the family shooed flies away from the open incision. That was over a hundred years ago, you understand. When my father began his practice, conditions had improved. He had an office in our front parlor, and he made house calls in a buggy or sleigh, and he had a full-time driver who lived in the stable and took care of the horses. The driver—Zack was his name—later went to work for the *Picayune* and achieved notoriety by killing Titus Goodwinter.

Do you know the circumstances?

To go back a bit, Zack's father was a miner, blown to bits in an underground explosion. Zack became a bitter and violent man who regularly beat his wife and two children. Father used to patch them up and report it to the constable, but nothing was done about it. Zack's young daughter worked at the *Picayune,* too, and Titus, who was a flagrant roué, seduced the poor girl. She drowned herself, and Zack went after Titus with a hunting knife. Not a pretty story.

Was the Picayune *a good newspaper in its early days?*

Well . . . I'll tell you . . . if you'll turn that thing off.

End of interview.

After Qwilleran snapped off the tape recorder, Mrs. Gage said, "I can speak to you confidentially because you're a friend of my favorite grandson. Junior speaks highly of you. The truth is: I have never thought well of that branch of the Goodwinter family, nor of the newspaper they published. Ephraim, the founder of the *Picayune,* was not a journalist. He was a rich mine owner and lumber baron who would do anything for money. It was his avarice and negligence that caused the terrible mine explosion, killing thirty-nine men. Eventually he took his own life. His sons were no better.

His grandson, Senior, was a strange one; he was interested only in *setting type!*" She rolled her eyes in derision.

"Why did your daughter marry him?" Qwilleran asked bluntly, since Euphonia was noted for blunt candor.

"Gritty had *always* wanted to marry a Goodwinter, and she *always* did exactly what she wanted. It was a strange match. She's a spirited girl who likes a good time. Senior had no spirit at all and was certainly not my idea of a good time. How they produced Junior, I can't explain. He's too small to be Gritty's offspring—she's such an amazon!—and too smart to be Senior's son."

"Recessive genes," Qwilleran said. "He resembles his grandmother."

"You are a charming man, Mr. Qwilleran. I wish Junior might have had you for a father."

"You are a charming woman, Mrs. Gage."

They both paused for a moment of mutual admiration, and he found himself wishing she were thirty years younger. Spirit—that's what she had—spirit! Probably the result of all that *breathing.*

"Do you think Junior shows promise?" she asked.

"Great promise, Mrs. Gage. You can be proud of him. Were you aware that the *Picayune* was failing?"

"Of course I was aware. I tried to help. I don't know what the man did with my money, unless . . ."

"Unless what, Mrs. Gage?"

"I'll be perfectly frank. Let it all hang out, as Junior says. You see, I learned in a roundabout way that Senior had been making frequent one-day trips Down Below. To Minneapolis, as a matter of fact. If my son-in-law had ever shown any *spirit,* I would have guessed it was another woman. Under the circumstances, I could only deduce that he was gambling as a last resort—gambling and losing."

"Has it occurred to you that his death may have been suicide?"

She looked startled. "Senior would not have the spirit, Mr. Qwilleran, to take his own life."

Upon leaving, he said, "You are an excellent subject for an interview, Mrs. Gage. I hope we can meet again—perhaps for dinner some evening."

"I shall be delighted to accept if the invitation is still good in the spring. I leave for Florida tomorrow," she said. "This has been *such* a pleasure, Mr. Qwilleran. Now don't forget to *breathe!*"

Qwilleran was in a good mood that evening as he lounged in his favorite leather chair in the library, stroking the cat on his lap and waiting for a book to hit the carpet. He had stopped remonstrating; the book trick was becoming a game that he and Koko played together. The cat pulled out a title; Qwilleran read aloud, accompanied by purrs, iks, and yows.

On this occasion Koko's selection was *The Life of Henry V*, a good choice, Qwilleran thought. He thumbed through the pages for a passage he liked: the king's pep talk to his troops. *"Once more unto the breach, dear friend; once more!"*

Koko assumed his listening position, sitting tall and attentive on the desktop, his tail curled around his front paws, his blue eyes sparkling black in the lamplight.

It was a powerful speech, filled with graphic detail. *"But when the blast of war blows in our ears, then imitate the action of the tiger!"*

"Yow!" said Koko.

With such an appreciative audience Qwilleran was not shy about dramatizing the script. With a terrible look in his eyes he wrinkled his brow, stiffened his sinews, bared his teeth, stretched his nostrils, and breathed hard. Koko was purring hoarsely.

Bellowing at full volume, Qwilleran delivered the last line: *"Cry God for Harry! England and Saint George!"*

"YOW-OW!" Koko howled. Yum Yum fled from the room in alarm, and Mrs. Cobb came running.

"Oh! I thought you were being murdered, Mr. Q."

"Merely reading to Koko," he explained. "He seems to enjoy the sound of the human voice."

"It's *your* voice he likes. Last night everyone was saying you should join the theater group," she said.

When the household returned to its normal calm, a name flashed across Qwilleran's mind—Harry Noyton. He had had dealings with Harry Down Below. The man was a reckless entrepreneur who was always searching for a new challenge or a financial gamble. No matter how absurd the proposition, Harry always made it pay. He was currently living alone in Chicago, in a penthouse atop an office tower he had built.

On an impulse Qwilleran dialed Noyton's apartment, and a subhuman voice stated that he could be reached at his London hotel.

"How's that for a coincidence?" Quilleran asked Koko. "Harry's in England!" He glanced at his watch. Ten-thirty. It would be the middle of the night in London. All the better! Noyton had often roused him from sleep at an unearthly hour, and without apology.

He dialed the London hotel, expecting it to be the Saint George, but it was Claridge's. When Noyton's voice came on the phone he sounded as vigorous as he did at high noon; his energy was phenomenal.

"Qwill! How's the boy? I hear you're living high on the hog since leaving the *Flux*. What's cookin'? I know you never spend a quarter on a phone call unless it's urgent."

"How would you like to be a newspaper tycoon, Harry?"

"Is the *Fluxion* up for sale?"

Qwilleran described the situation in Pickax, adding, "It would be a crime to prostitute a century-old newspaper as an advertising throwaway. The county needs a paper, and the *Picayune* name is part of everyone's life. It's had national publicity this week, and there's more to come. If someone made the widow a better offer, she might see the light."

"Hell, I'll talk to the widow. I'm good at talking to widows."

Qwilleran believed it. Noyton was a self-made man with a talent for attracting women as well as money, although he had never acquired any polish. Even in a tailor-made three-piece suit he succeeded in looking like a scarecrow. He had several ex-wives and was always looking for another.

"I'm flying home tomorrow," he said. "How do I get to Pickax? Never heard of the place."

"You fly to Minneapolis and then pick up a hedgehopper to Moose County. Sorry I don't know the schedule. Probably they've never had one."

"I'll charter something. I'll get there somehow. Nobody can keep me on the ground for long."

"Better get here before snow flies."

"I'll give you a ring from Minneapolis."

"Good! I'll pick you up at the airport, Harry."

With a comfortable feeling of accomplishment, Qwilleran began his nightly house check and, in so doing, found another pigskin book on the floor. This time it was *All's Well That Ends Well.*

"It hasn't ended yet, old boy," he told Koko as he dropped the two protesting cats into the wicker hamper.

He was right. At two o'clock in the morning he was roused from sleep by a telephone call from Jody.

"Mr. Qwilleran, I'm so worried. Juney hasn't come home."

"Maybe he went to his mother's house. Have you called there?"

"There was no answer. Pug has gone back to Montana, and Mrs. Goodwinter is probably staying . . . in Indian Village. I called Grandma Gage earlier, and she thought Juney was still Down Below. I even called Roger, his friend in Mooseville."

"Then we'd better notify the police. I'll call the sheriff. You sit tight."

"I'm going crazy, Mr. Qwilleran. I feel like going out and looking for him myself."

"You can't do that, Jody. You should call a friend and have her stay with you. How about Francesca?"

"I hate to call her so late."

"I'll call her for you. A police chief's daughter is used to emergencies. Now you hang up so I can call the sheriff. And drink some warm milk, Jody."

SEVEN

SATURDAY, NOVEMBER SIXTEENTH. "Possibility of snow squalls today with falling temperatures. Presently it's twenty-five degrees. Last night's low, fifteen. . . . And now for the news: A hunter reported missing early this morning has been found by sheriff's deputies aided by state troopers. Junior Goodwinter is listed in fair condition at Pickax Hospital, suffering from exposure and a broken leg."

As Qwilleran later learned from police chief Brodie, a deputy on routine patrol of side roads on the opening day of hunting season had spotted the red Jaguar parked near a wooded area. When Junior was reported missing, they were able to start the search at that point, using tracking dogs and the mounted posse, a volunteer group of farmers who were expert horsemen.

"It seems to me," Qwilleran said to Mrs. Cobb at the breakfast table, "that no one should go hunting alone. Too many hazards."

"Herb always goes alone," she said.

Qwilleran thought, That guy can't find anyone to go with him. Uncharitable thoughts came to his mind whenever Hackpole was mentioned. Aloud he said, "If he's taking you to dinner tonight, why not bring him in for a drink before you leave?"

"That would be nice," she said. "We'll have it right here in the kitchen. He'll be more comfortable here."

"Would he like a tour of the museum?"

"Well, to tell the truth, Mr. Q, he thinks art objects are dust catchers, but I'd like to show him the basement."

"You've never told me anything about his background," Qwilleran said, although he had heard about it from Junior.

"He grew up here. After a hitch in the army he worked on the East Coast, married, and had a couple of kids. They're grown-up now, and he doesn't even know where they are."

That fits the picture, Qwilleran thought.

"He came back to Moose County because of his wife's allergies, but she didn't like country life and she left him."

Ran off with a beer truck driver, Qwilleran had heard.

"He's a very lonely man, and I feel sorry for him."

"Has he shown you the farmhouse?"

"Not yet, but I know what I want to do—strip the wallpaper, paint the walls white, and stencil them."

"Would you like to have the big pine wardrobe? If so, it's your wedding present."

She gasped. "You mean the Pennsylvania German *schrank?* Oh, I'd love it! But are you sure you want to part with it?"

"My life will never be the same without it," he said. "I expect to have anxiety attacks and periods of great depression, and I may have to go into therapy, but I want you to have the *schrank.*"

"Oh, Mr Q, you're kidding me again."

"Have you set a date?"

"Next Saturday if it's all right with you. Herb just wanted us to go to the courthouse, but I told him I wanted to be married here. Susan Exbridge is standing up for me. Would you be willing to be best man?"

He controlled a gulp. "Be glad to, Mrs. Cobb. Do you have a guest list? We'll have a champagne reception."

"That's very kind of you, but I don't think Herb would care for a reception, Mr. Q."

"Let me know if you change your mind. I want you to have a memorable wedding. You've been a valuable asset here."

"There's one favor I'd like to ask, if you don't mind," she said. "Would you speak to Koko about the herb garden? He keeps moving it around."

"Did you ever try speaking to a cat about *anything?*" Qwilleran asked. "He crosses his eyes and scratches his ear and goes right on doing what he was doing."

"I wouldn't mention it, but . . . after I've moved the garden into a sunny spot, he moves it into a dark corner. I've seen him do it. He stands on his hind legs, puts his paws on the lower shelf, and pushes."

The corners of Qwilleran's mouth twitched as he pictured Koko wheeling the herbs across the stone floor of the solarium like a baby carriage. Sunlight was not plentiful in November, and that cat wanted the best patches of sun for himself.

"Why don't you ask Hackpole to devise some kind of brake for the wheels?" he suggested.

The doorbell rang.

"Oh, dear! I forgot to tell you," Mrs. Cobb said. "I guess I'm all discombobulated. Hixie Rice is stopping on her way to work. That's probably her at the front door." She jumped up.

"Sit still. I'll get it."

Hixie had parked her little car in the circular drive, and she was ogling the front door with its quantity of brass fittings polished to a dazzling brilliance by Mr. O'Dell.

"Everything is so grand, Qwill! You should have a butler," she said as her heels clicked across the white marble vestibule. "Here, I've brought you the latest delicacy in our frozen catfood line: lobster nuggets in Nantua sauce with anchovy garnish."

Koko made an immediately appearance in the foyer and stood staring at Hixie without expression, except for a fish-hook curve in his tail.

"I think he remembers me," Hixie said. "*Comment ça va, Monsieur Koko?*"

"Eeque, eeque," he replied. As Qwilleran gave Hixie a tour of the house, Koko followed like an overzealous security guard.

"Gorgeous rugs!" she said as they entered the drawing room.

The two large antique Aubussons were creamy in color, with borders and center medallions of faded pink roses.

"Watch Koko," Qwilleran said. "He always avoids stepping on the rose pattern."

"Weren't the old red dyes made from some kind of bug? Maybe he can smell it."

"After a hundred years? Don't try to explain it, Hixie. How about a cup of coffee?"

When they were settled comfortably in the library she gazed at the four thousand leather-bound books. "Did you find it traumatic, Qwill, to inherit a lot of money? Do you feel vulnerable or isolated or guilty?"

"Not particularly."

"Don't you find people envious or resentful or hostile?"

"You've been reading a book, Hixie. Actually, it's just a nuisance to have a lot of money, so I turn it over to a philanthropic trust, and they get rid of it quietly."

She started to light a cigarette, and he stopped her. "City ordinance. No smoking in museums. . . . How's your friend's mother?"

"Who?"

"You said Tony's mother had a stroke and he had to fly to Philadelphia."

"Oh, she's getting better, and he's back here, working on his cookbook," Hixie said airily. "I'm going to write a book myself, on the rest rooms in country restaurants. They're not to be believed!"

"Don't complain. You're lucky the facilities are indoors. What's your objection?"

"Well, let me tell you about the North Pole Cafe in Brrr. They have only one rest room, and you have to dodge a very busy cook and a three-hundred-pound female dishwasher to get there. When I found it, between a garbage can and a sour mop, the room was dark, and I couldn't find the light switch. So the cook came and pulled a greasy string hanging from the ceiling, and *voilà!* the rest room was flooded with light from a fifteen-watt bulb.

"My next problem: how to close the door. It was wide open—and apparently stuck. When I tried forcing it, a toilet brush and a bleach bottle fell down on my head. You see, they kept the door open by hooking it to a high shelf where they kept the cleaning stuff. I got the thing closed and started groping for the john. I could hear a gurgling sound underfoot, from some kind of drain in the floor. Every once in a while it choked and gurgled and bubbled. I worried about that.

"The john seat was anchored by one bolt, and it was riding sort of sidesaddle. The floor drain kept gurgling and bubbling. The rusty washbowl started gasping and erupting, so I got out of there fast and made a bush stop on the way home."

"Hixie, you always exaggerate," Qwilleran said. "How was the food?"

"Fabulous! I mean it! And now there's something I'd like to discuss with you. Would Koko endorse our line of frozen catfoods? We'd design a 'Koko's Choice' label and have

Koko T-shirts and other premiums. Maybe free bumper stickers saying, 'My Cat Loves Koko.' How does that go down?"

"I don't think he'd take kindly to exploitation. He doesn't go for anything unless it's his own idea."

"He could do TV commercials," she persisted. "Next week I'll bring a video camera and give him a screen test."

"That I've got to see," Qwilleran said. "How's everything at the Old Stone Mill?"

"My boss came in to dinner last night and said he's rewriting our contract, giving us a better deal."

"Congratulations!"

"He was feeling pretty good. He had some woman with him—not his wife—and they went through two bottles of our best champagne."

"I hear his divorce is now final."

"He's not wasting any time. The two of them were planning a southern cruise and hoping they could get away before snow flies."

"What did she look like?" Qwilleran asked.

"The hearty athletic type with a loud laugh—the kind I can't stand! Mr. X has an apartment in our complex, and I think she's moved in. Why is everyone around here so concerned about snow flying?"

Snow did not fly on Saturday, although it was still being predicted on the hourly weathercasts. Qwilleran was listening to the six o'clock news in the library when Mrs. Cobb peeked into the room.

"He's here," she said nervously.

Qwilleran followed her to the kitchen to greet the man who was stealing his housekeeper. He gave Hackpole a handshake intended to be hearty and sincere and found his fingers crushed in a powerful grip.

"They say we can expect some snow tonight," Qwilleran

said, employing Moose County's standard conversation opener.

"It won't snow for a few days yet," Hackpole said. "I've been out in the woods all day, and I can tell by the way the whitetails are acting."

"I hear you're an expert woodsman, and I'd like to hear more about that, but first . . . how about a drink? Mrs. Cobb, what is your pleasure?"

"Do you think I could have a whiskey sour?" she asked coyly.

"Shot and a beer for me," her date said. He was wearing his date-night attire: a corduroy sports coat with plaid flannel shirt. Koko had been circling him and finally ventured to sniff his shoes.

"Scat!" yelled Hackpole, stamping his foot.

Koko did not even blink.

"What's the matter with that cat? Is it deaf?" he asked. "I can make most cats jump two feet off the floor."

"Koko considers himself licensed to sniff shoes," Qwilleran said. "He knows you have dogs at home."

The three of them pulled up chairs around the ancient kitchen table imported from a Spanish monastery.

"Looks like you could use a new table," said the guest, surveying three centuries of carefully preserved distress marks. He tossed off the shot and then poked three fingers in the breast pocket of his sports coat.

Mrs. Cobb tapped his hand in an affectionate rebuke. "No smoking, dear. It's bad for the antiques, and it's forbidden by law in museums."

He left the cigarettes in his pocket and looked warily at Koko. "Why does it sit there staring at me?" he demanded with the irritability of a smoker who has been told not to smoke.

"Koko is evaluating you," Qwilleran said. "The data will be programmed in the minicomputer in his brain."

"We always used to have a pack of barn cats around," said the guest. "We'd tie a tin can to a cat's tail and have a swell moving target for a .22." He laughed, but he was the only one who did.

Qwilleran said, "If you tied a can to Koko's tail, he'd sit and stare at a point between your eyes until you began to feel dizzy. Soon there would be a dull ache under your left shoulder blade, then a stabbing abdominal pain. Your feet would get numb, and you'd find it hard to breathe. Then your blood would start to itch. Do you know what it feels like to have itching blood?"

Mrs. Cobb patted her friend's hand. "He's only kidding, dear. He's always kidding." She saw him fingering the cigarette pack again. "Oops! Musn't do!"

Hackpole threw the pack on the table.

"I hear you're pretty good with a deer rifle," Qwilleran said amiably.

"Yeah, I'm a pretty good shooter. I've hunted elk, moose, grizzlies—everything. The whitetail's my favorite, though. I've got some eight-point trophy bucks mounted, but the forkhorn gives the best meat. That's what I brought in yesterday. I always get my buck the first day."

Qwilleran thought, I'll bet he does some poaching the rest of the year.

"I made a clean kill and made sure it was well bled out. Then I gutted it, slung it over my back, and carried it to my pickup. I was home by noon. It weighed in at one ninety-eight."

Qwilleran mentally subtracted fifty pounds.

With a hint of pride Mrs. Cobb said, "Herb is a still-hunter."

"Yeah. You don't know about still-hunting, I bet."

Qwilleran had to admit his ignorance.

"Still-hunters, we don't sit behind a bush and wait for something to come down the trail. You hafta move around, looking for game—very slow, very careful, very quiet. When you sight your buck, you stalk it and wait for the best shot. You hafta move like a deer and make noise like a deer would. Like, no zippers, no cigarette lighters. You hafta have good eyes and a good running shot. Lotta satisfaction in still-hunting."

"I'm impressed," Qwilleran said as he poured another shot for his guest. "I understand you're also a volunteer fire fighter."

"I'm quittin'," Hackpole said, looking disgruntled. "A lotta women are joining up. I don't mind them running a canteen when it's an all-night fire, but they got no business driving a truck and hanging around the fire hall."

The bride-to-be said, "I'm glad he's giving it up. It's terribly dangerous."

"Yeah, smoke inhalation, for one thing. Or you're trying to vent a fire and the roof caves in. Once I saw a hose get away from the nozzleman and go whipping around, cracking heads and breaking bones. You don't know the power of water going through a hose! There's a lotta stuff people don't know."

"I've always wondered why firemen go crazy with the ax," Qwilleran said.

"We gotta vent the fire, so the smoke and heat can get out and we can go into the building and knock down the blaze."

"Any idea what caused the *Picayune* fire?"

"Started in the basement. That's all anybody knows. My shop did some repair work on those old presses. They had a drip pan underneath to catch the solvent when they cleaned off the ink. There was a lotta rags, a lotta paper. Bad business! The stairs acted like a flue, and the fire went right up to the roof."

"Well, dear," Mrs. Cobb said, "we ought to be going, but first I want you to see the pub in the basement."

The original builders of the mansion had imported an English pub from London, complete with bar, tavern tables and chairs, even wall paneling.

It was something Hackpole could appreciate. "Hey, you could get a liquor license and open a tavern down here," he said.

As they rode the elevator back to the main floor, Qwilleran asked where they were going to dinner.

"Otto's Tasty Eats. One price—all you can eat." He fingered his breast pocket. "Where's my cigarettes?"

"You left them on the kitchen table, dear," said Mrs. Cobb.

"I don't see the damn things," he called from the kitchen.

"Did you look in all your pockets?"

"It don't matter. I got another pack in the glove compartment."

Qwilleran extended his hand. "I'm glad we could finally meet, and let me congratulate you on finding a wonderful—"

He was interrupted by a loud crash. It came from the rear of the house. He and the housekeeper rushed into the solarium, followed slowly by their guest. The place was in darkness, but a pale, ghostly shape streaked out of the room as they entered.

When the lights were switched on, the catastrophe was revealed. In the middle of the floor stood the mobile herb garden, and nearby was a clay pot, smashed, with soil and foliage scattered in every direction. Other plants had been uprooted from their pots and flung about the room, and the floor was a gritty mess of soil and leaves.

"Oh dear! Oh dear!" said Mrs. Cobb in shock and dismay.

"It's our resident ghost," Qwilleran explained to Hackpole. "Did Mrs. Cobb tell you we have a ghost?"

Nobly she said, "Every old house should have a ghost," but there was a tremor in her voice, and she glanced around uneasily for a glimpse of the guilty cat.

"We'll replace everything," Qwilleran reassured her. "Don't worry. You two go to dinner, and I'll clean up the mess. Have a nice evening."

As soon as the couple had left, he went in search of the Siamese. As he expected, they were in the library, looking innocent and satisfied. He stepped on a small bump and found a cigarette under the Bokhara rug. That was Yum Yum's contribution to the occasion. Koko had his chin on his paw and his paw on the cover of a pigskin-bound book. He raised his head and turned bright expectant eyes on the man.

"I'm not going to read to you. You don't deserve it," Qwilleran said quietly but firmly. "That was a wicked thing to do. You know how much Mrs. Cobb loves her herb garden, and our food tastes better because of the things she grows. So don't expect any kind words from me! You lie there and contemplate your sins, and try to be a better cat in the future. . . . I'm going out to dinner."

He wrested the book away from Koko. It was *Hamlet* again. Before returning it to the shelf he sniffed it. Qwilleran had a keen sense of smell, but all he could detect was the odor of *old book*. He sniffed *Macbeth* and the other titles Koko had dislodged. They all smelled like *old book*. Then he compared the odor with titles that Koko had so far ignored: *Othello, As You Like It,* and *Antony and Cleopatra*. He had to admit they all smelled exactly the same—like *old book*. He went out to dinner.

EIGHT

SUNDAY, NOVEMBER SEVENTEETH. "Light snow turning to freezing rain," was the prediction. Actually, the sun was shining, and Qwilleran looked forward to taking a long walk.

Over the breakfast pancakes he apologized profusely to the housekeeper. "I'm really sorry about your herb garden, Mrs. Cobb. The pot he broke contained mint, which is related to catnip, I believe. Why he uprooted the others is a mystery. We'll replace them all."

"It won't be that easy," she said. "Four of them were started from seed in a cold fame at Herb's place. The others were plants, and we can't buy them at this time of year."

"There was no point in scolding him. Unless you catch a cat in the act and rap him on the nose, he doesn't connect the reprimand with the misdemeanor. That's what Lori Bamba said, and she knows all about cats. No doubt it was Yum Yum who stole the cigarettes. I found one under a rug and another behind a seat cushion."

"And I found the empty pack under a rug in the upstairs hall," Mrs. Cobb said.

"I'm afraid your evening got off to a bad start. Did you enjoy dinner?"

She pursed her lips, then admitted, "Well, we had a little argument. When he found out that cigarette smoke is injurious to antiques, he said I can't use them in the farmhouse. He's practically a chain-smoker."

"Could you use reproductions?"

"I hate copies, Mr. Q. I've lived too long with the real thing."

"There must be some compromise."

"I can think of one good compromise," she said crisply. "He can give up his smelly habit. You don't hear the surgeon general issuing any warnings against *antiques!*"

Qwilleran made sympathetic noises, then excused himself, saying he wanted to go out and buy a Sunday *Fluxion.*

He walked with a light step for two reasons. He sensed a rift between Mrs. Cobb and Hackpole that might forestall the marriage. And . . . he had received an invitation from Polly Duncan.

"Thursday is my day off," she had said. "Why don't you drive out to my cottage, and I'll do a roast with Yorkshire pudding? Come before dark; the house is easier to find in daylight."

He walked briskly. It was four miles around the periphery of Pickax, and on the way he met the fire chief, going into the drugstore for the Sunday *Fluxion.*

Qwilleran said, "Where's the snow that Moose County is famous for?"

"Couldna say, but this weather will do till the white stuff comes along."

"Explain something to me, Scottie. Pickax has a strange arrangement of streets. Nothing makes sense."

"It were laid out by two miners and a lumberjack on payday," said Scottie, "or so the story goes."

"How do the fire trucks ever find the right address? The city's bounded on the south by South Street—nothing wrong with that—but it's bounded on the north by East Street, on the west by North Street, and on the east by West Street. The ball field is at the corner of South North Street and West South Street. It could drive a logical mind crazy."

"Dunna look for logic up here, laddie," said Scottie, shaking his shaggy gray head.

"Did the fire marshal fly up to investigate the *Picayune* fire?"

"We needna call him unless it looks like arson, or somebody dies in the fire. And this one, it were accidental combustion caused by oily rags and solvents in the pressroom."

"How can you tell when a fire has been set?"

"Are you plannin' a little arson, laddie?"

"Not in the foreseeable future, Scottie."

"Weel, if you do, avoid leavin' a two-gallon jerry can on the premises, painted red and smellin' like gasoline. And dunna throw the match too soon. The explosion can throw you out the door."

"Can you tell when the fire starts with an explosion?"

"Aye. If the door is blown off the hinges—that's one way. And if the walls are charred deep."

Qwilleran finished his walk, stopping for a cup of coffee at a diner on N. North Street and the Sunday paper at a party store on S. West Street.

In the afternoon, as he was reading the *Fluxion* and counting typographical errors, the doorbell rang, and when he went to the front entrance he found an elderly face peering from the hood of a parka.

"Good afternoon," said the caller in a cheerful high-pitched voice. "Do you have any mouseholes you want plugged?"

"I beg your pardon?"

"Mouseholes. I'm good at plugging mouseholes."

Qwilleran was puzzled. Workmen always came to the service entrance; they never came on Sunday; and they were usually much younger.

"I was just taking my constitutional," said the old man. "It's a nice day for a walk. I'm Homer Tibbitt from the Old Timers Club."

"Of course! I didn't recognize you in the parka. Come in!"

"I saw your cat parading around with a mouse at the party, and I thought you might have some mouseholes you want plugged. I'd do it gratis."

"Let me take your coat, and we'll sit down and talk about it. Would you like a cup of coffee?"

"I'll take some if it's decaffeinated, and it won't hurt if you put a drop of brandy in it to start the old furnace working again."

They went into the library, Mr. Tibbitt walking vigorously with arms and legs flailing in awkward coordination. There was a fire in the grate, and he stood with his back to the warmth. "I'm used to old houses like this," he said. "I was volunteer custodian at the Lockmaster Museum in the county below. Have you heard of it?"

"Can't say that I have. I'm new up here."

"It was a shipbuilder's mansion—all wood construction—and I plugged fifty-seven mouseholes. In a stone house like this the mice have to be smarter, but we have smart mice in Pickax."

"What brought you up here to the Snow Belt, Mr. Tibbitt?"

"I was born here, and the old homestead was standing empty. There was another reason, too; a retired English teacher down in Lockmaster was chasing me. They like retired principals. I was principal of Pickax Upper School when I retired. I'm ninety-three. I started teaching school seventy years ago."

"You should have brought your English teacher to Pickax," Qwilleran said. "I've never heard so many butchered verbs and pronouns."

The principal gave an angular gesture of despair. "We've always tried our best, but there's a saying up here—if you'll pardon the grammar: Country folks is different, and Moose County folks is more different."

Despite his creaking joints, the old man was enormously energetic, and Qwilleran said, "Retirement seems to agree with you, Mr. Tibbitt."

"Keep busy! That's the ticket! Now, if you want me to do a survey on the mousehole situation . . ."

Qwilleran hesitated. "We have a janitor, you know. . . ."

"I've known Pat O'Dell since he was in the first grade. He's a good boy, but he hasn't made a study of mouseholes."

"Before we launch a campaign against *mus musculus,* Mr. Tibbitt, I'd like to get some of your recollections on tape for the oral history program—that is, if you would be willing."

"Turn on the machine. Ask me some questions. Just give me another cup of coffee with a drop of brandy—make it two drops—and be sure it's decaffeinated."

The following interview with Homer Tibbitt was later transcribed:

Question: What can you tell us about the early schools in Moose County?

Beginning way back when my mother was a schoolmarm, they were built of logs—just one room with desks around the walls, hard benches with no backs, and a potbellied stove in the middle. And they were drafty! She taught in one school where the snow blew through the chinks, and there were rabbit tracks in the snow on the floor.

What was required of a teacher in those days?

My mother walked three miles to school and got there

early enough to sweep the floor and start a wood fire in the stove. She taught eight grades in one room—without any textbooks! Her pay was a dollar a day plus free board and room with a farm family. Male teachers were paid two dollars.

How many students did she have in that one room?

Thirty or forty enrolled, but only half of them ever showed up for classes.

What subjects did she teach?

She was supposed to teach the three Rs, history, geography, grammar, penmanship, and orthography. She also organized games and special programs, and she was required to lecture on the evils of drink, tobacco, and tight corsets.

How about team sports? Was there athletic competition?

They played games at recess, and there was rivalry between schools, but it was over spelling matches, not football.

Had conditions improved when you started to teach?

We still had one-room schools, but they were well built, and we had textbooks. We still didn't have indoor plumbing. . . . Could I bother you for another cup of coffee? My mouth gets dry.

Did you know any of the Goodwinters connected with the newspaper?

I retired before Junior was born, but I had his father in my classes. Senior was a quiet boy with a one-track mind. I grew up with Titus and Samson, and I knew the old man. When I was eleven years old I worked as a printer's devil after school. Ephraim Goodwinter made plenty of money in mining, but he was greedy. Ever hear about the explosion that killed thirty-two men? The engineers had warned Ephraim, but he wouldn't spend the money on safety measures. After the explosion he tried to make it right by donating a public library.

Is it true he hanged himself?

Aha! That's one of Moose County's dirty little secrets. The

family said it was suicide, and the coroner said it was suicide, but everybody knew he was *lynched,* and everybody knew who was in the lynching party. The whole town turned out for his funeral. They wanted to be sure he didn't come back, the saying was.

What happened to Titus and Samson?

There was a cock-and-bull story about Samson's horse being frightened by a flock of blackbirds and that's how he was killed. Then Titus was murdered by the *Picayune* wagon driver. Died with his derby hat on his head.

Who was the wagon driver?

Zack Whittlestaff. This county is full of curious names: Cuttlebrink, Dingleberry, Fitzbottom—almost Elizabethan. I used to have a Falstaff in one of my classes, and a Scroop. Straight out of Shakespeare, eh?

Would you say there was a vendetta against the Goodwinters?

Well, the relatives of the explosion victims hated Ephraim, you can be sure of that. Zack was one of them. He was a ruffian. No good in school. Married a Scroop girl. I had their two children in my classes. The girl got into trouble and drowned herself. Left a suicide note addressed to her cat—probably the only living being that loved the poor girl.

End of interview.

The recording session was interrupted by a phone call from Minneapolis. Harry Noyton was on his way. His chartered plane would arrive at the Pickax airport at five-thirty.

"How's the weather up there?" Noyton asked.

"No snow, but it's cold. I hope you're bringing warm clothing."

"Hell, I don't own any warm clothes. I grab a heated taxi when I want to go somewhere."

"There are no taxis in Moose County," Qwilleran said. "We'll have to buy you some long johns and a hat with earflaps. Meet you at five-thirty."

He allowed plenty of time for driving. Airport Road ran through deer country. At dusk they would be feeding and moving around. Gun hunters had been in the woods for three days, stirring them up and making them nervous. Qwilleran drove cautiously.

While waiting for the plane to land he had a few words with Charlie. "Do you think we'll get any snow this winter?"

"It's kinda late, but when it comes it'll be the Big One."

"I hear you've lost a good customer."

"Who?"

"Senior Goodwinter."

"Yeah. Too bad. He was a nice fellah. Killed himself with work. Most people are always taking off for Florida or Vegas or somewhere, but all he ever did was fly down to Minneapolis on business and come back the same day. That's why I say he killed himself with work. Fell asleep at the wheel, most likely."

When Noyton galumphed off the plane, he had a light raincoat flapping around his lanky figure, and he carried a traveling bag just large enough for a razor and an extra shirt. That was his style. He boasted he could fly around the world with a toothbrush and a credit card.

"Qwill, you old rooster! You look like a farmer with those boots and that hat!"

"And you look like a visitor from outer space," Qwilleran said. "You'll frighten the natives with that three-piece suit. First thing tomorrow we'll take you to Scottie's Men's Shop and buy some camouflage. . . . Buckle up, Harry," he added as he turned on the ignition in his small car.

"Hell, I never fastened a seat belt in my life, except on planes."

Qwilleran turned off the ignition and folded his arms. "There are ten thousand deer in Moose County, Harry. This is the rutting season. At this time of evening all the bucks chase all the does back and forth across the highway. If we hit a buck, you'll go through the windshield, so buckle up."

"Jeez! The odds are better at the Beirut airport!"

"Last winter a buck chased a doe down Main Street in Pickax, and they both went through the plate-glass window of a furniture store. Landed in a water bed."

Noyton fastened his seat belt and stared anxiously at the road for the next ten miles, while Qwilleran scanned the cornfields and thickets for movement.

"If we encounter a buck, Harry, do you want me to hit him broadside and risk having his hooves come through the windshield, or shall I try to avoid him and land upside down in a ditch?"

"Jeez! Do I have a choice?" said Noyton, gripping the dashboard with both hands.

When they reached the outskirts of Pickax, Qwilleran said, "Here's the program. Tomorrow I turn you over to the mayor and the economic development people. He'll put you in touch with the widow—and she's a merry one, I might add. Tonight I'll take you to dinner at the Old Stone Mill. After that there's a bedroom suite awaiting you at the palace I inherited. You have your choice of Old English with side curtains on the bed, or Biedermeier with flowers painted on everything, or Empire with enough sphinxes and gryphons to give you nightmares."

"To tell the truth, Qwill, I'd be a helluva lot more comfortable in a hotel. It gives me more flexibility. I had a meal in Minneapolis, and now I'd like to turn in. Any objection?"

"None at all. The New Pickax Hotel is centrally located near the city hall."

"Building new hotels, are they?" Noyton said with obvious approval.

"The New Pickax Hotel was built in 1935 after the original hotel burned down. It has a part-time bellhop, color TV in the lobby, indoor plumbing, and locks on the doors."

He dropped Noyton at the hotel entrance. "Call me tomorrow when you're rested, and I'll pick you up for breakfast. I want a private talk with you before turning you over to the mayor."

At the end of the day Qwilleran and his two friends relaxed in the library for a while before lights-out. Yum Yum sat on his lap with her back in a convenient position for stroking, and Koko sat tall and alert on the desktop, awaiting conversation.

Qwilleran began in an even, conciliatory tone. "I don't know what to say to you, Koko. You're not usually destructive—unless you have a reason. Why did you ruin the herb garden?"

The cat squeezed his eyes and made a small sound without opening his mouth.

"It won't do any good to act contrite. The damage is done. If you're trying to alienate our splendid housekeeper, you're cutting off your whiskers to spite your face. You won't eat half so well when she's married and living somewhere else."

Koko hopped from the desk to the bookshelf and started pawing at the set of plays.

"No readings tonight. I've had a full day. But we'll play Mr. Tibbitt's tape and see how it sounds."

The small portable recorder made the old man's high-pitched voice even more nasal and shrill, and Koko shook his head and batted his ears with a paw.

There was the ring of a telephone bell on the tape, and the recording came to an abrupt end. Qwilleran stroked his moustache reflectively. "Ephraim was lynched," he said aloud. "Titus was knifed. The other brother—Samson—was probably ambushed. And Senior was . . . what? Was his death an accident? Or was it suicide? Or was it murder?"

"Yow!" said Koko, and Qwilleran felt a significant twinge in the roots of his moustache.

NINE

MONDAY, NOVEMBER EIGHTEENTH. "An unexpected cold snap brought temperatures as low as five degrees in Pickax last night, six below in Brrr, but a warming trend is indicated with a few snow flurries this afternoon."

Qwilleran snapped off his car radio with an impatient gesture. Despite the predictions, Moose County had yet to see even a light dusting of snow. He was driving to the New Pickax Hotel in the limousine that he had inherited from the Klingenschoen estate, the better to impress the visitor from Down Below.

When Noyton saw the long black vehicle, he said, "Jeez! Qwill, you've really got it made! How come? Did you marry oil? No one ever told me why you left the *Fluxion.* I thought you retired to write a book."

"It's a long story," Qwilleran said. "First I want to show you where I live and treat you to one of my housekeeper's memorable breakfasts."

"You—with a housekeeper as well as a limo? I remember when you lived in a furnished room and rode the bus."

"Actually I live over the garage, and I'm turning the house into a museum."

In a state of wonder Noyton walked into the K mansion

and said, "I know kings in Europe that don't live this good. One thing I want to know: Why am I here? Why don't you finance this newspaper yourself?"

It was a question that Qwilleran was tired of hearing. He explained his position. "I'm a writer, Harry, not an entrepreneur." He related the history of the *Picayune* and reiterated the county's crying need for a newspaper.

"Who's going to run it?" was Noyton's first question.

"Arch Riker has just left the *Fluxion*. He's a great editor and knows the business inside out. Junior Goodwinter is the last of a long line of newspaper Goodwinters. He's a trained journalist. His academic record is tops, and he has boundless energy and enthusiasm."

"Sounds like my kind of joe. Who's the widow?"

"Gritty Goodwinter . . ."

"I like her already!"

"She wants to sell the newspaper to a close personal friend who'll only exploit the name of the hundred-year-old publication. Of course, you could forget the *Picayune* and start something called the *Backwoods Gazette* or the *Moose Call,* but the *Picayune* had a million dollars' worth of publicity last week and is due for more in a national news magazine."

"I got the picture," Noyton said. "We'll get the paper away from those bastards."

"Mrs. Goodwinter also has a barnful of antique printing presses. You could start a newspaper museum."

"I like it!" Noyton exclaimed. "What made you think of me, anyway?"

Qwilleran hesitated. They were eating breakfast, and Koko was under the table hoping someone would drop a strip of bacon. "Well, it's like this: Your name just popped into my head." How could he explain to a man like Noyton that the cat had drawn his attention to a certain book? No, it was too farfetched.

After breakfast the two men paid a visit to Scottie's Men's Shop. The proprietor burred his *r*'s and sold Noyton a raccoon car coat, an Aussie hat, and some tooled leather boots. For the rest of the day the big ungainly man with a craggy face was highly visible in Pickax.

He was seen leaving the hotel, entering the city hall, driving around with the mayor, lunching with influential men at the country club, walking out of the law office, walking into the bank, dining with the Goodwinter widow, and eating a twenty-ounce steak with two baked potatoes.

It was rumored that he was a Texan buying oil rights that would make Moose County farmers rich. Or he was a speculator promoting offshore drilling that would ruin the tourist industry. Or he was the advance man for a nuclear power plant that would leak radiation, contaminate the drinking water, and kill the fish. Or he was a Hollywood scout for a major movie to be made in Moose County. The rumors were reported by Mrs. Cobb, who had heard them from Mrs. Fulgrove, who had been told by Mr. O'Dell.

Meanwhile Qwilleran made a morning visit to the hospital to see the young newspaper editor who was known for his boundless energy and enthusiasm. Junior was slumped in a chair with his leg in a cast, his face unshaven, and his expression disgruntled. Jody was flitting about, trying to be cheerful and useful, but Junior was being stubbornly morose.

"You idiot!" Qwilleran greeted the patient. "If you're going to break a leg, why not pick a more comfortable place?"

Jody said, "He caught a bad cold in the woods, but it didn't go into pneumonia. He wants to stay in the hospital until his beard grows."

"Nowhere else to go," Junior said hopelessly. "The farmhouse is sold. The furniture is being auctioned off

Wednesday. I can't stay with Jody; all she's got is a studio apartment."

"We have some spare beds you're welcome to use," Qwilleran said.

"I don't know. I just don't know what to do."

"Well, wipe that bleak look off your face. I have some good news. An acquaintance of mine from Down Below wants to buy a newspaper. He's prepared to offer your mother three times what XYZ has offered, and he'll sink a bundle into a new printing plant."

Junior looked wary. "Is he crazy?"

"Crazy and loaded. He owns office buildings, hotels, ball clubs, a chain of restaurants, and a couple of breweries in the U.S. and abroad, and he likes the idea of owning a newspaper. He might get into magazines later on."

"I don't believe it. I'm hallucinating. Or you're hallucinating."

Jody cried, "Oh, Juney! Isn't that fabulous?"

Qwilleran went on. "Noyton is here now. The city fathers are gung ho. The plan is for Arch Riker to be the publisher, and you'll be managing editor of a real newspaper. I know some young journalists Down Below who are disenchanted with the city, and they'll find this a good place to raise a family. They won't earn as much as they did Down Below, but it costs less to live up here. Who knows? We might get Noyton to finance a decent airport and buy an airline. We'll have to monitor his enthusiasm, though, or he'll build a fifty-story hotel in the middle of a cornfield."

Junior was speechless.

"Oh, Juney," his little friend kept squealing, "say something."

"Are you sure it's going through?"

"Noyton never backs down."

"But my mother has this . . . close connection with Exbridge."

"Connection! She's having an affair with Exbridge, and you know it. But if she's as hungry as it appears, she'll forget about XYZ and go for the larger fish. Not only will Noyton jingle hard cash in her ears; he'll turn on the charm. Women like him."

"Is he married?" asked Jody.

"Not at the moment, but he's too old for you, Jody."

She giggled.

"He's interested in buying the old presses in the barn also, to start a newspaper museum. Your father would be pleased, Junior."

"Oh, wow!"

"Jody," said Qwilleran, "would you get us some coffee from the cafeteria? And some of those oatmeal cookies made out of cardboard and sawdust?" He handed her a bill and waited for her to disappear. "Before she returns, Junior, answer a few questions, will you? Do you think your father's accident might have been suicide?"

Junior stared. "I don't think—he'd do—anything like that?"

"He had bankrupted the family. Your mother was having an affair. And there might be another reason."

"What do you mean?"

"Do you remember that stranger in a black raincoat who came up here on the plane? You thought he was a traveling salesman. I think he was an investigator of some kind. If your father was involved in anything shady, he might have known the man was coming. . . ."

"My dad wouldn't do anything illegal," Junior protested. "He didn't have that kind of mind."

"Next question: Could it have been murder?"

"WHAT!" Junior almost jumped out of his cast. "Why would . . . who would . . . ?"

"Skip that one. What was in the metal box you tried to save after the fire?"

"I don't know. Dad was very secretive about it, but I knew it was important."

"How big was it?"

Junior sneezed and reached for a tissue. "About as big as a tissue box."

"I hear Jody coming. Tell me this: Why was your father making frequent one-day trips to Minneapolis?"

"He never told me." Junior's face turned red. "But I know he wasn't getting along with my mother."

Jody returned with the coffee. "No oatmeal cookies left, so I brought molasses."

"They taste like burnt tires," Junior said after a couple of nibbles. "How was the turnout at the preview, Qwill?"

"Full house! I've started interviewing the Old Timers and taping oral histories. Got any suggestions? I've got your grandmother and Homer Tibbitt on tape."

"Mrs. Woolsmith," Jody said in a small voice. "She'd be a good one."

Junior scratched his emerging beard. "You should be able to find some who remember the mines and the pioneer farms and the fishing industry before powerboats."

"Mrs. Woolsmith lived on a farm," Jody said softly.

"I need a subject with a reliable memory," Qwilleran said.

"You'll still have to drag it out of them," Junior warned him. "The Old Timers like to talk about their blood pressure and their dentures and their great-grandchildren."

Jody said, "Mrs. Woolsmith has almost all her own teeth."

'Well, give it some thought," Qwilleran said to Junior. "There's no hurry."

"Wait a minute! I've got it! There's a woman in the senior care facility," Junior suddenly recalled. "She's over ninety, but she's sharp, and she spent all her life on a farm. Her name is Woolsmith. Sarah Woolsmith."

Jody picked up her coat and shoulder bag and walked quietly from the room.

"Hey, where's she going?" Junior yelled.

Following his session at the hospital, Qwilleran went to lunch at Stephanie's, wondering about Senior's metal box and his frequent trips to Minneapolis. Junior's red-faced embarrassment meant that he knew or suspected the reason. Young people who are quite casual in their own relationships can be strangely embarrassed by the sexual adventures of their elders. As he was musing about this curious reaction, he heard a familiar voice at the table behind him.

A man was ordering a roast beef sandwich with mustard and horseradish. "Trim the fat, please. And bring a tossed salad with Roquefort dressing and no cucumber or green pepper."

The voice had a clipped twang that Qwilleran had heard before. He rose and walked in the direction of the men's room, glancing at his neighbor as he passed. It was the so-called historian he had confronted in the library. The man had exchanged his buttoned-down image for more casual attire—less conspicuous in Moose County—but there was no doubt about his identity. He was the stranger whose previous visit had coincided with Senior's fatal accident—or suicide—or murder.

Qwilleran spent the rest of his lunch hour sifting the possibilities. He composed scenarios involving the metal box . . . adultery . . . gambling . . . the drug connection . . . espionage. In none of them did the mild-mannered typesetter seem to fit.

TEN

TUESDAY, NOVEMBER NINETEENTH. "Warmer today, with highs in the upper twenties. Some chance of snow this afternoon, with blizzard conditions developing Wednesday. Currently our temperature is nineteen."

"That's terrible!" Mrs. Cobb said. "Tomorrow's the auction, and it's way out in the country. They say the hotel's already full of out-of-town dealers. They came for the preview this afternoon."

"Don't worry. If they predict a blizzard, it'll be a nice day," Qwilleran said with the cynicism of a Moose County weather nut. "How will they handle an auction in a house like that? It's nothing but a series of small rooms."

"The actual auction will probably be in the barn. The posters and radio announcements said to dress warm. Foxy Fred is handling it, so everything will be done right. I'm going to the preview this afternoon to pick up a catalogue. What time is Miss Rice coming? The cats are hungry."

At Hixie's suggestion the Siamese had been given only a teaspoonful of food for breakfast—only enough to keep them from chewing ankles. The idea was that Koko should be ravenously hungry for this screen test, and Yum Yum had to suffer with him. They yowled constantly while

Qwilleran ate his eggs Benedict. They paced the floor, got underfoot, and screeched when a foot accidentally came down upon a tail.

Koko evidently knew that Hixie was responsible for this outrage. Upon her arrival he greeted her with a button-eyed glare and a switching tail.

"Bonjour, Monsieur Koko," she said. He turned and walked stiff-legged into the laundry room, where he scratched the gravel in his commode.

"Here's my scenario," she explained to Qwilleran. "We start with a shot of the front door, which denotes elegance and wealth at a glance. Then we enter the foyer, and the camera pans from the French furniture to the grand staircase to the crystal chandelier."

"It sounds like prime-time soap opera."

"Next we zoom to the top of the staircase, where Koko is sitting, looking bored."

"Who's going to direct this?" Qwilleran wanted to know.

Hixie ignored the question. "Then the butler announces in a starchy voice that pork liver cupcakes are served. That's voice-over. You can do the voice-over, Qwill. Immediately Koko runs downstairs, flowing in that liquid way he has, and the camera follows him into the dining room."

"Dining room?" Qwilleran muttered doubtfully. The Siamese were accustomed to meals in the kitchen and were reluctant to eat in the wrong location.

Hixie went on with her usual confidence. "Quick shot of the twenty-foot dining table with three-foot silver candelabra and a single elegant porcelain plate. We can use one of the Klingenschoen service plates with the blue border and gold crest and *K* monogram. . . . Then . . . cut to Koko devouring the pork liver cupcakes avidly. We may need to do several takes, so be prepared to grab him, Qwill. The trick is to avoid rear-end shots."

"That won't be easy. Cats are fond of mooning."

"Okay, you put him on the top stair."

Koko had been listening with an expression that could be described only as sour. When Qwilleran stooped to pick him up, he slipped from his grasp like a wet bar of soap, streaked down the foyer in a blur of movement, and sprang to the top of the Pennsylvania *schrank*. From this seven-foot perch he gazed down at his pursuers defiantly. He was sitting dangerously close to a large, rare majolica vase.

"I don't dare climb up and grab him," Qwilleran said. "He's taken a hostage. He probably knows it's worth ten thousand dollars."

"I didn't know he was so temperamental," Hixie said.

"Let's have a cup of coffee in the kitchen and see what happens when we ignore him. Siamese hate to be ignored."

In a few minutes Koko joined them, sauntering into the room with a swaggering show of nonchalance. He sat on his haunches like a kangaroo and innocently licked a small patch of fur on his underside. When this chore was finished he allowed himself to be carried to the top of the staircase.

Hixie directed from below. "Arrange him in a compact bundle on the top step, Qwill, facing the camera."

He lowered the cat gently to the carpeted stair, but Koko stiffened his body. His back humped, his tail curled into a corkscrew, and all four legs looked out-of-joint.

"Try it again," Hixie called up to them. "Tuck his legs under his body."

"You come up and tuck his legs under his body," Qwilleran said, "and I'll go down and take the pictures. Your scenario is good, Hixie, but it won't play."

"Well, bring him down, and we'll do a close-up with the catfood to see how he looks on camera."

Qwilleran lugged Koko into the dining room. By now the cat was a squirming, protesting, nasty, snarling bundle of flying fur.

"Ready, Mrs. Cobb!" Hixie shouted toward the kitchen.

The housekeeper, who was standing by as prop-person, trotted from the kitchen carrying a plate heaped with gray pork paste. "Is this going to be in color?" she asked.

Carefully Qwilleran placed Koko in front of the plate—profile to the camera—while Hixie moved in with her telephoto lens. Koko looked down at the gray blob, with his ears and whiskers swept backward in loathing. He picked up one fastidious paw and shook it in distaste. Then he shook the other paw and slowly walked away, switching his tail.

Qwilleran said, "If you ever need a picture of a cat slowly walking away, Koko is your subject."

"It was all new and strange to him," said Hixie, undaunted. "We'll try it another day."

"I'm afraid Koko will always be his own cat. He cares nothing for fame and fortune and media exposure. The word *cooperation* has never been in his vocabulary. Whenever I try to take a snapshot, he rolls over on his haunches, points one leg to heaven in a pornographic pose, and licks his intimate parts. . . . Let's go and finish our coffee."

Mrs. Cobb had a fresh pot waiting for them, and she served it in the library with a few of her apricot-almond crescents.

"What's new in the restaurant business?" Qwilleran asked Hixie.

"Not much. We've just hired a busboy named Derek Cuttlebrink. I love funny names. In school I knew a Betty Schipps, who married a man named Fisch, and they opened a seafood restaurant. Do you ever browse through the Moose County phone book? It's a panic! Fugtree, Mayfus, Inchpot, Hackpole . . ."

"I know Hackpole," said Qwilleran. "He's in used cars and auto repair."

"Then let me tell you something amusing. When I first

took this job I was trying to be ever so charming, remembering faces and greeting customers by name. I'd taken a course to improve my memory, and I was using the association technique. One day Mr. Hackpole came in with some frumpy woman that he was trying to impress, and I called him Mr. Chopstick. He didn't like it one bit."

"He has no sense of humor," Qwilleran said, lowering his voice, "and that 'frumpy woman' happens to be Mrs. Cobb, the housekeeper of my choice, whose apricot-almond crescents you're wolfing down."

"I'm sorry, but you have to admit she's frumpy," Hixie whispered.

"Not any frumpier than a certain advertising woman I used to know Down Below."

"Touché," she said. "Why don't you come to the Mill for lunch today?"

"What's the special?"

"Chili. Bring your own fire extinguisher."

Shortly before noon Qwilleran had another visitor. Nick Bamba, husband of his part-time secretary in Mooseville, dropped off a batch of letters to be signed. Nick was greeted effusively by two sniffing Siamese, who seemed to know that he shared living quarters with three cats and a person whose long braids were tied with dangling ribbons. The two men went into the library followed by two vertical brown tails, stiff with importance.

"Time for a drink?" Qwilleran asked. He welcomed the visits of the sharp-eyed young engineer who worked at the state prison and shared his interest in crime. "How's everything at the incarceration facility?"

"Quiet enough to have me worried," Nick said. "Make it bourbon. How do you like this weather?"

"It reached six below in Brrr the other night."

"Windchill factor was thirty-five below."

"How's the baby?" Qwilleran could never remember the name or sex of the Bamba offspring.

"He's fine. He's a good baby, and healthy, thank God!"

"That's good to know. Did you take Snuffles to the vet?"

"He says it's some kind of dermatitis that affects spayed cats. She's taking hormones now."

"I appreciated your report on the trespasser, Nick. I notified the sheriff as you suggested."

"I see you've got your property posted now."

"Mr. O'Dell hurried up there and covered all the bases: no trespassing, no hunting, no camping."

"He's a terrific guy," Nick said. "When I was in high school he bailed me out of some hairy scrapes."

"Anything new in Mooseville?"

"There's never anything new in Mooseville. But . . . you know that camper I spotted on your property last week? It was unusual for this area—sort of citified. Three shades of brown. Custom job. Since then I've seen it several times in the parking lot at the Old Stone Mill, back near the kitchen door. Just for the hell of it, I did a rundown on the plates. It's registered to someone by the name of Hixie Rice."

After Nick had left, Qwilleran reflected that Hixie was hardly the outdoor type; he had never seen her in heels lower than three inches.

He went to lunch early and ordered his bowl of chili.

"Did Koko get over his snit?" Hixie asked.

"Apparently. As soon as you walked out the door, he gobbled the pork liver cupcake. . . . Incidentally, who owns that good-looking camper on the parking lot?"

Hixie looked vague. "The brown one? Oh, it belongs to one of our cooks. Her husband works in Mooseville and has to commute sixty miles a day, so he drives their small car, and she drives the gas-guzzler to work."

What was she hiding? Qwilleran recalled that Hixie had

always been a glib liar, though not necessarily a successful one, and she always managed to get involved with a certain fringe element in the romance department. What else had she invented? The invisible chef? His cookbook? His sick mother in Philadelphia?

ELEVEN

WEDNESDAY, NOVEMBER TWENTIETH. When the telephone rang at six in the morning, Qwilleran knew it would be Harry Noyton. Who else would have the nerve or insensitivity to call at that hour? He managed a sleepy hello and heard an unbearably cheerful voice say, "Rise and shine! Gonna sleep all day? How about inviting me over for one of those he-man breakfasts?"

"Do you expect me to get the housekeeper out of bed in the middle of the night?" Qwilleran grumbled.

"I'm coming over there anyway. Want to talk to you. I'll grab a taxi and be there in five minutes."

"There are no taxis, Harry. You can walk. It's only three blocks."

"I haven't walked three blocks since they let me out of the infantry!"

"Try it! It's good for you. Don't go to the main house; come to my apartment over the garage."

Qwilleran pulled on some clothes and opened a closet door that concealed a mini kitchen. A mini sink produced instant boiling water for his culinary specialty, instant coffee. A mini microwave thawed breakfast rolls taken from a mini freezer.

In no time at all Noyton bounded up the stairs. "Is this where you live? I like this modern stuff better than the junk in the big house. Hey, this is a sexy sofa! Do you bring girls up here?"

Qwilleran was always grumpy before his morning coffee. "This is where I work, Harry. I'm writing a book."

"No jive! What's it about?"

"You'll have to wait and buy a copy when it's published."

"I like you newspaper guys," said Noyton with buoyant good humor. "You're independent! That's why I go for this idea of owning a paper. This neck of the woods is waiting for something to happen. There's a lot of money up here! People own their own planes, three or four cars, forty-foot boats, sable coats! You should see the rocks on the women at the country club!"

"You're looking at inherited wealth," Qwilleran said. "There's also poverty and unemployment, and too many kids aren't going to college. A newspaper with guts could stir up some civic consciousness and promote job training and job opportunities and scholarships. The Klingenschoen Fund can't do it alone—and shouldn't do it alone!"

"Dammit! You've got it all figured out. That's what I like about you newspaper guys."

Qwilleran placed mugs of coffee and a plate of Mrs. Cobb's cinnamon rolls on the travertine card table. "Pull up a chair, Harry. How do you like the hotel? Are you comfortable?"

"Hell, they gave me the bridal suite with a round bed and pink satin sheets!"

"What luck with your conferences yesterday?"

"No hitch! Everything's sewed up! That Goodwinter gal doesn't know what hit her! I wrote six-figure checks on three different banks for the rights to the *Picayune* name and the old printing equipment."

"How did you work it?"

"The mayor took us all to lunch at the club—her and the economic development guys—private conference room. It was upbeat all the way. When it was over, she was calling me Harry and I was calling her Gritty. My lawyers called her lawyer, her banker called my bankers, and we both had a deal. The city's behind it a hundred percent. It'll create jobs. We get a building tax-free for ten years. The paper can be job-printed until the plant is set up."

"What will happen to the old burned-out building?"

"The city's condemning it and paying her off. They'll resell it for a minimall. The county commissioners got in the act, too. The county will go fifty-fifty on a newspaper museum near Mooseville. Tourist attraction, you know. . . . Hey, these are damn good rolls!"

"What was XYZ Enterprises doing all the time you were outbidding them and buttering up the widow?"

"XYZ never had anything on paper. It was all hanky-panky with Gritty. So she wasn't obligated to do business with those robbers. If a poor widow can get three-quarters of a million instead of some piddling five-digit figure, who's going to take her to court?"

Qwilleran thought, The news won't go down well with Exbridge. She'll have to move out of Indian Village in a hurry. The news will be all over town by now.

Noyton was wound up and talking nonstop. "Some of the commissioners drove me around to see the lay of the land, and—hey, you faker!—they didn't say a word about rutting bucks coming through the windshield! I like Mooseville. Everything's built of logs. I'd like to build a hotel there. The town's ripe for a highrise. We could build it of poured concrete logs. How does that grab you?"

"Harry, you have no taste. Leave the design to the architects."

"Hell, it's my money! I tell the architects what to design."

"Well, when the newspaper is launched, don't try to tell the editors how to edit."

Noyton's face took on a confidential smirk. "Gritty rode with us to Mooseville, and we sat in the back seat and developed a little—what do you call it?"

"Rapport."

"Then she took me to dinner at the place with the wheel that rattles and creaks. I told them to give me an oilcan and a screwdriver, and I'd go out and fix the damn thing. But we had a good time, Qwill, and I mean a *go-o-od* time. We ended up in my suite at the hotel with a bottle of hooch. She didn't want to go home to where she's been living, so I made a little arrangement at the hotel. Couldn't let those pink sheets go to waste. She's my kind of woman, Qwill—with spunk and a little shape to her figure. Remember Natalie? My life was never the same after I lost Natalie. And do you know what? Gritty goes for me in a big way! I'm taking her to Hawaii for a little holiday. I've got some business down there. Nothing big. Just condos."

"You'd better get out of here before snow flies," Qwilleran said, "and before Exbridge comes after you with a shotgun. He just got a divorce because of Gritty."

"I'm not afraid of Exbridge," Noyton said. "I've handled smarter suckers than him. . . . Oh, by the way, I talked to your editor friend—found him down in Texas—and he's hot for it. Then Gritty took me to the hospital to meet Junior, and he went into orbit!"

Qwilleran said, "Find out if Gritty knows anything about a small fireproof box that disappeared in the *Picayune* fire. No one knows what it contains, but Junior thinks it's important. It could be buried in the rubble."

"No problem! We'll get a crew over there and start sifting. And did I tell you I made an offer for the Pickax Hotel?

We'll get a good decorator up here from Down Below and change the name to Noyton House."

"Don't do it that way. Use a local designer and keep the old name. Do you want these good people to think they're being invaded? The trick is to fit in, not take over."

"Okay, General. Yes *sir,* General. Sure you don't want to go on my payroll?"

"No, thanks."

"Now I've got to get out of here. Thanks for the coffee. I've tasted better, but it was sure strong! I've got a few loose ends to tie up before I leave for the airport. I've chartered a plane to Minneapolis."

"Need a ride to the airport?"

Noyton shook his head and looked smug. "Gritty's driving me, but do me a favor, will you? She'll leave her car keys at the terminal desk with Charlie. Somebody should pick it up before snow flies. She won't be needing it. She's not coming back till spring."

Noyton had just gone thumping down the stairs in his new boots when Junior telephoned. "Want to hear some news?"

"Good or bad?"

"Both. The deal for the *Picayune* is finalized. The money's in the bank. Arch Riker is on his way up here. I'm getting out of the hospital today. I've shaved off my beard, and Grandma Gage is going to Florida, so I'm house-sitting till she comes back."

"What's the bad news?"

"Jody's mad at me. I don't know what's wrong with her. All of a sudden she says I don't listen to her and I ignore her when other people are around."

"You'll have to start thinking from her viewpoint as well as your own if you two are going to get married," Qwilleran said. "I speak from sad experience. You don't know how much she worries about you. She worried about you when your father died, when you were fighting the *Picayune* fire, when you missed out at the *Fluxion,* and when you went out in the woods."

There was a pause, then, "Maybe you're right, Qwill."

At eight o'clock Qwilleran tuned in the morning weather report: "Storm warnings in effect for all of Moose County. . . . Repeat: Storm warnings in effect."

Mrs. Cobb buzzed him on the intercom. "Are you interested in breakfast, Mr. Q?"

"Not this morning, thanks, but I want to talk with you before you leave for the auction."

He put the Siamese in the wicker hamper, and the three of them crossed the yard to the main house.

"Did you hear the weather report?" Mrs. Cobbs said. "It sounds like the Big One. I hope it holds off until after the auction. Susan Exbridge is picking me up at ten o'clock. Herb told me not to buy anything, but you know how I am at auctions!"

"How was the preview?"

"They have some wonderful things, and I saw the farmhouse for the first time. I can hardly wait to get my hands on it. We solved our problem; Herb is going to have one wing of the house for smoking and guns and stuffed moose heads and all that. Are you going to the auction?"

"I might drop in for a while to see the action. When's the best time to go?"

"Not too early. They put up box lots in the morning and hold the good things till later. They'll have a lunch wagon around noon. Don't forget to dress warm, and don't wear your best clothes, Mr. Q."

After Mrs. Cobb had bustled off in great excitement Qwilleran loitered around the house until he could stand the suspense no longer. Who would be at the auction? What were they buying? How high were the prices? What were people talking about? What were they serving at the lunch wagon? Wearing his lumberjack coat, woodsman's hat, and duck boots, he headed for Black Creek Lane in North Middle Hummock.

The country roads were unusually heavy with traffic. Cars, vans, and pickups were heading north, and a few were returning, loaded. Half a mile from the farmhouse he began to see vehicles parked on both sides of the road. He pulled in where a pickup was pulling out and walked the rest of the way. Auction-goers were trudging to their cars lugging floor lamps and rocking chairs. One woman was carrying a fern stand made of bent twigs.

"I don't care, honey," she said to her frowning spouse. "I simply wanted something that belonged to a Goodwinter, even if it was only an old toothbrush."

Parked in the front yard was a moving van labeled Foxy Fred's Bid-a-Bit Auctions. Customers shuffled through rustling leaves, examining rows of household furnishings: blankets, bicycles, small appliances, glassware, laundry equipment, garden tools. Large pieces of furniture were still in the farmhouse; everything else was jammed into a large pole barn where the bidding was in full swing.

Foxy Fred, wearing a western hat and red down jacket, was on the platform, haranguing a hundred or more bidders who were packed in shoulder-to-shoulder. "Here's a genuwine old barn lantern complete with wick. Who'll gimme five? . . . Five? . . . Gimme four . . . Dollar bill over there. Gimme two. Gimme two. . . . Two I got. Gimme three. Do I see three? Three! No money! Wanna four, wanna four, wanna four."

In order to bid, customers were picking up numbered flashcards from a red-jacketed woman who was entering sales in a ledger and collecting money. Qwilleran had no intention of bidding, but he picked up a card anyway. It was number 124.

"Look up! Look up!" the auctioneer called out. Porters in

red Bid-a-Bit windbreakers were hoisting an upholstered chair high over their heads for audience inspection.

Bidding was slow, however. The customers were either bored or stifled by blasts of heat from portable electric heaters. Suddenly Foxy Fred jolted them to attention. After only two bids he allowed a ladder-back rocker to go for an outrageously low price. The audience protested.

"If you don't like it, wake up and bid!" he scolded them.

Qwilleran ambled out of the barn and found Mrs. Cobb and Susan Exbridge at the lunch wagon. "How's the food?" he asked.

"It's not exactly Old Stone Mill," said Mrs. Exbridge, "but it's good. Try the bratwurst. It's homemade."

"The new chef at the Mill has made a big difference," Qwilleran said. "Has anyone met him?"

"I've seen him in the parking lot at Indian Village," she said. "He's tall, blond, and *very* good-looking, but he seems rather shy."

Mrs. Cobb said, "You'll never guess what I bought! A handmade cherry cradle! I'm expecting my first grandchild soon."

"Are the out-of-state dealers bidding things up?" Qwilleran asked her.

"They're hanging back, waiting for the good items, but there's a lot of them here. I can always spot a dealer. They're sort of shrewd-looking but laid-back. See that short man with his hands in his pockets? See the woman with a fuzzy brown hat? They're dealers. The man in the shearing coat—I think he's security. He isn't bidding. He isn't even listening. He's just watching people."

Before turning to look, Qwilleran had a hunch it would be the stranger who claimed to be a historian. The man was wandering aimlessly through the crowd.

At that moment there was a general movement toward

the barn, as if on signal. Inside the building the chatter was loud and excited as the porters started to bring out the heavy artillery.

"Look up! Look up!" the auctioneer shouted in a voice that cut through the hubbub. "Victorian rococo chair, genuwine Belter, I think—part of a parlor suite—two chairs and a settee. Upholstered in black horsehair. Good condition. Who'll gimme two thousand for the set? Two thousand to start. Two thousand, anyone?"

A flash card was raised.

"HEP!" shouted a porter, who doubled as spotter.

"Two thousand I got. Gimme twenty-five gimme twenty-five gimme twenty-five. Waddala waddala waddala . . ."

"HEP!"

"Twenty-five! Gimme thirty."

"HEP!"

"Thirty! Gimme forty. Waddala waddala bidda waddala bidda bidda waddala . . ."

"HEP!"

The excitement was mounting. It was like the last half of the ninth inning with the score tied, two out, and the bases loaded, Qwilleran thought. It was like third down on the two-yard line with a minute to play.

When the furniture was finally knocked down for a figure that he considered astronomical, the audience deflated with groans and sighs.

Someone tugged at his sleeve, and a woman's voice said, "How come you didn't bid on that one, Qwill?"

"Hixie! I didn't know you liked auctions!"

"I don't, but my customers have been talking about this one, so I sneaked away when the lunch crowd thinned out."

"Quiet back there!" shouted Foxy Fred, and Qwilleran took Hixie's arm and steered her outside and across the yard to the farmhouse.

"The good stuff is in here," he said, picking up a catalogue. Among the large items still in the house were two General Grant beds, a parlor organ, a breakfront twelve feet wide, a large pine hutch, a black walnut sideboard with matching table, and a ponderous rolltop desk. "This desk is the only thing I'd be tempted to bid on," Qwilleran told Hixie.

She was not really interested in the antiques. "Have you heard the latest rumor?" she asked.

"Which one? The town is full of rumors this week."

"It's no false alarm. My boss's live-in friend is eloping with another man. They came in for dinner last night—a couple of middle-aged lovebirds acting like kids. I seated them at a good table over the waterwheel, and it drove the guy crazy. He asked for an oilcan."

"Does Exbridge know about the switch?"

"Apparently, because he's livid! When he came in for lunch today he was in a mood for murder. The Bloody Mary was warm; the soup was cold; the veal was tough. He threatened to fire Antoine."

"Who?"

"Well, he likes to be called Tony, but his name is Antoine."

Qwilleran was fingering the flash card in his pocket. "I've got to go back to the barn to see what's happening," he said. "See you later."

The mood in the barn was contagious. He was catching auction fever, the symptoms being nervous excitement and a reckless sense of adventure.

"It's getting hot now, folks," shouted Foxy Fred, and an oak icebox, an eighteenth-century candlestand, and a Queen Anne table went under the hammer in rapid succession. Then the parlor organ and pine hutch were auctioned by number from the catalogue.

"Next we have a six-foot rolltop desk in cherrywood,"

said the auctioneer. "Perfect condition. Dated 1881. Outstanding provenance. Belonged to Ephraim Goodwinter, mine owner, lumberman, founder of the Pickax *Picayune,* and donor of the Pickax Public Library. Shall we start at five thousand? . . . Five thousand? . . . *Four* thousand?"

"One thousand," said a woman near the platform. It was the dealer with the fuzzy brown hat.

"One thousand I've got. No money! Beautiful desk—seven drawers—lots of pigeonholes—maybe a secret compartment. Who'll bid two thousand?"

Qwilleran held up his card.

"HEP!" shouted the spotter.

"Two thousand now. Make it three. Three do I hear? Solid cherry. Lotta history goes with this desk."

"HEP!"

"Three thousand we got. Who'll bid three and a half? Waddala waddala bidda waddala bidda bidda bidda·waddala . . ."

The auctioneer's singsong gibberish had a mesmerizing effect on Qwilleran. He raised his card.

"Thirty-five hundred for this five-thousand-dollar desk, folks. No money. Make it four-triple-oh, four-triple-oh, four-triple-oh . . ."

"HEP!"

Qwilleran's turtleneck jersey was tightening around his neck. He slipped out of his coat.

"Four thousand. Make it fournahaff fournahaff fournahaff. It's a giveaway. Solid cherry. Cast brasses."

"HEP!"

"Four thousand five hundred. Do I hear five grand? It's going, folks. Are you gonna let 'em steal it?"

"Forty-six!" Quilleran called out.

"Four-six! Who'll gimme four-seven? Waddala waddala bidda waddala bidda bidda waddala . . ."

"HEP!"

The woman in the fuzzy brown hat wanted the desk and was inching up.

"Four-seven. Do I hear four-eight? Waddala waddala bidda . . ."

Qwilleran raised his card.

"HEP!"

"Four thousand eight hundred. It's going, folks—"

"Forty-nine!" said the dealer.

"Fifty!" shouted Qwilleran.

"That's the spirit! Do I hear fifty-one?"

All heads turned to the dealer in the fuzzy hat. The hat wagged a negative.

"Fifty-one do I hear? Fifty-one? Going for five thousand. Going going going . . . SOLD to number one twenty-four."

The audience applauded. Mrs. Cobb waved her catalogue in wild approval. Qwilleran mopped his brow.

After making arrangements to have the desk delivered, he drove home in a confused state of shock and agitation. Five thousand for a piece of furniture still seemed like a staggering sum to the former feature writer for the *Daily Fluxion*. At a restaurant in Middle Hummock he tried to phone Junior, but there was no answer at Grandma Gage's house.

Upon arriving home, he discovered why. There was a message on the answering machine. "Hi! We're flying Down Below to get married. Jody's parents live near Cleveland. Hope we get back before snow flies. And hey! They found Dad's lockbox!"

Mrs. Cobb had gone out to dinner with Susan Exbridge, so Qwilleran rummaged in the refrigerator and found some lentil soup and cold chicken. He heated the soup for himself and cut up the chicken for the Siamese.

"No readings tonight," he told Koko. "I've had enough stimulation for one day. '*The rest is silence.*' That's from *Hamlet*, in case you didn't know."

The tall case clock in the foyer bonged seven times, and he tuned in the weather report. Storm warnings had been in effect all day, and yet the weather had been fine. Dubiously he listened to the current prediction:

"Storm warnings were lifted late this afternoon, but a storm alert remains in effect. Winds are twenty-five miles an hour, gusting to forty. Present temperature: nineteen in Pickax, seven in Brrr. And now for a look at the headlines. . . . Two persons were killed in a car-deer accident on Airport Road at four forty-five p.m. Names are withheld pending notification of relatives. The westbound car struck and killed a large buck, then entered a ditch . . ."

"*Junior!*" Qwilleran cried. "No! No! The *Picayune* jinx! Fifth to die a violent death! And poor little Jody . . ."

TWELVE

THURSDAY, NOVEMBER TWENTY-FIRST. "Storm warnings are again in effect for Moose County," said the WPKX announcer, "with high winds continuing from the northwest and temperatures constant in the twenties. . . . And in the news . . . here's an update on yesterday's fatal accident in the Airport Road. Killed at four forty-five p.m. were Gertrude Goodwinter, forty-eight, of North Middle Hummock, and Harold Noyton, fifty-two, of Chicago. According to the sheriff's department, their car struck and killed a large buck, then entered a ditch and rolled over."

Qwilleran made an early visit to the police station that morning to see Andrew Brodie. Although the sheriff's deputies were courteous and cooperative, only the Pickax police chief could be depended upon for friendly conversation and off-the-record information.

Brodie was sitting at his desk, swamped with paperwork and complaining as usual. "And what's on your mind?" he asked, after a tirade about computer systems.

"Do you know anything about yesterday's fatal accident on Airport Road?"

"The sheriff and state police handled it," he said, "but we helped track down the next of kin. Wasn't easy, what with her husband just buried and her mother in Florida and

Junior on a plane somewhere and the other two kids out west. The fellah that was with her—they had to get lawyers and bankers out of bed to find out about him."

"At first I thought Junior and Jody had been killed. I knew Jody is a friend of your daughter's, so I tried calling your house last night but got no answer."

"The wife and I were out visiting," Brodie said, "and Francesca was rehearsing for that concert at the church, where they're going to wear all those old-fashioned costumes. It'll be a spectacle, all right. They're making their own costumes, and they're going all out!"

"I'm looking forward to it," Qwilleran said, after which he commented on the weather, the hunting season, and the Goodwinter auction before steering the conversation back to the accident. "Do you know who was driving?"

"No telling. They were both thrown from the car, as I understand it."

"I assume they weren't wearing seat belts."

"It would look like it, wouldn't it?"

"Does the sheriff think they were traveling fast?"

"According to the skid marks, pretty fast. And according to the coroner, they'd had a few. The buck was a big one, over two hundred pounds, eight-point. Don't suppose you know anything about the fellah she was with. The name's Noyton."

"All I know," Qwilleran said, "is that he's a one-man conglomerate with some greedy ex-wives and squabbling children, and they'll be challenging the will for ten years."

When he left Brodie's office, Qwilleran began wondering how Exbridge would react to Gritty's death, and how the ex—Mrs. Exbridge would react to her ex-husband's loss of his ex-mistress. His curiosity prompted him to have lunch again at the Old Stone Mill. Hixie was always good for some candid observations.

Today she seemed nervous and preoccupied, however. She

seated guests but avoided conversation. Qwilleran took a long time to consume his pea soup and corned beef sandwich, stalling until most of the customers had left. Then he offered to buy Hixie a drink, and she sat down at his table in a fretful mood.

"Hideous accident on Airport Road," he remarked. "Wasn't the woman your boss's former roommate?"

"I can't worry about his problems today," she snapped. "I have problems of my own."

"What's the matter?"

"Tony left suddenly this morning—right before the lunch rush! No explanation. He just went out the window."

"The window?"

"And he took *my car! My car* instead of that stupid camper!"

"I thought the camper belonged to one of your cooks."

Hixie dismissed the question with a wave of the hand. "It was in my name. That is, I bought it for *his birthday.* So why didn't he take the camper? Why did he take *my car?*"

"Perhaps he had some urgent errand to do."

"Then why did he go out the washroom window? And why did he take his *knives?* I see what it's all about, Qwill—the same old shaft for big-hearted Hixie. If Tony planned to come back, he wouldn't have taken his *knives.* You know how chefs are about their knives. They practically *sleep* with them."

"Did anything unusual happen to cause his quick exit?"

Hixie frowned at her glass of Campari before answering.

"Well, about eleven o'clock we were setting up for lunch, and a man hammered on the door. It was locked, and one of the waitresses went to see what he wanted. He asked for Antoine Delapierre. She told him we had no one by that name, but he barged right in. I was folding napkins at the serving station, and I could tell right away he wasn't just another *potato chip* salesman. He looked cold and determined."

"Was he wearing a shearling car coat and rabbit-fur hat?"

"Something like that. Anyway, I asked what he wanted, and he said he was a friend of Antoine Delapierre. Tony heard it, grabbed his knives, and bolted into the employees' washroom. That's the last we saw of him. He left the window open and blazed away in *my car!* Why did I ever give that jerk a duplicate set of keys?"

Because he was tall, blond, and very good-looking, Qwilleran thought. He felt sorry for her. Hixie, the born loser, had lost out again. But this time she wasn't weeping; she was furious.

"Then Tony Peters wasn't his real name?" he asked.

"A lot of people change their names for business purposes," she said casually, but her eyes were shifting nervously.

"Do you know what the incident was all about?"

"I haven't the *foggiest* idea. When the man walked into the kitchen, I got huffy and ordered him out."

Qwilleran refrained from pursuing the conversation. Sooner or later Hixie would blurt out the truth. He contemplated the new development with some satisfaction. His suspicion had checked out; the stranger in Pickax was actually an investigator.

Meanwhile, he had to go home and dress for dinner at Polly Duncan's cottage on MacGregor Road. Roast beef and Yorkshire pudding!

Mrs. Cobb was busy in the kitchen, baking hazelnut jumbles. "Do you think you should drive out in the country, Mr. Q?" she said. "They mentioned storm warnings on the radio."

"They mentioned storm warnings on the radio yesterday,

and nothing happened. I think their computer is malfunctioning. They've been reading last year's weather predictions all month. So there's nothing to worry about."

He took a handful of hazelnut jumbles and went looking for the Siamese. He made it a point to say goodbye to them whenever he left the house for a few hours—another of Lori Bamba's recommendations.

The cats were not in the library, but a copy of *The Tempest* lay on the floor beneath the bust of Shakespeare. It gave Qwilleran pause, but only for a moment. Koko had pulled out that threatening title once before, and there had been no stormy weather. Senior Goodwinter had crashed into the old plank bridge, but the weather remained fine.

Qwilleran headed north. It was cold, and there was a high wind, but he was wearing his suede car coat with beaver collar, a trooper's hat in the same fur, a wool shirt in the Mackintosh tartan, hunting boots, fur-lined choppers, and, of course, the long red underwear that was standard equipment in Moose County.

The sky was overcast, and the wind whistled, but his heart was light and his mind was fired with ambition. After this evening he would plunge into the writing of the book he had neglected; it would please Polly to know he was writing again.

Her invitation to dinner was auspicious; it meant, he hoped, that she was relaxing the mystifying behavior that kept him at arm's length. He thought he had discovered the reason for her reserve. At a recent meeting of the library board a grant from the Klingenschoen Fund was allocated to the purchase of books, video equipment, and a new furnace—not a dollar for personnel. Furthermore, he was appalled to learn how little the head librarian was paid. Polly's tiny cottage, old car, and limited wardrobe all suggested straitened circumstances. Qwilleran knew her to be a proud woman; did the discrepancy in their financial status embarrass her? He knew—and she undoubtedly knew—that the town gossips would enjoy labeling the head librarian a gold digger.

With these thoughts running through his mind as he drove, he hardly noticed the minuscule dots of white on his windshield. A little farther on, large snowflakes in crystalline designs reminded him of a childhood thrill—catching them on his tongue. Soon a light dusting of snow was visible on the pavement, and Qwilleran slowed his speed to allow for slippery patches.

By the time he turned off the main highway onto MacGregor Road, there was a veil of white over fields and evergreens—a beautiful sight, although swirling snow was obscuring his vision. Dusk seemed to be falling early. He was now traveling east, and the snow was whipping against the windshield fast enough to render the wipers ineffective. It was just a snow squall, he told himself. It wouldn't last long. He drove slowly and carefully.

Polly's house, he remembered from his previous, surreptitious visit, was three miles from the main highway—two miles of pavement, then a jog in the road, and a mile of gravel. There were no other cars in sight, and he was now driving through a tunnel of white—dense white. He hoped he could stay on the pavement; there were no tire tracks to follow. No one had passed that way since the snow had started to fall. Crossroads were indistinguishable from open fields.

Suddenly something loomed up in front of his car, and he stopped just before plunging into underbrush. He had reached the jog in the road. Now he had to turn left for a short distance and then turn right onto the unimproved continuation of MacGregor Road. He made several attempts before finding the actual turn. After that he knew it would be clear sailing—just a mile to the two rural mailboxes, MacGregor and Duncan. He checked the odometer.

The problem was to stay on the road; on each side of the roadbed would be the inevitable drainage ditch. The windshield wipers, though working furiously, were useless against the onslaught of snow. He was driving through a white blanket. The hood of the car was invisible. At least he didn't have to worry about deer; they would be driven to cover. He had learned that much from Hackpole. But he had no time to think about Hackpole, or even Polly. The problem was to drive in a straight line while blinded by snow.

Again a clump of vegetation loomed up ahead. He was off the road! Turning the wheel, he went into a skid. He babied it, but the car was sliding sideways. It was sliding down a slope, and it came to a stop at a dangerous angle. The drainage ditch! Another degree of tilt, and the car would roll over. He turned off the ignition and sat there, surrounded on all sides by walls of white.

He knew the car would never make it out of the ditch under those slippery conditions—and from that angle—even with front-wheel drive. He considered the options. The longer he hesitated, the more the snow banked up against the windshield and side window—an opaque layer, inches thick, and gray-white in the dust. Opening the door, he tested the terrain underfoot. Slush! It was the ditch. If he scrambled up the slope he would be on solid ground, and he could walk the rest of the way. It was now less than half a mile, he knew.

Putting on his hat, pulling down the earflaps, turning up his coat collar, tugging on the mittens, he prepared to face the elements. If he clambered up the bank and turned right, he would be headed toward the farm. He would have to proceed on blind faith. In the enveloping blizzard there was no sense of direction; the wind was hurling snow from all points of the compass.

Now he could feel something solid underfoot—the roadbed—but already there was an accumulation of five, ten, or fifteen inches, depending on the drifting. He moved forward, blinded by the snow, one thoughtful step at a time. He had a plan! If he found himself slipping down a slope to the right, he would be off the roadbed; he would veer to the left. It he slipped to the left, he would be headed for the opposite ditch.

In this way he zigzagged ahead, not daring to hope that a car would come along. Would he see the fog lights? Would he hear the motor above the howling wind? It was shrieking now, shrieking through trees that he couldn't see.

Though his coat collar and storm hat were snug, and though his trousers were stuffed into his boots, the relentless wetness found its way into every crevice. He banged the snow off his mittens and brushed the buildup from his face. It was no use; in another few seconds he was coated with freezing wet.

He had been walking for what seemed like an hour. Could he be traveling in a circle? If he had inadvertently done a right-about-face, thinking the right ditch was the left ditch, he would now be headed for the main highway, three miles back.

The blind groping was discouraging, frightening. He was totally disoriented. He held his mittened hands in front of him like a sleepwalker, but there was nothing to feel. He could hardly keep his eyes open. His eyelids were raw. Were they freezing shut? His cheeks and forehead were numb from the vicious wind and wet. He shouted, "Hello!" He shouted, "Help!" He was shouting into a void and swallowing snow.

What do I do now? he asked himself—not in panic but in

defeat. He had an overbearing desire to sink to his knees, roll up in a ball, and call it quits. Keep going, he told himself. Keep going!

He remembered the mailboxes. He had to bump into them, or he'd miss them entirely. He inched along, not seeing, not feeling, not knowing. The snow was getting deeper underfoot and piling inches thick on his clothing. He stood still and tried to breathe normally, but he was being smothered by the wind and drowned by the snow.

Suddenly, without warning, something rose up in front of him and he fell over two mailboxes, close together, with a foot of snow on top of each. He threw his arms around them like a drowning sailor clutching at floating debris. He bent over them, trying to catch his breath.

A few feet beyond would be the driveway. But how many feet beyond? It was trial and error. When he banged a knee on a concrete culvert, he knew he was there. He remembered a hedge that bordered the drive. He would follow the hedge, feeling his way. It worked until the hedge came to an abrupt end. The brick farmhouse would be on the left. The cottage should be straight ahead.

Once again he was stumbling blindly on what he hoped would be a straight course. It was dark now, and he realized that snow is not white in the black of night. Yet, he thought he detected a glow in the space ahead. He followed it, reaching for it, until he fell over steps buried in a drift. He scrambled up on hands and knees. There was a door directly in front of him. He leaned against it, pounding with both fists. The door opened, and he fell into a kitchen.

"Oh my God! Qwill! What happened? Are you hurt?"

He was on his hands and knees in an avalanche of snow jolted from his clothing when he fell. Polly was tugging at his arm. He crawled farther into the room and heard the door slam behind him, cutting off the noise of the storm. It was bright and quiet indoors.

"Are you all right? Can you get up? I didn't think you were coming. What happened to your car?"

He wanted to stay on the floor, but he allowed her to help him to his feet.

"Let me brush you off. Stand still."

He stood, silent and motionless, while she pulled off his hat and mittens and threw them on the kitchen table. With towels she removed the snow and ice from his moustache and eyebrows. She brushed a bushel of snow from his coat, pants, and boots. And still he stood, dumbly and numbly, in a flood of melting snow and ice.

Now she was untoggling his car coat. "Let's get you out of these wet clothes, and I'll get you a hot drink. Sit down. Let me pull your boots off."

She led him to a chair, and he sat obediently.

"Your socks are dry. Do your feet feel all right? They're not numb, are they? Your shirt is wet around the collar. I'll put it in the dryer. Your pants, too. They're soaking wet. Thank the Lord you wore long johns. I'll bring you some blankets."

And still he could say nothing. She wrapped him in blankets and led him to a sofa, convinced him to lie down, tucked him in, stuck a thermometer in his mouth.

"I'm going to make some hot tea and call the doctor to see if I'm doing the right thing."

Qwilleran closed his eyes and thought of nothing but warmth and dryness and safety. Vaguely he heard a teakettle whistling, a telephone being jiggled, water being sponged into a pail.

When Polly returned with a mug of hot tea on a tray, she said, "The phone's dead. The lines must be down. I wonder if I should bring you a warm footbath. How do you feel? Do you want to sit up and drink some tea?" She took the thermometer from his mouth and studied it.

Qwilleran was beginning to feel like himself. He rose to

a sitting position without assistance. He accepted the mug of tea with a grateful glance at Polly. He sipped it and uttered a long, deep sigh. Then he spoke his first words. *"For this relief, much thanks, for it is bitter cold."*

"Thank God!" She laughed and cried. "You're alive! What a fright you gave me! But you're all right. When you quote Shakespeare, I know you're all right."

She threw her arms around his blanketed shoulders and nestled her head on his chest. At that moment the power failed. Half of Moose County blacked out, and the cottage was thrown into darkness.

THIRTEEN

FRIDAY, NOVEMBER TWENTY-SECOND. Qwilleran opened his eyes in a small bedroom filled with dazzling light.

"Wake up, Qwill! Wake up! Come and see what's happened!" Someone in a blue robe was standing at the window, gazing rapturously at the scene outdoors. "We've had an ice storm!"

He was slow to wake, Groggily he remembered the night before: Polly . . . her tiny cottage . . . the blizzard.

"Don't lie there, Qwill. Come and see. It's beautiful!"

"You're beautiful," he said. "Life is beautiful!"

It was cool in the bedroom, although a comforting rumble and roar somewhere in the cottage indicated that the space heater was operating. Dragging himself out of bed, he wrapped himself in a blanket, and joined Polly at the window.

What he saw was an enchanted landscape, dazzlingly bright in a cold, hard November sun. The wind was still. There was a hush over the countryside, now glazed with a thin film of sparkling ice. Fields were acres of silver. Every tree branch, every twig was coated with crystal. Power lines and wire fences were transformed into strings of diamonds.

"I can't believe we had a howling blizzard last night,"

he said. "I can't believe I was wandering around in a whiteout."

"Did you sleep well?" she asked.

"*Very* well. And not because of tramping through the snow or eating too much roast beef. . . . I smell something good."

"Coffee," she said, "and scones in the oven."

The scones were dotted with currants and served with cream cheese and gooseberry jam.

"The hedge you followed in the blizzard," Polly said, "is a row of berry bushes, planted by the MacGregors years ago. He lets the people on the next farm pick them, and then they supply us with preserves. . . . Is something bothering you, Qwill?"

"Mrs. Cobb will be worried. Is the phone working?"

"Not yet. The power came on half an hour ago."

"Do the snowplows come down this road?"

"Eventually, but we're not on their priority list. They do the city streets and main highways first."

"Have you heard anything on the radio?"

"Everything's closed—schools, stores, offices. The library won't open until Monday. All meetings are canceled. They cleared the helicopter on the hospital roof and airlifted a patient this morning. Many cars were abandoned in snowdrifts. The body of a man was found in a car that had run off the road. He was asphyxiated. Do you carry a shovel in your trunk, Qwill?"

He shook his head guiltily.

"If you're stranded, you have to clear the snow away from the tail pipe, you know, so you can run the heater."

"If we're going to be snowbound," Qwilleran said, "I'd rather be snowbound here with you than anywhere else. It's so peaceful. How did you find this place?"

"My husband was killed on this farm while he was fighting a barn fire, and the MacGregors were very kind to me. They offered me the hired man's cottage rent-free."

"What happened to the hired man?"

"He's an extinct species. The farmers have *employees* now, who live in ranch houses in town."

"Don't you worry about your landlord in weather like this?"

"He's in Florida. His son drove him to the airport on Tuesday. I have to feed his pet goose during the winter. Did you ever hear of a goose-sitter?"

The kitchen was suddenly quiet. The space heater had done its job and clicked off. The refrigerator had finished rechilling. The pump had filled the tank and was silent. Then the silence indoors and out was broken by a distant rumble.

"The snowplow!" Polly cried. "How very unusual!"

From the west window they could see plumes of snow being blown as high as the treetops. Then the machine came into view, followed by a smaller plow and a sheriff's car. The convoy stopped in front of the farmhouse, and the small plow started on the driveway. Eventually the sheriff's car pulled up to the door.

"Mr. Qwilleran here?" the deputy asked.

Qwilleran presented himself. "My car's in the ditch somewhere along the road."

"Saw it," said the deputy. "I can take you into town . . . if you want to go," he added, glancing at the woman in a blue robe.

Qwilleran turned a disappointed face to Polly. "I'd better go. Will you be all right?"

She nodded. "I'll phone you as soon as the lines are repaired."

The deputy politely turned away as the two said goodbye.

Riding back to Pickax with the officer, Qwilleran said, "I guess this storm was the Big One."

"Yep."

"Did it do much damage?"

"The usual."

"How did you find me?"

"Just came looking. Got a call from the Pickax police chief and the mayor and the road commissioner." He picked up the microphone. "Car ninety-four to Dispatch. Got him!"

Pickax, the city of gray stone, was now smothered in white and glittering with ice. The Park Circle looked like a wedding cake. At the K mansion every window, door, and railing was crested with inches of snow, and Mr. O'Dell was riding the snowblower, clearing the driveways.

Mrs. Cobb greeted Qwilleran with a show of relief. "I was worried sick because of the way the cats were acting," she said. "They knew something was wrong. Koko howled all night."

"Where are they now?"

"Asleep on the refrigerator—exhausted! I didn't sleep a wink myself. It started to snow right after you left, and I was afraid you'd lose your way or get stuck. The phones were dead, but as soon as they fixed them I called everyone I knew, even the mayor."

"Mrs. Cobb, you're shaking. Sit down, and let's have a cup of tea, and I'll tell you about my experience."

When he had finished, she said, "The cats were right! They knew you were in trouble."

"All's well that ends well. I'll call Hackpole's garage to pull me out of the ditch. Now how about the wedding? Is everything going according to plan?"

"We-e-el," she said uncertainly, with her eyes lowered.

"Is anything wrong?"

"Well, Herb is starting to say he doesn't want me to work after we're married—at least, not here at the museum. He thinks I should stay at home and . . . and . . ."

"And what?"

She moistened her lips. "Do the bookkeeping for his business operations."

"WHAT!" Qwilleran shouted, "And waste your years of experience and knowledge? The man's crazy!"

"I told him there wouldn't be any wedding if I couldn't work at the museum," she said defiantly.

"Good for you! That took courage. I'm glad you asserted yourself." He knew how much she wanted a home of her own, and a husband. Not just a man. A husband.

"Anyway, he backed down, so I guess everything's okay. My wedding suit arrived—pink suede—and it's gorgeous! My son sent it from Saint Louis, and it doesn't need a single alteration. He'd be here for the wedding if the flying wasn't so iffy. Besides, they're expecting their baby any day now. I hope it's a boy."

Qwilleran preferred to avoid domestic details, but the housekeeper wanted to chatter about the wedding plans.

"Susan Exbridge is going to wear gray. I've ordered our corsages—pink roses—and pink rosebuds for you and Herb."

"I know you don't want a reception," Qwilleran said. "but we ought to crack a bottle of champagne and toast the bride and groom."

"That's what Susan said. She wants to bring some caviar and steak tartare."

At those words two sleeping brown heads on top of the refrigerator were promptly raised.

Qwilleran repressed a chuckle as he pictured Hackpole wearing a pink rosebud and reacting to fish eggs and raw meat. "How about background music?" he suggested. "We should put a cassette in the player."

"Oh, that would be lovely. Would you choose something, Mr. Q?"

The Bartered Bride, he thought. "And where do you want to hold the ceremony?"

"In the drawing room, in front of the fireplace. Let me show you what I have in mind."

They left the kitchen, followed by the Siamese, who liked to be included in domestic conferences.

"We could face the magistrate across a small table," Mrs. Cobb said. "A fire in the fireplace would make it cozy, and we'd put a bowl of pink roses on the table, to tie in with the roses in the rug."

At that moment there was an explosive snarl behind them. Koko was bushing his tail, arching his back, and showing his fangs. His ears and whiskers were sleeked backward, and his eyes had an evil slant.

"My heavens! What's wrong?" Mrs. Cobb cried.

"He's standing on the roses!" Qwilleran said. "He always avoids walking on the roses!"

"He gave me a fright."

"He's having a catfit, or seeing a ghost," Qwilleran said, but he felt an uneasy quiver on his upper lip, and he smoothed his moustache vigorously.

As they returned to the kitchen Mrs. Cobb said, "I'm so thankful that you brought me to Pickax, Mr. Q. It's been a wonderful experience, and I've met Herb, and I'm getting married among all the things I love. I'm very grateful."

"Don't get carried away, Mrs. Cobb. You've done a great job, and you deserve the best. Are you sure you don't want to take a week off?"

"No, we're just going to have dinner at the Pickax Hotel and spend our wedding night in their bridal suite," she said. "Then we'll have our honeymoon trip in the spring. Herb wants to take me fishing in northern Canada."

Qwilleran could not imagine her casting for trout any more than he could imagine Hackpole sleeping between pink satin sheets. "But you could take a week right now for rest and relaxation," he said.

"Well," she said almost apologetically, "there's a committee meeting Monday about the trimming of the Christmas tree, and Sunday night is the *Messiah* concert and reception in costume. I wouldn't miss that for anything!"

"What about Herb?"

"He won't mind. There's something on TV that he likes to watch every Sunday night."

Qwilleran had qualms about this marriage, and they were growing stronger. He would feel like a hypocrite, standing up for a man he heartily disliked, but he was doing it for Mrs. Cobb. She was always so generous with her time and effort and good cheer . . . so eager for approval and so embarrassed when praised . . . so knowledgeable in her field and yet so gullible in her emotions . . . so ready to please and adjust to the whims of others—especially a man with muscles and tattoos.

"You're still shaking, Mrs. Cobb," he said. "It's excitement and lack of sleep. Go upstairs and take it easy. I'll feed the cats and go out to dinner. And don't prepare any meals tomorrow; it's your wedding day."

She thanked him profusely and retired to her suite.

Qwilleran went into the library to select wedding music: Bach for the ceremony and Schubert with the champagne and caviar. Koko followed him and scrutinized each cassette, sniffing some and reaching for others with an uncertain paw.

"A feline librarian is bad enough," Qwilleran said. "Please! We don't want a feline disc jockey."

"Nyik nyik nyik," Koko retorted irritably, swiveling one ear forward and the other back.

The telephone rang, and the caller said, "The friendly telephone company has resumed service to the peasants on MacGregor Road."

The melodic voice made the back of Qwilleran's neck tingle. "I've been thinking about you, Polly. I've been thinking about everything."

"It turned out beautifully, Qwill, but I shudder to think of you in that whiteout."

"I've done a little shuddering myself. When can I see you again?"

"I'd like to drive in for the concert Sunday night."

"Why not pack an overnight bag? If you drive home after the concert, you'll only have to turn around and come back Monday morning. You can have your choice of suites upstairs: English, Empire, or Biedermeier."

"I think I'd like an English suite," Polly said. "I've always wanted to sleep in a four-poster bed with side curtains."

"YOW!" Koko said.

Replacing the receiver gently, Qwilleran said, "And you mind your own business, young man!"

FOURTEEN

SATURDAY, NOVEMBER TWENTY-THIRD. "Cloudy skies and another three inches of snow," the weatherman was predicting. Nevertheless, the sun was shining, and Pickax was shimmering under the blanket of white that had descended on Thursday. Snow stayed white in Pickax.

When Qwilleran went to the main house to prepare the cats' breakfast, Mrs. Fulgrove and Mr. O'Dell were on the job. "Nice day for a wedding," he remarked.

"Sure, now, when it comes to marryin', the devil take the weather," said the houseman. "When I wedded herself, the heavens thundered an' the dogs howled an' the birds fell dead in the road, but for forty-five year we lived together with nary an angry word between us. An' when she went, God rest her soul, she went sudden with nary a pain or tear."

Mrs. Cobb was nervous. With no meals to prepare and no rum-raisin squares to bake, she puttered aimlessly about the house, waiting for her hair appointment. The cats were restless, too, sensing an upheaval of some kind. They prowled ceaselessly, and Koko talked to himself with private yows and iks and occasionally shoved a book off the shelf. Qwilleran was glad to escape. At two o'clock he was scheduled to interview Sarah Woolsmith.

The ninety-five-year-old farm woman was a long-term resident at the senior care facility adjoining the Pickax Hospital, two modern buildings that seemed out of place in a city of imitation castles and fortresses.

The matron at the reception desk was expecting Qwilleran. "Mrs. Woolsmith is waiting for you in the reading room," she said. "You'll have the place all to yourselves, but please limit your visit to fifteen minutes; she tires easily. She's looking forward to your interview. Not many people want to listen to elderly folks talk about the old days."

In the reading room he found a frail little woman with nervous hands, sitting in a wheelchair and clutching her shawl. She was accompanied by the volunteer who had wheeled her down from her bedroom.

"Sarah, dear, this is Mr. Qwilleran," the volunteer said slowly and clearly. "He's going to have a nice visit with you." In an aside she whispered, "She's ninety-five and has almost all her own teeth, but her eyesight is not good. She's a dear soul, and we all love her. I'll sit near the door and tell you when the time is up."

"Where are my teeth?" Mrs. Woolsmith demanded in shrill alarm.

"Your partial is in your mouth, dear, and you look lovely in your new shawl." She squeezed the old lady's arm affectionately.

Wasting no time on preliminaries, Qwilleran said, "Would you tell me what it was like to live on a farm when you were young, Mrs. Woolsmith? I'm going to turn on this tape recorder." He held up the machine for her to see, but she looked blankly in several directions.

The following interview was later transcribed:

Question: Were you born in Moose County?
I don't know why you want to talk to me. I never did any-

thing but live on a farm and raise a family. I had my name in the paper once when I had a burglar.

What kind of farming did you do?

It was in the paper—about the burglar—and I tore it out. It's in my purse. Where's my purse? Take it out and read it. You can read it to me. I like to hear it.

Sara Woolsmith, 65, of Squunk Corners was sitting alone and knitting a sweater in her living room last Thursday at 11:00 p.m., when a man with a handkerchief over his face burst in and said, "Give me all your money. I need it bad." She gave him $18.73 from her purse, and he fled on foot, leaving her unharmed but surprised.

I used to knit in them days. We had seven children, John and me, five of them boys. Two killed in the war. John died in the big storm of '37. Went to bring in the cows and froze to death. Fifteen cows froze and all the chickens. Winters was bad in them days. I have a 'lectric blanket. Do you have a 'lectric blanket? When I was a young girl we slep' under a pile of quilts, my sisters and me. Mornings we looked up to see the frost on the ceiling. It was pretty, all sparkly. There was ice in the pitcher when we washed our face. Sometimes we caught cold. Ma rubbed skunk oil and goose grease on our chests. We didn't like it. (Laughs.) My brother shot wild rabbits, but I could chase 'em and catch 'em. Pa was proud of me. Pa didn't have a horse. He hitched Ma to the plow, and they tilled the land. I didn't go to school. I helped Ma in the kitchen. Once she was sick and I had to feed sixteen men. I was only *this big*. Harvesttime, it was. They was all neighbors. Neighbors helped neighbors in them days.

Did you ever have time for . . .

Us womenfolks, we scrubbed clothes in a washtub and made our own soap. I made vinegar and butter. We stuffed pillows with chicken feathers. We had lots of those! (Laughs.) Once a week we took a wagon to town and got the mail and bought a penny stick of horehound candy. I married John and we had a big farm. Cows, horses, pigs, chickens. We hired neighbor boys for huskin' and shellin'. Nickel an hour. The whitetails came and ate our corn. Once the grasshoppers came and ate everything. They ate the wash on the line. (Laughs.) The neighbor boys worked twelve hours a day, huskin' and shellin'.

What do you remember about . . .

Never locked our doors. Neighbor could walk in and borrow a cup of sugar. It was a neighbor boy took my money. I knowed who he was, but I didn't tell the constable. I knowed his voice. Worked on our farm sometimes.

Why didn't you tell the constable?

His name was Basil. I felt sorry for him. His father was in prison. Killed a man.

Was that the Whittlestaff family?

I peeked out the window when he took my money. It was moonlight. I saw him runnin' across our potato field. I knowed where he was headin' for. The freight train stopped at Watertown to take on water. You could hear the whistle two miles away. Boys used to jump the freight trains and run away. One boy fell on the tracks and was killed. I never went on a train.

End of interview

The volunteer interrupted Mrs. Woolsmith's monologue. "Time's up, dear. Say goodbye now, and we'll go upstairs for our nap."

The old lady put forth a thin trembling hand, and Qwilleran grasped it warmly in both of his, marveling that such fragile hands had once scrubbed clothes, milked cows, and hoed potatoes.

The volunteer followed him into the hallway. "Sarah remembers everything seventy-five years ago," she said, "but she doesn't remember recent events. By the way, I'm Irma Hasselrich."

"Are you related to the attorney for the Klingenschoen Fund?"

"That's my father. He was prosecutor when Zack Whittlestaff was convicted of killing Titus Goodwinter. Zack's boy, who robbed Sarah and ran away, came back years later and repaid the eighteen dollars and seventy-three cents, but she doesn't remember. He sends her chocolates every Christmas, too. He turned out to be quite a successful man. Changed his name, of course. If I had a name like Basil Whittlestaff, I'd change it, too," she laughed. "He sells used cars and runs a garage. He's ornery, but he does good work."

Qwilleran went home to dress for the wedding. He was not anticipating the occasion with any pleasure. He had been best man for Arch Riker twenty-five years before, when he was young and crazy and not always sober. On that occasion he had fumbled the ring, causing the groom to drop it and causing two hundred guests to titter.

And now he was going to be best man for Basil Whittlestaff. When Hixie called him Mr. Chopstick, she was not far off base.

At five o'clock the November dusk had painted the snowy whiteness of Pickax a misty blue. At the K mansion the draperies were drawn, crystal chandeliers were alight, and Mr. O'Dell had started a festive blaze in the drawing room fireplace.

The tall case clock in the foyer bonged five times. Mr. O'Dell dropped a cassette in the player, and the solemn chords of a Bach organ prelude resounded through the house. In the drawing room the magistrate was stationed in front of the fireplace. The bridegroom and his best man waited in the foyer. There was a moment of suspense, and then the bride and her attendant appeared on the balcony above and started their dignified descent.

Mrs. Cobb, usually seen in a smock or pantsuit or baggy jumper, was almost stunning in her pink suede suit. Susan Exbridge always looked stunning.

By the time the wedding party lined up in front of the

magistrate, he was red faced from the heat behind him. Flanking him on the hearth were two indignant Siamese whose territory in front of the fire was being usurped by a stranger.

Qwilleran felt uneasy; Hackpole fidgeted nervously; and the magistrate mopped his forehead before commencing the brief ritual: "We are gathered together to join together this man and this woman . . ."

Despite the tranquil beauty of the setting, the atmosphere was tense.

"If any person can show just cause why they may not lawfully be joined together, let him now speak or forever hold his peace."

"Yow!" said Koko.

Hackpole frowned; the two women giggled; and Qwilleran felt a mixed reaction of amusement and apprehension.

Herbert took Iris to be his wedded wife, and Iris took Herbert to be her wedded husband. Then it was time for the ring.

This was Qwilleran's moment. The ring was in his pocket, and he fumbled for it. Wrong pocket. Ah! He found the ring. And then he disgraced himself again. The wedding ring flipped out of his hand and rolled down the rug.

Yum Yum was after it in a flash. The resident thief of the Klingenschoen mansion, attracted by anything shiny and gold, batted her small treasure under the Chinese desk with Qwilleran in mad pursuit. Just as the trophy was within his reach, she chased it into the foyer—batting it with one paw, darting after it, batting with the other. She was pushing the ring under an Anatolian rug when the best man finally intercepted it.

At record speed the perspiring magistrate concluded the ceremony. "I pronounce you man and wife." Hackpole gave his bride an embarrassed kiss, and the rest was hugs, handshakes, congratulations, and best wishes.

The buoyant notes of Schubert piano music fitted the occasion, and Mrs. Fulgrove and Mr. O'Dell appeared with trays of champagne and hors d'oeuvres. Qwilleran, with crossed fingers and a glass of white grape juice, proposed a toast to the future happiness of the newlyweds.

The moment of celebration was brief. The magistrate gulped his champagne and left in a hurry, and the new Mrs. Hackpole coaxed her husband into the dining room to see the wild-game carvings on the massive German sideboard.

"I hope she'll be happy," Qwilleran said to Susan Exbridge. "Unfortunately I upheld my reputation as the worst 'best man' in nuptial history."

"But Koko did nobly as best cat," she said. "His well-timed declaration broke the tension."

The Hackpoles returned from their brief sight-seeing and expressed a desire to leave, the groom jingling his car keys and pushing his bride toward the back door.

"Wait a minute," Qwilleran said. "Give me your keys, and I'll bring your car to the front door. We're not throwing rice, but you ought to leave in style."

"But we have two cars," Hackpole objected. "Hers is in the garage."

"Pick it up tomorrow. No one ever heard of a bride and groom leaving in separate vehicles."

Qwilleran and Susan watched them drive away to the bridal suite in the new Pickax Hotel. "Well, there they go," he said, "for better or worse."

Susan accepted his invitation to dine at Stephanie's, where shaded candles glowed on tables draped to the floor, and soft colors and soft music created a romantic ambience. It was the night before the *Messiah* oratorio, and they discussed the plans for the gala reception at the museum following the performance.

"The Fitch twins are going to do videotapes," Susan said.

Qwilleran nodded his approval. "My friends Down Below refuse to believe the cultural activities in this remote county."

"I consider that we're the Luxembourg of the northeast central United States," Susan said with a dramatic flourish of her expressive hands. "And let me tell you about the surprise we've planned for the *Messiah* audience. Do you know why it's traditional to stand during the 'Hallelujah' chorus?"

"I've heard that the English king was so impressed when he heard it for the first time that he rose to his feet, and when the king stands, everyone stands. Isn't that the legend?"

"That's right! Around 1742. King George the Second will attend the performance tomorrow night, with the entire royal court in eighteenth-century regalia. Our theater group is staging it. . . . You ought to join the Pickax Thespians, Qwill. You have a good voice and a good presence. We could do *Bell, Book and Candle,* and Koko could play Pyewacket."

"I doubt whether he'd want to play a cat," Qwilleran said. "He's an insufferable snob. He'd rather play the title role in *Richard the Third,* I'm afraid."

Dinner with Susan was a pleasant sequel to a wedding he had found distressing. He gave her an armful of pink roses to take home, and she gave him a theatrical kiss. Temporarily he forgot his regret at losing a live-in housekeeper and his disapproval of her choice of husband. He forgot until he made his nightly house check before retiring to his apartment.

A slim volume lay on the library rug. It was a copy of *Othello,* and the best-known quotation came to Qwilleran's mind: *"Then must you speak of one who loved not wisely but too well."*

As he carried the Siamese across the yard in the wicker hamper, he remembered another line, and his moustache bristled. *"Kill me tomorrow; let me live tonight.*

FIFTEEN

SUNDAY, NOVEMBER TWENTY-FOURTH. Two more inches of snow fell during the night. When Qwilleran carried the wicker hamper to the main house on Sunday morning, the bronze bells in the tower of the Old Stone Church and the tape-recorded chimes in the Little Stone Church were announcing morning services. Mr. O'Dell, who had attended early mass, was busy with the snowblower.

"Sure, I'm after clearin' the driveway and parkin' lot for the party tonight," he said. "It won't snow any more today, I'm thinkin'."

Qwilleran turned up the thermostat in the house and was preparing the cats' breakfast when he heard the back door open and slam shut. It would be O'Dell, he thought, looking for a hot drink on a cold morning. When no one appeared, and when he heard a whimpering in the back hall, he went to investigate.

"Mrs. Cobb!" he exclaimed. "What are you doing here? What's happened to you?"

Her face was haggard and drained of color; her hair was wild; she was leaning weakly against the back door. At the sight of Qwilleran she burst into tears, covering her face with her hands.

He led her into the kitchen and seated her in a chair. "How did you get here? You've been walking in the snow. Where are your boots?"

"I don't know," she wailed. "I just . . . ran out. I had to get away."

"What went wrong? Can you tell me?" He pulled off her wet shoes and bundled her feet in towels.

She shook her head, and a sob turned into a groan. "I've made—I've made a terrible—mistake."

"I don't understand, Mrs. Cobb. Can't you tell me what's happened?"

"He's a monster! I married a monster! Oh, what shall I do?"

"Are you hurt?"

She shook her head, scattering a torrent of tears.

Qwilleran handed her a box of tissues. "Did he abuse you physically?"

"Oh-h-h-h! I can't talk about it!" She put her head down on the table and shook convulsively.

"Was he drinking heavily?"

She managed a tremulous yes.

"I'll make a cup of tea."

"I can't—it won't stay down," she whimpered. "I've been throwing up all night."

"You'd better drink some water, at least. You're probably dehydrated."

"I can't keep it down."

"Then I'm calling the doctor." He dialed the home telephone of Dr. Halifax, and the nurse who took care of the doctor's invalid wife said he was at church.

Qwilleran hurried outdoors and flagged down the houseman. "An emergency, Mr. O'Dell! Rush across to the Old Stone Church and get Dr. Hal. Look for a white head of hair, then walk down the aisle and beckon to him."

"I'll take the snowmobile," Mr. O'Dell said with a puzzled frown.

He roared away on the two-seater, and Qwilleran returned to the kitchen in time to see Koko rubbing against Mrs. Cobb's ankles. When she reached down to touch him, he jumped on her lap. She hugged him, and he allowed himself to be hugged, flicking his ears when her tears fell.

As soon as the noisy machine returned, Qwilleran went to the back door.

"Nice timing," said the old doctor. "You got me out right before they took up the offering. What's the trouble?"

Qwilleran explained briefly and directed him to the kitchen. In a moment Dr. Hal returned, "Better drive her to the hospital. Where's your phone? I'll order a private room."

"I don't know what it's all about," Qwilleran said in a low voice, "but her husband might be looking for her. I think you should specify no visitors."

He helped Dr. Hal walk the patient to the back door.

"I'll need—some things," she said faintly.

"We'll pack a bag and send it to the hospital. Don't worry about a thing, Mrs. Cobb." Qwilleran would never be able to call her Mrs. Hackpole.

The houseman brought the car up, and Qwilleran said to him, "While I'm gone, would you go to the Little Stone Church and catch Mrs. Fulgrove when the service is over? Ask her to come and pack Mrs. Cobb's personal things for a short hospital stay."

The drive to the hospital was done in silence except for an occasional sob. "I'm so much trouble for you."

"Not at all. You were wise to come back to the house."

When he returned from delivering the patient, Mrs. Fulgrove was bustling about with importance. "I packed all what I could think of," she said, "which it ain't easy seein' as how I never been in hospital myself, God be praised, but I put in what I thought was right and the little radio near her bed, and I looked for a Bible but I couldn't find one, which I packed my own and it should be a comfort to her."

"Had Mrs. Cobb asked you to work tonight during the reception, Mrs. Fulgrove?"

"That she did, but seein' as how it's Sunday—which I don't do work on the Lord's day—I couldn't take money for it, but I'll help out and pleased to do it, seein' as how the poor soul is in the hospital and I'm thankful for my health."

Qwilleran asked the houseman to deliver Mrs. Cobb's necessities to the hospital. "Do you think we can manage the reception without her, Mr. O'Dell?"

"Sure an' it's our best we'll be doin'. The club ladies will be after needin' help with the punch bowl and the likes o' that. And should I take the little ones across the yard before the party starts, now?"

"I don't believe so. The cats enjoy a party. Let them stay in the house."

"When the club ladies leave for the concert, I'll be lockin' up and goin' to the church for a little, but I'll be comin' back before it's over. Mrs. Cobb was for turnin' on all the lights and lightin' all the fireplaces. Too bad she won't be enjoyin' it now. What is it that's ailin' herself?"

"Some kind of virus," Qwilleran said.

Around noon the telephone rang, and a thick voice demanded, "Where is she? Where's my wife?"

"Is this Mr. Hackpole?" Qwilleran asked. "Didn't you know? She's in the hospital. She had some kind of attack, they say."

With an outburst of profanity the caller hung up.

Phoning the hospital in the afternoon, Qwilleran learned that the patient was resting quietly and holding her own, but no visitors were permitted, by order of Dr. Halifax.

In the afternoon Susan Exbridge and her committee arrived to prepare the punch and decorate the punch table. At the same moment Polly Duncan arrived with her overnight bag. The women greeted each other politely but not warmly, and the committee seemed surprised to see Polly on the premises.

On the way to the Old Stone Mill for dinner Qwilleran said to Polly, "I see you know Susan Exbridge."

"Everyone knows Susan Exbridge. She's *in* every organization and *on* every committee."

"She thinks I should join the theater group."

"You would find it *very* time-consuming," Polly warned him testily. "If you're serious about writing your book, it would definitely interfere."

She spoke with an acerbity that was unusual for her, and Qwilleran refrained from mentioning Mrs. Exbridge again.

At the restaurant the customers were standing in line, and Hixie was frantically trying to seat the crowd. She had no time for banter. Qwilleran and his guest had to wait for a table and wait for a menu. Judging from the tenor of the conversation in the dining room, everyone was headed for the concert, and everyone was thrilled.

Qwilleran said to Polly, "My mother used to sing in the *Messiah* choir every Christmas. My favorite number is the 'Hallelujah' chorus, especially if they pull out all the stops. I like that two-second rest before the last hallelujah—two seconds of dead silence and the POW!"

Hixie handed them menus with an apology for the delay. Clipped to the folder was a small card suggesting a ready-to-serve Concert Special. Clipped to Qwilleran's menu was another small card scribbled in Hixie's hand: "Want a private talk. Call you tomorrow."

Shortly after six-thirty the restaurant emptied, and the diners converged on the Old Stone Church. The lofty sanctuary was filled to overflowing, both the cushioned pews and the folding chairs in the side aisles. The first three pews were roped off, and the audience was mystified. Guesses and rumors circulated. The anticipation was palpable.

"Do you object to sitting in the back row on the side aisle?" Qwilleran asked Polly. "I want to leave right before the last note, so I can check the museum before the guests arrive."

At seven o'clock Mr. O'Dell slipped into a folding chair nearby, and the two men exchanged nods.

Then the performers appeared—first the orchestra in gray livery. The chorus filed in wearing powdered wigs and pastel costumes—the women in lace fichus and voluminous skirts; the men in knee breeches, waistcoats, and stocks. Finally the soloists made a dramatic entrance in jewel-toned velvets, creating a stir in the audience.

The conductor turned to face the expectant listeners. "Ladies and gentlemen, all rise for His Majesty, King George."

The doors to the rear were flung open, and while the orchestra played coronation music, the royal party moved down the center aisle in dignified procession—a panoply of red velvet, ermine, white satin, and purple damask. The audience gasped, then murmured in wonder, then applauded with delight.

Qwilleran whispered to Polly. "I wish my mother could have seen this. She would have flipped."

The church was noted for its excellent acoustics; the chorus was well rehearsed; the soloists and instrumentalists were professionals; the pipe organ was magnificent. It was a performance Qwilleran would never forget—for more reasons than one.

Toward the end of the oratorio Mr. O'Dell slipped out, giving an explanatory nod to Qwilleran. The orchestra played the opening bars leading up to the first explosive and spine-tingling hallelujah. The king and his royal party rose;

the audience rose; and Qwilleran lost himself in the majesty of the music and his own personal nostalgia.

The hallelujahs built up with mounting intensity and joyous celebration, ascending to that dramatic moment—that breathtaking pause—the two seconds of hollow silence!

In that fraction of a fraction of time Qwilleran heard a false note—the wail of a siren. Bruce Scott, seated several rows ahead, slid out of the pew and scuttled up the aisle. Two other men made quick exits. Qwilleran scowled. It was unfortunate timing for the fire siren.

The "Hallelujah" chorus ended, and an aria began. Then a door behind Qwilleran opened, and an usher tapped his arm and whispered.

Qwilleran was out of his seat instantly, running across the narthex and down the steps. On the other side of the park the museum was aglow—not with light but with a red glare.

"Oh, my God! The cats!" he yelled.

He dashed across the street, dodging traffic. He cut through the park, plowing frantically through deep snow. Flashing red and blue lights surrounded the building. More sirens were sounding.

"The cats!" he shouted.

Black-coated figures were unreeling lines and hoisting ladders. "Stay back!" they ordered.

Qwilleran dashed past them. "*The cats!*" he bellowed.

The red glare spread to the second-story windows. Glass exploded and tongues of flame licked out.

"Stop him!"

He was headed for the back door, nearest the kitchen.

"Keep him out!"

Strong arms restrained him. He looked up and saw the glare spreading to the third floor. Ladders went up. Windows shattered, and black smoke billowed out.

Qwilleran groaned in defeat.

SIXTEEN

MONDAY, NOVEMBER TWENTY-FIFTH. Qwilleran turned on the radio in the bedroom of his garage apartment. "Headline news at this hour: The Klingenschoen Museum on Park Circle was totally destroyed by fire Sunday night, the result of arson, according to fire chief Bruce Scott. A charred body found in the building, allegedly that of the arsonist, has not yet been identified. Thirty fire fighters, four tankers, and three pumpers responded, with surrounding communities assisting the Pickax volunteers. No firemen were injured. . . . We can expect warmer temperatures today and bright sunny skies—"

"Sunny!" Qwilleran muttered, snapping off the radio. He stared with mournful eyes at the gray scene outdoors: the cold, heavy, leaden sky . . . the ground black with frozen mud and soot . . . the smoke-damaged skeleton of a three-story fieldstone building that had once been a showplace. The windows, doors, and roof were gone, and the blackened stone walls enclosed a mountain of charred rubble. The acrid smell of smoke that hung over the ruin also seeped into his apartment.

Polly walked to his side and held his hand in silent sympathy.

"Thank you for helping me get through this ghastly night," he said. "Are you warm enough?" She was wearing a pair of his pajamas. "We didn't get heat until an hour ago. The power came on about five o'clock, but the phone is still dead. The last fire truck didn't leave until daylight."

Gazing at the depressing sight, Polly said, "I can't understand it."

"It's beyond comprehension. Would you like coffee? There's nothing here for breakfast except frozen rolls. What time are you due at the library?"

"YO-W-W-W!" came a loud and demanding howl from the adjoining room.

"Koko heard a reference to breakfast," Qwilleran said as he went to open the door of the cats' parlor.

They walked out with expectant noses and optimistic tails.

"Sorry," he said. "The only aroma this morning is stale smoke. There's no food until I go to the store. Just be glad you're alive."

"Here comes Mr. O'Dell," Polly said.

"Better go and get dressed."

She grabbed her clothes and disappeared into the bathroom as the houseman plodded up the stairs.

Qwilleran greeted him in a minor key. "It's a sad day, Mr. O'Dell, but we're thankful you saved the cats."

"That boy-o there, it was himself that did it, carryin' on like a banshee an' scratchin' the broom closet door that I waxed only a week since. I opened the door, and it was the picnic basket he was wantin' to get into. Scoldin' the little one, he was, till she jumped in after himself. You were wantin' me to leave them in the house, but it was a divil of a row he was makin', so I carried them over here before goin' to listen to the music a little. A wonder, it is!"

"Koko knew something was going to happen," Qwilleran

explained. "He sensed danger. Have you heard anything about the arsonist? On the radio they said he's still unidentified."

"That I did," said O'Dell. "My old friend Brodie I stopped to see this mornin'. It's himself been tryin' to get you on the phone."

"The line has been out of order all night. What did Brodie have to say?"

The houseman shook his head dolefully. "Sure an' I feel sorry for the poor woman—herself in the hospital and her new husband burned to death and a criminal."

Qwilleran was silent. It was the kind of thing that man would do—burn down the museum to stop his wife from working. He was a madman! He was crazy to think he could get away with it.

"I was there when they were after puttin' him in a canvas bag," the houseman said. "It's black, he was, like a burned hot dog, split open and pink inside."

"Spare us the details, Mr. O'Dell. Now it's Mrs. Cobb we have to worry about. We all know how much the museum meant to her."

"Is there anythin' I can do, now, for the poor soul?"

"You can take this money, buy some flowers, and deliver them to the hospital. *Not* pink roses! Wait a minute: I'll write a note to enclose.

The houseman left, and Polly emerged from the bathroom wearing the winter-white dress she had worn to the concert. "This is not what I usually wear for a hard day's work in the stacks," she said. "How can I explain that I lost my luggage in the museum fire?"

"I'm sorry about your luggage, Polly."

"I'm sorriest about those four thousand books."

"It's the library I'll miss most of all," he said. "I saved only one thing. When the auction van delivered the desk, I bribed the porters to bring Mrs. Cobb's wedding present out of the house, so the Pennsylvania *schrank* is in the garage along with Ephraim Goodwinter's old desk."

The telephone rang, a welcome sound after hours without service. Qwilleran grabbed it. "Yes? . . . It's been out of order, Dr. Hal. What's the situation? . . . That's bad, but there's worse to come. They've identified the arsonist. . . . Would it help if I went to the hospital and had a talk with her? . . . Okay, I'll let you know how it goes."

He replaced the receiver and gazed at it thoughtfully.

"What's the trouble, Qwill?"

"Mrs. Cobb was doing all right until she tuned in her radio and heard the news about the fire. Then it was hysteria-time all over again."

Polly left for work, and the telephone started to ring—and ring. Friends, associates, and strangers called to voice their horrified reactions and offer condolences. Prying busybodies wanted to know who had set the fire—and why. On Main Street a steady stream of motorists cruised around the Park Circle, gawking at the ruins.

Junior Goodwinter's phone call from Down Below came as a surprise. "Qwill! I can't believe it! Jody got a call from Francesca. She said they haven't identified the torch."

"It was Hackpole! One of your own fire fighters."

"Not anymore! They dumped him last spring for infraction of rules. When and if he showed up for training, he was half-shot."

Qwilleran said, "I'm greatly distressed about your mother's accident, Junior. That was a terrible thing."

"Yeah, I know. What can I say?"

"There's been no announcement about the funeral."

"No funeral. I talked to my brother and sister, and we decided to have a memorial service later."

"How will this affect the revival of the *Picayune?*"

"No one knows yet, but I have some good news. You know my dad's fireproof box—it had a key to a vault in Minneapolis. He'd been putting a hundred years of the *Picayune* on microfilm, and he didn't want anyone to know he was spending the money."

"And I have some good news for you," Qwilleran said. "Your great-grandfather's desk is in my garage, and it's yours when you marry Jody."

"Oh, wow!" Junior yelled.

The telephone kept on ringing. Hixie Rice called to inquire if the Siamese were safe and if they needed food. Shortly after, her high-heeled boots were clicking up the stairs, and she delivered a doggie bag of chicken *cordon blue.*

"I was absolutely *devastated* when I heard about the fire," she said, looking about for an ashtray. "Mind if I smoke, Qwill?"

"Okay with me," he said, "but don't blow smoke at the cats. It'll turn their fur blue."

She pocketed her cigarettes. "I should give them up. They say the damn things cause *wrinkles.*"

"Cup of coffee?" Qwilleran suggested.

"If it's your famous instant poison, no thanks."

"Any news about your chef and his knives?"

"Brace yourself," Hixie said. "Did you hear about the unidentified body found in a car stuck in a snowdrift? Well, that was Tony, fleeing to Canada in *my car!*"

"You really know how to pick 'em, Hixie."

"When I told you he escaped through the washroom window, I didn't tell you the whole story. Tony was a French Canadian living here illegally. He changed his name and bleached his hair. I could live with that, but . . . he tried to defraud the insurance company."

"That's bad."

"He sold his car to a chop-shop and reported it stolen. That man was an *insurance* investigator. The first time he came snooping around, Tony took off in the camper and spent a few days in the woods—"

"On *my property!* You told me he'd gone to see his sick mother in Philadelphia. And now what? Does the loss of your partner affect your job?"

"That's what I want to talk to you about, Qwill. My boss was planning a Caribbean cruise with the Goodwinter woman until she decamped with another man and got killed."

"So he wants you to go in her place," Qwilleran guessed.

"Well, he has the reservations and the tickets. . . ."

"Hixie, you're a one-woman true-story magazine. If you're looking for advice, I have no comment to make."

"That's okay. I just wanted to bounce off you. You're so sympathetic."

When Hixie had clicked down the stairs in her pencil-heeled boots, Qwilleran prepared for his visit to the hospital, wondering about Mrs. Cobb's wedding night: Did he threaten to torch the museum? Why didn't she warn us?

He found her sitting in an armchair in her pink robe, staring out the window without her eyeglasses. There were pink carnations and snapdragons on her bedside table, but her radio had been removed. A note propped against the flower vase read: "We miss you—Koko and Yum Yum."

"Mrs. Cobb," he said quietly.

She groped on the windowsill for her glasses. "Oh, Mr. Q! I feel so terrible about everything. I was afraid the cats were trapped in the fire, and I almost died! But now I know they're safe. The flowers are so pretty. I could cry, but I don't have any tears left. When I heard about the museum, I wanted to kill myself! I was sure Herb did it. Did he do it?"

Qwilleran nodded, slowly and regretfully. "The body has been identified. The evidence is all there. I'm sorry to bring you this sad news."

"It doesn't matter. The worst has happened. And I feel so guilty. It's all my fault. Why did I get involved with that man? He did it to spite me—to get his own way."

Qwilleran pulled up a chair and sat down. He spoke gently. "I know it's painful for you, Mrs. Cobb, but no one is blaming you."

"I'll go away when I get out of here. I can live in Saint Louis. I've called my son."

"Don't run away. Everyone likes you. They consider you a valuable asset to the Historical Society and the city. You could open an antique shop—do appraisals—set up a catering business—start a cookie factory. You belong here now."

"I don't have anywhere to go—anywhere to live. That was my *home.*"

"I imagine the Goodwinter house will be yours. . . ."

"Oh, I could never live there . . . not after what happened."

"It's Junior's ancestral home. He'd want it occupied by someone like you—with your love for old houses."

"You don't understand. . . ."

Qwilleran's drooping moustache and mournful eyes were compellingly sympathetic. "If you talk about it, you might feel better. Yesterday morning you came trudging through the snow in a weakened condition, after being ill all night. He did something grossly offensive to upset you."

"It was what he *told* me."

Qwilleran knew when to be silent.

"He was drinking. He always got talkative and boastful when he had a few. I didn't mind that."

Qwilleran nodded with understanding.

"He used to tell me about doing heroic things in the

army. I didn't believe half of it. But he liked to talk that way, and it did no harm. Once he told me that his father killed Senior's father in a fight, and his uncle helped to lynch Ephraim Goodwinter. He was *proud of it!* I was so stupid! I went along with it and flattered him." She sighed and looked out the window.

"And then . . . on Saturday night at the hotel . . ."

"He started bragging about killing deer out of season . . . overcharging customers . . . cheating on his taxes. He thought that was smart. He said he did the 'dirty work' for XYZ Enterprises. I didn't know what to say. I didn't know whether to believe him." She looked to Qwilleran for approval or disapproval.

He gave a neutral nod and looked encouraging.

"It was my *wedding night!*" she cried in anguish.

"I know. I know."

"Then he told me how his shop did repairs for the Goodwinter cars, and he knew Gritty very well. He kept a bottle in his office and they drank together. Him and a Goodwinter! He seemed to think it was an honor! I guess it's all right to tell you this; she's gone now. They're both gone."

There was a long pause. Qwilleran waited patiently.

After taking a deep breath, Mrs. Cobb said, "Gritty wanted to get rid of her husband and marry Exbridge, but Senior was broke, and she wouldn't get anything in a divorce. If he died accidentally there would be money from insurance and the sale of the newspaper and antiques and all that."

She had been calm at the beginning, but now she was clenching and unclenching her hands, and Qwilleran said, "Relax and take a few deep breaths, Mrs. Cobb. . . . This is a pleasant room. I had this room when I fell off my bike, but they've changed the hideous wall color."

"Yes, it's a pretty pink," she said. "Like a beauty shop."

"Is the food satisfactory?'

"I haven't any appetite, but the trays look nice."

"The cookies are terrible—take my word for it. They should get a few of your recipes."

She attempted a wan smile.

After a while Qwilleran asked, "Did Herb tell you what actually happened to Senior Goodwinter?"

Mrs. Cobb looked out of the window, then down at her hands. "Senior took his car to Herb's garage for winterizing." Her voice was shaking. "Herb did something to it—I've forgotten what it was—so it would go out of control and burst into flames . . ."

". . . when it hit a bad bump like the old plank bridge?"

She nodded.

"Is that how he bought the farmhouse cheaply?"

She gulped and nodded again.

"And torching the *Picayune* building was part of the deal?"

"Oh, Mr. Q! It was terrible! I told him he was a murderer, and he told me I was a murderer's wife and I'd better keep my mouth shut if I knew what was good for me. He looked terrible! He was going to hit me! I ran in the bathroom and locked the door and got sick. Then he went to sleep and snored all night. I wanted to run away! I got dressed and sat up until morning When he started to wake up, I ran out of the room—left my wedding suit, purse, everything."

"Then that's how he got the key to the museum."

She groaned, and her face—usually so cheerful—looked drawn and miserable.

When Qwilleran returned to his apartment he opened a can of tuna fish, flaked it, and arranged the morsels on a plain white china plate. "No more home-cooked food," he told the Siamese. "No more gourmet meals. No more antique porcelain dishes."

They gobbled the tuna with heads down and tails up, like ordinary cats. Yet Koko's behavior had been extraordinary. Two hours before the museum fire he had wanted to get out of the building; he *knew* what was coming. What else did he know?

Did he sense that Mrs. Cobb's marriage would end in disaster? How else could one explain his bizarre performance on the pink roses of the rug? And when he uprooted the herb garden, did he perceive some semantic connection with Herb Hackpole? No, that explanation was too absurd even for Qwilleran's vivid imagination. More likely, Koko was simply chewing the leaves as cats like to do, and he got a little high on an herb related to catnip. Yet, they were questions that would never be answered.

Even more perplexing was Koko's attraction to Shakespeare. Could he smell the pigskin covers, or the neat's-foot oil used to preserve the leather, or some rare nineteenth-century glue used in the bindings? If so, why did he concentrate on *Hamlet?*

Koko lifted his head from the plate of tuna and gave Qwilleran a meaningful stare that made his moustache quiver. What was the plot of the play? Hamlet's father had died suddenly; his mother remarried too soon; the father's ghost revealed that he had been murdered; the mother's name was Gertrude.

A shiver ran down Qwilleran's spine. NO! he told himself. The similarity to the Goodwinter tragedy was too fantastic; one could go mad pondering such a possibility. Koko's predilection for *Hamlet* was strictly a coincidence. That, at least, was what he told himself.

The Siamese had finished their dinner and were washing

up. The room now smelled of fish as well as acrid smoke. Opening the window a few inches for ventilation, Qwilleran was wounded by the tragic scene outdoors, the ghost of a noble building. Koko had been trying to communicate, and if he had read the cat's meaning, this senseless destruction could have been averted.

What happens next? he asked himself. We can't leave the building in ruins; do we tear it down? The gutted shell was three stories high, solid fieldstone, two feet thick at the base. It occupied a prominent location on Main Street, sharing the Park Circle with the courthouse, public library, and two churches.

Koko jumped to the windowsill, saying "ik ik ik" and wearing a bright-eyed expression of anticipation.

"I'm sorry we haven't had much conversation lately," Qwilleran apologized. "Too many distractions. You probably don't understand the fire and all its ramifications. Will you miss your Shakespeare game? Thirty-seven priceless little books went up in flame. And what shall we do with the remains of the museum?"

As he spoke, it began to snow softly and silently, whitening the frozen ruts and soot-encrusted ice, drawing a merciful white curtain across the ugly scene of devastation.

At the same time Qwilleran slapped his forehead in sudden realization. "I've got it! A theater!" he exclaimed.

"YOW!" said Koko.

"Pickax needs a theater. '*The play's the thing,*' as Hamlet said. We'll have a playhouse, Koko, and you can play Richard the Third. . . . Where are you?"

The cat had vanished.

"Where the devil did that cat go?" Qwilleran thundered with a frown.

Koko had returned to his feeding place and was trying to lick the ceramic glaze from the china plate.

The Cat Who Sniffed Glue

PROLOGUE

Yes, there really is a place called Moose County, 400 miles north of everywhere. The county seat is Pickax City, population three thousand.

There really is a busboy named Derek Cuttlebrink. And there is a barkeeper who looks like a bear and charges a nickel for a paper napkin. And there is a cat named Kao K'o Kung, who is smarter than people.

If they sound like characters in a play, that's because . . . "All the world's a stage, and all the men and women merely players." So, dim the lights! Raise the curtain!

ACT ONE

SCENE ONE

Place: A bachelor apartment in Pickax City
Time: Early one morning in late May
Cast: JIM QWILLERAN, former journalist, now heir to the Klingenschoen fortune—a big man, about fifty, with graying hair, bushy moustache and doleful expression

KAO K'O KUNG, a Siamese cat familiarly known as Koko

YUM YUM, another Siamese cat—Koko's constant companion

ANDREW BRODIE, Pickax chief of police

THE TELEPHONE RANG at an early hour, and Qwilleran reached blindly toward his bedside table. Half awake, he croaked a hoarse hello and heard an authoritative voice saying, "I want to talk to you!"

The voice was familiar, but the tone was alarming. It was Andrew Brodie, the chief of police in Pickax, and he sounded stern and accusing.

Qwilleran was always groggy before his first cup of coffee, and his mind groped for an explanation. Had he put a Canadian nickel in a parking meter? Tossed an apple core from his car window? Honked the horn within 500 feet of the hospital?

"Did you hear me? I want to talk to you!" The tone was not so gruff as before.

Qwilleran was getting his bearings, and he recognized the bantering style that passed for sociability among adult males in Moose County. "Okay, Brodie," he said. "Do I go to the station and give myself up? Or do you want to send the wagon and handcuffs?"

"Stay where you are. I'll be right there," said the chief. "It's about your cat." He hung up abruptly.

Again the possibilities churned in Qwilleran's mind. Had the Siamese been disturbing the peace? They were strictly indoor pets, but the male had a high-decibel yowl and the female had a shriek that could be duplicated only by a synthesizer. Either of them could be heard for blocks on a calm day if the windows were open. It was late May, and the windows were open to admit the sweet refreshing breezes for which Moose County was famous—sweet and refreshing except when they came from the direction of the Kilcally dairy farm.

Hurriedly Qwilleran pulled on some clothes, ran a wet comb through his hair, collected the newspapers cluttering the living room floor, slammed the bedroom door on his unmade bed, and looked out the window in time to see Brodie's police car pulling into the driveway.

Qwilleran lived in an apartment over a four-car garage, formerly the carriage house for the Klingenschoen estate. The carriage house was situated far back on the property; the mansion itself fronted on Main Street facing the park—a huge, square stone building now being remodeled as a theater for stage productions. Its broad lawns had been brutally torn up to accommodate trucks, piles of lumber, and a temporary construction shed. As the police car maneuvered around these obstacles, carpenters and electricians swarming over the site waved friendly salutes in the chief's direction. Brodie was a popular lawman, an amiable Scot with a towering figure, a beefy chest, and sturdy legs that looked appropriate with the kilt, tam-o'-shanter, and bagpipe that he brought out for parades and weddings.

As Brodie climbed the stairs to the apartment, Qwilleran greeted him from the top of the flight.

The chief was grumbling. He was always complaining about something. "They made the stairs too steep and too small when this place was built. There isn't room for a healthy man's foot."

"Walk up sideways," Qwilleran suggested.

"What's that thing?" Brodie pointed to a circle of ornamental wrought iron, a yard in diameter, leaning against the wall at the head of the stairs. Centered in the design were three cats rampant—scrappy animals—rearing on hind legs, ready to attack.

"That's from the gate of a three hundred-year-old Scottish castle." Qwilleran spoke with pride. "It's adapted from the Mackintosh coat of arms. My mother was a Mackintosh."

"Where'd you get it?" Brodie's envious manner indicated he would give anything for a similar memento of his own clan—or anything within reason; he was a thrifty man.

"From an antique shop Down Below. I left it in the city when I moved up to Pickax. Had it shipped up here last week."

"Looks heavy. Must've cost plenty for freight."

"It weighs about a hundred pounds. I'd like to incorporate it in my living room, but I don't know how."

"Ask my daughter. She has a lot of far-out ideas."

"Is that a commercial?" Qwilleran asked. Francesca Brodie was an interior designer.

With a bagpiper's swagger Brodie walked into the living room, giving it a policeman's quick once-over before flopping into a man-sized lounge chair. "You've got a comfortable roost here."

"Francesca's been helping me fix it up. When I lived in the mansion up front, this was an escape from too much opulence, but when I started living here full-time it suddenly looked bleak. How do you like what she put on the walls? Hand-woven Scottish tweed."

The chief turned to appraise the oatmeal-colored, oatmeal-textured wallcovering. "You shelled out plenty for that stuff, I bet. But I guess you can afford it." He then stared at the end wall. "You've got a lot of shelves."

"Francesca designed the shelf setup and had her carpenter build it. I'm starting to collect old books."

"With your bankroll you ought to be buying new books."

"I like old books. I bought a whole set of Dickens for ten bucks. You're a thrifty Scot; you should appreciate that."

"What's that picture?" Brodie pointed to a framed print over the sofa.

"An 1805 gunboat that used to sail the Great Lakes . . . How about a free cup of coffee?" Qwilleran stirred heaping spoonfuls of instant coffee into boiling water and handed a mug to Brodie. "Okay, what's the bad news, chief? What's so urgent that you have to get me out of bed?"

"Just got back from a law-enforcement conference Down Below," Brodie said. "Glad to be back where life is civilized. I tell you, those cities down there are jungles. They stole the mayor's car the first day of the conference." He took a swallow of coffee and choked. "Och! This is rugged stuff!"

"What was the conference about?"

"Drug-related violence. One of the speakers was a friend of yours. Lieutenant Hames. I talked to him at lunch."

"Hames is a brilliant detective, although he likes to play dumb."

"He told me some things about you, too. He said you gave him some good tips when you were writing for the *Daily Fluxion.*"

Qwilleran smoothed his moustache modestly. "Well, you know how it is. Things happen on a newspaper beat. I kept my eyes peeled and my ears flapping, that's all."

"Hames told me something else, too, and I thought he was putting me on, but he swears it's true. He says you have a very unusual cat. Very smart animal."

"He's right about that. Siamese are remarkably intelligent."

Brodie eyed his host keenly. "He says your cat is, like they say . . . psychic!"

"Wait a minute now. I wouldn't go that far, Brodie."

"He said your cat led the police to evidence that solved a couple of cases."

Qwilleran cleared his throat as he did before making a formal declamation. "You're a dog man, Brodie, so maybe you don't know this, but cats are the detectives of the animal world. They're naturally inquisitive. They're always sniffing around, scratching here and there, finding small places to sneak into, digging things out of holes. If my cat unearthed any clues, it was purely accidental."

"What's its name? I'd like to have a look at this cat."

"Koko is a seal-point Siamese, a neutered male, highly pedigreed. And don't call him 'it' or he'll put the whammy on you."

An imperious demand sounded from somewhere down the hall.

"That's Koko," Qwilleran said. "He heard his name mentioned, and he hasn't had his breakfast yet. I'll let him out. The cats have their own apartment."

"They do? I'll be damned!"

"With private bath and television."

"Television! You've gotta be kidding."

"Just a small black-and-white set. Cats don't see colors."

Enjoying Brodie's shock, Qwilleran excused himself and walked down the hall. The former servants' quarters over the garage provided him with a living room, writing studio, and bedroom. The fourth room—the one with the sunniest exposure—was reserved for the Siamese. It was furnished with soft carpet, cushions, baskets, scratching posts, and wide window sills facing south and west. In the bathroom were two commodes—his and hers. Originally they shared the same litter pan, but the female had developed a temperamental behavior pattern in recent weeks; she wanted her own facilities.

Qwilleran returned to the living room, followed by his two housemates, their body language demanding food. Two lean, fawn-colored bodies stretched to their longest; two brown masks with brown ears followed two brown noses uplifted in anticipation; two brown tails extended horizontally with a slight upcurve at the tip. They had the same kind of long, slender brown legs, but Koko walked with a resolute step while Yum Yum minced along daintily, a few paces behind him. At the living room entrance both animals stopped as if on cue and surveyed the stranger.

"They have blue eyes!" Brodie said. "I didn't know you had two. Are they from the same litter?"

"No, I adopted them from different sources," Qwilleran said. "Each one was left homeless under circumstances that Lieutenant Hames would probably remember."

The larger of the two sauntered into the room with a matter-of-fact gait and examined the visitor from a civil distance.

Qwilleran made the introductions. "Chief, this is Koko, the inspector general. He insists on screening everyone for security reasons. Koko, this is Chief Brodie of the Pickax police department."

The police chief and the cat stared at each other, the lawman with a puzzled frown. Then Koko leaped lightly to a bookshelf six feet off the floor. Squeezing between Benjamin Franklin's *Autobiography* and Boswell's *Life of Johnson,* he settled down to monitor the newcomer from an aerial vantage point.

Brodie said, "He looks like an ordinary cat! I mean, you can tell he's purebred and all that, but . . ."

"Did you expect him to have green fur and electronic eyes and rotating antennae? I told you, Brodie, he's just a pet who happens to be normally inquisitive and unusually intelligent."

Brodie relaxed and turned his attention to the smaller Siamese, who was slowly approaching with graceful, pigeon-toed steps, all the while concentrating on his shoes.

"Meet Yum Yum the Paw," Qwilleran said. "She looks fragile, but she has a lightning-fast paw like a steel hook. She opens doors, unties shoelaces, and steals anything small and shiny. Watch out for your badge."

"We used to have cats on the farm," Brodie said, "but they never came indoors."

"These never go outdoors."

"Then how do they find anything to eat? You don't buy that expensive stuff in *little cans,* do you?"

"To tell the truth, Brodie, Koko refuses to eat anything labeled 'catfood.' He wants his meals freshly cooked."

The chief shook his head in disbelief or disapproval. "Hames told me you spoiled your cat rotten, and I guess he wasn't just beating his gums."

"Did you learn anything about drug-related violence at the conference?"

"Like I told Hames, drugs and violence aren't our problem up here. He didn't believe me."

"Neither do I, although I've heard you say it before."

"Sure, we've pulled up some funny plants in a couple of backyards, and a few years back the kids were sniffing this here airplane glue, but we don't have drug rings or drug pushers. Not yet, anyway."

"How do you account for it?"

"We're isolated—400 miles north of everywhere, like it says on the sign at city limits. Crackpot ideas are slow in reaching us. Hell, the fast-food chains haven't even discovered Moose County yet." Brodie took another swallow of coffee with a grim expression. "Another thing: we have good family life up here. We have a lot of church activities and organized sports and healthy outdoor hobbies like camping and hunting and fishing. It's a good place to bring up kids."

"If drugs and violence aren't the problem, what do you do to keep so busy? Write parking tickets?"

The chief scowled at him. "Drunk drivers! Underage drinking! Vandalism! That's what runs us ragged. When my girls were in high school, them and my wife and I were always going to funerals—you know, the funerals of their classmates—kids getting themselves killed in car accidents. They'd be driving fast, horsing around in a moving vehicle, drinking beer illegally, hitting a patch of loose gravel, losing control. But now we've got another headache: vandalism in on the increase."

"I noticed that someone made power turns on the courthouse lawn last week."

"That's what I mean. There's a certain element—a few crazies—that don't have anything to do. They shot out two streetlights on Goodwinter Boulevard last night. When I was a kid we smashed pumpkins and strung trees with toilet paper on Halloween, but this new generation does it all year round. They pull up the flowers in front of city hall. They bash rural mailboxes with baseball bats. I don't understand it!"

"I haven't seen any graffiti."

"Not yet, but they poured a can of paint on the fountain in the park. We know the punks that are doing it, but we never catch 'em in the act." Brodie paused. He was looking hopefully at Qwilleran.

"Do you have a plan?"

"Well . . . after talking to Hames . . . I wondered if your cat . . . could tip us off to where they're going to strike next, so we could stake it out."

Qwilleran eyed him askance. "What were you guys smoking at that conference?"

"All I know is what Hames told me. He said your cat has ESP or something."

"Listen, Brodie. Suppose that little animal who is sitting on the bookshelf licking his tail—suppose he knew that vandals were going to heave a brick through the school window on June second at 2:45 A.M. Just how would he communicate this information? You're nuts, Brodie. I admit that Koko occasionally senses danger, but what you're suggesting is preposterous!"

"Out in California they're using cats to predict earthquakes."

"That's a whole different ballgame . . . How about more coffee? Your cup's empty."

"If I drank another cup of this battery acid, I'd be paralyzed from the neck down."

"After the suggestion you just made, I think you're paralyzed from the neck up. Who's the leader of this gang of hoodlums? Isn't there usually a leader? How old is he?"

"Nineteen and just out of high school. He comes from a

good family, but he runs with a pack from Chipmunk. That's the slummiest town in the county, I guess you know. They get a few cans of beer and go cruising in their broken-down crates."

"What's his name?"

Brodie seemed reluctant to reveal it. "Well, I'm sorry to say . . . it's Chad Lanspeak."

"Not the department-store heir! Not the son of Carol and Larry!"

The chief nodded regretfully. "He's been in trouble ever since junior high."

"That's really bad news! His parents are just about the finest people in town! Community leaders! Their older son is studying for the ministry, and their daughter is premed!"

"You're not telling me anything I don't know. Lanspeak is a good name. It's hard to figure out how Chad got off the track. People say the third child is always an oddball, and it may be true. Take my three girls, for instance. The two older ones got married right after school and started families. I've got four grandkids, and I'm not fifty yet. But Francesca! She was the third. She was determined to go away to college and have a career."

"But she returned to Pickax to work. You haven't lost her."

"Yes, she's a good girl, and she still lives at home. That's something we're thankful for. The family is still together. But she's all wrapped up in decorating and acting in plays."

"She has talent, Brodie. She's directing the next play at the Theatre Club. You should be proud of her."

"That's what my wife says."

"Francesca is twenty-four, and she has to make her own choices."

The police chief seemed unconvinced. "She could have married into the Fitch family. She dated David Fitch when they were in high school. That's another fine old family. David's great-grandfather struck it rich in the 1880s—in mining or lumbering, I forget which. David and Harley went to Yale, and now they're vice presidents at the bank. Their dad is bank president. Fine man, Nigel Fitch! I thought sure I was going to have one of the boys for a son-in-law."

Brodie looked away sadly. His disappointment was painful to witness.

"One of my daughters married a farmer," he went on, "and the other one married an electrician with his own business. Decent fellas, they are. Ambitious. Good providers. But Francesca could have married David Fitch. She used to bring him and Harley home after school to listen to that noise the kids call music. They were real gentlemen. 'Hello, Mr. Brodie' and 'How are you, Mr. Brodie?' They liked to hear me play the pipes. Nice boys. Nothing snobbish about them at all. Full of fun, too."

"They're fine young men," Qwilleran agreed. "I've met them at the Theatre Club."

"Talk about talent! They're in all the plays. They were the twins in a musical called "The Boys from Poughkeepsie" or something like that. Nigel is lucky to have sons like those two. Francesca really passed up a good chance."

"Yow!" said Koko in a sudden irritable commentary on the conversation, as if he were bored.

"Well, to get back to my suggestion," Brodie said. "Give it a thought or two. I'd like to break up this gang before they get into something worse, like torching barns or breaking into summer cottages or stealing cars. That can happen, you know."

"Did you ever talk to Carol and Larry about their son?"

The chief threw up his hands. "Many times. They keep up a brave front, but they're heartbroken. What parent wouldn't be? The boy doesn't live at home. He drifts around, shacking up wherever he can, partying all night. Never wanted to go to college."

"What does he do for money?"

"As I understand it, his grandmother left him a trust fund, but he doesn't get his monthly check unless he goes to college or works in the family store—Larry put him in charge of sporting goods—but he goofs off half the time and goes hunting or trapping. Poaching, most likely."

"I feel bad about this," Qwilleran said. "The Lanspeaks don't deserve this kind of trouble."

"You know, Qwill, you bachelors are lucky. You don't have any problems."

"Don't be too sure."

"What's your problem?"

"Women."

"What did I tell you!" Brodie said in triumph. "I told you they'd all be chasing after you. A fella can't inherit millions like you did and expect to live a normal life. If you don't mind some advice, I say you should get yourself a wife and get your name off the eligible list."

"I had a wife," Qwilleran said. "It didn't work out."

"So try it again! Marry a young woman and start thinking about heirs. You're not too old for that."

"When I go, I'm leaving everything to the Klingenschoen Memorial Fund. They'll distribute it right here in Moose County, where the money was made and where it belongs."

"I suppose all kinds of people are bugging you for handouts."

"The Fund takes care of that, too. I turn everything over to them. They dole it out to charities and good causes and give me a little to live on."

"Och! You're a little daft. Did anybody ever tell you?"

"I've never wanted a lot of money or possessions."

"I noticed that," said Brodie, glancing around the room.

"How many millionaires or billionaires live over the garage? Did you ever see how the Fitches live? Nigel and his wife have a double condominium at Indian Village, and Francesca says it's really fixed up! Harley and his bride have the old Fitch mansion that looks like a castle. Twenty-two rooms! David and Jill have a new house that's going to be on the cover of some magazine . . . I tell you, Qwill, Fran really blew it when she didn't marry David Fitch. But it's too late now."

After Brodie had made his departure, maneuvering down the stairs and complaining about the narrow treads, Qwilleran mixed another cup of instant coffee in the four-by-four-foot closet that served as his kitchen. He also warmed up some two-day-old doughnuts in the miniature microwave.

Koko jumped down from the biography shelf and started prowling like a caged tiger, yikking and yowling because his breakfast was late. Yum Yum sat hunched up in a bundle of self-pity for the same reason.

"Cool it," Qwilleran told Koko, after consulting his watch. "The chuckwagon will be here any minute."

When he and the Siamese lived up front in the mansion, they had a housekeeper who spoiled all three of them with home-cooked delicacies. Now Qwilleran took lunch and dinner in restaurants, and the cats' meals were catered by the chef at the Old Stone Mill. A busboy named Derek Cuttlebrink made daily deliveries of poultry, meat, and seafood that needed only to be warmed with a little of the accompanying sauce.

When Derek finally arrived with the shrimp timbales in lobster puree, he apologized for being late and said, "The chef wants to know how they liked the veal blanquette yesterday."

"Okay, except for the Japanese mushrooms, Derek. They don't like Japanese mushrooms. And tell him not to send marinated artichoke hearts—only the fresh ones. Their favorite food is turkey, but it must be off-the-bird—not that rolled stuff."

He tipped the busboy and sat down to finish his coffee and watch the Siamese devouring their food. Each cat was a study in concentration—tail flat on the floor, whiskers swept back out of the way. Then they washed up fastidiously, and Yum Yum leaped into Qwilleran's lap, landing as softly as a cloud and turning around three times before settling down. Koko arranged himself on the biography shelf and waited for the dialogue to begin.

Qwilleran made it a policy to converse with the cats; it seemed more rational than talking to himself, as he had a tendency to do after living alone so long. Koko in particular seemed to enjoy the sound of a human voice. He responded as if he understood every word.

"Well, Koko, what do you think of Brodie's ridiculous suggestion?"

"Yow," said the cat with an inflection that sounded like disdain.

"The poor guy's really disappointed that Fran didn't marry into the Fitch family. I wonder if he knows she's making a play for me."

"Nyik nyik," said Koko, shifting his position nervously. He had never been enthusiastic about any of the women in Qwilleran's life.

Qwilleran had first met Fran Brodie when he started buying furniture from Amanda's Studio of Interior Design. Amanda was middle-aged, gray-haired, dowdy, tactless and irascible, but he liked her. Her assistant was young, attractive and friendly, and he liked her also. Both women wore neutral colors that would not compete with the fabrics and wallpapers they showed to clients, but on Amanda the beige, gray, khaki and taupe looked drab; on Francesca's willowy figure they looked chic. More and more Amanda retired into the background, running the business while her vivacious assistant worked with the clients.

Fran was tall like her father, with the same gray eyes and strawberry-blond hair, but her eyes had a steely glint of ambition and determination.

"She knows I'm involved with Polly Duncan," Qwilleran said, "but it doesn't slow her down. Polly warned me about joining the Theatre Club and hiring Fran, but I thought it was just female cattiness . . ."

"YOW!" said Koko sternly.

"Sorry. I didn't mean that. Let's say it looked like an older woman's jealousy of a young rival, and Fran is really on the make! I don't know whether she's after me or the Klingenschoen money."

"Nyik nyik," Koko said.

"The aggressiveness of the new generation is hard for me to accept. I may be old-fashioned, but I like to do the chasing."

Francesca's strategy was all too transparent. She had asked for a key to his apartment, in order, she said, to supervise the workmen and the delivery of merchandise. She brought wallpaper-sample books and furniture catalogues for his perusal, entailing consultations in close proximity on the sofa, with pictures and patterns spread out on their laps and with knees accidentally touching. She timed these tête-à-têtes for the cocktail hour, when it was only polite for Qwilleran to offer a drink or two, after which a dinner invitation was almost obligatory. She suggested that they fly Down Below for a few days to select furniture and art objects at design centers and galleries. She wanted to do over his bedroom with draped walls, a fur bedcover, and mirrored ceiling.

Francesca was attractive without doubt. She bubbled with youthful vitality, wore enticing scents, and had legs that looked provocative with high-heeled sandals. Having turned fifty, however, Qwilleran was beginning to feel more comfortable with women of his own age who wore size 16. Polly Duncan was head librarian at the Pickax Public Library, and she shared his interest in literature as no other woman had ever done. Following the tragic death of her husband many years before, she was now rediscovering love, and her responses were warm and caring, belying her outward show of reserve. They were discreet about their relationship, but there were few secrets in Pickax, and everyone knew about the librarian and the Klingenschoen heir, and also about the interior designer.

"Polly is getting edgy," Qwilleran said to his attentive listener. "I don't like what jealousy does to a woman. She's intelligent and admirable in every way, and yet . . . the brainiest ones sometimes lose control. Sooner or later there's going to be an explosion! Do you think librarians ever commit crimes of passion?"

"Yow," said Koko as he scratched his ear with his hind foot.

SCENE TWO

Place: Downtown Pickax
Time: The following morning
Cast: HIXIE RICE, a young woman from Down Below
EDDINGTON SMITH, dealer in used books
CHAD, the black sheep of the Lanspeak family
Construction workers, pedestrians, clerks

QWILLERAN DECIDED TO take a casual walk downtown after hearing the 9 A.M. newscast on station WPKX. "Vandals opened fire hydrants during the night, seriously draining the city's water supply and impeding firefighters called to a burning building on the west side."

As a veteran journalist who had written for major newspapers around the country, Qwilleran despised the headline news on the radio—those twenty-five-word teasers sandwiched between two hundred-word commercials. They only fueled the feud between the print and electronic media. He stormed around his apartment, ranting aloud—to the alarm of the Siamese.

"How many hydrants were opened? Where were they located? What was the extent of water loss? What was the cost to the city? Whose building burned as a result? When was the vandalism discovered? Why did no one notice the gushing water?"

The Siamese flew about the apartment as they always did when Qwilleran went on a rampage.

"Well, never mind. Excuse the outburst," he said in a calmer mood, tamping his moustache. "In a few days we'll get our news from print coverage."

Moose County had been without a good newspaper for several years, and now the situation was about to be corrected. Thanks to the Klingenschoen Memorial Fund and some prodding from Qwilleran, a paper of professional caliber would hit the streets on Wednesday next.

Meanwhile, there were only two adequate sources of news. One could plug into the grapevine that flourished in the coffee shops, on the courthouse steps, and over back fences. Or one could wander into the police station when the talkative Brodie was on duty.

"I'm going downtown to do a few errands," Qwilleran informed his housemates. "Mr. O'Dell will be coming in to clean, and he has orders not to give you any handouts, so don't put on your phony starvation act. See you later."

Koko and Yum Yum listened impassively and then accompanied him to the head of the stairs, where they both rubbed jaws against the Mackintosh coat of arms until their fangs clicked on the wrought iron. Qwilleran often wondered about their silent farewells. Were they sorry to see him go, or glad? Were they worried or relieved? Who could tell what was behind those mysterious blue eyes?

He always walked downtown. Everything in Pickax was within walking distance, although few of the locals ever used their legs for transportation. As he walked down the long driveway, the construction crew working on the renovation of the mansion greeted him jovially, and the job supervisor tossed him a hard hat and invited him into the building to inspect their progress.

The Klingenschoen mansion, three stories high and built of fieldstone two-feet thick, had been completely gutted in preparation for the conversion, and the interior was redesigned to provide amphitheater seating, a thrust stage, a professional lighting system, and adequate dressing rooms. It would seat three hundred and would be the new home of the Theatre Club.

"Will it be finished on schedule?" Qwilleran asked.

"Hopefully, if the architects don't give us any flak," said the supervisor. "Someone's flying up from Down Below to make an inspection next week. I hope they don't send that girl architect. She's a tough baby."

Qwilleran chuckled at the remark. The architectural firm was a Cincinnati outfit specializing in small theater design, and the "tough baby" was Alacoque Wright, a flighty young woman he had dated Down Below before she eloped with an engineer. He resumed his walk, marveling at the quirks of fate and anticipating a reunion with Cokey.

The three blocks of Main Street that constituted downtown Pickax were unique. In its heyday the town had been the hub of the mining and quarrying industry in the county, and all commercial buildings were constructed of stone. What made the cityscape unusual was the design of the stores and office buildings, which masqueraded as miniature castles, temples, fortresses and monasteries, reflecting the flamboyant taste of nineteenth-century mining tycoons.

Walking past the public library (housed in a Greek temple), Qwilleran automatically looked for Polly Duncan's cranberry-red car in the parking lot. In front of the lodge hall (a small-scale Bastille) a volunteer shaking a canister for the "Save Our Snakes" fund flashed an irresistible smile, and he donated a dollar. As he passed Scottie's Men's Shop (a Cotswold cottage) a young woman breezed out of the store with her hair flying, her shoulder bag flying, and yards of skirt flying. It was Hixie Rice, the exuberant advertising manager of the new Moose County newspaper. She had been his neighbor Down Below, and he had been instrumental in bringing her to Pickax.

"Hi, Qwill!" she trilled.

"Morning, Hixie. How's it going?"

"Like you wouldn't *believe!* I sold Scottie a double spread for the opener, and he signed a twenty-six-week contract. Even that weird bookstore took a quarter page. And today I'm lunching at the country club with three bankers! Nigel Fitch is charming, and his sons are adorable, especially the one with a moustache. Too bad they're all married."

"I didn't know that made much difference to you."

"Forget my lurid past Down Below," she said with an airy gesture. "In Pickax I'm *totally* discreet. I've given up married men, cigarettes, and high heels. I bought seven pairs of skimmers at Lanspeak's, and I skim everywhere. What are you doing for dinner tonight? I'll buy."

"Sorry, Hixie, but I've got a date."

"Okay. Catch you later." She skimmed across Main Street in the middle of the block, dodging cars, vans, and pickups with deft footwork, throwing kisses to the drivers who whistled in appreciation or honked horns in annoyance.

Qwilleran headed for the bookstore that Hixie called weird. For once she had not exaggerated. It literally crouched on the backstreet behind Lanspeak's department store. Rough stones were piled up to simulate a grotto, and the stone was feldspar; on a sunny day it glittered like the front of a burlesque house. Hanging alongside the front door was a weathered sign, almost illegible: EDD'S EDITIONS. In the grimy front window were old books with drab covers, and one drooping potted plant.

The interior of the store was as dim as the feldspar exterior was dazzling. Coming in from the sunshine Qwilleran could see nothing at first, but he blinked until the scene took shape: tables loaded with haphazard piles of dingy books, floor-to-ceiling shelves jammed with grayish bindings and invisible titles, a shaky wooden stepladder, and a smoky-gray Persian cat walking across a table of old magazines, waving his plume of a tail like a feather duster. The place had a smell of old books and sardines.

Qwilleran's arrival had activated a tinkling bell on the front door, and soon the proprietor materialized from the shadows. Eddington Smith was a small, thin man with gray hair and a gray complexion and nondescript gray clothing. He reminded Qwilleran of someone else he had known, except for his bland smile—a permanent smile expressing utter contentment.

"Greetings," the man said, softly and pleasantly.

"Morning, Edd. Nice day, isn't it? How's Winston?" Qwilleran stroked the cat, and Winston accepted the attention with the dignity of a prime minister. "How old is this building, Edd? It's so hideous, it's fascinating."

"It's over a hundred years old—a blacksmith's shop originally. They say the mason who built it was strange in the head." He spoke gently and kindly.

"I believe it."

" 'We shape our buildings, thereafter they shape us,' to quote Mr. Churchill. I guess it's true. My grandfather said the blacksmith was a regular caveman."

"Apparently the building hasn't had the same effect on you," Qwilleran said genially.

"That's right," Eddington said, still smiling. "I feel like something that lives under a stone. Dr. Halifax says I spend too much time in the shop. He says I should get out and join a club and have some fun. I'm not sure I'd like fun."

"Dr. Hal is a wise man. You should take his advice."

" 'Work is much more fun than fun!' That's what Noel

Coward said . . . Is there something I can do for you today? Or do you want to browse?"

"I'm interested in finding a set of Brittanica published in 1910."

"The eleventh edition!" The bookseller nodded in approval. "I'll see what I can do. I'm still searching for your Shakespeare."

"Remember, I want the plays in separate volumes. They're easier to read."

Eddington's smile looked roguish. "A British scholar called Shakespeare the sexiest writer in the English language."

"That's why he's been popular for four hundred years." Qwilleran gave Winston two more strokes and started for the door.

Eddington followed him. "You belong to the Theatre Club, don't you?"

"Yes, I joined recently. I'm being initiated with a role in the next play."

"Harley Fitch invited me to join. Do you know Harley? He's a nice young man. Very friendly."

Qwilleran edged closer to the door.

"I wouldn't be good at acting," said the bookseller, "but I could open and close the curtain, I suppose—something like that."

"Once you get up on that stage, Edd, you might discover hidden talents." Qwilleran now had his hand on the door-handle.

"I don't think so. The others in the club are all smart and well-educated. Harley Fitch and his brother went to Yale. I've never been to college."

"You may not have a degree," Qwilleran assured him, "but you're a very well-read man."

Eddington lowered his head, smiling modestly, and

Qwilleran took the opportunity to escape into the sunshine. He wondered about the enigmatic little man. How did he stay in business? How did he earn enough to buy sardines for Winston? There were never any customers in the store. He sold no greeting cards or paper napkins or scented candles as a sideline. Just old, faded, dusty, musty books.

Qwilleran also gave some thought to the celebrated Fitch family, a name that everyone mentioned with respect, if not adoration. The Fitches were "friendly . . . charming . . . clean-cut . . . a fine old family . . . real gentlemen . . . fun-loving . . . clever." The adulation could become cloying.

He stopped for a cup of coffee at the luncheonette and then went to the police station, where he found Brodie on the sergeant's desk. "The kids went cruising again last night," he said to the chief.

"Och! It's no laughing matter," Brodie said. "It'll cost the city a few hundred in water revenue, and a family on the west side saw their house burn down to the ground for lack of water pressure."

"How many hydrants did the vandals open?"

"Eight. They used pipe wrenches, so there's no damage to the hydrants themselves. I suppose we should be grateful to the delinquents for being so considerate."

"Where were the hydrants located?"

"East Township Line—industrial area—deserted at night. It happened about three or four in the morning, judging by the amount of water wasted. Senseless! Senseless!"

"When was it discovered?"

"About six o'clock this morning. The low pressure set off a sprinkler alarm at the plastics factory, and that alerted the fire department. Right after that the call came in from the west side."

"Whose house burned down?"

"Young couple with three kids and no insurance. There

wasn't enough water in the tank to put the fire down. Mind you, two hundred and fifty thousand gallons lost! What gets me is this—we have plenty of floods and forest fires and tornadoes and hurricanes and droughts. We don't need man-made disasters as well."

"How come the prowl car didn't spot the gushing water during the night?"

Brodie leaned back in his chair wearily. "Listen. We have a force of six men, including me and the sergeant. There are seven days in the week and twenty-four hours in the day—and all this damned paperwork! That spreads us pretty thin. On Friday nights we have two cars out on the beat. That's payday, you know; the boozers whoop it up and sleep it off on Saturday. So we concentrate on the bars and party stores and school parking lot. There was a big dance at the school last night, and after that the kids went partying in the neighborhoods—making noise, raising hell, all the usual. We logged I don't know how many DPs. There were two brawls at taverns and three car accidents, and that's just within the city limits! Drivers and passengers all sloshed! Then there was a minor fire in a foster home for the elderly—some old geezer smoking in bed. No damage, but enough panic for a major earthquake! I tell you, Qwill, Friday night is hell-night in Pickax, especially in spring—just like it was a hundred years ago when the lumberjacks used to come into town and mix it up with the miners."

"I can see you had your hands full," Qwilleran said. "What were the state troopers doing all this time?"

"Oh, they assisted—when they weren't chasing drunk drivers all over the county. One high-speed chase ended up with the guy in the Ittibittiwassee River."

"It looks as if the vandalism is escalating, as you predicted."

"When they get tired of pulling up flowers, they look for

bigger kicks. This is Saturday. They'll be out again tonight." Brodie looked at Qwilleran inquiringly. "There should be some way to outguess them."

"Forget about cat power, Brodie. It won't work." Qwilleran saluted the chief and went on his way. He wanted to make one more stop before lunch. He wanted to meet the black sheep of the Lanspeak family.

The department store was the largest commercial building on Main Street—a Byzantine palace with banners flying from the battlements. That was the kind of dramatic touch that would appeal to Larry Lanspeak. He and his wife, Carol, were the lifeblood of the Theatre Club. Their energy and enthusiasm were legendary in Pickax; so was their store. In the 1880s it had served Moose County as a small general store, selling kerosene, gun powder, harnesses, crackers, cheese, and calico by the yard. Now the inventory included perfume and satin chemises, microwave ovens and television sets, fishing rods, and sweat shirts.

Sweat shirts! That was Qwilleran's cue. He headed for the men's casual wear in the rear of the store. It meant zigzagging through the women's department with their seductive aromas and silky displays. Clerks who had sold him sweaters, robes, and blouses in Polly Duncan's size brightened when they saw him.

"Morning, Mr. Q."

"Help you, Mr. Q? We just received some lovely silk scarfs. Real silk!"

In the sporting goods department a young man was leaning on a glass showcase, poring over a gun catalogue. His pigtail and Fu-Manchu moustache looked ludicrous for a conservative town like Pickax.

"Do you have any sweat shirts?" Qwilleran asked him.

"On the rack." The clerk jerked his head toward the casual wear with a look of boredom.

"Do you have any in green?"

"What's on the rack, that's what we've got."

"How much are they?"

"Different prices. Whatever it says on the tag."

"I'm sorry, but I didn't bring my reading glasses," Qwilleran said. "Would you be good enough to help me?" It was a lie, but he enjoyed irritating clerks who irritated him.

Reluctantly the young man left his gun catalogue and found a green sweat shirt in a large size and at a price that seemed fair. While the sale was being written up, Qwilleran looked at fishing rods and reels, bows and arrows, hunting knives, lifebelts, backpacks, and other gear that had nothing to do with his lifestyle. He spotted one item, however, that would be most inconvenient for a lazy clerk to reach: a pair of snowshoes hung high on the wall.

"Are those the only snowshoes you have?" he inquired.

"We don't stock snowshoes in spring."

"What are they made of?"

"Aluminum."

"I'd like to examine them."

"I'll have to get a ladder."

"That sounds like a good idea," Qwilleran said, enjoying his script and performance.

After some exertion and disgruntled muttering the young man brought down the snowshoes, and Qwilleran studied them leisurely.

"How do you keep them on your feet?"

"Bindings."

"Which is the back and which is the front?"

"The tail is the back."

"That makes sense," Qwilleran said. "Is this the only kind you ever carry?"

"In winter we have some with wood frames and cowhide lacing."

"Do you do any snowshoeing yourself?"

"When I check my traps."

"Do you use aluminum or wood?"

"Wood, but I make my own."

"You make your own snowshoes? How do you do that?" There was a note of sincere amazement in the question.

The clerk showed some slight signs of life. "Cut down a white ash to make the frames. Kill a deer to get the hide for lacing."

"Incredible! How did you learn to do it?"

The fellow shrugged and looked half-pleased. "Just found out, that's all."

"How do you make a curved frame out of a tree?"

"Cut it to the right size, steam it and bend it, that's all."

"Amazing! I'm new in the north country," Qwilleran said, "but snowshoeing is something I'd like to try next winter. Is it hard to do?"

"Just put one foot in front of the other. And don't be in a hurry."

"How fast do you go?"

"Depends on the snow—hardpack or soft—and whether you're in underbrush. Four miles an hour is pretty fast."

"Do they come in different sizes?"

"Different sizes and different styles. I've made all kinds—Michigan, Bear Paw, arctic—all kinds."

"Do you make them to sell?"

"Never did, but . . ."

"I'd like to buy a handmade pair, if I could see a selection."

"I have some at my folks' house. I guess I could get ahold of them next week."

"Would you bring some samples to my apartment?"

"Where do you live?"

"Behind the Klingenschoen mansion, over the garage. My

name is Qwilleran." He observed a spark of recognition in the clerk's hooded eyes. "And what's your name?"

"Chad."

"When could you bring the samples?"

"Tuesday, maybe. After work."

"What time do you quit?"

"Five-thirty."

"I have a Theatre Club rehearsal at seven. Could you get to my place not later than six?"

"I guess."

Qwilleran left the store in a good frame of mind. He didn't really want a pair of snowshoes or even a green sweat shirt; he wanted to satisfy his curiosity about Chad Lanspeak.

That was Saturday morning.

Late Saturday night or early Sunday, vandals broke into the Pickax high school and destroyed a computer.

SCENE THREE

Place: The rehearsal hall at the Pickax community center
Time: Late Monday evening
Cast: Members of the Theatre Club, rehearsing for *Arsenic and Old Lace*

"So long, kids, See you tomorrow night."

"G'night y'all. Anybody need a ride home?"

"Good night, Harley. Don't forget to bring your grandfather's bugle tomorrow night."

"Hope I can find it."

"Anyone want to stop at Bud's for a beer?"

"Darling, I'd love a beer . . . if you're buying."

"Listen, everybody, before you go! Have your lines tomorrow night. No excuses! We start work on the timing."

"Nighty-night, Francesca. You're a slave driver, but we love ya."

"Good night, David . . . Good night, Edd. Don't worry about anything. You're going to be just fine. Glad to have you in the company."

"Good night, Fran," said Qwilleran. "You're doing a good job of handling these clowns."

"Don't go yet, Qwill. I want to talk to you." She was watching the others leave—young and not so young, talented or simply stagestruck, affluent or working for the minimum wage—but they all looked alike in their nondescript rehearsal clothes: mismatched pants and tops, ill-fitting, well-worn, purposely ugly. Qwilleran felt too well-dressed in his new green sweat shirt. Even Fran, who was meticulously chic on the job, looked sloppy in faded tights, running shoes, and her father's old shirt. Eddington Smith was the only one who had reported for rehearsal in suit, white shirt, and tie.

Fran sat down next to Qwilleran and said, "Qwill, you're going to be the hit of the show when you roar 'Bully!' and 'Charge!' with your thundering voice. But I'd like to see a burst of energy when you gallop upstairs with an imaginary sword. Remember, you think you're Teddy Roosevelt charging up San Juan Hill."

"You don't know what you're asking, Fran. I'm laid-back by choice and by temperament, and getting more so every year."

"Make an adjustment," she said with the sweet smile she always employed to get what she wanted. "You'll be able to practice with the bugle tomorrow night if Harley remembers to bring it."

Qwilleran said, "The Fitch twins are the ones who'll steal the show—Harley in his Boris Karloff makeup, and David playing that slimy doctor like a perfect creep."

"They're two talented boys," Fran said, "and such good sports. They're really wasted on banking." She glanced at her watch, yet seemed in no hurry to leave.

"I'm glad you gave Eddington a part to play, even though he's terrified."

"He'll be perfect for old Mr. Gibbs, won't he? But I hope he learns to project. He speaks in a whisper."

"No one ever shouts in a bookstore, and that's where he's spent his whole life."

"Anyway, here's what I wanted to discuss, Qwill. We want to do *Bell, Book and Candle* for our summer show, and we'll need a cat to play Pyewacket. Do you think . . ."

"No, I don't think Koko would care for the role. He's extremely independent. He doesn't take direction. And he prefers his own script."

"Maybe we should announce a public audition and invite people to bring their cats."

"You'd have a riot!" Qwilleran said. "You'd have three hundred cat lovers with three hundred cats, all wailing and spitting and fighting and climbing up the curtain. And the humans would be even worse—pushy, indignant, belligerent. A company tried it Down Below, and they had to call the police."

"But it would generate publicity. When the newspaper starts publishing, we'll get all kinds of coverage. They've promised to review our productions."

"They're dreaming! Who'll qualify as a drama critic in Moose County?"

"You," she said with her sweet smile.

Qwilleran huffed into his moustache. "How can I sit in the fifth row, center, taking notes at the same time I'm onstage blowing the bugle and charging up San Juan Hill?"

"You'll figure it out." She could be infuriatingly illogical one minute and a frighteningly straight thinker the next. "Will the theater be ready on schedule?"

"They've promised, but anything can happen in the building trades: electricians are electrocuted; plumbers drown; painters inhale toxic fumes; carpenters bleed to death."

"What would you think of an original revue for the grand opening, instead of a Broadway play?"

"What kind of material?"

"Humorous skits . . . witty parodies . . . a chorus line . . . comic acts. Harley and David have a funny twin act that they do. Susan danced in college; she can do choreography."

"Do you have a theme in mind?"

"It should be a spoof of contemporary life, don't you think? I mean—politics, television, fashion, pop music, the IRS—anything. Preferably tied in with Moose County."

"And who would write these humorous skits and witty parodies?" he demanded.

"You!" There was that tantalizing smile again.

Qwilleran growled a protest. "That would take a lot of time and thought, and you know I'm writing a novel, Fran."

She looked at her watch. "Well, think about it. Now I've got to go home. I'm expecting a long-distance call from Mother. She's visiting my aunt Down Below. Thanks for your input, Qwill. See your tomorrow night at seven sharp."

Qwilleran walked home slowly, enjoying the soft breezes of a spring evening. On Monday nights the downtown area was always deserted, and an eerie silence fell upon Main Street. His footsteps echoed in the canyon created by the stone buildings.

The idea of an original revue began to appeal to him. He had written student shows in college. It might be fun to write parodies of well-known songs, one for each town in Moose County. The early settlers had given them outlandish names: Sawdust City, Chipmunk, Squunk Corners, Middle Hummock, West Middle Hummock, Wildcat, Smith's Folly, Mooseville, even a village named Brrr. (It was the coldest spot in the county.)

The parodies would be easy, he thought. He tried a few opening lines, and his rich baritone reverberated in the stone canyon:

"Everything's out of date in Sawdust City . . ."
"Way down upon the Ittibittiwassee . . ."
"Mid-dle Hum-mock, here I come! . . ."
"April in Chipmunk; ragweed in blossom . . ."
"When it's Big Mosquito time in Mooseville . . ."
"I'm just wild about Wildcat . . ."

All too soon he reached the Park Circle. Here Main Street divided and circled a small park, on the perimeter of which were two churches, the courthouse, the public library, and the future theater. There was a nightlight in the construction shed, but the long driveway to the carriage house was in darkness. The moon had ducked behind a cloud, and he had forgotten to turn on the exterior lights at the corners of the carriage house.

He unlocked the door leading to the upstairs apartment and reached inside to flick the wall switch. The light fixture did not respond; neither did the light at the top of the stairs. A power outage, he supposed. The local joke was that Pickax blacked out if the weatherman even predicted a thunder storm. He started to mount the stairs in the dark. Brodie was right; they were steep, and the treads were narrow. They seemed narrower and steeper in total darkness. Slowly and carefully he went up, gripping the handrail.

Halfway to the top Qwilleran stopped. There was a strong odor in the stairwell—almost like coffee—or something burning. Electrical wires? He had a fear of fire when the cats were home alone.

At that moment he heard a sound he could not identify. He listened hard. The cats were locked in their apartment at the far end of the building, and it was not an animal sound; it was a scraping, like metal on wood. He remembered the wrought-iron coat of arms leaning against the wall in the upper hallway. If it came crashing down the stairs, it would send him flying to the bottom of the flight. He flattened himself against the wall and slid upward, one cautious step at a time.

In the upper hall he paused and listened. He felt a presence. There was no sound, but someone was there—breathing. The living-room door was open, and he was sure he had closed it before leaving. The total darkness indicated that the blinds were closed, and he was sure he had left them open. Now he was positive he could hear breathing, and he saw two red eyes glowing in the blacked-out room.

Stealthily he groped for the light switch inside the door, hoping it was operative. His hand touched something hairy.

From his throat came a horrendous roar—like a trapped lion, a wounded elephant, and a sick camel. It was a curse he had learned in North Africa.

Instantly there was light, and a chorus of tremulous voices managed a weak "Happy birthday!"

There were two dozen persons in the room, looking either shaken or sheepish or guilty.

"Dammit, you knuckleheads!" Qwilleran bellowed. "You could give a guy a heart attack! . . . What's this?"

Towering above him was a black bear with glass eyes and gaping jaws, rearing on hind legs, one paw over the light switch.

The two glowing spots of red were lights on a small machine. It stood on the travertine card table, plugged in and bubbling.

"I'm sorry," said Francesca. "It was my idea. We used the key you gave me."

Harley Fitch said, "My clone gets credit for the dramatic staging."

"My clone unscrewed the lightbulbs," said his brother, David, the one with a moustache. "He stood on my shoulders and ruined my golf swing permanently."

Qwilleran confronted Francesca. "So that's why you kept

me overtime. I wondered why you looked at your watch every five minutes."

Larry Lanspeak said, "We needed a half hour to get set up. We had to park our cars out of sight and hike over here and wrestle the bear up those damn stairs and then hide Wally's van."

Wally Toddwhistle, a young taxidermist, said, "I happened to have the bear in my van. I'm delivering it to a customer."

"How did you guys know it's my birthday?"

Fran said, "Dad ran a check on your driver's registration."

"And what's that thing?" He pointed to the machine with the two red lights.

"That's a gift from all of us," said David's wife. "A protest against the lethal coffee you serve. You set it for the number of cups you want and the strength you prefer. A timer turns it on."

Then someone produced paper plates and cups, and someone else unveiled a sheet cake decorated with a bugle and the theater's traditional wish: "Break a leg, darling!"

As Qwilleran began to simmer down, the cast and crew of *Arsenic and Old Lace* relaxed. They were all there: Carol Lanspeak and Susan Exbridge, who were playing the wacky old sisters; Larry Lanspeak, a versatile character actor; Harley and David Fitch, who liked to do drunks, weirdos, and monsters; David's clever wife, Jill, who designed sets and costumes; Wally Toddwhistle, a genius at building sets out of orange crates, baling wire, and glue; Derek Cuttlebrink, who was attempting his first role; Eddington Smith, painfully ill at ease; and other members of the troupe whom Qwilleran knew only slightly. They were all talking at once:

Susan: "Darling, your entrance in the second act was marvelous!"

Fran: "An integrated actor thinks with his whole body, Derek."

Carol: "How's your wife, Harley?"

Harley: "Okay, but kind of grouchy. The doctor told her to quit smoking till after the baby comes."

Wally: "What's that big round iron thing in the hallway?"

Qwilleran: "It came from a castle in Scotland. Part of a gate, I think."

Larry: "At every performance she went up, and I had to ad-lib the whole scene. I could have killed her!"

David: "I grew a moustache to play the villain in *The Drunkard* because I'm allergic to spirit gum, and then I decided to keep it. Jill likes it."

Derek: "Where are the cats?"

Qwilleran: "In their apartment, watching the tube. Shall I let them out?"

Koko and Yum Yum made their entrance walking shoulder to shoulder like a team of horses. In the doorway they stopped abruptly, their ears, whiskers, noses, and blue eyes sensing the situation: noisy strangers, eating and dropping crumbs. In the next instant they sensed the black bear looming above them. Yum Yum bushed her tail, humped her back, sleeked her ears and whiskers, slanted her eyes, and made a wicked display of fangs. Koko crept cautiously toward the beast with his belly dragging the floor until convinced that it was harmless. Then he bravely sniffed its hind legs and rose up to paw the stiff-haired pelt. Next he turned his attention to the taxidermist, who was nervously guarding his handiwork. Koko subjected Wally Toddwhistle to a thorough inspection with his wet nose.

"He knows you work with animals," Qwilleran explained, by way of excusing Koko's impolite nuzzling.

Wally was flattered, however. "If a cat likes you," he said

earnestly, "it means you have a princely character. That's what my mother always says."

Harley Fitch raised his right hand in affirmation. "If Wally's mother says so, it's gospel truth, believe me!"

"Amen," said David.

"Who's buying the bear?" Qwilleran asked the young taxidermist.

"Gary Pratt—for his bar at the Hotel Booze. I have to deliver it tonight when I leave here. Do you know Gary? My mother says he looks more like a bear than the bear does."

"Hear! Hear!" said Harley.

Next, Koko discovered that some of the noisy strangers were sitting on the floor, which was his domain by divine right. He stalked them and scolded, "Nyik nyik nyik!"

Meanwhile, Yum Yum had calmed down and was checking out sandals, western boots, and double-tied running shoes, none of which interested her. Then she discovered Eddington Smith's laced oxfords. The bookseller stood shyly apart from the others, and Qwilleran went over to speak to him.

Eddington said, "I've found some Shakespeare comedies for you. An old lady in Squunk Corners had them in her attic. They're in good condition." He spoke softly, smiled blandly.

"I didn't know . . . the Bard had a following . . . in Squunk Corners," Qwilleran said absently as he kept an eye on the cats. Yum Yum was gleefully untying the man's shoelaces. Koko was exploring his socks and trouser legs with intent nose, forward whiskers, and a wild gleam in his eye.

"People up here," Eddington explained, "used to collect rare books, fine bindings, and first editions. Rich people, I mean. It was the thing to do."

"When the newspaper starts publishing they ought to send a reporter to your shop to get an interview."

"I don't think I'd be very good for an interview," said the bookseller. "I bought an ad, though—just a quarter page. I never advertised before, but a nice young lady came in and told me I should." Guiltily he added, " 'advertising is . . . a campaign of subversion against intellectual honesty and moral integrity.' Somebody said that. I think it was Toynbee."

"Your character won't be compromised by a quarter page," Qwilleran assured him.

At that moment Harley Fitch walked up with the cake tray, and Koko transferred his attention to the bank vice president, rubbing his ankles, nipping his jeans, and purring hoarsely.

"Have some cake, Edd," said Harley in his heartiest voice, as if the bookseller were deaf.

"I've had two pieces already. 'Reason should direct and appetite obey.' "

"Who said that, Edd?"

"Cicero."

"Cicero would want you to have another piece of cake. How often do you go to a birthday party?"

Wistfully Eddington said, "I've never been to a birthday party before."

"Not even your own?"

The little man shook his head and smiled his bland all-purpose smile.

"Okay! For your birthday we'll have a party on the stage of the new theater, with a ten-foot sheet cake. You can blow out the candles before an audience of three hundred."

Pleasure fought with disbelief in the bookseller's gray face.

"We'll have it proclaimed Eddington Smith Day in Pickax."

David, hearing the commotion, joined the act. "We'll have a parade with floats and the high-school band, and fireworks in the evening."

Jill Fitch drew Qwilleran aside. "Aren't they crazy?" she said. "But they'll do it! They'll have the parade, the fireworks, and a proclamation from the mayor—or even the governor. That's the way they are." She lowered her voice. "Want to come to a surprise housewarming for Harley and Belle on Saturday night? They've moved into the old Fitch mansion, you know. Bring your own bottle."

"How about a gift?"

"No gifts. God knows they don't need anything. Have you seen Grandpa Fitch's house? It's loaded with stuff. I don't know how Harley can live with all those mounted animals and marble nymphs."

"I've never met Belle," Qwilleran said. "Doesn't she ever come to rehearsals?"

Jill shrugged. "She doesn't feel comfortable with this crowd. I guess we come on a little strong. And now that she's pregnant, Harley says she feels self-conscious."

It was a noisy party, with twenty-four club members crowded into a room designed for one man and two cats. Carol Lanspeak laughed a lot. Larry did impersonations of his more eccentric customers. Susan Exbridge, a fortyish divorcée, invited Qwilleran to a dance at the country club, but he pleaded another engagement; she served on the library board, and he feared Polly would hear about it. Eddington Smith said he'd never had such a good time in his life. Harley Fitch was flattered by Koko's advances and asked if he could take him home.

After the crowd had departed, Qwilleran made another cup of coffee in the machine and finished the cake. Yum Yum curled up on his lap, and Koko disposed of the crumbs on the carpet. Sirens sounded, speeding north on Main Street, and Qwilleran automatically glanced at his watch. It was 1:35 A.M.

The next morning he remembered the sirens when he

tuned in the headline news on WPKX: “All dental appointments at the Zoller Clinic are cancelled today due to a fire that broke out sometime after one o’clock this morning. Arson is suspected, and police are investigating. Patients may call to reschedule.”

SCENE FOUR

Place: Qwilleran's apartment; later, the rehearsal hall
Time: Tuesday evening
Featuring: CHAD LANSPEAK

THE LANSPEAK DEPARTMENT store closed at 5:30, and Qwilleran wondered if Chad Lanspeak would appear as promised. If he were as irresponsible as Brodie thought, he would have forgotten about the appointment and gone fishing. At 5:45 there was no sign of the reputed black sheep. Qwilleran peered out the window toward Main Street and saw only the construction workers driving away in their trucks.

Finally at 6:15 a battered pickup turned into the driveway, coughing and shuddering as it came up to the carriage house, where it stopped with an explosive jerk. A young man jumped out and collected an armful of snowshoes from the truck bed. Qwilleran pressed the buzzer that released the door, and Chad Lanspeak struggled up the stairs with his load—gracefully shaped, honey-colored wood frames with a varnished sheen, laced with natural leather thongs in an intricate pattern.

"I brought 'em all," he said. "I didn't know I had so many. Hey, what's that iron thing?" He was staring at the Mackintosh insignia with the curious motto circling the rampant cats: TOUCH NOT THE CATT BOT A GLOVE.

"It came from the gate of a Scottish castle," Qwilleran said. "It's three hundred years old."

"It must be valuable."

"It has sentimental value. My grandparents came from Scotland."

Chad was hardly recognizable as the bored salesclerk at his father's store. He still sported the hirsute flourishes that made him conspicuous in Pickax, but he was as affable as any of the teens Qwilleran had met in that salutary environment. Country-bred youths, he had observed, possessed an easygoing, outgoing manner that bridged generation gaps.

"Line up the snowshoes on the living-room floor," Qwilleran suggested, "so I can compare styles and sizes."

"I've never seen a place like this," said Chad, appraising the suede sofa, square-cut lounge chairs, chromium lamps and glass-topped tables.

"I like contemporary," said Qwilleran, "although it doesn't seem to be popular in Pickax."

"That's an interesting picture. What is it?"

"A print of an 1805 gunboat that sailed the Great Lakes."

"It has sails and cannon and *oars!* That's funny! A gunboat with oars! Where'd you get it?"

"From an antique shop."

"Is it valuable?"

"An antique is worth only what someone is willing to pay for it."

Next Chad admired the state-of-the-art stereo components on the open bookshelves, and Qwilleran began to think he'd made a mistake in bringing the fellow to the apartment. He thought, Dammit! He's casing the joint! The cats were present, quietly washing up after their evening meal, and Qwilleran spirited them away to their own apartment. Strangers often admired them less for their beauty than for their obvious monetary value, and it was his constant fear that they might be stolen.

"Now let's get down to business," he said. "I have a rehearsal at seven o'clock."

Chad was still attracted to the gunboat print. "There's a guy around here that makes model ships like that. He's really good. He could sell them for a lot of money if he wanted to."

"No doubt," said Qwilleran. "Now which style would you recommend for a beginner?"

"Let's see . . . the Bear Paw is easiest to start with, but it doesn't have any tail, and the tail helps in tracking, you know. I brought some bindings so you can see how they work. What kind of boots do you have?"

Qwilleran produced a pair of logger boots and was duly strapped onto a pair of Bear Paws. Awkwardly he attempted to maneuver them down the long hallway.

"You don't have to lift your feet so high," Chad called out after him. "Lean forward . . . Swing your arms . . . Your feet are too wide apart."

Qwilleran said. "I like the look of the others better. These remind me of fruit baskets."

"Well, there's this Michigan style; it's larger and has a heavier tail for tracking. The arctic is the fastest; it's long and narrow. All depends what kind of snow you have and how much brush. You should start with something smaller than those. Maybe you should try the thirty-six inch Beavertail."

Strapped onto Beavertails, Qwilleran clomped uncertainly down the hall again.

"Drag your tail!" Chad called out. "Your feet are too far apart. You'll get sore legs."

"It's like walking on tennis rackets."

"You'll get used to it when you get out in the snow."

"How much for the Beavertails?" Qwilleran asked. "I'll write you a check."

"It's hard to get a check cashed. Do you have the . . . uh . . ."

"I don't keep money in the house, but if you'll drive me to the east-side drug store, they'll cash a check for me. Then you can drop me off at the rehearsal hall."

He helped Chad carry the snowshoes down the narrow stairs and into the decrepit truck. It was a terrain vehicle, riding high on huge tires. As they started off, he remarked, "There's nothing wrong with this truck that couldn't be improved with a muffler, some springs, a coat of paint, and a new motor."

"It's okay," Chad explained. "It's what I need when I go setting my traps. Ever do any trapping?"

"I'm a city boy," Qwilleran said. "I don't trap or hunt or fish, but I know they're popular sports around Moose County."

"You can earn good money trapping. You can go shoeing with me when snow flies, if you want, and I'll show you how to use your Beavertails. Maybe you'd like to see my traps."

The idea of trapping wild animals repelled Qwilleran. He had heard that a beaver caught in the jaws of a trap would chew off its own leg to get free. Since he had shared living quarters with the Siamese he had become highly sensitive about cruelty to animals. Even the thought of hooking a fish disturbed him, although he enjoyed trout amandine at the Old Stone Mill.

"I'd appreciate a lesson in *shoeing* in actual snow," he

said, trying to speak the lingo, "but I'm not sure I could warm up to the idea of trapping. Where do you go?"

"I get rabbits and squirrels in the Hummocks, and foxes out Ittibittiwassee Road. I use live traps mostly. That way the pelts aren't damaged."

Qwilleran stared ahead through the dirty windshield and said nothing. He didn't want to know what happened to the animals after they were trapped live.

"I got a skunk a couple of weeks ago. They're the trickiest. The safest thing is to drown them."

Qwilleran was glad when they arrived at the drug store. After the check was cashed and the Beavertails were paid for, they started off for the rehearsal hall with a rumble, a jolt, and a backfire, and he said casually, "What do you think of the vandalism in Pickax, Chad? It's getting pretty bad."

They had reached the main intersection and stopped for the traffic light—it was the only one in town—and Chad leaned out of the window and yelled "Hiya!" to the occupants of a noisy rustmobile. He didn't answer the question.

"When I was young," Qwilleran went on, "we used to overturn garbage cans in Chicago. For some strange reason that I can't remember at this stage of my life, we thought it was fun. What fun do they get out of breaking into the school and clobbering a computer?"

"I guess they didn't like school, and they're getting even," Chad said.

"And they didn't like having a tooth drilled so they set fire to the dental clinic. Is that the way it works?" Qwilleran asked him. "I don't understand it. You're young; maybe you can explain it to me."

"I wasn't anywhere near that place when it happened," Chad said defensively. "I was at a party in Chipmunk." He pulled up in front of the community center, jamming on the brakes hard.

"Thanks for the lift, fella. I'll get in touch with you when snow flies."

Chad nodded in sulky silence.

Qwilleran glanced at his watch; he was a half-hour late for rehearsal. The transaction had taken longer than he expected, and the detour to the drug store had wasted another twenty minutes. Francesca was strong on punctuality; she would not be happy.

When he walked into the rehearsal hall, the situation was worse than he expected. Several of the cast were absent without phoning in an excuse. Several, besides Qwilleran, had been tardy. Fran was vexed, and the general mood was tense. Reacting to her irritation the actors lost their concentration and missed their cues or fluffed their lines. In Qwilleran's vital scene he oozed up the stairway instead of charging like a madman. Eddington spoke his lines in a terrified stage whisper. The propman had forgotten to bring a sword, and Harley Fitch had never arrived with his grandfather's World War I bugle.

At one point the exasperated director waved them off the stage and tried coaching Eddington. The Lanspeaks took this opportunity to chat with Qwilleran. Larry said, "Our prodigal son paid us a surprise visit last weekend—in that truck he holds together with Band-Aids. He picked up all his snowshoes and said you wanted to buy a pair. He seemed almost human in spite of his alien genes."

Carol said, "And at the store today he was actually civil to customers. Everyone thought he must be sick."

It was the first time the Lanspeaks had ever mentioned their youngest, although they frequently boasted about the other two, who won math prizes, played the saxophone, captained the tennis team, and edited the yearbook.

Qwilleran said, "Chad brought the whole caboodle to my apartment and gave me a crash course in snowshoeing. I bought a pair of Beavertails."

"Quiet back there!" Fran shouted. "We're trying to rehearse." Later, when Carol got the hiccups and Susan got the giggles, she called out, "Break! That's all for tonight. We'll try again tomorrow, and if everyone isn't here at seven sharp, and if you don't know your lines and take the rehearsal seriously, there'll be no show!"

Qwilleran had never seen her so perturbed, and he mentioned the fact to Wally as they left the building.

"My mother would say it's because there's a full moon," said the taxidermist.

SCENE FIVE

Place: Office of the new Moose County newspaper
Time: Later the same evening
Cast: ARCH RIKER, publisher and editor in chief
JUNIOR GOODWINTER, managing editor
HIXIE RICE, advertising manager
ROGER MACGILLIVRAY, reporter

THE STONE BUILDINGS of downtown Pickax gleamed blue-white in the light of the full moon. Following the disastrous rehearsal, Qwilleran started to walk home but detoured by way of the newspaper office. It was the eve of the publication of the first issue, and he was as nervous as a prospective father. At his suggestion the Klingenschoen Fund had made the venture possible. At his urging his longtime friend, Arch Riker, had come up from Down Below to run the operation. Eventually a printing plant and office complex would be built; meanwhile, the paper was being job-printed, and the editorial and business functions were housed in a rented warehouse.

Qwilleran knew the staff had been working twelve or more hours a day, and he had stayed out of their way, but now it was the countdown; the new publication would be in the hands of readers Wednesday afternoon. He felt envious. It was a moment of excitement and tension, and he was an outsider.

As he expected, the lights were still on in the building, a former meat-packing warehouse, and he found Riker and Junior Goodwinter in the office they shared—with beer cans in their hands and with their feet propped on their desks. It was nothing like the slick, color-coordinated, acoustically engineered, electronically equipped work-station environment Riker and Qwilleran had known at the *Daily Fluxion*. In this temporary situation executives and cub reporters alike sat at secondhand desks and poked old manual typewriters in a barnlike workplace that still smelled of bacon, although Junior enjoyed the distinction of a rolltop desk that had been his great-grandfather's.

"The coffee's still hot," Riker said. "Grab a cup, Qwill, and find a chair. Put your feet up."

"Are you getting antsy?" Qwilleran asked.

"Everything's locked up except page one; we're still hoping for a banner headline for the kick-off. After the radio spots we got eighteen thousand subscriptions, and we've given a print order of thirty thousand. Hixie and her crew sold so many ads that we're going to forty-eight pages, twice what we expected."

Qwilleran had never seen him so animated. At the *Fluxion* Riker was the epitome of the jaded editor—a little paunchy, a little bored. Here, his ruddy face glowed with satisfaction and excitement.

The young, fresh-faced managing editor said, "We've got a lot of copy in type. Stories poured in from the stringers, but we still needed boilerplate to fill the holes. Roger MacGillivray quit his teaching job, and he's covering city hall, police, and general assignment. His mother-in-law is handling the food page; she teaches home ec, you know."

"I'm blissfully aware of her blueberry pies," Qwilleran said.

"Kevin Doone is writing a garden column for us. Do you know Kevin? He runs a landscape service."

"I know Kevin well. 'Call Doone to Prune!' I could live for a year on what he charged to prune a few apple trees on my property. Are you doing anything about the vandalism issue?"

"We're running a tough editorial," Riker said, "with a strong pitch for community involvement, parental responsibility, and more prowl cars after dark, even if they have to hire part-time officers. And the sheriff's got to keep an eye on those kids in Chipmunk. They think Pickax is a shooting gallery. It's time to turn off the indulgent grin and the sentimental attitude that boys will be boys."

"What happened at the dental clinic this morning?"

"They were apparently looking for narcotics and cash, and when they were disappointed they trashed the office and started a fire."

"I envy you guys. It's tough to be on the outside, looking in."

"I told you we could use your skills, Qwill," said Riker, "but you're busy writing that damned novel."

Qwilleran smoothed his moustache regretfully. "I'm beginning to think I'm miscast as a novelist. I'm a journalist."

"I could have told you that, you donkey!"

"And I don't have the temperament for free-lance work. I need the discipline of assignments and deadlines."

"Do you want to come on in?"

"What could I do?"

"Features. The kind of meaty, informative stuff you did for the *Fluxion*. We have a lot of space to fill and a lot of amateurs writing for it. We need all the professionalism we can get."

The front door slammed, and Hixie Rice suddenly appeared. "Quick, you guys! I need a beer, coffee, anything! I'm punchy! I've been hitting the restaurants all over the county. They all want to buy ads in the food section. These flat heels are *killing* me!" She kicked off her skimmers and turned to Qwilleran. "What are you doing here? You're supposed to be rehearsing or writing a novel or feeding your cats."

"If I haven't forgotten how," he said, "I'm going to write a column about interesting people who do interesting things."

"We're assuming," said Riker, "that such individuals exist in this outpost of civilization."

"There are no dull subjects," Qwilleran reminded him. "Only dull reporters who ask dull questions."

"Okay, so that's all settled! Now all we need is some hot-breaking news for page one. The opening issue is going to be a collector's item, and I want it to look like a newspaper."

Junior said, "Roger's at city hall covering the zoning-board meeting tonight, and if we're lucky, it'll break up in a fistfight, or something good like that."

"Don't you guys ever try any creative journalism?" Hixie taunted them. "Kidnap the mayor! Bomb city hall! Pull the plug on the Ittibittiwassee dam and flood Main Street!"

The three serious journalists scowled at her.

Qwilleran said to Riker, "What name have you picked for the paper?"

"That's got me stymied. I want it to be something like *Moose County Chronicle* or *Clarion* or *Crier* or *Caucus*. We've got to make a decision fast."

"You newspaper types have no imagination," Hixie objected. "Why not the *Moose County Cannonball* or *Crowbar* or *Corkscrew?*"

The three serious journalists groaned.

Qwilleran suggested, "Let the readers pick the name. Print a ballot on page one."

"But we've got to have some kind of flag for the first issue," Riker insisted. "We've got to call it something."

"Call it the *Moose County Something,*" Hixie said. "I dare you!"

The front door slammed again.

"That's Roger," Junior guessed.

A young man with a camera bag slung over his shoulder burst into the office. Roger had a pale complexion and stark black beard, and tonight he was paler than usual. He was also breathing hard. He stared at the four waiting staffers.

"What's the trouble, Roger?" asked Riker.

He gulped. "Murder!" His voice cracked on the word.

"Murder?!" Riker took his feet off his desk.

"Who?" demanded Junior, jumping to attention.

"Where?" Hixie put her shoes on quickly.

"At city hall?" Qwilleran asked, touching his moustache nervously.

Roger gulped again. "In West Middle Hummock! Two people shot! Harley Fitch and his wife!"

SCENE SIX

Place: The newspaper office
Time: The afternoon following the Fitch murder
Cast: Staff members

THE FIRST COPIES of the *Moose County Something* were coming off the press, and it should have been a time of hilarity and popping champagne corks in the city room, but the front-page news had deadened everyone's spirit. In a small town like Pickax, murder could not be an impersonal tragedy. Everyone was a friend or neighbor or relative or customer of the victim. Even Arch Riker, relatively new in town and a veteran of a thousand, big-city murder stories, was gloomy. "I wanted a sensational banner for page one," he said, "but I didn't want it that bad."

A bundle of papers arrived from the job-printer and the staffers grabbed. Blazoned across the front page was the grim news: HARLEY FITCH AND WIFE FOUND SHOT TO DEATH.

In the cities Down Below, Qwilleran reflected, the public would immediately assume it to be a drug-related execution. In Pickax, 400 miles north of everywhere, there was no glimmer of such a thought. Suspicion might come later—in the coffee shops and over back fences—but at this moment the reaction was one of shock and sadness and reluctance to believe it could happen in Moose County.

Early that morning Francesca had phoned. "Oh, Qwill! Isn't it a beast! I've been nauseated all night. I heard it on the midnight news. Dad wouldn't talk about it. I suppose the paper will be out this afternoon with more details. I'd like to call David and Jill, but I'm afraid. They must be horrified."

"It's going to be on the front page," Qwilleran said. "It's the banner story with a picture of Harley. No one could find a photo of his wife—at least, not on such short notice."

"Downtown is crowded with people, all standing around talking about it. Nobody can believe it! With them expecting a baby and everything! Nobody can settle down to business."

"It's hard to take. Who could possibly have done it?"

"It's got to be the Chipmunk gang. The tourist season hasn't started yet; we don't have those crazies wandering around the county looking for something to shoot. Yes, it's definitely those punks from Chipmunk."

Qwilleran touched his moustache with his knuckles. "When everything went wrong at rehearsal last night I had a feeling there was something in the air. Wally said it was because of the full moon."

With a whimper Fran said, "And I was cursing Harley and David and Jill for being absent without explanation. Now that I know the reason, I could cut out my tongue. We'll cancel the show, of course. No one will have the heart to go on with it. God! I can't work. I can't do anything! I think I'll go home and drink up Dad's supply of Scotch. Do you want to come with me?"

The story on page one was subheaded: BURGLARY OBVIOUS MOTIVE. It carried the byline of Roger MacGillivray.

The scion of a prominent Moose County family and his bride of a few months were found shot to death Tuesday evening at their home in West Middle Hummock. Harley Fitch, 24, and his 21-year-old wife, Belle, were victims of a gunman whose apparent motive was robbery, according to the sheriff's department. The couple were preparing to leave the house for a Theatre Club rehearsal in Pickax, family members said. The time of death was between 6 and 7 P.M., according to the coroner.

David and Jill Fitch, Harley's brother and sister-in-law, discovered the bodies at 7:15 P.M., when they arrived to pick up the couple for the drive to Pickax. They live a quarter mile from the Fitch mansion, recently occupied by the newlyweds who were reported to be expecting a child.

Jill Fitch told police, "We've been rehearsing five nights a week for a play. We usually share the ride, leaving at 6:30. I tried to phone Harley to say we'd be a little late because of a plumbing problem, but there was no answer. I thought they were probably outdoors and couldn't hear the phone, so we just hurried as much as we could. When we finally drove up to their house, we tooted the horn, but no one came out, so David went in, and that's when he found them."

A spokesman for the sheriff's department noted that Harley's body was found lying in the rear entrance hall; his wife's body was in an upstairs bedroom. There was no sign of a struggle, the spokesman said. The two were wearing jeans and sweat shirts, described as "rehearsal clothes" by family members.

There was evidence, according to the spokesman, that the murderer or murderers had started to ransack the house and either found what they wanted or were interrupted by the arrival of the other couple.

Jill Fitch informed police, "I remember seeing a vehicle pulling away as we approached. It was going fast down the dirt road and throwing up a cloud of dust." There are no other residences on the road in question.

The 22-room house was the ancestral home of the Fitch family, built in the 1920s by Harley's grandfather, Cyrus Fitch, and noted for its valuable collection of art objects, books, and curios.

Harley was the son of Nigel and Margaret (Doone) Fitch of Indian Village. Following his graduation from Yale university and a year of travel, he joined the Pickax bank where his father is president. Harley and his brother, David, were recently named vice presidents.

Harley graduated from Pickax high school before attending Yale. He maintained a better-than-average scholastic record in high school while playing on the tennis team, participating in student government, and acting in student plays. In college he majored in business administration and continued his interest in the dramatic arts.

Upon returning to Pickax he was active in the Boosters Club and the Theatre Club, where he was last seen as Dromio in *The Boys from Syracuse*. He was an avid sailor, who skippered the 27-foot *Fitch Witch* to several trophies. A builder of model ships since the age of 10, he exhibited his handiwork frequently, winning numerous prizes.

Harley married Belle Urkle in October of last year in Las Vegas.

A sidebar carried comments from persons who had known Harley Fitch: the high-school principal, the tennis coach, schoolmates, the president of the Boosters, bank personnel, and Larry Lanspeak, representing the Theatre Club. "A model student . . . always enthusiastic and cooperative . . . fun to be with . . . talented actor . . . a 100-percent team player . . . wonderful to work for . . . always so thoughtful . . . upbeat all the way."

Qwilleran read the story three times, massaging his moustache as he read. There were details that aroused his curiosity. Down Below, when he was writing for the *Fluxion,* such an event would have demanded a bull session at the Press

Club, with fellow journalists reviewing the story, analyzing, questioning, circulating rumors, airing suspicions, outguessing the police, exchanging inside information. Unfortunately there was no Press Club in Pickax, but he asked Arch Riker if he would like to have dinner at the Old Stone Mill.

For an answer Riker unlocked a desk drawer and withdrew a small box. He was looking smug. The box contained an impressive diamond ring. "I'm giving it to Amanda tonight," he said, his ruddy face virtually bursting with joy.

Qwilleran was nonplussed. This development accounted for Riker's uncharacteristically happy mien lately. Divorced after twenty-five years, he had been morose and introspective until he moved to Pickax, and Qwilleran was glad he had found a woman he liked. But *Amanda!* That was the shock.

"Congratulations," he managed to say. "This comes as a surprise."

"It will surprise Amanda, too. She's never been married, and we all know she's grouchy and opinionated, but what the hell! We're right for each other."

"That's all that matters," said Qwilleran.

Next he asked Junior to stay in town for dinner.

"I'm not a bachelor any more," said the managing editor with a happy grin, "and Jody's parents are up here from Cleveland to celebrate the kickoff. Jody's having leg of lamb and German chocolate cake."

Then Qwilleran broached the subject to Roger MacGillivray and offered to stand treat.

"Gosh, I'd like to," said Roger. "I don't often get a freebie. But Sharon's going to her cousin's bridal shower, and I promised to baby-sit. My life has changed a lot in the last couple of months."

Once again Qwilleran was the lonely bachelor surrounded by happy couples, and he thought regretfully of his failing friendship with Polly Duncan. There were others he could invite to dinner—Francesca, Hixie, Susan, even Iris Cobb—but none equalled Polly for stimulating conversation over the duck à l'orange. And yet she had been noticeably cool since he joined the Theatre Club and hired a designer. Suddenly there had been no idyllic Sundays at her little house in the country—no berry picking, morel gathering, nutting, birding, reading aloud, or other delights. Her chilliness was made more awkward by the fact that she was head librarian, and he was a trustee on the library board.

In desperation he telephoned her at the office. "Have you heard the news?" he asked in a somber voice.

"Isn't it dreadful? Do they know who did it?"

"Not that I'm aware. No doubt the police have suspects who are being questioned, but the authorities aren't giving out any information. You can't blame them. How have you been, Polly?"

"Fine."

"Could you have dinner with me tonight?"

She hesitated. "I suppose your rehearsal is canceled on account of . . ."

"The show is called off altogether, and I'm not getting involved in any more plays. You were right, Polly; they're too time-consuming. I'd like very much to see you tonight."

There was a weighty pause, then: "Yes, I'd like to have dinner. I've missed you, Qwill."

His sigh of relief was audible. "I'll pick you up at the library at closing time."

He walked home with a light step, stopping at Lanspeak's store to buy a silk scarf in Polly's favorite shade of blue, which he had gift-wrapped.

Returning home to shower and shave and dress for dinner, he bounded up the stairs three at a time, but lost his exuberance when the Siamese did not come to greet him. Where were they? He knew he had not locked them in their apartment. Mr. O'Dell had not been there to clean. He peered into the living room, but Koko was not on the bookshelves with the biographies, and Yum Yum was not curled up in her favorite chair.

Had someone broken in and stolen the cats? He rushed to their apartment. They were not there! He checked their bathroom. No cats! He called their names. No answer! In a panic he searched the bedroom. They were nowhere in sight. Were they shut up somewhere? He yanked open dresser drawers. On hands and knees he examined the back corners of the closet. He called again, but the apartment was silent as death. Fearfully he approached his writing studio. It was never tidy, but this time there were signs of vandalism: desk drawers open, papers scattered about the floor, desktop ransacked, paper clips everywhere!

It was then that he noticed two silent figures—one on top of the filing cabinet and the other on a wall shelf with *Roget's Thesaurus* and a bottle of rubber cement. Yum Yum was crouched on the shelf in her guilty position—a compact bundle with elevated shoulders and haunches. Koko was on the filing cabinet, sitting tall but without his usual confidence.

Qwilleran gazed down at the papers on the floor. To his surprise they were all envelopes. *New* envelopes. His stationery drawer was open. When he scooped up the scattered items he noticed fang marks in the corners, and all the gummed flaps had been licked clean.

Sitting down in his desk chair he swiveled to face the culprits. He surmised that Yum Yum had opened the drawers with her famous paw, and Koko, who was attracted to any kind of adhesive, had been on a glutinous binge. Once before, he had ungummed a whole sheet of stamps, and had paraded impudently around the apartment with an airmail stamp stuck on his nose.

"Well, my friends," Qwilleran began calmly, "do I have to start locking my desk drawers? What's the mater with you two? Are you bored? Unhappy? Is there something lacking in your life? Is your diet inadequate?"

Koko, the usual spokesman for the pair, had no comment.

"You have epicurean food and the recommended daily allowances of vitamins. Do you realize there are cats who have to scrounge for their food in garbage cans?"

There was no reply.

"Has the cat got your tongue?"

Still no answer. Qwilleran doubted that Koko was even listening.

"You don't know how lucky you are. Some cats live outdoors all year in snow and sleet and torrential rains. You have a steam-heated apartment with private bath, TV, wall-to-wall carpeting, and . . ."

Qwilleran huffed into his moustache as the truth dawned upon him. Koko—with a glazed expression in his eyes and a peculiar splay-legged stance—was high on glue!

"You devil!" he blurted. And then he had a second thought. Koko never did anything unusual without a good reason. But what could this reason be?

SCENE SEVEN

Place: Tipsy's Restaurant in North Kennebeck
Time: Later that evening
Introducing: POLLY DUNCAN
MR. O'DELL, Qwilleran's part-time houseman
LORI BAMBA, a friend of Koko and Yum Yum

WHEN QWILLERAN picked up Polly Duncan at the library he asked, "I'm glad you can have dinner with me. Do you mind if we drive out into the country? The bad news has made me restless and uneasy. I need to talk about it."

Her voice was soft and gentle, with a timbre that he found both soothing and stimulating. "I understand, Qwill. A tragedy like this makes people want to huddle together." She gave him a needful glance that was all too brief.

"I thought we might go to Tipsy's. Do you know anything about it?"

"The food is good, and it's very popular," Polly said brightly, as if determined to make this a cheerful evening. "Did you know the place was named after a cat? The founder of the restaurant was a cook in a lumbercamp and then a saloonkeeper. During Prohibition he went Down Below and operated a blind pig. After Repeal he came back up here with a black-and-white cat named Tipsy and opened a steakhouse in a log cabin."

"What was his name?"

"Gus. That's all I know. But he was legendary around here, and so was Tipsy. That was fifty or sixty years ago. The place has changed hands many times, but they always retain the name."

They drove through typical Moose County terrain: rolling pastureland dotted with boulders and sheep, dairy farms with white barns, dark stretches of woods, abandoned mines with the remains of shafthouses. At a fork in the road a signpost indicated that it was three miles to West Middle Hummock. The other branch of the road led to Chipmunk (2 miles) and North Kennebeck (10 miles).

"West Middle Hummock isn't far from Chipmunk, is it?" Qwilleran observed.

"A study in contrasts," Polly said.

The highway soon ran through a cluster of substandard dwellings: cottages with sagging porches and peeling paint, sheet-metal shacks, trailer homes hardly larger than gypsy wagons, and larger houses advertising rooms to rent.

"The rooming houses were brothels in the early days of Chipmunk," she said.

Youths were hanging around the burger palace and the party store, drinking from cans and blasting the atmosphere with their boomboxes. Qwilleran thought, Are these the rowdies who broke into the school, trashed the dental clinic, and opened the hydrants? Is this where Chad Lanspeak hangs out? Are the Fitch murderers holed up in this town?

North Kennebeck, on the other hand, was a thriving community with a grain elevator, condominiums, an old railway depot converted into a museum, and Tipsy's—a log-cabin restaurant that attracted diners from all parts of the county.

The exterior logs were dark and chinked; the interior was whitewashed and inviting, with rustic furnishings and a casual crowd of diners. Under a spotlight in the main dining room hung a portrait of a white cat with black boots and a black patch that seemed to be slipping down over one eye. It gave her the look of a tipsy matron.

Polly said, "She also had a deformed foot that made her stagger and added to her inebriated image. How are your cats, Qwill?"

"Koko is happy that I've started collecting old books. He prefers biographies. How he can distinguish Plutarch's *Parallel Lives* from Wordsworth's poems is something I don't understand."

"And how is dear little Yum Yum?"

"That dear little Yum Yum has developed an unpleasant habit that I won't discuss at the dinner table."

He ordered dry sherry for Polly and, for himself, Squunk water with a dash of bitters and a slice of lemon. (The village of Squunk Corners was noted for a flowing well, whose waters were said to be therapeutic.) Raising his glass in a toast, he said, "To the memory of a promising young couple!"

"Harley was an admirable young man," Polly said sadly.

"Koko took an instant liking to him. No one seems to know much about his wife. The paper said they were married in Las Vegas, and I thought that unusual. The affluent families around here seem to like big weddings at the Old Stone Church—with twelve attendants and five hundred guests and a reception at the country club."

"When David and Jill were married, their wedding cost a fortune."

"Harley's wife never came to the Theatre Club, yet the newspaper said both couples were going to the rehearsal and both couples were wearing rehearsal clothes."

Polly raised her eyebrows. "Did you ever read a news story that was completely accurate?"

They consulted the menu. It was no-frills cuisine at Tipsy's, but the cooks knew what they were doing. Polly was happy that her pickerel tasted like fish and not like seasoned bread crumbs. Qwilleran was happy that his steak required chewing. "I always suspect beef that melts in my mouth," he said.

The conversation never strayed far from the Fitch case. Polly worried about Harley's mother, who was a trustee on the library board. "Margaret has very high blood pressure. I'm afraid to think how she may react to the shock. She's such a wonderful person—so generous with her time, always willing to chair a committee or captain a fund-raising event—not just for the library, but for the hospital and school. Nigel is the same way. They're beautiful people!"

"Hmmm," Qwilleran mused, unsure how to react to this outpouring of sentiment—so unusual for Polly. "It will be rough on David," he ventured to say. "He and his brother were so close."

"Yes, and David was the more sensitive of the two, but Jill will give him the support he needs. She has a firm grip on her emotions. Did you notice that it was Jill who was quoted in the newspaper? When she and David were married, everyone in the wedding party was nervous except the bride."

"Didn't it surprise you to learn that we've had an armed robbery in Moose County?" he asked.

"It was bound to happen. Firearms are plentiful up here. So many hunters, you know, with rifles, shotguns, handguns. The majority are responsible, law-abiding sportsmen, but . . . these days anything can happen." She shot him a quick, inquiring glance. "I don't hunt, but I do have a handgun."

Qwilleran's moustache bristled. Her reserved personality, her gentle manner, her quiet voice, her matronly figure, her conservative dress—nothing suggested that she might have a lethal weapon in her possession.

"Living alone on a country road, I feel it's only prudent," she explained. "What's happening Down Below is beginning to happen here. I've seen it coming. I don't like it."

"Why don't you move into town?" he suggested.

"I've lived in that little house ever since Bob died. I adore my little garden. I like the wide-open spaces. I enjoy living on a dirt road and seeing cows in a pasture when I drive to work.

"Sometimes one has to compromise, Polly."

"Compromise doesn't come easily to me."

"I've noticed that," Qwilleran said.

Polly declined dessert, but he was unable to resist the lemon-meringue pie.

"Have you ever seen the Fitch estate?" he asked.

"Several times. When Margaret and Nigel lived in the big house, she gave a tea for the library board every Christmas. They have hundreds of acres—beautiful rolling country with woods and meadows and streams and a view of the big lake from the highest hill. The mansion that Cyrus Fitch built in the 1920s is a large rambling place. They say he designed it himself. He was a militant individualist! An avid collector, too. Harley and David grew up there—among big-game trophies, rare books, Chinese-temple sculpture, medieval armor, and all the exotic things that people collected in the twenties if they had money. When David married Jill, his parents built them a modern house on the property. When Harley married, he and his bride moved into the mansion and his parents took a condominium."

"Can one drive into the property?"

"It's a private road, but there's nothing to stop anyone from entering."

"What is there to attract burglars? I can't imagine that the thieves were interested in rare books or mounted rhinoceros heads."

"There was jewelry handed down in the family. I imagine Harley's wife received some of it after they were married."

Qwilleran stroked his moustache thoughtfully. "I have a feeling the killer or killers had been there before."

When they left Tipsy's and started the drive back to Pickax in the first pink of the sunset, he asked, "How do you like the *Moose County Something?*"

"I rejoice that we have a newspaper once more, but the name is appalling."

"It's only temporary until the readers cast their ballots."

"I was surprised at the size of it."

"It will settle down to twenty-four pages as time goes on. They plan to publish Wednesdays and weekends until the new plant is finished, then go to five days a week. I'm going to write a feature column."

"What about your novel?" Polly asked sharply.

"Well, Polly, I've reached the painful decision that I'm not geared for producing fiction. For twenty-five years my career was based on ferreting out facts, verifying facts, organizing facts and reporting them accurately. It seems to have stultified my imagination."

"But you've been working on your novel for two years!"

"I've been talking about it for two years," he corrected her. "I'm getting nowhere. Maybe I'm just lazy."

"You disappoint me, Qwill."

"You overestimate me. You were expecting me to be a north-woods Faulkner or a dry-land Melville."

"I was expecting you to write something of lasting value.

Now you will simply produce more disposable newspaper prose. Your columns in the *Daily Fluxion* were always well-written and informative and entertaining, but are you living up to your potential?"

"I know my limitations, Polly. You're setting a goal for me that's unrealistic." He was becoming annoyed.

"It was your idea to write a novel."

"It's every writer's idea to write a novel sooner or later, but not all of us have the aptitude. On my desk I have a bushel of notes and a fistful of half-written pages." Unfortunately his voice was rising. "I need the discipline of a newspaper job! That's why I'm writing a column for the *Moose County Something.*" His tone had a finality that implied: Like it or not!

Polly looked at her watch. They were nearing the center of Pickax. "I enjoyed having dinner with you."

"Won't you come up to the apartment for a nightcap?"

"Not tonight, thanks. I have things to do." Her voice was curt.

The last few blocks were driven in silence. With a brief good-night she transferred to her own car in the library parking lot—the cranberry-red two-door he had given her for Christmas during a surge of holiday spirit, grateful sentiment, and emotional delirium. When she drove away, the blue silk scarf in the gift-wrapped box was still on the back seat of his car, quite forgotten.

It was too good to last, he thought, as he drove around the Park Circle to his carriage house. His relationship with Polly was inevitably coming to an end. Once loving and agreeable, she had become critical. She thought their intimacy gave her license to direct his life, but he was his own man. That was why his marriage had failed a dozen years before.

As he unlocked the door of the carriage house, he heard

the telephone ringing, and he ran up the stairs, hoping . . . hoping that Polly had changed her mind . . . hoping she had driven a few blocks and had stopped at a phone booth . . .

The voice he heard, however, was that of Mr. O'Dell, the white-haired houseman who had been school janitor for forty years and now conducted his own one-man janitorial service.

"Sure, an' it's sad news tonight," said Mr. O'Dell. "Young Harley was a good lad, but he married the wrong colleen, I'm thinkin'. Will yourself be needin' me tomorrow, now? It's a new grandson I have in Kennebeck, and the urge is upon me to lay eyes on the mite of a boy."

"By all means take the day off, Mr. O'Dell," said Qwilleran. "Was everything all right when you were here?"

"All but the little one. Herself did her dirty outside the sandbox again. It's bothered about somethin', she is."

Qwilleran immediately phoned Lori Bamba in Mooseville, the young lady who seemed to know all about cats. He described the situation. "Yum Yum has always had good aim until recently. I bought a second commode, thinking she wanted facilities of her own, but she ignores the pan and bestows her souvenirs on the bathroom floor."

"It might be stress," Lori said. "Is she under stress?"

"*Stress!*" he shouted into the phone. "I'm the one who's under stress! She lives a life of utter tranquility. She has a comfortable apartment with all conveniences—two gourmet meals every day, brushing three times a week. She has a reserved seat on my lap every time I sit down. And I hold intelligent conversations with both of them, the way you recommended."

"Have you made any recent changes in her environment?"

"Only new wallpaper in the living room. I don't see why that should concern her."

"Well," said Lori, "you should observe her closely, and if any other symptoms develop, take her to the doctor."

Qwilleran did not sleep well that night. It worried him inordinately when anything was wrong with the Siamese. He regretted also what was happening between Polly and himself. In addition, he could not help grieving about the cold-blooded murder that had gripped the community with sadness and fear. As he lay awake, he heard the 1:30 A.M. freight train blowing its mournful whistle at unguarded crossings near the city limits. The weather was clear, and, with his ear on the pillow, he could hear the dull click of wheels on tracks, although it was almost half a mile away. When the 2:30 A.M. freight rumbled through town, he was still awake.

SCENE EIGHT

Place: Downtown Pickax
Time: The day before the Fitch funeral

Qwilleran tuned in the headline news on WPKX every half hour expecting to hear that suspects in the murder of Harley and Belle Fitch were being questioned, or that arrests had been made and charges brought, or that the murderer had given himself up, or that he had killed himself, leaving a confession in a suicide note. Despite the scenarios he composed, nothing of the sort happened. It was reported only that police were investigating.

It also was announced that the funeral would be held on Friday, and it was the wish of the family that it be private. Qwilleran knew the decision would disappoint most of the local citizens; funeral-going and funeral-watching were consuming interests in Pickax.

Further, it was announced that Margaret Fitch, mother of the slain man, had suffered a massive stroke and was in critical condition at the Pickax hospital.

All of this only aggravated Qwilleran's impatience to know exactly what was happening, and he walked to the police station to confront Brodie—walking less briskly than usual; after a sleepless night he lacked pep. They had not talked together since the incident in West Middle Hummock, but Brodie would know everything and would be willing to reveal a few facts, off the record.

"Bad business, Brodie," Qwilleran said upon entering the office.

"Bad business," echoed the chief without lifting his eyes from his paperwork.

"Any suspects?"

"That's not for me to say. It's not my case."

"I suppose West Middle Hummock is the sheriff's turf."

Brodie nodded. "And the state police are assisting."

"Off the record, Brodie, do you suspect the punks from Chipmunk?"

The chief looked Qwilleran straight in the eye and said coolly, "No comment."

This was a surprising response from the usually talkative lawman, but Qwilleran knew when to stop wasting his time. "Take it easy," he said as he left.

His next stop was the office of the *Moose County Something*. In a newspaper city room one could always count on hearing inside information, true or false. He discovered, however, that Junior Goodwinter was taking a day off, having worked seven days a week since the inception of the project, and Roger MacGillivray was out on the beat, pursuing a story on wild turkeys.

Arch Riker was on hand, huddled over his desk, but he had heard no rumors and could answer no questions.

Qwilleran said, "I'm curious about the background of Belle Fitch. My houseman says Harley married the wrong woman."

"You hound-dog!" Riker exploded, pushing his chair away from his desk in an impatient gesture. "You're never happy unless you're sniffing the trail of something that's none of your business!"

Surprised by his friend's acerbic comment, Qwilleran said teasingly, "What's eating you, Arch? Did Amanda refuse your ring?"

"That's none of your business either," the editor snapped. "When can we have your first column?"

"When do you want it?"

"Tomorrow noon for the weekend edition."

This was the kind of short deadline that heated Qwilleran's blood, concentrated his attention, and primed the flow of ideas. "How about a piece on the eccentric bookseller who does business in a former blacksmith shop?"

"What about pix? Do you have a camera?"

"Not good enough to shoot dark books and a dark cat in a dark store."

"Okay, line it up, and we'll assign our part-time photographer—if we can find him—and if he can find his camera."

Qwilleran left the office with restored pep. About Riker's late-blooming romance he had ambivalent reactions, however. The two of them had grown up together in Chicago, and he would be sorry to see his friend disappointed. On the other hand, it would mean that Riker would still be available for bachelor dinners at the Old Stone Mill and bull sessions at the Shipwreck Tavern in Mooseville.

He picked up a tape recorder and a notebook from the city room and walked briskly to the store called Edd's Editions. The bell on the door tinkled, and Eddington Smith appeared out of the gloom.

"A terrible thing," the little man said in a voice denoting grief. "Is there any more news about the murder?" At that moment Qwilleran realized for the first time that the perpetual smile on the bookseller's face was a masklike grimace.

"The police are investigating," he said. "That's all I

know. Perhaps you heard that Mrs. Fitch has had a stroke. She's in critical condition."

The bookman shook his head sorrowfully. "I knew the whole family. It doesn't seem like it's really happening. 'All the world's a stage, and all the men and women merely players,' as someone said."

There was a tiny "meow" in a dark corner, and Winston came into view, waving his plumed tail and jumping across tables—from medical books to biographies to mysteries to cookbooks.

Qwilleran stroked the fluffy smoke-toned back. "I'd like to write a column about your enterprise for the new paper, Edd. In your ad you mentioned book repair. Is there much repair work in a town like this?"

"Not much. The library gives me some work, though. Mrs. Duncan is very nice. And this morning a lady from Sawdust City brought me a family bible to be repaired. She saw my ad."

"Where do you do this work?"

"My bindery is in the back. Would you like to see it?"

"Yes, and I'd like to turn on my tape recorder and ask some questions."

Eddington led the way into the back room, and Winston jumped off the cookbooks and followed.

"Did you ever see a hand bindery?" the bookman asked with a show of pride. He pulled cords dangling from the ceiling, and fluorescent tubes illuminated a roomful of bookpresses, cutting machines, a grindstone, workbenches, stools of varying heights, a small gas stove, and unusual tools.

Qwilleran started making notes on what he was seeing, and Eddington saw him staring at the small stove.

"That's for heating the glue," he said. "And my soup."

The two men perched on stools, and Eddington handed

Qwilleran an open book. "Look at page seventy-two. I can repair a tear with transparent Japanese tape and some cornstarch paste, and the mend is invisible."

It was true. Page seventy-two looked flawless.

As Winston jumped onto the workbench where they were sitting, the bookman said, "He always comes into the bindery when I'm working. He likes the smell of glue and paste."

"Koko likes to sniff glue, too. What kind do you use?"

"Nothing synthetic. I make my paste out of wheat flour or cornstarch. The glue comes from animal hides. I buy it in sheets and melt it. Did you know it's the glue used in bookbindings that attracts bookworms?"

As Eddington talked about his craft, he was no longer the shy man who ran the bookshop with a soft sell and whispered his lines at the Theatre Club. He spoke softly but with authority and demonstrated book-binding operations with skilled assurance.

"How did you get interested in books?" Qwilleran asked.

"My great-grandfather was a book collector. You know the town called Smith's Folly? He founded it in 1856. His mine failed twice, but the third time he struck it rich."

"What happened to your great-grandfather's fortune?" Qwilleran asked as he glanced around the room. In the far corner there was an uncomfortable-looking cot, a folding card table with a solitary folding chair, a small sink with a mirror hanging on the wall above it, and a shelf of dishes and canned goods.

"I'm sorry to say the next generation spent it all on lovely ladies," said Eddington, blushing an unhealthy purple. "My father had to earn his living selling books from door-to-door."

"What kind of books?"

"Classics, dictionaries, encyclopedias, etiquette books—

things like that. People with no education wanted to improve themselves, and my father was like a missionary, telling them to read and live better lives. He never made much money, but he was honest and respected. As somebody said, 'Virtue and riches seldom settle on one man.' "

"And how did you get into the used-book business?"

"An old man died, and they threw his books on the dump. I carted them away in a wheelbarrow. I was only fourteen. Now I buy from estates. Sometimes there's an odd book in the lot that's worth something. I found a first of Mark Twain in a box with some old schoolbooks and etiquette books. And once I found a book that Longfellow inscribed to Hawthorne."

"In your ad you mentioned library care as one of your services. What does that entail?" Qwilleran asked.

"If a customer has a good private library, I go and dust the books and treat the leather bindings and look for mildew and bookworms. Most people don't even know how to put books on a shelf. If they're too far apart, they yawn, and if they're too close together, they can't breathe."

"Are there many good private libraries in this area?"

"Not as many as before. People inherit them and sell the books to buy yachts or put their children through college."

"Could you name some of your clients?"

"Oh, no, that wouldn't be ethical, but it's all right to say that I took care of the Klingenschoen library when the old lady was alive."

"How about the Fitch mansion? Off the record." Qwilleran turned off the tape recorder. "I've heard they have some rare books."

Almost in a whisper the bookseller said, "Cyrus Fitch's collection is worth millions now. If they sell it at auction, it'll be big news all over the world."

"Do you suppose the burglars who shot the young couple were after rare books?"

"I don't think so. Not around here. Unless . . ."

"Unless what?"

"Oh, nothing. Just a silly thought." Eddington looked embarrassed.

"Are there professional book thieves—like the art thieves who steal old masters—who might come up here from Down Below?"

"I never thought of that. I should check the books against the inventory. But first I'd better talk to the lawyer."

Qwilleran asked, "How long have you been making house calls to the Fitch mansion?"

"Almost twenty-five years, and when Mr. and Mrs. Fitch moved out, they told me to keep on taking care of the library."

"So you knew Harley's bride. What was she like?"

Eddington hesitated. "She had a pretty face—very pretty. A little-girl face. I don't like to say anything unkind, but . . . she used to say some words that I wouldn't repeat even in front of Winston."

"What was her background?"

"Her name was Urkle. She came from Chipmunk. Of course, I knew her before Harley married her. She was one of Mrs. Fitch's maids."

Qwilleran remembered Mr. O'Dell's remark: "He married the wrong colleen." To Eddington he said, "One wonders why Harley would choose a girl of that class."

" 'Love makes fools of us all,' as Thackeray said. I *think* it was Thackeray," said the bookseller.

Qwilleran stood up. "This has been an enlightening session, Edd. A photographer will come around tomorrow to get a few shots."

"Maybe I'd better clean the front window."

"Don't overdo it!"

On his way to the exit Qwilleran stopped and asked, "When would you normally make your next house call to the Fitch collection?"

"Tuesday after next, but I don't know what to do now. I'll have to talk to the lawyer. I don't want to bother Mr. Fitch, but the books should be taken care of."

"I'd appreciate it if you'd take me along," Qwilleran said. "I might learn something."

"Shall I ask the lawyer if it's all right?"

"No, just take me along as your assistant. I'm good at dusting."

As Qwilleran walked home he marveled at the knowledge of the modest, self-educated little man, at his complete joy in working with books, and at his shabby living quarters. He remembered the narrow cot, and the sad table and chair, and the shelf above the sink. On it were a cup and plate, a dented saucepan, some canned soup and sardines, a razor and comb, and a *handgun!*

Arriving at his apartment he knew there was a message on the answer-box even before he reached the top of the stairs. Koko's mad racing back and forth told him the phone had been ringing in his absence.

The message was from Francesca. She would drop in at five o'clock. She had some stunning wallpaper samples for his bedroom. She also had some news, she said.

SCENE NINE

Place: Qwilleran's apartment; later Stephanie's restaurant
Time: The same day

QWILLERAN WENT INTO his studio to organize his thoughts and compose a catchy lead for the Eddington Smith profile, taking care to confine the cats to their apartment. Ordinarily they assisted his creative process by sitting on his notes, biting his pen and stepping on the shift key of the typewriter, but this time he had a firm deadline. The Siamese were banished.

The job required concentration. In his workshop Eddington used a strange vocabulary: giggering and glairing; nipping up, blinding in, holing out, wringing down and fanning over; casing in, lacing in, and gluing up.

Eddington had said that Winston liked the gluing-up process. Was Koko smelling the glue when he sniffed the spines of books as if reading the titles? Could a cat possibly smell the glue on a seventy-five-year-old volume of Dickens or a century-old Shakespeare? It hardly seemed likely. But, ruling out glue as the attraction, why did Koko sniff books? Why did he sniff certain titles and not others? Were there bookworms in the bindings? Could he smell animal matter? When they spent the summer months in the country, the Siamese were always fascinated by ants, spiders, and ladybugs on the screened porch. Why not bookworms? Qwilleran decided he would ask Eddington to inspect Koko's favorite titles. The cat had suddenly become interested in *Moby Dick* and *Captains Courageous.*

These ruminations were not helping him meet his deadline, and when Francesca arrived with her wallpaper samples, he said, "Excuse me if I appear groggy. I've been working on a profile of Edd Smith, and I'm in a bookish fog. Tell me your news, Fran."

"First, a drink," she said, collapsing on the sofa.

"First the news," Qwilleran insisted, "and then a drink."

"Chad Lanspeak is a suspect! Carol and Larry are in a panic!"

"Hmmm," he said, tamping his moustache. "What time do the police think Harley was killed? Your father wouldn't tell me anything. I don't know why. Suddenly he clammed up."

"I know why," said Fran. "Last year he was reprimanded for talking about a case under investigation. Poor Dad! He loves to talk. I can probably find out for you. Why do you want to know?"

"Chad came to my apartment at 6:15 P.M. to sell me some handmade snowshoes. The transaction took longer than I expected, so it was 7:30 before he dropped me off at the community center. I know, because I looked at my watch and figured you'd give me hell for being a half-hour late. According to the newspaper account, David and Jill found the bodies at 7:15. Assuming Chad had put in a full day at the store, he couldn't be implicated."

"You should phone Carol and Larry and tell them that," said Fran. "They've called in their attorney. Do you know Hasselrich?"

"He's the attorney for the Klingenschoen Fund."

"Call Carol and Larry right away. It'll relieve their minds."

Qwilleran punched the number of the Lanspeak residence, visualizing their attractive country house as he waited for them to answer: split-rail fences, cedar shake roof, picturesque barn. "Hello, Larry? This is Qwill. I have some information for you that may be vital . . . Yes, I know. Fran told me, but assuming Chad worked a full day in the store, he's in the clear. He was with me from 6:15 to 7:30 and supposedly came directly from work. What time did he check out? . . . Well, then, he should be covered. You remember I told you he was selling me snowshoes. That's why I was late for rehearsal . . . That's right. He drove me downtown in his rattletrap truck and dropped me off at the rehearsal hall at 7:30 . . . Yes, I thought it might help. I even have a pair of Beavertails to prove it. Tell Hasselrich, and let him take it from there. I'm standing by if he wants me to do anything . . . So long, Larry. Chin up!"

As he poured Scotch for Fran, she walked around the living room, appraising it with a professional eye—moving a table three inches to the left, adjusting the blinds, straightening the picture of the 1805 gunboat. "How did this print get so crooked?" she asked. "We haven't had any earthquakes or sonic booms."

"Blame it on Koko," Qwilleran said. "He likes to rub his jaw against the corners of picture frames, and that one is easy to reach from the back of the sofa. If you knew anything about cats, that would be perfectly obvious."

She settled down with her drink. "I still can't believe we've lost Harley."

"No one says much about his wife. Did you know her very well?"

Fran shifted her eyes. "I met her a few times."

"Did she come from Chipmunk?"

"Somewhere out in that direction."

"What did people think about their marriage? Why were they married in Las Vegas?"

"Honestly, Qwill, I don't feel like talking about it. Harley isn't even buried yet. It's too painful. Mind if I smoke?" With gestures that had a practiced grace she shook out a cigarette, flicked the silver lighter he had given her for Christmas, and inhaled deeply.

Qwilleran waited for her to enjoy a few puffs before saying, "You and David were close friends, weren't you?"

"How did you know? It was just a high-school crush."

"Did you ever think you might marry him?"

"Did you ever think you might be a nosey bastard . . . *darling?*"

Archly he said, "I have a compassionate curiosity about my fellow beings. It's one of my noble traits." He produced a bowl of cashews and watched her gobble them hungrily. "Seriously, Fran, do you suppose the local investigators are competent to solve this case?"

"The state police have sent a detective up here, Dad says. A homicide expert. But don't underestimate our local cops. They've grown up here, and they know everyone. You'd be surprised how much they know about you and me and Chad and everyone else. They don't keep files on us; they just know."

Qwilleran poured another drink for her; her glass was emptying fast. "What's the Fitch mansion like?" he asked.

"Banana-split architecture at its gooiest!" she said. "A mix of Victorian Gothic, art deco and Italian. But it has a certain country charm. All those chimneys! All those rambling stone walls around the property!"

"I wonder if the killer or killers had time to find what they wanted before being interrupted. No doubt they had a lookout in their vehicle—someone who alerted them when David and Jill were approaching. What do you think they were looking for?"

"Money and jewelry, I suppose. They started ransacking the desk in the library and the dresser drawers upstairs. Harley's grandmother left jewelry in trust for Harley and David to give to their wives when they married. Belle had some pretty good things."

"What about books? Might they be looking for rare books?"

"Are you kidding? They were probably dropouts from Chipmunk who wouldn't know a rare book from a telephone directory."

"What kind of firearm did they use?"

"A handgun that's very common around here for hunting . . . Hey, don't let Dad know I'm telling you this. He's not supposed to discuss it, but he and Mother have a rap session at the kitchen table after every shift, and I have big ears."

"You have very lovely ears, if I may digress."

"Well, thank-you," she said amiably, looking surprised and pleased. "I just might go to dinner with you, if you extend the invitation."

"First I want to feed the cats," Qwilleran said. He released them and set out two bowls of the chef's *specialité du jour,* a kind of bouillabaisse without the mussel shells. "It would be interesting to know," he said, "if Harley knew the killer. I imagine it was someone who had been in the house and knew what they had. It was someone who knew their rehearsal schedule and expected them to be gone by 6:30. That is, if they were killed between 6:30 and 7:15. On the other hand, if they were killed before 6:30, it was by someone who picked a random time for robbery and murder."

"Qwill, this is giving me a headache. Can't we discuss the

wallpaper and then go to dinner? Come over here and let's look at the samples."

They sat together on the sofa, with the heavy wallpaper book on their collective knees. The Siamese, meanwhile, had declined to eat; it was the same stuff they had been served for breakfast, and soupy concoctions were not their favorites. The two cats sat across from the sofa, staring into space.

Fran said, "I'd really love to see you do your bedroom in aubergine, avocado and rose taupe."

"I like it the way it is—tan, brown, and rust," Qwilleran informed her.

"Well, if you insist! How do you like this one? It's a marvelous texture in rust."

"The color's too dull," he said.

"Here's one with more life but not so much surface interest."

"Too flashy."

"How about this one?"

"Too dark."

"The wallcovering is only for the upper half of the wall," she reminded him. (The lower walls were paneled with the narrow wood beading common in nineteenth-century railway depots.) "In other words, it's simply a background for prints and watercolors that will be framed in chrome to tie in with your chromium exercise equipment. That is, if you're sure you want to keep the bike and rowing machine in your bedroom. Couldn't they go in the cats' apartment?"

Qwilleran scowled at her.

"Okay, they couldn't go in the cats' apartment. However," she went on, "I definitely think we should get rid of those ugly old-fashioned radiators. You owe it to yourself to install a completely new heating system."

"Those ugly old-fashioned radiators give good, even

heat," Qwilleran said, "and they look right with the ugly, old-fashioned paneling. The plumber says they're over seventy-five years old and still in excellent operating condition. Show me any new invention that will still be good seventy-five years from now."

"You sound like my father," Fran said. "At least let me design an enclosure for the radiators—just a shelf on top and grillework in front. My carpenter can build them."

"Will it impair their efficiency?"

"Not at all. I also think we should shop for new bedroom furniture for you when we go to Chicago. The new lines are coming out, and I have some wonderful sources . . . Ouch! . . . The cat grabbed my ankle."

"I'm sorry, Fran. Are your stockings torn?"

She smoothed her leg experimentally. "I don't think so, but those claws are like needles. Which one did it?"

Qwilleran watched Yum Yum the Paw slinking guiltily from the room. "Let's go to dinner," he said.

He gathered up Fran's wallpaper samples, and she dropped her cigarette pack into her handbag. "Where's my lighter?"

"Where did you leave it?"

"I thought I put it on the coffee table."

She rummaged in her handbag, and Qwilleran searched the floor and looked behind the sofa cushions.

"It can't have wandered very far," he said. "It'll turn up, and I'll give it back to you. Meanwhile, this would be a good time to give up smoking."

"You're sounding like my father again," she said with a frown.

They drove to Stephanie's, one of the best restaurants in the county. It occupied an old stone mansion in an old residential section of Pickax, and although the exterior was forbidding, the interior had a hospitable ambience created by soft colors, soft textures, and soft lighting. Qwilleran always liked walking into a restaurant with Francesca. On this occasion, heads turned to admire the young woman with gray eyes, gray suit, gray paisley blouse, gray hose, and high-heeled gray sandals.

Perusing the menu, he suggested the herbed trout with wine sauce.

"I'd rather have the spare ribs," she said.

"The trout is better for you."

"Will you stop sounding like my dad, Qwill?"

They talked about her father's virtuosity on the bagpipe, Qwilleran's fondness for things Scottish, Edd Smith's esoteric enterprise, and the future of the Theatre Club without Harley.

Qwilleran asked, "Do you know how David is reacting?"

"I talked to Jill on the phone, and she said he's a basket case. Nigel, too. I wonder if they're resilient enough to cope. They'll need counseling, that's for sure. To lose someone through illness or accident is traumatic, but murder is so evil!"

"Are you a good friend of Jill's?" He had observed a remarkable similarity between the two young women—their figures, their manner of walking and talking, their stagey Theatre Club gestures and attitudes.

"We were clubby in high school," she said. "We double-dated, played basketball, went in for art. She's very clever. I'm smart, I think, but Jill is clever."

"Is her family well-heeled?"

"Not any more. They lost everything in 1929. Her great-great-grandfather owned a string of sawmills. Her great-grandfather was a Civil War hero. Her grandfather was mayor of Pickax for twelve years. Her maternal grandmother . . .

As Francesca related Jill's family history, a scenario began to take shape in Qwilleran's mind. He waited a suitable interval before saying, "That was bad news about Harley's mother. Have you heard any more details?"

"No." The brevity of reply confirmed what he was thinking.

"If Mrs. Fitch doesn't pull through, it will be a great loss to the community. She's done so much for the public library, the hospital, the school, and other good causes."

Francesca's attention suddenly centered on her dinner plate.

"I've met Mrs. Fitch at library board meetings, and she impresses me as a very gracious woman—certainly generous with her time and cooperation."

Francesca raised her wrist and tapped her watch. "Do you realize what time it is? I've got to go back to the studio and write up some orders."

"And I have to buckle down to work on the Edd Smith profile." Later, as they said good night and she gave him a theatrical kiss, he presented her with the gift-wrapped silk scarf he had bought for Polly. "I know I'm a difficult client," he apologized, "but here's a small thank-you for your patience. And I'll have a good look for your cigarette lighter."

Upstairs in his apartment he found that the few remaining cashew nuts had been fished out of the bowl and batted around the room. "Is this your work, madame?" he asked Yum Yum, who was licking her right paw. "And do you know anything about a missing cigarette lighter?"

To Koko he said, "Fran wouldn't comment on Margaret Fitch, and she didn't want to talk about her relationship with David. Put two and two together and what do you get? A manipulative mother who stopped her son from marrying a policeman's daughter?"

"Yow!" Koko replied.

SCENE TEN

Place: Qwilleran's apartment; later, the newspaper office
Time: The day of the Fitch funeral

IT WAS A private funeral in accordance with the wishes of the family. The obsequies were held in the Old Stone Church across the park from Qwilleran's property, and the police kept traffic moving and discouraged loitering in the vicinity. There were no photographers waiting on the sidewalk or lurking in the trees with their telephoto lenses.

Riker had wanted to give the event coverage, saying that Fitch was an important name in the county, the deaths were shocking, and the funeral was newsworthy.

Junior Goodwinter disagreed. "It's different in a town like this. We respect their feelings."

Riker insisted, and the argument became heated until Qwilleran was asked to mediate.

He agreed with Junior. "The public's right to be nosey won't be violated. Within an hour of the burial all the details of the funeral will be common knowledge. Telephones will be busy; the coffee shops will be buzzing. The Pickax grapevine is more efficient than any newspaper that publishes twice a week. So cool it, Arch."

On the morning of the funeral Qwilleran was typing the last paragraph of the Eddington Smith story and the Siamese were sitting on his desk when the telephone rang. Yum Yum flew away to parts unknown, while Koko jumped to the phone table and scolded the instrument.

"Qwill, this is Cokey," said the voice on the phone. Alacoque Wright, the young architect, sounded more mature than she had been during their brief fling Down Below. "I'm phoning from the construction shed on your front lawn."

"Good to hear your voice, Cokey. When did you arrive? How does the theater look?" Koko was now standing with his hind feet on the table and his forepaws on Qwilleran's shoulder, and he was snarling into the mouthpiece. Qwilleran pushed him away.

"The job is looking good. They've been following the specs more closely this time. Only one problem: the wall color in the dressing rooms doesn't match the sample. It was supposed to be a rose ochre of low saturation to flatter the actors and elevate their mood. It will have to be repainted at the contractor's expense."

"How long are you going to be here, Cokey?" Koko was biting the phone cord, and Qwilleran gave him another shove.

"Until tomorrow noon. I'm staying at the Pickax Hotel. It's not exactly the Plaza, but my room has a bed and indoor plumbing, for which I'm grateful."

"Let's have dinner tonight. Come to my apartment over the garage whenever you're through with your work. We'll have a drink, and you can say hello to Koko. He's making an unholy fuss at the moment for some obscure reason."

"See you later," she said.

Qwilleran turned to the cat sitting on the phone table just beyond arm's reach. "Now, what was that all about, young man? If you must monitor my phone calls, try to act with civility."

Koko scratched his ear with infuriating nonchalance.

Qwilleran returned to his typing, only to be interrupted by a phone call from Polly Duncan. The dulcet quality of her voice indicated that she had recovered from her peevishness, and his hopes soared.

"I'm embarrassed, Qwill," she said. "Monday was your birthday, and I didn't even mention it when we had dinner on Wednesday. If it isn't too late to celebrate, would you be my guest at Stephanie's this evening?"

"I'd like that," he said with warmth. "I'd like that very much, but unfortunately the architect for the theater project is here from Cincinnati, and I have to do the honors."

"How long will he be here?"

"Uh . . . until tomorrow noon." He decided not to point out the gender discrepancy.

"Then could you dine with me tomorrow evening?"

"Saturday? That's when the newspaper bosses are treating the staff to a victory bash. It's just an in-house celebration with drinks, bonuses and speeches, but I have to be there to represent the Klingenschoen Fund."

"You're really keeping busy, aren't you?" she said crisply.

He waited hopefully for an invitation to roast beef and Yorkshire pudding at her cozy little house on Sunday, but she merely signed off with polite regrets.

So Qwilleran was in a sober mood when he walked downtown to hand in his copy and photo request at the newspaper office. As he approached the building he saw a post-office vehicle parked at the curb and a mailcarrier dragging large sacks into the building. Their contents were being dumped on the floor in the middle of the city room, and everyone—publisher included—was slitting envelopes and counting ballots for the official name of the new publication.

"Come on, Qwill!" Junior called out. "Dig in and start counting. Help yourself to coffee and doughnuts."

Hixie said, "The write-ins are the best. Here's one for *The Moose County Claptrap.*"

By noon there were a few scattered votes for *Chronicle, Clarion* and *Caucus,* but 80 percent of the readers wanted to retain the flag used on the first issue: *The Moose County Something.*

"At least it's different," Riker acknowledged reluctantly.

"People around here like to be different," Junior explained. "My next-door neighbor hangs his Christmas tree upside down from the ceiling, and there's a restaurant in Brrr that charges a nickel for a paper napkin."

Roger said, "I know a farmer in Wildcat who doesn't believe in daylight saving time. He refuses to move his clock ahead, so he's an hour late for everything all summer."

"Okay, how about this one?" Hixie said. "I sold an ad to a little old lady in Smith's Folly who sells candy, cigarettes, and pornographic magazines, and she mentioned the Fitch funeral. She said she'd never been to a funeral. She said all her family were buried in the backyard *without any fuss.*"

Riker said, "I don't believe a word of this nonsense."

"In Moose County I'll believe anything," Qwilleran said, "but Hixie is exaggerating about the magazines. I've been in that shop."

"It's true!" she insisted. "The racy stuff is behind a curtain."

"Okay, you loafers, back to work," Riker ordered. "Here comes the mailgirl with another sack."

Qwilleran wanted to leave, until he heard they were sending out for deli sandwiches. "What news on the police beat?" he asked Roger.

"The investigation continues. That's all they'll say."

"That's all they ever say. Have you had any tips that they're closing in?"

"Well, everyone seems to think it's narrowing down to Chipmunk. That's what people said from the very beginning. You know, I hate to see a town get a reputation like that. When I was teaching, I had some good students from Chipmunk. There are decent working-class families living in those low-rent houses, but a few hoodlums give the town a black eye."

Qwilleran was smoothing his moustache, and Riker noticed the familiar gesture. "If the police can't solve the case, leave it to Qwill," he said with mild sarcasm.

"One thing I've been wondering," Qwilleran said. "Harley's wife never attended rehearsals at the Theatre Club. Didn't like the people, I guess. So why was she going to attend on Tuesday night?" He waited for an opinion, but none was forthcoming. "Did she want to be out of the house? Did she know what was going to happen?"

"Wow!" said Junior. "That's a pretty radical idea."

"We don't know what connections she might have had in Chipmunk. She might have collaborated in a plot to burglarize the house."

Roger said, "Her maiden name was Urkle, and they're not a bad family. Belle wasn't a good student; in fact, she dropped out. But she wasn't a bad girl."

"Go ahead, Qwill. What's your theory?"

"Let's say she supplied a key to the house and told her accomplices where to look for loot. But the timing was off, because David and Jill were delayed. When her confederates arrived, they were confronted by Harley. Maybe he recognized them, or maybe they were just trigger-happy and afraid he would identify them, so they killed him. Then Belle had to be silenced because she knew who had murdered her husband, and they feared she might crack under questioning."

"Wow!" said the young managing editor.

"How many do you think were involved in the break-in?" Roger asked. "Everyone refers to murderers, plural."

"In any conspiracy, the fewer the better. I would say there was one to stand look-out in their vehicle, and another for the inside work. Being alone, he might have been overpowered by Harley, so he had to shoot . . . I get a sad picture of poor little Belle Urkle in her so-called rehearsal clothes, waiting upstairs, realizing the plot has failed, playing a scene she never rehearsed."

"Shall we have soft music in the background?" Hixie suggested.

"She hears the shot downstairs. She's terrified, not knowing what will happen next. She hears the killer coming up the stairs . . ."

"You'd better go back to writing your novel, Qwill," said Riker.

Then Roger said, "One of the cops told me something interesting today—off the record, of course. In determining the time of death, they decided that Belle was shot first."

SCENE ELEVEN

Place: The Old Stone Mill
Time: Evening of the same day
Introducing: ALACOQUE WRIGHT, architect from Cincinnati

WHILE WAITING FOR Alacoque Wright to arrive, Qwilleran wrote two letters of condolence: one to Nigel Fitch on the loss of his son, and one to David and Jill on the loss of their brother. He had to work fast in order to seal the envelopes and affix the stamps before that maniac of a cat swooped in with his wet tongue. As soon as an envelope or stamp came out of the desk drawer, Koko stalked it with a quivering nose and an insane gleam in his eye.

Next, Qwilleran prepared for company. He straightened the gunboat picture over the sofa, removed used coffee cups and scattered newspapers, put on his best suit, and filled the ice bucket with cubes. "Cokey is coming," he said to the Siamese. "Try to be on your best behavior."

Koko made an ugly noise, halfway between a hiss and a snarl, and Qwilleran suddenly realized why. At that moment the doorbell sounded, and Cokey was admitted.

There were hugs and kisses appropriate under the circumstances, and then Qwilleran said, "I can't call you C-o-k-e-y any more. Koko will have a fit. He thinks it's his name being spoken. Cats are jealous of their names. Koko doesn't like anyone to touch his tail, pry open his mouth, or apply his name to any other entity—animal, vegetable or mineral. That's why we have only ginger ale around the house and not that other popular beverage."

"That's all right," said Alacoque. "Call me Al. That's what my husband always called me. How are you, Qwill? You're looking so healthy, it's indecent. I missed you the first time I was in town."

"I was Down Below, partying at the Press Club, inhaling polluted air and trying to get unhealthy again, so my old friends would recognize me."

"I must say there's something about country living that agrees with you."

"You've changed, too," Qwilleran said. "You're looking older and wiser, if you don't mind the dubious compliment." Formerly addicted to clothes that she made out of drapery samples, she was now the sleek, well-dressed, self-assured, city-bred, successful career woman—in pant-dressing suitable for climbing around a construction site.

"There's nothing like a good job and a bad marriage to make a girl look older and wiser," she admitted ruefully.

"I didn't know about your marriage. Are you divorced?"

"No, but I work in Cincinnati, and he's driving a truck in San Francisco, where he belongs."

She volunteered no details, and Qwilleran asked no questions. Walking to the small serving bar incorporated in the bookshelves, he remarked, "I suppose you're still drinking yogurt and prune juice."

"Lord, no! I'll take Irish neat, if you have it . . . Is that Koko? He looks older and wiser, too."

"The little one is Yum Yum. You've never met her."

"She's adorable. How's your current love life, Qwill?"

"I don't know, frankly. I've been rather happy with a woman of my own age—a librarian—but she's beginning to resent the young woman I've hired as my interior designer."

"Stick with the librarian, Qwill. You know how I feel about interior designers! Remember when I was a reluctant assistant in Mrs. Middy's studio with all those calico lampshades and mammy rockers?" Alacoque looked around the living room with approval. "I'm glad to see you've furnished in contemporary."

"I find it comfortable, especially with a few old books and old prints thrown in."

"Do you like living up here?"

"To my surprise, yes. I've always lived in big cities and had the big-city viewpoint, but people up here think differently and I find myself adjusting. Also, a town of this size has a human scale and a slower pace that I find comforting."

"That's the second time in a minute and a half that you've mentioned comfort. Is that a sign of growing older?"

"Older and smarter. In Pickax I walk a lot; I've lost weight, and I'm breathing better. We have fresh air, safe streets, minimal traffic, friendly people, boating in summer, skiing in winter . . ."

"Does Pickax need an architect? Young, talented, friendly female wishes to apply."

"I may need an architect soon," Qwilleran told her. "There's an old apple barn on my property that I'd like to convert into a place to live."

"I've always wanted to convert a barn."

"We're dining tonight at an old gristmill converted into a restaurant. I think you'll approve of it—both the food and the architecture. But first I'd like to give you a scenic tour of Moose County, whenever you're ready."

"Let's go," she said, draining her glass.

As they drove past farms, woods, lakes, and historic mine sites, Alacoque exclaimed over the grotesque shapes of weathered shafthouses, the stark remains of ghost towns, picturesque stone farmhouses, and a whole town of chinked log buildings on the lakeshore.

"And now we're coming into the Hummocks," Qwilleran said, "where the affluent families have their estates." The road swooped up and down nobby hills traced with miles of low, stone walls. Then he turned into a gravel road between stone pylons, marked PRIVATE. "This is the Fitch estate—hundreds of acres, in the family for generations. I've never been here before, but they say there are two interesting houses. One is a twenty-two-room mansion built in the twenties, and the other is a contemporary house that's been photographed for a national magazine."

The road curved around hills, ascended the rounded crests and dipped down again, winding between woodland and meadow.

"Gorgeous terrain!" Alacoque said. "Was it done by glaciers or bulldozers?"

They crested a hill, and suddenly in the valley below there appeared a sprawling stone house with many chimneys—and two police cars in the driveway.

"There was a murder here on Tuesday," Qwilleran explained.

"Was it a young banker and his wife?" Alacoque asked. "I heard the construction workers talking about it."

A sheriff's car backed out of the drive and blocked the road as Qwilleran approached, and a brown-uniformed deputy strolled over to speak to him. "This road is closed, sir. May I see your driver's license?" He glanced at the wallet Qwilleran offered, and his expression relaxed as he recognized the name and photograph of the richest man in the county, "Were you looking for someone, sir? There's no one here, and no one at the other house, either."

"My passenger is an architect from Cincinnati," Qwilleran replied. "She's merely interested in seeing the exterior of David Fitch's house. Its architecture has had national attention."

"I see," said the deputy slowly, as he thought about it, bobbing his head until the tassels on his broad-brimmed hat danced. "You can drive up there if you want to. I'll lead the way. There are some tricky forks in the road and some muddy spots."

The two cars proceeded slowly along the winding road. "Muddy spots!" Qwilleran said. "It hasn't rained for a week." There were no forks in the road, either.

Up and down the gentle hills they moved until the spectacular house came in view.

"Fantastic!" Alacoque cried. "It's inspired by those shafthouses at the old mines!"

The contemporary house was built of rough cedar. Five cubes, each smaller than the one below, were stacked to make an irregular five-story pyramid, until the top floor was merely a lookout over the valley below.

The sheriff ambled over. "You can walk along the terrace if you want to. It has a good view. You can see the big lake from here."

"Do you know who did the construction?" Alacoque asked.

"Caspar Young, ma'am."

"Do you know who designed it?"

"No, ma'am."

As she studied the house from all angles, she remarked on

the use of massive timbers, the cantilevered decks, the integration with the terrain, the fenestration, massing and site orientation, the planes and angles and voids. The deputy, who accompanied them closely, appeared to be impressed.

Qwilleran thanked him and then followed the official car back down the road. He looked at his watch. "I want to see," he said to Alacoque, "how long it takes to drive from here to the stone house, and exactly when and where it comes into view. I'm wondering how much warning the burglars had—how much time to pack their loot and make a getaway. David and Jill were late in picking up Harley and Belle. They said they had a plumbing emergency. If they had been on schedule, all this might not have happened. Did someone want them to be late? Was the plumbing emergency contrived?"

"I suspect the plumber," Alacoque said. "All plumbers look furtive to me."

The tour continued through Squunk Corners, the lakeside town of Brrr, and Smith's Folly. Then they arrived at the Old Stone Mill, and Alacoque was enchanted by the former gristmill built of stone and nestled in a wooded setting. The old millwheel turned and creaked and shuddered as if it were still supplying power to grind wheat and corn. Within the building, timbers and floors were artfully bleached to the color of honey, and pale-oak tables and chairs contributed to the cheerful feeling of well-being.

"Hello, Derek," Qwilleran said to the tall busboy who was filling the water glasses with the air of one who owned the place. "You seem to be busy tonight."

"Friday, you know," Derek explained. "How did the cats like the poached salmon this morning?"

"It was a big hit! They even ate the capers." Turning to his guest Qwilleran said, "This is Derek Cuttlebrink, purveyor of fine foods to Their Majesties, the Siamese, and a member of the Theatre Club."

"Hi!" said the busboy.

"My guest has come all the way from Cincinnati to try your famous poached salmon, Derek."

"I have a cousin in Cincinnati," he said.

"Cincinnati is full of cousins," Alacoque said with a disarming smile.

Qwilleran asked, "Where's my favorite waitress tonight?"

"She quit. We have a new girl at this station. This is her first day. She's pretty nervous, and she's kinda slow, so give her a break."

Eventually a thin, frightened girl presented herself at the table. "I'm S-s-sally, your s-s-server. Today's s-s-specials are clam chowder, oysters Rockefeller, and poached s-s-salmon. Would you like s-s-something from the bar?"

"Yes, Sally," Qwilleran said. "The lady will have Irish whiskey neat, and I'll have Squunk water with a dash of bitters and a slice of lemon."

"S-s-quunk water with . . . what?"

"A dash of bitters and a slice of lemon."

Alacoque was eager to talk about the theater—the two graceful stairways in the lobby, the rake of the amphitheater, the versatility of the staging area. "How good is your theater group?" she asked.

"A cut above most amateur companies," he said. "It was founded a hundred years ago and named the Pickax Thespians, but the present generation thought it sounded like deviant sex, so it was changed to the Theatre Club. The young man who was killed Tuesday was one of our best actors."

"What were the circumstances?"

"He and his wife were gunned down in their home—the stone house where we encountered the police cars."

"Were they into drugs?"

Qwilleran gave her a frigid glance. "No one is into drugs up here, Alacoque."

"That's what *you* think. Do they know who killed them?"

"They've been questioning suspects. Robbery was the obvious motive. They say the house is crammed with valuable collectibles, accumulated a couple of generations back. The family has old money, and they're very well liked. Harley and his brother have always been known as cooperative, outgoing guys with a lot of class."

"How about Harley's wife?"

"They'd been married only a short time. I never met her."

"I don't know whether I should repeat this, but . . . the construction gang said she was a tramp."

"Did they offer any corroborative detail?"

"No, but they all nodded and leered. Why would a man like Harley marry a girl with that reputation?"

"Pertinent question. I've been wondering about that myself."

Her attention was wandering. She said, "There's a woman over there who keeps looking at us. She's with another woman."

"Describe her."

"Middle-aged, intelligent looking, neat hair, pleasant face. Hair slightly gray. Plain gray suit, plain white blouse."

"Size 16? Walking shoes? That's my librarian," he said. "I told her I was having dinner with an architect from out of town, and she assumed you wore a beard and smoked a pipe. I didn't correct her. Now I'm in the doghouse for keeps."

"If you need consoling," Alacoque said, "young, talented, friendly female architect wishes to apply."

Suddenly there was a change of mood in the restaurant. The pleasant hum of diners' voices was interrupted by an excited hubbub in the rear of the room. The doors to and from the kitchen were rapidly swinging in and out. Waitresses were whispering to their customers, who responded with little cries of emotion and shocked exclamations. One waitress dropped a tray on the hardwood floor. It was Sally, who fell to her knees, frantically scooping up cheesecake.

Qwilleran flagged down the busboy. "What's happening here?"

"Sally heard the news and got all shook up, I guess. Lucky it was cheesecake and not soup or something."

"What news?" Qwilleran demanded.

"Did you know Harley's mother was in the hospital?"

"Of course I knew that," Qwilleran snapped impatiently.

Derek glanced toward the kitchen. "Our salad girl's mother is a nurse at the hospital. She just phoned and said Mrs. Fitch died."

"Oh, my God," Qwilleran moaned. To Alacoque he explained, "Mrs. Fitch had a massive stroke after her son was murdered."

"Yeah," said Derek. "Her husband was there at the hospital when she died, and he went out to the parking lot and sat in his car and shot himself."

SCENE TWELVE

Place: Editorial offices of *The Moose County Something*
Time: Saturday evening

THE READERS HAD GIVEN their mandate. With the publication of the weekend issue, *The Moose County Something* became the official name of the newspaper, although the decision grated on Arch Riker's better judgment and caused him acute embarrassment. He said, "I always wanted to be an editor in chief, but I never wanted to be editor in chief of something called *The Moose County Something!* Already I'm getting the raspberry—by mail, phone, and carrier pigeon—from the guys Down Below, and I'm afraid it's only the beginning."

Nevertheless he hosted the victory celebration on Saturday night with gracious hospitality. Desks in the city room were pushed together to serve as a bar and a buffet, and the former was dispensing everything from beer to champagne. Milling around the open bar were editors, reporters, columnists, one part-time photographer drinking enough for three, stringers from outlying towns, office personnel, adpersons, and the circulation crew.

Although exhausted after putting together the first forty-eight-page *Something*, the staff had managed to produce a weekend issue of thirty-six pages. It had gone to press too soon, however, to cover the deaths of Margaret and Nigel Fitch, and the banner headline on page one read: WILD TURKEYS RETURN TO MOOSE COUNTY.

Kevin Doone, who had been a pallbearer at the funeral of Harley and Belle, was doing justice to the open bar. "I need this," he said to Qwilleran, raising his martini glass. "Carrying that casket was the hardest thing I've ever had to do. Harley was my cousin, you know, and a super guy! When Brodie started playing the bagpipe as we were coming down the church steps, I really fell apart! David wanted a piper at the church and the cemetery because Harley always liked that kind of music. God! It sounded mournful! And now Aunt Margaret's gone. And Nigel! . . . I've got to get a refill."

Kevin dashed away to the bar, and the writer of social news, Susan Exbridge, caught Qwilleran's eye. *"Darling, why are we here?"* she cried, waving her arms and spilling her drink. Since getting a divorce and joining the Theatre Club she had become overly dramatic. "We should all be at home, privately mourning for Nigel—that beautiful man!"

Qwilleran agreed that the bank president was distinguished looking: tall, straight, perpetually tanned, with polished manners and affable personality. "How could he do it?" he asked Susan.

"He couldn't face life without Margaret," she said. "They were devoted! And, of course, everyone knows that *she* made him a success. He was a sweet man, but he would have been nothing without Margaret's push. She directed the whole show."

Qwilleran, carrying his glass of ginger ale on the rocks, moved amiably among the convivial drinkers, all complimenting each other on their contributions to the new paper. One of them was Mildred Hanstable, the buxom teacher from the Pickax high school, where she taught art and home economics, directed the senior play, and coached girls' volleyball. Now she was writing the food pages for the *Something*.

Qwilleran said, "Mildred, I read every word of your cooking columns, even though cubing and dicing and mincing are Greek to me. Everything sounded great, especially the Chinese chrysanthemum soup."

"When are you going to learn to cook, Qwill?"

"Sorry, but I'll never have the aptitude to boil an egg, understand an insurance policy, or file my own tax return."

"I could teach you to boil eggs," she said with her hearty laugh. "I give private lessons!"

Qwilleran's expression changed from genial to doleful. "This was the night there was supposed to be a housewarming party for Harvey and Belle. Tell me something, Mildred. Teachers and cops in small towns know everything about everybody. What do you know about Belle Urkle?"

"Well, I'm sorry to say she dropped out of school. She said she wanted to work for rich people and live in a big house. You could hardly blame her, if you'd seen how people live in Chipmunk. She was a maid in the Fitch house, but I can't understand what notivated Harley to marry her."

"Love? Lust? Biological entrapment?"

"But he didn't have to marry her and embarrass the family, did he? As soon as I heard about the murders, I got out the tarot cards and did a couple of readings. There's a deceitful woman involved!"

"Hmmm," Qwilleran said politely. He was skeptical of tarot cards. "May I replenish your drink, Mildred?"

When he returned with her Scotch and his ginger ale, he inquired casually about Harley's scholastic record.

"Both boys were good students—and so talented!" she

said. "David did excellent pen-and-ink sketches, and Harley built model ships with exquisite detail. They were both in school plays, and I guess they became quite serious about drama in college. You may not know this, Qwill," she said, stepping closer, "but Harley disappeared for a year!"

"What do you mean by that?"

"Both boys were expected to come home after graduating from Yale—to work in the bank. Harley didn't show up."

At that moment Junior Goodwinter interrupted. "Don't you guys want any food? We've got turkey and corned-beef sandwiches."

"We'll be right there," Qwilleran assured him. "Mildred is divulging some cooking secrets."

"I always put a teaspoon of bitters in my lime pie," she said, picking up her cue, and when Junior moved away she said to Qwilleran, "No one really knows what happened to Harley. The family said he was traveling for a year, but of course there were many rumors."

There was another intrusion. Mildred's son-in-law said, "What are you two subversives plotting?"

"We're helping the police solve the Fitch case," Qwilleran informed him.

"Excuse me," Mildred said, "I'm going to get another drink."

Roger said, "I heard something interesting this afternoon, Qwill. A few hours before Nigel shot himself, he dictated letters of resignation from the bank—for David as well as himself. His suicide was evidently premeditated."

"But why would David have to resign?" Qwilleran asked.

Before Roger could think of an answer, Hixie breezed into their midst with her usual breathless enthusiasm. "You'll never believe what happened this afternoon. I was having my hair done at Delphine's, and a huge deer crashed through the front window. He ran right through the shop and out the back window. Broken glass everywhere! And utter panic!"

Qwilleran looked doubtful. "Do you have this story copyrighted, Hixie?"

"It's true! Ask Delphine! The windows are boarded up now, and a sign says, THE BUCK STOPPED HERE. I can't understand why he didn't gore a couple of customers."

Roger said, "Why don't these things happen on our deadline? All we get is a flock of wild turkeys."

Arch Riker was circulating and playing the genial host. Amanda was there, too, drinking bourbon and scowling and complaining. She was wearing a conspicuous diamond ring on her left hand.

Riker, beaming, took Qwilleran aside. "We're taking the plunge, old sock. She may be cantankerous, but I admire her. She ran a successful business for twenty-five years and served on the city council for the last ten. And she doesn't take guff from anyone!"

"She's a remarkable woman," Qwilleran said.

Amanda stepped forward, frowning. "Who called me a remarkable woman?" She demanded belligerently. "You never hear of a remarkable man! He's successful or intelligent or witty, but if a woman is any of those things, she's 'a remarkable woman' like some kind of female freak."

"I apologize," Qwilleran said. "You're absolutely right, Amanda. It's a lazy cliché, and I'm guilty. You're not a remarkable woman. You're successful and intelligent and witty."

"And you're a liar!" she growled. Riker grinned and dragged her away, confiscating her glass of bourbon.

Qwilleran looked around for Mildred. He wanted to hear the rest of her story about Harley's disappearance, but she was in earnest conversation with the stringer from Mooseville, so he went to the buffet. While he was eating his second corned-beef sandwich, he spotted Homer Tibbitt, official historian for the *Something,* leaving the city room. "Homer! Where are you going? The party's only begun!"

"I'm going home. It's 8:30—past my bedtime," said the ninety-four-year-old retired school principal in a high-pitched reedy voice. "My days keep getting shorter. When I'm a hundred, I'll be going to bed before I get up."

"I just wanted to know how well you knew the Fitch family."

"The Fitches? The boys came along after I retired, but I had Nigel in math and history when I was teaching. I knew Nigel's father, too. Cyrus was a character!"

"Is he the one who built the big house in Middle Hummock?"

"Cyrus? Yes indeed! He was a big spender, a big-game hunter, a big collector, a big bootlegger, a big everything."

"Did you say bootlegger?"

"That was something he did on the side," Homer explained plausibly. "The family money came from mining. Cyrus built his house in West Middle Hummock so he could see the big lake from the top of one of the hills. Rumrunners brought the stuff over from Canada and landed on his beach."

"How did he get away with it?"

"Get away with it? One night he didn't get away with it! The sheriff confiscated the whole shipment and poured it on the dump in Squunk Corners. That's why Squunk water is so good for you! . . . Well, it's past my bedtime. Good night."

Qwilleran watched the old man making his exit with vigorous maneuvers of angular arms and legs. Then he caught Mildred alone at the bar. "You were telling me something interesting about Harley when we were interrupted," he said.

"Was I?" She paused to think. "I've had a few drinks . . . Was it about the tarot cards?"

"No, Mildred. It was something about Harley's disappearance after his graduation from Yale."

"Oh! . . . Yes . . . He was traveling . . . That's what the family said . . . Nobody believed it."

"Why didn't they believe it?"

"Well . . . you know . . . people around here . . . gossipy."

"Where did they think he was?"

"Who?"

"Harley."

"Oh! . . . Let's see . . . Ask Roger . . . I've got to sit down."

Qwilleran guided her to a chair and offered to bring her a sandwich and coffee. "How do you like it?"

"What?"

"The coffee."

"Oh! . . . Black."

When he returned with the food, someone told him that Mildred had gone to lie down in the staff lounge, so he ate the sandwich himself and sought out her son-in-law. "Better look after Mildred, chum. She's had too much to drink."

"Where is she?"

"Lying down for a while. She was mentioning Harley's mysterious disappearance a couple of years ago. Know anything about that?"

"Oh, sure. The family said he was traveling, but you know how we are up here. We get bored with the truth and have to invent something. Some people thought he was doing undercover work for the government. I thought he shipped out as a deckhand on a tramp steamer. He liked boats, and that's the kind of offbeat thing he'd do—probably grow a beard, wear a patch over one eye and stomp around like Deadeye Dick."

"He married Belle in Las Vegas. Was he a gambler?"

"I've never heard anything to that effect. If he had one consuming passion, it was sailing. The *Fitch Witch* was a neat boat—twenty-seven feet. He and Gary Pratt used to sail her in races and win trophies."

"Hmmm," Qwilleran said, as suspicion tickled the roots of his moustache. In the last few days—since Harley's murder, to be exact—Koko had taken a sudden interest in things nautical. Several times he had tilted the gunboat picture that hung over the sofa, sometimes violently. And the titles he had started sniffing on the bookshelves were sea stories. First it was *Moby Dick* and then *Two Years Before the Mast.* Most recently it was *Mutiny on the Bounty.* Qwilleran had explained to himself and others that all cats tilt and sniff; they like to rub a jaw on the sharp corners of picture frames and smell the glue used in bookbinding.

Nevertheless, the nautical connection was a curious coincidence, he thought. And there was another mystifying detail: Koko had been excessively attentive to Harley at the birthday party . . . less than twenty-four hours before his murder—almost as if he knew something was going to happen.

SCENE THIRTEEN

Place: Qwilleran's apartment
Time: Early Monday morning . . . and TOO early Tuesday morning
Introducing: PETE PARROTT, a paperhanger from Brrr

THE PHONE RANG early. It was Francesca. "Is Pete there yet?" she inquired.

"Who?"

"Pete, the paperhanger. He has the wallcovering for your studio, and he's going to deliver it this morning. He can install it today or hold off for a couple of days if you wish."

"The sooner the better," Qwilleran decided. "I'll be needing to use my studio the rest of the week. What's Pete's last name?"

"Parrott. Pete Parrott. He's the one who did your living room when you were out of town. He's the best in the county."

"And the most expensive, I suppose."

"You can afford it," she said, with a flippancy that irritated him. He had always disliked being told what to do with his money, whether he had much or little.

Quickly he started tidying his studio, stuffing papers into

desk drawers and removing the debris of bachelor living: two coffee mugs, a tie, waste paper that had missed the basket, a pair of shoes, old newspapers, another coffee mug, a sticky plate, a sweater. He also locked up the cats in their apartment despite their vociferous objections; the busboy had not yet delivered their breakfast.

Then Qwilleran sat down to listen for the doorbell. When it finally rang at 9 A.M., it ushered in Derek Cuttlebrink, delivering chicken liver pâté and two boned froglegs for the howling Siamese. The busboy was in no hurry to return to his place of employment; he wanted to talk about the Theatre Club.

"Too bad they canceled the show just because Harley wasn't in it any more," he said. "I had a pretty good part—the policeman, you know. I even had my cop's uniform fitted. They had to lengthen the pants and sleeves."

"There'll be another play in the fall, and you can audition again," Qwilleran informed him.

"I'm thinking of going back to school in the fall and getting into law enforcement. It's a whole lot better than stacking dirty dishes. Wearing a uniform and riding around in a car all day—that's for me!"

"There's more to police work than wearing a uniform and riding around in a car, Derek, but it would be a good idea to complete your education in any event. By the way, how's our nervous waitress who dropped the tray of cheesecake Friday night?"

"Sally? She's okay. She's getting the hang of the job. But she's going to school in the fall—art school—somewhere Down Below. I wish I had her luck. Her tuition's all paid for—by Mr. Fitch."

"Harley Fitch?" Qwilleran asked with sudden interest.

"No, his father. That's why she was all shook up when he shot himself, although she's already got the money."

In his mind Qwilleran was matching up the suave, sophisticated, handsome banker with the timid, scrawny, stuttering waitress, and trying to imagine some kind of illicit connection.

As if reading his mind, the busboy explained, "Sally's dad is janitor at the bank."

"That's a unique fringe benefit," Qwilleran said. "Perhaps you should consider being a janitor instead of a cop."

At 10 A.M. the paperhanger had still not arrived. . . . Eleven o'clock . . . One o'clock . . . Not until 2:30 did the white commercial van pull up to the carriage house. The driver was a burly young man in white coveralls and white visored cap, with thick blond hair bushing out beneath it. Healthy-looking young men with blond hair were in good supply in this north country.

"Sorry I'm late," he shouted from the bottom of the stairs. "Something came up, and I had to take care of it."

"I wish you had phoned."

"Tell the truth, I didn't even think of it. I was sort of messed up in an emergency."

At least he's honest, Qwilleran thought, and he has an honest face.

"Well, I'd better bring up my gear," he said.

The Siamese, released from their apartment hours before, watched with interest as stepladders, a folding table, buckets, and boxes of tools came up the stairs.

Qwilleran said, "I was out of town when you papered the walls in the living room. You did a first-rate job."

"Yeah, I do good work."

"How long will it take you to do my studio?"

Pete appraised the room with a brief, professional glance. "Not long. Just short strips above the dado, and the plaster's in good shape. A little touch-up with spackle. Sizing dries in nothing flat. And there's no matching. One job I did was all stripes—even on the ceiling, and they had to be mitered. Worst thing about it, the whole room was out of whack. Not a plumb line anywhere! When I finished I was cock-eyed and walking lopsided."

"Was that Fran Brodie's idea?"

"Yeah, she comes up with some doozies, but this stuff is easy." The wallcovering was natural tan cork—thin slices over a rust-colored backing. "Well, I better get started."

"I'll get the cats out of your way." Koko was inspecting everything, and Yum Yum was studying the paperhanger's shoes.

"They don't bother me. They were around the last time I was here. The big one had his nose in everything I did."

"Koko has a healthy curiosity. Do you mind if I watch, too?"

Pete wielded yardsticks, shears, knives, brushes, and rollers with swift assurance.

"You seem to know what you're doing," Qwilleran said in admiration. "I'm a confirmed don't-do-it-yourselfer."

"Been hanging wallpaper since I was fourteen," said Pete. "I papered some of the best houses in the county. Never had a complaint."

"That's a good track record. Did you ever paper the Fitch mansion in the Hummocks?"

Pete stopped abruptly and laid down his shears. The expression on his face was difficult to interpret. "Yeah, I been there, three or four times."

"That was a shocking incident Tuesday night."

"Yeah." Qwilleran noticed that he gulped.

"The police haven't made any arrests, but I understand they're questioning suspects."

"Yeah, they're doing their job." Pete went back to work but not as energetically as before.

"I've never seen the Fitch house," Qwilleran said. "What kind of wallpaper did they like?"

"Raw silk—very plain. I hung a lot of raw silk when Mr.

and Mrs. Fitch lived there. Then they moved to Indian Village and wanted the same thing in their condo. They're got some spread!"

"Did you do any work for Harley and his wife when they moved in?"

"Yeah, I did the breakfast room in a crazy pattern with pink elephants. She liked everything jazzy. I did their bedroom, too—all red velvet."

"Would you like a cup of coffee or a cold drink or beer?" Qwilleran asked.

"I wouldn't mind something to drink. Coffee, I guess. Gotta stay sober on this job, even if it isn't all stripes."

Qwilleran thawed some frozen coffee cake in the microwave, pressed buttons on the computerized coffeemaker, and served the repast in the studio, among the ladders and paste buckets. Pete sat on the floor with the plate between his legs. Koko watched him with whiskers curled forward and then applied his nose to the man's shoes and pantlegs with the concentration of a bloodhound on a hot scent.

"Shove him away," said Qwilleran, who was also sitting on the floor with his coffee.

"He's okay. I like animals. This is good coffee cake."

"A friend of mine made it. Iris Cobb. She manages the Goodwinter Farmhouse Museum."

"Yeah, I know her. I did some work for the museum. She's a good cook. I gained about ten pounds before the job was done."

"I wonder if they'll make the Fitch mansion into a museum now," said Qwilleran, edging back into the topic that interested him. "I doubt whether David Fitch wants to live there."

"Yeah, he has that crazy house up on the hill. I can't figure it out, but I guess they like it. They don't go in for wallpaper."

"Harley will be missed at the Theatre Club. He was a good actor and always high-spirited. I never met his wife. What was she like?"

Pete shook his head slowly in silent awe. "She had *everything!*" When Qwilleran registered surprise, he added, "She used to be my girl." There was another gulp.

Qwilleran waited for details, but none was forthcoming, so he said, "You knew her for quite a while?"

"Ever since she went to work for the Fitches—housework, you know. She lived there at the house. That's when I was hanging the raw silk."

"Then you have a personal reason to resent this crime."

"Yeah," he said moodily.

"Why did you let her get away?"

"She didn't want a paperhanger, although I make good money. She wanted a rich man—someone to take her to Vegas and Hawaii and places like that. Well, she got him, but it didn't do her any good."

"A damn shame, Pete."

"Yeah, I really went for that girl." He turned an unabashed face to Qwilleran. "The reason I was late today—the police wanted to ask some questions."

"I'm sure they're questioning everyone who knew Belle. That's the way it's done."

"Yeah, but I guess they thought I had reasons for . . . killing them both."

After the work was finished and Pete had cleared out his ladders and buckets, it was late. Qwilleran had no desire to go out to a restaurant, so he thawed some frozen stew for himself and gave the cats the rest of their chicken liver pâté. Yum Yum nibbled it daintily, but Koko lacked appetite. He prowled the living room nervously, as if a storm might be brewing, although nothing but fine weather was predicted.

"You liked the paperhanger, didn't you?" Qwilleran said

to him, "and I think he liked you. He seems like a decent guy. I hope the police don't find a way to pin something on him."

Qwilleran was restless, too. He tuned in and rejected four out-of-county radio stations before settling on WPKX for the local news:

> A North Kennebeck motorist driving west on Ittibittiwassee Road narrowly escaped injury when a vehicle behind him, which had been speeding and weaving across the yellow line, passed recklessly, forcing him off the pavement. Following this and other similar incidents, the sheriff's department has announced a new war on drunk driving . . . In other news: Pickax will have posies this summer. Fifty flower boxes on Main Street have been planted with petunias . . . Sports news at this hour: The Pickax Miners beat the Brrr Eskimos in softball tonight, eight to three.

Next Qwilleran tried the out-of-town newspapers, but even the *Daily Fluxion* and *Morning Rampage* failed to capture his attention. He made a cup of coffee and drank only half of it. He wanted to phone Polly but was reluctant to do so; he would have to explain the female architect.

In desperation he pulled *Moby Dick* off the shelf—a book he had not read since college days—and the first three words grabbed his attention: "Call me Ishmael." Halfway through the first paragraph he settled down with enjoyment. This was the kind of literature that he and Polly used to read aloud during lazy weekends in the country. He was still reading when the 2:30 A.M. freight train sounded its mournful whistle on the north side of town. The Siamese had long since fallen asleep.

And he was still reading when a succession of sirens screamed up Main Street. It sounded like three police cars and two ambulances. A major accident, he told himself. Another drunk driver leaving a bar at closing time. Reluctantly he closed the book and turned out the lights.

Qwilleran slept well that night and dreamed richly. He was embarking on a whaling voyage . . . *seeing the watery part of the world . . . a sailor aloft in the masthead, jumping from spar to spar like a grasshopper.* He was not ready to give up his dreaming when the telephone jolted him awake.

"Qwill, have you heard the news on the radio?" It was Francesca. She and her father had a habit of phoning at an unreasonable hour.

"No," he mumbled. "What time is it?"

"Seven-thirty. There was a car-train accident last night."

"Did you wake me up to tell me that?"

"Wake up, Qwill, and listen to me. Three youths were killed when they rammed their car into the side of a moving freight train."

Qwilleran grunted. "Someone's going to get sued if they don't do something about those dark crossings: no street lights; no red warning lights; no barricades." He was fully awake now. "Kids get a few beers, drive seventy in a forty-five-mile zone, with the radio blasting so they can't hear the train whistle. What does anyone expect?"

"Please, no soliloquy, Qwill. I called to tell you that the victims were three teenagers from Chipmunk, and one of them was Chad Lanspeak!"

Qwilleran was silent as he sorted out his reactions and groped for words.

"I know it's going to be rough on Carol and Larry," Fran went on, "but here's the significance of the accident. Dad says it winds up the Fitch case! The other two kids were the prime suspects!"

Still he said nothing.

"Qwill, have you gone back to sleep?"

"Sorry, Fran, I haven't had my coffee yet. I'll have to think about this for a while. We'll talk about it later."

He replaced the phone gently and touched his moustache almost reverently. It was tingling as it did in moments of intuitive premonition. It was telling him that the car-train accident, no matter what others might say, had no bearing on the investigation of the Fitch murders.

ACT ONE—CURTAIN

INTERMISSION

FOLLOWING THE DEATH of the prime suspects, the concerned citizens of Moose County were noticeably relieved. It was over! Everyone knew the homicide detective had returned to his headquarters in the state capital.

Furthermore, it was June, and they had weddings, graduations, parades, fireworks, picnics, family reunions, and camping trips to think about. Conversation in the coffee shops returned to normal: the weather, fishing conditions off Purple Point, and the selection of a beauty queen for the Fishhook Festival in Mooseville.

Qwilleran alone failed to share their relief. The state detective, he told himself, had left town to catch the real criminals off-guard. It might take time, but someone, somewhere, would be deluded into a false sense of security. Someone would return to the scene of the crime. Someone would talk too freely in a bar. Someone would inform the police.

An uneasy sensation on Qwilleran's upper lip convinced him that the final curtain had not fallen on the Fitch murder case.

ACT TWO

SCENE ONE

Place: Qwilleran's apartment; later, Stephanie's restaurant
Time: Late afternoon on the day following the car-train accident

QWILLERAN SAT AT the big desk in his cork-lined studio, writing a letter of condolence to Carol and Larry Lanspeak. The Siamese were sitting on his desk in parallel poses—Yum Yum waiting to grab a paper clip and Koko hoping to lick a stamp, a quarter inch of pink tongue protruding in anticipation.

Yum Yum had leaped to the desktop first, arranging her parts in a tall, compact column. She sat on her haunches with forelegs elegantly straight, forepaws close together, tail wrapped around her toes clockwise. Koko followed suit, arranging himself alongside the female in an identical pose, even to the direction of the tail. They were almost like twins, Qwilleran thought, although Koko's strong body and noble head and intelligent eyes and imperious mien gave him a masterful aura that could not be mistaken.

"I feel sorry for the Lanspeaks," he said to the Siamese. His voice sounded rich and mellow, thanks to the cork wallcovering, and the cats liked a rich, mellow, male voice. "I can provide Chad's alibi for the night of the murder, but the Chipmunk stigma will always link him to the killers in the public memory. As the saying goes . . . 'lie down with dogs; get up with fleas.' "

Koko scratched his ear in sympathetic agreement.

"I'm not convinced that the Chipmunk hoodlums killed Harley; there are too many alternatives. I may be beating the drum for an unpopular cause, but I'm going to follow my instincts." He groomed his moustache with his fingertips.

"Harley disappeared for a year after graduation, and no one really knows where he went or what he was doing. He could have been mixed up in almost anything. Just because he was an admirable figure in Pickax, it doesn't follow that he played that role out of town. He was a versatile actor, and he liked to play against type. That Boris Karloff bit he was rehearsing was his kind of number."

Koko blinked in apparent acquiescence; Yum Yum maintained her wide-eyed, baffled, blue stare.

"His year of sowing wild oats, if that's what it was, could have led to blackmail. He could have made enemies. He might have experimented with drugs and become involved with a drug ring. And a sexual escapade with some questionable character, male or female, is not beyond the realm of possibility."

Both cats squeezed their eyes, as if this were heady stuff.

"There's no telling what a young man will do when he cuts loose from his family and hometown. He might have run up gambling debts that he couldn't pay. It was odd that he married Belle in Las Vegas instead of at the Old Stone Church."

Qwilleran was swiveling his chair back and forth as he spoke. Abruptly he stopped and caressed his moustache.

"And another possibility! David may have been a silent partner in Harley's adventure. Their grandfather was a bootlegger. Rumrunners from Canada used to land their goods on his beach. Perhaps something else has been landing on that beach. David's house would make a good lookout station."

Both cats now had their eyes closed and were swaying slightly.

"I hope I haven't bored you," he said. "I was just airing a few theories."

He finished writing his note to the Lanspeaks. His messages of sympathy were always beautifully worded; a sincere fellow-feeling had always been one of his assets as a newspaper reporter.

As he was addressing the envelope the telephone rang, and he swiveled to reach it on the table behind him. It was a call from Iris Cobb, manager of the Goodwinter Farmhouse Museum. In her usual cheery voice she asked, "Would you like to come over and see the museum, Mr. Q, before it opens to the public? You could come to dinner, and I'd make pot roast and mashed potatoes and that coconut cake you like."

"Invitation accepted, Mrs. Cobb," he replied promptly, "provided the coconut cake has apricot filling."

She had been his housekeeper when he and the Siamese lived in the big house, and the old formality of address still existed between them. It was always "Mr. Q" and "Mrs. Cobb."

"You could bring Koko and Yum Yum," she suggested. "I miss the little dears, and they'd enjoy prowling around this big place after being cooped up in your apartment."

"Are you sure they'd be welcome in the museum?"

"Oh, yes, they never do any damage."

"Except for an occasional ten thousand–dollar vase," Qwilleran reminded her. "What day did you have in mind?"

"How about Sunday at six o'clock?"

"We'll be there!" He made a mental note to buy a pink silk scarf at Lanspeak's. Pink was Mrs. Cobb's favorite color. He missed his former housekeeper's cooking. Now, as live-in manager of the museum, she had one wing of the farmhouse as a private apartment—with a large kitchen, she said. The invitation sounded promising.

Qwilleran turned back to his desk and found the desktop strewn with paper clips; the envelope he had been addressing was gone, and two cats were missing. A telltale slurping under the desk led him to Koko and a limp, sticky envelope.

"Okay, you scoundrels," he said as he crawled under the desk. "I consider this antisocial behavior. Shape up, or you'll get no pot roast on Sunday."

When the telephone rang a second time, he stowed the envelope in a drawer. It was five o'clock, and he knew who would be on the line.

"I'm about to leave the studio, Qwill. Do you mind if I drop in to check on Pete's work?"

"Sure, come along, Fran. It's a big success. The cork gives the room a good acoustical quality."

"I knew it would, and your voice sounds perfectly magnificent!" she said. "See you in five minutes." She sounded gayer than usual.

Francesca has been to lunch with a client, Qwilleran thought. To the Siamese he said, "She's coming for a drink, and I don't want anybody grabbing her ankle or stealing her personal property."

Shortly after, the designer turned her own key in the lock downstairs and bounced up to the apartment in high spirits.

"Scotch?" he asked.

"Make it light. I had a lo-o-ong lunch date with a new

client. Don Exbridge! I'm doing his new condo in Indian Village."

Qwilleran huffed silently into his moustache. The recently divorced Exbridge was a developer and one of the most eligible catches in town; women melted at his smile.

They carried their drinks into the studio, and Qwilleran sat at his writing desk while Francesca curled up in the big lounge chair where he did his creative thinking and occasionally a little catnapping. She curled up with more abandon than usual, he noted. He said, "The cork walls were a good choice for this room, Fran."

"Thank you. Pete did a great job. He always does."

"Even with mitered stripes?"

"Ah! The Brrr Blabbermouth has been telling tales!" she said with a grimace. "That stripe job was one of my early mistakes. At lunch today Don Exbridge asked for plaid wallcovering in his den, and I vetoed it in a hurry. I told him his whole condo development is out-of-square. He just smiled his enchanting smile. He's very easy to get along with. We're going to Chicago to choose some things for his place."

Qwilleran frowned. "When are you and I flying Down Below to choose my bedroom furnishings?"

Fran reacted with surprise and pleasure. "How about next week? There's a new king-size four-poster I want you to see."

"I don't want anything that looks as if George Washington slept in it," he objected.

"This bed is contemporary. Stainless-steel posts with brass finials. And there are some new case pieces from Germany that you'll like—very neo-Bauhaus. Do you mind if I make the hotel reservations? I know a cozy place near the showroom district—expensive, but it'll go on your bill, and it won't hurt a bit. How about next Wednesday? If we catch the morning shuttle to Minneapolis, we can be in Chicago for lunch."

Qwilleran thought, When Polly finds out about this, it will be the coup de grace.

Fran said, "What else did Big Mouth tell you?"

"About the pink elephants and red velvet that he installed for Harley and Belle. Was that one of your mistakes?"

"NO!" she thundered in her best stage voice. "My boss handled that transaction. Amanda will sell clients anything they want, whether it's bad taste or utterly impractical or illegal. She's corrupt, but I like her."

"Arch Riker is going to marry Amanda."

"I hope he has a sense of humor. He'll need it!"

"Have you heard how the bank will replace Nigel and the boys?"

"Nothing official, but the rumor is that two women officers will be elevated to VP, and a new president will come in from Down Below. I hope he'll need an interior designer."

"Where were you when you heard about the suicide?" he asked.

"At the hairdresser's. Everyone cried. People really loved Nigel. He was so suave and good-looking and charming!"

"I was having dinner at the Old Stone Mill," Qwilleran said, "and one of the waitresses dropped a tray when she heard the news. I presume Nigel was suave, good-looking, charming, and a big tipper."

"Now you're playing the cynical journalist. Bravo!" she said. "Did you hear that Margaret's place on the library board is going to be filled by Don Exbridge?"

Qwilleran grunted in disapproval. Exbridge was the developer who had tried to have the historic courthouse demolished. He said, "Exbridge will convince the city to tear down our historic public library, so he can build a new one for $9.9 million."

"Now you're being vicious as well as cynical!" There was an amused glint in her steely, gray eyes. She liked to goad him. "Don would also like to replace Nigel on the Klingenschoen board of trustees."

"Perfect!" Qwilleran said. "He can manipulate Klingenschoen grants to buy political favors, like rezoning, tax abatement, sewers, and other benefits for his private enterprises . . . May I freshen your drink? Then we'll go to Stephanie's for dinner." Mischievously he added, "I heard some curious news last week. I heard that Harley disappeared for a year after finishing college." He knew it would ruffle her.

"He didn't *disappear!* He traveled for a year. For centuries young men have taken the grand tour before settling down. Nothing unusual about that!" She was on the defensive now.

"The consensus is that he did something unconventional during his year of freedom."

"Stupid gossip!" she said testily.

"Did he travel by plane, motorcycle, or camel?"

"Frankly, I never thought it important to ask."

"Did he discuss his itinerary?"

"The Fitches would consider it tacky to bore people with their travels. And he didn't bring home any color slides or French postcards or plastic replicas of the Taj Mahal. . . . What am I getting? The third degree?"

"Sorry . . . How's David? Have you seen him, or talked with him?"

"I talk to Jill on the phone every day," Fran said, relaxing after her brief flurry of annoyance. "She thinks David's on the verge of a breakdown. They're going away for a few weeks—to a quiet place in South America where they spent their honeymoon."

"I suppose David will inherit everything."

"I really don't know." She looked at her watch. "The restaurant stops serving at nine o'clock."

"Okay, let's go . . . as soon as I feed the cats."

"Did you ever find my cigarette lighter?"

"No, but Mr. O'Dell has been alerted to look for it when he cleans."

The Siamese had retired to their apartment and were studiously watching birds from the windowsill. Qwilleran put a plate of tenderloin tips on a placemat in their bathroom, turned on the TV without the audio, and quietly shut the door to their apartment.

On the drive to Stephanie's he said, "Is it true that Harley's grandfather was a bootlegger?" He expected another indignant rebuttal.

"Yes!" she said with delight. "He believed people were going to drink anyway, and if he smuggled in good stuff from Canada, they wouldn't go blind from drinking rotgut. He didn't believe in Prohibition, income tax, or corsets for women."

The draped tables at Stephanie's were placed in the original rooms of the old house, and Qwilleran and his guest were seated in the second parlor. The late sun was still beaming through the stained-glass windows, turning the beveled mirrors and wine glasses into rainbows. Over dinner they discussed the new theater.

Qwilleran said, "They're installing the seats this week. It should be available for rehearsals in August. Do you still want to open with an original revue?"

"Well . . ." Fran said indecisively, "under the circumstances we thought of doing a serious play and asking David to take a role. Something challenging and worthwhile might renew his interest in life. He's so depressed that Jill is afraid he'll follow his father's example."

Qwilleran thought, If David is involved in the situation that led to Harley's execution, he has good reason to be depressed. He could be the next victim. To Fran he said, "Do you have any particular play in mind? Nothing Russian, I hope; it would push him over the brink."

"And nothing too bloody," she said.

"And nothing about two brothers."

A mellifluous voice could be heard in the front parlor, where there were four or five tables for diners. It was a man's voice, talking earnestly, then laughing heartily.

"I recognize that voice," Qwilleran said. "But I can't place it."

Fran peered over his shoulder. "It's Don Exbridge!" she said brightly. "And he's with a woman. I think it's Polly Duncan! They seem to be having a go-o-od time." She looked teasingly smug. "Aren't you going to send drinks over to their table?"

Qwilleran scowled as a ripple of pleasant laughter came from the front parlor. It was Polly's gentle voice. After that he was impatient with the rest of the dinner: the salad was limp; the hazelnut torte was soggy; the coffee was weak. He was impatient with Fran's conversation. He was impatient to send her on her way, impatient to get home to the sympathetic Siamese. Not once, he recalled, had she mentioned Koko and Yum Yum during the evening; he doubted whether she even knew their names. Not once had she remarked about the new newspaper or commented on the column he was writing. On the whole he was sorry he had agreed to fly Down Below to look at a stainless-steel bed and some neo-Bauhaus chests. There was nothing wrong with his present bedroom furniture. He felt comfortable with it. He had always felt comfortable with Polly, too. He had never felt entirely comfortable with Francesca.

On arriving home he went first to the cats' apartment to

check on possible drafts from an open window and to turn off the TV. They were both asleep in one of the baskets, curled up like yin and yang. Then he flicked on the light in the bathroom to see if they had finished their dinner, and to give them fresh water.

The scene was one of havoc! Yum Yum's commode was overturned, and its contents had been flung about the room. A shiny object, half-buried in a damp mound of kitty gravel, proved to be a silver cigarette lighter.

Something, Qwilleran thought, is radically wrong with that cat! She used to be so fastidious! Tomorrow she goes to the doctor!

SCENE TWO

Place: Qwilleran's apartment
Time: The morning after Yum Yum's demonstration
Featuring: AMANDA GOODWINTER

AS HE DIALED the animal clinic to make an appointment for Yum Yum, Qwilleran thought, It was stupid of me to buy her a plastic dishpan; she wanted equal rights! She wanted an oval roasting pan like Koko's.

He was explaining the situation to the receptionist at the clinic when the doorbell rang—three insistent rings. Only one person in Pickax rang doorbells like that.

Amanda Goodwinter clomped up the stairway complaining about the weather, the truckdrivers on the construction site, and the design of the stairs—too steep and too narrow. The love of a good newspaperman had done nothing to improve her disposition or her appearance. Wisps of gray hair made a spiky fringe under the brim of her battered golf hat, and her washed-out khaki suit looked unfitted and unpressed.

"I came to see if my free-loading assistant is making any progress," she said, "or is she just taking long lunch hours with clients?"

"I think you'll be pleased with what she's done," Qwilleran said.

"I'm never pleased with anything, and you know it!" She trudged around the apartment, glaring at the wallcoverings and built-ins and accessories, mumbling and grumbling to herself.

"Francesca plans to design some enclosures for the radiators," he said.

"Planning it is one thing; doing it is another." She straightened the gunboat picture, which Koko had tilted again. "Where did you get this print?"

"From an antique shop in Mooseville that's run by an old sea captain."

"It's run by an old flimflam artist! He never went farther than the end of the Mooseville pier! There are ten copies of this picture floating around the county—all cheap reproductions, not original prints. The only original is in the Fitch mansion, and it's there because I sold it to Nigel as a birthday present for Harley. Never did pay me for it!"

"I understand you helped the family with their decorating," Qwilleran said.

"There's nothing anyone could do with that place except burn it down. Did you ever see the junk old Cyrus collected? They're supposed to be treasures. Half of it's fake!"

"The paperhanger told me they have some pretty wild wallpapers."

"Arrgh! That tramp Harley married! I gave her what she wanted, but I made sure it's peelable wallpaper. I hope somebody has the sense to peel it off! They should go in with a backhoe and shovel out all the crap! All those mangy stuffed animals and molting birds and phony antiques! Don't know what they'll do with the old mausoleum now. Might as well dynamite the whole thing and build condos."

"Would you like to sit down, Amanda, and have a cup of coffee?"

"No time for coffee! No time to sit down!" She was still tramping back and forth like a nervous lioness. "Besides, that stuff you call coffee tastes like varnish remover."

"With the Fitch family virtually wiped out," Qwilleran said, "this community has suffered a great loss."

"Don't waste any tears over that crew! They weren't as perfect as the lunkheads around here like to think."

"But they were civic leaders—active in all the service clubs and all the fund-raising drives. They served the community unselfishly." He was aware that he was baiting her.

"I'll tell you what they were up to, mister; they were polishing their egos! Fund-raising—pooh! Just try to get any money out of their own pocketbooks, and it was a different story. And were they ever slow to pay their bills! I should've charged 'em the same interest the bank charges!"

Qwilleran persisted. "The daughter of the janitor at the bank is going to art school, and Nigel Fitch personally paid her tuition."

"The Stebbins girl? Hah! Why not? Nigel's her natural father! Stebbins has been blackmailing him for years! . . . Well, I can't stay here all day, completing your education." She started down the stairs. Halfway down she said, "I hear you're going to Chicago with my assistant."

"We have to choose some furniture for my bedroom," Qwilleran said. "By the way, when's the wedding?"

"What wedding?" she shouted and slammed the front door.

SCENE THREE

Place: Black Bear Café
Time: Evening of the same day
Introducing: GARY PRATT, barkeeper, sailor, and friend of Harley Fitch

QWILLERAN HAD three reasons for driving to the Hotel Booze in Brrr on Thursday evening. He had a yen for one of their no-holds-barred hamburgers. Also, he wanted another look at the black bear that had scared the wits out of him at his birthday party. But mostly, he wanted to talk with Gary Pratt, the barkeeper who had sailed with Harley on the *Fitch Witch*.

He telephoned Mildred Hanstable, who lived a few miles west of Brrr, to ask if she would like to meet him for a boozeburger. She would, indeed! Women never declined Qwilleran's invitations.

She said, "I'd like to see what Gary's done to the hotel since his father let him take over."

"I hope he hasn't cleaned it up too much," Qwilleran said. "And I hope Thumbprint Thelma hasn't quit. I wonder if they still set ant traps under all the tables."

The Hotel Booze was built on a sandhill overlooking the

lakeside town of Brrr. It was an old stone inn dating back to pioneer days when there were no frills, no room service, no bathrooms, and (on the third floor) no beds. In its "Publick Room" miners and sailors and lumberjacks gathered on Saturday nights to drink red-eye, eat slumgullion, gamble away their pay, and kill each other. From those turbulent days until the present the hotel had been distinguished by its rooftop sign. Letters six feet high spelled out the message: BOOZE ROOMS FOOD.

Most of Moose County considered the Hotel Booze a dump. Nevertheless, everyone went there for the world's best hamburgers and homemade pie.

Qwilleran and his guest met in the parking lot and walked together into the Publick Room, now renamed the Black Bear Café. At the entrance the bear himself stood on his hind legs, greeting customers with outstretched paws and bared fangs.

"The room looks lighter than before," Mildred observed.

Qwilleran thought it was because they had washed the walls for the first time in fifty years. "And they repaired the torn linoleum," he said, looking at the silvery strips of duct tape crisscrossing the floor. "I wonder if they reglued the furniture."

He and Mildred seated themselves cautiously on wooden chairs at a battered, wooden table. A sign on the empty napkin dispenser read: PAPER NAPKINS ON REQUEST, 5¢.

Behind the bar was a hefty man with a sailor's tan, an unruly head of black hair and a bushy black beard, lumbering back and forth with heavy grace, swinging his shoulders and hairy arms as he filled drink orders calmly and efficiently.

Mildred said, "Gary's getting to look rather formidable. I'm glad he's taking an interest in the business. He didn't show much promise in school, but he made it through two years of college and stayed out of trouble, and now that his father is ill he seems to be showing some initiative."

Towering boozeburgers were served by a young waitress in a miniskirt. "Where's Thelma?" Qwilleran asked, remembering the former waitress who ambled out in a faded housedress and bedroom slippers.

"She retired."

Thelma had always served the toppling burgers with her thumb on top of the bun; now they were skewered with cocktail picks.

Mildred said, "I hope I didn't disgrace myself at the office party Saturday night."

"They were pouring the drinks too stiff. I had three corned-beef sandwiches and two dill pickles and regretted it later."

"I liked your column on Edd Smith, Qwill. It's about time he had some recognition."

"He's amazingly well-read. He quotes Cicero and Noel Coward and Churchill as easily as others quote the stars in a TV serial. But how does he make a living in that low-key operation? Does he have a sideline? Extortion? Counterfeiting?"

"I hope you're only trying to be funny, Qwill. Edd is an honest, sweet-natured, pathetic little man . . ."

". . . who keeps a deadly weapon next to his toothbrush."

"Well, I have a handgun, too. After all, I live alone, and in summer all those batty tourists come up here."

"Speaking of handguns," he said, "I was having dinner at the Old Stone Mill when we heard that Nigel had shot himself, and one of the waitresses reacted very emotionally. I hear she's an art student. Her name is Sally."

"Yes, Sally Stebbins. She received a scholarship from the Fitch family, and I imagine she felt the loss deeply."

"How did she rate a scholarship? Is she a good artist?"

"She shows promise," Mildred said. "Fortunately her father works at the bank, and Nigel has always taken a paternal interest in employees and their families." She regarded him sharply. "I hope you're not resurrecting the old gossip."

"Is it worth resurrecting?"

"Well, I may as well tell you, because you'll dig until you find out anyway. There was a rumor that Nigel was Sally's real father, but it was a despicable lie. Nigel's integrity has always been beyond reproach. He and Margaret were simply wonderful people."

Qwilleran gazed at her intently and fingered his moustache. Did she believe what she was saying? Was it the truth? What could anyone believe in this northern backwoods where gossip was the major industry? He asked her, "What was your reaction to the car-train accident?"

Mildred shook her head sadly. "I regret the loss of human life, but it seems like poetic justice if they're the ones who killed Harley and Belle. Roger says the police haven't found the jewels. Did you know some valuable pieces are missing? They're hushing it up, but Roger has a friend in the sheriff's office."

The waitress in the miniskirt announced the pie of the day: strawberry. It proved to be made with whole berries and real whipped cream, and Qwilleran and his guest devoured it in enraptured silence. Then Mildred inquired about the Siamese.

"Koko's okay," he said, "but I had to take Yum Yum to the vet. I phoned him about her problem, and he told me to bring her in with a urine sample."

"Interesting! How did you manage that?"

"Not with a paper cup! I had to buy a special kit—a minuscule sponge and some tiny tweezers—and then sit in the cats' apartment for five hours, waiting for Yum Yum to cooperate. When the mission was finally accomplished I took her to the clinic with the sponge in a plastic bag the size of a Ritz cracker. I felt like a fool!"

"How did Yum Yum feel?"

"Hell hath no fury like a female Siamese who hates the vet. As soon as she saw the cold, steel table, the fur began to fly. Cat hairs everywhere! Like a snowstorm! She was probed and poked and squeezed and stuck with a thermometer. The vet was murmuring soothing words, and she was howling and struggling and snapping her jaws like a crocodile."

"Did he find anything wrong?"

"He said it's all psychological. She's objecting to something in her life-style or environment, and I don't think it's the new wallpaper. In my opinion she's jealous of the interior designer."

"Really?" said Mildred. "How does Koko react to the designer?"

"He ignores her. He's too busy sniffing glue."

Over the coffee Mildred said, "Confidentially, Qwill, is Roger doing all right at the paper?"

"He's doing fine. He has a history teacher's nose for accurate facts, and he writes well."

"I worried about his giving up a good teaching position—with a new baby in the family and Sharon not working. But I guess his generation is more daring than ours."

"Speak for yourself, Mildred. I, for one, like to make daring decisions."

"Have you decided to get married again?" she asked hopefully.

"Not *that* daring!"

After she said good night, adding that she wanted to be

home before dark, Qwilleran moved to a stool at the bar. He had been there before, and Gary Pratt remembered his drink: Squunk water with a dash of bitters and a slice of lemon.

"How do you explain your policy on paper napkins?" Qwilleran asked him.

"Everything costs money," Gary said in a surprisingly high-pitched voice. "The bank stopped giving me free checks, and the gas station stopped giving me free air. Why should I give them free napkins?"

"I admire your logic, Gary."

"The thing of it is, when I kept the dispensers full of napkins they were always disappearing. My customers used them to blow their nose, clean their windshield, and God knows what else."

"You've convinced me! Here's my nickel. I'll take a napkin," Qwilleran said. He nodded toward the mounted bear at the entrance. "I see you've employed a new bouncer."

"That's Wally Toddwhistle's work. He's the best in the business."

"I'm interviewing Wally tomorrow for the paper."

"Mention the Black Bear Café, will you?" Gary said. "Give us a plug. Tell them the hotel is over a hundred years old, with the original bar." He ran a towel over its scarred surface with affection. "My old man let the place run down, but I'm fixing it up. Not too fancy, you know. We get a lot of boaters, and they like the beat-up look."

Qwilleran glanced around the room and noticed boaters with striped jerseys and tanned faces, farmers in feed caps, men and women in business suits, and elderly folks with white hair and hearing aids. All were eating boozeburgers and strawberry pie and looking happy—with one exception. A sandy-haired man seated a few stools down the bar was drinking alone, hunched over his beer in a posture of dejection. Qwilleran noticed he was wearing expensive-looking casual clothes and a star sapphire on his little finger.

"How long has the big sign been on the roof?" Qwilleran asked Gary.

"Since 1900, as far as I can trace it. It's visible from the lake. In fact, if sailors line up the steeple of the Brrr church with the *Z* in 'Booze,' it'll guide 'em straight through the channel west of the breakwall." He filled an order for the barmaid and returned to Qwilleran. "Some folks in town object to 'Booze' in such big letters, but, the way I see it, it's a friendly word. Boozing means sitting around, talking and taking it easy while you sip a drink. It goes back to the fourteenth century, only it was spelled b-o-u-s-e in those days. I looked it up."

Gary had professional aplomb. His black eyes roamed about the café constantly, all the while he talked and worked. He would pour a shot of whiskey, greet a newcomer, ring up a tab, nudge a boisterous customer on the shoulder, wipe the bar, mix a tray of martinis for the barmaid, draw a pitcher of beer, caution a masher, wipe the bar again.

"The thing of it is," he explained to Qwilleran, "Brrr is a harbor of refuge for boats, the only one this side of the lake. I want the café to be a place where everyone can come and feel comfortable and at home."

"I understand you're a sailor yourself."

"I've got a catamaran. She's been in a few races. I used to sail with Harley Fitch, but those days are over. Too bad! Harley and David used to come in here a lot, and we'd talk boats. Not David so much; he's a golf nut. Shoots in the low seventies. Ever see Harley's model ships?"

"No, but I've heard about them. Pretty good, I guess."

"I tried to buy one of his America's Cup racers for the café, but he wouldn't part with it. The thing of it is, he was getting kind of funny toward the end."

"How do you mean—funny?"

"There was his marriage, for one thing. That was all wrong. But there were other things. When he went to work for the bank, I tried to get a loan to improve this place. If I'm gonna rent the rooms, I gotta put in an elevator and bring everything up to code. All that takes money—a lot of money. His father was president of the bank, you know, and I thought we were good friends and could work out a deal."

The barkeeper moved away to refill a glass. When he returned, Qwilleran said, "Did the loan go through?"

Gary shook his shaggy black hair. "No dice. I was really teed off about that, and I gave it to him straight from the shoulder. We had a row, and he never came in here again . . . I didn't care. The thing of it is, he was never the same after he came home."

"Came home from where?" Qwilleran asked with a display of innocence. "From college?"

"No, he was, uh . . . David came home and went into the bank with his father, but Harley spent a year in the east before he came home."

Qwilleran ordered another Squunk water and then leisurely inquired what Harley was doing in the east.

Gary's black eyes roamed the room. "The family didn't want anybody to know, and people made a lot of wild guesses, but Harley told me the truth. When you get out there on the lake with a blue sky full of sail and only the whisper of a breeze, it's easy to talk. It's like going to a shrink. That was before things turned sour between us, you know. I promised to keep mum about it."

Qwilleran sipped his drink and glanced idly at the backbar with its nineteenth-century carvings and turnings and beveled mirrors.

Gary said, "I didn't say anything about it when the police were here. After the murder they were talking to everybody that knew him."

Qwilleran said, "Do you think Harley's secret mission may have had some bearing on the murder?"

Gary shrugged. "Who knows? I'm no detective."

"Personally," Qwilleran said in his best confidential manner, "I'm not convinced the Chipmunk kids were responsible for the crime, and I think we should do everything we can to bring the real criminals to justice. At the moment I'm wondering if Harley made enemies during his year away from home. Did he get mixed up in gambling or drugs?"

"Nothing like that," said the barkeeper. "I could tell you, I suppose. It doesn't make any difference now that he's dead, and his folks are dead."

Qwilleran's mournfully sympathetic eyes were fixed on Gary's shifting black ones.

Gary said, "But I'd be crazy to tell a reporter. I know you're writing for the paper. Are you digging up some dirt about the Fitches?"

"Nothing of the kind! I'm concerned because Carol and Larry Lanspeak are good people, and I hate to see their boy falsely linked to the murder."

Gary was silent and thoughtful as he wiped the bar for the twentieth time. He glanced around the room and lowered his voice. "Harley's folks said he was traveling out of the country. The thing of it is . . . he was doing time."

"He was in jail?"

"In prison—somewhere in the east."

"On what charge?"

"Criminal negligence. Car accident. A girl was killed."

"Did Harley tell you this?" Qwilleran asked.

"We were still friendly then, and he wanted to get it off his chest, I guess. It's tough living with a secret in a tight little place like Moose County."

"And there's always the chance that someone from outside will come into town and reveal it."

"Or some skunk of a newspaper reporter will dig it up and make trouble."

"Please!" Qwilleran protested.

"Maybe I shouldn't have told you."

"In the first place, I don't consider myself a skunk of a reporter, Gary, and in the second place, my only concern is to find a clue to the identity of the killer—or killers."

"Can you make anything out of it—the way it stands now?"

"One possibility comes immediately to mind," Qwilleran said. "The victim's family may have thought Harley paid too small a price for his negligence. They obviously knew he was affluent. So they came gunning for him. An eye for an eye . . . and a little jewel robbery on the side. I understand the Fitch jewels are missing."

"If you talk to anybody about it," Gary said, "don't get me involved. I can't afford to stick my neck out. When you have a bar license, you know, you have to walk on eggs."

"Don't worry," Qwilleran said. "I protect my sources. Actually, I suspect the police already know about Harley's prison term, but I'm glad you told me . . . It is a far, far better thing that you do than you have ever done—to paraphrase a favorite author of mine."

"That's from an old movie," Gary said.

"Ronald Colman said it. Dickens wrote it."

The barkeeper became affable. "Do you sail?"

"You're looking at a one hundred-percent landlubber."

"Any time you want to go out, let me know. There's nothing like sailing."

"Thanks for the invitation. What's my tab? I've got to be going."

"On the house."

"Thanks again." Qwilleran slid off the bar stool and then

turned back to the bar. "Did anyone ever tell you, Gary, that you look like a pirate?"

The barkeeper grinned. "The thing of it is, I'm descended from one. Ever hear of Pratt the Pirate? Operated in the Great Lakes in the 1800s. He was hanged."

On the way out of the café Qwilleran gave the black bear a formal salute. Then he sauntered out of the hotel, pleased with the information he had gleaned. He ambled to the parking lot, unaware that he was being followed. As he unlocked the car door he was startled by the shadow of someone behind him. He turned quickly.

The man standing there was the blond barfly with the star sapphire and the melancholy mood. "Remember me?" he asked sullenly.

"Pete? Is that you? You startled me."

"Wanted to talk to you," the paperhanger said.

"Sure." When Pete made no move to begin, Qwilleran said, "Your car or mine?"

"I walked. I live near here."

"Okay. Hop in." They settled in the front seat, Pete slumped in an attitude of despair. "What's bothering you, fella?"

"Can't get her off my mind."

"Belle?"

Pete nodded.

"It will take time to get over that horrible incident," Qwilleran said, going into the sympathy routine that he did so well. "I understand your grief, and it's healthy to grieve. It's something you have to muddle through, one day at a time, in order to go on living." He was in good form, he thought, and he felt genuinely sorry for this hulk of a man whose tears were beginning to trickle down his face.

"I lost her twice," Pete said. "Once when he stole her

away from me . . . and once when he got her murdered. I always thought she'd come back to me some day, but now . . ."

"The shooting wasn't Harley's fault," Qwilleran reminded him. "Both of them lost their lives."

"Three of them," Pete said.

"Three?"

"The baby."

"That's right. I had almost forgotten that Belle was pregnant."

"It was my kid."

Qwilleran was not sure he had heard correctly.

"That was my kid!" Pete repeated in a loud and angry voice.

"Are you telling me that you were sleeping with Belle after her marriage?"

"She came to me," Pete said with a glimmer of pride. "She said he wasn't doing her any good. She said he couldn't do anything."

Qwilleran was silent. His fund of sympathetic sentiments was not equipped for this particular situation.

"I'd do anything to get the killer," said Pete, snapping out of his dejected mood. "I heard you talking in the bar. *I'd do anything to get him!*"

"Then tell me anything you know—anyone you suspect. Frankly, it might save your hide. You're in a sticky situation. Were you doing any work for Harley and Belle at the time of the murder?"

"Papering a bedroom for a nursery."

"Were you working that day?"

"Just finishing up."

"What time did you leave?"

"About five."

"Was Harley there?"

"She said he was out sailing. He did a lot of sailing. He had a boat berthed at Brrr—a twenty-seven-footer."

"Who was with him? Do you know?"

Pete shook his head. "He used to go out with Gary from the Booze. Then Gary got his own boat, and Harley stopped coming into the bar. I saw him at the Shipwreck Tavern a coupla times, though—with a woman."

Qwilleran remembered Mildred's tarot cards. *A deceitful woman involved!* "Do you know who she was?"

Pete shrugged. "I didn't pay that much attention."

"Okay, Pete. I want you to think about this. Think hard! Think like a cop. And if you come up with anything that might throw suspicion in any direction, you know how to reach me. Now I'll drive you home."

Qwilleran dropped the paperhanger at a terrace apartment halfway down the hill and waited until the man was indoors. Then he drove home, wondering how much of the story was true.

That Pete hated Harley for stealing his girl was undoubtedly a fact. That Pete hated Belle for deserting him was a possibility. That Harley proved to be impotent and that Belle turned to Pete for solace might be a wild fantasy in the mind of a disappointed lover. In that case, Pete was a logical suspect. He had the motive and the opportunity, and in Moose County everyone had the means. Belle was the first to be killed, according to the medical examiner. She and Pete might have argued in the bedroom, and he might have shot her in a fit of passion. But he was cool enough to wreck the room and make it look like burglary. One would suppose that he was about to leave the house with the smoking gun and a few jewels in the pocket of his white coveralls, when Harley returned from sailing. They met in the entrance hall. Perhaps they had a few words about the fine weather for sailing and the difficulty of hanging wallpaper in an old house with walls out-of-square. Then Pete presented his bill and Harley wrote him a check. Perhaps Harley offered him a drink, and they sat in the kitchen and had a beer, after which they said "Seeya next time" and Pete pulled out his gun and eliminated Harley.

There was a flaw in this scenario, Qwilleran realized. Harley would be wearing sailing clothes, and the newspaper account stated that both victims were in their "rehearsal clothes." Also, it was 7:30 when David and Jill approached the mansion and saw a vehicle speeding away on the dirt road, creating a cloud of dust.

More likely, Pete was innocent. He left at five o'clock with his ladders and paste buckets. Harley came home and changed into rehearsal clothes while Belle (who was also in rehearsal clothes for some unexplained reason) put a frozen pizza in the microwave. And then the murder vehicle arrived.

Qwilleran was too tired to figure out how the murderers first killed Belle upstairs and then killed Harley downstairs. Furthermore, there was the possibility that Roger's information from the medical examiner had been distorted by the Pickax grapevine. Slowly and thoughtfully he mounted the stairs to his apartment. At the top of the flight the Siamese were waiting for him, sitting side by side in identical attitudes, tall and regal, their tails curled around their toes—counterclockwise this time. He wondered if the direction had any significance.

SCENE FOUR

Place: The Toddwhistle Taxidermy Studio in North Kennebeck
Time: The next morning
Introducing: MRS. TODDWHISTLE

IN MAKING HIS appointment with Wally Toddwhistle, Qwilleran asked for directions to the studio.

"You know how to get to North Kennebeck?" Wally asked. "Well, we're east of Main Street . . . I mean west. You know Tipsy's restaurant? You go past that till you get to Tupper Road. I think there's a street sign, but I'm not sure. If you get to the school, you've gone too far, and you'll have to turn around and come back and turn right on Tupper—or left if you're coming from Pickax. You go quite a ways down Tupper. There's a shortcut, if you don't mind a dirt road—not the first dirt road; that one dead-ends somewhere. There's another dirt road. . ."

A woman's voice interrupted—a throaty voice with a great deal of energy behind it. "I'm Wally's mother. If Wally stuffed owls the way he gives directions, he'd have the feathers on the inside. Got a pencil? Write this down: Two blocks past Tipsy's you turn left at the motel and go nine-tenths of a mile. Turn left again at the Gun Club and we're the third farmhouse on the right—with a sign out in front. Pull in the side drive. The studio's out back."

On the way to North Kennebeck Qwilleran visualized Mrs. Toddwhistle as a large woman with football shoulders, wearing army boots. Wally himself always looked hollow-eyed and undernourished, but he was a nice kid—and talented.

He allowed an hour for lunch at Tipsy's and even had time to stop at the Gun Club. The pro shop, open to the public, was stocked with rifles, shotguns, handguns, shells, scopes and camouflage clothes. Here and there were mounted pheasants, ducks, and other game birds.

"Help you, sir?" asked the brisk man in charge.

"Just passing by and stopped for a look," Qwilleran said. "Are the birds Wally Toddwhistle's work?"

"Yes, sir! Certainly are!"

"The sign in the window says you teach the use of firearms."

"Certainly do! We don't sell anything to anybody unless they know how to use it. We have classes for children and adults, ladies included. Safety is what we stress, and care of the firearm."

"Do you sell many handguns?"

"Yes, sir! A lot of hunters are using handguns."

"Do you find people buying them for personal protection?"

"Our customers are sportsmen, sir!"

Qwilleran priced the handguns and then went on his way to the taxidermy studio. There was a neat, white farmhouse with lace curtains in the windows and the usual lilac bush by the door and a modern pole barn in the rear. That was the studio.

He was greeted by Mrs. Toddwhistle, with Wally two

steps behind her. She was not what he expected, being short and chunky and aggressively pleasant. "Have any trouble finding us, honey?" she asked. "How about a cup of coffee?"

"Later, thanks," he said. "First I'd like to talk to Wally about his work. I saw the stuffed bear at the Hotel Booze last night."

"*Mounted* bear, honey," the woman corrected him in a kindly way. "We don't stuff animals any more, except birds and small mammals. Wally buys or builds a lightweight form and pulls the skin over it like a coat. It's more accurate and not so goshdarned heavy . . . is it, Wally? When they used to stuff animals with excelsior, mice got into them and built nests. My husband was a taxidermist."

"I stand corrected," Qwilleran said. "Be that as it may, the bear looks great! They've got it spotlighted."

"Very bad to have a mounted animal under a spotlight or near heat," she said. "Dries it out . . . doesn't it, Wally? And all the smoking in Gary's bar is going to ruin the pelt. It's beautiful work. A shame to spoil it! Wally didn't charge half enough for that job."

They were in an anteroom with several specimens on display: a bobcat climbing a dead tree, a pheasant in flight, a coyote raising its head to howl. Qwilleran directed a question to the silent taxidermist. "How long have you been doing this work?"

His mother was relentless. "He probably doesn't even remember . . . do you, Wally? He was only a few years old when he started helping his daddy scrape skins. Wally always loved animals—didn't want to hunt them—only preserve them and make them look real. I help him with scraping the meat off the hides, getting the burrs and straw out of the pelts—things like that."

"May I ask you a favor, Mrs. Toddwhistle?" Qwilleran

began amiably but firmly. "I have a problem. I've never been able to interview two persons at the same time, even though I've been a reporter for twenty-five years. I have an unfortunate block. Would you mind if I interviewed your son first? After that I'd like to sit down with you and get your story—and have that cup of coffee."

"Sure, honey, I understand. I'll go back to the house. Just give me a buzz on the buzzer when you're done." She bustled from the studio.

When his mother had gone, Wally said, "I haven't heard from Fran. What's the club going to do about a summer show?"

"No summer show, but they plan to do a serious play in September, with rehearsals beginning in August. No doubt you'll be called upon to build the sets, although I don't know who'll design them. Jill is taking David to South America for a few weeks. He's having difficulty adjusting, and she wants to get him away for a while."

"I'm having a hard time accepting it, too," said Wally. "After I heard about the murder, I couldn't work for days; I was so nervous. I'm glad it's all over."

"I'm not convinced of that. New evidence may come to light."

"That's what my mother says. She used to work for the family when Mr. and Mrs. Fitch lived in Grandpa Fitch's house."

"She did?" Qwilleran patted his bristling moustache.

"She cooked for them after my dad died. That's why the murder hit me so hard, and then Mrs. Fitch's stroke and Mr. Fitch's suicide! It was terrible!"

Following this revelation Qwilleran had to struggle to keep his mind on the interview. Wally conducted him into a barnlike area that was a bewildering combination of zoo, furrier's workroom, animal hospital, butcher shop, catacomb, and theater backstage. There were freezers, oil drums, a sewing machine, a wall of bleached animal skulls, a skeletonic long-legged bird. A shaggy, white wolf, not yet fitted with eyes and nose, lay stiffly on its side, its forelegs wrapped in bandages. A brown bear hide was being stretched on a board to make a rug. Fox, skunk, owl, and peacock, were in various stages of dress and undress.

Some of the animals were alive: dogs with wagging tails, a cage of small fluttering birds, a menacing macaw chained to a perch. An orange cat was curled up on a cushion, asleep.

Wally was eager to show and tell: A box of glass eyes included eleven kinds for owls and twenty-three for ducks. "We have to be authentic," he said . . . Plastic teeth, tongues, and palates were for animals being mounted with open mouths. Real teeth, Wally explained, would crack and chip . . . There were ear-liners for deer. He showed how he turned the ears inside out and glued the liners in to stiffen them . . . Also in evidence were animal forms in yellow plastic foam. "They're manikins." Wally said. "They're good because I can sculpture the foam to fit the skin, then coat the manikin with skin paste, pull the skin over it, fit it and adjust it."

Qwilleran said, "You seem to do a lot with adhesives."

"Yes, it takes all kinds—glue, skin paste, and epoxy for things like putting rods in leg bones. I repaired a damaged eyelid by gluing on a piece of string and painting it. You could never tell anything was wrong."

The young man was an artist at reconstructing animals, making them lifelike, bringing out their natural beauty, but Qwilleran was impatient to see his mother again. The buzzer brought her running from the house with coffee and freshly made doughnuts. He edged into the subject of the Fitch family diplomatically.

"I was their cook for seven years," Mrs. Toddwhistle said with pride. "Practically a member of the family."

"I hear the house is a virtual museum."

She rolled her eyes in disapproval. "Grandpa Fitch was a collector. They have tons of stuff all over the house and it all had to be dusted and vacuumed. They even have a man come in to dust the books."

"Why did you leave their employ?"

"*Well!*" she said with an emphasis that promised a significant story. "The mister and missus moved to a condominium, and they wanted me to stay and cook for Harley and his bride, but I said *no way!* Belle was the girl who did the dusting, and I certainly wasn't going to take orders from her! All she liked was pizza! She had eyes set close together. Some men think that's sexy, but I say you can't trust anybody with eyes set close together. Harley only married her to spite his parents. He knew it would embarrass them."

Wally said, "Mother, do you think you should talk about that?"

"Why not? They're all dead. Everybody knows it anyway."

Quickly Qwilleran put in, "Why was Harley antagonistic to his family? He seemed like such an agreeable guy."

"Well, you see, Harley was away for a while, and when he came back he found that David had married his girl! Way back in high school it was always Harley and Jill, David and Fran—football games, proms, sailing and everything. It was quite a shock to everybody when Jill married David."

"How did Mr. and Mrs. Fitch feel about it?"

"It was okay with them! They paid for a big wedding. Jill's folks couldn't have afforded such a blast, although they used to have money. Jill comes from good stock."

"I wonder how Fran reacted to the switch."

"I don't know. She didn't come around any more after that. She's a nice girl, with a lot on the ball, but I guess the missus thought she wasn't good enough for David."

Qwilleran combed his moustache with his fingertips. "I didn't know parents dictated their kids' lives any more. It sounds archaic."

"*Money,* honey," said Mrs. Toddwhistle, making a "gimme" gesture with her fingers. "Mister and missus got the boys hooked on high living—boats and cars and all—then doled out just enough money so they'd heel and sit up." (One of the dogs trotted over and sat up, expecting a crumb.) "Yes, they gave Harley a big sailboat, but it wasn't in his name. The fancy house that David and Jill live in—it's not theirs, not a stick of it."

"Wally says you don't subscribe to the Chipmunk theory about the murder."

"I sure don't! The police ought to talk to that old boyfriend of Belle's. He was plenty mad when he got jilted."

"The paperhanger?"

She nodded. "He's a quiet kind of fellow, but still waters run deep . . . Another doughnut, honey?"

After his third doughnut, Qwilleran thanked them for the refreshments and the interview and left, saying, "That's a beautiful cat you have. I have a couple of Siamese at home."

"Oh, the orange one?" Mrs. Toddwhistle said. "It was killed on the highway, and Wally found it and brought it home. He didn't want to see such a beautiful animal wasted . . . did you, Wally?"

Later in the afternoon Qwilleran sat at his desk in the studio and tried to organize what he had learned about the art of taxidermy. There was something about salting fresh hides to draw out moisture and tie in the hairs, removing skunk scent with tomato juice or coffee grounds, freezing skins until they could be scraped and tanned. Yet, his mind kept returning to Mrs. Toddwhistle's gossip. It threw some light on the Fitch family and explained Francesca's ruined romance, but it did nothing to further Qwilleran's unofficial investigation. He was hearing conflicting tales from all sides, and he never knew whether his informants were lying or guessing or talking through their hats. Koko, his silent partner in so many previous adventures, seemed to be of no help in pinpointing the truth.

Yum Yum sensed his frustrated mood and sat on the desk with hunched posture and worried eyes. Koko was elsewhere, probably in the living room on the bookshelves.

Qwilleran said to her, "All that cat does is sniff bookbindings and hang around waiting for an envelope to lick. I think your friend Koko is hooked! And it's affecting his senses."

"YOW!" came a loud comment from the living room, and Qwilleran went to track it down. Koko was perched on the back of the sofa, tilting the gunboat picture again.

Qwilleran patted his moustache with sudden comprehension. He would visit the decrepit antique shop in Mooseville, where a bogus sea captain had sold him an "original print" that was only a copy!

SCENE FIVE

Place: The Captain's Mess, an antique shop in Mooseville
Time: Saturday afternoon
Introducing: CAPTAIN PHLOGG

ON SATURDAY MORNING Qwilleran took the gunboat print off the wall and drove to the resort town of Mooseville to follow up Koko's obvious clue.

The evening before, he had phoned Mrs. Cobb at the museum. "What do you know about The Captain's Mess?" he asked. "What do you know about Captain Phlogg?"

"Oh, dear, I hope you didn't buy anything from that old quack," she said.

Qwilleran mumbled something about wanting to write a column on the shop. "Do you know when it's open? There's no listing in the phone book."

"It's open when he feels like it. Saturday afternoon would be the safest."

"See you Sunday," he said. "I have two friends here who are looking forward to your pot roast."

Driving up to the lakeshore he recalled buying the gunboat print from the fraudulent Captain Phlogg. The living room needed a large picture over the sofa, and the two-by-three-foot print was the best he could find for the money. The captain's asking price was twenty-five dollars, but Qwilleran had talked him down to five, including frame.

The shop occupied an old building that was ready to collapse. Both the fire department and the board of health wanted it condemned, but local history buffs declared it a historic site, and the chamber of commerce considered it a tourist attraction. After all, "the worst antique shop in the state" was a distinction of sorts. Collectors came from miles away to visit the crooked little shop run by a crooked little sea captain. Only a town like Mooseville would take pride in an establishment famous for infamy.

Qwilleran arrived at noon on Saturday, hoping for a chance to talk with Captain Phlogg before customers started dropping in, but it was 1:30 before the proprietor approached the premises with unsteady gait and unlocked the door with shaking hand.

The interior reeked of mildew, stale tobacco, and whiskey. A lightbulb dangling from a cord illuminated the collection of dusty, broken, tarnished, water-stained, dirt-encrusted artifacts of marine provenance. Captain Phlogg himself—with his ancient pipe and stubble of beard and battered naval cap—blended into the mess.

Qwilleran showed him the gunboat. "Do you remember this?"

"Nope. Never see'd it afore."

"You sold it to me last summer."

"Nope, it never come from here." The captain had an all-sales-final, no-money-back policy that caused him to disclaim everything he had ever sold.

Qwilleran said, "You sold it to me for five dollars, and I've just found out it's worth hundreds. I thought you'd like to know." Qwilleran enjoyed fighting falsity with falsity.

The captain took the foul-smelling pipe from his mouth. "Lemme look at it . . . Give ye ten for it."

"I wouldn't part with it. It's one of two very rare prints, according to art historians. The other is in the Cyrus Fitch collection. Does that name ring a bell?"

"Never heard of it."

"It's in West Middle Hummock. There was a murder there, week before last. A young sailor named Harley Fitch."

"Never heard of 'im."

"His boat was the *Fitch Witch.*"

"Never heard of it."

"He docked around here and hung out at the Shipwreck Tavern."

"Never go there."

"He also built model ships."

"Never heard of 'em."

"Do you know a sailor by the name of Gary Pratt in Brrr?"

"Nope."

"If the model ships come on the market, would you be interested in buying any of them?"

"How much he want?"

"I don't know. He's dead. But the estate might be willing to sell."

"Give 'em ten apiece."

"Is that a firm offer?"

"Take it or leave it be." The captain poured an amber liquid from a flask into a mug and took a swig.

Qwilleran departed with his gunboat picture, grumbling at Koko for giving him a false clue. It never occurred to him that he might have misinterpreted Koko's maneuver.

SCENE SIX

Place: The Goodwinter Farmhouse Museum
Time: Sunday evening
Introducing: Iris Cobb, resident manager of the museum

Qwilleran carried a wicker picnic hamper into the cats' apartment. "All aboard for the Goodwinter Museum!" he announced. The Siamese, who had been sunning drowsily on a windowsill, raised their heads—Koko with anticipation, Yum Yum with apprehension. While the male hopped eagerly into the hamper, the female—suspecting another visit to the clinic—raced around the room faster than the eye could see. Qwilleran intercepted her in midair, dropped her into the travel coop and closed the lid.

Koko scolded her with macho authority and she hissed with feminist spunk as Qwilleran carried the hamper downstairs to the energy-efficient two-door that served his transportation needs. He also transferred the cats' commodes to the car. They now had a matched pair of oval roasting pans with the handles sawed off to fit the floor of the back seat.

It was a half-hour drive to the museum in North Middle Hummock—out Ittibittiwassee Road and across the Old

Plank Bridge, then past the Hanging Tree, where a wealthy man once dangled from a rope. Beyond were prosperous farms and country estates. At the end of a lane lined with maple trees stood the rambling farmhouse, sided with cedar shakes that had long ago weathered to a silvery gray. Qwilleran had visited the house before, when it was occupied by the socially prominent Mrs. Goodwinter. Now the property of the Historical Society, it had been restored to the way it looked one hundred years before.

He drove to the west wing and unloaded the two roasting pans. "Where shall I put these?" he asked without ceremony when his former housekeeper greeted him at the door.

"Oh, you have *two* litterpans now!" she said in surprise.

"A new arrangement—at the request of our Siamese princess."

"Put the pans in the bathroom," she said. "I put a bowl of water in there and a placemat for their dinner. They always loved my pot roast."

"Who didn't?" Qwilleran said over his shoulder as he returned to the car for the hamper. When he opened the lid two necks stretched upward and two heads swiveled to survey the scene. Then the cats emerged cautiously and began a systematic exploration of the resident manager's apartment.

With these important matters concluded, Qwilleran observed the amenities. "You're looking very well," he told his hostess. "Your new responsibilities agree with you."

Her cheerful face, framed by a ruffled pink blouse, was radiant as she peered through the thick lenses of pink-rimmed glasses. "Oh, thank you, Mr. Q!"

"How are your eyes, Mrs. Cobb?"

"No worse, thank heaven." She was a plump and pleasant woman, overly good-hearted, inclined to be sentimental, and brave in the face of the tragedies that had marked her life.

"How do you feel about living out here alone? Do you have a good security system?"

"Oh, yes, I feel very safe. Our only problem, Mr. Q, is mice. We've been thoroughly inspected by the carpenter, mason, plumber, and electrician, and none of them can figure out how the mice are getting in. There's an ultrasonic thing, but it doesn't discourage them. I've set traps with peanut butter and caught three."

"I hope they haven't done any damage to the museum."

"No, but it's something we worry about . . . Would you like to look around the apartment while I wash the salad stuff?"

The focus of her living quarters was the country kitchen, where a round oak table and pressed-back chairs were ready for dinner. (Dinner for three, Qwilleran noticed. Nothing had been said about another guest.) There was a small bedroom with an enormous bed—the kind Lincoln would have liked. And there was a parlor with wing-back chairs in front of the fireplace, a rocker in a sunny window, and a large Pennsylvania German wardrobe that had been in the Klingenschoen mansion at one time. Koko soon discovered the sunny window. He even recognized the wardrobe. Yum Yum stayed in the kitchen, however, where the pot roast was putting forth tantalizing aromas.

Mrs. Cobb said, "I invited Polly Duncan because she helped with research for the museum, but she had a previous engagement. So I called Hixie Rice. She's been advising us on publicity, you know. She had a date to go sailing this afternoon, but she'll be here a little later."

"Hixie is always good company," Qwilleran said, wondering if Polly really had another engagement, or if she was avoiding him.

"You'll never recognize the main part of the house when you see it," Mrs. Cobb said as she twirled the lettuce in a salad basket. "Remember all that decorator-type wallpaper?

When we removed it, we found the original walls had been stenciled, so we did some research on stenciling and got the paperhanger to restore it for us. He was very cooperative. He's a nice young man but down in the dumps because his girl jilted him and married someone wealthy. I told him to forget his old flame and find a girl who'll appreciate him. He's almost thirty; he should get married . . . Now prepare for a surprise!"

She led the way into a section of the house built in the mid-nineteenth century and now restored to the simplicity of pioneer days. Furnishings such as a rope bed, trestle table and pie safe had come from the attics of Moose County residents.

"We want it to look as if our great-great-grandparents still live here," she said. "Can't you just imagine them cooking in the fireplace, reading the evening prayers by candlelight, and taking Saturday night baths in the kitchen?"

The floors sloped; the floorboards were wide; the six-over-six windows had some of the original wavy glass. Mrs. Cobb conducted the tour with professional authority while Qwilleran and Koko tagged along, the latter sniffing invisible spots on the rag rugs and rubbing his back against furniture legs. Yum Yum stayed in the kitchen, guarding the pot roast.

"And now we come to the east wing, added in 1890. We use these rooms to exhibit collections. Here's the Halifax Goodwinter Room with the doctor's collection of lighting devices—from an early rush lamp to an elegant Tiffany lamp in the wisteria pattern—very valuable."

At this remark Qwilleran kept a close watch on Koko, but the cat was not attracted to art glass. He merely rubbed his jaw against the corner of a showcase.

"The Mary Tait MacGregor Room is all textiles. Old Mr. MacGregor gave us his wife's quilts, hooked rugs, jacquard coverlets and so on, all handed down in her family." Koko rolled on a hooked rug done in a distelfink pattern.

The Hasselrich Room featured Moose County documents, which Qwilleran said he would like to study at some future date: land grants, early birth and death certificates, journals of nineteenth-century court proceedings, and ledgers from old general stores, itemizing kerosene at a nickel a gallon and three yards of calico for fifteen cents.

"It breaks my heart to show you the next room, considering what happened," said Mrs. Cobb. "Nigel was president of the Historical Society, and he didn't even live to see it dedicated. That rolltop desk belonged to Cyrus Fitch, and in one of the drawers we found a list of his bootleg customers. Imagine! He was smuggling whiskey during Prohibition! They're all dead now, except Homer Tibbitt."

The cut glass, she said, was donated by Margaret Fitch. A punch bowl, decanters and other serving pieces were dazzling under artfully placed spotlights, but not dazzling enough to capture Qwilleran's full attention. He was getting hungry. Nigel had contributed his collection of mining memorabilia: pickaxes, sledgehammers, miners' caps, lanterns, etc., and David had done pen-and-ink sketches of the shafthouses at the old mines.

Qwilleran tried to subdue his rumbling stomach and then realized that the disturbance was actually a low growl coming from Koko's chest. The cat had discovered a tiered platform exhibiting three model ships. He stood on his hind legs and pawed the air, weaving his head from side to side and looking exactly like one of the rampant cats on the Mackintosh coat of arms.

"Oh, look at him!" cried Mrs. Cobb. "Isn't that touching? Those models were made by Harley Fitch! The three-masted schooner is a replica of one that sank off Purple Point around 1880."

"I think Koko smells the glue," Qwilleran said. "He's a fiend for glue. We'd better get him out of here before he launches a naval attack."

A car drove into the yard, and Qwilleran grabbed Koko while Mrs. Cobb went to greet Hixie Rice.

Sunburned and windblown and clad in sailing stripes, shorts and deck shoes, Hixie breezed into the house. "I hope you don't mind how I look. I've been sailing with one of my customers. He has a catamaran. I never knew sailing could be so *divine!"*

"You should put something on that sunburn," Mrs. Cobb advised as she served Hixie a Campari.

Qwilleran said, "I wondered why the Black Bear Café was running such large ads in the *Something.* You've been cozying up to the proprietor. I hope you know he's descended from a pirate."

"I don't care if he's descended from a dinosaur! He has a beautiful boat. We're going out again next Sunday."

"He used to sail with Harley Fitch. Did he mention the *Fitch Witch?"*

"No, he talked mainly about himself . . . and how a blue skyful of sail and a whispering breeze touches the soul of a man."

The pot roast was succulent; the mashed potatoes were superlative; the homemade bread was properly chewy; the coconut cake was ambrosial. So said the guests, and Mrs. Cobb basked in their compliments.

Hixie summed it up. "Forget about the museum, Iris, and open a restaurant. Half the places that run ads in our paper are vile! The ethnic restaurants are the best bet. There's a super little eatery in Brrr called the North Pole Café, where they serve the best *zupa grzybowa* and *nerki duszone* I've ever tasted. North *Pole!* Get it?"

"How about Italian food?" Qwilleran asked.

"There's a fabulous place in Mooseville that's a real mama-and-papa operation. He cooks, and she waits on table. When I went there to pick up their ad order, I went to the restroom and got locked in. I hammered on the door, and I heard Mrs. Linguini yell, 'Papa, lady locked in the toilet! Bring a toothpick!' After a while there was a picking sound in the lock, and Mr. Linguini opened the door, looking cross. He said, 'You do it wrong. I show you.' And he came into the washroom and locked the door. Of course, the mechanism didn't work, and I was locked in the ladies' room with Mr. Linguini!"

"How did you get out?" asked Mrs. Cobb, seriously concerned.

"He hammered on the door and yelled, 'Mama, bring a toothpick!' Oh, it's lots of fun selling ads for the *Moose County Something.*"

Qwilleran said, "Hixie, you should write a guide to the restaurants and restrooms of the county."

"Don't think I haven't thought of it! All I need is a snappy title that's fit to print."

After coffee she excused herself, saying she wanted to get home before dark, although Qwilleran suspected she was going back to the Black Bear Café. He walked her to her car.

"Since you're so keen on creative journalism," he said, "why don't you ask your sailing partner if he killed Harley and Belle in order to finance the remodeling of the hotel. A skyful of sail and a whispering breeze and thou might loosen his tongue."

"You want me to accuse him of murder while we're five miles out in the lake and I'm ducking the boom? No thanks!" She gunned the motor and took off.

Qwilleran chuckled. Hixie had always dated men on the shady side of respectability. He returned to the house where

Mrs. Cobb was touching a match to the kindling in the fireplace.

"We'll have our second cuppa here," she said. "It'll be cozy. That Hixie is a clever girl, isn't she? And nice looking. I wonder why she doesn't get married."

They sat in the wing chairs. Koko, stuffed with pot roast, went to sleep on the hearth rug. Yum Yum still preferred the kitchen.

"Wonderful little animals," she said. "I miss them."

"And they miss your cooking . . . I do, too," he added with more feeling than he usually displayed before his former housekeeper.

She breathed a heavy sigh that summed up all the misadventures they had survived at the Klingenschoen mansion. She was looking prettier than usual in her pink ruffled blouse, with the dancing flames lighting her face. He remembered the pink scarf and dashed out to the car for the Lanspeak giftbox tied with pink ribbon.

"Oh, real silk!" she cried. "And my favorite color. You remembered!" Her tear-dampened eyes were enlarged by the strong lenses in her eyeglasses, and Qwilleran felt a surge of compassion for her. She liked male companionship, and yet all three of her marriages had ended sadly. Although she claimed to be happy, he knew she was lonely. Sometimes he wondered about himself. He had been a bachelor for ten years, telling himself it was the best way to live. Life had been agreeable while Mrs. Cobb was his housekeeper, and the meals had been superb. Now he ate in restaurants and was constantly looking for a dinner companion. His best friend, Arch Riker, would soon be married and staying home evenings. Most of the women he knew were either too aggressive or too frivolous for his taste. The head librarian was the exception, but he and Polly had played their last scene, and he knew when to bring down the curtain.

He was quiet, lulled into contentment by good food, pleasing environment, and the domestic tranquility of the moment. Mrs. Cobb seemed to sense his mood, and her eyes smiled hopefully. Only the crackling of the fire and Koko's heavy breathing broke the silence. Qwilleran wanted to say something, but for once he was at a loss for words. She was an amenable woman, a comfortable companion. He had only to say "Iris!" and she would say "Oh, Qwill!" with tears streaming down under her thick glasses.

Suddenly there was a rushing, bumping, scrambling, thumping burst of noise from the adjoining room. The man and woman ran to the kitchen. Yum Yum was lying on her side at the base of the gas range with her famous paw extended under the appliance while her tail slapped the floor.

"She's got a mouse!" Qwilleran said. He reached for her and received a snarl in response.

"Leave her alone," Mrs. Cobb said. "She thinks you want to take it away from her."

"That's where the mice are getting in—where the gas lines come into the house," he said. "No wonder she was watching the range all evening. She could hear them."

"Oh, she's a good kitty—a real good kitty!"

"She's smarter than your plumber, Mrs. Cobb."

The tail-thumping slowed and then stopped, and Yum Yum wriggled across the floor, withdrawing her long foreleg with the prize clutched in the sharp claws of her famous right paw. Koko walked into the room and yawned.

Mrs. Cobb looked at him in consternation. "Just like a man!"

Her comment took Qwilleran by surprise. It was out of character for the docile, male-worshipping widow he had known.

"Time to go home," he said, opening the picnic hamper. "It was a wonderful dinner, Mrs. Cobb, and you're to be complimented on the museum. Let me know if there's anything I can do."

With the hamper on the backseat and the two commodes on the floor, Qwilleran tooted a farewell to his hostess on the doorstep and headed the car toward Pickax. He was thankful that Yum Yum had caught her mouse at an auspicious time, saving him from an amorous slip of the tongue. He needed no more women on his trail—least of all, his former housekeeper, who was marriage oriented and tragedy prone. All three of her husbands had died violent deaths.

He drove past the Hanging Tree and across the Old Plank Bridge and then west on Ittibittiwassee Road. There was little traffic. The county had built the road—at great expense—to accommodate Exbridge's condominium development. Most motorists preferred the shorter, more commercial route, however, and the local wags called the new highway Ittibittigraft.

Darkness was falling as he passed the site of the old Buckshot Mine. It was here, he recalled, that he had suffered a serious bicycle accident a year before—a highly questionable accident.

And now . . . it all happened again.

SCENE SEVEN

Place: A lonely stretch of Ittibittiwassee Road
Time: Later the same evening

IT WAS LATE Sunday night, and the traffic on Ittibittiwassee Road was sparse. Westward bound, Qwilleran met no cars approaching in the opposite direction, and he drove with his country brights illuminating the yellow lines on the pavement. On either side darkness closed in over the patches of woods, abandoned mine sites and boulder-studded pastureland. Now and then a half-moon accentuated the eeriness of the landscape, then retired behind a cloud.

Eventually headlights appeared in Qwilleran's rearview mirror—country lights excessively bright until he flicked the mirror to cut the glare. The vehicle was gaining on him. Its pattern was erratic: swerving into the eastbound lane as if planning to pass—falling back into line—coming closer—swerving again to the left. It was a van, and when it came alongside, it was too close for a prudent driver's peace of mind. Qwilleran edged to the right. The van crowded closer.

He's drunk, Qwilleran thought, and he steered close to the shoulder and eased up on the pedal. The van loomed over the small car. Another inch and it would bump him off the road. He steered onto the shoulder . . . Easy! Loose gravel! . . . Skidding! Easy! Turn into the skid! Baby the brake! . . . And then the little car hit a boulder and flipped over . . . still traveling, sliding along the edge of the ditch . . . another jolt, another rollover, twice, before it came to a shuddering halt in the dry ditch.

There was a moment of stunned disorientation—pedals and dashboard overhead—seat cushions and roasting pans everywhere—a shower of kitty gravel.

Why was there no cry from the cats?

Qwilleran unbuckled and climbed out of the door that had been thrown open by the impact. Then he crawled back into the dark car and groped for the hamper. It was lying on the upside-down ceiling, jammed under a seat cushion, its cover open, the cats gone!

"Koko!" he yelled. "Koko! Yum Yum!"

There was no answer. He thought, They might have taken flight in terror! They might have been flung from the car! In panic he searched the ditch in the immediate vicinity, looking for small light-colored bodies in the darkness. He called again. Utter silence.

Then headlights illuminated the landscape as a car approached from the east, stopping on the shoulder of the road. A man jumped out and ran to the scene. "Are you okay? Anybody hurt?"

"I'm all right, but I've lost my cats. Two of them. They may have been thrown out."

The motorist turned and shouted toward his own car, "Radio the sheriff, hon, and bring the torch!" To Qwilleran he said, "Have you tried calling them? It's heavily wooded along here. They might be hiding."

"They're indoor cats. They never go out. I don't know how they'd react to the accident and unfamiliar surroundings."

"Your car's totaled."

"I don't care about the car. I'm worried about the cats."

"The guy was drunk. I saw him weaving before he crowded you off the road. Seemed like a light-colored van."

The man's wife arrived with a high-powered flashlight, and Qwilleran started beaming it in the ditch and along the edge of the thicket.

The man said to her, "He had two cats in the car. They escaped or were thrown out."

"They'll be all right," she said. "We had a cat fall from a third-floor window."

"Quiet!" Qwilleran said. "I thought I heard a cry."

The wail came again.

"That's some kind of night bird," the woman said.

"Quiet! . . . while I call them and listen for an answer."

Headlights and a flashing red rooflight appeared in the distance, and a sheriff's car pulled up. The deputy in a brown uniform said, "May I see your operator's license?" He nodded when Qwilleran handed it over. "How did it happen, Mr. Qwilleran?"

The other motorist said, "I saw it all. A drunk driver. Crowded him off the road, and then skipped."

Qwilleran said, "I had two cats in the car, and I can't find them."

The deputy flashed a light around the wreck. "Could be underneath."

The woman said, "We'd better go, honey. The baby-sitter has to leave at 11:30."

"Well, thanks," Qwilleran said. "Here's your flashlight."

"Keep it," the man said. "You can get it back to me where I work. Smitty's Refrigeration on South Main."

The deputy wrote his report and offered Qwilleran a ride into Pickax.

"I can't leave until I find them."

"You could be out here all night, sir."

"I don't care. After you leave they may come crawling out of the bushes. I've got to be here when they do."

"I'll check back with you on my next round. We're watching this road. I nabbed four DWIs last night."

He left, and Qwilleran resumed his search, calling at intervals and hearing nothing except the night noises of the woods, as some small animal scurried through the underbrush or an owl hooted or a loon cackled his insane laugh.

He extracted the wicker hamper from the wreckage—out of shape but intact. He found the two commodes, also. The roasting pans had fared better than the body of his car. He was grateful for the flashlight.

Another vehicle stopped. "Anybody hurt?" asked the driver, walking over to view the car in the ditch. "Anyone call the police?"

Qwilleran went through the same script. "No one hurt . . . The sheriff's been here . . . No, thanks, I don't need a ride. I've lost two cats and I have to wait . . ."

"Lots of luck," the man said. "There are coyotes out there and foxes, and an owl can carry off a cat at night."

"Just go on your way, please," Qwilleran said firmly. "When it's quiet, they'll come back."

The car left the scene, but the Siamese did not appear. He snapped off the torch. It was totally dark now—totally dark with the moon behind a cloud. He called again in desperation. "Koko! Yum Yum! Turkey! Turkey! Come and get it!" . . . There was absolute silence.

Once more he combed the ditch with the beam of the flashlight, each time venturing a few yards farther from the wreck. After half an hour of fruitless searching and calling, he groaned as another car pulled up.

"Qwill! Qwill, what are you doing out here?" a woman's voice called out. She left her car and hurried toward him. "Is that your car? What happened? Has anyone called the sheriff? I have a CB." It was Polly Duncan.

"That's not the worst," he said, shining the torch on the wreck. "The cats are lost. They may be hiding in the woods. I'm not leaving here till I find them, dead or alive."

"Oh, Qwill, I'm so sorry. I know how much they mean to you." It was the quiet, soothing voice that had appealed to him during their happier days.

He recounted the entire story.

"But you can't stay here like this all night."

"I'm not leaving," he repeated stubbornly.

"Then I'll stay with you. At least you'll have some shelter and a place to sit. I'll turn my lights off. Maybe they'll sense your presence and come out . . ."

"If they're still alive," he interrupted. "The sheriff thought they might be pinned under the car. They don't answer when I call their names. Another guy said there are predators out there."

"Don't listen to those alarmists. I'll pull my car farther off the highway, and we'll sit and wait . . . No! I won't listen to any protests. There's a blanket in my trunk. It gets chilly after midnight at this time of year. Put those things in the backseat, Qwill."

He put the commodes and hamper in her car, and then he and Polly settled in the front seat of the car he had given her for Christmas. His gloom was palpable. "I don't mind telling you, Polly, how much those two characters have meant to me. They were my family! Yum Yum was getting more lovable and loving every year. And Koko's intelligence was incredible. I could talk to him like a human, and he seemed to understand every word I said. He even replied in his own way."

"You're speaking in the past tense," Polly rebuked him. "They're still alive and well—somewhere. I have enough faith in Koko to know he'll be able to take care of himself and Yum Yum. Cats are too agile to let themselves get trapped under the car. Flight is their forte, and their best defense."

"But the Siamese have lived a sheltered life. Their world is bounded by carpets, cushions, windowsills, and laps."

"You're not giving them credit for their natural instincts. They might even walk back to Pickax. I read about a cat whose family took him to Oklahoma for the winter, and he walked back to his home in Michigan—over 700 miles."

"But he was accustomed to the outdoors," Qwilleran said.

The sheriff's deputy stopped again, and when he saw Qwilleran's companion, he said, "Do you need any potatoes, Mrs. Duncan?" They both laughed. To Qwilleran he said, "Glad you've got company. I'll keep an eye on you two."

As he drove away Polly said, "I've known Kevin ever since he was in junior high, bringing his homework assignments to the library. His family had a potato farm."

Gradually she talked him out of his pessimistic mood by introducing other subjects. Nevertheless, every ten minutes Qwilleran left the car and walked up and down the roadside, calling . . . calling.

Returning from one disappointing expedition he said to Polly, "You were out late tonight."

"There was a party at Indian Village," she explained. "I usually go home early when I'm driving alone, but I was having such a good time!"

Qwilleran considered that statement in silence. Don Exbridge had a condo in Indian Village.

"The party was given," she went on, "by Mr. and Mrs. Hasselrich, honoring the library board. They're charming hosts."

"I hear Margaret Fitch's place on the board will be filled by Don Exbridge," he said glumly.

"Oh, no! Susan Exbridge is a trustee, and it would hardly

be appropriate to have her ex-husband on the board. Where did you hear that?"

"I don't recall," he lied, "but I noticed you were dining with him at Stephanie's, and I assumed you were briefing him on his new duties."

Polly laughed softly. "Wrong! The library needs a new roof, and I was trying to charm him into donating the services of his construction crew. But since you bring up the subject, I saw you dining with a strange woman after you told me you were dining with your architect from Cincinnati."

"That strange woman," Qwilleran said, "happens to be the architect from Cincinnati. You get two black marks for assuming the profession is limited to males."

"Guilty!" she laughed.

The sheriff's car was coming down the highway again, and it stopped on the opposite shoulder. When the deputy stepped out, he was carrying something small and light-colored. He was carrying it with care.

"Oh my God!" Qwilleran said and tumbled out of the car, hurrying across the pavement to meet him.

"Brought you some coffee," the deputy said, handing over a brown paper bag. "From the Dimsdale Diner. Not the best in the world, but it's hot. Temperature's dropping to fifty tonight. Couple of doughnuts, too, but they look kinda stale."

"It's greatly appreciated," Qwilleran said with a sigh of relief as he pulled out his bill clip.

"Put that away," the officer said. "The cook at the diner sent it."

The kindness of Polly and the deputy and the cook at the diner and the motorist with the flashlight did much to relieve Qwilleran's depression, although he still felt a numbness in the pit of his stomach. He wanted to talk about the cats. He said to Polly, "They're always inventing games. Now their hobby is posing like bookends."

"Does Koko still recommend reading material for you?"

"He was pushing biographies until a few days ago. Now he's into sea stories."

"Has he lost interest in Shakespeare?"

"Not entirely. I saw him nuzzling *The Comedy of Errors* and *Two Gentlemen of Verona* the other day."

"Both of those plays involve sea voyages," Polly reminded him.

"I'm sure it's the glue he's sniffing. The subject matter is coincidental. But you have to admit it's uncanny."

"There are more things in Koko's head than are dreamt of in your philosophy," said Polly, taking liberties with one of Qwilleran's favorite quotations.

And so they talked the night away.

Qwilleran said, "Now that I'm dropping out of the Theatre Club, Polly, I'm going to review plays for the paper."

"You'll make a wonderful drama critic."

"It means two passes to every opening night, fifth row, center. I hope you'll be my steady theatre date."

"I'll be happy to accept. You know, Qwill, your columns have been very good. I'm sorry I scolded you about your journalism. I especially liked your profile on Eddington Smith."

"Incidentally, when Edd and I were discussing the Fitch case, I mentioned the possibility of rare-book thieves, and he hemmed and hawed—never would say what was on his mind."

"Well, it's a possibility," she said. "I've heard that Cyrus Fitch owned some pornographic books that certain collectors would commit any crime to possess. They're said to be locked up in a small climate-controlled room along with

George Washington's Farewell Address and Gould's *Birds of Great Britain.*"

"If Edd lets me go to the mansion to help him dust books, I'll check out the hot stuff," Qwilleran said.

And then she told him something that caused him to wince. "I'm leaving for Chicago Wednesday. A library conference. I'm catching the morning shuttle."

She added a questioning glance. It was customary for him to drive her to the airport, but . . . he and Fran were also leaving on the Wednesday morning shuttle! He thought fast.

"Wait! I think I heard something!" He jumped out of the car and walked a few paces, stalling for time. Here was a ticklish situation! He and Polly were rediscovering their old camaraderie; they had shared the blanket during the chilly hours before dawn; he had hoped for reconciliation. How would she react to a jaunt to Chicago with her rival? As far as he was concerned, it was a business trip to select furniture. Would Polly accept that explanation graciously? Did Fran—with her "cozy hotel"—contemplate it as a business trip? She had made the hotel and travel reservations and would add the charges to his bill—plus an hourly fee for her professional advice, he surmised.

It was awkward at best. One half of his brain ventured to suggest canceling the trip. The other half of his brain sternly maintained his right to schedule a business trip anywhere, at any time, with anyone.

The sky was beginning to lighten in the east, and he walked back to the car. "You stay here. I'm going to look around," he said. "If they holed up for the night, they'll start getting hungry when the sun rises, and they might come crawling out. Watch for them while I go searching."

"Will the glasses help?" Reaching under the seat, Polly handed him the binoculars she used for birding.

The woods that had been a black, incomprehensible mass

in the dark of night were becoming defined: evergreens, giant oaks, undergrowth. He walked along the highway to a spot where five, tall elm trees grew in a straight line perpendicular to the road. They were obviously trees that had been planted many years before, possibly to border a path or sideroad to some old farmhouse long since abandoned. He was right. An unused dirt road, almost overrun with weeds, followed the line of trees. If the Siamese had discovered it the night before, they might have sheltered in the remains of the old farmhouse.

A light breeze rustled the lofty branches of the elms and blew strands of spiderweb across his face. Everything was wet with dew. A faint, rosy glow appeared in the east. He found the site of the house, but it was now only a stone foundation tracing a rectangle among the grasses.

He stopped and called their names, but there was no response. He walked on slowly. Now he was reaching the end of the road. Ahead were the withered trees of a long-neglected orchard, rising in grotesque shapes from a field of weeds. He scanned the orchard with the binoculars, and his heart leaped as he saw a bundle of something on the branch of an old apple tree. He walked closer. The sky was brightening. Yes! The indistinct bundle was a pair of Siamese cats, looking like bookends. They were peering down at the ground, wriggling their haunches as if preparing to leap.

He lowered the field of vision to the base of the tree and his eyes picked up something else, half concealed in the grasses. A ghastly thought flashed through his mind. Could it be a trap? A trap like those that Chad Lanspeak used for foxes? In horror he edged closer. No! It was not a trap. It moved. It was some kind of animal! It was looking up in the tree! The cats were wriggling, ready to jump down!

"Koko!" he yelled. "No! Stay there!"

Both cats jumped, and Qwilleran fled back to the car,

shouting to Polly, "I need your car! Radio the sheriff to pick you up! I've found the cats. I'm taking them to the vet!"

"Are they hurt?" she asked in alarm.

"They've had a run-in with a skunk! Don't worry . . . I'll buy you a new car."

SCENE EIGHT

Place: Qwilleran's apartment
Time: The day after the accident on Ittibittiwassee Road

QWILLERAN'S CAR HAD been towed to the automobile graveyard; Polly's cranberry-red car was at Gippel's garage, being deodorized; the Siamese were spending a few hours at the animal clinic for the same purpose.

In his apartment Qwilleran paced the floor, chilled by the realization that they might have been lost forever in the wilderness. They might have suffered a horrible death, and he would never have known their fate. The sheriff's helicopter and the mounted posse and the Boy Scout troop would hardly go searching for those two small bodies. He shuddered with remorse.

It was all my fault, he kept telling himself. He was convinced that it was no drunk driver who ran him off the road; it was someone who was out to get him because he had been asking questions about the murderer of Harley and Belle. Why did he have this compulsion to solve criminal cases? He was a journalist, not an investigator. Yet, he was aware, few journalists accepted their limitations. The profession was teeming with political advisors, economic savants, critics and connoisseurs.

No more amateur sleuthing! he promised himself. From now on he would leave criminal investigation to the police. No matter how strong his hunches, no matter how provocative the tingling sensation in the roots of his moustache, he would play it safe. He would interview hobbyists and sheep farmers and old folks in nursing homes, write a chatty column for *The Moose County Something,* read *Moby Dick* aloud to the Siamese, take long walks, eat right, live the safe life.

And then the telephone rang. It was Eddington Smith calling. "I talked to the lawyer, and he said I should check the books against the inventory. You said you'd like to help with the dusting. Do you want to come with me tomorrow?"

Qwilleran hesitated for only the fraction of a moment. What harm would there be in visiting the Fitch library? Everyone said it was an interesting house—virtually a museum.

"You'll have to pick me up," he told the bookseller. "I've wrecked my car." When he turned away from the phone he was finger-combing his moustache in anticipation.

After lunch Mr. O'Dell drove to the clinic in his pickup and brought home two bathed, deodorized, perfumed and sullenly silent Siamese in a cardboard carton punched with airholes. When the box was opened they climbed out without a glance one way or the other and stole away to their apartment, where they went to sleep.

"A pity it is," said Mr. O'Dell. "The good souls at the clinic were after doin' their best, but sure an' the smell will come back again if the weather turns muggy. It'll just have to wear off, I'm thinkin' . . . And is there anythin' I can do for you or the little ones, since you're lackin' a car?"

"I'd appreciate it," Qwilleran said, "if you'd go to the hardware store and buy a picnic hamper like the old one that was smashed."

The Siamese slept the sleep that follows a horrendous experience. Every half hour Qwilleran went to their apartment and watched their furry sides pulsating. Their paws would twitch violently as if they were having nightmares. Were they fighting battles? Running for their lives? Being tortured at the animal clinic?

Earlier Fran Brodie had telephoned. "I hear you rolled over last night, Qwill."

"Where did you hear that?"

"On the radio. They said you weren't seriously hurt, though. How are you?"

"Fine, except when I breathe. I get a stitch in my side."

"Now you'll have to drive that limousine you inherited." She enjoyed teasing him about the pretentious vehicle in his garage.

"I got rid of it. It was a gas guzzler and hard to park, and it looked like a hearse. It was only standing in the garage, losing its charge and drying out its tires, while I was paying insurance and registration fees every year. I sold it to the funeral home."

"In that case," Fran said, "we can drive my car to the airport Wednesday. We should leave about eight AM to catch the shuttle to Minneapolis. I made the hotel reservations for four nights. You'll love the place. Quiet, good restaurant—and that's not all!"

Qwilleran hung up the phone with misgivings. Burdened with other concerns, he had given no thought to this particular dilemma.

Shortly after that, Polly had called to inquire about the cats.

He said, "It's been a blow to their pride. They usually

carry their tails proudly, but today they're at half-mast. Gippel is working on your car, Polly, but I want you to have a new one, and I'll drive the red job."

"No, Qwill!" she protested. "That's tremendously kind of you, but you should buy a new car for yourself."

"I insist, Polly. Go over to Gippel's and look at the new models. Pick out a color you like."

"Well, we'll argue about that when I return from Chicago. You can use the 'red job' while I'm away. What time do you want to pick me up Wednesday morning? I'll be staying in town at my sister-in-law's."

Feeling like a coward, he said, "Eight o'clock." Not only had he failed to resolve his dilemma, he had compounded it with his dastardly acquiescence.

SCENE NINE

Place: Fitch mansion in West Middle Hummock
Time: A Tuesday Qwilleran would never forget

WHEN EDDINGTON SMITH'S old station wagon rumbled up to the carriage house Tuesday morning, Qwilleran went downstairs with the new picnic hamper.

"You didn't need to bring any food," the bookseller said. "I brought something for our lunch."

"It's not food," Qwilleran explained. "Koko is in the hamper. I hope you don't object. I thought we could conduct an experiment to see if a cat can sniff out bookworms. If so, it would be a breakthrough for some scientific journal."

"I see," said Eddington with vague comprehension. Those were his last words for the next half hour. He was one of those intense drivers who are speechless while operating a vehicle. He gripped the wheel with whitened knuckles, leaned forward, and peered ahead in a trance, all the while stretching his lips in a joyless grin.

"My car flipped over in a ditch on Ittibittiwassee Road Sunday night, and it's totaled," Qwilleran said and waited for a sympathetic comment. There was no reaction from the mesmerized driver, so he continued.

"Fortunately I had my seat belt fastened, and I wasn't hurt except for a lump on my elbow as big as a golf ball and a stitch in my side, but the cats were thrown from the car. They disappeared in the woods. By the time I found them, they'd had an altercation with a skunk, and I had to drive them to the animal clinic. Did you ever spend fifteen minutes with two skunked animals in a car with the windows closed?"

There was no reply.

"I didn't dare roll the windows down more than an inch or two, because the cats were loose in the backseat, and I didn't know how wild they'd be after their experience. I couldn't breathe, Edd! I thought of stopping at the hospital for a shot of oxygen. Instead I just stepped on the gas and hoped I wouldn't turn blue."

Even this dramatic account failed to distract Eddington's concentration from the road.

"When I got home, I took a bath in tomato juice. Mr. O'Dell raided three grocery stores and bought every can they had on the shelf. He had to burn my clothes and the cats' coop. Their commodes were in the car when it flipped, and they rattled around like ice cubes in a cocktail shaker. One of them conked me on the head. I'm still combing gravel out of my hair and moustache."

Qwilleran peered into Eddington's face with concern. He was conscious, but that was all.

"The cats were deodorized at the clinic, but there's no guarantee it'll last. I may have to buy a gallon of Old Spice. I'm trying to keep them downwind."

After a while Qwilleran tired of hearing his own voice, and they drove in funereal silence until they reached the Fitch mansion. Eddington parked the car at the backdoor in a service yard enclosed by a high, stone wall.

If the murderers had parked there, Qwilleran observed,

their vehicle would not have been visible from either of the approach roads; on the other hand, if they had stationed a lookout in the vehicle, he could not have seen David and Jill approaching. The lookout may have been patrolling the property with a walkie-talkie, he decided.

Eddington had a key to the back door, which led into a large service hall—the place where Harley's body had been found. Doors opened into the kitchen, laundry, butler's pantry, and servants' dining room. Qwilleran was carrying the wicker hamper; Eddington was carrying a shopping bag, and after groping in its depths he produced a can of soup and two apples and left them on the kitchen table. Then he led the way to the Great Hall.

Although lighted by clerestory windows 30 feet overhead, the hall was a dismal conglomeration of primitive spears and shields, masks, drums, a canoe carved from a log, shrunken heads, and ceremonial costumes covered with dusty feathers. Qwilleran sneezed. "Where is the library?" he asked.

"I'll show you the drawing room and dining room first," Eddington said, opening large, double doors. These rooms were loaded with suits of armor, totem poles, stone dragons, medieval brasses, and stuffed monkeys in playful poses.

"Where are the books?" Qwilleran repeated.

Opening another great door Eddington said, "And this is the smoking room. Harley cleared it out and moved in some of his own things."

Qwilleran noted a ship's figurehead, carved and painted and seven feet tall, an enormous pilot wheel, a mahogany and brass binnacle, and an original print of the 1805 gunboat, signed, and obviously better than his reproduction. There were several sailing trophies. And on the mantel, on shelves and on tables there were model ships in glass cases.

The hamper that Qwilleran was clutching began to bounce and swing.

He said, "Koko is enthusiastic about nautical things. Would it be all right to let him out?"

Eddington nodded his pleasure and approval. " 'Enthusiasm is the fever of reason,' as Victor Hugo said."

It was the liveliest display of spirit that Koko had shown since his ordeal. He hopped out of the hamper and scampered to a two-foot replica of the HMS *Bounty,* a three-masted ship with intricate rigging and brass figurehead. Then he trotted to a fleet of three small ships: the *Niña,* the *Pinta,* and the *Santa Maria,* all under full sail with flags and pennants flying. When he discovered a nineteenth century gunboat with brass cannon, Koko rose on his hind legs, craning his neck and pawing the air.

"Now where's the library?" Qwilleran asked as he returned a protesting cat to the hamper.

It was a two-story room circled by a balcony, with books everywhere. Although there were no windows—and no daylight to damage the fine bindings—there were art-glass chandeliers that made the tooled leather sparkle like gold lace.

"How many of these do we have to dust?" Qwilleran wanted to know.

"I do a few hundred each time. I don't hurry. I enjoy handling them. Books like to be handled."

"You're a true bibliophile, Edd."

" 'In the highest civilization, the book is still the highest delight.' That's what Emerson said, anyway."

"Emerson would have a hard time explaining that to the VCR generation. Let me close the doors and release Koko from his prison. He'll flip when he sees these books. He's a bibliophile himself."

Koko leaped from the hamper and surveyed the scene. On three walls there were banks of bookshelves alternating with sections of fine wood paneling, each with a curio cabinet containing small collectibles in disorganized array.

There were Indian arrowheads and carved ivories, seashells and silver chalices, chunks of quartz and amethyst mixed with gold figurines that might have been smuggled from an Egyptian tomb. (Amanda had said a lot of them were fakes.) Above each cabinet was a mounted animal head or a gilded clock or an elaborate birdcage or a display of large bones like relics of some prehistoric age. Koko inventoried all of this, then discovered the spiral staircase, which he mounted cautiously. It was different from any of the staircases he had known.

Meanwhile, Eddington had pulled a bundle of clean rags from his shopping bag. "You can start in that corner with *S*. I left off at *R*. Slap the covers together gently, then wipe the head and sides with a cloth. Dust the shelf before you put the books back."

By this time Koko was whirling up and down the spiral stairs in a blur of pale fur and using the balcony as an indoor track.

Eddington opened the shallow drawer of the library table, a massive slab of oak supported by four carved gryphons. He removed the drawer entirely, and, after groping inside the cavity, brought out a key. "The rare books are in a locked room with the right temperature and humidity," he said. " 'Infinite riches in a little room,' as Marlowe said." Carrying his shopping bag he unlocked a door in a paneled wall and stepped inside. Qwilleran heard the lock click.

As he started dusting he pondered how much of Eddington's time in the locked room was spent with Cyrus Fitch's torrid literature. He himself had to exercise severe self-discipline to resist reading everything he dusted: Shaw, Shelley, Sheridan, for starters.

Koko busied himself here and there, and his activity and excitement caused his deodorant to lose its effectiveness. "Go and play at the other end of the room," Qwilleran told him. "Your BO is getting a little strong."

At noon Eddington reappeared and said somberly, "Time for lunch." He looked worried.

"Anything wrong in there, Edd?"

"There's a book missing."

"Valuable?"

The bookseller nodded. "There might be more missing. I won't know till I finish checking the whole inventory."

"Could I help you? Could I read off the listings or anything like that?" Qwilleran had a great desire to see that room.

"No, I can do it better by myself. Do you like cream of chicken soup?"

Koko was now examining the far end of the room—the only wall without bookshelves. It was richly paneled, and it sealed off one end of the library under the balcony. Koko always discovered anything that was different, and this wall looked like an afterthought; it destroyed the symmetry of the room.

"Start heating the soup," Qwilleran said. "I want to finish dusting this bottom shelf."

As soon as Eddington had left, he rapped the odd wall with his knuckles. This had been a bootlegger's house, and bootleggers were known to like secret rooms and subterranean passages. He studied it for irregularities or hidden latches. He pressed the individual sections, hoping to find one less stable than the others. While he was systematically examining the wall, the library door opened.

"Soup's ready!"

"Beautiful paneling!" Qwilleran said. "Just by touching it anyone could tell it's superior to the stuff they use nowadays."

He bundled Koko into the hamper, apologizing for his scent, although Eddington insisted he didn't notice anything, and the three of them went to the kitchen for lunch.

"It isn't much," the little man said, "but 'We must eat to live and live to eat.' Fielding said that."

"You are exceptionally well-read," said Qwilleran. "I suspect you do more reading than dusting when you disappear into that little room. What kind of books do you have in there?"

The bookseller's face brightened. "*The Nuremberg Chronicle, 1493* . . . a Bay psalm book in perfect condition—the first book published in the English colonies in America . . . a first of Poe's "Tamerlane" . . . the first bible printed in America; it's in an Indian language."

"What are they worth?"

"Some of them could bring a price in five or six figures!"

"If one were stolen, would it be difficult to sell? Are there fences who handle hot books?"

"I don't know. I never thought about that."

"Which book is missing?"

"An early work on anatomy—very rare."

"A family member may have borrowed it to read," Qwilleran suggested.

"I don't think so. It's in Latin."

"I'm amazed at your knowledge of books, Edd. I wish I could remember everything I've read and come up with a trenchant quote for every occasion."

Eddington looked guilty. "I haven't done much reading," he confessed. "I took Winston Churchill's advice. He said: 'It's a good thing for an uneducated man to read books of quotations.' "

After the meagre lunch (Koko had a few bits of chicken from the soup) the party returned to the library. Eddington locked himself in the little room while Qwilleran resumed his dusting (Tennyson, Thackeray, Twain) and Koko resumed his explorations.

The hush in the library was almost unnerving. Qwilleran

could hear himself breathe. He could hear Koko padding across the parquet floor. He could hear . . . a sudden creaking of wood at the far end of the room. Koko was standing on his hind legs and resting his paws on the paneled wall that was different from the others. A section of it was moving, swinging open. Koko hopped through the aperture.

Qwilleran hurried to the spot. "Koko, get out of there!" he scolded, but the inspector general had found something new to inspect and was totally deaf. The secret door opened into a storage room—windowless, airless, stifling, and dark. Qwilleran groped for a light switch but found none. In the half-light slanting in from the library chandeliers he could see ghostly forms in the shadows: life-size figures of marble or carved wood, a huge Buddha, crude pottery ornamented with grotesque faces, a steel safe, and . . . a brass bugle! It was the one he would have used in the Theatre Club production if the show had not been canceled, and he resisted the impulse to shatter the silence with a brassy blast.

In the close atmosphere Koko's unfortunate aroma was accentuated. He was prowling in and out of the shadows, and one of the items that attracted him was an attaché case. Qwilleran had learned not to take Koko's discoveries casually, and he grabbed the case away from the purring cat. Kneeling on the floor in a patch of dim light he snapped the latches, opened the lid eagerly, and sucked in his breath at the sight of its contents. As he did so, a shadow fell across the open case, and he looked up to see the silhouette of a man in the doorway—a man with a club.

Lunging for the bugle, Qwilleran raised it to his lips and blew a deafening blast. At the same moment the man came through the door, swinging the club. Qwilleran bellowed and struck at him with the bugle. In the semidarkness both weapons missed their mark. The club descended again, and Qwilleran ducked. He swung the bugle again with both hands, like a ballbat, but connected with nothing. The two men were flailing blindly and wildly. Qwilleran was breathing hard, and the stitch in his side felt like a knife-thrust.

Dodging behind a cigar store Indian he waited for the right moment and slashed again with all his strength. He missed the man, but he struck the club. To his amazement it crumbled! Instantly he swung the brass bugle at his assailant's head, and the man sank dizzily to the floor.

Only then did Qwilleran see his face in full light. *"David!"* he shouted.

Outside the door a hollow voice roared, "Stop or I'll shoot!"

Qwilleran froze and slowly raised his hands. From the corner of his eye he could see a handgun; it was pointed at the crumpled figure on the floor.

"Edd! Where'd you get that?" he gasped.

"It was in my shopping bag," said the little man, reverting to his usual shy delivery. For the first time in his life he had projected his voice.

"Keep him covered while I call the police, Edd. He might come around and start trouble again."

As he spoke, Koko emerged from the shadows and stalked the supine figure on the floor. He was purring mightily as he rubbed his head against the sprawled legs. He climbed on the man's chest and sniffed nose to nose. The man stirred and opened his eyes, saw two blue eyes staring into his own, caught a whiff of Koko's aroma, and passed out again.

SCENE TEN

Place: Back at Qwilleran's apartment over the garage
Time: Later the same day

NO ONE TALKED on the way back to Pickax. Eddington Smith was frozen to the wheel; Qwilleran was still aghast at his recent discovery; and Koko was asleep in the hamper, which was placed at the extreme rear of the station wagon, with all the windows open.

"Thanks for the ride, Edd. Thanks for the good lunch," Qwilleran said when they arrived. "Don't forget to report that missing book to the lawyer."

"Oh, I found it! It was on the wrong shelf!"

"Well, it was an exciting afternoon, to put it mildly."

" 'Excitement is the drunkenness of the spirit,' as somebody said."

"Uh . . . yes. I'm glad you didn't have to use your gun."

"I am, too," said Eddington. "I didn't have any bullets."

It was then that Qwilleran noticed Francesca's car in the drive, and it reminded him that his troubles were not over. He carried the hamper into the garage. "Sorry, Koko. I've got to keep you down here until Fran leaves. You're smelling pretty ripe."

As he climbed the stairs to his apartment, his nose told him that Yum Yum also needed another shot of deodorant spray, and his eyes notified him that something was missing in the hallway. The Mackintosh coat of arms was not leaning against the wall in its accustomed place.

"Hello!" he called. "Fran, are you here?"

When there was no reply, he checked the premises. In the living room, lying in the middle of the floor, was the heavy circle of ornamental iron. In the cats' apartment he found Yum Yum huddled in a corner, with a pathetic expression in her violet-blue eyes. In his studio he found a red light glowing on the answer-box. He punched a button, listened to the message and then hurriedly called Francesca at home.

"Qwill, you'll never believe what happened!" she said. "I wanted to incorporate the Mackintosh thing in one of your radiator enclosures, so I went over to measure it and see how it would look. I was halfway across the living room with it . . ."

"You *lifted* that piece of iron?"

"No, I was rolling it like a hoop when I accidentally stepped on a cat, and it screeched like seven devils. I was so spooked that I rolled the damn thing over my foot!"

"Yum Yum's screech could raise the dead," he said. "I hope you're not hurt, Fran."

"Hurt! I was wearing sandals and broke three toes! A police car took me to the hospital. Dad will pick up my car later. But Qwill," she wailed, "I won't be able to go to Chicago tomorrow!"

Qwilleran heaved a sigh of relief that activated the stitch in his side, but he extended sympathy and said all the right things. After that he went to the cats' apartment, picked up Yum Yum and stroked her smelly fur. "Sweetheart," he said, "did you trip her accidentally, or did you know what you were doing?"

Immediately he telephoned Polly at the library to remind her that he was driving her to the airport in the morning. "I may board the plane with you," he added. "I know some good restaurants in Chicago."

He sprayed the cats and was serving them a small shrimp cocktail and a dish of veal Stroganoff when he happened to glance out the front window. A police car was in the driveway, and the burly figure of the chief was stepping out of the passenger's door and approaching Francesca's car with a bunch of keys.

Qwilleran opened the window. "Brodie! Come on up for a cup of coffee!"

The chief was more amiable than he had been when questioned about the Fitch case. He clomped up the stairs saying, "I hope it's not the same witch's brew you gave me once before."

Qwilleran locked the cats in their apartment, set the automatic coffeemaker for extra strong, and handed the chief a mug. "You're in a better frame of mind than the last time I saw you."

"Arrgh!" growled Brodie.

"Is that a comment on the coffee or the state investigation?"

"The case is settled now, looks like. So maybe I can talk without getting in hot water. That evidence you found in the closet cracked it wide open. It was the kind of evidence they were hoping for."

"You don't need to repeat this, but . . . it was Koko who found it! First, he discovered how to get into the secret closet."

"What did I tell you? I told you we could use him on the force."

"I never did buy the Chipmunk theory, and when I opened the attaché case, I knew it was an inside job. I figured that David had killed Harley, rifled the safe, and stashed the money and jewels and murder weapon in the closet, intending to pick it up later. That was a lot of cash for a banker to have in the house."

Brodie nodded. "The bank examiners are in town. They'll find a few shortages, I'll bet."

"I didn't know who it was when he attacked me in the dark storage room, but I knew I was fighting for my life. He had killed twice, and I had found the evidence. After I stunned him with his grandfather's bugle, I began to collect my wits, and I thought, Why would David kill his twin? What possible motive? At that moment Koko walked over to him, purring like a helicopter. When he sniffed the guy's moustache, I said to myself, That's not David on the floor; that's Harley." Qwilleran paused and caressed his moustache with satisfaction. "Koko could smell the spirit gum! The moustache was false—glued on the guy's upper lip."

"YOW!" came a stentorian cheer from down the hall.

"He knows we're talking about him," said Qwilleran.

Brodie said, "So you think you know the motive now?"

"I'm pretty sure. From what I've heard on the Pickax grapevine I've constructed a scenario. See if you think it'll play:

"Scene 1: Margaret Fitch, a manipulative mother, encourages David to marry Harley's girl, while Harley is serving time in prison for criminally negligent homicide.

"Scene 2: Harley returns home and marries a tramp to spite David, Jill, and his meddlesome parent.

"Scene 3: Harley is still carrying the torch for Jill, however, and she realizes she's still in love with him. They can't afford to divorce their mates because Margaret dominates them with an iron fiscal policy. She gives them a taste for luxuries but keeps them poor.

"Scene 4: Jill plots the embezzlement of bank funds, the murders, and Harley's exchange of identities with his twin.

"Scene 5: On the night of the murder David and Jill arrive at Harley's house at 6:30 as usual. Harley has already shot Belle, and he turns the gun on his brother. Then he exchanges their jewelry and wallets—and shaves off David's moustache. Meanwhile, Jill is staging the ransacking of the library and bedroom, packing the attaché case with money, jewels, and the murder weapon.

"Scene 6: Despite Harley's acting talent and his false moustache, his parents know he isn't David. His mother has a fatal stroke, and his father can't face the choice he has to make—either to inform the police that his son has been murdered by his twin brother, or to become an accessory after the fact and live with a heinous secret.

"Scene 7: Harley and Jill plan to disappear in South America, but their getaway is foiled."

The chief grinned and shook his head. "Even Lieutenant Hames won't believe the one about the cat and the glued-on moustache."

When the news of the showdown at the Fitch mansion leaked out, the Pickax grapevine worked overtime, and Qwilleran's phone rang all evening.

Arch Riker said, "We're remaking page one for tomorrow's paper, but there's one statement from Edd Smith that won't wash. He says you were hit on the head with a club and it shattered. We all know you're a hardhead, Qwill, but even *your* skull isn't hard enough to shatter a club."

"It wasn't a club, Arch. It looked like the thighbone of a camel. It was one of the bizarre relics on display in the library. There we were—in a dark closet—lunging at each other like Hamlet and Laertes, only those guys had rapiers, and all we had was a bone and a brass bugle. We must have looked like a couple of baggy-pants comics. When I whacked the bone with the bugle, it crumbled, and I realized it was made of plaster. Amanda says they have a lot of fakes in that place."

When Amanda herself called, she growled, "This whole stink wouldn't have happened if that family hadn't been so damned stingy with their money—and so phony about everything! Mr. and Mrs. Perfect, they thought they were! And they conned the whole county into believing it."

Gary Pratt also telephoned. "Jeez! I'm glad it's over. I probably knew more about Harley than anybody else did, sailing with him all the time. When he came home from his year in the clink, he was full of hate. He couldn't forgive David for stealing his woman."

Pete Parrott's message was brief. "I hope that SOB gets what he deserves!"

Roger MacGillivray, who had written the breaking story on the murder, said, "You know, Qwill, if it's true that Jill planned it all, she had a neat script—almost too neat. The plumbing emergency . . . the vehicle going fast down the dirt road and throwing up a cloud of dust . . . all those convincing details!"

Polly Duncan was the last to call. "Your phone has been busy all evening, Qwill. Are the rumors true? How did you know it was Harley and not David?"

"It started at my birthday party, Polly. Koko took an instant liking to Harley, Edd Smith, and Wally Toddwhistle—and later, my paperhanger. This theory may sound farfetched, but . . . they were all men who regularly worked with adhesives, and Koko is a fiend for glue. When he saw Harley's model ships, he pranced on his hind legs like the Mackintosh cat. And at the Fitch library, when he showed such an avid interest in the man on the floor, I knew it wasn't David."

Late that night, when the freight train whistled at crossings north of town, Qwilleran sprawled on the sofa and reviewed the events of the last two weeks. Yum Yum was asleep on his chest, and Koko was balancing on the back of the sofa.

"Why were you so interested in sea stories all of a sudden?" Qwilleran asked him. "Why did you keep tilting the gunboat picture? Did you sense the identity of the murderer? Were you trying to steer my attention to a sailor and builder of model ships?"

Koko opened his mouth in a wide yawn, all teeth and pink gullet. It was, after all, 2:30 A.M., and he had had a hard day.

"Was it a coincidence that you and Yum Yum started acting like bookends? Or were you pointing a paw at the *twins?*"

Koko squeezed his eyes sleepily. He was sitting tall but swaying slightly. He almost toppled off the sofa back.

"You rogue! You pretend you haven't the slightest idea what I'm talking about," Qwilleran said. "We'll try it once more . . . Would you like some turkey?"

Koko's eyes popped open, and Yum Yum raised her head abruptly. With one accord the two of them jumped to the floor, yikking and squealing as they raced to the refrigerator, where Qwilleran found them arranged in identical poses, like twins, as they stared up at the door handle.

EPILOGUE

THE PROSECUTOR IS seeking a change of venue for the trial of Harley and Jill, arguing that it will be impossible to seat an objective jury in Moose County, where the citizenry is still under the spell of the Fitch mystique.

According to Jill, who is cooperating with investigators to save her own neck, they staged the vandalism at the dental clinic to destroy the twins' dental records.

Qwilleran no longer employs the services of Francesca Brodie, and Yum Yum has reverted to her fastidious habits in the commode.

The Siamese, using their own built-in deodorant applied with long pink tongues, have dispelled the memory of the black-and-white kitty on Ittibittiwassee Road.

Qwilleran is reading *Moby Dick* aloud to the cats and spending weekends at Polly Duncan's cozy house in the country.

The Klingenschoen Theatre will open with an original revue written by Qwilleran and Hixie Rice. The hit number is sure to be "I Left My Heart in Pickax City."

Koko is learning how to turn the television off.

FINAL CURTAIN

The Cat Who Went Underground

ONE

If Jim Qwilleran had read his horoscope in the daily paper on that particular morning, perhaps none of this would have happened. But astrology had never been one of his interests.

As he drank his third cup of coffee in his bachelor apartment over the garage, he glanced at the floor, which was strewn with out-of-town newspapers. He had devoured the national and international news, studied the editorials, scoffed at the viewpoints on the Op-Ed page, and scanned the sports section. As usual he skipped the stock market reports and the comics, and he never thought of looking at the horoscope column.

The advice he failed to read was portentous. The *Daily Fluxion* said, "This is not an auspicious time to change your life-style. Be content with what you have." The *Morning Rampage* said, "You may feel restless and bored, but avoid making impulsive decisions today. You could regret it."

Comfortably unaware of this counsel from the constellations, Qwilleran sprawled in his overscale lounge chair with a coffee mug in his hand, a cat on his lap, and another on the bookshelf nearby. They were an unlikely threesome. The man was a heavyset six feet two, fiftyish, sloppily attired, with graying hair and mournful eyes, and his exceptionally luxuriant moustache needed trimming. His companions, on the other hand, were aristocratic Siamese with elegantly sleek lines and well-brushed coats, who expected pampering as their royal prerogative.

Qwilleran's ragged sweatshirt and cluttered apartment gave no clue to his career credentials or his financial status. He was a veteran journalist with worldwide experience, now retired and living in the small northern town of Pickax, and he had recently inherited millions, or billions, from the Klingenschoen estate; the exact figure had not yet been determined by the battery of accountants employed by the executors.

Qwilleran had never cared for wealth, however, and his needs were simple. He was content to live in an apartment over the Klingenschoen garage, and for breakfast on that particular morning he had been satisfied with coffee and a stale doughnut. His roommates had more discriminating palates. For them he opened a can of Alaska king crab, mixing it with a raw egg yolk and garnishing it with a few crumbles of fine English cheddar.

"Today's special: Crustacean à la tartare fromagère," he announced as he placed the plate on the floor. Two twitching noses hovered over the dish before tasting it, like oenophiles sniffing the bouquet of a rare wine.

After breakfast the Siamese huddled as if waiting for something to happen. Qwilleran finished reading the newspapers, drank two more cups of coffee, and drifted into introspection.

"Okay, you guys," he said as he finally roused himself from his caffeine reverie. "I've made a decision: We're going up to the lake. We're going to spend three months at the log cabin." He made it a policy to discuss matters with the cats.

It was more satisfying than talking aloud to himself, and his listeners seemed to enjoy the sound of a human voice making conversational noises in their direction.

Yum Yum, the amiable little female, purred. Koko, the male, uttered a piercing but ambiguous "Yow-w-w!"

"What did you mean by that?" Qwilleran demanded. Receiving only an incomprehensible blue-eyed stare in reply, he smoothed his moustache and went on: "I have three reasons for wanting to get out of town: Pickax is a bore in warm weather; Polly Duncan is away for the summer; and we're out of ice cubes."

For two years he had been living in Pickax—not by choice but in accord with the terms of the Klingenschoen will—and the old stone buildings and stone-paved streets seemed dull in June. The nearby resort town of Mooseville, on the other hand, was burgeoning with leaf, flower, bird, sunshine, blue sky, rippling wave, lake breeze, and hordes of carefree vacationers.

The second reason for Qwilleran's discontent was more vital. Polly Duncan, the head librarian in Pickax, around whom his life was beginning to revolve, was spending the summer in England on an exchange program, and he was feeling restless and unfulfilled. Although he knew little about the outdoors and cared even less for fishing, he conjectured that a log cabin on a lonely sand dune overlooking a vast blue lake might cure his malaise.

There was a third reason, less sublime but more pertinent: the refrigerator in his apartment was out of order. Qwilleran expected appliances to function without a hitch, and he showed irrational impatience when equipment broke down. Unfortunately the Pickax refrigeration specialist had gone camping in northern Canada, and the only other serviceman in the county was hospitalized with a herniated disc.

Altogether, a summer in Mooseville sounded like an excellent idea to Jim Qwilleran.

"You probably don't remember the cabin," he said to the cats. "We spent a few weeks there a couple of years ago, and you liked it. It has two screened porches. You can watch the birds and squirrels and bugs without getting your feet wet."

The seventy-five-year-old log cabin, with its acres of woodland and half mile of lake frontage, was among the far-flung holdings Qwilleran had inherited from the Klingenschoen estate, and it was being managed by the executors until the terms of the will could be fulfilled. He had only to express his wishes to the attorneys, and the property-management crew would turn on the power, activate the plumbing system, restore phone service, and remove the dust covers from the furniture.

"You don't need to worry about a thing!" attorney Hasselrich assured him with his boundless optimism. "You'll find the key under the doormat. Just unlock the door, walk into the cabin, and enjoy a relaxing summer."

As circumstances evolved, it was not that easy. The summer vacation started with a dead spider and ended with a dead carpenter, and Jim Qwilleran—respected journalist, richest man in the county, and card-carrying good guy—was suspected of murder.

But in his blissful ignorance, he had taken the attorney at his word. Preparing for the trip to the lakeshore, he packed his small car with a few summer clothes, a box of books, a turkey roaster filled with gravel that served as the cats' commode, a computerized coffeemaker, his typewriter, and the Siamese in their travel coop. This was a wicker picnic hamper outfitted with a down-filled cushion, and Yum Yum hopped into it with alacrity. Koko hung back. He had some covert catly reason for not wanting to go.

"Don't be a wet blanket," Qwilleran chided. "Jump in and let's hit the road."

He should have known that Koko's whims were not to be taken lightly. The cat seemed to have a sixth sense that detected precarious situations.

When they embarked on their jaunt to Mooseville—it was only thirty miles—the occasion had the excitement of a safari. The skies were sunny, the June breeze was soft, and the temperature was warm enough for Qwilleran to wear shorts and sandals. To avoid tourist traffic he drove north on Sandpit Road instead of the main highway, waving a friendly hand to strangers in pickup trucks and tooting a friendly horn at any farmer on a tractor. Within minutes he had shed the tensions of the City of Stone, for although the population of Pickax was only three thousand, it had the commercial bustle of a county seat. With growing elation he planned his summer. He would do plenty of reading, take long walks on the beach, go canoeing whenever the lake was calm. He also had a writing commitment: two features a week for the Moose County newspaper, to be given thumb position on page two. His column, called "Straight from the Qwill Pen," would be enjoyable to write (the editor was giving him carte blanche) and challenging enough to keep the creative juices percolating.

"Is everybody happy back there?" he called out over his shoulder without, however, hearing any reply from the hamper.

Qwilleran had only one regret about the forthcoming summer: Polly Duncan would not be there to share it with him. Her substitute, a librarian from the English Midlands, had already arrived in Pickax. Young, brash, brisk in her manner, and clipped in her speech, she was far different from Polly, who had a gentle nature and a soft, low musical voice. Polly's figure was matronly, and there were traces of gray in her unstyled hair, but she was stimulating company. Animated discussions enlivened their dinner dates, and weekends at her country hideaway made him feel twenty years younger.

As Qwilleran brooded about the absence of Polly, a car approached from the north, far exceeding the speed limit. He recognized the driver. It was Roger MacGillivray, a young reporter for the county newspaper. Qwilleran presumed wryly that Roger was rushing to the office to file a breaking story on some momentous news event in Mooseville: Someone had caught a whopping big fish, or someone's great-grandmother had celebrated her ninety-fifth birthday. Stop the presses!

Roger was a likable young man, and he had a mother-in-law who was an interesting woman. She spent summers at a cottage half a mile down the beach from the Klingenschoen cabin. Mildred Hanstable taught home economics and art in the Pickax schools, wrote the food page for the Moose County newspaper, and happened to be a superlative cook. It occurred to Qwilleran that he might expect a few dinner invitations in the forthcoming weeks. Mildred had a husband, but he was "away" and no one ever mentioned him.

Soon the potato farms and sheep ranches and sandpits were left behind, and the road plunged through lush evergreen forests. A commotion in the wicker hamper indicated that the Siamese could smell the lake air, still a mile away. Qwilleran himself noticed something different in the atmosphere—an invigorating buoyancy. It was the Mooseville magic! Every summer it attracted droves of tourists from polluted, crime-ridden urban centers in the southern part of the state, which the locals called Down Below.

"It won't be long now," he told his passengers.

The lake burst into view, a body of water so vast that its

blue met the blue of the sky at some invisible point. At the side of the road a chamber of commerce sign welcomed visitors to "Mooseville, 400 miles north of everywhere!" Here the highway ran along the shoreline, ascending gradually to the top of Mooseville's famous sand dunes. Qwilleran frowned when he encountered unusual conditions: mud on the pavement, dump trucks coming out of the woods, the whine of chain saws, the grinding din of a backhoe. He regretted the symptoms of lakefront development, while realizing it was inevitable. Next came the rustic arch marking the entrance to the Top o' the Dunes Club, a private community of summer people, Mildred Hanstable included.

Half a mile farther along he turned into a dirt road marked with the letter K on a cedar post. The wicker hamper started to bounce with anticipation. The Siamese knew! It had been two years ago, yet they remembered the scent; they sensed the environment. The private drive meandered through the woods, past wild cherry trees in blossom, through a stand of white birches, up and down over gentle dunes created by lake action eons ago and now heavily wooded with giant oaks and towering, top-heavy pines.

The drive ended in a clearing, and there was the picturesque old cabin, its logs and chinking dark with age, virtually dwarfed by the massive fieldstone chimney.

"Here we are!" Qwilleran announced, opening the top of the hamper. "You stay here while I take a look around."

While the Siamese hopped about inside the car and stood on hind legs to peer out the windows, he walked to the edge of the dune and surveyed the placid lake. Gentle waves lapped the sandy beach at the bottom of the dune with seductive splashes. The breeze was a mere caress. Flocks of tiny yellow birds were flitting in the cherry trees. And here, in this quiet paradise, he was to spend the entire summer!

As Hasselrich had promised, the key was under the mat

on the screened porch, and Qwilleran unlocked the door eagerly. The moment he opened it, a blast of frigid air slapped him in the face—the musty breath of a cabin that had been closed for the winter. He shivered involuntarily and retreated to the porch and the warmth of a summer day. Something had gone wrong! Hasselrich had failed him! Tentatively he reached a hand around the door jamb and found a wall switch; the hall light responded, so he knew the cabin had power. And someone had been there to remove the sheets shrouding the living room furniture. Qwilleran retreated hastily to the warm porch to think about this unexpected setback.

From his previous visit he vaguely remembered a heating device installed unobtrusively on one wall of the living room. Grabbing a jacket from the car and wishing he had not worn shorts and sandals, he once more braved the dank chill. Hurriedly he switched on lights and opened the interior shutters that darkened the place. The wall-heater lurked in a dim corner—a flat metal box with louvers and knobs, and a metal label that had the effrontery to read *Komfort-Heet.*

Qwilleran huffed angrily into his moustache. The thermostat was set for seventy degrees, but the thermometer registered fifty, and to him it felt like a damp thirty. He dialed the thermostat to its highest limit, but there was no rush of heat, not even a reassuring click. He gave the heater a kick, a primitive technique that worked with old steam radiators, but had no effect on the *Komfort-Heet.*

Qwilleran had spent his life in apartments and hotels, where one had only to notify the manager and a dripping faucet would be fixed or a loose doorknob tightened. About space heaters he was totally ignorant. Of one thing he was certain, however: He could not expose the Siamese to this bone-chilling cold. They were indoor cats, accustomed to central heat in winter and sunny windowsills in summer.

There was a fireplace, of course, and there were logs in the wood basket, but he could find no matches. Automatically he felt in his jacket pocket, although he had given up pipe-smoking a year before. He checked the other utilities and found that the plumbing functioned and the telephone produced a dial tone. He gave the space heater another kick and reviled its obstinacy.

At that moment he heard an impatient yowl from the car. Spitting out a suitable expletive, he looked up a number in the slim phone book that listed Mooseville subscribers.

"Good morning!" chirruped a woman's pleasant voice.

"Mildred, this is Qwill," he said abruptly. "I'm at the cabin. I just drove up with the cats to spend the summer."

"That's ducky!" she said. "You can come to the beach party tomorrow night."

"Forget parties," he snapped. "There's something wrong with the blasted heater! The cabin's like a subterranean cave! What do I do? Is there someone I can call?"

"Perhaps the pilot light's out," she said helpfully. "Did you look to see if the pilot light's out?"

"I don't even know where it is or what it looks like."

"There should be a little access door on the front—"

Qwilleran sneezed. "Just tell me who repairs these things, Mildred. I'm on the verge of double pneumonia."

"Are you on Glinko's list?" she asked.

He was losing patience. "Glinko! Who's Glinko?"

"Didn't anybody tell you about Glinko? You can call him any hour of the day or night, and he'll send a plumber, electrician, or any kind of repairman you need. It's a wonderful convenience for—"

"Okay, what's his number?" he cut in, shivering and stamping his feet.

"Not so fast, Qwill. First you have to go to his shop, sign up, pay a fee, and give him a key to your cabin."

"I don't like the idea of handing out keys indiscriminately," he said with irritation.

"People around here are perfectly honest," she said with a note of gentle reproach. "You've lived Down Below too long. You suspect everyone."

Thanking her briefly, Qwilleran dashed out to the car and dropped the cats into their travel coop again. "Sorry. You're going for another ride," he announced.

They headed for downtown Mooseville, three miles to the west, where the Huggins Hardware Store made duplicate keys.

The proprietor said, "Spending the summer up here, Mr. Q?"

"Only if I can get the chill out of the cabin, Cecil. Where can I find a repairman for a wall-heater?"

"Glinko's got 'em all tied up," said the storekeeper. "See Glinko."

Mildred had said that Glinko's place of business was right behind the post office, and Qwilleran found only one building in that location: a garage—a greasy, shabby garage with a large door standing open. There was a car inside, with its hood raised. Under the hood a pair of spindly legs in old ragged trousers could be seen waving aimlessly, while the torso was buried among the valves, spark plugs, and cylinders. There was no visible head.

"Excuse me," Qwilleran said to the waving feet. "Where can I find Glinko?"

The torso reared up, and the head came into view—a face almost obscured by a wild set of whiskers, a rat's nest of hair under a greasy beret, and a pair of bright, merry eyes. The gnomelike character slid across the fender and landed nimbly on the concrete floor. "Standin' right here," he said with a toothless grin. "Who be you?"

"My name is Qwilleran, and I'm staying at the Klingenschoen cabin near Top o' the Dunes."

The gnome nodded wisely. "That be the place with a K on a post."

"Correct," said Qwilleran. "I have a heating problem. I need a repairman."

"See the wife," said the little man, nodding toward the house in the rear. "She be the one does all that."

Qwilleran grunted his thanks and found his way to the house, picking his way through tall weeds, chunks of concrete, and auto parts. Three other cars were parked in the weedy lot, waiting for Glinko's attention, and they were all in the $40,000 class.

The house was no less dilapidated than the garage. The front steps had caved in, and Qwilleran climbed cautiously through the remaining boards and rapped on the torn screened door. The woman who waddled over to greet him, ample flesh bouncing and tentlike dress billowing, was all smiles and affability.

He introduced himself and said, "I understand you operate a service network."

"Network!" she hooted, her plump cheeks trembling with merriment. "That's a good one! Wait'll I tell Glinko. Ha ha ha! Come in and join the club. You wanna beer?"

"Thank you, but I have two friends waiting for me in the car," he declined.

She ushered him into a dingy living room where there was nothing to suggest a business operation. "Two hun'erd to join," she stated. "Fifty a year dues, or a hun'erd if you wanna be on the fast track."

Qwilleran thought the fee exorbitant, but he gave his name and the address of the cabin and opted for priority service. "Right now I need a wall-heater repaired in a hurry. How quickly can you dispatch a repairman?"

"Dispatch!" she cried with glee. "That's a good one! Gotta use that! . . . Lemme see . . . In a hurry for a plumber, eh?" She gazed upward as if reading file cards on the water-stained ceiling. "Ralph, he went off to Pickax for a load o' pipe . . . Jerry, he come down with hay fever so bad he can't see to drive . . . Little Joe's workin' out your way, puttin' in a new toilet for the Urbanks. I'll radio out there."

"Do you bill me for the work?" Qwilleran asked.

"Nope. You pay Little Joe when the work's done. But you gotta gimme a key."

He handed over the new key with reluctance. "I'll write you a check for three hundred. Is that right?"

Mrs. Glinko shook her head and grinned. "Gotta have cash."

"In that case I'll have to go over to the bank. Do you want to write down my name and address? It's spelled Q-w-i-l-l-e-r-a-n."

"Got it!" she said, tapping her temple. "I'll *dispatch* Little Joe after dinner. Dispatch! Ha ha ha!"

"Not until after dinner?" he protested.

"We eat dinner. You folks eat lunch. Ha ha ha!"

After picking up some cash at the bank for Mrs. Glinko, Qwilleran drove to a parking lot overlooking the municipal marina. There he released the cats from the hamper. "No point in going home yet," he told them. "We'll give the guy time to fix the heater. Let's hope the Glinko system works."

He bought a hot dog and coffee at the refreshment stand and consumed it behind the wheel, offering the Siamese a few crumbs which they delicately declined. Together they watched the craft rocking at the piers: charter fishing boats, small yachts, and tall-masted sailboats. There was plenty of money rolling into Mooseville, he concluded. Soon the natives would get rich and start spending winters in the South. He wondered where the Glinkos would idle away the winter. Palm Springs? Caneel Bay?

At two o'clock he drove slowly to the cabin, skeptical

about Mrs. Glinko's reliability and efficiency. To his relief he found a van parked in the clearing—a rusty, unmarked vehicle with doors flung wide and plumbing gear inside.

The cabin doors were also open, front and back, and warm June air wafted through the building. Little Joe had been smart enough to ventilate the place. Good thinking on his part, Qwilleran had to acknowledge. Why didn't I do that?

The access door on the front of the heater was open, and in front of it a body lay sprawled on the floor. Qwilleran first noticed the muddy field boots, then the threadbare jeans. By the time his eyes reached the faded red plaid shirt, he knew this was no repairman.

"Hello," he said uncertainly. "Are you the plumber?"

The body rolled over, and a husky young woman with mousy hair stuffed into a feed cap sat up and said soberly, "There was a dead spider in the pilot light. Whole thing's dirty inside. I'm cleanin' it out. Gotta broom? I made a mess on the floor." This was said without expression in her large, flat face and dull gray eyes.

"You surprised me," Qwilleran said. "I was expecting some fellow named Joe."

"I'm Joanna," she said. "My daddy was Joe, so we were Big Joe and Little Joe." She lowered her eyes as she spoke.

"Was he a plumber, too?"

"He was more of a carpenter, but he did all kinds of things."

Noticing the past tense, Qwilleran sensed a family tragedy. "What happened, Joanna?" he asked in a sympathetic tone that was part genuine interest and part professional curiosity. He was thinking that a female plumber would make a good subject for the "Qwill Pen."

"My daddy was killed in an accident." She was still sitting on the floor with her eyes cast down.

"I'm sorry to hear that—very sorry. Was it a traffic accident?"

She shook her head sadly and said in her somber voice, "A tailgate fell on him—the gate on a dump truck."

"Terrible!" Qwilleran exclaimed. "When did it happen?"

"Coupla months ago."

"You have my sympathy. How old was he?" Joanna appeared to be about twenty-five.

"Forty-three." She turned back to the heater as if wanting to end the painful conversation. She lighted the pilot, closed the door and scrambled to her feet. "Where's the broom?"

Qwilleran watched her sweep, noting that she was very thorough. Joanna was a strong, healthy-looking young person, but she never smiled.

"Be right back," she said as she carried a small toolkit to her van. When she returned, she mumbled, "That'll be thirty-five."

Assuming that she, like Mrs. Glinko, preferred cash, he gave her some bills from his money clip and accepted a receipt marked "Paid—Jo Trupp." He thought the charge was high, but he was grateful to have the heater operating.

Next she handed him a yellow slip of paper. "You gotta sign this," she said without looking at him. "It's for Mrs. Glinko."

It was a voucher indicating that he had paid Jo Trupp for the heater job—that he had paid her twenty-five dollars. Twenty-five? He hesitated over the discrepancy for only a moment before realizing he was dealing with corruption in low places. He would not embarrass the poor girl for ten dollars. Undoubtedly she had to pay Glinko a kickback and liked to skim a little off the top.

Once the plumber's van had disappeared down the long undulating driveway and the indoor climate was within reason, Qwilleran was able to appreciate the cabin: the white-washed log walls, the open ceiling crisscrossed with log trusses, the oiled wood floors scattered with Indian rugs, two white sofas angled around a fieldstone fireplace, and the incomparable view from the bank of north windows. A mile out on the lake, sailboats were racing. A hundred miles across the water there was Canada.

He carried the wicker hamper indoors and opened the lid slowly. Immediately two dark brown masks with wide, blue eyes and perky ears rose from the interior and swiveled like periscopes. When assured that all was clear, they hopped out: lithe bodies with pale fawn fur accented by slender brown legs, whiplike brown tails, and those inquisitive brown masks. Qwilleran apologized to them for their protracted confinement and the unconscionable delay, but they ignored him and went directly to the fireplace to sniff the spot where a white bearskin rug had warmed the hearth two summers before; bloodied beyond repair at that time, it had since been replaced by an Indian rug. Next, Koko stared up with interest at the moosehead mounted above the mantel, and Yum Yum flattened herself to crawl under the sofa where she had formerly hidden her playthings. Then, within minutes they were both overhead, leaping across the beams, landing on the mantel, swooping down to the sofas, and skidding across the polished floor on hand-woven rugs.

Qwilleran brought his luggage indoors and quickly telephoned Mildred Hanstable. "Mildred, I apologize for my bad manners this morning. I'm afraid I was rather curt when I talked with you."

"That's all right, Qwill. I know you were upset. Did it work out all right?"

"Amazingly well! Thanks for the tip. Glinko took care of the matter in no time at all. But I've got to talk to you about that extraordinary couple and their unorthodox way of doing business."

Mildred laughed. "It works, so don't disturb it. Why don't you come over here for dinner tonight? I'll throw together a casserole and a salad and take a pie out of the freezer."

Qwilleran accepted promptly and made a special trip into Mooseville for a bottle of Mildred's favorite brand of Scotch and a bottle of white grape juice for himself. He also laid in a supply of delicacies for the Siamese.

When he returned from town, Koko was in the back hall, busily occupied with a new discovery. The hallway functioned as a mudroom, with a mud-colored rug for wiping feet, hooks for hanging jackets, a cleaning closet, and other utilitarian features. Koko had tunneled under the rug and was squirming and making throaty sounds.

Qwilleran threw back the rug. Underneath it there was a trap door about two feet square, with a recessed metal ring for lifting. The cat eagerly sniffed its perimeter.

Qwilleran had visions of underground plumbing and wiring mysteries, and his curiosity equaled Koko's. "Get out of the way, old boy, and let's have a look," he said. He found a flashlight in the closet and swung back the heavy slab of oak. "It's sand! Nothing but sand!" Koko was teetering on the brink, ready to leap into the hole. "No!" Qwilleran thundered, and the cat winced, retreated, and sauntered away to lick his breast fur nonchalantly.

By the time Qwilleran set out for Mildred's cottage, his companions had been fed and were lounging on the screened porch overlooking the lake. They sat in a patch of sunshine, utterly contented with their lot, and why not? They had consumed a can of red salmon (minus the dark skin) and two smoked oysters. Now they relaxed in leisurely poses that prompted Qwilleran to tiptoe for his camera, but as soon as they saw him peer through the view-finder, Yum Yum started scratching her ear with an idiot squint in her celestial blue eyes, while Koko rolled over and attended to the base of his tail with one leg pointing toward the firmament.

They were chased off the porch and locked in the cabin before Qwilleran set out on the half-mile walk to Mildred's place. A desolate stretch of beach bordered his own property, lapped by languid waves. Next, an outcropping of rock projected into the water, popularly known as Seagull Point, although one rarely saw a gull unless the lake washed up a dead fish. Beyond Seagull Point a string of a dozen cottages perched on the dune—a jumble of styles: rustic, contemporary, quaint, or simply ugly, like the boatlike structure said to be owned by a retired sea captain.

The last in the row was Mildred's yellow cottage. Beyond that, the dune was being cleared in preparation for new construction. Foundations were in evidence, and framing had been started.

A flight of twenty wooden steps led up the side of the dune to Mildred's terrace with its yellow umbrella table, and as Qwilleran reached the top she met him there, her well-upholstered figure concealed by a loose-fitting yellow beach dress.

"What's going on there?" Qwilleran called out, waving toward the construction site.

"Condominiums," she said ruefully. "I hate to see it happen, but they've offered us clubhouse and pool privileges, so it's not all bad. The lake is too cold for swimming, so . . . why not?"

Handing the bottles to his hostess, he volunteered to tend bar, and Mildred ushered him into the house and pointed out the glassware and ice cubes. Their voices sounded muffled, because the walls were hung with handmade quilts.

Traditional and wildly contemporary designs had the initials M.H. stitched into the corners.

"These represent an unbelievable amount of work," Qwilleran said, recognizing an idea for the "Qwill Pen."

"I only appliqué the tops," she said. "My craftworkers do the quilting." Besides teaching school, writing for the local newspaper, and raising money for the hospital, she conducted a not-for-profit project for low-income handworkers.

Qwilleran regarded her with admiration. "You have boundless energy, Mildred. You never stop!"

"So why can't I lose weight?" she said, sidestepping the compliment modestly.

"You're a handsome woman. Don't worry about pounds."

"I like to cook, and I like to eat," she explained, "and my daughter says I don't get enough real exercise. Can you picture me jogging?"

"How is Sharon enjoying motherhood?" Qwilleran asked.

"Well, to tell the truth, she's restless staying home with the baby. She wants to go back to teaching. Roger thinks she should wait another year. What do you think, Qwill?"

"You're asking a childless bachelor, a failed husband, with no known relatives and no opinion! . . . By the way, I saw Roger on my way up from Pickax. He was hightailing it back to the office to file his copy for the weekend edition, no doubt."

Mildred passed a sizzling platter of stuffed mushrooms and rumaki. "I liked your column on the taxidermist, Qwill."

"Thanks. It was an interesting subject, and I learned that mounted animal heads should never be hung over a fireplace; it dries them out. The moosehead at the cabin may have to go to the hospital for a facelift. Also, I'd like to do something with the whitewashed walls. They'd look better if they were natural."

"That would make the interior darker," Mildred warned. "Of course, you could install skylights."

"Don't they leak?"

"Not if you hire a good carpenter."

"Where do I find a good carpenter? Call Glinko, I suppose. Has anyone figured out his racket, Mildred? He has a monopoly, and I suspect price-fixing, restraint of trade, and tax evasion. They don't accept checks, and they don't seem to keep written records."

"It's all in Mrs. Glinko's head," said Mildred. "That woman is a living computer."

"The IRS frowns on living computers."

"But you have to admit it's a wonderful convenience for summer people like us."

"I keep wondering what else they supply besides plumbers and carpenters."

"Now you're being cynical, Qwill. What was wrong with your space heater?"

"A dead spider in the pilot light—or so the plumber said; I'm not sure I believe it. Glinko sent me a *woman* plumber!"

Mildred nodded. "Little Joe."

"She isn't so little. Do you know her?"

"Of course I know her!" Mildred had taught school in the county for more than twenty years, and she knew an entire generation of students as well as their parents. "Her name is Joanna Trupp. Her father was killed in a freak accident this spring."

Qwilleran said, "There's a high percentage of fatal accidents in this county. Either people live to be ninety-five, or they die young—in hunting mishaps, drownings, car crashes, tractor rollovers . . ."

Mildred beckoned him to the dinner table.

"Is Little Joe a competent plumber?" he went on. "I thought of writing a column about her unusual occupation."

"I don't know what it takes to be a competent plumber," Mildred said, "but in school she was always good at working with her hands. Why she decided to get a plumber's license, I haven't the faintest idea. Why would any woman want to fix toilets and drains, and stick her head under the kitchen sink, and crawl under houses? I don't even like to clean the bathroom!"

The casserole was a sauced combination of turkey, homemade noodles, and artichoke hearts, and it put Qwilleran in an excellent frame of mind. The Caesar salad compounded his pleasure. The raspberry pie left him almost numb with contentment.

As Mildred served coffee on the terrace she said, "There's a party on the dunes tomorrow night. Why don't you come as my date and meet some of the summer people? Doc and Dottie Madley are hosting. He's a dentist from Pickax, you know. They come up weekends."

"Who will be there?"

"Probably the Comptons; you've met them, of course . . . The Urbanks are retired; he's a chemist and a golf nut and a bore . . . John and Vicki Bushland have a photo studio in the next county. He's an avid fisherman. Everyone calls him 'Bushy,' which is funny because he doesn't have much hair . . . The attorney from Down Below is newly divorced. I don't know whether he'll be coming up this summer . . . There's a young woman renting the Dunfield cottage . . ."

"How about the retired sea captain?"

"Captain Phlogg never mixes, I'm glad to say. He's a stinker in more ways than one."

"I'd like to write a column on that guy, but he's a disagreeable old codger. I've been in his antique shop a couple of times, and it's a farce!"

"He's a fraud," Mildred said in a confidential tone. "He's never been to sea! He was just a ship's carpenter at the old shipyard near Purple Point."

"What is he doing in a social enclave like the Dunes Club?"

"Want to hear the story that's circulating? Phlogg bought lakefront property when it was considered worthless. He scrounged lumber from the shipyard and built the house with his own hands, and now lake frontage is up to two thousand dollars a foot! A word of warning, Qwill—don't ever let your cats out. He has a dog that has a reputation as a cat-killer. The Comptons took him to court when their cat was mauled."

There was a muffled ring from the telephone, and Mildred excused herself. Just inside the sliding doors she could be heard saying, "Hi, Roger! I hear you're babysitting tonight . . . No, what is it? . . . Who? . . . Oh, that's terrible! How did it happen? . . . What will his family do? They have three kids! . . . Well, thanks for letting me know, Roger, but that's really bad news. Maybe we can raise some money for them."

She returned to the terrace with a strained expression. "That was Roger," she said. "There's been a drowning—a young man he went to school with."

"How did it happen?" Qwilleran asked.

"He went fishing and didn't come home. They found his body at the mouth of the river. It'll be in the paper tomorrow."

"Boat accident?"

"No, he was casting from the bank of the river. I feel awful about it. After being out of work all winter, he'd just been hired for the construction gang at the condo development."

Mildred offered more coffee, but Qwilleran declined, saying he wanted to be home before the mosquitoes attacked. The true reason was that he felt a peculiar sensation on his upper lip—a twitch in his moustache that, in some inexplicable way, had always presaged trouble.

He covered the half mile along the beach more briskly than before. For the last few hundred yards he felt compelled to run. Even as he climbed up the dune to the cabin he could hear Koko yowling violently, and when he unlocked the door he smelled gas!

TWO

When Qwilleran returned from Mildred's cottage and smelled the noxious fumes in the cabin, he telephoned the Glinko number.

"Glinko *network!*" a woman's voice said, with emphasis on her new word.

He described the situation quickly with understandable anxiety.

"Ha ha ha!" laughed Mrs. Glinko. "Don't light any matches."

"No advice," he snapped. "Just send someone in a hurry." He had opened doors and windows and had shut the cats up in the toolshed.

In a matter of minutes an emergency truck pulled into the clearing, and the driver strode into the cabin, sniffing critically. Immediately he walked out again, looking up at the roof. Qwilleran followed, also looking up at the roof.

"Bird's nest," said the man. "It happens all the time. See that piece of straw sticking out of the vent? Some bird built its nest up there, and you've got carbon monoxide from the water heater seeping into your house. All you have to do is get up there on a ladder and clean it out."

Qwilleran did as he was told, reflecting that the Glinko

network, no matter how corrupt, was not such a bad service after all. Two crises in one day had been handled punctually and responsibly. He found a stepladder in the toolshed, scrambled up on the roof, and extracted a clump of dried grass and eggshells from the vent, feeling proud of his sudden capability and feeling suddenly in tune with country living. Up there on the roof there was an intoxicating exhilaration. He was reluctant to climb down again, but the long June day was coming to an end, the mosquitoes were moving in, and remonstrative yowls were coming from the toolshed.

Settling on the screened porch with the Siamese, he relaxed at last. The yellow birds were swooping back and forth in front of the screens as if taunting the cats, and Koko and Yum Yum dashed to and fro in fruitless pursuit until they fell over in exhaustion, twitching their tails in frustration. So ended the first hectic day of their summer sojourn in Mooseville. It was only a sample of what was to come.

Qwilleran forgot about the drowning of Roger MacGillivray's friend until he bought a newspaper the next morning. He was in Mooseville to have breakfast at the Northern Lights Hotel, and he picked up a paper to read at the table. Headlined on page one was Roger's account:

MOOSEVILLE MAN DROWNS IN RIVER

Buddy Yarrow, 29, of Mooseville Township, drowned while fishing in the Ittibittiwassee River Thursday night. His body was found at the mouth of the river Friday morning. Police had searched throughout the night after his disappearance was reported by his wife, Linda, 28.

According to a spokesperson for the sheriff's department, it appears that Yarrow slipped down the riverbank into the water. There was a mudslide at the location where his tackle box was found, and the river is deep at that point.

Yarrow was a strong swimmer, his wife told police, leading investigators to believe that he hit his head on a rock when he fell. A massive head injury was noted in the coroner's report. Police theorize that the strong current following last week's heavy rain swept the victim, stunned or unconscious, to the mouth of the river, where his body was caught in the willows overhanging the water.

"He always went fishing at that bend in the river," said Linda Yarrow. "He didn't have a boat. He liked to cast from the bank."

Besides his wife, the former Linda Tobin, Yarrow leaves three children: Bobbie, 5; Terry, 3; and Tammy, 6 months. He was a graduate of Moose County schools and was currently employed in the construction of the East Shore Condominiums.

There were pictures of the victim, obviously snapshots from a family album, showing him as a high school youth on the track team, later as a grinning bridegroom, still later as a fisherman squinting into the sun and holding a prize catch.

On page two of the newspaper, in thumb position, was the column "Straight from the Qwill Pen" about a dog named Switch, assistant to an electrician in Purple Point. Switch assisted his master by selecting tools from the toolbox and carrying them up the ladder in his mouth.

Qwilleran noted two typographical errors in his column and three in the drowning story. And his name was misspelled.

He had several ideas for future columns, but the subject that eluded him was the infamous Mooseville antique shop called The Captain's Mess, operated by the bogus Captain Phlogg. The man was virtually impossible to interview, being inattentive, evasive, and rude. He sold junk and, worse yet, fakes. Yet, The Captain's Mess was a tourist attraction—so bad it was good. It was worth a story.

On Saturday morning—after a fisherman's breakfast of steak, eggs, hashed browns, toast and coffee—Qwilleran devised a new interview approach that would at least command Phlogg's attention. He left the hotel and walked to the ramshackle building off Main Street that was condemned by the county department of building and safety but championed by the Mooseville Chamber of Commerce. He found Captain Phlogg, with the usual stubble of beard and battered naval cap, sitting in a shadowy corner of the shop, smoking an odoriferous pipe and taking swigs from a pint bottle. In the jumble of rusted, mildewed, broken marine artifacts that surrounded the proprietor, only a skilled and patient collector could find anything worth buying. Some of them spent hours sifting through the rubble.

The captain kept an ominous belaying pin by his side, causing Qwilleran to maintain a safe distance as he began, "Good morning, Captain. I'm from the newspaper. I understand you're not a retired sea captain; you're a retired carpenter."

"Whut? Whut?" croaked the captain, evidencing more direct response than he had ever shown before.

"Is it true that you were a carpenter for a shipbuilder at Purple Point—before you made a killing in land speculation?"

"Dunno whut yer talkin' about," said the man, vigorously puffing his pipe.

"I believe you live in a house on the dunes that you built with your own hands, using lumber stolen from the shipyard. Is that true?"

"None o' yer business."

"Aren't you the one who has a vicious dog that runs loose illegally?"

The old man snarled some shipyard profanity as he struggled to his feet.

Qwilleran started to back away. "Have you ever been taken to court on account of the dog?"

"Git outa here!" Captain Phlogg reached for the belaying pin.

At that moment a group of giggling tourists entered the shop, and Qwilleran made a swift exit, pleased with the initial results. He planned to goad the man with further annoying questions until he got a story. The chamber of commerce might not approve, but it would make an entertaining column, provided the expletives were deleted.

Returning to the log cabin, Qwilleran was met at the door by an excited Koko, while Yum Yum sat in a compact bundle, observing in dismay. Koko was racing back and forth to attract attention, yowling and yikking, and Qwilleran cast a hasty eye around the interior. Living room, dining alcove, kitchen and bar occupied one large open space, and there was nothing abnormal there. In the bathroom and bunkrooms everything appeared to be intact.

"What's wrong, Koko?" he asked. "Did a stranger come in here?" He worried about Glinko's duplicate key. There was no way of guessing how many persons might have access to that key. "What are you trying to tell me, old boy?"

For answer the cat leaped to the top of the bar and from there to the kitchen counter. Qwilleran investigated closely and, in doing so, stepped in something wet. On the oiled floorboards a spill usually remained on the surface until mopped up, and here was a sizable puddle! The idea of a catly misdemeanor flashed across Qwilleran's mind only briefly; the Siamese were much too fastidious to be accused of such a lapse.

Opening the cabinet door beneath the sink, he found the

interior flooded and heard a faint splash. He groaned and reached for the telephone once more.

"Ha ha ha! A drip!" exclaimed the cheerful Mrs. Glinko. "Allrighty, we'll *dispatch* somebody PDQ."

In fifteen minutes an old-model van with more rust than paint pulled into the clearing—the same plumber's van as before—and Joanna swung out of the driver's seat.

"Got a leak?" she asked in her somber monotone as she plunged her head under the sink. "These pipes are old!"

"The cabin was built seventy-five years ago," Qwilleran informed her.

"There's no shutoff under the sink. How do I get down under?"

He showed her the trap door, and she pulled open the heavy slab with ease and lowered herself into the hole. Koko was extremely interested and had to be shooed away three times. When she emerged with cobwebs on her clothing, she did some professional puttering beneath the sink, went down under the floor again to reopen the valve, and presented her bill. Qwilleran paid thirty-five dollars again and signed a voucher for twenty-five. It made him an accomplice in a minor swindle, but he felt more sympathy for Joanna than for Glinko. He rationalized that the ten-dollar discrepancy might be considered a tip.

"What's under the floor?" he asked her.

"The crawl space. Just sand and pipes and tanks and lots of spiders. It's dusty."

"It can't be very pleasant."

"I ran into a snake once in a crawl space. My daddy ran into a skunk." She glanced about the cabin, her bland face showing little reaction until she spotted Koko and Yum Yum sitting on the sofa. "Pretty cats."

"They're strictly indoor pets and never go out of the house," Qwilleran explained firmly. "If you ever have occasion to come in here when I'm not at home, don't let them run outside! There's a vicious dog in the neighborhood."

"I like animals," she said. "Once I had a porcupine and a woodchuck."

"What are those yellow birds that fly around here?"

"Wild canaries. You have a lot of chipmunks, too. I have some pet chipmunks—and a fox."

"Unusual pets," he commented, wondering if vermin from the wildlife might be tracked into the cabin on her boots.

"I rescued two bear cubs once. Some hunter shot their mother."

"Are you allowed to keep wild animals in captivity?"

"I don't tell anybody," she said with a shrug. "The woodchuck was almost dead when I found him. I fed him with a medicine dropper."

"Where do you keep them?"

"Behind where I live. The cubs died."

"Very interesting," Qwilleran mused. Eventually he might write a column on Joanna the Plumber, but he would avoid mentioning Joanna the Illegal Zookeeper. "Thanks for the prompt service," he said in a tone of farewell.

When she had clomped out of the cabin in her heavy boots, he recalled something different about her appearance. The boots, the jeans, the faded plaid shirt and the feed cap were the same as before, but she was wearing lipstick, and her hair looked clean; it was tied back in a ponytail.

He settled down to work on his column for the midweek edition—about Old Sam, the gravedigger, who had been digging graves with a shovel for sixty years. He had plenty of notes on Old Sam as well as a catchy lead, but there was no adequate place to write. For a desk the cabin offered only the dining table, which was round. Papers had a way of sliding off the curved edges and landing on the floor, where the cats played toboggan on them, skidding across the oiled floorboards in high glee. They also liked to sit on his notes and catch their tails in the carriage of his electric typewriter.

"What I need," Qwilleran said to Yum Yum, who was trying to steal a felt-tip pen, "is a private study." Even reading was difficult when one had a lapful of cat, and the little female's possessiveness about his person put an end to comfort and concentration. Nevertheless, he made the best of an awkward situation until the column was finished and it was time to dress for the beach party.

As the festive hour approached, the intense sun of an early evening was slanting across the lake, and Qwilleran wore his dark glasses for the walk down the beach to Mildred's cottage. He found her looking radiant in a gauzy cherry-colored shift that floated about her ample figure flatteringly and bared her shoulders, which were plump and enticingly smooth.

"Ooooh!" she cried. "With those sunglasses and that moustache, Qwill, you look so sexy!"

He paid her a guarded compliment in return, but smoothed his moustache smugly.

They walked along the shore to the Madleys' contemporary beach house, where a flight of weathered steps led up the side of the dune to a redwood deck. Guests were gathering there, all wearing dark glasses, which gave them a certain anonymity. They were a colorful crew—in beach dresses, sailing stripes, clamdiggers and halters, raw-hued espadrilles, sandals, Indian prints, Hawaiian shirts, and peasant blouses. Even Lyle Compton, the superintendent of schools, was wearing a daring pair of plaid trousers. There was one simple white dress, and that was on a painfully thin young woman with dark hair clipped close to her head. She was introduced as Russell Simms.

The hostess said to Qwilleran, "You're both newcomers. Russell has just arrived up here, too."

"Are you from Down Below?" he asked.

Russell nodded and gazed at the lake through her sunglasses.

"Russell is renting the Dunfield house," Dottie Madley mentioned as she moved away to greet another arrival.

"Beautiful view," Qwilleran remarked.

Russell ventured a timid yes and continued to look at the water.

"And constantly changing," he went on. "It can be calm today and wildly stormy tomorrow, with raging surf. Is this your first visit to Moose County?"

"Yes," she said.

"Do you plan to stay for the summer?"

"I think so." Her dark glasses never met his dark glasses.

"Russell . . . that's an unusual name for a woman."

"Family name," she murmured as if apologizing.

"What do you plan to do during the summer?"

"I like to . . . read . . . and walk on the beach."

"There's a remarkably good museum in town, if you're interested in shipwrecks, and a remarkably bad antique shop. How did you happen to choose the Dunfield cottage?"

"It was advertised."

"In the *Daily Fluxion?* I used to write for that lively and controversial newspaper."

"No. In the *Morning Rampage.*"

Qwilleran's attempts at conversation were foundering, and he was grateful when Dottie introduced another couple and steered Russell away to meet the newly divorced attorney.

Everyone at the party recognized Qwilleran—or, at least, his moustache. When he was living Down Below and writing for the *Fluxion,* his photograph with mournful eyes and drooping moustache appeared at the top of his column regularly. When he suddenly arrived in Pickax as the heir to the Klingenschoen fortune, he was an instant celebrity. When he established the Klingenschoen Memorial Fund to distribute his wealth for the benefit of the community, he became a local hero.

On the Madleys' redwood deck he circulated freely, clinking ice cubes in a glass of ginger ale, teasing Dottie, flattering the chemist's wife, asking Bushy about the fishing, listening sympathetically as a widower described how a helicopter had scattered his wife's ashes over Three Tree Island.

Leo Urbank, the chemist, flaunted his academic degrees, professional connections, and club affiliations like a verbal résumé and asked Qwilleran if he played golf. Upon receiving a negative reply he wandered away.

Bushy, the photographer, invited Qwilleran to go fishing some evening. He was younger than the other men, although losing his hair. Qwilleran had always enjoyed the company of news photographers, and Bushy seemed to fit the pattern: outgoing, likable, self-assured.

The superintendent of schools said to Qwilleran, "Have you heard from Polly Duncan since she escaped from Moose County?"

Qwilleran knew Lyle Compton well—a tall, thin, saturnine man with a perverse sense of humor and blunt speech. "I received a postcard, Lyle," he replied. "She was met at the airport by the local bigwigs, and they gave her a bunch of flowers."

"That's more than we did for the unfortunate woman who came here. I think Polly's getting the better part of the deal. Since she's so gung ho on Shakespeare, she may decide to stay in England."

Qwilleran's moustache bristled at the suggestion, although he knew that Compton was baiting him. "No chance," he said. "When Polly airs her theory that Shakespeare was really a woman, she'll be deported . . . By the way, do you know anything about that young man who was drowned?"

As superintendent of schools Compton knew everyone in the county, and was always willing to share his information, though taking care to point out that he was not a gossip, just a born educator. "Buddy Yarrow? Yes, he was well-liked at school. Had to struggle to keep his grades up, though. Married the Tobin girl, and they had too many kids too fast. He had a tough time supporting them."

Mildred overheard them. "I'm applying to the Klingenschoen Fund for financial aid for the Yarrows," she said. "I hope you'll put in a good word, Qwill."

Dottie Madley said, "Buddy built our steps down to the beach, and he was very considerate—didn't leave any sawdust or nails lying around. Glinko sent him to us."

"Did someone mention Glinko?" asked Urbank. "We had some plumbing done this week, and Glinko sent us a *lady plumber!*"

"I suppose she fixes everything with a hairpin," said Doc.

Qwilleran concealed a scowl. He had long ago curbed his tendency to make jocular remarks about hairpins and bras.

"Doc!" said Mildred in her sternest classroom voice. "That is an outmoded sexist slur. Go to the powder room and wash your mouth out with soap."

"I'll stop quipping about hairpins," Doc retorted, "when you gals stop calling the john the powder room."

"Objection!" said John Bushland. "Derogatory reference to a minority!"

It was then that Qwilleran made a remark that exploded like a bomb. It was just a casual statement of his summer intentions, but the reaction astonished him.

"Don't do it!" said the host.

"You'll be sorry," his wife warned, and she wasn't smiling.

"Only mistake I ever made in my life," said the attorney. "We tried it last summer, and it broke up our marriage."

"When we did it, my wife almost had a nervous breakdown," said the chemist.

Bushy added seriously, "For the first time in my life I felt like *killing someone!*"

Qwilleran had simply mentioned that he would like to build an addition to the log cabin. Everyone at the party, he now learned, had encountered infuriating or insurmountable obstacles while building an addition or remodeling a kitchen or adding a porch or putting on a new roof.

"What seems to be the problem?" he asked in mild bewilderment.

"All the good contractors are busy with big jobs in the summer," explained Doc Madley. "Right now they're building the condos on the shore, a big motel in Mooseville, senior housing in North Kennebeck, a new wing on the Pickax Hospital, and a couple of schools. For a small job like yours you have to hire an underground builder."

"If you can find one," Urbank added.

"Pardon my ignorance," Qwilleran said, "but what is an underground builder?"

"You have to dig to find one," said Compton by way of definition.

"What about Glinko? I thought his service was the bright and beautiful answer to all problems great and small."

"Glinko can send you someone for an emergency or a day's work, but he doesn't handle building projects."

"Do these underground builders advertise in the phone book?"

"Advertise!" Bushy exclaimed. "They don't even have telephones. Some of them camp out in tents."

"Then how do you track them down?"

"Hang around the bars," someone said.

"Hang around the lumberyard," someone else said. "If you see a guy buying two-by-fours and nails and plywood and *being refused credit,* grab him! That's your man."

"Don't give him a nickel in advance," Compton warned. "Pay him for the hours worked."

"And hope to God he comes back the next day," said Urbank. "We spent one whole summer waiting for a man to finish our job, and then we found out he was in jail in some other county."

"Ours lived in a trailer camp," said Dottie, "and Doc went out there every morning at six o'clock to haul him out of bed."

"If you're interested in bargains," Doc said, "the underground builder is a good bet. He may never finish the job, but he comes cheap."

"And you'll have to watch him every minute, or he'll put the door where the window should be," Bushy warned.

"Hmmm," said Qwilleran, unable to muster any other verbal reaction after the astonishing tirade.

"On the whole," said Compton, "they know their craft, but they're damned casual about it. They don't bother with blueprints. You tell them what you want, draw a picture in the sand with a stick, and wave your hands."

"Of course, if the worst comes to the worst," said Doc, "there's always Mighty Lou."

Everyone laughed, and the discussion died a merciful death as the hostess invited them to the buffet.

The guests pocketed their sunglasses, went indoors, and served themselves cold chicken, potato salad, and carrot straws. Some found small tables. Others balanced plates on their knees. Compton stood up with his plate on the fireplace mantel.

The attorney, sitting next to Qwilleran, said under his breath, “Have you tried talking to that new girl? I’m brilliant in the courtroom, but I couldn’t get a blasted word out of that woman!”

Mildred said in her classroom voice, “Did anyone see the visitors last night?”

“What time?” Bushy asked.

“About two in the morning.”

“That’s when they usually come around,” Sue Urbank remarked.

“Let me tell you what happened to me,” the photographer said. “I took my boat out last night for some twilight fishing, and I was baiting my hook when I felt something shining over my head. I knew what it was, of course, so I reached for my camera—I never go anywhere without it—but when I looked up again, the thing was gone!”

“What was it?” Qwilleran asked.

“Another UFO,” Bushy replied in a matter-of-fact way.

Qwilleran searched the other faces, but no one seemed surprised.

“Ever get a picture of one?” the photographer was asked.

“Never had any luck. They scoot off so fast.”

“Have any abductions been reported?” Qwilleran inquired with the smirk of a skeptic.

“Not yet,” answered Doc, “but I’m sure Mildred will be the first.”

Calmly she retorted, “Doc, I hope all your patients sue you!”

Sue Urbank said, “It’s a funny thing. I didn’t see a single visitor last summer, but this year they’re out there almost every night.”

“We can expect abnormal weather—with all that activity over the lake,” Dottie predicted.

Qwilleran continued to stare at them with disbelief.

Mildred observed his reaction and said, "Shall I phone you, Qwill, some night around two o'clock when they come around?"

"That's kind of you," he said, "but I need all the beauty sleep I can get."

During the small talk Russell Simms was silent, staring at her plate and chewing slowly. Once Qwilleran glanced suddenly in her direction and caught her studying him from the corner of her eye. He preened his moustache.

Urbank said, "Did everyone read their horoscope this morning? Mine said I'd make a wise investment, so I went out and bought a new set of clubs."

"Mine said I should cooperate with my mate," said the attorney. "Unfortunately I don't have one at the moment. Any volunteers?"

Bushy said, "Today's *Fluxion* told me to go out and have a good time. The *Rampage* told me to stay home and get some work done."

"I don't read horoscopes," Compton announced.

"That's true," said his wife. "I have to read them to him while he's shaving."

"Lyle, I always knew you were a hypocrite," said Doc.

"A hypocritical superintendent is more to be trusted than a painless dentist," said Compton. "Never trust a dentist who doesn't hurt."

"Qwill, what's your sign?" asked Mildred.

"I don't think I have a sign," he said. "When the signs were handed out, I was overlooked."

Three persons asked his birthdate and decided he was a Gemini on the cusp of Taurus. Mildred said it would be an interesting year for Gemini. "You can expect the unexpected," she added.

When coffee was served and guests returned to the deck, Compton wandered down to the beach to smoke a cigar. Qwilleran followed him and said, "Doc is a great kidder."

"He's good at shooting the breeze," Compton said, "but if you want your teeth fixed, you might better go to an auto mechanic."

"How did you react to all that chatter about UFOs and horoscopes?"

"Don't expect any rational conversation from this beach crowd," said the superintendent. "They're all intelligent folks, but they get a little giddy when they come up here. Must be something in the atmosphere."

"I assume Captain Phlogg never comes to any of these parties."

"No, he's an antisocial fellow. He has a big dog that wanders around the dunes like the hound of the Baskervilles, and I've got my shotgun loaded. If I ever catch him doing his business *on my beach,* he's going to get it! Right between the eyes!"

Qwilleran said, "I opened a can of worms when I mentioned building an addition."

"You don't really intend to do it, do you?"

"I'm badly in need of more space. The cabin is okay for weekends or a brief vacation, but it's inadequate for the whole summer. Did you ever hire an underground builder?"

"About two months ago," said Compton. "He poured a slab for a two-car garage and roughed it in, and then he never came back. I've done everything but hire a private detective. He was one of the itinerants who come up here during the resort season, you know, and the only way I could get hold of him was to leave a message at the Shipwreck Tavern. They haven't seen him for five weeks, and we're sitting there with a half-built garage. Can't get anyone else to finish the damn thing."

"This is not very encouraging," Qwilleran said.

"You have to live through it to believe it."

"Someone mentioned Mighty Lou . . ."

"Forget him! You may have seem him swaggering around town—a weight lifter who thinks he's a builder. He has a fortune in tools, but he doesn't know which end of the nail to hit."

"How does he make a living?"

"He doesn't need to make a living. His family used to own all the sandpits in the county."

There was a spectacular sunset—a ball of fire sinking into the lake and turning it blood red. Then the mosquitoes swooped in, and the guests went indoors to play cards. Qwilleran suggested to Mildred that they leave.

"Let's go home and make a sundae," she said. "I'm still hungry. Do you realize there were thirteen of us at that party? That's unlucky."

"We'll all get food poisoning from the potato salad," Qwilleran predicted cheerfully. "Did you get a chance to talk to the young woman in the white dress? Her first name is Russell. She acts like a sleepwalker."

"I don't know what she's all about," Mildred said. "Did you see her eyes when she took off her sunglasses? Weird!"

"Maybe she landed from one of your extraterrestrial aircraft."

"You don't believe in the visitors," Mildred reproached him. "But just wait till you see one!" When they got to Mildred's she served homemade French vanilla ice cream with strawberries and a sprinkling of something crunchy. "What do you think of the topping?"

"It looks like dry catfood," he said, "but it's good!"

"It's my homemade cereal—wonderful in the morning with milk and sliced bananas. What do you eat for breakfast, Qwill?"

"I haven't eaten cereal since I was twelve years old."

"Then I'm going to give you some to take home." Mildred was always mothering her friends with homemade food. "Now tell me about the addition you want to build."

"Nothing very large—just a room for sleeping and writing, and a lavatory, and an apartment for the cats. Could you make a rough diagram? Something I could show the builder?"

"That will be easy," she said. "I'll make elevations, too. You'll never be able to match the log walls, but you can use board-and-batten and stain it to harmonize with the logs."

She made sketches, and they discussed details, and he stayed longer than he had intended. When he finally left for home, Mildred gave him a plastic tub of cereal and lent him a flashlight for the beach. "Watch out for the rocks at Seagull Point," she warned as she sprayed him with mosquito repellent. "And watch out for visitors!" she added mischievously.

Walking back to the cabin, he was confident he could line up a reputable builder without resorting to workmen on the fringe. He had contacts in Pickax; the Klingenschoen money was at his disposal; and he had done many favors for individuals and organizations. He could foresee no problem.

Arriving at the cabin, he scrambled up the side of the dune, walked around the building and let himself in the back door. "I'm home!" he called out. "Where's the welcoming committee? . . . Damn!" He tripped over a crumpled rug that was supposed to cover the trap door.

Switching on lights, he searched for the Siamese. As soon as he saw Yum Yum sitting on the sofa in her worried pose, he knew something was amiss, and then he noticed the shower of confetti on the hearth rug. An entire page of the newspaper had been torn to bits! Completely destroyed was the story on page one about the drowning of Buddy Yarrow, and that included Qwilleran's own column on the reverse side—the story about Switch, the electrician's dog.

"Where the devil are you?" Qwilleran shouted. There was a slight movement overhead, and his gaze moved slowly up the face of the stone fireplace to the high mantel—a huge timber hewn from a twenty-foot pine log. Koko was not on the mantel or on the crossbeams. He was on the moosehead, sitting tall between the antlers and radiating satisfaction in every whisker.

"Don't sit there looking smart!" Qwilleran barked at him. "Whatever you're trying to tell me, your mode of communication is not appreciated. Furthermore, you rolled up that rug in the hall and I tripped over it! I could have broken my neck!"

Koko squeezed his eyes and looked angelic.

"You devil!" Qwilleran said as he collected the bits of paper, wondering why Koko had done what he did.

THREE

IF QWILLERAN HAD READ his horoscope Monday morning, he could have saved a few phone calls. Most vacationers consulted their stars in the *Morning Rampage,* which was flown to Mooseville daily from Down Below. On Monday morning the *Rampage* had this to say to Gemini readers: "Listen to the advice of associates. Don't insist on doing things your own way."

Qwilleran never read the horoscopes, however. First he telephoned XYZ Enterprises in Pickax, and Don Exbridge said, "I wish we could accommodate you, Qwill, but we're having labor trouble, and it'll be a miracle if we can meet our contract deadlines. We're in danger of losing a whole lot of money." Then he called Moose Country Construction, second largest contractor in the area, and was assured they would be glad to do the work for him—next summer. Finally, the owner of Kennebeck Building Industries declared it would be a privilege and a pleasure to build an addition to the Klingenschoen log cabin—after Labor Day.

Qwilleran wanted the new wing in July, not September, and his disappointment was aggravated by two other developments. First, a cluster of insect bites had suddenly appeared on his left buttock, and they were driving him crazy despite applications of an expensive preparation recommended by the Mooseville druggist. And that was not all: The kitchen sink was leaking again!

Irately he made another emergency call to Glinko and then stormed out of the house in frustration and annoyance, hoping the lonely half-mile stretch of sand between the cabin and the dune cottages would restore his perspective.

As he walked he began to realize that he had lived contentedly with very little money during his entire adult life; now that unlimited funds were available, he was reacting like a spoiled child. He sat down on a log tossed up on the beach by a recent storm, sitting carefully to avoid the cluster of bites. The lake rippled gently, and the water lapped the shore with soothing splashes. Sandpipers ran up and down the beach. Gulls were squawking.

An unusual number of gulls filled the sky to the east, wheeling and diving and screaming. Something special was happening beyond the clump of rocks and willows known as Seagull Point. He walked slowly toward the promontory lest he disturb their fun, and when he reached the willows he saw a woman on the beach, a drab figure in fawncolored slacks and sweater. She was standing at the water's edge, taking food from her sweater pockets and tossing it to the hysterical birds. He recognized Russell's dark clipped hair and her dreamlike movements. The gulls were going berserk, skreeking and chattering, fighting each other for scraps in midair, swooping in and taking the food from her fingers. And she was talking to them in a language he could not interpret. He watched the spectacle until her pockets were empty and she walked slowly east toward the cottages.

As Qwilleran sauntered back toward the cabin his pique was somewhat soothed by the tranquility of the beach and the performance of the gulls. Climbing the slope of the dune was an awkward exercise. In the fine dry sand he climbed three steps upward and slid two steps backward. Avalanches of sand cascaded down to the beach. Other beach-dwellers had installed steps to combat the erosion. He really would need to find a carpenter . . .

A familiar van stood in the clearing, and Joanna was in the kitchen repairing the second leak under the sink.

"How did it happen so soon after you fixed it?" he demanded with a hint of accusation.

"You need new pipe. This old stuff is no good."

"Then why didn't you tell me? Why didn't you install some new pipe?"

"I just did," she said simply, lying on the floor, propped on one elbow, with her head under the sink.

When Qwilleran saw the bill, he said, "What kind of pipe am I buying? Gold-plated?"

"It's plastic," she said in her humorless way. "Could I have a drink of water?"

He handed her a glass. "Help yourself. I think you know where it is."

"You gonna be here all summer?" She was wearing lipstick again—a purplish red.

"That's my intention," he said with pointed brevity, thinking she might be planning to pay daily social visits.

She looked around the cabin, staring at the Indian throw rugs with their splashes of red. "Pretty rugs."

A raucous voice was coming from her van. "I believe your short-wave radio wants your attention," he said.

After she had driven off in her van to the next job, Qwilleran began to suspect the entire Glinko method of doing business. When Joanna fixed the sink the first time, could she have left a fitting loose so that it would start dripping again? Was this a Glinko technique? Did Mrs. Glinko train her people, like a north-country Fagin?

Suspicious, frustrated, and disgruntled, he needed the

therapy of a long lunch hour at the Press Club with half a dozen fellow journalists, but there was no Press Club within four hundred miles of Moose County. There was, however, his old friend Arch Riker. He made a call to the newspaper office in Pickax.

After years without an adequate newspaper, Moose County now had a publication of professional caliber that reached the reading public twice a week, answering their need for local news and local advertising. It was called the *Moose County Something,* a name that had started as a joke and had persisted. Editor and publisher of the *Something* was Qwilleran's lifelong friend from Down Below. He telephoned Arch Riker. "Are you free for dinner tonight, Arch? It's been a long time."

"Sure has!" said Riker. Because of his approaching marriage and the pressures of launching a new publication he had not been available for bachelor dinners for many weeks. "I'm free, and I'm hungry. What did you have in mind?"

"I've moved up to the cabin for the summer. Why don't you meet me here, and we'll go to the Northern Lights Hotel. They have spaghetti on Mondays . . . How's your lovely fiancée?"

"Lovely, hell! We broke it off this weekend," Riker growled into the phone. "I'll see you at six o'clock . . . Wait a minute! Where's your cabin? I've never been there."

"Take the main highway north to the lake, then left for three miles until you see a K on a cedar post."

The editor's car pulled into the clearing shortly after six, and Qwilleran went out to meet his paunchy, red-faced, middle-aged friend.

"Man, this is my idea of the perfect summer place!" Riker exclaimed as he admired the weathered logs, hundred-foot pine trees, and endless expanse of water.

"Come in and mix yourself a martini," Qwilleran said. "We'll relax on the porch for a while."

The editor entered the cabin in a state of awe and envy as he saw the massive stone fireplace, the open ceiling trussed with logs, the moosehead over the mantel, and the bar top made from a single slab of pine. "You're one lucky dog!"

He mixed his drink with the concentration of a research chemist while Qwilleran leaned on the bar, watching the process, knowing enough not to interrupt. Then, "What happened between you and Amanda?" he asked with the genuine concern of an old friend.

"She's the most cantankerous, opinionated, obstinate, unpredictable woman I've ever met," Riker said. "Enough is enough!"

Qwilleran nodded. He knew Amanda Goodwinter. "Too bad. She's losing a good man. Do you ever hear from Rosie?"

"She writes to the kids, and they keep me informed. Rosie married again, and they say she has to support him."

"Rosie lost a good guy, too. How do you feel about living up here? Have you adjusted?"

Riker gave his martini a trial sip, winced, and nodded approval. "Yes, I'm glad to be here. I was relieved to cut loose from the *Fluxion,* and after the divorce I wanted to get out of the city. I never thought I'd like living in the hinterland, so far from everywhere, but my attitude is changing. My viewpoint is changing."

"In what way?"

"Remember our front-page story about the chicken coop fire last week? It destroyed 150,000 chickens. When I was working Down Below I would have written a flippant headline about the world's largest chicken barbecue, assuming the place was fully insured and no particular loss." He took another sip of his martini. "Instead, I empathized with the farmer. I've never met Doug Cottle, but I've driven past his farm—the neat house, well-kept barnyard, huge facility for chickens. And when it happened, I felt real agony over the loss of his property and the fate of all those birds trapped in a burning building. I could imagine his dreams and years of work going up in flames in the middle of the night! . . . Ironic, isn't it? I've edited copy for hundreds of fires Down Below, and I never felt that way before. Am I getting old?"

They carried their drinks to the lakeside porch, where the armchairs were made of three-inch logs hammered together by some anonymous carpenter at some date unknown.

"Sit down, Arch. They're more comfortable than they look."

Riker slid cautiously into a hollowed-out seat and breathed a deep sigh of contentment. "Beautiful view! I'll bet you get some spectacular sunsets. You have a lot of goldfinches."

"What do you know about birds, Arch?"

"When you raise a family you learn a lot of things you didn't want to know."

"My plumber said they're wild canaries."

"Your plumber didn't have three kids working on merit badges in ornithology. What do you hear from Polly, Qwill? Does she like England?"

"I've had a couple of postcards. They've asked her to give talks to civic groups."

"I suppose you'll be seeing a lot of Mildred while Polly's away."

Qwilleran's moustache bristled. "If you're thinking what I think you're thinking, the answer is no! Mildred lives half a mile down the beach; we both write for the newspaper; her son-in-law is one of my best friends; she's a great cook. But that doesn't mean I intend to jeopardize my relationship with Polly. And, for what it's worth, Mildred has a husband."

"Okay, okay!" said Riker, throwing up his hands in surrender. He and Qwilleran had grown up together in Chicago, and their friendship had survived fistfights in grade school, arguments in high school, competition in college, and bickering ever since.

Qwilleran said, "Now that you've broken up with Amanda, there's no reason why you couldn't take Mildred out to dinner yourself, Arch. On a scale of one to ten I'd give your ex-fiancée a two and Mildred a nine."

"Not bad!"

"And I'd rate you six-plus."

Riker threw him a sour look. "Don't forget I'm your boss."

"Don't forget I'm your financial backer." The *Moose County Something* had been made possible by a loan from the Klingenschoen Fund, engineered by Qwilleran behind the scenes. "And if you don't start spelling my name right in my column, the interest rate is going up."

"I apologize. We gave the typesetter twenty lashes and an hour to get out of town." Riker looked around the porch. "Where's that supercat? Has he read any minds lately? Predicted any crimes? Sniffed out any dead bodies?"

"Mostly he's too busy being a cat—laundering his tail, chattering at squirrels, eating spiders—all that kind of stuff. But yesterday he tore up the front page of your newspaper, Arch. That should tell you something about the *Something*. He may be protesting the number of typos."

Koko was a legend among newsmen Down Below—the only cat in the history of journalism to be an honorary member of the Press Club. In addition to feline curiosity and Siamese intelligence he possessed an intuition that could put him on the scent of a crime. With a sniff here and a scratch there he could dig up information that astounded humans who had to rely on brainpower alone.

"He would have made a great investigative reporter," Riker said. "We always had cats at home, but never any to compare with Koko. I think it has something to do with his whiskers. He has a magnificent set of whiskers."

"Yes," Qwilleran agreed quietly, stroking his ample moustache.

Riker leaned forward suddenly and squinted at a small mound of sawdust on the porch floor. "You've got carpenter ants!"

"Carpenter *what?*"

"Ants that chew their way through old wood. You'd better get a fumigator out here."

Qwilleran groaned. He envisioned another call to Glinko.

Riker misunderstood the reaction. "Well, you don't want the porch to fall down around your ears, do you? You should get a carpenter out here to examine the logs."

Qwilleran groaned again. "Let me tell you about the joys of living in a seventy-five-year-old log cabin—the perfect summer place, as you call it." He explained the Glinko system, described the couple who operated it, and recounted the visits of Joanna Trupp. "Three visits from a plumber in four days!"

"Sounds to me as if she goes for your moustache," Riker said. "You know how women react to that brush on your lip! Are you going to take her to lunch?"

Qwilleran ignored that quip. "It sounds to me as if the whole Glinko network is a racket. I'll know more at the end of the summer. If my suspicions are correct, the *Something* should run an exposé!"

"Put Koko on the investigation," the editor said with a grin.

"I'm serious, Arch! The whole operation stinks!"

"Oh, come on, Qwill! You're making a mountain out of a molehill. You'd suspect your own grandmother."

Qwilleran shifted his position uncomfortably.

"What's the matter? You're doing a lot of wriggling tonight. I think the porch posts aren't the only place you've got ants."

"They're insect bites that itch like hell," Qwilleran said testily. "About a dozen bites in one spot, and they don't go away."

His friend nodded wisely. "Spider bites. Our kids used to get them at summer camp. They last about a week."

At that moment Koko swaggered onto the porch with a show of authority and stared pointedly at Qwilleran.

"Excuse me while I feed the cats," he said. "Mix yourself another drink, Arch, and then we'll go into town for dinner."

The resort town of Mooseville was two miles long and two blocks wide, strung out along the shoreline at the foot of the sandbluffs.

"One of these days," Riker predicted, "some horny buck will chase a sexy doe across the top of that hill, and all that sand will come sliding down. We'll have another Pompeii. I only hope it's on our deadline."

At the village limits the lakeshore highway became Main Street, with the municipal docks, a marina, and the Northern Lights Hotel on the north side. Across the street were civic buildings and business establishments built entirely of logs, or concrete poured to resemble logs. Post office, town hall, bank and stores acted out the charade, and only the Shipwreck Tavern deviated from civic policy. The town's noisiest and most popular bar occupied what appeared to be the wooden hull of a beached ship.

Qwilleran said, "We'll stop at the tavern for a quickie and then go over to the hotel to eat."

The interior of the bar emulated the hold of an old sailing

vessel with sloping bulkheads and massive timbers, but instead of creaking hull, slapping waves, and singing whales, the sound effects were of television, jukebox, video games, and shouting, laughing patrons.

"Like the pressroom at the Fluxion!" Riker yelled. *"Who are they?"*

"Tourists! Summer people! Locals!" Qwilleran shouted back.

A busy waitress with a talent for lip-reading took their order: one martini straight-up with an anchovy olive, and one club soda with a lemon twist. When the bartender received the order, he waved in the direction of their table. Only Qwilleran ever ordered club soda with a twist.

Excusing himself, Qwilleran ambled over to the crowded bar to wedge in a few words with the man who was pulling beer. What followed was a pantomime of frowns, headshaking, shrugs, and other gestures of helplessness.

"What was that?" Riker shouted.

"Tell you later."

A whiskered old man in a battered naval cap lurched into the tavern and climbed on a stool; the nearby barflies moved away.

"Who's that?"

"Antique dealer!" Qwilleran pointed out another colorful ancient in overalls—red-cheeked, bright-eyed, nimble as a monkey. *"Gravedigger!"*

They were soon blasted out of the Shipwreck Tavern and across the street to the hotel, where the dining room was so quiet, Riker complained, that it hurt his ears. Plastic covers on the tables and paper bibs on the customers identified it as spaghetti night.

"Now I'll explain," said Qwilleran. "That perfect summer place of mine that you admire so much is too small for everyday living. I want to build a small addition. I've talked to Hasselrich, and it's approved by the estate, but now comes the problem: finding a builder."

"That shouldn't be difficult," said Riker. "The county has some big contractors."

"Unfortunately they're tied up with major projects in the warm months, and they won't take a small job. The summer people have to resort to itinerant carpenters who drive into town in rusty crates and live in tents."

"Are they licensed?"

"They get away without a license because they're a necessary evil. The township looks the other way."

"I never heard of such a thing!"

"There are plenty of things you never heard of, Arch, until you came to Moose County. It's like living on another planet . . . Speaking of planets, do you hear any talk about UFOs?"

"Occasionally from the wire services, but that's old stuff."

"I mean—have you heard reports of recent activity over the lake?"

"No," said the editor with amused interest. "Are there rumors?"

"The summer people discuss visitors from outer space the way you talk about the Chicago Cubs. Why don't you assign Roger to do a story?"

"Why don't you do the story yourself? It's your lead."

"I'm a nonbeliever. You and I know it's some kind of meteorological phenomenon, but Roger swears it's interplanetary, and Mildred acts as if she's on first-name terms with the crews."

The salad was crisp, the garlic bread was crusty, and the spaghetti was al dente. "It's the best thing they do," Qwilleran said. "All the locals come on Mondays. They let the tourists have the gray pork chops and gray baked potatoes and gray broccoli on the other nights."

A young couple at a nearby table waved to Qwilleran, and when Riker said he had to go back to the office, Qwilleran went over to speak with Nick and Lori Bamba. "Who's baby-sitting tonight?" he asked.

"My mother-in-law," said Lori. "Thank God for mothers-in-law. I've given up trying to get you to do it, Qwill."

"Pull up a chair," Nick invited. "Have dessert with us."

Lori was Qwilleran's part-time secretary. Working out of her house, she answered his mail with one hand and held the formula bottle with the other. "Your mail has doubled since you started writing the 'Qwill Pen,' " she said. "I can hardly keep up with it."

"Start typing with two hands," he suggested.

"How are the cats?"

"They're fine. We've moved up to the cabin for the summer, and I want to build an addition. Know where I can find a good builder?"

Lori and Nick exchanged significant glances. "Clem Cottle?" Nick suggested.

"Perfect! Clem needs the work."

"And he's not so busy on the farm since the fire . . . Qwill, we're talking about Doug Cottle's son," said Nick. "They're the ones had the big chicken coop fire."

Lori said, "Clem's getting married, and he could use some extra money."

"Is this guy any good?" Qwilleran asked.

"Very good, very reliable," Nick said. "When would you want him to start? I'll phone him right away. We're in the same softball league."

"For starters I'd like him to build a flight of steps down to the beach."

"Sure, he can do that with one hand!"

Nick excused himself and went to the phone, and Lori said to Qwilleran, "I wish Nick could find another job that would use his skills and experience—and still allow us to live here—and still pay a decent salary. Being an engineer at the state prison isn't the most elevating occupation. He sees so much that's sordid and just plain wrong."

"But he has a built-in verve that keeps him riding on top. He's always up."

"That's his public posture," Lori said. "I see him at home . . . Here he comes."

"Clem's interested," Nick said. "He wants to talk to you."

The voice on the phone had the chesty resonance of a man who has spent his life on a farm—and on a softball field. "Hello, Mr. Qwilleran. I hear you want a carpenter."

"Yes, I have several jobs in mind, but the most urgent is a set of steps down to the beach before my cabin slides down into the lake. Do you know the kind I mean?"

"Sure, I helped Buddy Yarrow build those a couple of years ago for some people at the Dune Club. I know what lumber to order without any waste."

"When could you start?"

"How about tomorrow?"

"I couldn't ask better than that. Do you know where to find me?"

"It's the drive with a K on a post. I've passed it a million times."

"See you tomorrow then." Qwilleran tamped his moustache with satisfaction and returned to the Bambas' table. "I'm indebted to you kids," he said, and picked up their dinner check.

When Qwilleran returned home, the Siamese greeted him with a look of hungry eagerness, and he scouted for a small treat that they might enjoy. Mildred's tub of homemade cereal was still unopened. "This may look like catfood," he explained, "but it's breakfast cereal for humans." (They normally objected to anything produced especially for cats.) They gobbled it up. Then he sprawled on the sofa with a news magazine, while Yum Yum snuggled on his lap and Koko perched on the sofaback, both waiting to hear him read aloud about the trade deficit and the latest hostile takeover.

At midnight it was time to lock the doors and close the interior shutters. Daybreak came early in June, and unless the louvered shutters were closed, the pink light of sunrise illuminated the cabin and gave the cats the erroneous idea that it was time for breakfast.

The lakeshore could be very dark and very quiet on a calm, moonless night, and Qwilleran slept soundly until two-thirty. At that hour a sound of some kind roused him from sleep. It was alarming enough to cause him to sit up and listen warily. Again he heard it: a deep, continuous, rumbling moan that rose louder and angrier and ended in a high-pitched shriek. Recognizing Koko's Tarzan act, reserved for stray cats, Qwilleran shouted "Quiet!"

He lay down again. Then he became aware of intermittent flashes of light. He swung out of bed and hurried into the living room. A greenish light so powerful that it filtered through the louvered shutters was coloring the white walls, white sofas, and even Koko's pale fur with a ghastly tint. The cat was on the arm of the sofa, his back humped, his tail bushed, his ears back, his eyes staring at the front window.

Qwilleran threw open the shutters and was blinded by a dazzling, pulsating light. He rushed to the front door, struggled with the lock, dashed out on the porch shouting *"Hey, you out there!"*

But the light had disappeared, and there was not a sound, although a breeze sprang up and swished through the cherry trees. He groped his way back indoors, still blind from the intensity of the flashes.

It was a joke, Qwilleran decided, as he regained his vision, and as Koko's tail resumed its normal shape, and as Yum Yum came crawling out from under the sofa. It was that photographer from the Dune Club, he decided. He had been flashing his strobe lights to play a trick on a nonbeliever, and no doubt Mildred was the one who gave him the idea.

FOUR

THE WHINING OF an electric saw and the sharp blows of a hammer interrupted Qwilleran's sleep on Tuesday morning. He looked at his bedside clock with one eye open; it was only six-thirty. He was a late riser by preference, but he realized that the carpenter was on the job and the beach steps were being built. He pulled on a warmup suit and went out to the top of the dune.

There was a light blue pickup in the clearing—one of five thousand of that color in Moose County according to his private estimate. This one was distinguished by a cartoon on the cab door: a screeching, wing-flapping chicken. On the door handle hung a softball jacket: red with white lettering that spelled out COTTLE ROOSTERS. Lumber was stacked in the clearing, and a table-saw was set up. The carpenter himself was halfway down the sandbank working at top speed, driving home each nail with three economical strokes of the hammer. *Bang bang bang.*

"Morning," said Qwilleran sleepily when the hammering stopped.

The young man looked up from his work. "Hope I didn't wake you up."

"Not at all," said Qwilleran with amiable sarcasm. "I always get up at six o'clock and run a few miles before breakfast."

The humor was lost on the carpenter. "That's good for you," he said. "Oh, I forgot—I'm Clem Cottle." He scrambled up the sandbank, holding out a calloused hand.

He was one of five thousand big, healthy, young blond fellows in Moose County—again a private estimate. "Your face looks familiar," Qwilleran said.

"Sometimes I help out behind the bar at the Shipwreck." Clem wasted no time on conversation, but returned to building the steps.

"What kind of wood are you using?" The lumber had a greenish tint like the bilious light that had seeped into the cabin in the middle of the night.

"It's treated so it doesn't have to be painted. Everybody's using this now." *Bang bang bang.*

As one who could smash a finger with the first blow, Qwilleran watched the carpenter with admiration. Every nail went in straight, in the right place, with an economy of movement. "You're a real pro! Where did you learn to do that?"

"My dad taught me everything." *Bang bang bang.* "I'm building a house for myself. I'm getting married in October."

"I was sorry to hear about the fire. That must have been a devastating experience."

Clem stopped hammering and looked up at Qwilleran. "I hope I never have to live through anything like that again," he said grimly. "I woke up in the middle of the night and thought my room was on fire. The walls were red! The sky was red! The volunteers came out from Mooseville and some other towns, but it was too late."

"What will your father do now?"

Clem shrugged. "Start all over again."

"Would you care for a cup of coffee or a soft drink?"

"No, thanks. Too early for a break yet." *Bang bang bang.*

Qwilleran prepared coffee for himself and astounded the Siamese by serving their breakfast two hours ahead of schedule—a can of boned chicken topped with a spoonful of jellied consommé. Unable to believe their rare good fortune, they pranced in exultant circles, yikking and yowling.

"You deserve this," he told them. "You've had a disturbing vacation so far . . . leaks, plumbers, crazy lights in the night, and now that noisy carpenter!" He watched them devour their food. They seemed to enjoy an audience; there were times when Yum Yum refused to eat unless he stood by, and it gave him pleasure to observe them crouching over the plate with businesslike tails flat on the floor, ears and whiskers swept back, heads jerking and snapping as they maneuvered the food in their mouths. When he offered them a few nuggets of Mildred's cereal for dessert, Koko rose on his hind legs in anticipation.

Qwilleran was so intent on studying his companions that the telephone startled him. It was Mildred's excited voice on the phone. "Qwill, have you heard the news?"

"I haven't turned on the radio," he said. "What happened? Did a flying saucer splash down in front of the Northern Lights Hotel? Probably needed a few repairs at Glinko's garage."

"You're being funny this morning, Qwill! Well, listen to this: Roger called me a couple of minutes ago. Captain Phlogg was found dead in his shop!"

"Poor fool finally drank himself to death. The chamber of commerce will be distraught. Who found the body?"

"A Mooseville officer making the rounds at midnight. He saw a light inside the shop and the door open. The captain was slumped in his chair. But here's the chief reason I'm calling," she said. "His dog has been howling all night. Do you think I should go over and feed it?"

"Do you want to lose an arm? I suggest you call the sheriff. I wonder if the old guy has any relatives around here."

"Not according to Roger. I wonder what will happen."

"The state will bury him and search for heirs and assets. Do you think he had money stashed away? You never know about miserly eccentrics . . . Well, anyway, Mildred, you'd better call the sheriff about the dog. It's good of you to be concerned."

Qwilleran hung up the receiver gently, thinking warm thoughts about his kind, considerate neighbor . . . and wondering why he had received no long letter from Polly Duncan.

On the dune, where construction was nearing completion, he said to Clem, "Would you be interested in building an addition to this cabin?"

Clem appraised the weathered logs. "You'd never match that old logwork."

"I'm aware of that, but I'd settle for board-and-batten with the proper stain."

"And the old foundation is fieldstone. The last stone mason died two years ago. You'd have to have concrete block under the new part."

"No objection."

"How would you connect the old and the new?"

Qwilleran showed him the sketches, with the new wing right-angled to the cabin, and a door cut through into the back hall. Clem took them to his truck, figured costs, and presented an estimate in writing.

He said, "You're outside the village limits, so you won't need a permit. I mean, you're supposed to have one, but nobody ever does. So I could start digging for the footings tomorrow and pour them the next day. They'll set over the weekend."

"I'll give you a deposit."

"Forget it! I've got credit at the lumberyard. The Cottles have been here since 1872."

"One question," Qwilleran said. "Do you know anything about carpenter ants? They're getting into the porch posts."

"Just get a bug bomb and spray 'em good," Clem advised.

After the blue truck with the frantic chicken on the door had pulled away, Qwilleran recalled the transaction with satisfaction. The bill for the steps had been reasonable, and Clem had accepted a check with no hemming and hawing about cash. The young man was not only honest and skilled but remarkably industrious. He worked on his father's farm, moonlighted at the Shipwreck Tavern, and was building himself a house. Now Qwilleran was inclined to discount the alarmist gossip about building problems. Lyle Compton had called the dune-dwellers a giddy bunch, and their chitchat about UFOs and horoscopes confirmed that opinion. It had been a mistake to believe their cocktail conversation about underground builders.

On the whole he was feeling so elated about the latest turn of events that he agreed to act as a judge for the Fourth of July parade when someone called him from the county building in Pickax. It was a civic chore he ordinarily would have sidestepped, but the caller was a woman with a voice like Polly Duncan's. She said that the countywide parade would be held in Mooseville and Mildred Hanstable had agreed to be a judge, with a third yet to be announced. She said that Qwilleran's name on the panel of judges would add greatly to the prestige of the event. She added that she always read "Straight from the Qwill Pen" and it was the best thing in the paper. Grooming his moustache modestly, Qwilleran agreed to help judge the floats on the Fourth of July.

For lunch he went into town to the Northern Lights Hotel, and as he walked through the lobby he recognized something out of the corner of his eye. It was the picture of a young man. The hotel had a quaint custom of announcing social news on a glorified bulletin board in the lobby. A gilt frame and some ribbons and artificial flowers were intended to glamorize the display. Qwilleran usually walked past quickly with averted eyes, but this time he stopped for a closer look. A photo of a young couple was displayed with a neatly printed card reading, "Mr. and Mrs. Warren Wimsey announce the engagement of their daughter, Maryellen, to Clem Cottle, son of Mr. and Mrs. Douglas Cottle, all of Black Creek. An October wedding is planned." Clem was stiffly posed in a collar and tie. The girl looked wholesome and intelligent and country-pretty.

Wimsey! The name was familiar to Qwilleran. There were dozens of Wimseys, Goodwinters, Trevelyans, and Cuttlebrinks in the slim directory of Moose County telephone subscribers. Families had a tendency to stay in the area for generations, and the annual family reunions were attended by a hundred members of the clan, or even more. In the cities where Qwilleran had lived and worked, such family get-togethers were unheard of, and he thought, Ah! Another idea for the "Qwill Pen."

After lunch he walked to Huggins Hardware to buy insect spray as Clem had suggested. It was a brilliant summer day, and Main Street was teeming with tourists, always distinguishable from the locals by their clothing, speech, and attitude. The young vacationers were as boisterous and as naked as the law would allow. The middle-aged tourists from the city stared at the natives with amused superiority. Busloads of white-haired day-trippers followed tour guides in and out of the shipwreck museum and gazed obediently at a certain spot in the lake where, they were told, a shipful of gold bullion had sunk a hundred years ago and was still there! Qwilleran made another mental note for his column.

The hardware merchant was taking advantage of the traffic by displaying minnow pails, beach balls, bicycles, and life preservers on the sidewalk.

Qwilleran, in his present elevated mood, had a taste for adventure. "How much for a lightweight ten-speed, Cecil?" he asked.

"Where do you plan to ride, Mr. Q? The traffic is murder on the highway this summer. You'd be better off to get a trail bike and stick to the dirt roads. Much safer!"

"They look like the clunkers I pedaled when I was delivering newspapers."

"Just take one out and try it, Mr. Q. You won't be disappointed. Head for the riverbank," Cecil Huggins advised. "Go out Sandpit Road half a mile and then get off the asphalt onto Dumpy Road till it dead-ends at Hogback. If you cut across the fields to the river, there's a dandy trail there. Be careful of mudslides. That's where Buddy Yarrow slipped in."

The seat and handlebars were adjusted to Qwilleran's six feet two, and he set out on Cecil's proposed route. He had to admit that the bike negotiated the uneven terrain in exhilarating fashion. Leaping over ruts and roots and washouts, he felt like an intrepid twelve-year-old, and there were no trucks, no electric signs, no whiffs of carbon monoxide.

Dumpy Road was a benighted colony of substandard housing, but it led to the bank of the Ittibittiwassee, which bubbled into eddying bays and babbled on the pebbles like Tennyson's brook. To Qwilleran all was enchantment: the splash and gurgle of the rapids; the willows weeping over the water's edge; the wildflowers, birds, and scurrying animals that he could not identify, never having bothered to learn about nature. He envied the country-smart locals who rescued bear cubs and built their own houses. They were descendants of the pioneers who had settled this north country, chopping down trees to build their log cabins and picking wild herbs to make their own medicines. Qwilleran wondered what they did about spider bites in the old days. Much of his biking was done standing up on the pedals.

Around each bend there was another surprise: a deer having a drink; a solitary fisherman in waders; something sleek, brown and flat-tailed, swimming and diving. There was one discordant note: Ahead he could see a jumble of junk marring the natural beauty of the riverbank—a series of boxlike structures built of chickenwire and scrap lumber. He dismounted and wheeled his bike cautiously closer. They were ramshackle cages. In one of them an animal was sleeping, rolled up in a ball; it looked like a fox. In another enclosure some tiny creatures with striped backs were chasing each other and climbing over a wheel that rotated. An old bathtub sunk in the ground was filled with rainwater, and ducks waddled in and out of their pool.

It was obviously Joanna's zoo, and Qwilleran hoped she was not there. Her house—no better than a large box with windows, perched on concrete blocks—fronted on the dirt road called Hogback, and it was surrounded by plumbing fixtures. Broken or rusted sinks, toilets, oil tanks, and water heaters were dotted about the yard like tombstones in a plumbing graveyard. To add to the funereal effect there was a row of wooden crosses marking small graves.

He was contemplating these crosses when a van careened down Hogback Road in a cloud of dust. It jerked to a stop, and Joanna jumped out.

"I was biking on the riverbank and saw your interesting zoo," he explained, unhappy to be caught prowling about her property.

"Didja see my chipmunks?" she asked with more spirit than she usually mustered. "I built 'em an exercise wheel."

"What do you feed them?" he asked in a lame attempt to show intelligent interest.

"Sunflower seeds and acorns. You should see 'em sit up and eat and wash their face. Wanna hold one? They like being stroked."

"No, thanks," he said. "Anything that eats acorns probably has very sharp teeth. What happens to them in winter?"

"I give 'em straw, and they sleep a lot."

"Those crosses—are they graves?"

"That's where I buried the bear cubs. The woodchuck, too. And some chipmunks."

Appraising the yardful of retired fixtures, he asked, "What made you decide to be a plumber, Joanna?"

"My daddy showed me how to do all that kind of stuff, so I took a test and got my license." She saw Qwilleran looking at her house. "Someday I'm gonna get somebody to build me a real house, when I get enough money. Wanna beer?"

"No, thanks. I borrowed this bike, and if I don't return it soon, the sheriff will come gunning for me. What's the quickest way back to Mooseville?"

She pointed down Hogback Road, and he rode off through the dirt ruts at top speed, gripping the handlebars, concentrating on his balance, certain that she was watching, hoping he would not take an embarrassing header.

The following days were eventful for both Qwilleran and the Siamese. Clem Cottle and his younger brother staked out the new east wing and went to work with shovels, digging like madmen, then building wooden forms. The next morning the cement mixer truck rumbled into the clearing, and the two young men ran back and forth trundling wheelbarrows filled with wet concrete. Yum Yum hid under the sofa, and even brave Koko retired discreetly under a bunk in the guestroom, slinking out to peek once in a while.

Qwilleran went for another ride on his new bike, this time taking a back road to an abandoned nineteenth-century cemetery that he had visited two years before. To his surprise the vandalized tombstones had been restored, the weeds were under control, and there was hardly a beer can to be seen. A new sign announced: PIONEER CEMETERY. NO PICNICS. He suspected the preservation program had been instigated by the tireless Mildred Hanstable, and he telephoned her when he returned home.

"Hi, Qwill!" she said in her exuberant style. "I saw you out riding on one of those funny-looking bikes."

"I am now a demon on wheels," he replied. "The terror of the countryside. I visited the old cemetery. Who's been cleaning it up?"

"The student history clubs. They're restoring all the abandoned cemeteries and cataloguing the family graveyards around the county. The early settlers used to bury their dead on their own land, you know, and the sites are protected by law, but first they have to know where they are."

Another idea for the "Qwill Pen," he thought. "I understand you're one of the judges for the parade. How about dinner afterward? At the Fish Tank."

"I'd love it!" she said. "Their navy grog is fabulous, and I always need a stiff drink after a Moose County parade. How did you like the cereal?"

"It's delicious," he said, speaking for the others. "Great wonders come out of your kitchen, Mildred. And another great wonder: I've found a carpenter without resorting to the underground."

"Who?"

"Clem Cottle from Black Creek."

"You're lucky!" Mildred said. "Clem is a good carpenter and a fine young man. He's marrying Maryellen Wimsey, and she used to be in my art classes. She's a lovely girl."

During the next few days Maryellen drove into the clearing daily at noon in a small yellow car, bringing a hot lunch and staying long enough to pick up stray nails and stack the scraps of wood in tidy heaps.

Clem reported for work every morning at six-thirty—sometimes with his younger brother, but more often alone. He laid the foundation blocks, installed the basic drainage, put in the joists and subfloor, and started the framing.

There were other visitors besides Maryellen. Dune-dwellers who had never cared to walk on the beach suddenly began to take exercise. Attracted by the sounds of industry or compelled by curiosity or driven by envy, they strolled casually past the cabin, waved to Qwilleran on the porch, and climbed the new wooden steps to check the carpenter's progress. Mildred Hanstable and Sue Urbank were the first visitors, applauding Qwilleran's good fortune in finding a decent builder. Mildred brought him another tub of cereal.

Leo Urbank robbed valuable time from his golf game to inspect the new structure, predicting that it would never be completed. "Take it from me," he warned. "They're hot at the beginning, but they drop out halfway through."

The Comptons were unexpected callers. Lisa Compton was a jogger who regularly pounded the shoreline in a green warmup suit, but her husband considered the beach solely as a place to smoke a cigar. Yet, there he was, plodding through the sand and climbing the steps.

"When the guy finishes your place," he said, "maybe he could come over and work on our garage."

"I'll line him up for you," Qwilleran said. "I suppose you know Clem Cottle."

"Oh, sure," said the superintendent. "We had thirteen Cottles going through the school system at one time. Clem was the brightest. Too bad he didn't go to college for more than two years. But they were all conscientious—all good stock. I wish I could say the same for all the old families. There's a lot of inbreeding in a tight community like this."

One evening John and Vicki Bushland sauntered down the beach to take pictures of the sunset, and Qwilleran invited them to view the spectacle from the screened porch, minus mosquitoes. "Where's your studio?" he asked them.

"In Lockmaster. It's been there for eighty years."

"I'm not familiar with that town."

"It's sixty miles southwest of here—a county seat like Pickax, only bigger," Bushy said.

"What kind of work do you do?"

"The usual: portraits, weddings, club groups. When my grandfather started the business he photographed a lot of funerals. At the cemetery they'd open the coffin and prop it up on end, with the mourners gathered around the corpse. You can still see those gruesome group pictures in family albums. He was a great guy, my grandfather. He took two kinds of pictures—what he called vertical-up-and-down and horizontal-sideways."

Qwilleran asked, "Do you shoot animals?"

"A few. Some people want their kids taken with the family pooch."

"How about cats?"

"Lockmaster isn't big on cats," said the photographer. "Mostly dogs and horses."

"But cats make wonderful models," said Vicki. "They never strike a pose that isn't photogenic."

Qwilleran huffed lightly into his moustache. "I dispute that. Every time I think I'm getting a good snapshot, my cats yawn or turn into pretzels, and nothing is less picturesque than a cat's gullet or his backside."

Knowing they were being discussed, the Siamese sauntered onto the porch and posed as a couple—Yum Yum sprawled in a languid posture with chin on paw and ears tilted forward; Koko sitting tall with tail curved gracefully around haunches.

"See what I mean?" cried Vicki.

"Look at those highlights!" said Bushy as he raised the camera to his eye, but before he could snap the picture, both cats dissolved in a blur of fur and were gone. Challenged, he said, "I'd like to get those two characters in my studio and work with them. Could you bring them down to Lockmaster?"

"I don't see why not," Qwilleran said. "They're good travelers."

"You could bring them down some evening when the studio's closed, and I could spend time with them. Just give me a ring." He gave Qwilleran his business card. "I'd like to enter them in a calendar competition."

Not all the visitors were dune-dwellers during those exciting days of construction activity. One afternoon Joanna's van pulled into the clearing.

"Whatcha doin' over there?" she asked.

"Building an addition to the cabin," Qwilleran said.

She stared at it wordlessly for a while. "No more leaks?" she said finally.

"So far, so good."

"Did you find my lipstick?"

"I beg your pardon?" Qwilleran said.

"My lipstick. I thought maybe it rolled out of my pocket when I was here."

"I haven't seen it," he said, noting that her face had the original washed-out appearance.

"It could be under the house."

"Feel free to have a look, but don't let Koko go down there."

Joanna went indoors, and the trap door slammed twice. She returned, looking disappointed. "I'll hafta buy another."

After she had left, Qwilleran wondered why she had waited so long to ask about her missing lipstick. Was it simply an excuse to pay a social call? He felt sorry for the girl—so plain, and with so few advantages. But he was not going to take her to lunch! He had lunched his doctor and his interior designer, but Joanna was getting a ten-dollar tip for every plumbing job; she could buy her own lunch.

By July third the roof trusses had been erected, and the roof boards were in place. Clem had been working fast. "Trying to get it under cover before it rains," he explained when he collected his tools on Thursday night.

"Are you taking a long holiday weekend?" Qwilleran asked him.

"Can't afford to. I'll be here bright and early Saturday, but tomorrow I'll be in the parade. The boss at the Shipwreck came up with a good idea, and I said I'd do it."

"Are you riding on a float?"

"Nothing like that," said the young man with a wide grin. "I'm just gonna walk down the middle of the street. Then after the parade there's a softball game—Roosters against the state prison team. If you like ballgames, you oughta come and see us play."

Qwilleran liked the young carpenter, and he gave him a parting salute as the Frantic Chicken drove away. It was prophetic. That was the last time he ever saw Clem Cottle.

FIVE

THE FOURTH OF JULY dawned with the sunshine of a flag-waving holiday, and Qwilleran was in good spirits, despite some soreness following his last bike ride. The east wing with its roof boards in place was beginning to look like a habitation.

"Well, chums, we're on our way!" he told the Siamese. "You'll have your own apartment in a few weeks. What would you like for breakfast? Turkey from the deli? Or cocktail shrimp from a can?"

Koko was not present to cast his vote, but Yum Yum was rubbing against Qwilleran's ankles in anticipation and curling her tail lovingly around his leg, and he knew she preferred turkey. He began to mince slices of white meat.

"What's that noise?" He set down the knife and looked up. "Did you hear a tapping noise? . . . There it is again!"

Tap tap tap.

With a sudden drop in his holiday mood he envisioned another leak or mechanical breakdown. "There it goes again!" Possibilities flashed through his mind: the electric pump; the water heater; the refrigerator. It would mean another emergency call to that laughing hyena in Mooseville.

Tap tap tap.

Qwilleran followed the sound. It led him past the mudroom, past the bathroom, and into the guestroom. The tapping had stopped, but Koko was sitting on the windowsill overlooking the building site, and the morning sun made glistening shafts of every whisker, every alert hair over his eyes.

"Did you hear that, Koko?"

The cat turned his head to look at Qwilleran, and at that moment his brown tail slapped the windowsill three times. *Tap tap tap.*

Qwilleran uttered a sigh of relief. "Okay, Thumper, come and get your breakfast, and please don't play tricks like that."

The parade was scheduled to start at two o'clock, and he dressed in what he considered appropriate garb: white pants and open-neck shirt with a blue blazer. He was sure the judges would be required to wear some absurd badge of office, and he was prepared for the worst. Mildred, when he picked her up at her cottage, was wearing one of her fluttery sundresses in a blue-and-white stripe.

"Keep your fingers crossed," she said, as she stepped into his car.

"What should I deduce from that cryptic remark?"

"Maybe you didn't see the parade last year."

"I did not. I'm not a parade-goer by choice."

"Well, I went with Sharon and Roger last year, and I was appalled! It was nothing but a candy-grab! Politicians rode in new-model cars, throwing candy to the crowd. Beauty queens rode in convertibles, throwing candy to the crowd. The used-car dealer rode in a three-year-old car *with a price tag!* And he was throwing candy to the crowd. There were no floats and no marching bands—just sound trucks blaring pop music, and commercial vehicles advertising the Mooseville video arcade and the Friday night fish fry in

North Kennebeck. But worst of all, there was not a single flag in the parade! This was Independence Day, and there was not an American flag to be seen!"

"How did the crowd react to all of this?"

"All that free candy? Are you kidding? They loved it!"

"I'd say you had reason to be disturbed," Qwilleran said.

"Disturbed! I was *furious!* When the holiday weekend was over, I got on my horse and went into battle. You don't know me, Qwill, when I get mad! That was before the *Something* started publication, so I couldn't write an irate letter to the editor, but I wrote to every elected and appointed official, every civic leader, every chamber of commerce, every citizens' group, and every school principal in the county. I spouted off at meetings of the county commissioners and the village councils. I really made myself a public nuisance. You know, Qwill, every veterans' organization and fraternal lodge has a big flag and a color guard. The two high schools and three junior highs have marching bands. Their uniforms don't fit, and they hit some wrong notes, but they march, and they beat drums, and they blow trumpets. Where were they on Independence Day? That's what I wanted to know."

"What happened after your outburst?"

"We'll soon find out. They appointed a county committee to organize this year's parade, and—wisely, perhaps—I wasn't asked to serve. Apparently they laid ambitious plans, but you know what happens when a committee takes charge. Sometimes nothing!"

The sidewalks in Mooseville were already crowded with parade-goers, and the parking lots were filled. Police had barricaded several blocks of Main Street, detouring traffic, but Qwilleran found a place to park near Glinko's garage. He and Mildred pushed their way through the crowds to a reviewing stand built in front of the town hall. A committeewoman wearing a tri-color bandoleer guided them to the judges' table, and gave them scorecards and straw boaters with tri-color hatbands. Mildred wore hers straight-on, and Qwilleran said she looked saucy. He tipped his at a rakish angle, and Mildred said he looked dashing, especially with that big moustache.

"The floats," the committeewoman explained, "are to be rated on originality, execution, and message, using the suggested point system."

The third judge had not arrived. Mildred guessed it would be an announcer from WPKX. Qwilleran thought it might be the superintendent of schools; Lyle Compton was always the most visible official in the county.

"He says it's part of his job," Mildred confided, "but I think he's getting ready to run for the state legislature."

"My carpenter is going to be in the parade," Qwilleran said. "It's some kind of stunt sponsored by the Shipwreck Tavern."

"I hope the parade won't be so commercial this year."

Their conversation was interrupted by the arrival of the third judge, who was creating a commotion as she complained about the steps, fell over the folding chairs, and upset the tripods that held the public-address speakers.

"Who wants to drive thirty miles for a parade?" she grumbled. "It should have been held in the county seat!"

The committeewoman tried to explain. "It was thought that Mooseville is the center of population on a big holiday, Miss Goodwinter. All the tourists are here."

"Tourists, bah! Why don't they stay home? Let them go to their own parade and leave some parking spaces for the citizens. I had to walk three blocks!"

It was Amanda Goodwinter, Pickax interior designer, city council member, and former fiancée of Arch Riker. She was wearing her usual colorless, shapeless clothing with a man's golf hat jammed over her spiky gray hair. "I don't know why I'm here!" she added grouchily. "I hate parades! And I'm not going to wear that silly straw hat!" She banged the boater down on the table and looked at the scorecard. "Originality, execution, and *message?* What does that mean? A parade is a parade. Why does it have to have a *message?*" Scowling and fussing, she settled herself in a folding chair. "Five minutes of this will give me a backache."

"Good afternoon, Amanda," said Qwilleran graciously.

"What are you doing here? You're as big a fool as I am!"

The beat of drums could be heard in the distance, and voices below the reviewing stand drifted up to the judges' table:

Excited youngster: "I think they're coming!"

Police officer: "Back on the curb, sonny."

Child: "Are they gonna throw candy?"

Mother: "Don't forget to salute the flag, the way your teacher said."

Old Man: "The band's getting ready to play."

Screaming child: "He took my sucker!"

Another screaming child: "Lift me up! I can't see!"

With a stirring flourish one of the high school bands swung into "The Stars and Stripes Forever," the sun glinting on their brass instruments two blocks away. A sheriff's car with flashing rooflights led the way at four miles an hour. Then there was a breathless wait as heads turned and necks craned.

The wait was long enough to solemnify the marching of the color guard—a tall, beefy flag-bearer flanked by two men and two women in uniform, arms swinging and eyes straight ahead. As if on cue a breeze sprang up when they reached the reviewing stand, and the stars and stripes rippled over the heads of the stern-faced marchers.

When the guard of honor had passed and the officials on the reviewing stand had resumed their seats, tears were rolling down Mildred's face. "This really gets to me," she said in a choked voice.

"Congratulations!" Qwilleran said. "You won your battle."

"Not yet. I'm waiting for the candy."

There was no candy. Before the afternoon was over the onlookers had seen a grand marshal on a proud-stepping horse with nodding plumes and glittering harness brasses; seven color guards from organizations around the county; four student bands, plus Scottish pipers from Lockmaster, sixty miles away; ten floats, two drill teams, three fire trucks sounding their sirens; and fourteen dogs from the St. Bernard Club, pulling their owners on leashes.

Each municipality in Moose County sponsored a float. Pickax honored the men who had worked the mines in the nineteenth century: Moving silently past the viewers was a tableau of grimy miners wearing candles in their hats and carrying pickaxes, coils of rope, and sledgehammers.

Sawdust City, once the hub of the lumbering industry, staged a lumbercamp scene on a flatbed truck—with a cook flipping flapjacks, loggers brawling over a card game, and someone in a bear costume stealing the flapjacks.

Then came the Mooseville entry—a flatbed crowded with sportsmen and outdoor-lovers; fishermen with rods and reels, boaters with binoculars and lifejackets, golfers with their clubs, and campers grilling hot dogs. Presiding over them all was the reigning queen of the annual Fishhook Festival, her formal ballgown fashioned of camouflage fabric and her crown of deer antlers.

"Confused! Cluttered!" Amanda growled. "No organization!"

"But it's graphic," Mildred said.

"It projects a message," Qwilleran added.

"It's a mess!" Amanda insisted.

The lakeside town of Brrr, so named because it was the coldest spot in the county during the winter months, presented a plastic snow scene with a papier-mâché igloo and papier-mâché polar bear. Lounging in the synthetic snowdrifts were male and female sunbathers in bikinis. Judging by the whistles, this float was the popular favorite.

"No taste!" Amanda objected. "But what do you expect of that godforsaken town?"

Even the dreary little village of Chipmunk managed to enter a float. Known as the moonshine capital of the county during Prohibition, and notorious for the lethal nature of its white lightning, Chipmunk had resurrected a homemade still and displayed it on a flatbed draped in black. The visual punch line was the scattering of bodies on the truck, lifeless or comatose.

"Now *that one* shows some wit!" Amanda said, "and if you want a message, that says it all."

The judges agreed, and first prize went to the much maligned village of Chipmunk.

Relegated to the end of the two-hour parade were the commercial exhibits with their advertising slogans. A tow truck pulling a wrecked car was sponsored by Buster's Collision Service, "Where We Meet by Accident."

The Pickax Auto Repair and Radiator Shop advertised "A Good Place to Take a Leak."

Then a solitary man walked down the middle of Main Street, leading a donkey. There was laughter from the crowd.

"Can't see what it says!" Amanda complained.

Qwilleran read her the lettering on the animal's saddle blanket. "Get Your Donkey over to the Shipwreck Tavern."

Amanda snorted.

The last flatbed in the parade was sponsored by Trevelyan Plumbing and Heating—an arrangement of old-fashioned bathroom fixtures, with Grandpa Trevelyan sitting in the footed bathtub smoking a corncob pipe. The banner read, "If It Wasn't for Your Plumber, You'd Have No Place to Go."

The parade was over. The watchers swarmed across the parade route. Only then did Qwilleran realize that Clem Cottle had not marched. The man leading the donkey was the regular daytime bartender from the Shipwreck Tavern.

"Fabulous parade!" Mildred said. "They didn't throw a single piece of candy! And I love those Scottish pipers! Don't they have wonderful legs? You'd look good in kilts, Qwill."

"They did a good job of pacing the units," he said. "No long waits and no pileup and no overlapping bands."

"Whole thing was too long," Amanda groused.

Mildred said, "Mighty Lou made the grandest grand marshal I've ever seen. He has all those expensive leather clothes with silver nailheads, you know, and that was his own horse. Wasn't it a beauty?"

Qwilleran and Mildred raced the crowds to the Fish Tank and had an early dinner. It was a new restaurant in an old waterfront warehouse on the fishing wharves, and the old timbers creaked with the movement of the lake. They ordered the Fish Tank's famous clam chowder and broiled whitefish—from a waiter named Harvey who had once been in Mildred's art class.

"How's everything at the Top o' the Dunes?" Qwilleran asked her.

"Well, the animal-rescue people picked up Captain Phlogg's dog right away . . . And Doc and Dottie are buying a boat, which they'll berth at the marina in Brrr . . . And the Urbanks (don't repeat this) are splitting up, I happen to know. They got along fine until they retired, but that's the way it goes. Frankly, I don't know how Sue could stand him all these years."

"How about your next-door neighbor?"

"Russell? I've tried to be neighborly, but she doesn't respond. She's a strange one."

"I've seen her on the beach, feeding the gulls," Qwilleran said. "She talks to them."

"She's lonely. Why don't you talk to her, Qwill? You're always so sympathetic, and she might warm up to an older man."

"Sorry, Mildred. I've had enough complications with younger women. Even my plumber is getting a little too friendly."

"In what way?"

"She's started wearing lipstick and washing her hair. I recognize the early warning signals."

"Did you read your horoscope this morning?"

"You know I don't buy that nonsense, Mildred."

"Well, for your information, the *Morning Rampage* said your charisma will make you very popular with the opposite sex, and romance is just around the corner."

Qwilleran huffed into his moustache. "I'd be happier if they'd give practical advice, such as 'Don't order fish in a restaurant today; you could choke to death.' My whitefish is full of bones."

"Send it back!" Mildred said. "Don't eat it! Mine is filleted to perfection."

Qwilleran summoned the waiter and voiced his complaint.

"All fish has bones," the waiter said.

"But not all waiters have brains," Mildred snapped. "Harvey, take that plate out to the kitchen and bring Mr. Qwilleran a decent filet of whitefish—and no excuses!"

The waiter scuttled away with the plate.

Qwilleran asked, "How long does your authority over these kids continue? Harvey is at least twenty-five. Is there a statute of limitations?"

"Anyone who goes through my classes gets me for life," she stated flatly.

"There must be advantages and disadvantages in knowing everyone. How long do I have to live in Moose County before I know the entire population?"

"It's too late for you, Qwill. You have to be born here, grow up here, and teach school for a couple of decades."

There was a flurry of activity at the entrance as the parade's grand marshal entered and was seated at a table by himself, still glittering with silver nailheads.

"I wonder why he's alone," Qwilleran said.

"He's a loner," said Mildred.

But the waiter, serving the fresh plate of whitefish, said with a wicked grin, "Because they won't let his horse in."

Mildred reached across the table and rapped his knuckles with the handle of her table knife. "That was uncalled for, Harvey. Don't expect a tip!" To Qwilleran she added, "Mighty Lou is one of our town characters—colorful and harmless. If you were thinking of writing a column about him, don't! Let sleeping dogs lie."

"I was considering a column on family reunions. Are they closed sessions, or could a reporter barge in?"

"They'd be thrilled to have someone from the newspaper! They really would!"

"What do they do at these affairs?"

"They have a business meeting and elect officers for the coming year, but mostly they just visit and eat and play games."

"There was an announcement in the paper that the Wimsey family is having a reunion this Sunday on someone's farm."

"They're the largest family in the county, next to the Goodwinters," Mildred said. "Do you know Cecil Huggins at the hardware store? He's related to the Wimseys by marriage. Just tell Cecil you'd like to cover the reunion. And when you get there, look up Emma Wimsey. She's real old but still sharp, and she has the most wonderful cat story to tell! When she told me, I got shivers!"

When the waiter brought the dessert menu he said, "I'm sorry if I made a boo-boo, Mrs. Hanstable. It just slipped out."

"Your apology does you credit, Harvey. You're back in my good graces." To Qwilleran she said, "Why don't we go home for dessert? I could build a parfait with homemade orange ice and fresh raspberries."

They set out for the Dune Club, but not until Qwilleran had ordered a freshly boiled lobster tail to take home to the cats. On the way, Mildred made a critical appraisal of his posture at the wheel. "Do you have a stiff neck or something, Qwill?"

"Just some soreness in my shoulders—from biking, I suppose. I'm using a different set of muscles, or else I jarred something loose when I bounced over an exposed tree root."

"Take off your shirt," she ordered when they arrived at her yellow cottage. "I have a wonderful Swiss oil that Sharon got for me, and I'll give you a rub."

As she rubbed in all the right places, his thoughts flew across the Atlantic to Polly Duncan. In England the Fourth of July would be only "4 July," and Polly would have worked all day at the library, stopping for tea and seedcake at four o'clock. Perhaps she went to an early theater performance after work and then had fish-and-chips with a new friend. (What kind of new friend? he wondered.) And now she would be home in her flat, watching the telly and drinking cocoa—and writing him another postcard.

"Now you can put your shirt on," Mildred said. "The oil won't stain. It's wonderful stuff."

After the parfait Qwilleran admitted that he felt better, outwardly and inwardly, but he declined to stay longer, saying that he had to feed the cats before they started chewing the table leg. On the way back to the cabin he reflected on Mildred's charitable nature and her spunk. Singlehanded she had turned the Fourth of July celebration around—from a travesty to a spectacular success. The firm way she handled the whitefish situation; her concern for the lonely girl next door; her initiative in raising money for Buddy Yarrow's family; everything she did was admirable. And she was a superb cook! He could forgive her silliness about horoscopes and UFOs.

When Qwilleran let himself into the cabin, the rug over the trapdoor was askew as usual. He straightened it automatically and greeted the Siamese, who knew he was carrying something edible, aquatic, and expensive.

"How was your day?" he asked them. "Any excitement? Any phone calls?"

Yum Yum rubbed against his ankles, and Koko pranced in figure eights while he diced the lobster meat. After the feast all three of them went to the lakeside porch, where Koko emulated an Egyptian sculpture and Yum Yum languished in her seductive Cleopatra pose. Stealthily Qwilleran went indoors for his camera, but as soon as he returned, Yum Yum crossed her eyes and scratched her ear, and Koko assumed a grotesque position to wash a spot on his belly that appeared to be perfectly clean.

It was still daylight, and somewhere along the shore the gulls were squawking again. Qwilleran went down the wooden steps and walked toward the clamor. Scores of soaring wings were wheeling over Seagull Point. Moving in slowly, he photographed the performance without disturbing the woman who was feeding them. Then he sat on a boulder until she tossed the last morsel of food.

"Good show!" he applauded. "Fantastic aerial ballet. I snapped some pictures."

"Oh," said Russell, walking hesitantly toward him.

"Pull up a rock and sit down." He indicated a boulder a few feet from his own seat, and Russell sat down dutifully. "Did you go to the parade today?"

"I don't like crowds," she said sadly, addressing the lake.

"You missed an exceptional spectacle." He picked up a stone and flung it into the water. "Are you enjoying your vacation?"

She nodded without enthusiasm.

"I hope you've been to the museum."

"It was interesting," she said.

Clenching his teeth, he waited for an inspiration . . . The subject of food, he remembered, was a foolproof ice-breaker in difficult social situations. He said, "Have you discovered any good restaurants in town?"

After a pause she said, "I never go to restaurants."

"Do you prefer to cook?"

"I don't eat much."

That explained her pencil-thin figure and perhaps her low-energy level. He found a few flat stones and skipped them across the surface of the lake. Then he tried a desperate quip. "Read any good books lately?"

"Nothing special," she said.

"There's a small library in Mooseville, and also a woman who operates a paperback book exchange, in case you run out of reading material."

There was no comment from the other rock, and he skipped a few more stones.

"How do you like the Dunfield cottage?"

Russell squirmed on the rock. "I don't know."

"What's the trouble?"

"I feel uncomfortable." She appeared to shrink.

"If anything worries you," he said, "feel free to talk it over with your neighbor, Mildred Hanstable. She's a kind and understanding woman. And if you need help of any kind, call Mildred or me."

"You're a nice man," said Russell suddenly.

"Well, thank you!" he said. "But you really don't know me. I turn down the corners of pages in books. I sometimes split an infinitive. And once I wore brown shoes with a black suit."

She almost smiled, but not quite. Waving a hand toward the log cabin, she said, "You're building something."

"I'm building an addition. Walk over and look at it some day. All our neighbors are interested in the process."

Russell stood up. "I have to go before it gets dark."

Without further civilities she walked toward the east, and Qwilleran ambled into the setting sun, wondering about this reticent young woman who never really looked at him. Obviously no one had told her the history of the Dunfield cottage, and yet she felt uncomfortable there. In a way she was like Koko; she could sense a sinister influence.

Back at the cabin Qwilleran detected mischief. Yum Yum was darting insanely about the living room while Koko looked on with magisterial calm from the top of the moosehead. Yum Yum seemed to have something small and gray in her mouth.

"Drop it!" Qwilleran shouted, and this was her cue to take flight. Around and around the cabin she flew with the thing in her mouth, while Qwilleran pursued with the grace of a Neanderthal, using all his wits to intercept her and being outwitted at every pass. Tired at last, she hopped on the dining table and dropped the dead mouse in his typewriter.

"Thank you!" he said. "Thank you very much!"

SIX

To the disappointment of holiday weekenders it rained on Saturday—rained hard. The bare roofboards on the east wing provided little protection from the downpour, which funneled between the boards and descended in sheets to drench the exposed subfloor. Qwilleran hardly expected Clem to work, and yet the carpenter failed to telephone. Previously he had been punctilious about reporting any change of plan, a businesslike practice that Qwilleran appreciated.

"That young man has a good head on his shoulders," he said to the Siamese. "He's bound to be a success. In a few years from now—if he quits the chicken business and sticks with contracting—he'll be giving XYZ Enterprises some competition."

Koko merely maneuvered his tail in reply. *Tap tap tap.* Much of the morning he spent in the window overlooking the building site. Nothing was happening, but he was waiting. *Tap tap tap.* The cat had always shown an interest in human occupations. He watched Joanna do plumbing repairs, and in Pickax he had supervised Pete Parrott's paperhanging and Mr. O'Dell's window washing and carpet cleaning, as well as Qwilleran's pecking on the typewriter.

Koko regarded each operation studiously, like an alert apprentice learning the trade. Now it appeared that he wanted to be a carpenter.

Qwilleran's first order of business on Saturday was to dial the phone number that he knew so well. "This is Qwilleran at the K cabin on the east shore."

"Ha ha ha! Don't need to tell me," laughed Mrs. Glinko. "Whatcha done now?"

He wanted to say, Dammit, do you think I sit around all day thinking of things to destroy? But she was so relentlessly cheerful and so conscientiously accommodating that he could not be angry with her. He explained, "It's like this, Mrs. Glinko. I'm afraid mice are getting into this seventy-five-year-old cabin. Is there anyone who could advise me how to stop the invasion?" One mouse hardly constituted an invasion, but he thought it wise to dramatize the urgency of the situation.

"Allrighty. I'll dispatch Young Jake," she said. "He'll know what to do. He goes to college. Ha ha ha!"

Young Jake arrived promptly—another of the big blonds indigenous to Moose County, driving another of the ubiquitous blue pickups. "We're having a little trouble here?" he asked with the kindly manner of an old country doctor.

Qwilleran explained the episode of the previous evening. "That's the first mouse I've seen, but it might be only the reconnaissance detail."

"Has your cat been showing interest in any particular part of the cabin?"

"She's spent a lot of time watching the stove and refrigerator in the last couple of days. I thought she was dropping broad hints about the meal service."

"We'll have a look," said Jake. "How do I get into the crawl space?" When shown the trapdoor he handed Qwilleran a flashlight. "I'll scout around down below, and you shine the light in the corners of the rooms and behind the appliances where pipes or cables come into the house. If I see a pinpoint of light, I'll close the crack with a sealant. Those little rascals can squeeze through even a hairline crack."

Jake dropped through the trapdoor with practiced ease and proceeded to shout orders. "Move east. That's right . . . Hold it! . . . All tight here. Move on . . . Hold it! . . . False alarm. Move on. Cables coming up. Not too fast! Hold it! . . . Ah! This is it! Hold steady!"

When the job was done, the expert emerged from the hole, draped with cobwebs. "The mice had an open invitation where the power lines come into the house," he said. "Excuse me. I'll step outside to brush myself off."

"You seem to know what you're doing," Qwilleran said when he returned and presented his bill.

"The job's guaranteed. If you have a problem, I'll come back. No extra charge."

"Fair enough. Is this your specialty?"

"No, I'm a general practitioner, but I've had plenty of cases like this at the beach cottages. I work during summer vacation."

"If you're Young Jake, I presume there's an Old Jake," Qwilleran said.

"My father. Maybe you know him. Dr. Armbruster, surgeon at the Pickax hospital. I'm in pre-med myself. I'm going into surgery."

Another idea for the "Qwill Pen," Qwilleran thought as the GP drove away. He released the Siamese from the guestroom where they had been confined while the trapdoor was open. "Thank you for your quiet and courteous cooperation," he said. "You've earned a treat. Cereal!" Yum Yum bounded to the kitchen, and Koko pranced on his hind legs.

When the rain stopped around noon, Qwilleran half expected to see the Frantic Chicken pulling into the clearing; Clem never wasted an hour, never missed an opportunity to earn a dollar for his forthcoming marriage to Maryellen. She was a fine young woman, and she was getting a good man.

There was no action on Saturday afternoon, however, and no phone call. Now everything would have to wait until Monday.

On Sunday the sun was shining, the temperature was pleasant, and Qwilleran dressed with the anticipation of a cub reporter assigned to a good story; in more than twenty-five years of newspapering he had never lost that element of challenge and expectation, though it were only a family reunion. There are no dull stories, he told himself—only dull reporters.

He sang in the shower, he soaped lavishly, and then the water suddenly ran cold. It was more than a shock to his wet body; it was a vexation to his equanimity. Wrapped in a bathtowel, he padded to the mudroom, where the water heater shared a closet with the washer-dryer combination. The heater gave no clue to its failure; it was neither dripping nor clanking nor blowing off steam. The cylindrical tank was silent and baffling.

Cursing the ill-advised timing of the mishap, Qwilleran called Glinko once more.

"You again!" Mrs. Glinko said in great glee. "What's buggin' you this time?"

"The water heater."

"Allrighty. I'll try to find Little Joe. Maybe she's at church. Ha ha ha!"

"I'm going out on assignment for the newspaper," Qwilleran said, "but you have the key, and she knows where everything is."

Unhappy about this latest emergency but resigned to the eccentricities of old plumbing, he said goodbye to the Siamese, cautioning them to behave well, and drove to the Wimsey centennial farm on Sandpit Road. He had seen it before—a vast complex of barns, sheds, coops, fences and acreage, with a plaque stating that it had been in the same family for a hundred years. It included a large oldfashioned stone farmhouse with flowerbeds and kitchen garden, a spacious front lawn with ancient lilac bushes, and a farmyard with parking space for the thirty or more cars that were piling in for the reunion.

Long rows of picnic tables were set up, and families arrived with hampers, coolers, and folding lawn chairs.

Cecil Huggins was watching for Qwilleran and he introduced him to the elected officers of the family. "What do you want us to do?" they asked.

"Whatever you normally do," Qwilleran said. "Forget I'm here."

"Well, dive in and get some grub when the dinner bell rings," they said, "and if you like to pitch horseshoes, there's always a coupla games going, down by the corn crib."

There were all ages in attendance: infants in arms, tots in strollers, oldsters in wheelchairs, pregnant women, children playing with Frisbees, beer-drinking husbands, and older men pitching horseshoes. Qwilleran noticed that men were inclined to talk to men, women talked to women, and mothers of small children talked to mothers of small children, while the elderly sat on lawn chairs under a large spreading tree and talked to each other. Yet, when the dinner bell rang, the entire clan came together in one lively, noisy mix of ages and sexes. Qwilleran counted a hundred and eleven persons, and he imagined that the genealogical tree of this family would resemble the circuitry of a computer.

There were a few celebrities in the crowd. A young serviceman, home on furlough after completing basic training, was welcomed like a brigadier general. Homage was paid to a new baby as if he were the firstborn of a crown prince. A couple who had recently announced their engagement were showered with effusive sentiments. Qwilleran expected to see Clem and his fiancée accorded the same star treatment, but they were not in evidence.

Wandering from group to group, listening and observing, he began to speculate that life might have cheated him. He saw cousins and second cousins and third cousins jabbering about family affairs and so happy to see each other. His only "family" consisted of an alienated ex-wife in Connecticut, some hostile in-laws in New Jersey, and two Siamese cats.

Cecil Huggins asked Qwilleran how he was enjoying his new bike and suggested some back roads to explore. "Try MacGregor Road," said the merchant. "There's a mighty pretty stretch after the pavement ends."

Qwilleran was well aware of that pretty stretch; Polly Duncan's hideaway was on MacGregor Road.

"And then, if you're feeling ambitious," Cecil said, "someday you might try the Old Brrr Road. It was abandoned after they built the lakeshore highway in the twenties, and it's all gone back to nature. Totally! My grandfather used to have a general store on Brrr Road at what they called Huggins Corners. Not a stick of it left! But it was a thriving emporium in its day. I guess that's how I got into the hardware business. Storekeeping is in my blood."

Mrs. Huggins joggled her husband's elbow. "Tell Mr. Q about Grandpa and the loaf of bread."

"Yes, that's a good one!" Cecil laughed. "I should write some of these down. You see . . . Grandma used to bake bread to sell in the store, and Grandpa always lined up the fresh loaves on the counter near the door, where customers could smell 'em as soon as they walked in. The bread was right next to the 'chawin' terbaccer' and the penny candy. Don't tell me they didn't know about merchandising in those days . . . Well, there was an old geezer who used to come in to swipe crackers out of the barrel—or a dill pickle when he thought no one was looking."

"He had a pile of money buried in his backyard," Mrs. Huggins said, "but he hated to spend a penny."

"That's right. Josh Cummins, his name was. And on his way out of the store after a game of checkers with his cronies around the stove, he'd always pick up a loaf of bread—the one nearest the door—and never pay for it. It griped Grandpa more and more every time, but he didn't want to collar the old guy and accuse him. You don't do that in a small town. So he thought of a scheme. He told Grandma to bake a loaf of bread with a dirty sock in it."

"And I guess socks really got dirty in those days," put in Mrs. Huggins.

"So Grandma baked the bread, and Grandpa put that loaf nearest the door when Josh was about to leave the store," Cecil said. "And sure enough, the old guy picked it up and walked out . . . Never stole another loaf!"

"They never found the money buried in his backyard," said Mrs. Huggins.

"That's right," said her husband, "and they never will. It's paved over now, for the high school parking lot. And they never found what old Mr. Klingenschoen buried on his property at the lake. All kinds of valuables, they say—back in the 1920s—just before he died, when he was a little tetched in the head. You ought to start digging, Mr. Q."

"Sorry, Cecil. I don't want to pay any more income tax."

"There goes the dinner bell!" said Mrs. Huggins, as

someone tugged at a rope and clanged a large cast-iron farm bell mounted on a high post.

The long tables were loaded with fried chicken, baked beans, and Cornish pasties; ham sandwiches, deviled eggs, potato salad, homemade pickles, and gelatine molds of every color; chocolate cakes, berry pies, and molasses cookies.

When the dinner bell rang a second time, there was a brief business meeting, and prizes were awarded to the oldest person in attendance, the youngest, and the family traveling the farthest distance. Then they all scattered—the elderly back to their chairs under the tree, the young ones to a field for softball, a few men to the front porch for a big league broadcast, and the young mothers to the farmhouse where they bedded down their tots for naps.

Qwilleran sauntered among the crowd, eavesdropping, as they talked about fishing, crops, television, funerals, babies, recipes, accidents, surgery, and the good old days.

Two women were arguing about the right way to make Cornish pasties. "My grandfather," said one, "went to the Buckshot Mine every day with a pasty in his lunch bucket, and my grandmother made pasties every day of her life. I have her recipe, and I know for a fact that she never used anything but meat and potatoes and a little onion."

The other said, "Well, in my family a pasty wasn't a pasty unless it had a little turnip."

"Never!" said the first. "My grandmother would sooner poison the well!"

Among the elderly men reminiscences were flying like the bees buzzing around the lilacs. A white-haired man wearing a blue ribbon labeled "Oldest" ventured to say, "When I started comin' to these shindigs, there was always a lineup at the outhouse, or the Cousin John as they used to call it. Now they rent a coupla them portable things. Times sure has changed."

One of his listeners said, "How about banks? Used to be you could go see the banker at home after supper, and he'd walk downtown with you and open up the bank if you was strapped for cash. Didn't have any of them time locks and alarms and cameras and such."

Eventually Qwilleran found Maryellen Wimsey among a group of young women. "Where's Clem?" he asked.

"He couldn't be here," she said simply.

"He's not ill, I hope. He didn't report for work yesterday, and he wasn't in the parade on Friday."

"He's out of town," the girl said, her gaze wavering.

"Will he be back tomorrow? I'm expecting him at the cabin. We've got to get the shingles on that roof."

"I hope so," she said uncertainly.

Qwilleran glanced at the group under the big tree. "Do you know which one is Emma Wimsey?"

"Yes," said Maryellen brightly, as if glad to change the subject. "She's in a wheelchair. She's the one with a blue sweater."

As he approached the congregation of oldsters he was hailed by an exuberant woman wearing a yellow blazer with a "We Care" emblem. "Mr. Qwilleran, you probably don't remember me. I'm Irma Hasselrich."

"Of course," he said. "You're the attorney's daughter, and you're a volunteer at the Senior Care Facility in Pickax."

Among the casually dressed picnickers she was conspicuous for her well-styled hair, her careful makeup, and the good cut of her clothes. Ms. Hasselrich was not young, but she was strikingly attractive.

"Oh, aren't you wonderful to remember!" she exclaimed. "You came to the facility last year to interview one of the ladies."

"A farmwife, as I recall. Mrs. Woolsmith, I believe her name was. How is she?"

"The dear soul passed on," said Ms. Hasselrich sweetly. "She was ninety-five and had nearly all her own teeth."

"And what brings you here today?" Qwilleran asked.

"I chauffeured three of our residents in the lift-van. I brought Abner Huggins, who won the prize for the oldest, and Emma Huggins Wimsey, eighty-nine, and Clara Wimsey Ward, eighty-two."

"I'd like to meet Emma Wimsey. They say she has an interesting story to tell. I'd like to get it on tape."

"She'll be delighted!" said the volunteer. "She used to teach school, and you'll find her very articulate. Her heart is weak now, but her memory is good . . . Emma! Emma, dear! You have a visitor!"

"Who is it? Who is it?" cried a faltering voice in great expectation.

"A reporter from the newspaper. I think he wants to hear your story about Punkin."

"Oh, dear! I've never been written up in the paper except when I married Horace. Do I look all right?"

"You look lovely . . . Emma, this is Mr. Qwilleran."

Emma Wimsey was a frail woman with thinning white hair, whose cheeks had been lovingly blushed, probably by Ms. Hasselrich. Though she appeared fragile, she was very much alive, and on her sweater was an enamel pin in the shape of a cat with a long curved tail. "Pleased to meet you," she said.

Qwilleran took her tiny hand warmly. "Mrs. Wimsey, it is my pleasure," he said. He had a courtly manner with persons over seventy, and it always pleased them.

Ms. Hasselrich suggested wheeling the chair to a quiet place, and they found a shady spot on the far side of the lilacs. "Are you warm enough, dear?" asked the volunteer.

Qwilleran brought lawn chairs and set up his tape recorder. "Why did you call your cat Punkin, Mrs. Wimsey?" he began.

"She was orange, and she came to me on Halloween. I was six years old. We were such good friends! We had a secret game that we played . . ." Her voice faded away, wistfully.

"What was your secret game, Mrs. Wimsey?"

"Well, after my mother put me to bed every night and closed the bedroom door, Punkin would come and scratch under the door, as if she was trying to get in. I'd jump out of bed and grab her paw. She'd pull it away and stick another paw under the door. Oh, we had such fun, and we never got caught!"

"How long did this secret game continue?" Qwilleran asked. "I mean, for how many years?"

"All the time I was growing up. Let me see . . . Punkin died before I went away to teachers college. Normal school, they called it then. Schoolteaching was the most respectable work a respectable young lady could do in those days. My grandfather had the first sawmill in Sawdust City, and we were supposed to be very respectable." Her eyes twinkled.

The volunteer said, "Emma, dear, tell Mr. Qwilleran about the fire at the college."

"Yes, the fire. I lived in a dormitory and studied hard and forgot all about Punkin's game. Then one night I suddenly woke up because I heard scratching under the door! For a minute I thought I was back home and Punkin wanted to play. But Punkin was dead! Then I smelled smoke. I ran down the hall shouting, 'Fire! Fire!' and pounding on everybody's door." She stopped to recall it in her mind's eye.

"Did you all escape safely?"

"Yes, and the firemen came and put the fire out."

"Did you tell anyone how you happened to wake up?"

"Oh, no! They would have laughed at me. But another time I heard the scratching again."

"When was that?"

"After I married Horace. We lived on a farm and had five

children, four of them boys . . ." Her concentration wavered as nostalgia swept over her face. She was smiling to herself.

Ms. Hasselrich said gently, "Tell Mr. Qwilleran about the windstorm, dear."

"It was a tornado!"

"Yes, dear. Tell what happened."

"Well, one night while I was carrying my fourth child, I woke up and thought I heard scratching under the door, the way Punkin used to do. I sat up and listened, and the wind was howling something fierce! I woke up Horace, and he jumped out of bed and said, 'Get the children down in the cellar!' It was a real tornado, and it blew the roof off our farmhouse. But we were all safe in the cellar." There was a long pause, and her eyes glazed.

Qwilleran asked, "Was that the last time you heard scratching under the door?" He waited patiently until she collected her thoughts.

"No," she said. "There was one more time, after Horace died and the children were all gone. I sold the farm and bought a little house in the town—Black Creek, it was. I lived alone, you see, and one night that scratching noise woke me up again. I listened hard, and I could hear someone moving around in the kitchen. So I got out of bed and tiptoed to the door, and I could see a flashlight! I don't remember if I was scared or not. I don't think I was."

"What did you do?"

"I closed the bedroom door very softly and called the police on my bedroom phone. My sons made me have a bedroom phone. I'd never had one before."

"Who was it in the kitchen?"

"A burglar. They caught him. That was the last time I ever heard the scratching." Emma turned to the volunteer. "Wasn't that the last time?"

"Yes, dear," said Ms. Hasselrich, "that was the last time you heard the scratching."

"Thank you, Mrs. Wimsey," said Qwilleran. "That's a remarkable story. How do you explain it?"

"It was the Lord's work," said the little woman, her eyes shining. "The Lord works in mysterious ways."

Emma Wimsey's story haunted him as he drove back to the cabin. As a journalist he was conditioned to scoff at supernatural tales, but as the daily companion of a Siamese who could sense danger and sometimes transmit such information, he had second thoughts. There was something in this north country—a kind of primeval force—that unsettled one's educated beliefs.

When he reached the cabin, he unlocked the door and called out, "Where's the gang? I've brought fried chicken right from the farm!"

Yum Yum came running.

"Where's your sidekick?" he asked her with a glance at the moosehead. "Where are you, Koko? Fried chicken!"

He expected to hear yikking and yowling, or at least a thump as Koko jumped down from a high place, but there was no audible response.

"Cereal!" That was their new buzzword.

Still there was no reply. Suddenly concerned, Qwilleran checked the bunkrooms, searched under bunks, opened closets and kitchen cabinets, opened the shower door—all with mounting anxiety.

As a chilling thought crossed his mind, he felt tension in his throat and a flush spreading over his face. Joanna had been there to fix the water heater, *and she had let Koko get out!*

He tested the hot-water faucet. Yes, she had been there.

"Oh, God!" he groaned as he rushed from the cabin.

SEVEN

KOKO WAS LOST!

Qwilleran ran from the cabin, calling his name. He looked up in the trees. He searched the toolshed. He combed the woods. He plunged down the steps to the beach, calling . . . calling . . .

Then in panic he ran back to the cabin and grabbed the phone book. Hands trembling, he looked up Joanna Trupp on Hogback Road. She was not listed. He might have guessed as much. He dialed the Glinko number, thinking they could radio her.

The Glinko telephone rang once . . . twice . . . but before they could answer, Qwilleran heard a distant yowl. He slammed down the receiver and rushed outdoors again.

"Koko!" he bellowed and then listened. There was no answer. Again he searched the grounds, fearing that the cat might be injured—mauled by a dog or wild animal—lying helplessly in the brush, too weak to cry out. How could he be found in these acres of woods?

Again he called Koko's name and listened to the answering silence. Had he imagined Koko's yowl, just as Emma Wimsey had imagined the scratching?

Defeated, he returned to the cabin, aware that his heart was pumping fast. He sat down on the sofa and put his head in his hands . . . Did he hear a faint yowl? It seemed to come from the fireplace! He tried to look up the chimney, but the damper was jammed. He looked in the woodbox. On a wild hunch he ran to the toolshed and brought the ladder, climbed up on the roof and looked down the chimney. There was no cap on the flue, no screening. A small animal could fall down and be trapped! If Koko had run out of the house and then found himself locked out, he might climb a tree, drop onto the roof and try to enter the house by way of the chimney. It would be good thinking—up to a point. How would Koko know the damper was closed—and jammed?

Qwilleran slid down the ladder, ripping his hands and tearing his trousers. He ran into the cabin, stuck his head in the fireplace and shouted up the chimney.

There was a distant answer, but this time it came from the opposite end of the cabin.

Qwilleran made a dash for the guestroom. "Koko!"

Once more he heard the ghostly reply. It was driving him mad, and Yum Yum was racing about the cabin and shrieking hysterically.

"Shut up!" he yelled at her.

Calm down, he told himself. Think carefully. Listen unemotionally. He's got to be here—somewhere. "Koko!"

This time the answer came from the rear of the cabin. He rushed to the mudroom, kicked the rug aside and hoisted the heavy trap door.

"YOW!" said Koko as he jumped out of the hole and shook the cobwebs from his fur.

Qwilleran let the door drop with a crash. "How long have you been down there?" he demanded.

"Yow!" said Koko, batting the cobwebs from his whiskers. He walked calmly to his water bowl in a corner of the kitchen and took a long drink.

Qwilleran washed and bandaged his hands. "Don't ever

do that to me again!" he said sternly. Now it was clear what had happened: Joanna had gone down under the cabin to deal with the defective water heater; Koko followed without her knowledge and was probably exploring some remote corner when she closed the trap door, locking him in the crawl space. Then she replaced the rug and left the premises. Koko had been down there for how long? An hour? Two hours? Three hours? It would teach him a lesson!

Qwilleran apologized to Yum Yum for shouting at her and then chopped the fried chicken for them, although his right hand was still shaking and he gripped the knife with difficulty. After placing the plate of chicken on the floor, he went for a walk on the beach to calm himself.

The loneliness of the shore, the gentle lapping of the water, the vast expanse of lake and sky . . . all these natural tranquilizers worked together to quiet his nerves. *Nerves?* He had never in his entire life exhibited nervous symptoms. And yet, his hands had been trembling when he consulted the phone book; they were still shaking when he chopped the chicken. During his career as a crime reporter he had faced life-threatening crises without flinching. Of course, he had been younger then. Now he was fiftyish, and it had been two years since his last physical examination. Perhaps he had been drinking too much coffee. Polly Duncan had urged him to cut down. Every woman he had known in recent years had nagged him about his health. Every woman except Mildred, that is. They hovered about his life like a Greek chorus, chanting, "Eat right . . . Get more exercise . . . Quit smoking!" He had given up his pipe. He had bought a bicycle. He ate broiled fish. And now Polly was campaigning to limit his caffeine.

Slowly he ambled along the beach, breathing deeply, stopping at intervals to gaze across the placid lake. Even before he reached Seagull Point he saw Russell walking toward him, wearing sunglasses and her usual drab attire.

"Hi!" he said. "Where are your feathered friends today?"

"I fed them early," she said.

"Just taking a walk?"

She nodded.

"I'm walking to lower my blood pressure," he told her. "I've just had a traumatic experience."

She looked at his bandaged hands. "You're hurt."

"That's nothing, but it's part of the story. You see, I thought my cat was lost in the woods. I have two cats, and they're not supposed to go out. In fact, they *never* go out. When I came home and found one of them missing, I don't mind telling you that I panicked! My cats mean a great deal to me. Actually, they're all the family I have. I worried about roving dogs, wild animals, hawks, even kidnappers. It turned out that the plumber came in my absence and opened the trap door to the crawl space. Koko went down under the floor and was trapped. He's the male. The female is Yum Yum. They're Siamese. Would you like to meet them?"

He realized he was babbling like a simpleton, but it helped him to talk about the distressing experience.

After a moment's hesitation Russell answered his question with a timid yes. He continued to talk all the way to the cabin.

She accepted a chair on the lake porch, sitting on the edge of it.

"Would you care for a ginger ale?" he asked.

"No, thank you."

"The cats are around somewhere," Qwilleran said. "They'll come out when they hear us talking about them. They're incredibly vain, and they like to be admired. Yum Yum is a lapcat, very affectionate, with all kinds of catly traits. Koko is something else, though! He's a remarkable animal with a keen intuition about people, situations, and events . . . I wonder where they are. Excuse me a moment."

He found the Siamese in deep slumber on the guestroom bunk—Koko evidently exhausted after his ordeal in the crawl space, Yum Yum glad to curl up in companionable proximity, and both of them stuffed with fried chicken. Picking them up in two hands, he carried them to the porch, one under each arm, their legs and heads and tails drooping, their bodies a dead weight. He set them down gently on the porch rug.

Yum Yum shook herself awake and looked at Russell with mild curiosity, then speculated on the laces in her canvas shoes. Koko, on the other hand, froze in the spot where he had been deposited, bushed his tail, and chattered at the visitor with the hostility he usually reserved for squirrels and stray cats.

"Koko! Watch your manners!" Qwilleran scolded.

"They're interesting," Russell said.

The tail gradually resumed its normal shape, and Koko walked back into the cabin with one or two backward glances at the stranger.

In embarrassment Qwilleran said quickly, "Would you like to see the new addition?"

They walked around to the back of the cabin. "Big chimney," Russell remarked as they passed the huge block of fieldstone. "Another porch," she commented when she saw the one in the rear.

"It's handy to have porches fore and aft. One is always cool, and one is always sheltered."

"Tall trees," she said, looking up at the hundred-foot pines.

"Very old," he said, nodding and looking wise.

As they stood in front of the east wing, he explained the

floor plan, discussed the method of connecting it to the original cabin, and described the proposed exterior of board-and-batten.

Russell observed everything in silence, nodding noncommittally, and when he had completed the prospectus, she said in a hollow voice, "I hope . . . they . . . get it finished."

As soon as Russell had headed down the steps to the beach, Qwilleran felt an urge to talk with Mildred Hanstable. "Thank you for steering me to Emma Wimsey," he said. "That's a good cat story, and it makes one think. I'll have to fix it up a little, but I think the readers will like it."

"And how about the reunion? Did you find it worthwhile?"

"Quite! It's enlightening to see how the other half lives. While I was there I felt envious, but now that I'm home, I find the idea of all those relatives somewhat suffocating."

"How long were you there?"

"About three hours, and when I reached the cabin, I got a real shock. I thought I'd lost Koko."

"What!"

"The plumber had let him get down into the crawl space, and I had some uneasy moments until I found him."

"How dreadful, Qwill! I know how you feel about those kitties."

"After that, I had a visit from your next-door neighbor. We spent a half hour together, and she said all of fifteen words in that time."

"I'm glad to hear she's loosening up," Mildred said.

"Who is this woman?" he demanded. "Where did she come from? Why is she here? She seems to be in her late twenties, but she dresses like 1935. Apparently she can afford a thousand dollars a month for a cottage."

"Maybe she's a poor girl who inherited some money from an old uncle."

"And inherited the wardrobe from an old aunt. When Koko met her he reacted as if she'd come from outer space. I think he knows more than we do . . . And another curious thing about that girl, Mildred: She detects something unsavory about the Dunfield house. Did you tell her what happened there?"

"Not a word!"

"And when I showed her the new addition, she said she *hopes it gets finished!* I'm beginning to worry."

"What is there to worry about?" Mildred said. "You have a splendid young man working for you."

"That's what I worry about. He's too good to be true." Qwilleran combed his moustache with his fingertips. "Clem didn't march in the parade Friday; he didn't show up for work yesterday; he didn't attend the reunion with his fiancée today. Maryellen's excuse was that Clem was out of town, but she wasn't very convincing."

"Oh, Qwill! You're always so suspicious. It's not unthinkable that a person would go out of town on a big holiday weekend."

Qwilleran huffed into his moustache, mumbled something about hoping for the best, and said goodnight. He refrained from mentioning that Koko had been tapping his tail in a significant way for the last three days.

EIGHT

QWILLERAN HAD BECOME accustomed to six-thirty reveille on weekday mornings, sounded by the rumble of Clem's truck, the whine of the table saw, and the staccato blows of the hammer. On Monday he slept until eight o'clock, however, and only the weight of two cats on his chest caused him to open his eyes.

His doubts about the carpenter's whereabouts proved to be well-founded; Clem did not appear. Qwilleran kept glancing at his watch and smoothing his moustache anxiously. Finally he telephoned the Cottle farmhouse.

A weary-voiced woman answered—Clem's mother, he assumed.

"Hello, Mrs. Cottle? This is Jim Qwilleran. I'd like to speak with Clem, if he's there."

There was a breathless pause. "You want . . . to talk to . . . Clem?"

"Gimme that phone," said a gruff male voice. "*Who is this?*"

"Mr. Cottle? This is Jim Qwilleran. Clem is doing some construction work for me, and he didn't show up on Saturday. I'm wondering when I can expect him."

"He's out of town," the man snapped.

"Do you know when he'll be back?"

"Don't know. I'll tell him to call you." The chicken farmer hung up.

Here was a situation that called for the moral support of caffeine, and Qwilleran made himself a cup of coffee—weaker than usual, in the wake of his nervous shakes the night before. How long should he wait for Clem to return? Would Clem ever return? An uneasy sensation on his upper lip was intensifying. When should he start hunting for a substitute? Would anyone want to finish a job started by another builder? Where would he find anyone to equal Clem? And then the burning question: What had happened to Clem Cottle?

The Siamese had finished their three-hour morning nap and had not yet settled down for their four-hour afternoon siesta. It was their Mischief Hour. Yum Yum was batting a pencil she had stolen from the writing table, and Koko was parading around with a sweat sock that Qwilleran used for biking.

"What shall I do, Koko?" he asked. "You have a lot of good ideas. Tell me what to do."

Koko ignored him pointedly as he staggered about the cabin, dusting the floorboards with the sock dragging between his forelegs.

"Are you telling me the house is dirty?" Qwilleran noted the fluffballs in the corners and the dust on almost everything. "Well, maybe it is." He ran the dustmop around the edges and flicked a duster half-heartedly over several tabletops.

The sock brought to mind Cecil's story about Grandpa Huggins and the loaf of bread. They had a sly wit, those early settlers. Grandpa's General Store had completely disappeared. Not a stick of it left, Cecil had said. It had been on the Brrr Road at Huggins Corners. The county was dotted with ghostly memories of villages and hamlets that had vanished without a trace, and they held a singular fascination for Qwilleran. He retrieved his sock, found its mate, changed into shorts and T-shirt, and set out on his bike to find the site of Grandpa Huggins's General Store.

Only a trail bike or a vehicle with four-wheel drive could negotiate the sandy furrows of the Old Brrr Road, and there was not enough traffic to keep the weeds from growing in the ruts. Yet, this had once been the only thoroughfare between Mooseville and Brrr, traversed by wagons, carriages, doctors on horseback, and pedestrians who thought nothing of walking ten miles to exchange a catch of fish for a few dozen eggs. Here and there one could see the remains of a collapsed barn or a stone chimney rising from a field of weeds. A crude bridge crossing the Ittibittiwassee River was nothing more than a collection of rattling planks.

Qwilleran passed a clearing with a circle of charred ashes in the center. Hunters had made camp here, or Scouts had pitched tents. He saw the rear end of a blue truck ahead, parked off the road with the front end in a shallow ditch. A varmint hunter, he surmised, but when he biked abreast of the pickup, he saw the frantic chicken painted on the door.

He threw down his bike and approached the truck warily, fearful of what he might find. The windows were open, and the cab was empty, but the key was in the ignition—not an unusual circumstance in the north country. When he flipped the key, the motor turned over, so the truck was not out of gas. But where was the driver? Qwilleran touched his moustache tentatively. Clem was not "out of town" as his father and fiancée had insisted.

After making this mystifying discovery, Qwilleran lost all interest in Grandpa Huggins's General Store. He turned the bike around and headed back to the dunes, thinking what a coincidence it was—and how fortunate it was—that Koko had stolen his sock. All that remained now was to determine an appropriate course of action.

As he pedaled up the snaking drive to the cabin, a small yellow car was leaving the clearing. He dropped his bike and walked to the driver's window. "Looking for me, Maryellen?"

"I wanted to talk to you," she said in a small voice.

"Back up," he said, "and come into the cabin."

He wheeled the bike to the toolshed and met her at the door to the back porch. "Let's sit out here. It's a little breezy on the lakeside. May I get you a drink?"

"No, thanks," she said, studying her hands clenched in her lap.

"What's the problem?" Qwilleran asked, although he could guess.

"I'm worried about Clem."

"So am I, but yesterday you told me he was out of town."

"That's what Mr. Cottle told me to say."

"What's his line of reasoning?"

"He says a young man has to have a last fling before he settles down. He says he did it himself when he was Clem's age. But Mrs. Cottle doesn't think that's what happened to Clem, and neither do I. It's not like him to go away without letting us know—not like him at all! He's too thoughtful to do that."

"From my brief acquaintance with him, I'm inclined to agree, but why did you come to me?"

"I didn't know who else to go to. I don't want to upset my parents. Dad has a heart condition, and Mom goes to pieces easily. Clem always said you were an important man in the county, so that's why I came." She looked at him appealingly.

"You're not going to like what I have to say, Maryellen,

but . . . I've just been biking on the Old Brrr Road, and I saw Clem's truck."

Her face and neck flushed a bright red.

"It's not wrecked," he went on. "The keys are in the ignition, and it's not out of gas. It's just parked off the road, halfway in the ditch. Would he have any reason for using the old road?"

She shook her head slowly. "He's not a hunter. Only hunters go back in there." Her eyes grew wide. "What do you think it means?"

"It means that Clem's father should stop kidding himself and report the disappearance to the sheriff."

In Qwilleran's early days as a newsman, when he covered the police beat for newspapers Down Below, he had a good rapport with the law-enforcement agencies, and he could always discuss cases with fellow journalists at the Press Club. In Moose County he had no such connections. There was Arch Riker, of course, but his old friend only kidded him about his suspicions. And there was Andrew Brodie, but the Pickax police chief dried up when the case was outside his jurisdiction, and the Cottle farm in Black Creek was on the sheriff's turf.

Under the circumstances, Qwilleran's only contact was Mildred's son-in-law, who covered the police beat for the *Moose County Something*. Having quit a teaching job to join the paper, Roger MacGillivray was hardly a seasoned reporter, but he was a willing listener, and he had enthusiasm.

Qwilleran telephoned Roger at the office. "Could you shirk your parental duties for one night," he asked the new father, "and meet me somewhere for dinner?"

"Right! Sharon owes me one. I baby-sat twice last week while she went out," said Roger. "Want to meet me in Brrr for a boozeburger?"

"Sure," Qwilleran said, "or we could try that new restaurant if you like red-hot food."

"I'm willing to give it a try. I have some red-hot news for you."

The new restaurant was called the Hot Spot, and it advertised in the *Something* as "the cool place to go for hot cuisine." It occupied a former firehall in Brrr, with thirty tables jammed into space that once housed two firetrucks. The original brick walls and stamped metal ceiling had been retained, and there was nothing to absorb sound except the sweating bodies that swarmed into the place for Mexican, Cajun and East Indian dishes.

"Noisy, isn't it?" Qwilleran observed as he and Roger stood in line for a table.

"Noisy is what people like," Roger said. "It makes them think they're having a good time."

A flustered host seated them at a small table squeezed between two others of the same limited dimensions. On one side were a pair of underclad beachcombers, shouting at each other in order to be heard. On the other side were two shrill-voiced women in resort clothes.

"This is not the place for exchanging confidences," Qwilleran said.

"Let's just eat and get out," Roger suggested. "Then we can have pie and coffee at the Black Bear and do some talking."

Waiters scurried about, bumping the chairs of the closely packed diners and colliding with each other. Qwilleran felt something splash on the back of his neck and dabbed at it with a napkin; it was red.

A harried waiter came to take their orders.

"Enchiladas!" Qwilleran said loudly.

"How hot d'you want the sauce?"

"Industrial strength!"

"Cajun pork chops!" Roger shouted.

After ordering they stared at each other dumbly, defeated by the high-decibel din. Qwilleran saw—seated across the table—a pale, slender, eager young man whose neatly clipped black beard and trimmed black hair accentuated his white complexion. Roger saw a robust fifty-year-old whose luxuriant salt-and-pepper moustache was known throughout Moose County and in several cities Down Below.

Although they found it difficult to communicate, nearby voices came through with amazing clarity. A woman's strident voice said, "My cat is always throwing up hairballs as big as my thumb."

Qwilleran frowned. "How's Sharon?" he shouted to Roger.

"Itching to go back to work!"

"How old is Junior?"

"Six months, two weeks, three days!"

Qwilleran became aware of a large bare foot, probably size fifteen, rising from the floor alongside him, as the beachcomber at the next table said to his companion, "Look at this toenail. D'you think I'll lose it? It turned black after I dropped the anchor on it."

The shrill voice on the other side was saying, "Her husband's in the hospital. They cut him from ear to ear and took out a tumor as big as a brussels sprout."

At that moment two dinner plates were banged down on the table without warning. Qwilleran sniffed his and said, "This isn't Mexican food. This is Indian curry."

"I ordered pork chops," said Roger, "but this is some kind of omelette."

"Let's get out of here!" Qwilleran seized both plates and carried them to the entrance, where he handed them to the astonished host. "Warm these up and serve them to somebody else," he said. "Come on, Roger, let's go to the Black Bear."

The Black Bear Café in the century-old Hotel Booze was

famous for its boozeburgers and homemade pies. The atmosphere was dingy and the furniture sleazy, but one could converse. Qwilleran and Roger seated themselves cautiously in two rickety chairs and were greeted by Gary Pratt, the shaggy black-bearded proprietor. He had a stevedore's shoulders and a sailor's tan.

"Looks like you've been out on your boat," Qwilleran remarked.

"Every Sunday!" said the big man in a surprisingly high-pitched voice.

"Is the Hot Spot cutting into your business?"

"All my customers went there once, when the place first opened, but they've all come back. What'll you have?"

"Boozeburger and a beer for me," said Roger.

"Boozeburger and coffee," Qwilleran said. "Okay, Roger, let's have your hot news."

"Do you know Three Tree Island?"

"Only by name. It's out in the lake in front of my place, I believe, but not visible from shore."

"It's several miles out—just a flat, sandy beach with a hump in the middle and a clump of trees. It belongs to a guy who owns some charter fishing boats, and he has a dock and fishing shack out there. Fishermen tie up to do a little drinking and clean their catch. Kids go sunning on the sand and use the shack for God-knows-what."

"So what's the news? He's decided to build condominiums?"

"The news is—and I got it from the pilot of the sheriff's helicopter—that there's been a UFO landing on the beach!"

Qwilleran regarded Roger with scornful disbelief. "He's putting you on."

"He's serious. I know the guy well. He spotted a large burned patch on the island—perfectly round."

"Some kids had a bonfire," Qwilleran said.

"Too big for that."

"What does the sheriff say?"

"The pilot hasn't made an official report. It might affect his credibility in the department."

"What are you leading up to?"

"I thought we could get a Geiger counter or something and go out there, and I'd write a story for the paper. Bushy has a boat, and he's game."

Qwilleran was temporarily speechless. In his early days, however, as a reporter he had followed wilder leads than this one. Roger was young. He should not be discouraged.

"Would you like to come with us?" the younger man asked.

Qwilleran smoothed his moustache thoughtfully. Although he placed no stock in the rumor, he hated to be left out of the investigation. "I wouldn't mind going along for the ride."

"As a disinterested third party you could corroborate our findings, and it would add weight to the story."

"Don't trap me into endorsing any harebrained adventure tale, m'boy. What's Bushy's reaction?"

"He's ready to go! I just wanted to get some input from you."

A waitress served the boozeburgers, six inches in diameter, four inches high, and famous throughout the county. The two men munched in silence for a while. This mountain of food required the utmost concentration and several paper napkins, and it so happened that the Black Bear charged a nickel for a paper napkin, not of the best quality.

"Everything okay?" asked Gary Pratt, prowling around the dining area like the black bear that he resembled.

"Next time I'm bringing my own paper napkins," said Qwilleran. "What's the pie today?"

"Chocolate meringue, but it's going fast. Want to order a couple of pieces?"

"It all depends on how you're cutting the pie—with an

inch-rule or a micrometer. I know your game, Gary. What you lose on the burgers, you make up on the pie and the paper napkins."

"For a couple of healthy guys like you," Gary said, "I'd suggest two slices apiece, and I won't charge for the napkins."

"It's a deal!"

Gary shuffled away, cackling his high-pitched laugh.

By the time the four slices of pie were served to the two men, it was Qwilleran's turn to launch a rumor of his own. He said, "Instead of chasing UFOs, Roger, you should be investigating a rash of criminal activity in Mooseville."

Roger gulped and set down his fork.

NINE

"How's the pie?" asked the proprietor, making his rounds.

"Best I ever tasted, Gary," said Qwilleran. "Is your grandmother still making your pies?"

"No, the old lady died, but my aunt has her recipes."

"It's rich but not cloying, creamy but not viscid."

"I should raise the price," Gary said as he walked away to ring up a sale on the antique brass cash register.

Qwilleran said to Roger, "There's something satisfying about the sound of an old cash register: the thump of the key, the ring of the sale, the scrape of the drawer popping out . . . How come you're not eating your pie?"

"You threw me a curve," said Roger, who had been staring into space. "What kind of criminal activity do you mean? Is something going on that I don't know about?" Like most natives of the county he considered it his privilege to know everything that was happening, and as a reporter he considered it his duty to know it first.

"It's happening right in front of your eyes. If you're going to be a journalist, you've got to start thinking as well as reporting."

"Gosh! Give me a clue!"

"I ran into a similar case in Rio fifteen years ago, but you expect that sort of thing in South America; you don't expect it in Mooseville." Qwilleran was purposely prolonging the suspense.

Roger stared at him expectantly, with his fork poised in midair.

"I seriously suspect," said Qwilleran, taking time to groom his moustache, "that someone in the Mooseville area has put a curse on carpenters."

Roger relaxed. "What's the joke, Qwill? Give me the punch line."

"It's no joke. Carpenters are dying and disappearing at an ungodly rate. Anyone who believes in UFOs should be able to accept the age-old mystique of the curse—an evil spirit exerting influence in an otherwise healthy community."

Roger put down his fork. These statements were coming from a veteran journalist whom he admired and respected. "Where do you get your statistics, Qwill?"

"It's common knowledge. We've had two accidents, one death from so-called natural causes, and a couple of disappearances. And it's all happened in the last two months. Joe Trupp appears to have been the first."

"Everybody knows the tailgate of a truck fell on him," Roger said. "It was an open-and-shut case of accidental death. That's what the coroner ruled."

"That's the beauty of a curse. Everything looks so natural, so normal, so accidental. Then there was the underground builder who was putting up Lyle Compton's garage. He vanished completely, and all efforts to trace him have failed."

"Well, you know those itinerants," said Roger. "They come and go. Half the time I suspect they're fugitives, and when the law starts to catch up with them, they take off!"

"Then how about Buddy Yarrow, drowned in a fishing accident? He was neither an itinerant nor a fugitive. He was a family man and highly respected craftsman. Also an experienced fisherman. Also a strong swimmer."

"Yeah, I know," Roger said with regret. "I knew Buddy well. But the coroner ruled that he slipped on the muddy bank of the river—after that big rain we had—and hit his head on a rock."

"And how about Captain Phlogg," Qwilleran persisted. "He masqueraded as a sea captain, but actually he was a ship's *carpenter.*"

"We all knew he'd drink himself to death sooner or later."

"Roger, if you're not going to eat your chocolate pie, push it over this way."

The young man applied himself to the dessert, consuming it but not necessarily enjoying it. "That's four victims," he said. "Are there more?"

"I suspect the fifth is Clem Cottle."

"Clem Cottle! What happened to him? Nothing has been reported."

Qwilleran finished his second piece of pie before continuing. "I don't know what happened to him. He'd been building a new wing on the cabin for me and doing a great job. When he left Thursday night he told me he'd be marching in the parade the next day. He also said he'd be on the job Saturday. Now listen to this: He wasn't in the parade, and he didn't work Saturday, nor did he attend the Wimsey reunion with his fiancée yesterday. Again this morning he failed to show up, so I called his folks. His father said Clem was out of town, and he had no idea when he'd be back."

"There's nothing unusual about that, is there?"

"Only that Maryellen was looking worried and Mrs. Cottle was sobbing when she answered the phone."

"Do you suppose he got in some kind of trouble?"

"Wait a minute. Here's the clincher: This afternoon I

went biking on the Old Brrr Road, and I found Clem's truck, headed into a ditch. There was no sign of a crash; it was simply parked there—abandoned—with the key in the ignition!"

"What did you do?"

"I told Maryellen it was time for the family to notify the authorities. So we may not be dealing with a curse in the old sense of the word, but you have to admit that something bizarre is happening in Mooseville. The town has a few peculiar characters. I won't mention any names. You know them as well as I do. Perhaps better. You've lived here all your life."

"Jeez!" said Roger in a daze. "You wouldn't think anything like that could happen in Mooseville."

"Think about it," Qwilleran said. "Keep your eyes open when you cover your beat. Don't believe everything you hear. Cogitate beyond the obvious . . . And finish your pie. I'll get the check."

After Roger had left for home, Qwilleran thought, That'll give the kid something to ponder while he's baby-sitting. It'll take his mind off UFOs.

He moved over to the bar where Gary was filling drink orders.

"Squunk water and a twist?" asked the barkeeper. Mineral water from a flowing well at Squunk Corners was Qwilleran's regular drink at the Black Bear. Gary trucked demijohns to the well and filled them without charge, then retailed the precious stuff in his bar at an incalculable markup.

Qwilleran said to him, "Considering what you make on Squunk water and paper napkins, you could afford to buy new chairs—or at least glue the old ones."

"The place would lose all its character. The boaters especially like the shabby atmosphere."

"Do you ever sail out to Three Tree Island, Gary?"

"Nah! What's there? Nothing but a stinkin' fish shack. The beach is okay for sunning, but I get all the sun I need on deck. And the water's too cold for swimming. That's the only thing wrong with this lake. Don't fall overboard, or you're an instant ice cube."

"Do you ever see any UFOs over the lake?"

"Oh, sure. All the time. They like us. I don't know why."

A few stools down the bar a man in a silk designer shirt and alligator Loafers joined the conversation. "I've seen seventeen this year." Among the come-as-you-are crowd he was highly conspicuous.

Gary said, "Mighty Lou is the official scorekeeper for extraterrestrial activity. Do you know Mighty Lou?"

Qwilleran turned and nodded at the man who had ridden in the parade as grand marshal. The man ignored the introduction but said, "I write them down in a book."

Gary moved away to serve a customer, and Qwilleran went to the men's room. When they resumed their conversation, Qwilleran said to the barkeeper, "Do you happen to know a good carpenter who would take on a small job? I've been building an addition to my cabin, but the guy let me down."

"They're hard to find in summer. They sign on with the big firms."

"I'd even consider an underground builder."

"Funny you should mention it," said Gary. "Iggy's back in town. He came in last night."

"Iggy?" Qwilleran repeated. "Can you recommend him?"

"He's a good craftsman, I guess, but he's lazy. You have to keep on his tail."

"Does he have a job lined up?"

"I doubt it. He just got in on his broomstick last night."

"Is he that bad?"

"Nah, I'm kidding. Want me to send him out to your place? He'll probably come in the bar later tonight. Write down your address."

Qwilleran wrote the information on a bar check. "Ask him to come early tomorrow morning."

"I'll try, but I doubt whether 'early' is in his vocabulary."

"Can you tell me anything about him?" Qwilleran asked.

"For one thing, he's the skinniest guy I ever saw—with a nicotine habit that won't stop. But he's strong as an ox! Can't understand it. He hardly ever eats."

"But he drinks?"

"He does his share of boozing, but the thing of it is, he's just lazy. And wait till you see his truck! I swear the only thing that holds the body onto the chassis is the brake pedal." Gary got a signal from a customer down the bar and moved away.

Mighty Lou settled his tab and threw a large bill on the bar for a tip. Then he approached Qwilleran with a chesty air of importance. "You need a builder?" he asked. "I can handle a few small jobs between contracts. Here's my card." He handed over a business card with engraved lettering on good stock: MIGHTY LOU, CONTRACTOR. There was a telephone number but no address.

"Thank you," said Qwilleran, putting the card in his wallet. "I may get in touch." He looked questioningly at Gary as the big man left the restaurant.

The barkeeper shrugged in a gesture of sympathy. "Harmless," he said. "Another Squunk?"

"No, thanks. I'm driving." As Qwilleran left the restaurant, he was hailed by diners at one of the tables. Lyle and Lisa Compton were lingering over coffee.

"Sit down and have a cup," said the superintendent.

Qwilleran lowered himself carefully into one of the wobbly chairs. "You're just the people I wanted to see! What was the name of the fellow who was building your garage?"

"Mert," said Compton. "He never told me his last name, and I was afraid to ask. These underground characters are very suspicious. They value their privacy."

"I'm hiring a guy named Iggy."

"What happened to Clem Cottle?" asked Lisa. "We were counting on him to do our garage when he finished with you."

"Clem . . . uh . . . hasn't come around lately, and I'm not going to fool around any longer. I'm going underground and hoping for the best."

"Let me give you some advice," said Lyle. "Don't give this Iggy fellow any money in advance. Have the lumberyard bill you directly for supplies. And keep a record of the hours he works."

"Also," said Lisa, "don't irritate him or he'll walk off the job."

"And one more thing," said the superintendent. "There's a law in the county against using an unlicensed builder unless he's related to you. So let it be known that Iggy is a close relative."

Qwilleran returned to the cabin, where he was greeted vociferously by the Siamese. "Guess who's coming tomorrow?" he said without enthusiasm. "Cousin Iggy."

TEN

ON TUESDAY MORNING Qwilleran was awakened by the bouncing of his mattress and the pummeling of his body. The Siamese were having a morning scrimmage on his bed and on his person. He hoisted himself out of bed and stretched, wincing as certain muscles reminded him of the bike ride on the Old Brrr Road.

"This is the day we're supposed to meet our new builder," he said to the cats as he coated some sardines with cheese sauce and garnished them with vitamin drops and crumbled egg yolks. "Let's hope he shows up. Keep your whiskers crossed."

"Yow," said Koko, tapping his tail on the floor three times.

In preparation Qwilleran called the lumberyard and alerted them that a fellow named Iggy would be picking up building materials, which should be charged directly to the Klingenschoen office in Pickax.

"Old horse-face? Is he back again?" said the man on the phone with a laugh. "Lotsa luck!"

The Siamese tossed off their breakfast and looked hopefully at Qwilleran for a chaser.

"Oh, all right," he said and gave them a few crumbles of

Mildred's cereal. Thus far they had consumed one-sixteenth of a tub of the stuff. "You have one-and-fifteen-sixteenths of a tub left," he told them.

At nine o'clock there was no sign of the builder. At ten o'clock Qwilleran was getting fidgety. When he heard the quiet rumble of a vehicle making its way up the winding, hilly drive, he went to the clearing to wait for it, although he knew it was hardly the sound of a truck held together by the brake pedal. He was quite right; the car that drove into the clearing was Mildred's little white compact.

She rolled down the window. "I'm on my way to a hair appointment and can't stay, but I brought you some more cereal." She handed him a plastic tub. "I toasted a new batch this morning."

"Thank you," he said, with more enthusiasm than he actually felt. He thought, I'll have to get another cat. The stock on hand was now two-and-fifteen-sixteenths of a tub. "Sure you won't come in for a cup of coffee?"

"Not today, thanks. But tell me—is there any more news about Clem Cottle? Roger called last night and said he's been reported missing. It'll be in tomorrow's paper."

"I haven't heard anything further." When the Moose County grapevine is functioning, he thought, who needs a newspaper?

"What will you do about your new addition, Qwill?"

"I've hired an underground builder. He's due here this morning."

Mildred said, "I don't know whether to say this or not, because I know you're skeptical about such things, but I've been wondering . . ." She bit her lip. "I really feel terrible about Clem's disappearance, you know. He had such a promising future. Sharon used to date him when they were in high school."

"What have you been wondering, Mildred?"

"Well, I have a friend who might throw some light on the mystery."

"Does your friend have evidence?"

"No, she's a clairvoyant. Sometimes she gets messages from the spirit world."

"Oh," said Qwilleran.

"Mrs. Ascott is quite old, and she lives in Lockmaster, but if I could get her to come up here for a brief visit, she might be able to tell us something." Mildred waited for an encouraging sign from Qwilleran. Receiving none, she went on. "Mrs. Ascott came up earlier this year for my grand-child's christening—she's godmother, you see—and while she was here I invited a few friends to meet her, and she was kind enough to answer questions . . . How do you feel about it, Qwill?"

"You do whatever you think is . . . uh . . . worthwhile, Mildred."

"Would you be available Saturday evening?"

"Me? What would you want me to do?"

"Just attend the meeting, and if you feel like asking a question, do so. Sharon and Roger will be there. They're quite enthusiastic about Mrs. Ascott's powers."

Uh-huh, Qwilleran thought. And about UFOs. And about horoscopes. And about tarot cards.

"It might be an idea for the 'Qwill Pen,' " Mildred said.

"All right," he said. "I'll go as an observer. Who'll be there?"

"Just some people from the Dunes. Now I must dash off for my appointment."

It was almost noon when Qwilleran heard what sounded like rifle shots in the woods, or a small cannon. The blasts became louder and the onslaught came closer until a ramshackle truck chugged into the clearing and stopped with one final backfire and a rattle of loose parts.

"Good morning," said Qwilleran pleasantly as he sauntered over to the vehicle, a rusty pickup with camper top.

Out stepped an emaciated man in a dirty T-shirt and torn jeans. What jarred Qwilleran was the man's teeth—the largest set, real or false, that he had ever seen. Thirty-two jumbo-size teeth grinned as the man approached, with a cigarette in hand, appraising the property as if he considered buying it.

Qwilleran's first thought was: They can't be real. His second thought was: They're not even *his!* "Are you Iggy?" he asked in the same hospitable tone.

"That's what they CALL ME!" the man said. He gestured toward the skeleton of a structure adjoining the cabin. "That the job you WANT DONE?" He had a peculiar speech pattern, starting almost inaudibly and ending in a shout.

"That's the job," Qwilleran said. "It's ready for shingles, and I hope you can get them on before it rains again. You have to pick them up from the lumberyard. The previous builder ordered them to match the ones on the main cabin."

"Can't match them old suckers," Iggy said. "Shingles CHANGE COLOR!"

"The people at the lumberyard understand the problem, and they're giving us the best match they can."

Iggy stood there with his thin body curved in a concave slump, one hand in a hip pocket, a cigarette in the other, and a seeming reluctance to leave.

"Gotta have some GREEN STUFF," he said, lipping the cigarette and rubbing his fingers together.

"The shingles will be billed directly to me, and I'll pay you for your labor at the end of each work day."

Still Iggy lingered.

"Is there any question?" Qwilleran asked.

"Got any CIGARETTES?"

"Sorry, I don't smoke."

"Can't work without SMOKE IN MY EYES," he said with a squinting grin.

Qwilleran handed him a few dollar bills. "Better get on your horse. The lumberyard closes for lunch from noon to one o'clock."

"See ya LATER."

How much later was a question that Qwilleran would have been wise to ask. As soon as the truck had spluttered down the drive with explosive reports every thirty seconds, he thawed a frozen deli sandwich in the microwave and gulped it down in order to finish by the time Iggy returned with the load of shingles. After all, the lumberyard was only two miles away, on Sandpit Road. As it evolved, there was no need to hurry. It was three hours before Iggy's truck returned, gasping and choking and backfiring.

"Couldn't find the sucker of a LUMBERYARD," he explained with his horsy grin that stretched the skin over the bones of his face. He started to unload bundles of shingles, and Qwilleran marveled at the weight the scrawny fellow could lift.

He went indoors to work at the typewriter and had barely inserted a sheet of paper around the platen when Iggy appeared in the doorway with a toothy question. "Where's the NAILS?"

"Didn't you pick up nails when you picked up the shingles?" Qwilleran asked in astonishment.

"You didn't say nothin' ABOUT NAILS."

"Then beat it back to the lumberyard before they close. They open at six in the morning and close at four in the afternoon."

"Won't get *this sucker* up at no six o'clock in THE MORNING," Iggy said with his leathery grimace.

"Go! Go!" Qwilleran ordered. And he returned to his

typewriter, growling at the cats who were sitting placidly on his notes without a worry in their sleek heads.

In two minutes the set of teeth appeared in the doorway again. "Gotta LADDER?"

Qwilleran drew a deep breath and counted to ten. "Don't you have a ladder in your truck? I never heard of a carpenter without a ladder."

"The sucker's too big to TOTE AROUND!"

"There's a stepladder in the toolshed."

"Need an EXTENSION LADDER!"

"Then buy one at the lumberyard and tell them to put it on my bill, and hurry before they close. Let's get some slight amount of work done today!" He was feeling snappish.

Trying to resume his writing, Qwilleran concentrated with difficulty until the truck returned, fracturing the silence with its ear-splitting racket. After that, reassuring noises could be heard on the roof. *Bang bang bang.* At least the man knew how to use a hammer.

After a while, consumed with curiosity, Qwilleran went outdoors to inspect the carpenter's progress. What he saw sent him sprinting to the building site, shouting and waving his arms. "Wrong color! Wrong color!" The shingles were bright blue.

"The suckers was on sale," Iggy called down from the roof. "You can PAINT 'EM!" *Bang bang bang.*

"Stop! I don't want to paint them. I want the right color! They're supposed to be brown. I'll phone the lumberyard . . . No, it's too late. They're closed . . . Take them off! Take them off! I'll phone the yard in the morning."

So ended the first day. Qwilleran computed the man's time: half an hour of work, five hours of travel back and forth.

"This is going to be worse than I thought," he told the cats, who sensed his discomposure and remained sympathetically quiet. "I've paid him for five and a half hours, and we have nothing to SHOW FOR IT! Dammit! I'm talking like Iggy."

When the carpenter reported for work on Wednesday morning—or, rather, when he arrived and observed the ritual of smoking several leisurely cigarettes—Qwilleran told him to return all unopened bundles of blue shingles to the lumberyard and bring the brown ones previously ordered. Iggy was quite agreeable. He flashed his teeth and nodded to everything, then smoked another cigarette.

The lumberyard was five minutes away, even in a junk vehicle like Iggy's spastic truck, but it was two hours before the man returned with the correct shingles. "Got a HAMMER?" he asked.

"A hammer! What happened to yours?" Qwilleran demanded. "You were using it yesterday."

"Had to hock the sucker FOR BREAKFAST."

Qwilleran huffed into his moustache with impatience. There was a hammer in the mudroom closet, but the idea of lending his own hammer to a carpenter hired to do carpentry was something he found offensive. "Here, take this money," he said. "Get your hammer out of hock."

It was a matter of two more hours before Iggy returned, grinning and puffing smoke, and after an inexplicable delay he tackled the shingles. *Bang bang bang.* Qwilleran listened with one ear as he tried to concentrate on his writing at the dining table. The carpenter had an eccentric habit of talking to himself as he worked.

All the time he was pounding he was mumbling, "Get in there, you sucker! . . . Whoa! Not there. Wrong place . . . Attaboy! Now y'got it . . . Need another nail . . . Where's that shingle?"

There were also long stretches of silence during which he

lighted up and inhaled deeply and enjoyed the landscape from his perch on the roof. During each interruption Koko's tail went *tap tap tap*.

"Cut it out!" Qwilleran yelled at him. "You're making me NERVOUS!"

To escape from the exasperating performance Qwilleran went into Mooseville for lunch, picking up the midweek issue of the *Moose County Something* and noting that rain was predicted. Making his usual stop at the post office he found two items of interest—one of them a postcard from Polly Duncan.

> Dear Qwill—Very busy meeting people, giving talks, seeing the beautiful countryside. "This other Eden . . . This precious stone set in the silver sea . . . This blessed plot . . . This England." But I think wistfully of your quiet summer in Mooseville. Love—Polly

Qwilleran huffed into his moustache. He had hoped for a long letter, not a postcard, with less Shakespeare and more personal news and a few endearments, but it was better than no word at all. Also in his post-office box was the following note:

> Dear Mr. Qwilleran,
>
> I'm writing you in behalf of Mrs. Emma Wimsey who so much appreciated your time and kind attention on Sunday. You were so gracious! It's safe to say that your visit was one of the highlights of her long life. She talks about you constantly.
>
> Sincerely,
> Irma Hasselrich, MCSCF
> Chief Canary

He read this note twice. In the middle of a day that was less than satisfactory, Ms. Hasselrich's flattery made him feel good. The acronym he could decipher: Moose County Senior Care Facility. But what was a Chief Canary?

When Qwilleran returned to the cabin, the roof was half-shingled, but Iggy was not on the site and not in his truck. Iggy, he soon discovered, was on the screened porch, asleep on the redwood chaise. He had removed his shoes and covered his face with a piece of shingle-wrapping. He had holes in his socks. He was snoring gently.

Qwilleran kicked the man's feet. "Up! Up! What do you think this is? A summer resort? I'm not paying you to sleep! Let's get that roof shingled before it rains!"

Iggy sat up, grinned, and felt for his cigarettes.

Now Qwilleran was as grouchy as he had been before going to lunch. He returned to his writing table and started a fretful letter to Polly. A "quiet summer," she had said. He'd give her an enlightening rundown on his "quiet summer." Then his eye fell on Irma Hasselrich's note. He read it once more and telephoned the Senior Care Facility in Pickax. Ms. Hasselrich answered from the reception desk.

"This is Jim Qwilleran," he said. "I've just received your thoughtful note, and it brightened an otherwise frustrating day. But I'd like to ask a question: What is the function of a Chief Canary?"

She trilled a tuneful laugh and said, "Our volunteers wear yellow smocks when they're on duty, and they're called canaries—a cheerful image, don't you think? I'm president of the volunteers this year, and so I'm entitled to wear a yellow blazer—as chief canary." She had the kind of voice he liked in a woman—cultivated, well-modulated, melodic. He remembered the yellow blazer she had worn at the reunion, and how well it had looked with her shining dark hair and shining dark eyes and artful makeup. She was a goodlooking woman, and she had her father's upbeat personality. Qwilleran had lunched with Hasselrich several times; he thought he would like to have dinner with his daughter. She was the right age—not too young but still youthful.

He said, "Tell Mrs. Wimsey that her story about Punkin will be in the paper this weekend."

"How wonderful! Thank you so much for alerting us."

Qwilleran went back to work in a more productive mood and maintained his equanimity until four o'clock, when Iggy wanted to quit for the day.

"Get back on that roof!" Qwilleran barked. "You don't get a nickel until those shingles are on. I don't care if you have to pawn your truck to buy your dinner! Finish that roof! It's going to rain tonight."

It was eight o'clock when Iggy drove the last nail and collected his earnings. "Before you go," Qwilleran said, "let me show you the sketches of the addition." He explained where the doorway would be cut in the existing cabin wall—to connect the old and the new. He explained that the cut-through would be left until the very last—for several reasons. He explained the choice of exterior siding and the style of window. "The lumberyard has the dimensions and will have the siding ready for you tomorrow morning. Don't come here first. Go to the lumberyard. Pick up the siding *and the nails* and bring them here."

The unflappable Iggy drove off, waving a friendly farewell, and Qwilleran strolled about the premises in peace, trying to imagine the finished wing, climbing between the studs to experience the orientation of rooms, gazing through the openings that would be windows, picturing the view. There was only one annoyance; the backyard was littered with cigarette butts, and rain would turn them into a soggy pudding. He found a sack and filled it with the unsavory litter. He had smoked pipe tobacco himself until recently, and he voiced no objection if his friends smoked, but

Iggy's non-stop habit represented sloth and delay, for which he was paying by the hour. As a journalist he had always done ninety minutes' work for an hour's pay, and he deplored Iggy's laxity, even though the Klingenschoen estate was paying for it.

On Thursday morning he handed the carpenter a coffee can and said, "For every butt that lands on the ground instead of in this can, I deduct a dime from your pay." He realized he risked alienating the man and losing his services, but Iggy was always tractable. He would merely grin with those extraordinary teeth and light another cigarette.

Despite weather predictions, the rain held off, and the exterior siding went up slowly, at the rate of three boards per cigarette, with plenty of conversation at the same time: "Where's that sucker? . . . Get in there! . . . Gimme the hammer. Where's the hammer? . . . There we go! Right size . . . Need another nail . . . That'll fix the sucker."

Before installing a board, Iggy would stand back, look up at the studding, then saw the proper length and nail it in place. Smaller lengths he measured with his foot or the spread of his hand.

Qwilleran said, "Don't you ever measure?"

"Don't need to measure," the carpenter said with his ivory grin. "I just EYEBALL THE SUCKER!"

With mixed amazement and disapproval Qwilleran went indoors to make a cup of coffee, but when he plugged his computerized coffeemaker into the wall outlet, sparks flew! The radio went dead. The refrigerator stopped humming. Without a moment's hesitation he reached for the phone and called Glinko for an electrician.

"Allrighty," said Mrs. Glinko. "I'll dispatch Mad Mac. He's out on the east shore, puttin' in circuit breakers for somebody—another one of you rich people. Ha ha ha!"

"This rich person would also like a chimney sweep,"

Qwilleran said. "There's something wrong with the fireplace."

"Allrighty. I'll dispatch Little Harry if he ain't busy."

Mooseville natives were fond of honorifics, which were bestowed on certain persons by consensus: Old Sam, Big Joe, Crazy Marvin, Mighty Lou, Fat William, and so on.

Little Harry was a young man of slight build who wore a tall silk topper, the traditional badge of his profession, somewhat incongruous with his smudged T-shirt and jeans. He quickly discovered why the damper was jammed; a raccoon had built a nest in the chimney.

"The chimney top should be screened," he said. "It looks like you had a screen up there, but something knocked it off. And I don't see a fire extinguisher anywhere. You should have a fire extinguisher. You wouldn't want to burn down a nice old cabin like this, would you?" he asked patronizingly. "What kind of wood do you burn?"

"I haven't burned any wood," Qwilleran said. "I couldn't get the damper open. That's why you're here."

"My job is to educate, not just to clean chimneys," said the young man haughtily. "If you burn green wood, it builds up creosote and you can have a chimney fire. Hot ashes are another common cause of fire. What do you use to take out ashes, and where do you dump them?"

"I haven't taken out any ashes, because I haven't burned any wood, because I couldn't get the damper open!" said Qwilleran, raising his voice. "If you'll come back next week, when I'm not so busy, I'll be glad to sign up for Basic Fireplace Technique 101. But now, if you'll excuse me . . ."

He was in a vile mood by the time the electrician arrived. Mad Mac—a hulking individual with bulging biceps and no neck—found a loose connection in the wall outlet and pronounced the entire wiring system obsolete.

"Y'oughta have the whole house checked. A mouse or

chipmunk gets in, chews on the wires, and you have a fire. These old logs—they're dry as tinder, burn like matchsticks. Whole place can go up quicker'n you can spit."

He lumbered about the cabin like a bulldozer, checking exposed wires, knocking over furniture, frightening the Siamese. "You got cats," he observed as they flew about the rafters. "With this kind of wirin' they could electrocute themselves."

Qwilleran clenched his teeth and kept his mouth shut.

Just before leaving, the electrician said, "Who's the carpenter out there? One of them hoboes? Don't know why you summer people hire them bums. I was wirin' a garage for some folks down the shore, and the damn carpenter stole my tools and took off! I ain't got no use for carpenters. Plumbers, they're okay, but carpenters! If I was president, I'd have 'em all shot at sunrise!"

Shortly afterward it started to rain, and Iggy had an excuse to quit for the day. His teeth flashed a thank-you when Qwilleran paid up, and he headed toward the rattling gypsy wagon that served as a truck.

"Wait a minute!" Qwilleran yelled. "You didn't put the boards under cover!"

"Won't do the suckers NO HARM," said Iggy.

"Nevertheless, I want the siding INSIDE!"

Iggy finished his cigarette, flipped the butt on the ground, and carried the lumber into the new wing.

"Koko, you and I are the only sane ones left," Qwilleran said when the carpenter's truck had coughed and exploded its way down the drive. "And it won't be long before I go off the deep end."

Koko was prowling irrationally, as he did before a violent storm, and his instincts were on target. High winds soon lashed the lake into a fury. Trees bent to the ground, and even the tall pines swayed alarmingly. The cabin windows were drenched with rain, July hail pelted the roof, and sheets of water blew through the new addition, only half of which was sided. Then a black cloud looming over the dune dumped bolts of lightning and volleys of thunder. The entire cabin shuddered, and . . . the submersible pump stopped pumping.

So, it was back to the telephone. "Mrs. Glinko, this is Qwilleran."

"Don't tell me! Somethin' blew out!"

"Whatever. All I know is—we're not getting any water."

"Drink beer. Ha ha ha."

"No jokes, please."

"Allrighty. Keep your hair on. We'll dispatch somebody."

As Qwilleran was scurrying about with bath towels, mopping up the horizontal downpour that forced its way through closed doors and windows, Arch Riker phoned from Pickax and asked casually, "Getting any rain up there?"

"Rain! We're inundated!" Qwilleran said. "The lake's rising! Tree branches are dropping like bombs! And the pump has conked out. The plumber's on the way over here. We've already had the electrician and the chimney sweep today . . . I don't know, Arch. I've had it with country living. I'm ready to throw in the towel."

"How's your building project progressing?"

"In slow motion. It's a long story. I could cheerfully murder the guy who's working on it now."

"Can you stand some good news?" asked the editor. "The whole staff thinks your copy for the weekend edition is great stuff—especially the story about the old lady and her cat. It's better than fiction. Why don't you do more memoirs?"

"I knew I'd wind up on the geriatric beat," Qwilleran said sourly.

"It was your choice," Riker reminded him. "You could have been an investigative reporter Down Below, but you opted for Pickax and the Klingenschoen bucks."

"Why don't you get the Historical Society to do oral histories for you?"

"Because you do 'em better."

"Well, I can't talk now, Arch. Here comes the plumber."

Joanna swaggered into the cabin in her heavy boots. "Your pump get hit?"

"I don't know. You're the plumber. All I know is—there's no water."

"Prob'ly burned out the motor." She kicked aside the mudrug, swung open the heavy trapdoor as if it were a cereal boxtop, and disappeared into the crawl space. Minutes later she emerged from the lower depths, covered with cobwebs. "Gotta go and get something," she said. She drove away mysteriously, returned with whatever it was, sank down under the floor once more, and soon shouted, "Try the tap!"

Water gushed from the faucet, and Qwilleran was grateful. Unlike Iggy, Joanna had done the work with no stalling, no mistakes, no excuses, no mumbling, no cigarette butts. Then she surprised him by saying, "I haven't seen Clem lately. He did the drains under the new place. Want me to do the finish plumbing?"

"It sounds like a good idea, but I have a different builder now. I'll mention it to him when he comes tomorrow," Qwilleran said. But Iggy did not report the next day . . . nor the next . . . nor the next.

ELEVEN

A DAY WITHOUT Iggy should have blessed the cabin with tranquility, but Qwilleran felt only anxiety when the carpenter failed to appear on Friday morning. Where was he? Why had he not returned? Would he *ever* return? The skeleton of the east wing was rain-soaked and forlorn. Qwilleran spent the morning glancing frequently at his watch and listening for the explosive arrival of Iggy's truck, but he found the woods surrounding the cabin disappointingly quiet except for peeps amd chirps, buzzing and chattering, as birds, insects, and small animals went about their daily business, whatever it might be; Qwilleran did not pretend to know.

Following the storm of the night before, the wind had subsided and the lake was settling down. The woods still had the verdant aroma of a rain forest; trees were dripping, the ground was scattered with fallen tree branches, but the sun was making an effort to shine through a milky sky.

Qwilleran was in no mood to write. He passed the time by picking up the storm's debris—piling large branches behind the toolshed and breaking twigs into suitable lengths for fireplace kindling. The carpenter had left scraps of shingles strewn about the property, and Qwilleran stacked them in neat piles along with their discarded wrappers. Every time a heavy truck rumbled down the distant highway he stopped to listen, regretting that he had spoken harshly to Iggy.

In midday, before he had taken time to drive into Mooseville, he was surprised to receive a phone call from Nick Bamba. "Say, Qwill, do you know you're blockaded?"

"Blockaded! What do you mean?"

"I just drove past your place, and there's a big tree down across your driveway. Also, the K sign has blown away."

"That explains it!"

"Explains what?"

"It's like this," Qwilleran said. "I was expecting a workman, but he didn't show up today. It's obvious now that his truck couldn't get through."

"But wouldn't he call you?"

"Not this one! He wouldn't have the common sense, or he wouldn't have the coins to put in the phone box. And without the K on the post, I doubt whether he could even find the driveway. It took him half a day to find the lumberyard, and they have a sign that's ten feet high. So thanks for telling me about the tree, Nick."

"That's okay, Qwill. Here's Lori. She wants to talk to you."

Lori Bamba was not only Qwilleran's part-time secretary; she was his advisor in matters pertaining to cats. She had three of her own, and Koko and Yum Yum knew it. Whenever she telephoned, Koko sensed who was on the line. Now he jumped on the bar and purred throatily.

"Hello, Lori," said Qwilleran. "Koko wants to say a few words."

He held the receiver to the cat's head, and there were yowls and musical yiks and cadenzas that Lori seemed to understand.

"Okay, that's enough," Qwilleran said, pushing Koko away. "What's on your mind, Lori?"

"I just wanted you to know I'm taking a vacation and won't be able to do any typing for about ten days. Do you want me to find a substitute?"

"No need. If there's anything urgent, I'll handle it myself. Everything else can wait till you get back. Where are you going?"

"I'm flying Down Below so the baby can meet his two sets of grandparents. They've never seen him. Nick will drive down later to pick us up, and we'll do some camping on the way home."

"Isn't the baby rather young for tents and ants and canned beans?"

Lori laughed. "We have an RV—not a big one—just enough for camping in comfort. You can borrow it if you ever want to go camping with Koko and Yum Yum."

"I appreciate the offer, and I'll mention it to them, but I don't think they'd care for roughing it." Koko knew he was being discussed and started pushing the receiver away from Qwilleran's ear. "Have a good trip, Lori, and let me speak to Nick again."

Koko lost interest when Lori's husband came on the line.

Qwilleran said, "You've heard the news about Clem Cottle?"

"I couldn't believe it!" said Nick. "What do you think happened?"

"Nobody knows. He built my steps to the beach, and I was grateful to you for recommending him. Then he started on my new addition. Did he play ball on the Fourth of July?"

"No, now that you mention it. The Roosters lost to us, twelve to three. He's their best pitcher."

"It appears that he hasn't been seen since he left my place

Thursday night. Of course, we don't know what the police have found, if anything. Let me know if you hear." Nick's status at the state prison made him a good source of scuttlebutt. "And thank you again, Nick, for telling me about the tree."

Qwilleran lost no time in calling Glinko. "Please dispatch a crew to remove a fallen tree," he requested. "It's a big one, blocking my driveway."

"Ha ha ha! That'll keep you home tonight," said the cheerful Mrs. Glinko. "What d'you want 'em to do with it? Chop it up for firewood? That'll cost extra."

"Tell them to take it away," Qwilleran said. "Immediately."

Fallen trees, vanishing builders, raccoons in the chimney, leaking sinks, birds' nests in the vents, spider bites on the seat! He was beginning to yearn for his dull apartment in Pickax.

The next morning he walked down the long drive to the highway and was pleased to see that the Glinko crew had spirited away the fallen tree. He drove into town for breakfast and bought a large letter K at the hardware store.

The hardware merchant said, "I read in the paper about Clem Cottle. They said he was last seen building something for you."

"That's true. You can't believe everything you read in the paper, but they get some of it right."

"He was engaged to marry one of the Wimsey girls, you know. I can't imagine what happened."

"The police are investigating, Cecil. They probably know more than they're telling."

The hardware man frowned. "It makes me wonder if it's connected with that big fire on Doug Cottle's farm."

"In what way?"

"I haven't figured it out yet, but it bothers me. The

chicken operation was fully insured, I happen to know. Clem and his father weren't getting along together. My wife got that from her sister; it's her daughter that was going to marry Clem . . . I don't know. I keep trying to put two and two together, and I come up with six-and-a-half. Do you have any theories?"

"Not a one," said Qwilleran. "I leave police work to the police."

After nailing the new letter K to the cedar post—with eight hammer strokes for each nail instead of three—he settled down to wait apprehensively for Iggy. Was the man on a binge? Had he found another job that was more congenial? And then the crucial question: Had he suffered the fate of five other carpenters?

Iggy, he reflected, was not a bad fellow. He was skilled in his craft when he chose to work, and he was neither sulky nor fractious nor dishonest—simply lazy and short on common sense, and his personal habits were annoying.

Briefly, Qwilleran considered notifying the sheriff's department about the missing carpenter. They would listen politely, but—considering the reputation of underground builders—how could they take the report seriously? And how could he identify Iggy? A skinny guy with prominent teeth and a truck that backfired a lot? What was the license number? What, for that matter, was Iggy's last name? He had no idea.

Instead, Qwilleran telephoned the Black Bear Café in Brrr and asked Gary Pratt if Iggy had been around.

"Not since I sent him to your place last week," the barkeeper said. "How's he doing?"

"When and if he works, he does a good job, but he needs constant prodding and supervision, and I never wanted to be a construction boss. By the way, do you know his last name?"

"Never heard it. And he doesn't use a credit card," said Gary with a laugh.

"I don't suppose you know where he's living."

"Sleeps in his truck, the chances are, on some back road."

"If you see him, Gary, tell him my driveway is clear now. It was blocked by a large tree as a result of the storm, but it's been trucked away."

"Sure thing," said Gary. "When are you coming in? Today's special is barbecued ribs and pecan pie—my grandma's recipe."

"I'll catch it the next time around," Qwilleran said.

On a wild hunch he jumped on his trail bike and explored the dirt roads surrounding Mooseville, where Iggy might park his truck and pass out for a couple of days. He even tried the Old Brrr Road where he had spotted Clem's abandoned pickup. The vehicle with the frantic chicken had been removed, and he saw no sign of Iggy's truck.

On another wild hunch he stopped at the lumberyard and asked if Iggy had charged any building materials to the Klingenschoen office since Thursday.

Three good-natured brothers ran the lumber business. "Hey, Joe," said brother Jim, "has old horse-face been in here the last coupla days?"

"Ain't seen him," said Joe. "Couldn't hardly miss that set of teeth."

"Ain't heard him either," said Jack. "Every time his jalopy pulls into the yard, I think we're being attacked by some nut with an Uzi."

When Qwilleran arrived at the cabin, there was a car parked in the clearing—a familiar tan four-door—and Roger was prowling around the building site.

"Trespassers will be prosecuted!" Qwilleran called out.

"Hey!" Roger greeted him. "This is the first I've seen of

your building project. It's neat! And you've got a new K on the signpost."

"The old one blew away. I lost a big tree, too."

"Lucky you've got five thousand others."

"Wait till I put my horse in the stable."

Qwilleran wheeled his bike into the toolshed and hung it on padded hooks, then conducted Roger through the framework of future rooms. "And this one, with south and west windows, is the cats' apartment. There are times when we all need our privacy. Will you come in for a drink?"

"I don't think I should," Roger said. "I'm on my way to Lockmaster to pick up Mrs. Ascott, and she doesn't approve of anything stronger than hot water with lemon. She's got bad eyes but a very good nose, and Mildred doesn't want us to offend her. You're attending the meeting tonight, aren't you?"

"In a weak moment I said I would," said Qwilleran with a lack of animation.

"How would you like to come along for the ride? It's an hour's drive to Lockmaster, and we can stop for dinner on the way down. I know a good place. Coming back, she'll sit in the backseat and not say a word. Frankly, she gives me the creeps. So I'd be glad of the company."

That was all Qwilleran needed to hear: Stop for dinner at a good place.

"I'll have to shower and feed the cats," he said. "How much time do we have?"

"We ought to leave by six o'clock."

"Then would you be good enough to give them their food?"

"Me! I've never fed a cat in my life!" Roger professed to a fear of felines, and he looked about apprehensively as he entered the cabin. "Where are they?"

Qwilleran pointed to Koko on the moosehead and Yum Yum on a crossbeam spanning the dining table.

"I'd feel more comfortable, Qwill, if they were down on the floor. Isn't that where cats are supposed to hang out?"

"Not Siamese! But I'll get them down in a hurry. Watch this! . . . CEREAL!"

Koko thumped from the moosehead to the mantel to the woodbox to the floor, and Yum Yum swooped through the air from the beam to the top of the bar, causing Roger to duck and retreat toward the exit. For their prompt response they were rewarded with a few of Mildred's tasty crumbles.

"Now here's a can of salmon," Qwilleran explained, "and here's the can opener and a spoon. Just spread it on this plate, mashed up, with the dark skin removed. They don't like the dark skin."

"At our house we eat the dark skin—if we're lucky enough to have canned salmon," said Roger. "Hey, it's *red salmon!* Mostly we buy tuna, when it's on sale."

Qwilleran said, "I notice you're wearing a coat and tie."

"Mrs. Ascott doesn't approve of casual."

"Okay, I'll be ready before six. If you want music, put a cassette on the stereo. Koko likes Brahms."

In the allotted time he emerged—coated, cravatted, and spiffily groomed except for his flamboyant moustache which always looked wayward. "I'll be glad to drive my car," he offered.

"Thanks, but Mrs. Ascott will fit better in the backseat of my four-door. She's rather large."

"How will she get home?"

"She'll stay over, and Mildred and Sharon will drive her back in the morning."

The route to Lockmaster was sixty miles straight down the main highway, and as soon as Roger went into overdrive, Qwilleran asked, "Have the police any leads on Clem Cottle's disappearance?"

"Not that they're telling."

"Do you know his father?"

"I've met Doug Cottle, but I don't know him very well."

"What is he like? He sounded curt when I talked to him on the phone."

"Oh, he's curt, all right. Curt is something he does very well. So different from Clem. I guess Clem takes after his mother. She's nice."

"Do father and son get along together?"

"Not too good, I hear. He blamed Clem for the fire—something he said Clem did, or didn't do, in connection with the electrical system."

"Did the state fire marshal investigate?"

"He didn't have to. No one was killed, and the fire chief didn't report any evidence of arson."

After crossing the Moose County line, the road led into hunting country with its rolling hills, opulent horse farms, and miles of fences dipping and curving across the green terrain. In the landscape and the dwellings there was an air of sophistication that Moose County lacked, and the restaurants were said to be better. Roger pulled into the parking lot of a place called the Palomino Paddock.

When Qwilleran noted the hostess in a long dress and several diners in dinner jackets and a wine steward wearing heavy chains, he began to think he should pick up the check for this meal. When they were seated (with pomp) and the menus were presented (with a flourish), he knew the Palomino Paddock was not for a young man on a tuna-fish budget. "Since you're driving tonight, Roger, dinner is my treat," he said.

They started with vichyssoise, and Qwilleran said, "What do you know about Mrs. Ascott?"

"Not much. She and my mother-in-law have been good friends for years. Mildred reads the tarot cards, you know, and I guess they have something in common. Did she ever read the cards for you?"

"Once, a couple of years ago. I hate to admit it, but she was right about everything—although I didn't think so at the time. You said Mrs. Ascott is a big woman?"

"She's huge! Not fat, just monumental, as Sharon says. There's something about a huge old woman that's more formidable than a huge young woman. Her eyes are always half closed, but they're long! Sharon thinks she uses eye makeup to make her eyes seem longer, like they do in India. She doesn't talk much in company, just monosyllables in a tiny voice. But when she goes into action and starts predicting the future, she's frightening. She sounds like a drill sergeant. I wouldn't mention this to Sharon or Mildred, but sometimes I think she's really a man."

Both men had ordered the prime rib, and Qwilleran declared it to be real beef without the hypodermic needle or irradiation or blood transfusion.

"Speaking of Mrs. Ascott," Roger said, "do you want to hear something weird? . . . When the baby was born, we asked her to be godmother. She came up here for the christening, and Mildred had a get-together for some friends, with Mrs. Ascott delivering spirit messages. It was spooky. She had a message for Sharon and me from a spirit named Harriet. This Harriet said we should move the baby's crib to another room. That's all—just move it to another room."

"How did you react?"

"I felt like a fool, but Sharon insisted, so we moved the crib from the nursery to our own bedroom, which was pretty crowded. Two nights later . . . the whole plaster ceiling of the nursery fell down!"

"Did you ever know anyone named Harriet?"

"Sharon never did," said Roger, "but that was the name of my great-great-grandmother."

Qwilleran threw a quick, incredulous glance across the dinner table. "Do you expect me to believe that?"

"It's true! Ask Sharon. Ask Mildred."

Lockmaster had been the home of wealthy lumber barons in the nineteenth century, and their mansions were fanciful examples of Victorian architecture. At one of these, which appeared to be an exclusive boarding house, Qwilleran and Roger picked up Mrs. Ascott. In her long black dress, with black crepe draped over her dyed black hair, she moved slowly and majestically to the waiting car with Roger at her elbow. They wedged her into the backseat with some embarrassment on the part of the men, and a few artfully controlled giggles from Roger. She sat in the center of the seat, staring straight ahead through eyes long and slitted.

"Are you comfortable, Mrs. Ascott?" Qwilleran asked.

"Mmmmm," she replied.

In the front seat, during the ride back to Mooseville, there were animated discussions about baseball, politics, and the prevalence of violent crime Down Below. Arriving at Mildred's cottage, the two men eased Mrs. Ascott out of the car and guided her indoors like two harbor tugs maneuvering an ocean-going liner into its berth. There she was greeted with adulation by Mildred and Sharon and ushered to a seat of honor in the middle of the living room sofa—the flowered sofa that Mildred had recently reupholstered with hours of sweat and tears. Qwilleran thought, I hope she reinforced the springs.

Seated in a half circle, facing the sofa, were the guests, speaking in hushed tones: John and Vicki Bushland, Sue Urbank without her husband, the Comptons, and others Qwilleran had not met. It was still daylight, but the traverse draperies had been drawn across the window-wall, and lamps were lighted. A hint of incense gave the assembly a mystical aura.

Mildred welcomed the group, saying, "We're privileged to have Mrs. Ascott with us this evening. She has so much to tell us about matters beyond our perception that I'll waste no time in introducing this renowned woman whose revelations speak for themselves."

The guests were asked to write their initials on slips of paper, fold them, and drop them in a basket, which was then placed on the coffee table in front of the seer. There was a breathless pause. Mrs. Ascott, ignoring the contents of the basket, gazed at a distant point above and beyond the heads of the assemblage. Finally she started to speak in a booming voice, addressing her pronouncements to the initials in the basket.

"To SFU . . . I am receiving the impression . . . of a mistake . . . You have made a drastic decision . . . not for the best . . . Is it too late to change your plans?"

"No," said Sue Urbank in a small frightened voice.

"Then do so!"

A murmur of surprise rippled through the audience.

"To RJM . . . You have changed careers . . . with some trepidation . . . Have no fear . . . You have acted wisely."

Roger and Sharon exchanged happy glances.

"Remember your responsibilities . . . Avoid unnecessary risks."

"Yes. Thank you," said Roger.

Mrs. Ascott continued to stare at the opposite wall through heavy-lidded eyes. "To LMC . . . I see pain . . . Remember your age and use discretion . . . You could have trouble with . . . your knees."

Lisa Compton groaned while nodding her head.

"To SKM . . . In my mind's eye . . . I see you tormented . . . by indecision . . . Duty first, desire later."

Again the MacGillivrays exchanged glances, not happy ones.

"To JWB . . . I have a vision . . . of great loss . . . material loss . . . but you will save what really matters."

Bushy passed a nervous hand over his nearly hairless head.

"To LFC . . . I see a dwelling . . . Are you selling property?"

"I'm trying to," said Compton.

"Don't be impatient . . . Bide your time . . . A good offer is on the way."

"Thank you."

"To VRB . . . My dear . . . something you have long wanted . . . will be yours."

Vicki Bushland barely suppressed a little shriek.

At that point Mrs. Ascott asked for a glass of water, and there was a brief intermission as guests whispered to each other and Qwilleran thought, Mildred could have briefed this woman on the concerns of her friends: Sue Urbank's pending divorce, Roger's career crisis, Lisa Compton's "jogging knees." Everyone knew that Lyle wanted to sell his house in Pickax and buy a condominium, and Sharon wanted to hire a baby-sitter and return to teaching school, and Vicki desperately wanted a successful pregnancy.

Mrs. Ascott resumed with a message for MTH: "It would be wise . . . to have a complete physical examination . . . without delay!"

Qwilleran thought this a cruel pronouncement to make so abruptly and in public, and he turned to see Mildred's reaction. Her lips were pressed together.

When the session ended, there had been messages for everyone except JQ, and Qwilleran surmised that the psychic had sensed his skepticism, or Mildred had warned her.

At this point the hostess rose and said, "Mrs. Ascott has

consented to answer a few direct questions if anyone cares to ask."

There was silence until, in a challenging voice, Qwilleran asked, "Can you tell us anything about the whereabouts of a young man named Clem Cottle?"

Mrs. Ascott stared at the upper wall with unseeing eyes. Finally she said, "I have a sense of distance . . . a long distance. He is very far away. Is he in the armed services?"

"No," said Qwilleran, "he's a local carpenter."

"He wishes to return . . . but he is unable."

She's bluffing, Qwilleran thought, but then the enigmatic woman added, "Are you JQ? I have a message for you . . . from a female spirit . . . Her name is . . . Joy . . . Take precautions . . . to protect your family. Do you have two . . . children?"

"No, ma'am, I have two cats."

There was a suppressed tittering in the audience.

"There is another message . . . from Joy . . . not quite clear . . . about an excavation . . . The message is . . . fading out . . . It's gone . . . That is all."

"Thank you," said Qwilleran, somewhat shaken.

She went on with other messages from other spirits for other guests, but he could think only of the cryptic tidings from Joy, his boyhood sweetheart, who had been dead for two years.

TWELVE

On Sunday morning Qwilleran recalled Mrs. Ascott's messages with mixed reactions. He suspected she had received no vibrations whatever about Clem Cottle and was only trying to save face. He resented her ominous reference to Mildred's health; there were less frightening ways of urging a friend to have a physical checkup. On the other hand, the idea of a spirit message from Joy Wheatley, with whom he had been so close for so many years, was disturbing. He remembered Roger's story about Harriet and the nursery ceiling.

He was on the porch with the Sunday papers, throwing each section on the floor as he finished reading it. Yum Yum liked to roll on them, kicking and squirming and having a good time. At one point he went indoors to call Mildred and discuss the events of the previous evening. There was no answer, of course; she and Sharon were chauffeuring Mrs. Ascott back to Lockmaster. While he was letting the phone ring the recommended number of times, however, he heard the unmistakable sound of ripping paper. Koko was standing on a newspaper with his front end down and his hind end elevated and his tail stiffened into a question mark. With teeth and claws he was shredding the

Moose County Something. It was the second time Koko had attacked the "Qwill Pen" column.

"This has got to stop!" Qwilleran scolded. "Shape up, or we'll ship you to Washington. You can get a job at the Pentagon."

Why did that cat never shred the *Daily Fluxion* or the *Morning Rampage* or the *New York Times?* Did it have something to do with the quality of the paper or the smell of the ink? Patiently he gathered the torn scraps of newsprint. Koko had destroyed Emma Wimsey's story about Punkin.

Qwilleran had met many old-timers since moving to Moose County: the incredible Aunt Fanny; Grandma Gage, who did push-ups and headstands; Homer Tibbitt, still doing volunteer work at ninety. When he was with them, he felt he was talking with his own grandparents, whom he had never known. Now he had a sudden strong urge to drive to Pickax and visit the Senior Care Facility. He could scout the possibilities of more memoirs. He might take some flowers to Emma Wimsey. He wondered if the Chief Canary would be on duty. Smugly he groomed his moustache with his fingertips.

Sunday afternoon was a popular visiting day at the Facility. Cars filled the parking lot, and relatives were chatting with residents in the lounge, the lobby, and the dining room. The "canaries" flitted about in their yellow smocks, bringing the elderly down from their rooms, watching lest they became overtired or overexcited, then wheeling them back to the elevator.

Irma Hasselrich, in her yellow blazer, was on duty at the reception desk. "Oh, Mr. Qwilleran!" she greeted him. "We've all been reading your column about Emma and Punkin. It's delightful!"

"Thank you," he said, "but I can't take credit. It was Emma's story."

"We read it to her three times, and it brought tears to her eyes. I myself thought it was beautifully written—with such sincerity and compassion."

Qwilleran preened his moustache with pleasure. Although he affected modesty, he relished compliments about his writing. "Is she allowed to have flowers?" He was carrying a bunch of daisies in a florist's green tissue.

"Of course. She'll be thrilled! I'll have someone bring her down to the reading room, where it's quiet. We're getting awfully busy today. By the way, Emma had some discomfort this week, and the doctor is limiting her visits to ten minutes."

When Emma's wheelchair rolled into the reading room, she reached forward to clasp Qwilleran's hand with both of her shrunken ones, her thin lips trembling in a smile. "Thank you . . . for that beautiful . . . write-up," she said, her speech faltering and her voice noticeably weaker. More than ever she appeared fragile and wispy.

"It was a pleasure to write," he said, "and here's a small thank-you for sharing your story about Punkin."

"Oh!" she cried. "I never had any . . . flowers in . . . green paper. We never had . . . money for . . . fancy things."

"May I ask, after you went to college, did you teach school?"

"Yes. The school had . . . one room. There was . . . a potbellied stove . . . and oil lamps . . ."

He tried to ask questions that would focus her attention and jog her memory, but her answers were hesitant and vague. "You told the story of Punkin very well. Do you remember any other tales?"

"I used to know . . . a lot of stories. . . . I wrote them down . . . I don't know where they are."

"Emma, honey," said the volunteer, "they're safe and sound in your room upstairs." She caught Qwilleran's eye and tapped her watch. Emma was looking weary.

"We'll have another visit someday," he said. "Until then, goodbye." He clasped her cold hands in his.

"Goodbye," she said in a wisp of a voice.

As Emma was wheeled away, clutching her daisies, he went to the reception desk to speak with Irma Hasselrich. "She seems to be failing," he said.

"But you never know!" she said brightly. "These farm-women have tremendous stamina." Optimism was the policy of the canaries.

"The newspaper is interested in running more memoirs of old-timers. How many residents do you have?"

"Sixty-five, and others on the waiting list."

"Would it be possible to screen them? The volunteers probably know who has a reliable memory and who has a story to tell."

"I'll raise the question at a staff meeting this week," she said, "but we wouldn't want to discriminate, would we? We might hurt the feelings of some of these dear folks. They're like children."

Her gentleness was attractive, Qwilleran thought, yet she had a cultivated sophistication. He was curious about this stunning woman, probably about forty, who had never married, who dedicated her life to helping others, and who still lived with her parents in Indian Village. This much he had gleaned from her father, the jovial attorney for the Klingenschoen Fund.

He said, "You could help a great deal with this project, if you could be good enough to give me some background information on policies of the facility. Perhaps you would be free for dinner some evening."

"Unfortunately," she said, "I'll be on the desk every evening this week, but it's charming of you to ask."

"How about Saturday night?"

"I would really love it, but it's Father's birthday."

Before Qwilleran could huff into his moustache, a voice called out, "Mr. Qwilleran! Mr. Qwilleran! I'm glad I caught you." It was Emma's canary, waving a shopping bag. "Emma wants you to have these things—to keep."

"What are they?"

"Just little mementoes, and some stories about her life."

"Shouldn't she give them to her family?"

"Her family isn't really interested, but Emma says you'll think of something to do with them. There's a candybox that was a valentine from her husband, probably seventy years ago."

"Give her my thanks," he said. "Tell her I'll write her a letter."

When he turned back to finish his conversation with the Chief Canary, she had walked away from the desk, replaced by a lesser canary in a yellow smock. "Ms. Hasselrich was needed in a meeting," she said. "Is there a message?"

There was no message. He carried Emma's keepsakes to the parking lot, thinking, What am I doing here? I could have been an investigative reporter Down Below.

At the cabin Koko was immediately attracted to the shopping bag and its contents. He took a vital interest in anything new, anything different, any addition to the household, and Mrs. Wimsey's mementoes—having been on a farm for seventy years—probably retained an enticing scent. Among the notebooks and envelopes and loose papers was the candybox, covered in faded pink brocade that was almost threadbare and topped with a heart outlined in yellowed lace—a pathetic reminder of bygone happiness. Qwilleran stuffed the documents back into the shopping bag and added the candybox to the clutter on the dining table, where Koko applied his inquisitive nose to every inch of the old silk and lace, all the while tapping the table with his tail. *Tap tap tap*.

THIRTEEN

ON MONDAY MORNING as Qwilleran was preparing to serve the Siamese their minced beef mixed with cottage cheese and laced with tomato sauce, there was an explosion in the woods, and a rusty pickup with camper top lurched into the clearing.

"Iggy's back!" Qwilleran proclaimed in a tone of excitement mixed with dread. "He must have run out of cigarette money."

Although eager to confront the man with questions and rebukes, he restrained his urges. He waited until the carpenter oozed out of the truck. As Iggy ambled toward the building site at the pace of a tired snail, Qwilleran followed. "Nice day!" he remarked to the prodigal workman.

"Should be able to finish THEM SUCKERS TODAY," said Iggy.

"To which suckers are you referring?" Qwilleran asked politely.

"Them boards!" He pointed to the siding.

"Good! And I wish you'd dispose of that rubbish." Qwilleran indicated the scraps of shingles and torn wrappings. "I have business in Pickax today, but I'll be back in time to pay your day's wages. See you after lunch."

He strode back to the cabin to finish working on the cats' breakfast but found them on the kitchen counter, finishing the job themselves. Before leaving for Pickax he glanced automatically around the interior, checking for feline temptations, locking up toothbrushes, hiding copies of the *Moose County Something,* closing all drawers, hiding the telephone in a kitchen cabinet, and leaving no socks lying around.

"Keep an eye on the carpenter," he told them. "Don't let him burn down the house."

He locked the doors, front and back, as he left. There was no need for Iggy to have access to the cabin.

The business in Pickax was the monthly luncheon meeting of the trustees for the Klingenschoen Fund. He stopped at his apartment to pick up some more books, dropped into the newspaper office to trade comradely insults with the staff in the city room, then reported to the meeting place in the New Pickax Hotel, built in 1935. Since that time it had never been redecorated, and the menu had never changed. The natives of Pickax were creatures of habit and tradition.

At the luncheon table Qwilleran remarked, "I see they've warmed up the 1935 chicken à la king again." His humor brought no response from the bankers, accountants, investment counselors, and attorneys who administered the fund, but the high-spirited Mr. Hasselrich said he thought the chicken was rather good.

Following the luncheon the trustees reviewed the Fund's philanthropies and considered new applications for grants and loans. It was Qwilleran's money, in the long run, that they were handling, but his mind wandered from the business at hand. He kept combing his moustache with his fingers; something was calling him home to the lakeshore.

He drove back to the beach faster than usual, with the car windows wide open, and the closer he came to the lake, the fresher and more invigorating the air. When he started up the driveway, however, the atmosphere changed. His eyes started to itch and smart unaccountably. At the same time he became aware of a foul odor . . . It was smoke! But not wood smoke! He detected noxious fumes from something burning—something toxic. He took the curves and hills of the drive like a roller coaster and jammed on the brake at the top of the dune. The clearing was filled with black, acrid smoke. Iggy's truck was there, and the carpenter was behind the wheel, blissfully asleep.

"Crazy fool!" Qwilleran muttered, coughing and choking. He jumped out of his car and banged the door of the pickup. "Wake up! Wake up! I didn't tell you to *burn* the stuff!" he yelled between fits of coughing.

Iggy climbed slowly out of the cab. The asphyxiating smoke had no effect on his leather lungs.

"Quick! Help me douse it with sand! I'll get shovels!" Qwilleran ran to the toolshed and threw open the door. What he saw was too improbable to comprehend. Staring at him from the darkness were two pairs of eyes.

"YOW!" came a voice from the depths of the shed, accompanied by a female shriek.

"How did you get out here?" Qwilleran shouted.

"YOW!" said Koko in indignation.

Qwilleran grabbed a couple of shovels and slammed the toolshed door shut in the faces of two astonished animals.

Working fast, with an occasional assist from Iggy, he smothered the smoldering pile of asphalt shingles and their waterproof wrappers.

When the job was done, he leaned on his shovel, breathing hard. "How did the cats . . . get into the shed?" he gasped.

"Cats?" asked Iggy. "WHAT CATS?"

"My cats! How did they get out here in the shed?"

"I never seen NO CATS."

"I'll show you. Get out there to the shed. Move it!"

With some persuasive shoving Iggy trotted down the narrow path to the toolshed.

Qwilleran threw open the door. "Now what do you call those animals?"

The two elegant creatures were pacing back and forth with resentment, their muscles rippling expressively under their silky fur, their whiskers bristling, their ears swiveling, their tails pointed like rapiers.

"*What do you call those?*" Qwilleran repeated.

"Funny-lookin' suckers, AIN'T THEY?"

Qwilleran wanted to grab the man by the seat of the pants and throw him out, but he gritted his teeth and paid him for five hours' work, after which Iggy drove away in his snorting, battered truck with a debonair wave of the hand and a toothy grin.

Seizing the two cats about the middle, Qwilleran carried them from the toolshed, opened the rattail latch of the porch door with an elbow, and tossed the two culprits on the redwood chaise. They froze in the position in which they landed and glared at him.

"Don't give me that insolent stare!" he said. "You two have some explaining to do!"

He unlocked the cabin door, stepped into the mudroom—and yelped! There was a hole in the wall, roughly three feet wide and seven feet high. Below it there was a liberal sprinkling of sawdust, with pawprints clearly defined.

"What? What?" Qwilleran spluttered, in the most inarticulate moment of his entire life.

Gradually the facts became clear. Beyond the opening was the roughed-in skeleton of the east wing. Iggy had cut a hole for the connecting door. After that, the lazy loafer had easy access to the cabin and could have napped on a white sofa or, worse yet, in Qwilleran's bed. Meanwhile, the cats had access to the east wing. Calmly they had walked through the newly sawed opening; casually they had jumped out an unframed window. But how did they end their journey in the toolshed?

In whatever way they managed the feat, it appeared that they had enjoyed the experience, because they were now peering between Qwilleran's legs, toe-deep in sawdust, ready to repeat the adventure. Grabbing them, he locked them up, announcing with a declamatory flourish, "Once more into the guestroom, dear friends!" While they howled their protests, he found a sheet of plywood left over from the subfloor and nailed it across the rectangular aperture with angry blows, smashing his thumb in the process.

Between erratic strokes of the hammer he thought he heard coughing outdoors.

Russell Simms was standing in the backyard with her hand over her nose and mouth. "Something's burning," she said in a muffled voice.

"Go around to the lake porch," he said. "I'll meet you there."

On the lake porch the air was fresh and clear, and he inhaled deeply. "Have a chair," he said to Russell, "and I'll tell you a story you won't believe. I came home from Pickax and found that idiot burning shingles! He also cut a hole in the wall of the cabin, and the cats got out."

"I saw them," she said quietly.

"You *saw them?* Where were they?"

"In the yard."

"Where was the carpenter?"

"I don't know."

"He was probably in the cabin, sleeping in my bed—that

blockhead! So you're the one who put the cats in the toolshed! That was smart thinking! But how did you manage it?"

She put a hand in her sweater pocket and drew out a few morsels of the dry catfood that she fed to the seagulls.

"Fishy Fritters!" Qwilleran said in amazement. "You actually lured them into the shed with Fishy Fritters? If I try to feed them Fishy Fritters, they throw a catfit . . . Well, Russell, it's a miracle that you happened along when you did. If I had lost those cats, I would have killed that man!"

"I had a feeling I should come," she said shyly.

"I don't know how to thank you. How can I thank you?"

Hesitantly she said, "Will you tell me something?"

"Of course."

"Honestly?"

"Of course!"

"What's wrong with my cottage?" She removed her dark glasses and looked at him directly for the first time, her eyes half closed and the pupils contracted. No wonder Mildred said her eyes were weird!

Having paused too long, he said quickly, "I don't think . . . that is, I was unaware of anything wrong with the cottage. When the Dunfields lived there, it seemed to be . . . rather comfortable."

"Why are they renting it?"

"Mr. Dunfield died, and his wife doesn't care to live at the beach any more."

"When did he die?"

"About two years ago."

"What happened to him?" Her piercing eyes searched his.

"Well . . . it was most unfortunate, you see. He was a fine

man, a retired police chief, a friend of mine . . . I'm sorry to say, he was murdered."

"*I knew it!*" Russell said with a shudder. She jumped up, rushed from the porch and ran down the steps to the beach. He watched her head for home along the shoreline, faster than she had ever traveled before.

FOURTEEN

"I SWEAR I COULD kill that guy!" Qwilleran said with vehemence. He was having lunch with Roger and Bushy and relating the events of the previous afternoon—how the underground builder had burned the shingles and allowed the cats to get out of the cabin. "If they had been lost in the woods, I would have clobbered him with a two-by-four—and I mean it!"

The photographer said, "When we were building our addition two years ago, our guy painted the whole thing a sick green while we were away. Our house is white, you understand! He painted the addition green because—he explained afterwards—the green paint was on sale! My wife was so upset, she almost had a miscarriage . . . What's your guy's name?"

"Iggy. That's all I know."

"Cripes! He's the one who painted us green! You have to watch him every minute."

"I know. He started to shingle my roof in a poisonous blue."

They were having a sandwich at the FOO, a down-at-the-heel restaurant on the west side of Mooseville. At some point in recent history the restaurant's large sign had lost the letter D in a wind storm, and it had never been replaced. Fishermen and boaters patronized the place because it was close to the docks, the food was cheap and plentiful, and the unlicensed establishment served illegal beverages in coffee cups. It also appeared to be popular with the sheriff's deputies, leading Qwilleran to deduce that the restaurant was under suspicion or the local law enforcers were corrupt.

The three men ate with their hats on, in accordance with FOO custom—Qwilleran in the orange hunting headgear that he liked, Roger in a Mooseville baseball cap, and Bushy with his skipper's cap at a dapper angle.

"Iggy was on the job when I left this morning," Qwilleran said, "but this time I've taken the precaution of locking up the cats in the guestroom. He's supposed to start framing the windows today. No doubt it will take him a week, allowing for catnaps and cigarette breaks."

Bushy nodded wisely. "If you ask me, it's not only tobacco he smokes."

"I wouldn't tolerate him, but he's my last resort . . . Any news about Clem, Roger?"

"Police are investigating. That's all I can find out," said the young reporter.

"That's what I guessed. Anyway, I'm stuck with Iggy. He's not only lazy and infuriating; he makes stupid mistakes, but I can't ride herd on him every minute. I'm glad to get away for a few hours."

"Have you spent much time on the lake?" the photographer asked.

"Last time was two years ago. I went out on a chartered trawler and hooked something I wasn't supposed to, and all hell broke loose. What's on the agenda, Bushy?"

"I thought we'd take off for the island right after lunch and spend a couple of hours over there investigating the situation on the shore, then do some fishing and fry up our catch on the beach. I've got a portable stove on the boat and a coffee pot, and we can slice potatoes and throw 'em in the pan."

"I brought the beer and ginger ale," said Roger.

"Have you checked the weather?" Qwilleran asked. "I hear they're having heavy winds in Canada."

"Luckily they're going to miss us," said Bushy, "but it gets cool out there on the island. You might need a sweater under your windbreaker."

"I brought one," said Roger.

"So did I," said Qwilleran.

"Then we're all set!"

The photographer's boat was a modest cabin cruiser called *Say Cheese,* and he was an experienced skipper. As they sped across the water, Qwilleran looked back at the receding shoreline, nestled at the foot of the sandhills and fringed with wharves and the masts of boats. Mooseville looked as quaint as an Italian fishing village, and he experienced a tingle of nostalgia for other times, other places, other friends.

It was one of those days when the sky was blue and the clouds were puffy, moving proudly like tall ships. They were moving fast, Qwilleran noted. The skipper had the motor wide open, and no one tried to talk against the roar. Soon the island appeared to rise out of the lake—just the tops of trees at first, then the wide beach, and then the small, flat-roofed fishing shack near the trees. He counted. There were actually three trees on Three Tree Island.

Bushy cut the motor, and they putt-putted toward a prefabricated metal pier. "They take the pier down in winter and store it in the shack," he explained. "The shack isn't much, but it's shelter. Mostly they use it to clean fish, so you won't want to spend much time inside unless you brought a clothespin." He pinched his nose.

With the boat tied up at the pier, they walked ashore. It was a low-lying island, and the beach was wide and smooth.

"Good place for a spaceship to land," Roger said. "The landing site is on the opposite side of the island, the pilot told me. Anyone want a drink before we start exploring?"

He brought a cooler from the boat, and they stretched out on the sand. Bushy and Qwilleran stripped off their shirts, but the white-faced Roger said, "Not me! I burn!"

As Qwilleran lay on the sand he heard a whistling sound high overhead. He sat up and listened, smoothing his moustache as he vaguely remembered hearing it once before when he was vacationing at the cabin. On that occasion it was followed by a violent storm. He said nothing about it; after all, he was a city-bred landlubber, while Roger and Bushy had known this lake all their lives. Since they showed no concern, Qwilleran lay down again.

"Okay, team," said the skipper after a half hour. "Let's hit the trail. Better put the cooler back on the boat and take your sweaters. Bring mine, will you, Rog?"

"Do we proceed clockwise or counterclockwise?" Qwilleran asked. They tossed a coin and started westward. It seemed like a small circle of land when viewed from the approaching boat, hardly larger than a cartoonist's idea of a desert island, but it proved to be a long way around when they trudged along the shore. The beach that appeared so hard and smooth was in actuality an expanse of deep, fine sand, and every step was a slide backward as well as a push forward. After tramping for half an hour there was still no hint of a scorched spot on the beach or even among the beach grass that covered the crown of the island.

The photographer had his camera ready. "Don't give up! We're not halfway around the island yet."

"How can you tell?" Roger asked. "It feels like we've been around twice."

They trudged on. Soon they put on their sweaters, having reached the windward side of the island. The breeze was coming from Canada across a hundred miles of water.

"Look! Did you see that?" Roger asked excitedly. "A water spout!"

"Is that a freak of nature?" Qwilleran asked. "Or does it have something to do with plumbing?" Since arriving in Mooseville he had become uncomfortably aware of plumbing.

"It's the tail of a cloud spinning around and picking up water like a fountain."

"That doesn't sound good."

Bushy had to admit that the clouds were moving faster than he would like, and Qwilleran pointed out that the sky was an unusual color in the north.

"I don't like it," said Bushy. "I think we should head back to the boat on the double and cut loose for the mainland. Storms come up fast on this lake. Let's go!"

They attempted the return trip at a trot, but the deep sand and the rising wind fought them every step of the way. The sky had changed to a yellow-gray, and the lake was whipping up a surf.

Bushy shouted against the wind, "We may have to stay on the island overnight!"

Qwilleran thought, The cats won't get their dinner. They'll be starved by morning, and they're locked up in that small bunkroom. They'll be furious.

When they arrived within sight of the boat it was thrashing in the waves and crashing against the metal pier. Even as they watched helplessly, the lines snapped, and the *Say Cheese* shot into the air on the crest of a wave and capsized.

"Oh, my God!" the skipper groaned.

The wind caught it under the bow, and it rolled and tossed wildly like a dying shark. Bushy ran to the edge of the water and watched it go, until a giant wave caused him to dash back to safety.

"Damn shame!" Qwilleran said.

"Rotten luck!" said Roger.

The dejected skipper said, "Let's get out of this wind."

Heads down and caps jammed on, they forged up the slope to the fishing shack, a makeshift hut of wood and corrugated metal that rattled in the wind. There were two windows, but they had been boarded up for the winter and not yet uncovered. The men entered the shack and leaned against the door to close it, so strong was the force of the gale. There was no light, with the windows covered, and it was drafty. The fishy aroma was the least of their concerns. Qwilleran stumbled over a wooden crate.

"There's a wood-burning stove here somewhere," Bushy said, groping around the interior, "but I don't know if there's any wood. Do we have matches?"

The matches, unfortunately, were on the boat along with the portable cookstove and coffee pot and fishing rods and radio. And none of the three men was a smoker.

"If I can fall over two more crates, we can all sit down," said Qwilleran.

Wooden boxes scraped on the uneven floor, and the three men sat down in the dark. They were silent for a few minutes, each with his thoughts.

"Who brought the dominoes?" Qwilleran asked.

Bushy laughed. "I loved that boat, but luckily it's insured, so let's get our chins up off the floor and figure out something to do for the next few hours. When I don't show up by nightfall, my wife will call the sheriff, and they'll come looking for us with the helicopter, but it could be a long wait."

"It's four-thirty," said Roger, whose watch glowed in the dark shack.

"Time for the Happy Hour!" said Bushy. "I could use a double martini right about now."

"How long do these big blows usually last?" Qwilleran wanted to know.

"Fifteen minutes or fifteen hours."

"If I have a choice, I'll take the abbreviated version."

"I'm never going to eat fish again," Roger said. "This place is putrid!"

"Any guess about the wind velocity?"

"I'd say fifty miles an hour."

"More like sixty, if you ask me."

"Listen! Did you hear something?" Bushy said with an anxious hitch in his voice. "It sounds like a splash right outside the shack!" He opened the door a crack and peered outside. "Hell! The lake's rising!"

Qwilleran wondered if the island had ever been entirely submerged. He wondered if the others were thinking the same thing. In the total darkness faces and emotions were invisible.

In another half hour the spray was hitting the shack and water was running under the door. Waves began slamming against the building.

No one was talking. They were all waiting—waiting for the next giant wave. The apprehension was palpable. Qwilleran had faced life-and-death situations before—with a dogged resolve to survive or a numb resignation. Only where Koko and Yum Yum were concerned did he ever succumb to gut-wrenching worry. Now, with mounting anxiety, he wondered what would happen to them. Would Mildred adopt them? Would they miss him? Koko would adjust, but Yum Yum would stop eating; she was emotionally dependent on Qwilleran, and she would pine away.

Another wave pounded the building, and it tilted.

"We're moving!" Bushy yelled as the shack shuddered and creaked.

"We're going to be swept into the lake!" Roger screamed. It was the first vocal evidence of fear. "I'm getting out!"

"Wait! Don't panic!" Qwilleran shouted. "Let's see what's the best thing to do. Bushy, got any ideas?"

"Which way are we moving?"

"My guess is . . . toward the center of the island."

With another watery crash the cabin moved again.

"Oh, God!" Roger said with a whimper.

Qwilleran said, "If you're praying, ask for suggestions."

There was another crash, followed by another shudder, and then the shack stopped with a bump.

"What's that?"

"We hit something!"

"I think we hit a tree!"

The waves pounded and roared, and the building quaked, but its journey stopped. It was wedged between the three trees of Three Tree Island.

"We're stuck!" cried Bushy. "Now what?"

A wave pushed the door open, and water gushed into the shack.

"Get on the roof," Qwilleran said. "We can't sit here like trapped animals. The water can't rise that high . . . Can it?" he asked when the other two were silent.

"How do we get up there?"

"Pile up the crates."

"Wait until after a big wave, and then act quick before the next one."

"Okay, here goes! Somebody give me a boost."

Qwilleran was the tallest and heftiest. Standing in ice water up to his knees, he boosted Bushy and then Roger. They reached down and gave him a hand just as the next surge of cold water soaked him to the armpits. The three sprawled on the roof like drowning sailors cast upon a reef. The shack was fast between the three trees and had tilted, so the flat roof had a precarious slant.

"Make yourselves comfortable," Bushy said.

"It's cold up here," Roger whined.

"It's colder down there. Flap your arms. Flex your knees, kid, but don't rock the boat."

The wind howled and whistled; the surf crashed. As time wore on, ominous clouds could be seen scudding toward the mainland.

"It smells better up here, if anyone cares," Roger said.

"At least we can see what's happening," said Qwilleran. "The sensory deprivation in that dark shack was giving me the willies." He had turned down the flaps of his hunting cap and was trying not to think about the cold. Compared to the frigid dunking he had suffered, the wind was not that chill, but he was soaked to the skin.

"Six o'clock. We've been marooned over an hour."

"Feels like a week," said Bushy. "I could use a shot of brandy."

"I'd settle for a cup of coffee," Qwilleran said. "Even one from the Dimsdale Diner."

"If I hadn't given up smoking, now is when I'd want a cigarette."

They clung to the roof, passing the time with meaningless chatter and attempts at brave humor.

"Seven fifteen," Roger announced.

"Am I numb from exposure, or is the wind subsiding?"

"It's dropping a little, but it's still cold."

"It's going to get colder before it gets warmer, so keep moving, fellas."

Qwilleran pictured the Siamese clamoring for their supper. Or did they raise the roof only when they had an audience? What did they do when no one was around? . . . What else was happening on shore? Soon it would be dark. Bushy's wife would notify the sheriff. Sharon would call her mother, and Mildred would call the sheriff, Mooseville police, and state troopers; she was a woman of driving action. Would it occur to her to drive to the cabin and feed the cats? She was thoughtful that way; she had even worried about Captain Phlogg's unpopular dog. But how would she get into the cabin? There was an extra key, but it was hidden under the log rack on the porch. She might look under the doormat or over the door frame, but who would think of looking in a hollow log at the bottom of the log rack? . . . Qwilleran was getting hungry. He wished he'd had the deluxe half-pound cheeseburger with fries, instead of the quarter-pounder with salad.

At eight-thirty the surf was less menacing, but the island was still flooded. An unhealthy yellow light illumined the sky, and gray funnel clouds could be seen over the mainland.

Bushy said, "I should have paid some attention to my horoscope this morning. It told me to stay home and do chores that I'd been putting off."

Roger said, "My horoscope said I'd take a trip, and this is one trip I'll never forget—that is, if I live. Something tells me I'm a candidate for pneumonia."

"Maybe I'd better start reading those things," Qwilleran said grimly.

"When I was born," Bushy said, "my parents had a neighbor who could write horoscopes, and she was supposed to be quite good. My parents had her do one for me, and she said I'd live a long life, so there's nothing for you guys to worry about tonight."

"That's your horoscope, not mine," said Roger. "I'm ready for an oxygen tent."

"This astrologer also said I'd be a portrait-painter (that's not too far off-base) and I'd marry a Capricorn (that's Vicki's sign) and my weak point would be my head. It sounded like I wouldn't have all my marbles, but I turned out to have a pretty good IQ and no hair!"

Qwilleran asked, "How did you react to Mrs. Ascott's session on Saturday night?"

"How about that?" Bushy said belligerently. "Did you get what she said about a material loss? She knew I was going to lose my boat, so why didn't she tell me to stay on dry land? I don't pretend to know how these things work, but all three of us were at that meeting and planning to embark on this damned trip. Why didn't she receive some kind of vibrations and tip us off?"

Roger said, "The girls still think she's wonderful, but I think she's slowing down. She told Mildred emphatically to get a physical checkup, and Mildred had just had her annual physical last week—the whole works—and nothing was wrong except her weight. It makes you wonder about Mrs. Ascott's other advice."

"She was off-the-track about Clem Cottle's whereabouts," Qwilleran said, "but that message from Joy rocked me back on my heels. We used to be very close."

"She said something about an excavation," Roger said. "Do you suppose she meant old Mr. Klingenschoen's buried treasure? Maybe she wants you to dig."

"You dig, Roger, and I'll split it with you."

They had hours ahead of them, and they talked to keep their teeth from chattering. Roger talked about the crazy kids in his classes when he was teaching history. The photographer talked about his customers who wanted to look like cover girls when they really looked like prunes.

Qwilleran talked about the Siamese: how they had taken an inordinate liking to Mildred's homemade cereal . . . how Koko shredded newspaper, but only the *Something* . . . and how he had an obsession with the trap door. "He got down into the crawl space once when the plumber was working on the water heater. I don't know what he finds so engrossing down there."

Roger said, "There could be mice or chipmunks. The chipmunks could tunnel under the foundation and come up in the crawl space and spend the winter there with a few bushels of acorns."

"For all you know," said Bushy, "you've got the Chipmunk Hilton under your floor . . . Say, I read your story about the woman who heard her cat scratching under the door after it was dead. How do you explain that?"

"I don't try," Qwilleran said, "and I'll tell you something else I can't explain. You know Russell Simms, who's been renting the Dunfield cottage? She had an urge to visit my cabin yesterday, and she arrived just in time to rescue my cats. A bloody miracle! She also had bad vibrations about the Dunfield cottage."

"Did you tell her about the murder?"

"Yes, but I should have kept my mouth shut. I had a phone call from Mildred this morning; Russell moved out of the cottage suddenly last night, forfeiting a whole summer's rent."

"Strange girl," said Roger. "Did you ever notice her eyes?"

"I'll tell you one thing," said Bushy. "I'd hate to be marooned on this island with Russell Simms and Mrs. Ascott."

Roger started to giggle and laughed until he was on the verge of hysteria.

"Cut it out," Bushy ordered. "You're shaking the shack."

"Let him laugh," Qwilleran said. "It'll warm him up."

"But the shack will cut loose from the trees and float away to Canada, and I don't have my birth certificate!"

At nine-thirty dusk was beginning to fall, and the wind dropped to a stiff breeze.

"I could use a blanket," Bushy said.

"I could use a sleeping bag and hot-water bottle," Roger said.

Qwilleran said, "I could use the *Komfort-Heet.*"

On the corrugated metal roof of the shack they did push-ups to keep warm and massaged their arms and legs. At ten-thirty they were still talking.

Bushy said, "I'll tell you a true story that's kind of spooky. It happened to my aunt during the Depression. Her husband got a job in a steel mill Down Below, and they were living in a one-room furnished apartment. That's all they could afford. Her husband worked hard, came home tired, went to bed, and snored. He snored so loud and so non-stop that it drove her crazy. She couldn't sleep. It was torture! Cotton in her ears didn't help, it was so loud. She felt like killing him! One night she dreamed she beat him to death with a table lamp, and she woke up in a cold sweat. Her husband was dead in the bed beside her. He'd had a coronary thrombosis."

In the thoughtful silence that followed Bushy's story they heard the throb of the sheriff's helicopter and saw the searchlight. The pilot dropped a ladder and picked them off the roof. "Blankets there! Hot drinks in the jug!" he shouted above the noise as the craft veered toward the mainland. "Taking you to Pickax! Landing on the hospital roof!"

There was not a word from the passengers. Qwilleran felt he might never wish to talk again.

"Tornado hit the shore!" the pilot shouted. "Lots of damage! I'll buzz the beach!"

They flew low over the dune, and the searchlight exposed the destruction: large trees uprooted and the condominium site reduced to splinters.

"Down there!" the pilot shouted. His passengers looked

down. The roof of the Dunfield cottage had been blown off, leaving the interior a maelstrom of rubble.

Lucky girl, Qwilleran thought. She got out just in time.

The helicopter followed the shoreline until it reached Seagull Point and the Klingenschoen property. Nestled in the trees, the cabin was not easy to spot, but he could distinguish the brown roof, the huge chimney, the two porches—all as solid as a rock, as it had been for seventy-five years. But . . .

"Where's the new addition?" Qwilleran yelled. "It's gone!"

FIFTEEN

THE THREE MEN snatched from the flooded island were treated for exposure at Pickax Hospital, but Qwilleran refused even a thermometer until he had telephoned Mildred and arranged for her to pick up the key and feed the cats. When he was released on Thursday it was Mildred who drove him home through the torrential rain that was the aftermath of the windstorm.

She said, "You and Bushy must be in excellent physical shape, or they wouldn't have let you go home today. Roger has to stay in for further observation. What a horrible ordeal for you poor dears! Did you know it was in the out-of-town newspapers yesterday?"

"I didn't see a paper or use the phone after Dr. Halifax gave me his knockout drop." Qwilleran spoke in a voice more subdued than usual.

"The *Morning Rampage* had a story on page three, saying three boaters were missing, and in the afternoon the *Daily Fluxion* reported the rescue on page one: *Former Flux Staffer Rescued from Lake.*"

"I hope they didn't say we were looking for the site of a UFO landing. How did they get the news? Moose County hasn't made headlines since the 1913 mine disaster."

Driving rain was beating against the windshield until the glass was virtually opaque, and Mildred pulled off the road to wait for some degree of visibility.

She said, "This is very unusual weather for July. Of course, we all know what's causing it."

"What's causing it?" he asked in all innocence.

"Why, the visitors from out there, of course!"

"You're not serious, Mildred."

"You can't expect aircraft to barge in from outer space without disturbing the atmosphere."

Earnestly he said, "Mildred, a couple of weeks ago there was a bright light pulsating outside my window at two o'clock in the morning. Do you know anything about that? Was it a trick?"

Mildred was incensed. "What do you mean?"

"I thought it might be a practical joke."

"You're really awful, Qwill, to say a thing like that . . . Are you sure you feel all right?"

"I'm okay. A little weary, that's all. The medication is sapping my energy."

The rain showed signs of abating. Mildred started the car and pulled onto the highway. "I'm sorry about what happened to your new addition, Qwill."

"Is it totally destroyed?"

"The foundation is intact, but the rest is rubble. Some of the boards have blown half a block away. And the Dunfield house is a wreck! What a blessing that the poor girl got out in time. I suppose we'll never know who she was, or where she came from, or why she was here."

They drove in silence for a few minutes, listening to the rain attack the car. Then Qwilleran said, "I nailed some plywood over the opening between the cabin and the east wing. I hope it didn't blow out."

"It's still in place. You're a better carpenter than you

think you are. The tornado didn't even ruffle a shingle on the cabin. They're crazy that way. A tornado will demolish a house without touching the lilac bush at the front door."

"Imagine the cats having to live through that! They'd be terrified! They say a tornado sounds like a jet when it tears through one's property."

Mildred said, "They were still holed up in the bedroom when I went there yesterday morning, but they were like wild animals. I don't know whether they were unnerved by the storm or just plain hungry. I took them some turkey, and last night they had meatloaf, and this morning some leftover salmon mousse. They liked it."

"They'd been imprisoned in the guestroom for almost twenty-four hours," Qwilleran said. "Luckily they had their commode and drinking water. Cats hate a closed door, you know, regardless of which side they're on. If they're out, they want to get in, and if they're in, they want to get out."

The K signpost came in view, and Mildred turned on her right-turn signal.

"My car's at the FOO. Would you mind dropping me off there?" he said. "I left it in their parking lot when we took off for Three Tree Island."

"Are you sure you should drive?" she asked. "If you feel drowsy, I'll get Sharon to drive your car back to the cabin."

"Thanks, Mildred, but I'm all right. Don't worry."

"All three times I went to your cabin there was a truck in the clearing. I suppose it belongs to your carpenter, but I didn't see him around."

"He was putting in window frames on the day of the tornado. I hope he wasn't hurt. He's so thin, a heavy wind could blow him away."

At the FOO she declined Qwilleran's invitation to have coffee and a doughnut, saying that FOO doughnuts would make better boat anchors.

"Thanks for the ride, Mildred, and it was good of you to take care of the cats."

"No trouble at all. In fact, I enjoyed doing it."

Qwilleran bought a copy of the midweek *Something,* which had gone to press before the tornado hit. Then he drove slowly to the cabin, thinking that Mildred was a wonderful woman who would make someone a good wife if only she would unload her absentee husband. When he turned into the K driveway, he was beginning to dread the first glimpse of the destruction, but he was eager to lay eyes on the Siamese. There had been times during those long, cold, wet hours when he thought he might never see them again. He shivered at the recollection.

The scene was exactly as Mildred had described it. Iggy's truck was in the clearing, and the east wing was a shambles, but Qwilleran didn't care; he was only glad to be alive. Although the drenching rain was turning the clearing into a lake, he waded through the puddles without noticing them. After what he had been through, what was an inch of rainwater?

He unlocked the door and said dully, "I'm home."

The Siamese regarded him from a distance with an expression of silent resentment.

"You can be glad your meal ticket wasn't drowned," he said. "CEREAL!"

The two ingrates bounded across the floor, Koko walking the last few feet on his hind legs, to receive their treat.

Qwilleran made coffee for himself and was sipping it with gratitude and relief when Arch Riker phoned.

"Thank God you were all rescued, Qwill," the editor said. "I heard about it on the radio Tuesday night and called the papers Down Below. It was too late for our midweek edition. Why doesn't anything ever happen on our deadline? What were you doing out on that island anyway?"

"You may not believe this, Arch, but we were looking for scorched earth where a UFO was said to have landed."

"You're cracking up, Qwill!"

"Be that as it may," he answered wearily, "I'm thinking of moving back to Pickax and crossing off this summer as a lost cause. The east wing is ruined. The sky is gray. The lake is even grayer. The rain is beating on the roof and flooding the windows, and the rotten weather is expected to continue. And it's all on account of those lousy UFOs."

There was a brief pause before Riker asked, "What kind of medication did they give you at the hospital, Qwill?"

"Ask Dr. Halifax. It's his secret formula. Is Pickax flooded?"

"Main Street looks like the Grand Canal. All the creeks and rivers in the county are swollen, and some of the bridges may wash out. Better stay put till the rain stops. You sound tired. Get some rest. Catch up on your reading. Forget about the 'Qwill Pen.' But when you get back to normal, you can write a hair-raising column about your ordeal."

And still it rained, pounding the roof, flattening the beach grass. "Damn those visitors!" Qwilleran said, shaking his fist at the dreary sky.

He went to the back porch and looked at Iggy's pickup in the clearing. The man might be living in it! He might be asleep in the truck-bed right now! Qwilleran realized he should investigate, but the rain was descending noisily, and he felt lethargic.

After a while Yum Yum forgave him for abandoning her, for shutting her up in a small room without food, for smelling like a hospital. When he stretched out on the sofa, she leaped lightly to his chest and uttered the seductive wail that meant she wanted to be petted. Koko, on the other hand, prowled about the cabin irritably, exploring remote corners, looking for a newspaper to shred, jumping on and off the moosehead repeatedly in a reckless waste of energy.

It was only when Koko crumpled the mudroom rug and started nosing the trap door with moist snorts that Qwilleran snapped to attention. His moustache bristled as a possibility flickered through his mind: Iggy might be under the floor, asleep! He might have seen the funnel-shaped clouds and gone under the cabin to safety. But how would he get into the cabin? The door was securely locked. . . . Well, he would knock out the temporary partition, step through the opening into the mudroom, and then nail the plywood back in place to keep out the gusting wind. He would know that all such beachhouses have crawl spaces, so he would find the trap door, go down in the hole, and close it after him. Then he would stretch out on the sand and go to sleep. Iggy could sleep anywhere! It was an interesting theory, but not plausible, Qwilleran decided. Even a somnolent carpenter wouldn't sleep thirty-six hours. Nevertheless, he shoved Koko away from the trap door, opened it a few inches, and shouted the man's name. There was no answer from Iggy but an ear-shattering yowl from Koko.

Qwilleran was aware he was not thinking clearly. He felt groggy. As he watched the rain cascading off the cabin roof, he thought, Iggy might have been injured when the roof of the east wing collapsed; he might have been killed; his body could be lying under the rubble; or it might have been blown into the woods, along with sections of the roof and siding. Qwilleran realized he should investigate, but the rain deterred him, and he lacked ambition.

His curiosity began to overwhelm his weariness, however, when Koko's behavior caused his moustache to quiver, ever so slightly. The cat was sniffing the trap door eagerly, passionately. Qwilleran remembered seeing a flashlight—somewhere—and he fumbled in drawers and cabinets before finding it in the mudroom. Koko, sensing his intention, pranced with long legs and rampant tail.

Qwilleran swung open the trap door and flashed the light into the dark hole. There was nothing in sight but sand. He tried sprawling on the mudroom floor with his head hanging over the edge in order to flash the light in several directions. He saw sand everywhere—a few rocks—a few pipes leading who-knew-where.

Koko had been racing around the mudroom, yikking and yowling at the spectacle of this large man lying on the floor. Now he peered down into the hole with his four feet tightly bunched, teetering on the edge.

"No!" Qwilleran commanded.

"Yow!" said Koko defiantly as he jumped down into the crawl space.

"Koko! Get out of there!"

The cat had disappeared into the shadows and failed to reply, much less obey.

Qwilleran tried the magic words, "Cereal! Cereal!" Yum Yum came trotting, but there was no response from Koko, the most obstinate creature he had ever encountered, and that included an ex-wife and two case-hardened editors. He flashed the light again, speculating on the feasibility of following the cat. There was about a two-foot clearance, in some spots less, between the sand and the floor joists of the cabin.

"Dammit, I'm not going after you!" he shouted to the miscreant under the floor. "You can stay there all day! I was marooned on an island; I came close to death; I narrowly avoided pneumonia; and I've lost the east wing. I'm not going to belly-crawl in the sand after a cat!"

Qwilleran scrambled to his feet, closed the heavy oak

door with a crash and straightened the rug over it, leaving Koko alone in the dark. Then he drove into Mooseville for lunch, first giving Yum Yum some affectionate stroking and a tidbit of bacon salvaged from his breakfast tray at the hospital.

"I hope he can smell this bacon," he said to Yum Yum. "Let him eat his heart out!"

Qwilleran was in no mood for conversation, and he found a secluded table at the Northern Lights Hotel. Even so, the waitress wanted to know all about his experience on the island. She had heard the news on the radio and had read about it in the *Daily Fluxion*.

Qwilleran pointed to his throat and mouthed the words, "Can't talk."

"You caught cold!" she said.

He nodded.

"It must have been freezing out there, with your clothes all wet and the wind blowing fifty miles an hour!"

He nodded.

"How about some cream of mushroom soup? That should feel good going down."

He nodded and also pointed to the half-pound cheeseburger with fries and cole slaw. When he had fortified himself with solid food and three cups of coffee, he felt alive once more.

Back at the cabin the rain was still hammering the roof, soaking the remains of the east wing, drenching the woods, and blotting out the lake view. Yum Yum greeted him nervously. She disliked being alone. She cried piteously.

"Okay, sweetheart," Qwilleran said, "we'll give him another chance."

He opened the trap door, expecting a contrite Koko to bound out of the hole, shake himself, and spend the next hour cleaning his fur, but the cat did not make an appearance. Once more Qwilleran sprawled on the floor, hanging his head over the edge—a maneuver of discomfort as well as indignity. It was then that he heard a distant rumble—the kind of noise that Koko made when he was busy with some engrossing task. He was talking to himself under his breath.

"What are you doing, Koko?"

There was more mumbling, almost a growl.

Qwilleran had been born with the same kind of curiosity that has killed centuries of cats, and he threw off his waterproof jacket and lowered himself into the hole. The opening was about two feet square, and he was a big man. He made several attempts before learning the knack: squat down, slide the legs forward while chinning on the edge, then roll over. Now he could flash the light to all corners of the crawl space. It was, as he had previously surmised, mostly sand, but now he noticed some lumps of concrete or hardened mortar, a sprinkling of acorn shells left there by tunneling chipmunks, and a beer can. He hoped there would be no snakes or skunks. It was dusty, and he sneezed a few times. Cobwebs tickled his face and were vastly unpleasant when they caught on his moustache.

He had no time to wonder about the beer can. Koko's behavior was disconcerting. The cat was in the center of the crawl space, approximately under the dining table, and he was digging industriously.

With Mrs. Ascott's message ringing in his mind, Qwilleran started a torturous belly-crawl toward him. The chunks of mortar had sharp corners, and the seventy-five-year-old joists were four-by-sixes, hard and unyielding. Ahead of him, sand was flying, propelled by the cat's frantic paws.

Qwilleran's moustache prickled as he approached Koko, and he felt a peculiar sensation in his scalp. "What have you found?" he called out.

Koko ignored him and kept on digging. Qwilleran crawled closer, trying to keep the beam of the flashlight on the scene of the excavation. The cat was uncovering something that he could not identify. It was something solid, with a shape that was becoming more defined. Qwilleran inched forward. And then the light went out. He shook the flashlight, joggled the thumb-switch and cursed the thing, but the battery was obviously dead. He threw it aside.

Now he was operating in total darkness. He knew he was within reaching distance of the cat, and he extended his right arm and grabbed a handful of furry hide. Koko struggled and yowled in protest as Qwilleran hauled him back and used his other hand to feel for the treasure.

It was a shoe—a canvas shoe with shoelaces. Inside the shoe was a foot, and connected to the foot was a leg.

SIXTEEN

Upon discovering the body Qwilleran notified the sheriff, though not until he had tipped off the *Moose County Something*. Once more two protesting Siamese were locked in the guestroom as police maneuvered Koko's grisly treasure from its burial place and up through the trap door—no simple operation! There were grunts, shouts, arguments, and muttered maledictions during the process. The rain continued, and the vehicles of the sheriff department, state police, coroner and technicians churned the driveway and clearing into mud.

Unofficial visitors were stopped by a roadblock at the entrance to the K property, Arch Riker being one of these. The editor and publisher of the *Something* chose to cover the incident himself, since Roger MacGillivray was still in the hospital. Also, Riker thought, Qwilleran might need moral support in his present medicated condition. The night on Three Tree Island and the destruction of the east wing, followed by the discovery of a dead body under the house, would be enough to shake even a veteran journalist if he happened to be taking Dr. Halifax's potent pills. The editor, showing his press card, was allowed to park on the shoulder of the highway and walk up the long muddy driveway in the rain. Upon arriving at the cabin, he was restricted to the back porch.

Indoors the mudroom was living up to its name, as feet came and went in the course of grim, official business. The atmosphere was one the cabin had never known: the awesome hush of a murder scene under investigation, punctuated by the terse comments and orders of lawmen at work, not to mention the occasional complaints of offended Siamese issuing from the guestroom. Qwilleran was asked to stand by but keep out of the way, as samples of sand were collected and the premises were photographed, measured, and dusted for prints.

Dr. Halifax's formula notwithstanding, Qwilleran's energy and alert curiosity were miraculously renewed by the excitement of the crime. When asked to identify the body, he was able to say it was the carpenter known as Iggy, an appellation that tallied with the name on the driver's license found in the pickup truck. It surprised him that Iggy possessed anything so conventional as a driver's license, and it disturbed him—now that the man was dead—that he had never known his full name, had never asked, had never needed to ask. Despite obnoxious work habits and unattractive personal habits, Iggy was a fellow human who deserved more than a dog's name. He was Ignatius K. Small.

In Qwilleran's opinion the cause of death had been a smashing blow to the skull, although no one bothered to inform him of the coroner's decision. Today Qwilleran was not the richest man in the county; he was not the leading philanthropist; he was not the star writer for the *Something*. He was merely the occupant of a house in which the body of a murdered man had been found.

When the investigators were ready to question him, he motioned them to the pair of white sofas, but the suggestion made the occasion too social. The red-headed detective from the state police post in Pickax preferred to sit at the dining table, and the sheriff's deputy preferred to remain standing. The table was cluttered as usual with writing paraphernalia: typewriter, papers, books, files, pens and pencils, scissors, staple gun, paper clips, and rubber cement—plus the recent addition of a faded pink brocade candybox adorned with a lacy heart. It caught the detective's attention, and Qwilleran thought, Let him make of that what he will.

Everyone in Moose County knew the Klingenschoen name, the Klingenschoen property, the identity of the Klingenschoen heir, and the size and droop of his moustache. Nevertheless, the detective asked routine questions in a polite, non-threatening way, and Qwilleran answered promptly and briefly.

"Your full name, sir?"

"James Qwilleran, spelled with a w. No initial."

"May I see your driver's license?" The detective accepted it and handed it back with barely a glance at the moustache on the card and the moustache on the face. "What is your legal address?"

"Number 315 Park Circle, Pickax."

"How long have you resided at that address?"

"Two years and one month."

"Where did you live before that?"

"Chicago, New York, Washington, San Francisco . . ."

"You moved around, Mr. Qwilleran. What kind of work did you do?"

"I was a journalist assigned to various bureaus."

"What is your occupation now?"

"Semi-retired, but I write for the *Moose County Something.*"

"What are you doing in Mooseville?"

"My plan is—or was—to spend the summer months here."

"Have you changed your plans now?"

"It will depend on the weather."

"When did you arrive?"

"About three weeks ago."

"Is anyone else living here, Mr. Qwilleran?"

"Two Siamese cats."

"Do you own this property?"

"I'm heir to the property, which is currently held in trust by the Klingenschoen estate."

"What was your connection with Ignatius Small?"

"I hired him to build an addition to the cabin."

"How long have you known him, Mr. Qwilleran?"

"About ten days."

They were routine questions designed to put him off-guard, and Qwilleran was waiting for the old one-two. Finally it was delivered:

"*Who buried him under your house?*"

"I have no idea," said Qwilleran without missing a beat. "I would have preferred Mr. Small to be buried elsewhere, and I imagine your men feel the same way."

"When was the last time you saw him, Mr. Qwilleran?"

"Tuesday morning."

"Under what circumstances?"

"He reported for work shortly before I left to have lunch in town. He said he was going to start framing the windows, and I paid him in advance for the day's work."

"Did you pay him in cash?"

"Yes."

"What was the amount?"

Qwilleran reached for a notebook on the table. "Fifty-five dollars."

"Were you expecting any other workmen on Tuesday?"

"No."

"And where were you between the time you left for the lunch and the time you found the body?"

"I had lunch with friends—John Bushland and Roger

MacGillivray at the FOO. Then we boarded Bushland's boat and went out to Three Tree Island. For some fishing," he added. "But a storm came up, and we lost our boat. After being marooned for several hours, we were rescued by the sheriff's helicopter. All of this is on record in the *Morning Rampage* and *Daily Fluxion.*"

"When did you return to this house?"

"About four hours ago."

"Where were you between the hour of your rescue and your return this morning?"

"In the Pickax Hospital under the care of Dr. Halifax."

"Have you any knowledge of what happened in your absence?"

"I certainly have! A tornado wrecked the new addition I was building."

"How did you happen to find the body?"

"My male cat was acting suspiciously, scratching the floor and trying to get down into the crawl space. I opened the trap door to see what was bothering him, and he jumped into the hole and refused to come out, so I left him under the floor and went to lunch."

There was a sharp cry from the guestroom. Koko knew he was the subject of the discussion.

"How long were you gone?"

"About an hour."

"And what happened when you returned?"

"The female was making a fuss about the male being underground, so I opened the trap door and found him digging in the sand and growling. I went after him and discovered he had disinterred a foot."

The trooper turned to the sheriff, who exhibited a chrome flashlight in a clear plastic bag. "Have you seen this flashlight before, Mr. Qwilleran?"

"It's a common style, but it looks like the one I was using

in the crawl space until it suddenly blacked out. Dead battery."

The sheriff removed the flashlight from its bag gingerly and pressed the thumb-switch; the light flashed on.

Qwilleran shrugged. "Well, that's the way they manufacture everything these days."

"When you came home from the hospital, Mr. Qwilleran, did you find the plywood panel nailed up as it is now?"

"Exactly."

"Is that how you left it on Tuesday?"

"Exactly."

"When you left on Tuesday, did you lock the door?"

"Yes. I always take great care to lock up."

"Does anyone else have a key?"

"I subscribe to the Glinko service, so they have a key. Also, there's a spare hidden on the screened porch in case I lose my keycase or lock myself out."

"Where is it?"

"Follow me."

They trooped out to the porch where Riker was waiting patiently and straining his ears to hear. Qwilleran—with a wink at the editor—reached toward the top of the doorframe.

"Don't touch it," said the sheriff, and he climbed up to look. "It's not here," he announced.

"Look under the doormat," Qwilleran suggested.

"Not there either," said the deputy.

"That's unusual."

The detective made a note. "Are you going to be around for a while, Mr. Qwilleran?"

"Around where?"

"Here at this address."

"I may move back to Pickax if the weather doesn't improve."

"Please keep us informed of your whereabouts. You might be able to help us further. And we'd appreciate it if you'd come in for prints, to check against those we've found . . . One more thing," he added, glancing over his shoulder at Riker. "Please don't discuss this case with anyone."

Taking the flashlight, beer can, mudrug, and other evidence in plastic bags, the officers left, only to be intercepted by the editor, who fired questions.

Meanwhile Qwilleran released the long-suffering animals from their prison. "You've lost your rug," he said to Koko.

He poured a double Scotch for his friend, a glass of white grape juice for himself, and a saucer of the same for Koko. "Care to wet your whiskers?" he asked as he placed the saucer on the floor.

The police cars soon pulled away, and the editor shambled into the cabin, dropping disconsolately on a sofa. "They wouldn't talk."

"Just tell your readers that the police are investigating."

"You dirty rat! For this I walked half a mile up your drive in rain and mud?"

"If a dead body turned up in your basement," Qwilleran told his old friend, "you too would keep your mouth shut."

"They don't suspect *you,* do they?"

"They suspect everyone, including the little green men in the UFOs."

"I'm your oldest friend," Riker continued persuasively. "You've always discussed cases with me."

"Heretofore, I was never personally involved. This is the first time I've had a dead body of my own. But I'll tell you one thing: Someone around here hates carpenters!"

The editor drained his glass and stood up. "How do *you* feel about carpenters, Qwill?"

"The same way I feel about editors. There are times when I've wanted to *kill them!*"

It was still raining, and Qwilleran drove Riker to his car parked on the highway. "How about having dinner somewhere tonight, scout?"

"Well, it's like this," said Riker. "My horoscope in today's *Rampage* said I'd resume relations with an estranged friend, so I'm taking Amanda to dinner tonight."

When Qwilleran returned to the cabin, he took care of one small detail. He reached into the lograck on the porch and withdrew a doorkey. After eradicating Mildred's fingerprints and replacing them with plenty of his own, he returned the key to its niche in a hollow log. Then he telephoned Mildred. "How's Roger?"

"He's one sick boy. Sharon is at the hospital now, and I'm keeping the baby. How do you feel?"

"I'm fine, thanks." The murder had not yet been announced on the radio, and Qwilleran had no intention of breaking the news. "Do you have today's papers from Down Below?" he asked her.

"I have the *Fluxion.*"

"What's my horoscope for today?"

"Hold the line. I'll get it." There was a rustling of newspaper pages. "Here it is. For Gemini it says, 'Don't complain about the lack of excitement today. Take a trip! Visit a friend! Do something you've been wanting to do.' How about that?"

After thanking Mildred and hanging up, Qwilleran pondered the advice for a while and telephoned Bushy, but the answering machine said that he and Vicki had gone back to Lockmaster and could be reached there. He found the photographer's business card and dialed the number. Bushy answered, sounding none the worse for a night on Three Tree.

"How are you doing?" Qwilleran asked.

"I'm so glad to be warm and dry and alive, I'm walking two feet off the ground. How about you?"

"No more than nineteen inches."

"That's true, you lost part of your house, didn't you? How were the cats when you got home?"

"They were in good shape. Mildred had fed them an epicurean menu."

"Don't forget, you're going to bring them down here for a studio portrait. How about tonight? It's only an hour's drive. We can talk about Three Tree. It'll do us both good to get it off our chests."

Qwilleran agreed. After all, his horoscope had suggested it.

"How would you like to go for a ride?" he asked the Siamese as he thawed two cartons of beef stew for his dinner and theirs. "You can have your picture taken by a professional photographer and entered in a calendar contest. You'll win hands-down."

They approached their share of the feast fastidiously, gobbling the meat and licking up the gravy but leaving the carrot and potato and onion high and dry on the rim of the plate. Then they washed up in perfect unison like a well-rehearsed chorus line: lick-the-paw three four . . . over-the-nose three four . . . over-the-ear three four. When the wicker picnic hamper appeared, they hopped into it and settled on the down-filled cushion as if they knew they were about to pose for calendar art. By the time they reached Lockmaster they were both comfortably asleep.

The lumber barons' mansions in Lockmaster had been lavished with turrets, gables, oriel windows, and verandas. Now they housed a funeral home, a museum, two insurance companies, three real estate agencies, a clinic, and the Bushland Photo Studio.

Bushy and his wife met Qwilleran at the door and clutched him in a triangular embrace as if the ordeal had made them old friends.

Vicki said, with tears in her eyes, "I was almost out of my mind Tuesday night."

"At least you were warm and dry," Qwilleran reminded her.

"It's amazing that you and Bushy pulled through better than Roger, although he's much younger."

Bushy said, "Roger is anemic. He needs a good slug of red wine every day. My mother was Italian, and that was her cure for everything. Why didn't I rub some on my head?"

"Bring the cats into the studio, Qwill," said Vicki.

The front parlor was furnished in updated Victorian, to provide quaint settings for contemporary photos. Qwilleran set down the hamper in front of the marble fireplace and opened the lid. Everyone was quiet, waiting for the Siamese to emerge, but not so much as an ear appeared above the rim of the hamper. Qwilleran peered into its depths and found both cats curled up like a single fur pillow with heads, legs, and tails tucked out of sight.

"Wake up!" he shouted at them. "You're on camera!"

Two heads materialized from the fur pillow—Koko bright-eyed and instantly alert, Yum Yum groggy and cross-eyed.

Bushy said, "Let's go in the other room and have a drink and leave them to get familiar with the place."

For the next half hour he and Qwilleran re-lived the horrors of the island experience.

"Now that I recall," Qwilleran said, "I pulled through with more fortitude than I showed when there was a dead spider in the *Komfort-Heet.*"

Bushy said, "I felt a kind of inner force fighting the cold."

The more they talked, the less horrifying it became. The ironic humor of the situation emerged. They could laugh about it and probably would, for years to come. When they returned to the front parlor to start the photo session, the Siamese were still asleep in the bottom of the hamper.

"Okay, you guys, cooperate!" Qwilleran said. He reached in with both hands and grasped Koko about the middle, thinking to lift him out, but Koko's claws hooked into the wicker and could not be dislodged.

"Come on, sweetheart," he said, putting his hands gently under Yum Yum's body, but she also had eighteen functional hooks that engaged the open weave of the hamper. "I'm going to need help," he said.

Vicki reached into the hamper, murmuring soothing words, and carefully unhooked Yum Yum's left paw from the wicker while Qwilleran did the same for the right paw. Then they lifted, but her rear claws were firmly anchored. By the time they disengaged the rear end, the front end was again attached to the hamper.

Qwilleran's back was beginning to ache. He stood up, stretched his spine, and took a few deep breaths. "There must be a way," he said. "Three intelligent adults can't be outwitted by two cats who don't have university degrees and don't even have drivers' licenses."

"Let's turn the thing upside-down and shake them out," Bushy suggested.

They tried it, and the down cushion fell out but not the cats.

"I say we should go back and have another drink," said Bushy. They did, and Koko and Yum Yum remained riveted to their travel coop for the remainder of the evening.

On the way home Qwilleran tuned in WPKX for the eleven o'clock news and heard this: "Police report that the body of a man identified as Ignatius K. Small, itinerant carpenter, was found buried under a lakeside residence east of Mooseville. According to the medical examiner, death was caused by a blow to the head, and the time of death was established as four o'clock Tuesday. The property is owned by the Klingenschoen estate. James Qwilleran of Pickax is currently living there."

"Dunderheads!" Qwilleran said. "They make me sound like the number-one suspect!"

SEVENTEEN

After WPKX had broadcast the news of the carpenter's murder every half hour, Qwilleran's telephone began to ring and he found himself fielding calls from concerned friends and friendly kidders. "No, I didn't do it, and if I did, do you think I'd tell you?" . . . "Thanks, but I'm not ready for an attorney yet; go chase an ambulance." There were crank calls also, but he had learned how to handle those when he worked for big-city newspapers.

While watching the Siamese eat their breakfast, he reconstructed the murder scene from their viewpoint. They were locked in the guestroom with their water dish and commode. For a while they sat on the windowsill and watched the carpenter, Koko probably tapping his tail in unison with the hammer. They had a couple of drinks of water, scratched the gravel in their commode, and catnapped on the guestbed . . . Perhaps a vehicle of some kind arrived and alerted them—alerted Koko, at any rate. Had he heard that particular motor before? What did he hear next? Voices? An argument? A fight? Did he see anything through the window? Did he hear the door being unlocked? The trap door being opened? After that there were indistinct noises under the floor. Eventually the trap door banged again and the vehicle drove away . . . Or did the murderer arrive on foot via the beach? That was a possibility . . . Everything was quiet, and Koko had another drink of water, after which he slept until wakened by the roar of the tornado and the terrifying crash of the east wing. Both cats scuttled under the bed. Later they heard the rain slamming the roof. It was dark, and they were hungry.

That had happened three days ago. Now they were satiated with white meat of tuna and were perched somewhere overhead, communing with their contented innards. Koko was on the moosehead, while Yum Yum crouched on a crossbeam overlooking the dining table where Qwilleran often did interesting things with typewriter, scissors, and rubber cement. The cats stayed at their posts even when the two state police officers were admitted to the cabin.

This time the red-haired detective from the Pickax post introduced an inspector from Down Below, evidently a homicide specialist. He explained that they needed a little more information. Qwilleran found it unusual that the state would fly a man four hundred miles north to investigate the murder of an itinerant carpenter, while hundreds of murders in the state capital itself went unsolved. With a cynical huff into his moustache he suspected that the homicide man wanted to get away from city heat for a while and possibly do a little fishing.

"Have a seat," said Qwilleran, pushing back some of the clutter on the table. The inspector pulled up a chair, while the local officer remained standing.

After some repetitious preliminaries the inspector asked, "Was Ignatius Small a good carpenter in your estimation, sir?"

"He seemed to know his craft."

"Was he recommended to you?"

"No. He was an itinerant carpenter and the only one

available. There's a shortage of carpenters in this neck of the woods during the summer months."

"How did you find him, sir?"

"These underground builders, as they're called, hang around the bars. A barkeeper sent him over here."

"Could you describe his personality?"

"He smiled a lot . . . and accepted orders and suggestions well enough."

"Did he always carry out orders?"

"To the best of his ability, I would say. He wasn't a sharp thinker, and he had very little energy."

"Would you say he was . . . *lazy,* sir?"

"If that denotes falling asleep while shingling the roof, yes, you could say he was lazy, or narcoleptic."

"How did you feel about that, sir?"

Qwilleran thought, He's fishing; watch your step . . . To the inspector he said, "I was grateful to find anyone at all to do my work. Beggars can't be choosy."

"Did he ever make mistakes?"

"Occasionally, but it was always something that could be corrected."

"Did he ever cause you to lose your temper?"

"What do you mean?"

"Did you ever threaten him physically?"

Qwilleran looked at the detective with expressionless eyes, mournfully lidded. "Would you elucidate?"

"Did you ever . . . threaten to . . . *clobber him with a two-by-four?*"

Instantly Qwilleran recalled lunch at the FOO with Bushy and Roger. They had been overheard!

At the same moment the telephone rang, and a fur body dropped from the overhead beam, landed on the table, panicked, kicked wildly, scattered papers and pens, flew past the inspector's head to a nearby bookshelf, leaped to the bar and collided with another fur body that had swooped down from the moosehead, bounced off the sofaback, whizzed past the dining table, skimmed across the chairbacks, and crashed into a lamp. The phone continued to ring. Fur bodies were flying in every direction. Zip! Whoosh! The three men were ducking. Then the ringing stopped, and the two cats came to rest on the sofa, where they engaged in mutual licking of imaginary wounds.

"Sorry," Qwilleran said. "They were having a catfit."

"The phone scared them," said the local officer.

The inspector stood up. "Thank you for your cooperation, sir. We may want to talk to you again."

When the detectives had left, Qwilleran said to the cats, "You two have never been scared by the telephone in your lives!" He gave them a few crunchy crumbles for a treat.

After starting a blaze in the fireplace to dispel the gloom of an overcast sky and the dampness of two non-stop rainy days, he sprawled on the sofa with a cup of coffee. The Siamese arranged themselves in cozy bundles on the hearth rug nearby—their backs to the warmth and their blue eyes fixed on his face, waiting for conversation.

"The thought occurs to me," said Qwilleran, stroking his moustache, "that Mooseville might be in the grip of a serial killer—an out-and-out sociopath."

There was a decisive "YOW!" from Koko.

"Thank you, sir, for your vote of confidence. Unlike you, the chamber of commerce will resist the idea; it's a bad image for a tourist town. But I suspect the police are on to something. Otherwise, why would they bring in their big guns? There's plenty for them to do Down Below. It's my belief that they suspect, as I do, that several isolated incidents up here are actually serial killings."

"YOW!" said Koko again, showing an unusual interest in the topic.

"Sorry, old boy," Qwilleran said to him, "one body is enough. You'll do no more excavating!" He massaged his moustache intently. "Where will they look for suspects? It could be an ordinary individual with a hidden personality disorder who kills and doesn't even know he's killing. That's happened elsewhere. It could be the superintendent of schools; it could be the president of the chamber of commerce! That's why it's hard to catch this kind of criminal. I say the police have a tricky job ahead of them. The killer could be someone who's had a twisted relationship with a specific carpenter and proceeds to transfer his animosity to all carpenters. Or he could be another carpenter—a monomaniac who wants the field all to himself. If this is the case, where was he when I needed a builder?"

Qwilleran got up to refill his coffee mug. The cats remained where they were.

Returning he said, "It's the logistics of this latest crime that boggle my mind: how to lower the body through the trap door, convey it to the middle of the crawl space without leaving a distinct trail, and bury it under loose sand—all with only two feet of headroom, or less. Of course, Iggy was as thin as a potato chip; he can't have weighed more than ninety pounds."

Qwilleran began to massage his moustache vigorously. "Could it be that Iggy was already in the center of the crawl space when he was attacked? Could it be that the killer lured him down there with the story of the Klingenschoen treasure? . . . Koko, did you hear two voices under the floor? If the answer is yes, tap your tail three times."

There was not even a whisker stirring on the hearth rug; both cats were having their afternoon nap.

Qwilleran screened the fireplace without disturbing them and drove to Mooseville to pick up his mail and replace certain items confiscated by the police.

In the post office he found the patrons talking about the murder as they licked their stamps and unlocked their boxes, but they quickly changed the subject when he approached. His mail was plentiful—too plentiful, considering that his secretary had gone on vacation. It always happened that way. And now his narrow escape on Three Tree Island would bring another flood of letters from well-wishers, and the publicity on the murder would result in yet another wave of correspondence.

When Qwilleran entered the hardware store he was aware he was being ogled by other customers. To the proprietor he said, "Thanks for turning off the rain, Cecil." Huggins was president of the chamber of commerce, and he regarded the weather as one of his responsibilities of office.

"Too late!" he said dolefully. "The tourists are leaving in droves, and the fishermen are giving me hell. We haven't seen the sun for three days . . . Say," he added in a lower voice, "is it true what they said on the radio?"

"Sad but true."

"Murder is bad for business, you know. Even worse than rain. Tourists don't like the idea of a killer running around loose. How'd the body get underneath your house, Mr. Q?"

"I wish I knew."

"Are the police bothering you?"

"I daresay they're bothering everyone."

"Do they have any suspects?"

Another customer barged into the conversation—a big man in a flashy cowboy outfit and expensive boots. "Hey, are you the fella with a dead body under the floor?" he asked with a pudding-face smile.

"I'm glad to say," Qwilleran said politely, "that it's no longer under the floor."

"How'd it get there?"

"Lou," said the storekeeper gently, taking the man's arm,

"look over there in the tool department. There's a new kind of saber saw that we just got in stock. You'll like it. I'll give you a five-percent discount as a good customer."

The big man drifted away to the other side of the store.

The hardwareman shook his head and said to Qwilleran, "He's a nuisance sometimes, but he spends a lot of money on tools, so I try not to offend him. Sometimes I feel guilty, because I know he never uses them, but a fella with his money is going to spend it on something, so let him spend it on electric saws. That's what I say. Am I right?"

"It makes sense," said Qwilleran. "What do you hear about the flooding?"

"Worst ever! The creeks in three counties are dumping into the Ittibittiwassee. It's flooding farms and washing out bridges. Very bad! They're announcing on the radio which roads are closed."

Qwilleran bought a new flashlight and had another key made. "Do you keep a record, Cecil, of people who buy duplicate keys?"

"Not a chance, Mr. Q. With all the records I have to keep for the government, I can't keep tabs on folks who lose their keys." The storekeeper accompanied Qwilleran to the door, and when they were beyond earshot of the clerks and customers he said, "There's something I should tell you, Mr. Q. Certain local folks are talking about you this morning in a way I don't like. You're a great guy when you're giving the K money away, but get a little mud splashed on your trouser cuffs, and they're ready to trample you in the gutter."

"Interesting observation," said Qwilleran, "but I don't get the point."

Cecil glanced hastily around the store and whispered, "A certain element around here—troublemakers and not very bright—would like to think you're the one who killed the carpenter and buried the body. If they don't know the truth, they invent it, and they like to do mischief."

Qwilleran took it lightly. "Perhaps I should call Glinko and requisition a bodyguard."

"If I were you, Mr. Q," said Cecil, "I'd go back to Pickax until it blows over. There's something else, too, that's being whispered: When Clem Cottle was last seen, he was working for you."

Qwilleran thanked him for his concern and left the store. This, he thought, is a new slant on Mooseville society—an idea for the "Qwill Pen."

When he arrived at the cabin, however, he momentarily lost his detachment. The interior was a wreck! Cecil's words flashed into his mind . . . until he recognized the nature of the damage and identified the culprits. The dining table had been swept clean, except for his typewriter; all the Indian rugs had been pushed into corners, their fringes chewed; Emma Wimsey's shopping bag was overturned and the contents scattered.

"Bad cats!" Qwilleran bellowed. Yum Yum went slinking under the sofa; Koko leaped from floor to woodbox to mantel to moosehead in a swift, guilty blur of light-and-dark brown. Scolding would accomplish nothing. This was a Siamese protest against the incarceration and neglect of the last few days. Perhaps the cats were even blaming him for the lack of sunshine.

Patiently Qwilleran collected the desktop clutter from the floor. Patiently he straightened the rugs. Patiently he collected Emma's papers. "I hope you cats know," he said, "that I'm bucking for sainthood when I do this with such forbearance."

Half the pens and pencils were missing, but he knew where they were. With a broom from the mudroom he made several swipes under Yum Yum's favorite sofa and retrieved the following:

A few balls of cat hair.

A toothbrush with a red handle.

Two felt-tip pens and one gold ballpoint.

Three pencils.

A postcard from Polly Duncan, perforated with fangmarks.

A cheap lipstick case, evidently Joanna's.

A white sock with green sports stripe.

Qwilleran assuaged his own damaged feelings with a cup of coffee and a session with the letter opener. First he read the latest postcard from Polly Duncan. She was having difficulty adjusting to the English climate; she was having respiratory problems. "She thinks *she's* got problems!" he said to anyone who cared to hear. Next he opened a letter from the Senior Care Facility:

> Dear Mr. Qwilleran,
> I think you will want to know this. Yesterday our dear Emma Wimsey celebrated her birthday. She had a birthday cake with candles and wore a paper hat. As the aide was putting her to bed, Emma said, "I hear scratching under the door." Shortly after, she passed away quietly in her sleep. She had just turned ninety.
>
> Sincerely,
> Irma Hasselrich, MCSCF
> Chief Canary

Emma Wimsey had lived a long life, Qwilleran reflected. She had secured an education, raised a family, performed her farm chores, worshipped her Lord, collected her little stories, and passed her final days among those caring canaries in yellow smocks. Only when he visualized the diminutive woman in a paper hat on her ninetieth birthday did he feel a degree of sorrow. Opening her valentine box, he regretted that none of her family wanted this paltry legacy. If she had left a grandfather clock and a rosewood piano, they would have fought for their inheritance—a bitter idea for the "Qwill Pen."

The box contained trinkets and scraps of paper, including one yellowed clipping from the old *Pickax Picayune,* probably seventy years old:

NUPTIALS CELEBRATED

> Emma Huggins and Horace Wimsey of Black Creek were united in marriage at the Mooseville Church Saturday at four o'clock. There were six in the wedding party. Refreshments were served in the church basement.

Among the mementos were a buffalo nickel and a Lincoln-head penny; a tiny locket; a blue ribbon won at a county fair for home canning; a thin ring set with a few garnets, one missing; a bit of ivory that could be nothing but a baby tooth, probably that of her firstborn.

The Siamese had come out of seclusion to watch the excitement, and when Qwilleran tackled the contents of Emma's shopping bag, they wriggled in anticipation. They knew reading material when they saw it, and they liked him to read aloud. In the bag were school notebooks filled with daily thoughts and bundles of hand-written manuscripts on lined paper.

"This appears to be," Qwilleran told his listeners, "the lifework of a north-country farmwife who attended teacher's college, taught school for a while, and retired to raise a family. She never forgot how to spell and punctuate and compose a good sentence, and she obviously had an urge to write."

Leafing through the collection, he found one tale titled

"The Face at the Bridge." It was footnoted, "A true story which I told to my children many times. It always scared them."

"Here's a story that will curl your whiskers," he said to the cats, and he read it aloud.

THE FACE AT THE BRIDGE

When I started teaching in a one-room schoolhouse near Black Creek, I lived with a farm family and had to walk three miles to school in all kinds of weather. I always went early because I had to make a fire in the wood stove and trim the lamps and wash the glass chimneys and sweep the floor.

One day in late November before snow had started to turn the brown landscape white, I set out for school in pitch-darkness. There was a covered bridge over the creek, and oh! how I dreaded crossing that bridge in the dark! On this particular day, as I entered the dark tunnel, I saw something that made my knees shake. There was a white object at the far end—small and round and white and floating in the air. I stood stockstill with my mouth open as it came closer, bobbing gently. I wanted to turn around and run, but my feet were rooted to the ground. And then I realized it was a FACE—no body, just a white face! It started to make noises: "U-u-ugh! U-u-ugh!"

I tried to scream, but no sound came from my mouth. Then two white hands reached for me. "U-u-ugh! U-u-ugh!"

As the white face came close to mine, I was about to faint, but then I recognized it. I recognized a pale young girl from our church. She was wearing black garments and a black shawl over her head, and she was trying to tell me not to be afraid. She was a deaf-mute.

Qwilleran smoothed his moustache with satisfaction. This was the kind of stuff his readers would enjoy, and it actually happened in Black Creek; the bridge might still be there. With his interest piqued, he delved into the bagful of manuscripts, reading how Emma's son had been attacked by a swarm of wild bees who chased him all the way home, and how Emma's cousin had caught her hands in the wringer of an early electric washing machine. There were local legends, mining and lumbering adventures, and the account of Punkin, the cat who scratched under the door.

The possibilities raced through Qwilleran's mind. The *Moose County Something* could feature these country tales with Emma's by-line on page two alongside the "Qwill Pen"; he would write an introduction for each one. Arch Riker might be able to syndicate them; there was a growing interest in country lore. If the Klingenschoen Fund would publish them in book form, the royalties could establish an Emma Wimsey Scholarship—unless greedy heirs tried to get into the act; Hasselrich would have to deal with that aspect.

"If we publish a book, that little lady will be dancing in her grave," Qwilleran told the cats, "and I hope her insensitive relatives choke on it!"

As he read on, he was able to identify the early and late periods of Emma's writing. In the older manuscripts the paper was yellowed and the ink was fading. Those of a later date were written by a hand that was beginning to shake with age or infirmity.

There was one work in poignant contrast to the others in the collection. Scribbled on the stationery of the Senior Care Facility, it was apparently written after Emma entered the nursing home. The handwriting was almost illegible, and Emma's story-telling talent had faded. Titled "A Family Tragedy," it was a mere statement of facts without style or grace or emotion. Qwilleran had no desire to read it aloud.

> My husband was a farmer. We had four sons and one daughter. She was beautiful. Her name was Violet. She could have had a fine young man, but she fell in love with a rough fellow. Her brothers pleaded with her, but she wouldn't lis-

> ten, so her father disowned her. Violet's husband never built her a proper house. They lived in a shack. Their little girl went to school in rags. My menfolk wouldn't let me visit them. I used to peek in the school window to look at my granddaughter. I gave the teacher clothes for her to wear. One day the girl went to school crying. Her mother was sick and all black and blue. The teacher called the sheriff. He arrested Violet's husband for beating her. He wasn't in jail long. Violet was pregnant. She died when the baby came. The older girl had to keep house and tend the baby. The teacher said she changed overnight from a child to a woman. There was a lot of gossip. The baby grew to be a beautiful child. I knew something terrible was happening. When the child was twelve she shot herself with her father's gun. I prayed that the Lord would punish him. My prayers were answered. The back of a dump truck fell on him and killed him.

Qwilleran lost no time in phoning the hardware merchant, who was related to the Wimseys by marriage. He put a blunt question to Cecil.

"Yes," was the answer. "Little Joe is Emma's granddaughter. Her real name is Joanna. Joanna Trupp. She doesn't have anything to do with the Wimsey or Huggins family—just keeps pretty much to herself. I don't know why. We've never given her any cause. All the relatives feel sorry for her. It's a sad case. But she's a pretty good plumber, I hear."

"Why do you call it a sad case?" Qwilleran asked.

"Well, you know, Big Joe abused both his daughters sexually after his wife died. That's probably why the younger girl killed herself. She was only twelve. Did it with her daddy's gun. Big Joe was just no good! Everybody knew that. God knows every family tree has one branch that's unhealthy and withers away. I hope Little Joe makes it."

EIGHTEEN

As soon as Qwilleran confirmed that Joanna was Emma Wimsey's granddaughter, he knew what to do with the valentine box. She might not care about it, but it included two small items of jewelry, and he ought to offer it to her. Adding the lipstick that Yum Yum had hidden under the sofa, he put the box in his bicycle knapsack.

Joanna lived on Hogback, one of the roads officially closed by the swollen river, but with his trail bike he could skirt the inundated areas. He had never experienced a flood. During his career as a newsman he had covered fires, riots, plane crashes, earthquakes, and the fringes of war, but never a flood. It was difficult to imagine the friendly Ittibittiwassee overflowing its banks, going crazy, drowning farms and destroying bridges. Now he could make a firsthand observation, and it might be a subject for the "Qwill Pen."

He biked up the paved Sandpit Road and east on the gravel Dumpy and was still a quarter-mile from the riverbed when he noticed a change in the atmosphere. The chirping, rustling, cawing, chattering sounds of dry land were deadened and replaced by the silence of flooded fields under a heavy sky. When the Ittibittiwassee came into view, it was no longer a river; it was a lake with trees and barns and sheds tilting far out on its glassy surface. Hawks were circling over the wetlands, looking for drowned carrion. The scene was unhealthily quiet.

Hogback Road was impassable, but he cut through the woods on the high ground that paralleled it. As he zoomed up over the last sandhill he had a view of the plumbing graveyard. Most of the old plumbing fixtures in the yard were submerged. The animal cages had washed away entirely, and Joanna's flat-roofed shack was dangerously tilted and about to collapse. The van was not there; neither was she. Still he felt compelled to call her name two or three times, and his voice sounded eerily loud across the counterfeit lake.

A spongy margin at the edge of the flood indicated that the water was beginning to recede or drain into the sandy soil, leaving debris in its wake: sodden papers and rags, bits of wood, food wrappers, beer cans, and a muddied plaid that looked like Joanna's everyday shirt. He picked up a crude wooden cross that had marked an animal's grave and lifted a large red rag from the mud. Then he jumped back on his bike and plunged back into the woods, heading for town.

Dumpy Road with its dreary trailer homes surrounded by junk cars was even more depressing on a gray day. It was rutted and treacherous after the rain, and he had to concentrate on the roadbed. Just then something whizzed past his ear, alarmingly close, and he saw a rock as big as a grapefruit hitting the ground. He turned to find its source, and a second rock grazed his shoulder. At the same time he saw two figures ducking behind a shed.

Qwilleran did no more sightseeing that day. He pedaled back to the cabin and telephoned Mrs. Glinko. "Have you seen Little Joe lately?" he asked.

"You got another leak?" she said with her perpetual good humor.

"No, but her house was destroyed by the flood, and I'm worried about her. We wouldn't want to lose a first-rate plumber, would we?"

"She's okay. She's around somewheres. Want me to dispatch her for anything? Ha ha ha!"

"No, thanks."

Qwilleran turned to the Siamese, who were attending him closely as if concerned—or hungry. "This is not the vacation paradise I envisioned," he told them. "I'd like to read my horoscope for today."

He picked up the phone again and called Mildred Hanstable. "Qwill here. How's Roger? . . . That's good. I was worried about him . . . No, not a thing. No mention of suspects. When Roger gets back on the beat, we may hear something. By the way, do you have any papers from Down Below? . . . Good! What's my horoscope for today?" There followed a long wait and a sound of rustling newsprint. He listened and then said, "Well, thanks, Mildred. And let's have dinner one night next week."

He tamped his moustache. In the *Morning Rampage* the forecast read, "Interesting developments are in the offing. Hang in there a little longer." The *Daily Fluxion,* on the other hand, advised, "Know when to wash your hands of a bad situation. Cut your losses."

Qwilleran gave the contradictory counsel some serious thought as he heated two cartons of chili for himself and opened a can of crabmeat for the Siamese, and he was inclined to go along with the *Rampage*. His ruminations were interrupted by the sound of a vehicle moving up the drive. He went to the back porch to investigate. It was a recreation vehicle of modest size, and the driver in camping attire who jumped out of it was Nick Bamba.

"Hi!" he said. "I'm on my way Down Below to pick up Lori and the baby, and I decided to drop by and see how you're doing. Hey! What happened to your new addition?"

"It was redesigned by the tornado," Qwilleran informed him. "Come in and have a bourbon. Have you had dinner?"

"No, I'll grab something on the road."

"I'm thawing some packaged chili. How about a bowl? It's not bad. Even Koko will eat it in a pinch." Qwilleran poured the drinks and set out some cheese and crackers. "Who'll take care of your cats while you're gone?"

"One of our neighbors at the condo. Mighty Lou."

Qwilleran looked dubious. "You mean the one-and-only original Mighty Lou? Is he reliable?"

"Oh, sure. He's very good with cats."

"He doesn't resemble your average cat-sitter."

"No, but he's a good guy—brushes them, talks to them, and everything. The cats like him." Nick took a sip of his drink, expressed satisfaction, and then said, "You came up with a couple of shockers this week, Qwill. First you're marooned on a desert island, and then you find a dead body under your house! Are there any suspects?"

"All I know is what I hear on the radio. The police don't confide in me."

"But you must have some noodles of your own." Nick knew that Qwilleran's suspicions had paid off in the past.

"I don't know. I'm up a tree. Someone must have had a key to get in and bury the body. I subscribe to the Glinko service, and all their service personnel have access to my key—and God knows who else can borrow it. What do you know about the Glinko operation, Nick? Is it all legal and aboveboard?"

"As far as I know."

"They're raking in the dough—dues from summer people

and commissions from their workers. What do they do with all their money? They live like paupers."

"They've got a lot of expenses," Nick said, "what with three kids in college, one of them in Harvard."

Qwilleran tried not to appear stunned. "Harvard, did you say? Harvard University?"

"Those eastern schools don't come cheap."

Qwilleran put the bourbon bottle and ice bucket on the coffee table. "Help yourself, Nick."

"Are you going to stay in Mooseville?" the young man asked.

"If the weather doesn't get any worse."

"I wasn't thinking about the weather."

"What's on your mind? Out with it!"

Nick hesitated before saying, "I think you'd be wise to pack up the cats and beat it back to Pickax. We have some riffraff around here, and I've heard some nasty rumblings. Don't forget, I work at the state prison, and there's no better place to hear rumblings."

Qwilleran stroked his moustache. Cecil had warned him; a small boulder had been aimed at him on Dumpy Road; and there had been several crank calls on the phone. "What is this riffraff you mention?"

"They hate the summer people, because they think they have money. The chamber of commerce keeps the lid on them in tourist season, but the town has emptied out since the storm, and the troublemakers are more visible. They gang together, get a few drinks, and cut loose. I'm warning you, Qwill. Go back to Pickax tonight!"

"I have yet to run away from a situation, my boy, and I've lived through some hairy ones."

"You're isolated here. There's only one driveway and no escape route. They can vandalize the cabin—start a fire—do something to the cats."

At the mention of the Siamese—Koko perched on the moosehead, Yum Yum looking fragile and precious on the sofa—Qwilleran grew pensive. He was so deep in thought that he jumped when the telephone rang. "Hello?" he said warily.

"Hey, Qwill, this is Gary at the Black Bear," said the barkeeper.

Qwilleran responded with some surprise. Gary had never phoned him before.

"How's everything in Mooseville?"

"Apart from the rain, the mosquitoes, and the tornado, everything's fine."

"Sorry to hear about Iggy. He wasn't a bad guy. Dumb, but not bad."

"Yes, it's unfortunate," said Qwilleran with less than his usual verve.

"Are you moving back to Pickax?"

"I haven't made any plans."

"I would if I were you," said Gary, his voice muffled as if he were cupping his hand around the mouthpiece. "A bunch of rowdies are gathering around here, and they've got something cooking. Take my advice and get out! . . . Gotta hang up now."

Qwilleran replaced the receiver slowly, and Nick observed his mood. "Trouble?" he asked.

"Another warning—from Gary Pratt."

"See? What did I tell you? If you don't leave," Nick said vehemently, "I'm staying here tonight. I've got a police radio, and I'm going to block the drive with my RV and sit up with my shotgun." Without waiting for an objection he dashed out to the clearing and moved his camper. When he returned, he had a portable spotlight, a shotgun, and a rifle. "I've alerted the sheriff," he said.

They ate chili and drank coffee, and Qwilleran recounted

his adventure on Three Tree Island, his tribulations with the underground builder, and Koko's discovery of the body. The sky darkened early at the end of that gloomy day, and he turned on some lamps.

"No lights!" Nick ordered. "And we'll close the inside shutters."

The Siamese sensed the mood of watchful waiting; they too watched and waited. As they all sat there in the dark Qwilleran asked, "What do you know about the buried treasure on this property?"

"I've heard that rumor all my life. Some think the old man buried jewelry or gold. Some say it was stock certificates that would be worthless now."

"Has anyone tried to dig it up?"

"Where would they dig? You've got about forty acres of woodland here and half a mile of beach."

"Wouldn't the crawl space be a logical place to bury the stuff?"

"Hey, man! You've got something there," said Nick. "Gotta shovel?"

Qwilleran smoothed his moustache. "Suppose some local person, who guessed the loot might be under the house, lured the carpenter down there with the promise of a split, got him digging for the treasure, hit him on the head after he found it, and pushed him into the hole he had dug!"

"And then left with the whole caboodle! Neat trick!" Nick said.

"If it's true, it might explain how Iggy's body got down there. But if it's true, I suspect it's only part of the story," Qwilleran said. "It's my guess that the murderer is a serial killer operating in Mooseville."

"What!"

"YOW!" came a voice from the moosehead.

"Koko agrees with me. I contend that the victims were

not only my builder but Clem Cottle and Buddy Yarrow and—"

He was interrupted by a triple-thump as the cat came down from his lofty perch, growling a gutteral threat.

"What's that?" Nick snapped. "He hears someone coming up the drive!"

"No, look at him! He's sniffing the trap door. It's the same performance he staged before he found Iggy's body."

Nick jumped to his feet. "There's something else down there. Want me to go and see?"

"I'll go," Qwilleran said.

"No, I'll go. I'm smaller." Nick grabbed his spotlight, threw open the trap door, and slipped through the hole nimbly. Koko streaked after him.

Yum Yum approached the scene cautiously, but Qwilleran intercepted her and shut her up in the guestroom. "Sorry, sweetheart. This is no business for a sensitive cat."

Down in the crawl space Nick was talking to Koko and getting an occasional "ik ik ik" in reply.

"Find anything?" Qwilleran shouted. "What's he doing?"

"He's at the far end," Nick yelled. "Come on, Koko ol' boy. Whatcha got over there?"

"YOW!"

"Is he digging?"

"No. Not digging. But excited." Nick's voice became more and more remote as he worked his way toward the far end of the crawl space.

The wait seemed interminable. "Any luck?"

There was no answer.

"Nick! What's going on down there?"

"Hey, Qwill!" shouted a muffled voice. "Come on down here!"

Qwilleran lowered himself through the trap door, thrusting his legs out as he had learned to do, chinning on the edge, then rolling over. The far end of the crawl space was brightly illuminated by the high-powered light. Nick and Koko had progressed as far as they could go. They were up against the fieldstone foundation, the man staring at the floor joists above him and the cat on his hind legs, pawing the air.

Qwilleran scudded across the sand like a lizard, amazed at his own agility, ignoring the cobwebs that clung to his face, and inching through tight spots with only a twelve-inch overhead.

"Get a load of this!" Nick said as Qwilleran approached. "You have to squeeze in between the foundation and the first joist, or you can't see it. Only a cat could have found it!"

Qwilleran twisted his body into the tight space and looked up as Nick swept his spotlight across the overhead timber. There were marks on the joist, but the wood was dark with age, and they were hard to decipher.

"It's written in *blood!*" Nick said. "Koko must have smelled the *blood!*"

"I was right!" Qwilleran exulted as he spelled out the obscure message. "They were serial killings!"

"YOW!" said Koko, racing across the sand to the trap door and hopping out of the crawl space.

"Let's get out of this damned hole," Nick said. "The cobwebs make me itch all over. You bring the spotlight."

He started to belly-crawl across the sand, and Qwilleran followed with the light, but not until he had reached up and touched the lettering on the joist. It wasn't blood; it was lipstick.

The two men brushed the sand off their clothing, then sprawled on the white sofas, talking and drinking coffee and listening for prowlers, their firearms close at hand. The Siamese, sensing the tension, sat on the sofas with their haunches elevated as if ready to spring. Twice the sheriff's helicopter buzzed the shoreline and searchlighted the Klingenschoen property.

At dawn Nick announced he would continue his journey Down Below if Qwilleran would promise to return to the safety of Pickax. "And when are you going to report to the police what we found?"

"As soon as I've put some food in my stomach and splashed some cold water on my face," said Qwilleran, who was adept at inventing false replies when the occasion demanded.

As soon as the camper pulled away from the cabin he telephoned the Glinko night number. "Qwilleran again," he said with the clipped speech of urgency. "We've got a plumbing emergency!"

"Allrighty. I'll dispatch Ralph," said Mrs. Glinko as if 5 a.m. emergencies were routine.

"Couldn't you dispatch Little Joe? She knows the plumbing setup here."

"Oh, so you want Little Joe, do you?" the woman said with a leering laugh. "You want her in a hurry, eh?"

"The toilet's backed up," Qwilleran said sternly.

"Okay, I'll try to find her. No tellin' where that babe is shackin' up now."

By the time Qwilleran had pacified the Siamese with an early breakfast and had started a blaze in the fireplace to dispel the dawn chill, Joanna's van pulled into the clearing. Although her attire was never neat, at this hour it looked slept-in, and her eyes were bleary. "Toilet backed up?" she asked with a yawn.

"I have to apologize," he said. "It was a false alarm. It corrected itself, but I appreciate your quick response, and I'll pay your bill for an after-hours housecall."

"I was sleepin' in my van on the Old Brrr Road when she buzzed me. My house washed out."

"I'm sorry to hear that. Will you rebuild?"

"Yeah, I'm gonna build a nice place like this." She swept admiring eyes over the cabin interior.

"May I offer you some breakfast? Coffee and a cinnamon roll?"

"Sure," she said, suddenly more awake.

"Or would you prefer an apple turnover?"

"Can I have both?"

"Why not? I can make them in a jiffy. How do you like your coffee?"

Joanna was fascinated by the microwave oven and computerized coffeemaker, and Qwilleran knew how to play the gracious host. They ate at the bar, and she talked about the tornado, and her animals, and how the flood had swept away their cages. When he suggested a second cup of coffee in front of the fire, she hesitated, looking at the white linen sofas and then down at her work clothes. "I'm too dirty."

"Not at all. Sit down and make yourself comfortable. And prepare for a surprise." He handed her Emma Wimsey's valentine box. "This belonged to your grandmother. Perhaps she never visited you, but she loved you very much. It contains some keepsakes she would want you to have."

She examined the trinkets and souvenirs in the box and glowed with pleasure. If she found Qwilleran's sudden hospitality a suspicious right-about-face, she gave no indication. After all, she was having breakfast with the richest man in the county—in a setting that was the epitome of glamor to a resident of Hogback Road.

Qwilleran, on the other hand, dreaded the confrontation that was coming and deplored the means he had taken to accomplish it. Finally he said, "I'm not going to rebuild my new addition. My carpenter was murdered. Did you know he was murdered?"

"Iggy?" she said without surprise.

"Ignatius K. Small was his name. And a few days before that, Clem Cottle disappeared. Yesterday I biked out Hogback Road to look at the flood damage, and I found Clem's jacket in the mud near your house." When she looked bewildered, he added casually, "Clem's red softball jacket with the rooster on it. How do you suppose it got there?"

"Mmmm . . . Clem was going to . . . build a new house for me," she said uncertainly. "He came out to tell me . . . how much it would cost."

In the same conversational tone Qwilleran went on. "Well, I'm afraid you've lost a good carpenter. I'm sure Clem is dead. Buddy Yarrow was another fine young man who was killed; he fell in the river near your house. And then there was a carpenter named Mert who disappeared, although they found his truck in a junkyard. And didn't you tell me your father was a carpenter?" He waited for a reaction but none came. Altering his tone to one of accusation and looking steadily into her eyes, he said, "Doesn't it seem strange, Joanna, that so many carpenters have died or disappeared? How do you explain it?"

Her eyes shifted as she tried to find an answer. "I don't know," she said in a small voice.

"I think you know how Clem's truck ended up in a ditch on the Old Brrr Road. Did you bury his body on your property?"

Joanna gazed at him, paralyzed with shock.

"And how about Mert? Did you invite him home for a beer and hit him on the head with a lead pipe?"

"NO!" She was looking frightened.

"Did you have the hardware store make a duplicate key to my cabin so you could go down into the crawl space? I think you got Iggy to go down there during the tornado—for safety—and he never came out."

Her expression changed from fright to menace—she was

a big strong girl—and Qwilleran thought it wise to move toward the fireplace in reach of the poker. As he paced back and forth on the hearth he said, "You know all about this, Joanna! Down in the crawl space there's a list of all five carpenters and the dates they were murdered."

Her eyes were moving wildly. "I didn't do it!"

"But you know something about it. Did you have a partner?"

"I didn't have nothin' to do with it!"

"The police are going to suspect you because the names in the crawl space are written with your lipstick."

"Someone else did it!" she cried. "She stole my lipstick!"

"Who?"

"Louise!" She was moistening her lips anxiously.

"Who's Louise?"

"A girl. She does . . . bad things."

"Why would she kill five carpenters?"

Her voice became hysterical. "They're bad! Her daddy was a carpenter! He was a bad man!" Suddenly she jumped up and rushed to the door.

"Don't forget your grandmother's box," Qwilleran said.

Joanna ran from the cabin and drove away in her van, spraying gravel.

Slowly and with regret Qwilleran dialed the number of the state police.

NINETEEN

THE SUN WAS SHINING, Pickax was drying out, and bells in the Old Stone Church on Park Circle were ringing joyously as Qwilleran arrived at his apartment over the Klingenschoen garage. In his car were his typewriter, summer clothes, coffeemaker, the Siamese in their travel coop, and of course their turkey roaster.

He consulted his horoscope in the weekend edition of the *Moose County Something,* which now carried a syndicated astrology column in response to reader demand. "You have some explaining to do, Gemini," said the anonymous astrologer. "Socialize with an old friend and get it off your mind."

Qwilleran telephoned Arch Riker. "Okay, boss, I'm back in Pickax and ready to talk. Why don't you come over for a drink tonight? The refrigerator man came back from vacation, and we have ice cubes."

"Do you mind if I bring Amanda with me?"

"If you can stand her, I can stand her," said Qwilleran with the breezy candor of a lifelong friend. "I assume your off-again romance is on again."

"We're having dinner with the Hasselriches at six, so we'll have to see you later, about ten. And do me a favor,

Qwill. I'd appreciate it if you'd water her drinks. She's bad enough when she's sober."

"Tell me one thing, Arch. How come you broke down and bought a horoscope column for the *Something?*"

"I read a survey. The horoscopes get a larger percentage of readership than anything else in the paper, including the weather."

At ten o'clock the couple climbed the stairs leading to the former servants' quarters over the garage, Amanda scowling and grumbling about the narrowness of the treads and the steepness of the flight.

Riker said confidently, "I knew you wouldn't last long in Mooseville, Qwill. You've lived too long with concrete sidewalks, traffic lights, and fire hydrants."

"How could you stand the damned mosquitoes?" Amanda said. "And all that sand! And all those noisy birds! They'd drive me crazy! And all that water! Who wants to look at a flat body of water all the time?"

"I'm glad my return has your blessing," said Qwilleran cheerfully as he served the refreshments with a flourish of cocktail napkins, coasters, and nut bowls.

"You're in a good mood tonight," the editor said.

"I talked to Polly in England. The doctors have advised her to cut her visit short. She's got a bad case of bronchitis and asthma. Wrong climate, I guess."

"Too bad she had to lose such a good opportunity," said Riker, "but for your sake I'm glad she's coming home. A woman with bronchitis and asthma is better than no woman at all." He chuckled, and Amanda glared at him.

Qwilleran asked, "How did you enjoy your dinner with the Hasselriches?"

"They're charming hosts," Riker said. "No doubt about it."

"They're so charming, I could throw up!" his companion growled.

"Was their unmarried daughter there?"

"Irma? Yes, she's just as cordial as her parents," the editor said. "Attractive woman, too."

Amanda made an unpleasant noise.

Qwilleran said, "Irma is a mystery to me. I wish I knew what she's all about."

"I'll tell you what she's all about," said Amanda with her usual belligerence. "When she was eighteen she killed her boyfriend, and old Judge Goodwinter—before he went off his rocker completely—sentenced her to twenty years in prison, but the Hasselriches made it worth his while to reduce the sentence. She got probation in the custody of her parents, plus orders to do ten years of community service. She's been serving the community *ad nauseam* every since!"

Riker glanced at Qwilleran and rolled his eyes expressively. "So, let's have the latest news on the Mooseville murder beat, Qwill. As usual it happened after our weekend issue had gone to press. I'll be glad when the new building's finished and we can start printing five days a week."

"First I'll let the cats out of their apartment. Otherwise Koko will raise the roof when he hears us talking about him." He opened a door at the end of a hall, and two proud Siamese paraded into the living room with tails and whiskers perpendicular. Yum Yum commenced an investigation of shoelaces. Koko rose effortlessly to a bookshelf six feet off the floor and settled down between Simenon and Conan Doyle.

"Well, Nick Bamba came over Friday night," Qwilleran began, "and we were having a quiet evening with the lights out and loaded firearms across our knees, in case anything happened, when Koko suddenly started making an ungodly fuss. He wanted to go underground! We let him go, and he led us to the names of the five carpenters who are alleged murder victims: Joe, Mert, Buddy, Clem, and Iggy— together with the dates of their demise. Captain Phlogg wasn't included; apparently the old soak really drank himself to death, as everyone thought."

"Where were the names?" Riker asked.

"Daubed on a floor joist in a tight spot where only a cat would find them. Nick thought the names were written in blood, but it was lipstick. That's when I knew the killer was Joanna Trupp."

Amanda snorted in disdain. "What's to stop a man from buying a lipstick if he wants to write on joists?"

"True," said Qwilleran, "but the first three names matched the purplish-red lipstick that Joanna lost in my cabin. Yum Yum had hidden it under the sofa. The last two names, apparently written after she bought a new lipstick, were in a different color—more orange."

"Why do you suppose she wrote with lipstick?" Riker asked. "Or is that question too naive?"

"For the same reason that people use lipstick to write farewell messages on bathroom mirrors: It's handy. If Little Joe were a house-painter instead of a plumber, she might have used red enamel. Don't overlook the significance of the color . . . The question next arises: Why did she keep a tally of her victims?"

"Because women like to make lists," Riker said archly, and Amanda scowled at him.

"Because each murder boosted her ego. It was a scorecard of her victories in a private war she was waging."

Riker said, "I'll bet she conked those guys with a lead pipe or a monkey wrench."

"We can assume she conked her father with the tailgate of a dump truck. Mert and Clem are unaccounted for; there'll be a search for their buried bodies on her property when the water recedes. Their trucks were found within walking distance of her private graveyard. Likewise, the mudslide where Buddy Yarrow went into the river was nearby."

"Question!" said Riker. "Since the first four were reported as accidents or missing persons, when did you first suspect murder?"

"Subliminally, I suppose, when Koko started tapping his tail. He'd been watching the carpenter drive nails *bang bang bang,* and when the man failed to report for work, Koko's tail started going *tap tap tap.*"

"Sounds like hogwash to me," Amanda muttered. "How about a refill, Sherlock? The Squunk water was delicious, but don't forget the bourbon this time."

Qwilleran refreshed her drink but not without a wink at Riker. "Perhaps it was none of my business," he said, "but I went around asking questions yesterday. Cecil Huggins remembers making a duplicate key for Joanna; it could have been a key to my cabin. The guys at the lumberyard remember Clem saying he was going to build a house on Hogback Road. The night bartender at the Shipwreck Tavern remembers the last time Mert came into the bar; Joanna was buying his drinks."

"Convenient recall!" Amanda protested. "Hearsay! Circumstantial evidence!"

"I admit it, but you can be sure that the mortality rate for carpenters will decline now that Joanna—and Louise—are in custody."

"Louise! Who's Louise?" Riker asked.

"Ah! Now we come to the curious part. Little Joe didn't know she was killing. She had invented another self—another girl—to do the dirty work. No doubt it was the only way she could cope with her intolerable homelife. For years both she and her sister were sexually abused by their father. When the younger girl killed herself—out of desperation, guilt, self-loathing, or whatever—it must have triggered a murderous hate in Joanna. Shortly after, 'Louise' engineered the tailgate accident that killed Big Joe. Little Joe's twisted reasoning would go something like this: Big Joe was a carpenter; he was a bad man; therefore all carpenters are bad men. It became the holy mission of 'Louise' to wipe them out, one by one."

"Shocking!" said Riker.

"That's what serial killers are all about," Qwilleran said. "Their motivation doesn't make sense. That's why they're so hard to catch."

"YOW!" came a loud voice from the bookshelf, and three heads turned to look.

Qwilleran said, "Koko no longer taps with his tail, now that the carpenter-killer has been apprehended. And I'm glad it's over. My only regret is that the murderer turned out to be Little Joe."

"What will happen to her?"

"Her fate now, I suppose, is in the hands of the courts and the doctors. It will take a lot of psychiatric treatment to straighten her out and get some answers to questions."

In the moment of silence that followed, a faint but distinct sound came from the Conan Doyle shelf: *tap tap tap*.

Amanda crowed with delight. "I always knew you were a windbag, Qwill, but I like your moustache."

After his guests had gone, Qwilleran made coffee for himself, poured a saucer of white grape juice for Koko, and gave Yum Yum a crumb of cheese. Then he sprawled in the big chair in his writing studio, while the Siamese arranged themselves on his desk in photogenic poses, waiting for the conversation to begin.

"Now that we're back in Pickax," he said, "I can't believe we spent those three lunatic weeks in Mooseville. There's something intoxicating about the atmosphere up there that distorts reality. It should be investigated by the narcs . . . Or even the EPA; it could be radioactivity from those UFOs."

Koko squeezed his eyes in agreement.

"And the behavior of you two was enough to unhinge a rational mind. When you staged your catfit, were you really alarmed by the ringing phone? Or were you trying to distract the inspector in a tense moment?"

Koko blinked innocently, and Yum Yum yawned.

"I'd also like to know, young man, why you reacted to Russell Simms in such an ungentlemanly manner. You embarrassed me! It's true there was something weird about her; she moved like a cat and had eyes like a cat, and she seemed to have a sixth sense . . . Hey, where are you going? Come back here!"

Koko had jumped down from the desk and was walking from the room with that particular stiff-legged gait that denoted supercilious disapproval. He paused in the doorway only long enough to switch his tail contemptuously—twice—before completing his haughty exit.

"I guess I offended him," Qwilleran said to Yum Yum. "He's temperamental, but we have to make allowances for genius, don't we? Koko was obsessed by the trap door long before Iggy was murdered and even before Clem disappeared, and it wasn't because of mice in the crawl space; he knew something *abnormal* was going to happen down there. Koko could teach Mrs. Ascott a thing or two."

Yum Yum purred delicately.

"That rascal made a fool of me when Arch and Amanda were here. He's developing a mischievous sense of humor. But I still maintain that his tail-tapping had something to do with the serial killings."

"YOW!" Koko reappeared in the doorway, standing on his hind legs and pawing the air.

"I said s-e-r-i-a-l," Qwilleran told him. "Not c-e-r-e-a-l."

Both cats stared at him with expectation in every whisker.

Qwilleran looked at his watch. "Okay, you guys, it's time for your bedtime treat!" He gave them a handful of Mildred's crunchy breakfast food.